EPIC

FAERIES & NYMPHS MYTHS & TALES

ANTHOLOGY OF CLASSIC TALES

Foreword by Dr. Jennifer Larson

FLAME TREE PUBLISHING

TALES

This is a FLAME TREE Book

Publisher & Creative Director: Nick Wells
Editorial Director: Catherine Taylor
Project Editor: Simran Aulakh
Special thanks to Michael Kerrigan

FLAME TREE PUBLISHING
6 Melbray Mews, Fulham,
London SW6 3NS, United Kingdom
www.flametreepublishing.com

First published 2026

26 28 30 29 27
1 3 5 7 9 10 8 6 4 2

ISBN: 978-1-83562-780-8
Special ISBN: 978-1-83562-921-5

The cover image is created by Flame Tree Studio, featuring artwork by Slava Gerj and Gabor Ruszkai, as well as the fairy from *Spirit of the Night* (1879) by John Atkinson Grimshaw (1836–1893). Internal decorations are courtesy Shutterstock.com and the following artists: fajarhidayah11, Belayet2288, kawsar4, and Karlionau (story headers).

Publisher's Note: Due to the historical nature of the classic text, we're aware that there may be some language used which has the potential to cause offence to the modern reader. However, wishing overall to preserve the integrity of the text, rather than imposing contemporary sensibilities, we have left it unaltered.

A copy of the CIP data for this book is available from the British Library.

Printed and bound in China

Represented in the EU for product safety and compliance by Authorised Rep Compliance Ltd, Ground Floor, 71 Lower Baggot Street, Dublin, D02 P593, Ireland. Contact at www.arccompliance.com

EPIC TALES

FAERIES & NYMPHS MYTHS & TALES

ANTHOLOGY OF CLASSIC TALES

Foreword by Dr. Jennifer Larson

FLAME TREE PUBLISHING

Contents

Monsters, Deities & Legendary Figures

Magic, Adventure & Quests

Love, Death & Tragedy

Foreword

IN 2001, when I was an early-career faculty member in Classics, I published an academic book about nymphs. Over the years, none of my other publications has brought so many comments, questions and thanks from readers. Clearly, something about nymphs captures the imagination, carrying us off to the mountain glade where long-lived tree nymphs cared for the infant Aeneas, or the pleasant and shady cave of the nymphs in Odysseus's Ithaca, with its furnishings cut into the living rock, and fragrant stores of honey.

In ancient Greek, the word *numphē* meant 'bride', conveying the lovely, youthful appearance and sexual desirability of these mythic females. There were other names too: *naias*, or 'flowing one', for the spring nymphs; *druas* or 'she of the tree' for the dryads whose lives were bound up with those of their trees, especially the beeches and holm oaks; and *nērēis* or 'daughter of Nereus' for the nymphs of loud-roaring sea.

Part of the enduring appeal of the nymph is her placement in the wild, undomesticated lands: the mountains, woods, meadows and sea. Despite her name, she is more free and untamed than any human bride, yet she shares some of the delights of human culture, above all music and dance. While nymphs were usually friendly toward humans, they occasionally caused harm, as in the myth that naiads pulled the beautiful youth Hylas into their pond, drowning him in order to make him their playmate.

The Old French word *fae*, the source of our word 'faerie' or 'fairy', has its roots in the Classical world too, for it derives from *fatum*, 'fate'. In European folklore, the *fae* were supernatural beings, both male and female, associated with enchantment and magic; the elves (Norse *Álfar*) of Northern European mythologies were similar figures who overlap with faeries in English lore. In Shakespeare's *A Midsummer Night's Dream*, for example, the word 'elf' is used as a synonym for 'faerie.'

According to European lore, faeries appear (more or less) human in form, and they possess their own land, an otherworld known as Faerie. A human might find herself in Faerie if she enters an ancient stone circle or burial mound (such as the *Sidhe* of Irish lore), wanders into an old-growth forest or falls asleep in a fairy ring of toadstools, particularly at certain liminal times: midnight, noon, cross-quarter days and solstices. Entering Faerie is dangerous, for the *fae* live up to their connection with fate or doom. Faerie lore developed under the influence of Christianity, which taught that they lacked souls. Although they might be superficially beautiful, they were deceitful, mischievous, and sometimes deadly.

Folklore the world over tells of supernatural fairy- and nymph-like beings, particularly in connection with natural features such as mountains, springs, rivers and caves. Water spirits are encountered everywhere, and include the Japanese *kappa*, Pania of the Reef in Māori myths of New Zealand, the Yacuruna or Water People of the Amazon basin, the Apsaras of Hindu tradition, and the mermaid-like female *jengu* of Cameroon. Across cultures, we find that faerie-like beings may help or harm humans, they may be invisible or change shape, and they may test or trick those who encounter them.

The tale of Melusine, one of the most famous in medieval French lore, presents a figure who resembles both nymph and faerie. In the literary version by Jean d'Arras (1393), Melusine is banished from the island of Avalon and cursed to take half-serpent form one day of every week. Raymondin meets and marries her, agreeing to her condition that he must never see her on a Saturday; in return she brings him good fortune, sons and wealth. But when Raymondin grows suspicious because Melusine never attends Mass, he spies on her in her bath, and sees the snaky lower half of her body. With the promise broken, Melusine abandons him forever, flying off in the form of a dragon. The story echoes Greek myths, Arthurian romance and European folktale.

This book will introduce you to many more legends from the inexhaustible store of world cultures. Enjoy!

Dr. Jennifer Larson

Publisher's Note

FAERIES AND NYMPHS share similarities as benevolent or mischievous spirits that are deeply connected to the natural world. Their alluring nature has inspired many fascinating tales from across the globe, featuring in European, Greek, Arabian and Persian mythologies to name a few. They also appear in folklore and literature from various cultures, ranging from Chinese to Roman, Slavic to Korean. These multifaceted creatures can be good or bad, guardians or protectors, but are generally depicted with magical abilities, such as enchantment, shape-shifting and flying. This truly is a wonderful collection of tales which brings together these two captivating supernatural forces.

We must remind the reader that, as tales from mythology and folklore are principally derived from an oral storytelling tradition, their written representation depends on the transcription, translation and interpretation by those who heard them and first put them to paper, and also on whether they are recently re-told versions or more directly sourced from original first-hand accounts. The stories in this book are a mixture, and you can learn more about the sources and authors at the back of the book. Due to the historical nature of such texts, we're aware that there may be some language used which has the potential to cause offence to the modern reader. However, wishing to preserve the overall integrity of the writing, rather than imposing contemporary sensibilities, we have left it largely unaltered.

EPIC

FAERIES & NYMPHS MYTHS & TALES

ANTHOLOGY OF CLASSIC TALES

Foreword by Dr. Jennifer Larson

FLAME TREE PUBLISHING

TALES

Faeries & Nymphs Myths & Tales

Introduction

Up the airy mountain,
Down the rushy glen,
We daren't go a-hunting
For fear of little men …

WILLIAM ALLINGHAM'S famous verses (1850) remind us of two vital faery facts: they aren't all female (as nymphs are) and neither are they all benign. In the west of Ireland, as recently as the 1920s, people dressed their young sons in skirts to fool the fairies into thinking they were female. Along with their myriad other faults, the Little People were irredeemably sexist and didn't see girls as worth the trouble of abducting. A more respectful view was available, though – had been at very least since 1589, in Sir Edmund Spenser's *The Faerie Queene*. Apart from allegorizing everything from Protestant theology to the European politics of the time, Spenser's enormous epic poem presents England's Elizabeth I as 'Gloriana', a Queen of surpassing grace and supernatural prestige.

From Nightmare to Dream

Spenser's contemporary, William Shakespeare is generally considered to have introduced the more miniature, butterfly-winged, delicately-feminine and basically benevolent fairy to English culture with the exquisite retinue he invented for Titania in his *A Midsummer Night's Dream* (c. 1595). The Fairy Queen herself, however, seems to be more of a standard human size; as does her husband Oberon. And his servant Puck – who, additionally, is frequently malevolent; not just mischievous but gratuitously cruel. If he's also known as 'Robin Goodfellow', that seems to be for the same reasons as American gangsters have been called 'Goodfellas' – a name used by frightened people in hopes of appeasing away potential harm.

Shakespeare showed ambivalence about fairies, then, holding on to the more authentically 'folk' belief in their (at best) untrustworthiness ("They are fairies; they that speak to them shall die," says a frightened Falstaff in *The Merry Wives of Windsor* (1602)) even as he promoted a more courtly, cutesy image for them. The latter was the view that, taken up by J.M. Barrie in his stories of Peter Pan, told modern mass audiences that fairies were mild, gentle and generous.

The Spirit of Childhood

And, in their delicacy, desperately fragile. Simply not to believe in them was to kill them – quite literally. 'Whenever a child says "I don't believe in fairies",' he wrote, 'there's a little fairy somewhere that falls right down dead.' Outside the wrap-around warmth of his plays and stories, this view sounds preposterously precious. That said, Barrie is surely right in his implicit sense that his fairies represent a personification of that capacity to wonder which the modern world has for the most part lost completely and which clings on, precariously, in the open minds of the very young.

It goes without saying that even the most innocent child has a sense of mischief: only a grown-up could have conceived Barrie's fantasy in its purest form. Real children may be every bit as ingenuous as he imagines, but – like their elders – they can show a callous streak. Hence the appeal of the Korean spirit Tokgabi's Puckish pranks; and of the rough justice shown 'The Twin Hunchbacks' in the Hungarian tale. One brother, coming upon a group of dancing fairies, shows them respect and courtesy. They respond by curing his deformity for him. When his twin seeks them out for similar treatment, he treats them with mockery and insult: they pay him back by making his hunchback twice as bad.

Spirits of Nature

Nymphs are different: by definition female, they were seen as minor deities by the ancient Greeks, and after them the Romans. That said, their close association with identifiable places suggests that, like the Celtic fairies – and those of a great many other cultures – they were a vestige of older animistic traditions. The earliest communities lived narrowly circumscribed lives and saw their fortunes governed by the moods of local deities. The Olympian pantheon, with its fractious little family of gods and goddesses was a product of more economically-developed and politically-ordered times. They represented general principles (like love or war) or elements (the sky, the sea). But coexisting with this universal order was an anarchy of locally-associated divinities.

Mostly these were nymphs, keeping a proprietary and protective watch over every significant spring or stream or stretch of sea (water nymphs were known as Naiads, while there were Oceanids for salt water). Mountains had Oreads to mind them; Epimelides protected upland pastures; Auloniades lower-lying pastures and valley floors. Dryads lived in oak trees; Daphnae in laurels. There were other classes of nymphs as well, associated with everything from breezes to stars. The Hesperides were associated with the evening and sunset.

Like the fairies, the nymphs of ancient times were to some extent to be sanitized in later tradition. Those of the Greeks were often sexually promiscuous and aggressive. That said, the gluttony and bloodthirst that drive the sometime-sea-nymph Scylla (in the story 'Scylla and Charybdis') to lurk along her rocky coast and snatch passing sailors to gorge on seems to have been the result of a curse imposed on her by the sorceress Circe, whom she had crossed in love.

A different kind of curse was placed on the wood nymph Echo by the goddess Hera, when she learned that her sometime friend had betrayed her trust. Echo had been talkative, bubbling over with chat, a natural raconteuse and storyteller. Hera could have listened to her for hours. Sometimes, indeed, she had done – discovering only afterwards that her errant husband Zeus had paid Echo to distract her while he was off philandering with others. Enraged, she had hit Echo where she knew it would hurt her most, in her voice, and her creative way with words. From now on, the Queen of Olympus decreed, Echo would have no ability to speak on her own part; only to repeat the last words she heard another say.

Hence her powerlessness when she saw and fell in love with the young Narcissus, though he's too wrapped up in himself and his own beauty to respond. No one he sees is worthy of his love – until one day he happens on his own reflection looking back up at him from a silver stream. Echo has to look on helpless as he cranes over to kiss the gorgeous youth – so far that, finally, he topples in and drowns. A slim and elegant flower, the Narcissus, sprang up in his memory. As for Echo, left alone, she fled that forest to wander aimlessly, 'searching for her lost love, and, of course, her voice'.

This is the Echo who's remembered; not the unscrupulous trickster who schemed against Hera, her supposed friend. And fair enough: this one is unquestionably more appealing. For the most part, indeed, the classical nymphs in the stories that have survived are relatively demure. If Barrie's fairies met a need in modern life for a sense of childlike innocence and wonder, these idealized nymphs met a yearning – at least among the overwhelmingly male custodians of folkloric literature – for a more soft-focus femininity, quiet and yielding.

A Disappearing Difference

The same might be said of a good many fairies. Indeed, as time went on and over the centuries the old myths and stories went through a more or less continuous process of collecting and editing, the original distinction between nymphs and fairies was gradually lost. It endured in works of scholarship and in anthologies of classical myth. Elsewhere, though, it ceased to be observed. In fairness, in important ways, the narrative function of these two types of spirit had been broadly similar, whatever differences there might have been.

Blessings, Boons...

The idea that the fairies may be benign is not of course confined to the modern Western tradition. Consider Kahukura in the Maori fairy tale. Walking out one night, he sees a fairy band straining to land a catch of fish from the heaving ocean. He pitches in and helps them drag the heavy net ashore. Finally realizing that they have a mortal human in their midst, the fairies take fright and run off in all directions. Not, however, before Kahukura has seen the special stitch they've used to make their net; a stitch the Maori were to use from that day on.

One function of the fairy in folktale is indeed to shower virtuous mortals with the blessings that their harsh realities do not generally afford them. Kahukura's workaday benefit is echoed in the dreamier gifts bestowed on La Cenerentola ('Cinderella', in the English tradition), whose 'Fairy Godmother' belongs to a long tradition of such magical benefactors. Ambrose has another such protector in the Hungarian story of 'The Three Princes, the Three Dragons, and the Woman with the Iron Nose'. She'll be balefully balanced by the old woman of the story's title, who as the dragons' mother will do her best to persecute him, but finally – of course – will see that right prevails. The Buddhist sage Sam-Chung, in the Chinese folktale, is helped by fairies to vanquish the Water Demon – and consequently to free human mortals from the curse of death.

...And Curses

The converse can hold too. Uletka, in the Hungarian story, is barred from her birthright by the bad fairy, Muta, who has murdered her mother and made her an orphan but still won't relent in her wicked vendetta against the young princess. Fortunately, like Snow White, she'll be protected by a group of gnomes. In 'Helga', a tale of Iceland, bad fairy has placed the curse on the young prince Torquil. When the story's heroine meets him, he's a hideous three-headed giant – made that way by the wicked fairy Gondomar. But Helga, a Nordic Cinderella, used to being bullied and disparaged by her family, is unfazed. She helps free him and – inevitably – they fall in love.

Alasdair MacEachern's family, in 'The Fairies and the Blacksmith' – a tale from Islay in Scotland's Western Isles – are also accursed by the fairies who gain a hold on them when, 'Alasdair of the Strong Arm' is away, his son Neil neglects to hang a rowan branch above their door. They carry him off and – as is the way with the wild Faeries – leave a child of their own as a changeling in its place. Alasdair divines what has happened but is unable to break the spell. Fearlessly, he decides he'll descend to the Faery realm to retrieve his son: he finds him at a forge where he is fashioning a fairy sword – with its strong edge he'll be able to sever the evil spell.

Escaping the Everyday

For many a folk protagonist a beautiful spirit provides not just an enchanting but a romantically alluring port in a storm. The time he spends with her, like that which the Confucian student spends with the old man's daughter in the Korean tale 'The Home of the Fairies', she offers an escape from the harsh realities of his real home. (In this particular case, of course, fairyland becomes a literal sanctuary for him and his family from a village which will be burned and pillaged by the invading Manchu the following year.)

In the Indian story 'Samvarana and Tapati', King Samvarana finds a refuge of this kind in Tapati, the 'matchless maiden' he finds awaiting him on a lonely hillside. Making her his bride, he has a dozen years' freedom from care and toil amidst the beauty of the mountains, but duty calls him back when drought afflicts his kingdom. He returns home, with his wife, to resume his reign. The mountains, it doesn't take a diviner to see, are the realm of idyllic happiness we can't help hankering after; but with things in life to attend to, we mustn't try to stay indefinitely.

So it certainly is with 'Calypso's Island' – an episode of Homer's ancient Greek epic poem, *The Odyssey*. A beautiful nymph, Calypso bombards Odysseus with affection, tenderness and care: so much so that for fully seven years he's 'drunk on luxury and love'. So completely does Calypso cater to his every need that he feels no need to look beyond her spellbinding company and pretty much forgets that he has a life (and obligations) in the outside world.

'Man's Meat'

A more grotesque take on this basic narrative is to be found in 'The Goblin City', one of the *Jataka* tales, a body of Buddhist 'birth stories' based on the prior lives of Gautama Buddha. This one describes a city in Sri Lanka populated by goblin women, who use their erotic allure and wicked wiles to trap those unwary male travellers who stray into their reach. Their voracity isn't just sexual: once they've worn their new husbands out, they kill and make a meal of them:

"Man's meat, man's meat,
That's what goblins like to eat!"

Sheen, 'star-bright and beautiful', the enchanted storm queen in the Irish legend, 'Murtough and the Witch Woman', doesn't even try to transport her victim, the High King Murtough, to another realm. Instead, she deploys her skills in love and magic (the two aren't clearly distinguished in this story) to have him change his own world, sending away his wife and family and his trusted counsellors. Though they will fight to win him back, it'll be too late for the hapless Murtough – but they'll live to dig a grave for her running crossways over that of their late king.

A Different Dimension

Such narratives often see Fairyland as not so much a place as an entire dimension, beyond our own; a philosophical plane, rather than a geographical one. And a realm whose very existence ushers in ideas of other possibilities, alternative lives. So we see with the Scottish story of 'Thomas the Rhymer', Thomas Learmont, Laird of Ercildoune, a castle in rural Berwickshire, in the Borders. Thomas was a poet in his own right, hence his name, though he's more famous from the works of others writing later like Sir Walter Scott. A semi-legendary figure, Thomas seems to have lived in the thirteenth century. His ballad has him lying down to nap one afternoon under a tree on the grassy slopes of Eildon Hill, near his home. In his vision he's approached by a beautiful lady, riding a grey palfrey.

She wore a hunting dress of glistening silk, the colour of the fresh spring grass; and from her shoulders hung a velvet mantle, which matched the riding-skirt exactly. Her yellow hair, like rippling gold, hung loosely round her shoulders, and on her head sparkled a diadem of precious stones, which flashed like fire in the sunlight.

Her saddle was of pure ivory, and her saddle-cloth of blood-red satin, while her saddle girths were of corded silk and her stirrups of cut crystal. Her horse's reins were of beaten gold, all hung with little silver bells, so that, as she rode along, she made a sound like fairy music

Ironically, he takes her for the Blessed Virgin Mary. She divines as such, and smiles as she tells him she's the 'Queen of Elfland'. She begs him for a kiss, and he can't resist, but the. moment her lips touch his she withers away to haglike hideousness before his very eyes.

It's too late now for him to change his mind, though: he's committed to her service for the next seven years. She carries him off to Elfland, a lovely country bathed in sunshine, where once again he sees her restored to youthful bloom. As it turns out, so is he himself, ready to enjoy the pleasures of this enchanted kingdom. Just being here is an intoxication. He's disappointed to be sent home after three days. Waking on his bumpy hillside, though, he finds he's actually been away for seven long years.

And been left with the gift of prophecy. 'True Thomas' predicts, among other things, his country's victory at the Battle of Bannockburn (1314) and, it's been suggested, the crowning of Scotland's James VI as James I of England (1603). Though back in Berwickshire with his people, he's been subtly yet profoundly changed by his experience in Elfland and in some ways still seems to inhabit a separate plane.

Waterworld

Deep and mysterious, the sight of water seems instantly to suggest to us a ready-made wonderland. Many ancient cultures believed there was another world down there, mirroring our own. So it seems to be in another Indian story: that of 'The Prince and the Procuress'. Prince Kandarpa-ketu of Sri Lanka ventures beneath the ocean waves to wed the ravishingly beautiful and graceful Princess Ratnamanjari. His life is blissful but – committing the cardinal fairy-tale sin of disobedience, placing his hand upon a painting his young wife has begged him not to touch – he's whirled away by magic and dumped unceremoniously back onshore.

Sometimes the situations are reversed and, rather than a mortal sojourning in fairyland, a spirit steps into his realm for an ecstatic while. So it is for the kind young man who catches a water-spirit in the Polish story 'The Good Ferryman and the Water Nymphs': she comes ashore and makes him a devoted and loyal wife. Such transitions aren't necessarily easy or smooth, as Hans Christian Anderson's 'Little Mermaid' was to find in her life ashore. But then the journey in the opposite direction has its traumas too. Glory, the girl in the Ugandan story 'The River Fairy', has to have her feet cut off so she can grow the tail that will make her a true 'fish-maiden'. Despite her fears, she decides that this is preferable to the cold and lonely life she lives ashore and eventually takes to her new environment with no regrets.

A Different Dimension

We too travel to a different place – are in some ways changed ourselves, as Glory is, when we immerse ourselves in the sort of stories we find here. Almost as important as the spirits themselves is the idea they bring of 'Fairyland' as a place apart. Fairytales transport us to a wholly different dimension. All stories do – all reading is in this sense at least 'escapism' – but tales of magic make the idea explicit. In every story here, we find the potential for change, for a different life, a different construction of reality.

Animals, Enchanting Creatures & Worlds Beyond Our Own

Introduction

"THERE ARE, SIR," the so-called 'Boy of Leith' is said to have told Captain George Buxton, in 1649,

> *"a great company both of men and women, and they are entertained with many sorts of music ... They have, besides, plenty of variety of meats and wine, and many times we are carried into France or Holland in the night, and return again, and whilst we are there, we enjoy all the pleasures the country doth afford."*

Leith, the port of Edinburgh, abuts on the lower slopes of Calton Hill, into whose granite mass the Boy claimed regularly to walk through a fairy portal. His account gives every indication of being inspired by wish-fulfilment but still strikes a chord with its evocation of another world, adjacent to our own. Its proximity enthralls us as much as its alienness, and makes us wonder what other enchantments may be so close at hand. Could that pond in its pine grove be the gateway to Fairyland as it is in the Korean story 'Home of the Fairies'? Might not that donkey be the emperor's brother, transformed by a spell as in the Roman story? And where is the wishing skin which, in the Hungarian tale, the fairies have been weaving for three hundred years. All these questions – and countless others – are answered here.

Fairy Elizabeth

THERE WAS ONCE SOMEWHERE, I don't know where, beyond seven times seven countries, and even beyond them, a poor man who had a wife and three children. They were awfully poor.

One day the eldest son said: "Dear mother, bake me some ash-cake and let me go into service." His mother at once baked the cake, and the lad started, and went on and on till he came to a high snow-clad mountain, where he met a grey-haired man and greeted him: "May the Lord bless you, my good old father." "The Lord bless you, my son. What are you after?" asked the old man. "I am going out to service, if the Lord will help me to some place." "Well, then, come to me," said the old man, "I will engage you." So they went to the house of the grey-haired old man, and the very next day they went out ploughing but they only ploughed up some grass-land, and sowed it with seed. Now let me tell you, that the old man promised him a bushel of seed for sowing. Two days passed, and at dawn of the third day the old man said: "Well, my son, today you can go out ploughing for yourself; get the plough ready, yoke the oxen in, and in the meantime I will get the bushel of wheat I promised." So the lad put the oxen to the plough and the old man got the bushel of wheat and placed it on the plough. They started, the old man accompanying him. Just at the end of the village he said to the lad: "Well, my son, can you see that place yonder covered with shrubs? Go there, and plough up as much of it for yourself as you think will be enough for the bushel of wheat." The lad went, but was quite alarmed at the sight of the shrubs, and at once lost heart. How could he plough there? Why, by the time he had grubbed up the shrubs alone it would be night. So he ran off home, and left the plough there, and the oxen then returned of their own accord to the old man's place – if I may interrupt myself, they were the oxen of a fairy.

When the lad arrived at his father's house, his other brothers asked him: "What sort of a place have you found?" "What sort of a place!" replied he, "go yourself, and you will soon find out." The middle son set out, and just as he was going over the snow-clad mountain he met the old man, who engaged him on the spot as his servant, and promised him a bushel of wheat, as he had done before. They went to the old man's home, and he fared just as his elder brother had done. At dawn on the third day, when he had to plough for himself, he got frightened at the sight of the vast number of shrubs, which no human being could have ploughed up in the stated time. So he went home too, and on his way he met his younger brother, who asked him: "What sort of a place have you found, my dear elder brother?" "What sort of a place had I? Get up out of the ashes, and go yourself, and you will soon find out."

Now let me tell you that this boy was continually sitting among the ashes. He was a lazy, ne'er-do-well fellow; but now he got up, and shook the ashes from him and said: "Well, my mother, bake me a cake also: as my brothers have tried their fortune let me try mine." But his brothers said: "Oh! You ash-pan! Supposing you were required to do nothing else but eat, you would not be good enough even for that." But still he insisted, that his mother should bake something for him. So his mother set to work and baked him a cake of some inferior bran, and with this he set out.

As he went over the boundless snow-clad mountain, in the midst of it he met the old man and greeted him: "The Lord bless you, my old father!" "The Lord bless you, my son! Where are you going?" "I am going out to service, if I can find an employer." "Well, you are the very man I want; I am in search of a servant." And he engaged him on the spot, promising to make him a present of a bushel of wheat for sowing. They went home together, and after they had ploughed together for two days, the lad set out on the third day to plough up the land allotted to him for his own use: while the youngster was putting the oxen to the plough the old man got the wheat and placed it on the plough. On the dyke there was a big dog, who always lay there quietly; but this time he got up, and started off in front of him. The old man also accompanied him as far as the end of the village, from whence he showed him where to go ploughing. The youngster went on with the plough, and soon saw that he was not able to plough a single furrow, on account of the thick bushes. After considering what to do, he bethought himself, and took his sharp hatchet and began to cut down a vast quantity of shrubs and thorns, the dog carrying them all into a heap. Seeing that he had cut enough, he began to plough. The two oxen commenced to drag the plough and cut up the roots in a manner never seen before. After he had turned three times, he looked round and said: "Well, I'm not going to plough any more, but will begin to sow, so that I may see how much seed I've got." He sowed the seed, and noticed that it was just sufficient, and therefore he had to plough no more. In great joy he set the plough straight and went home. The old man met him and said: "Well, my son, thanks to the Lord, you have now finished your year, and in God's name I will let you go. I do not intend to engage any more servants." Before I forget to tell you, I may mention it here, that the year had three days then. So the lad went home, and his brothers asked him: "Well, then, what sort of a place have you found?" "Well, I believe I've served my master as well as you did."

One day, a year after, he went into the field to look at his wheat crop. There he saw an old woman reaping some young wheat, so he went home and said to his father: "Well, my father, do you know what we have to do? let's go reaping." "Where, my son?" "Well, father, for my last year's service I had a bushel of wheat given to me for sowing, it has got ripe by this time, so let us go and reap it." So all four (his father, his two brothers, and himself) went; when they came to the spot they saw that it was a magnificent crop, a mass of golden ears from root to top, ready and ripe; so they all started to work and cut down every head.

They made three stacks of it, each stack having twenty-six sheaves. "Well my son," said the father, "there are three stacks here and there are three of you to guard them, so while I go home to hire a cart, guard them well, so that the birds may not carry away a single stem." The father went home, and the three sat down (one at the foot of each stack) to watch them, but the youngest was the most anxious, as it was his own, and ran to and fro continually to prevent his brothers falling asleep. Just as he had awakened them and was going back to his own stack he saw a woodpecker dragging away, by jerks, a golden ear along the ground, so he ran after it in order to get it back, but just as he was on the point of catching it the woodpecker flew off further and further, and enticed him, until at last it got him into the very midst of the boundless snow-clad mountains. All of a sudden the youngster discovered where he was, and that it was getting dusk. Where was he to go? And what was he to do? So he thought he would go back to the stacks, but as he had kept his eye on the woodpecker and the wheat-ear, he had taken no notice of the surroundings, and knew not which way he had come. So he determined to climb the highest tree and look round from there. He looked about and found the highest tree, climbed it, and looked East but saw nought, South and saw nought, North, and far, very far away he saw a light as big as a candle; so he came down, and started off in the direction in which he had seen the light and went straight over ditches, woods, rocks, and fields till at last he came to a large plain, and there he found the fire which he had seen before, and lo! it was such a heap of burning wood that the flames nearly reached heaven. He approached it and when he drew near the burning heap he saw that a man was lying curled round the fire, his head resting on his feet, and that he was covered with a large cloak. Then thought the lad, "Shall I lie down inside or outside of the circle formed by the body of the man?" If he lay outside he would catch cold; if he lay inside he would be scorched, he thought; so he crept into the sleeve of the cloak, and there fell asleep.

In the morning when the sun arose, the big man awoke, he yawned wide, and got up from the fire; as he rose the youngster dropt out of his sleeve on to the ground: the giant looked at him (because I forgot to tell you it wasn't a man, it was a giant), and was very much pleased at the sight; he quickly picked him up, took him into his arms, and carried him into his palace, (and even there put him into the best room) and put him to bed, covered him up well, and crept out of the room on tiptoe lest he should wake him. When he heard that the youngster was awake, he called to him through the open door, "Don't be afraid, my dear son, I am a big man it is true, but notwithstanding I will be to thee like thy father, in thy father's place; like thy mother, in thy mother's place." With this he entered the room, and the poor lad stared into the giant's eyes, as if he were looking up to the sky. Suddenly the giant asked him how he got there, and the lad told him the whole tale. "Well, my dear little son, I will give you everything that your heart can think of, or your mouth name, I will fulfil your every wish, only don't worry yourself;" and he had all sorts of splendid clothes made for him, and kept him on costly food; and this lasted till the lad became twenty years of age, when one day the lad became very sad, and his giant father asked him, "Well, my dear son, tell me why you are so sad, I will do all your heart can think of, or your mouth name; but do tell me what's the matter with you?" So the lad said, after hesitation, "Well! well! well! My dear father, I am so sad because the time has come when I ought to get married, and there's nobody here to get married to." "Oh! My son, don't worry yourself over that, such a lad as you has but to wish and you will find plenty of womankind, the very prettiest of them, ready to have you; you will but have to choose the one your heart loves best." So saying he called the lad before the gate and said: "Well, my son, you can see that great white lake yonder: go there at noon prompt and hide yourself under a tree, for every noon three lovely fairy girls come there who are as handsome as handsome can be: you can look at the sun, but you can't look at them! They will come disguised as pigeons, and when they arrive on the bank they will turn somersaults, and at once become girls: they will then undress, and lay their dresses on the bank: you must then glide up, and steal the dress of the one your heart loves best, and run away home with it, but be careful not to look back, however they may shout: because if you do, believe me, she will catch you, box your ears, and take her clothes from you."

So he went to the lake and hid himself under an oak, and all at once three white pigeons came flying, their wings flapping loudly as they came, they settled down on the bank, and went to take a bath. The lad wasn't slow to leave his hiding-place, and pick up the dress of the eldest fairy girl and run away with it; but she noticed it at once, rushed out of the lake, and ran after him, shouting: "Stop! sweet love of my heart. Look at me; see how beautiful my skin is; how pretty my breasts are. I'm yours, and you're mine!" So he looked round, and the fairy snatched her dress away in a moment, slapped his face, and returned to the others in the lake. Poor lad! he was very sad, and went back and told his giant father all that had happened, and his giant father answered, "Well; wasn't I right? Didn't I tell you not to look back? But don't fret; three in number are the divine truths, and three times also will you have to try. There are two yet left, go again tomorrow at noon. Take care you don't look back, or pick up the same dress that you picked up yesterday, because, believe me, if you do, there will be the mischief to pay." So he went early next day (he couldn't wait till noon) and hid himself under a tree, when all of a sudden the pigeons appeared, turned somersaults, and became three beautiful fairy girls. They undressed, laid their dresses on the bank, and went into the lake; in short, the lad fared with the second as with the first – he couldn't resist the temptation of looking back when the beautiful fairy kept imploring him, as the sweet love of her heart, to gaze at her beautiful skin and breasts. He looked back, was slapped in the face as before, and lost the fairy dress. He went home again, very sad, to his giant father, and told him how he had fared; and the giant said in reply: "Never mind, don't bother yourself, my son, three are the divine truths; there is one more left for you; you can try again tomorrow, but only be very careful not to look back this time." Next day he couldn't wait till noon, but went and hid himself under the oak very early, and had to wait a long, long time. At last the white pigeons arrived, turned somersaults as before, and put their dresses on the bank, whilst they themselves went into the lake. Out he rushed from his hiding-place, snatched up the youngest's dress, and ran away with it. But the fairy noticed that her dress was gone, and rushed out of the lake after him like a hurricane, calling out incessantly: "Stop! sweet love of my heart, look how beautifully white my skin is! See how beautifully white are my breasts. I am yours, and you are mine." But the lad only ran faster than ever, and never looked behind once, but ran straight home to his giant father, and told him that he had got the dress this time. "Well, my dear son," said he, "didn't I tell you not to worry yourself in the least, and that I would do all for you that your heart could desire, or your mouth name?" Once after this the lad was very sad again, so his giant father asked him: "Well, my son, what's the matter this time, that you are so sad?" "Well, my dear father, because we have only got a dress, and that is not enough for a wedding. What's the use of it? What can I do with it?" "Never mind, don't worry about that. Go into the inside closet, and on a shelf you will find a walnut, bring it here." So the lad went and fetched the nut, and the giant split it neatly in two, took out the kernel, folded up the dress (and I may mention it here the dress consisted of only one piece), put it inside the nut-shell, fitted the two halves together, and said to the lad: "Well, my son, let me have your waistcoat, so that I may sew this nut into the pocket; and be careful that no one opens it, neither thy father, nor thy mother, nor any one in this world, because should any one open it your life will be made wretched; you will be an outcast."

With this, the giant sewed the nut into the pocket, and put the waistcoat on him. As they finished this, they heard a great clamping noise, and a chinking (as of coins) outside. So the giant bade him to look out of the window, and what did he see? He saw that in the courtyard there was a lovely girl sitting in a carriage drawn by six horses, and about her beautiful maids and outriders, and the giant said, "You see, it is Fairy Elizabeth, your ladylove." So they went out at once, and helped Fairy Elizabeth out of her carriage, then she ordered the carriage and horses to go back, at once, to where they had come from, and in a moment they disappeared, and there was no trace of them left. They then went into the house, but the giant remained outside, and he drew in the dust figures of a priest, and a cantor, and guests, and they appeared at once. All went into the house, and the young folks got wed, and a great wedding feast was celebrated. There was the bridegroom's best man, and the groom's men, and the bride's duenna, and all her bridesmaids, and the wedding feast lasted three full days. They ate, drank, and enjoyed themselves, and when all was over the young couple lived together in quiet happiness. Once more, however, the lad became very sad, and the giant asked him: "Well, my dear son, why are you sad again? You know that I will do all your heart can desire, or your mouth name." "Well, my dear father," replied he, "how can I help being sad; it is true we live together happily, but who knows how my father and mother and brothers and sisters are at home? I should like to go to see them."

"Well, my dear son," said the giant, "I will let you go; you two go home, and you will find your relations keeping the third anniversary of your death: they have gathered in all the golden corn, and become so rich that they are now the greatest farmers in the village: each of your brothers have their own home and they have become great men (six-ox farmers) and have a whole flock of sheep." So the giant went outside, and drew in the dust the figures of horses and carriage, coachman, footmen, outriders, and court damsels, and they at once appeared; the young couple sat in the carriage, and the giant told the lad if ought happened to him he had only to think of one of these horses, and it would at once bring him back here.

With this they started, and they arrived at home and, saw that the courtyard of his father's house was full of tables, crowded with people sitting round them, but no one spoke a word; they all were speechless so that you could not even hear a whisper. The couple got out of the carriage, in front of the gate, walked into the yard, and met an old man; it happened to be his father. "May the Lord give you a good day, Sir!" said he; and the old man replied, "May the Lord bless you also, my lord!" "Well sir," asked the young man, "what is the meaning of all this feasting that I see, all this eating and drinking, and yet no one speaks a word; is it a marriage or a funeral feast?" "My lord, it is a burial feast," replied the old man; "I had three sons, one was lost, and today we celebrate the third anniversary of his death." "Would you recognize your son if he appeared?" Upon hearing this his mother came forward and said, "To be sure, my dearest and sweetest lord, because there is a mark under his left armpit." With this the lad pulled up his sleeve and showed the mark, and they at once recognized him as their lost son; the funeral feast, thereupon, was at once changed into a grand wedding festival. Then the lad called out to the carriage and horses "Go back where you have come from," and in a moment there was not a trace of them left. His father at once sent for the priest and the verger and they went through all the ceremonies again, and whether the giant had celebrated them or not, certainly the father did: the wedding feast was such a one as had never been seen before! When they rose from the table they began the bride's dance: in the first place they handed the bride to the cleverest dancer, and whether he danced or not, most certainly the bride did: as she danced her feet never touched the ground, and everyone who was there looked at the bride only, and all whispered to each other, that no man had ever seen such a sight in all his life. When the bride heard this she said, "Hum, whether I dance now or whether I don't, I could dance much better if anyone would return to me the dress I wore in my maiden days." Whereupon they whispered to each other, "Where can that dress be?" When the bride heard this she said, "Well, my souls, it is in a nutshell, sewn into my husband's waistcoat pocket, but no one will ever be able to get it." "I can get it for you," said her mother-in-law, "because I will give my son a sleeping-draught in wine and he will go to sleep," and so she did, and the lad fell on the bed fast asleep; his mother then got the nut from his pocket and gave it to her daughter-in-law, who at once opened it, took the dress out, put it on, and danced so beautifully, that, whether she danced the first time or not, she certainly danced this time; you could not imagine anything so graceful.

But, as it was so hot in the house, the windows were left open, and Fairy Elizabeth turned a somersault, became a white pigeon, and flew out of the window. Outside there was a pear tree, and she settled upon the top of it, the people looking on in wonder and astonishment; then she called out that she wanted to see her husband as she wished to say a word or two to him, but the sleeping draught had not yet lost its power, and they could not wake him, so they carried him out in a sheet and put him under the tree and the pigeon dropped a tear on his face; in a minute he awoke. "Can you hear me, sweet love of my heart?" asked the pigeon, "If you ever want to meet me seek for me in the town of Johara, in the country of Black Sorrow," with this she spread her wings and flew away. Her husband gazed after her for a while and then became so grieved that his heart nearly broke. What was he to do now? He took leave of all and went and hid himself. When he got outside of the gate he suddenly remembered what the giant had told him about calling to memory one of the horses; he no sooner did so than it appeared all ready saddled; he jumped upon it and thought he would like to be at the giant's gate. In a moment he was there and the giant came out to meet him. "Well, my dear son, didn't I tell you not to give that nut to anyone?" The poor lad replied, in great sorrow, "Well, my dear father, what am I to do now?" "Well, what did Fairy Elizabeth say when she took leave of you?" "She said that if ever I wished to meet her again I was to go to the town of Johara, in the country of Black Sorrow." "Alas, my son!" said the giant, "I have never even heard the name, so how could I direct you there? Be still, and come and live with me, and get on as well as you can." But the poor lad said that he would go, and he must go, in search of his wife as far as his eye could see. "Well, if you wish to go, there are two more children of my parents left, an elder brother and an elder sister. Take this; here's a mace. We three children couldn't divide it amongst us, so it was left with me. They will know by this that I have sent you; go first to my elder brother, he is the king of all creeping things; perhaps he may be able to help you." With this he drew in the dust the figure of a colt three years old, and bade him sit on it, filled his bag with provisions, and recommended him to the Lord.

The lad went on and on, over seven times seven countries, and even beyond them; he went on till the colt got so old that it lost all its teeth; at last he arrived at the residence of the king of all creeping things, went in, and greeted him, "May the Lord give you a good day, my dear father!" And the old man replied, "The Lord has brought you, my son. What is your errand?" And he replied, "I want to go to the country of Black Sorrow, into the town of Johara if ever I can find it." "Who are you?" asked the old man. With this he showed him the mace, and the king at once recognized it and said, "Ah, my dear son, I never heard the name of that town. I wish you had come last night, because all my animals were here to greet me. But stay, I will call them together again tomorrow morning, and we shall then see whether they can give us any information." Next morning the old man got up very early, took a whistle and blew it three times, and, in the twinkling of an eye all the creeping things that existed in the world came forward. He asked them, one by one, whether they knew aught of the town of Johara in the country of Black Sorrow. But they all answered that they had never seen it, and never even heard its name. So the poor lad was very sad, and did not know what to do. He went outside to saddle his horse, but the poor brute had died of old age. So the old man at once drew another in the dust, and it was again a colt three years old. He saddled it for him, filled his bag with provisions, and gave him directions where to find his elder sister.

With this the lad started off, and went over seven times seven countries, and even beyond them, till at last, very late, he arrived at the elder sister's of the giant and greeted her. She returned it; and asked him, "What is your errand?" he replied that he was going to the town of Johara in the country of Black Sorrow. "Well, my son," said the old woman, "and who has sent you to me?" "Don't you know this mace?" and she recognized it at once, and said, "Alas! my dear son, I am very pleased to see you, but I cannot direct you, because I never even heard of the place. Why did you not come last night, as all the animals were here then. But as my brother has sent you, I will call them all together again tonight, and perhaps they will be able to tell you something." With this, he went out to put his horse in the stable, and found that it had grown so old that it hadn't a single tooth left; he himself, too, was shrivelled up with age, like a piece of bacon rind, and his hair was like snow. At eve the old woman said to him, "Lie down in this bed!" when he lay down she put a heavy millstone upon him; she then took a whip, went outside the door, and cracked it. It boomed like a gun and the poor man inside was so startled that he lifted up the millstone quite a span high. "Don't be afraid, my son," called out the old woman, "I'm only going to crack it twice more," and she cracked it again; whether it sounded the first time or not, it certainly did this time, so that the poor man inside lifted the millstone quite a yard high, and called out to the old woman not to crack that whip again, or he should certainly die on the spot. But she cracked it again, notwithstanding, and it sounded so loud, that whether the first two sounded or not, this time it sounded so loud that the poor man kicked the millstone right up to the ceiling. After that the old woman went in and said to him, "You can get up now, as I am not going to crack my whip any more." So he got up at once, and she went and opened the window, and left the door wide open too. At once it became quite dark, the animals came in such clouds that they quite obscured the sunlight; she let them in one by one through the window, and read out the name of each one of them from a list, and asked them if they knew where the country of Black Sorrow was, but nobody knew it; so she dismissed them and shut the window and door. The poor man was very sad now; he didn't know what to do next or where he was to go. "There is nothing more to be done," said the old woman; "but I will give you a colt, and fill your bag full of provisions, and in heaven's name go back where you have come from."

They were still consulting when somebody knocked at the window and the old woman called out, "Who's that?" "It is I, my dear queen," replied a bird; and she began to scold it for being so late; but still she let it in, hoping that it might tell them something. Lo! it was a lame woodpecker. "Why are you so late?" she demanded, and the bird replied that it was because it had such a bad foot. "Where did you get your leg broken?" inquired the old woman. "In Johara, in the country of Black Sorrow." "You are just the one we want," said the old woman; "I command you to take this man on your back without delay and to carry him to the very town where you have come from." The woodpecker began to make excuses and said that it would rather not go there lest they should break the other leg also; but the old woman stamped with her foot, and so it was obliged to obey and at once set off with the man on its back, whose third horse had already died; on they went over seven times seven countries, and even beyond them, till they came to a very high mountain, so high that it reached to heaven.

"Now then," said the woodpecker, "you had better get down here, as we cannot get over this." "Well, but," said the poor man, "how did you get over it?" "I? Through a hole." "Well then, take me also through a hole." Then the woodpecker began to make excuses, that it could not take him, first urging this reason and then that; so the poor man got angry with the woodpecker, and began to dig his spurs into the bird's ribs saying, "Go on, you must take me, and don't talk so much; it was you who stole the golden wheat-ear from my stack." So what could the poor woodpecker do but carry him. They arrived in the country of Black Sorrow, and stopped in the very town of Johara. Then he sent the woodpecker away, and went straight into the palace where Fairy Elizabeth lived. As he entered Fairy Elizabeth sat on a golden sofa; he greeted her, and told her he had come to claim her as his wife. "Is that why you have come?" replied she. "Surely you don't expect me to be your wife; an old bent, shrivelled-up man like you. I will give you meat and drink, and then in heaven's name go back to where you have come from." Hearing this the poor man became very sad and didn't know what to do, and began to cry bitterly; but in the meantime (not letting him know) Fairy Elizabeth had ordered her maids to go out at once and gather all sorts of rejuvenating plants, and to bring some youth-giving water, and to prepare a bath for him as quickly as possible. Then she turned to the old man again, and, in order to chaff him, said, "How can you wish a beautiful young girl like me to marry such an ugly old man as you? Be quick, eat, drink, and go back to where you have come from." In his sorrow the poor man's heart was nearly broken, when all at once Fairy Elizabeth said to him, "Well, dearest love of my youth, so that you may not say that I am ungrateful to you for having taken the trouble to come to me, and made all this long journey for me, I will give you a bath." She motioned to the maids, they at once seized him, undressed him, and put him into the tub; in a moment he was a young man again a hundred times handsomer than he was in his youth; and while they were bathing him they brought from a shop numerous costly dresses and clothed him with them and took him to Fairy Elizabeth; man and wife embraced and kissed each other again and again, and once more celebrated a grand marriage festival, going through all the ceremonies again; after all this was over they got into a carriage drawn by six horses, and went to live with the giant, their father, but they never went again, not even once, to the place where he had been betrayed. The giant received them with great joy, and they are still alive to this day, if they haven't died since. May they be your guests tomorrow!

Uletka and the White Lizard

IN A CERTAIN COUNTRY, there dwelt a prince whose name was Elkàbo. He had a dear little daughter called Uletka, who was a most sweet child. She and her father lived quite alone in an old castle with four towers, that stood in a beautiful glade in the centre of a great forest.

Uletka was a most dainty and lovely little maid, her wings – she had wings, being related to a fairy – had grown quite strong, and glistened in the sunshine, reflecting all the colours of the rainbow. So sweet and graceful was little Uletka, that perhaps you would imagine she had no faults. Unfortunately she had one, which a wicked and revengeful fairy, who was offended with Nastia, her mother, had endowed her with, and this was the dreadful fault of Curiosity.

This wicked fairy, whose name was Mutà, had done even worse than this. She it was who had lured poor Nastia to destruction. In the forest was a great lake, overshadowed by trees, and covered over with water-lilies and lotus, while round its edge grew tall rushes. One day, when Nastia was walking by the shore of this lake, Mutà hid herself in the water, and calling out for help, pretended she was in danger of drowning. Nastia crept out on the great leaves of the water-lilies and grasped Mutà's hands, whereupon the spiteful fairy dragged her down to the bottom. Poor Nastia could not swim, besides which, Mutà held both her hands. She tried to struggle and to call for help, but it was useless, and thus she drowned. Prince Elkàbo, her husband, and all the neighbours, searched for her everywhere, and when they reached the edge of the lake they saw her body floating far off among the lotus flowers. As they watched she slowly changed into a most beautiful snow-white water-lily.

Elkàbo wept bitterly, and even the birds ceased to sing. A kingfisher, who was sitting on a flag-leaf, cried out to him that it was the work of the wicked fairy, Mutà. Then Elkàbo mounted his horse and quickly sought audience of the Queen of the Fairies, who lived at the furthest end of the country in a palace of crystal that had been erected among the mountains. He told her and all her courtiers, wise men and magicians, what misfortune had befallen him. Mutà's evil deed excited general indignation throughout the court, and the Queen ordered that the fairy should be transformed into a white lizard, which her head magician immediately proceeded to do. Then Her Majesty decreed that if Elkàbo could catch the lizard, he might be allowed to retain it captive until his little daughter, Uletka, who was then a baby, should release it with her own hands. In the event of this happening not even the Fairy Queen herself could prevent Mutà from resuming her natural form, together with her evil powers.

So Elkàbo returned home and searched day and night, travelling far and wide, until, at last, far away in Japan, he found the white lizard, hidden away under a cluster of orchids. He captured it and fastened it in a little cage made of silver wire, and every day he fed it himself, and would let no one else come near it. But as time went on Elkàbo grow afraid that Uletka might open the cage, as she was such a very inquisitive little girl. So he built a small tower near the edge of the lake, and there hung the cage, and every day he went down to the tower and fed the lizard with his own hands. The key of the tower he always wore suspended from his neck by a little gold chain, and no one but himself knew the secret of the tower by the lake.

Now Uletka was excessively curious, and often she would wander round the tower and turn the handle of the door, and fret because she always found it locked. She dared not ask her father any more about it, for she had done so once, and then she thought that she never had seen her dear, kind father so angry before.

At last, one day, Elkàbo was obliged to go on a journey, and as Uletka was getting quite a big girl, he felt he could safely entrust her with the key of the tower. He was going to be away two or three days, and told her that in the meanwhile she must go up every day to the tower and take with her a small bowl of bread. Uletka promised to obey her father implicitly, and really meant to keep her promise. Nevertheless, no sooner had Elkàbo departed than Uletka, unable to check her curiosity, started off to see the wonderful lizard in the tower by the lake. She opened the door with a trembling hand, and there, in a cage made entirely of silver wire, was the loveliest lizard she had ever seen. It ran up and down the cage and played with a straw that Uletka held out. She was quite enchanted, and remained a long time watching it play.

"What a lovely fairy you are," the lizard said suddenly.

Uletka was not at all astonished at hearing the lizard talk. It was so very pretty, that she at once knew it must be a fairy in disguise.

"Oh! I am not a fairy," said Uletka, modestly. "I am only a little girl, and am living with my father, Prince Elkàbo, at the palace yonder."

"How funny," said the lizard, "I made sure you were a fairy, you had such pretty wings; I am a fairy you know, my name is Mutà. What is yours?"

"My name is Uletka."

"What a pretty name," said the wily lizard. "I am sure I could easily make you into a fairy if I only had my magic cloak here. I would throw it over your shoulders, and you would become one immediately, and have the power to appear or disappear at will, turn into a tiny mouse, or a monstrous giant, and, in fact, go anywhere, and see everything just as you chose."

"Oh!" said Uletka, excitedly, "tell me where our magic cloak is, I will fetch it for you. I do so long to be a fairy. Do you really think I could become one?"

"There is no doubt about it," said the lizard; "my cloak would soon turn a pretty little girl like you into a fairy. Dear me, dear me, if I only could get out, I know exactly where to find it, together with the necessary wand. Hobo, the king of the gnomes, once hid it in a rose-bush, out of spite, and changed me into a lizard, and locked me up in a cage, so that I should not be able to get at it. But I know where it is, and if you will help me to get out you shall become a great and powerful fairy."

In one moment Uletka quite forgot her promise to her father, and only thought of the delights of becoming a real fairy, and being able to go where she liked, and see and know everything. She opened the cage, and the lizard jumped out. In an instant it changed into a fairy, with raven hair, and great flashing eyes, dressed in a garment of black gauze, all covered over with golden stars. She turned on Uletka, tore her pretty clothes, and broke her dainty wings. Laughing at her for her vanity and curiosity in thinking she could ever become a fairy, she drove her along into the forest, right to the other side of the lake, all among the dark trees, where she had never been before; then the wicked fairy vanished, and left her lying on the ground, weeping bitterly.

After poor little Uletka had been there some time she thought she heard her name softly whispered by the wind; then it sounded more distinctly, breathed in a sweet, sad voice, like a flower sighing. Uletka stalked gently towards the sound, and it grew louder and louder, until it seemed as if the trees murmured her name, one to another, and as she reached again the enchanted lake the voice rose from the waters, calling "Uletka! Uletka!"

As she stood listening, spellbound, the petals of a magnificent water-lily unfolded, and disclosed a fairy form of exquisite beauty, the spirit of her mother – Nastia. She beckoned to Uletka to approach, which the little girl did, stepping on the great flat leaves of the lilies. Nastia then told her to go into the forest, past the silver poplars and the enchanted palm-tree, till she found a great beech standing all alone. There she would find friends, and be safe from the power of the cruel Mutà, who otherwise would be certain to pursue her.

Uletka then knelt on the lily-leaves, and kissed her mother among the silver petals, then slowly saw them fold, hiding her mother from her view.

Away she sped, quickly past the poplars and the enchanted palm tree, till she was so tired and her feet so sore that she could hardly walk, but at last she came up to the tall solitary beech, standing towering above all the other trees of the forest. She went round it, and there in the very centre of the trunk, she discovered a little door. She knocked, but no one came; only the squirrels chattered together and called, "Who is that knocking at the Gnomes' door? whilst a blackbird echoing, said, "Yes; who can that be knocking at the Gnomes' door?"

At last, Uletka, tired of knocking, turned the little handle and went in. There, right in the very heart of the tree was a room with nine little chairs, and a table carved out of the wood of the tree, and on the table were dishes and spoons of wood, and a great feast of nuts, berries and other kinds of fruit, and large bowls full of delicious honey.

So, as Uletka was very hungry, she sat down and ate some honey and nuts, after which, feeling much better, she lay down on the floor and fell asleep...

When she awoke she was surrounded by a number of little men, with funny faces all laughing and looking at her; some of them were pulling her hair and saying, "Yes, yes, we know you; you are Uletka, you have let the wicked fairy, Mutà, escape. If she finds you she will kill you, but you are quite safe with us, therefore with us you must stay."

And the birds outside sang in chorus, "Yes, yes; it is little Uletka, Prince Elkàbo's child!" and then twittered all the more to show their gratification at her safety.

Uletka stayed with the Gnomes in the tree. Mutà could not hurt her there, for it belonged to Hobo, the King of the Gnomes, who reigned supreme in the forest. Every day the little Gnomes gathered nuts and acorns for their dinner. The shells of these they cut into cups and goblets. Sometimes the grass-elves would come and dine with them, and after dinner they all danced round the tree in the moonlight, while the white owl on the tree-top called "te-whit, te-whoo! te-whit, te-whoo!"

The little Gnomes manufactured a chair for Uletka, and carved a plate for her out of the shell of a hazelnut. They made her a spoon of white fir-wood, and wove garments for her out of cobwebs. She lived in the tree with the good little fellows, and made their garments from the fibres of dead leaves, which looked like the finest lace, using the thorn of a wild rose for a needle. Every day she laid the table for their dinner, and did all the house-work. She was kept busy all the day, though sometimes she would lie in the grass and talk to the violets, who smiled and nodded their dainty heads. She was good friends with every one in the forest; even the tall fox-glove nodded to her as she ran past him. The squirrel who lived at the top of the tree would crack nuts for her. A green and gold beetle was her particular friend. He would carry her on his back as he flew about the wood. But the blackbird loved her most of all, and sat and sang to her all day.

The good little Gnomes were continually trying to invent new games and pastimes in order to distract her thoughts. They composed new music, which they played on their funny little instruments made of wood, with fibres for strings, and danced new dances for her all day long. They also built her a most beautiful little summer house, thatched with rose leaves, where she could rest after having seen to the wants of her kind protectors. But poor little Uletka was not happy, for she could not help thinking of her poor mother and father, who would no doubt be so anxious and lonely without her, and she bitterly repented her curiosity which had placed her in this fearful position. She also thought of the wicked old fairy Mutà, who had been so cruel to her and caused her all this pain; and then she would cry bitterly, and wonder whether she would ever see her beautiful home with the four towers.

As her kind protectors did everything they could to make her feel contented, she did not let them see that she was pining for her home, as she knew that if they thought she was not happy, they would be quite miserable.

One day King Hobo called together a lot of his subjects and told them that early in the morning he intended starting on a grand beechnut hunting expedition in a distant part of the wood, where he had never been before, and commanded them to get ready so as to make an early start. Uletka was up betimes to see her little friends start, and promised to have a nice supper ready for them on their return.

King Hobo led his little army deep into the forest, and soon all were busy looking for the nuts. Suddenly one of them called out: "Oh, I have found such a beautiful stone, but it is so large I cannot move it, come and help me!" Some friends ran up to help him and after much digging, puffing and blowing they managed to dig it up. When Hobo saw it he exclaimed, "Why, that is a Diamond, and the largest I have ever seen. We will carry it home and give it to Uletka." But the diamond was so heavy that it took two of the strongest gnomes to carry it.

As it was the largest diamond ever discovered they held a great feast in honour of the event. The tables, covered with the good things prepared by Uletka, were spread all round the pine trees, and invitations were at once sent out to all their friends.

Among the guests who came were the frogs from the pond by the willows, who were accompanied by their fat cousins, old Mr and Mrs. Toad, a lot of grass-elves and little wood goblins; then there also came the large family of mice and the squirrels, all the birds and beetles, to say nothing of all the moths, the butterflies, the bees and the ants.

After every one had satisfied their hunger (and very little was left on the tables) a great concert was held, at which all the birds sang, but Uletka's friend, the blackbird, sang louder than any of the others to try and cheer her up, for he saw she did not feel quite happy. Then King Hobo asked Uletka to dance with him, the Gnomes keeping time by clapping their wooden cymbals. And so they kept up the gaiety until the bats and the white owl came out, when every one hurried off home, especially the mouse family, who were afraid that the owl might take a liking to one of them for supper. So soon everything was quiet in the forest and no one could guess that just before there had been such goings on under the pine trees.

Yet, in spite of all this gaiety, Uletka's sadness daily increased. She seemed to long more intently than ever for her home. At last her friend the blackbird, could not help noticing this, and determined, if possible, to help the little girl to whom he was so attached; so, one day, he flew to the palace of the Fairy Queen, far away beyond the great mountains.

And as Her Majesty was sitting at supper with all her court the blackbird arrived, and humbly begged she would graciously hear his request. Then he told her that he had a very dear little friend, Uletka, the daughter of Prince Elkàbo. She was so sweet, so loving, and so winning that all the birds and beasts in the forest were in love with her, and entirely devoted themselves to making her happy. But Uletka was a dear affectionate little girl, and although she was made so much of, as the guest of Hobo, King of the Gnomes, and was worshipped there almost like a queen, yet she could not manage to be happy, for she loved her father dearly, and knew he was longing for her company again. He (the blackbird) could not bear to see his little friend pining away like this, and had come to beg Her Majesty, the Queen of the Fairies, to help him.

Prince Repto, the Queen's son, heard the blackbird's story with wonder and delight, he thought he never heard anything so beautifully romantic. Immediately he begged his royal mother to allow him to go off with the blackbird, and bring little Uletka home with him, and make her his wife. The queen, who was very kind-hearted, and quite genuinely interested in Uletka, and in frustrating the wicked Mutà's plans, readily gave her consent, and Prince Repto, accompanied by the blackbird, started off for the kingdom of Hobo and his gnomes.

When he arrived it was late at night, the moon was shining brightly, and there, at the foot of the pine-tree he suddenly caught sight of Uletka. She was sitting on a large toadstool, while all the little gnomes were dancing round her, to the tune of harps played by the grass-elves, and the tinkling of the blue bells. Prince Repto had never seen such a beautiful princess before, and at once fell in love with her. Just at that moment Uletka looked up and saw the Prince, she gave a little cry in which fear and admiration were mingled at seeing such a handsome stranger. "Do not be alarmed, Princess," said Prince Repto, advancing and doffing his cap, "I have come to your aid," and then seating himself on a little toadstool at her feet he told her who he was, and how if she would consent he would marry her, when she would be one of the highest in Fairyland, and live with him in a palace of gold, where the wicked Mutà would be powerless to harm her.

This was rather premature for the first meeting, and Uletka was a little startled; but the Prince looked so very handsome, and was dressed so charmingly, the prospect also was so dazzling, that she did not hesitate long, more especially as it was so natural for her to love him, when, in addition to all these good qualities, he had taken so much trouble to win her. She therefore soon consented, much to the delight of the Prince and all the gnomes.

Prince Repto gave Hobo a crown of gold, and made him king of all the woods in the world, to reward him for his kindness to Uletka; all the gnomes clapped their hands, which sounded like twigs crackling, and the elves played a tune of joy, and sang a love song. There never was such rejoicing in the forest. And although it was long after their usual bedtime, all the birds stayed up and sang the most beautiful songs, so glad were they that dear little Uletka would at last be free from trouble; the nightingale and lark had a special duet together, which was the most beautiful music that is possible. But the sweetest song of all and the one that Uletka enjoyed the most, was the one that was sung by her little friend the blackbird, who had been the happy means of bringing her this good fortune. And in after years the blackbird was always a welcome guest in Uletka's home.

The next morning when the sun was shining brightly, the prince brought a beautiful coach made of a seashell; it was drawn by six white doves; he placed Uletka in it, then sat beside her, and all the gnomes gave a loud cheer as the coach rose high in the air, bearing the happy pair to the fairy kingdom beyond the trees. On the way they stopped, so that Uletka might kiss her dear father, who still dwelt in the castle with the four towers. They took him with them to Fairyland, where there were more festivities and rejoicings in honour of the wedding, and Repto and Uletka have lived happily together ever since. Hobo and the gnomes, and the frogs, and the squirrels, and the blackbird often go to see them, but nothing more has been heard of the wicked fairy Mutà.

Forget-me-not

IN THE GOOD OLD DAYS, many many thousands of years ago, you must know that this world was inhabited by various little fairies, gnomes, elves, and such-like funny little creatures; beasts could talk like rational human beings, even better than most human beings can talk now-adays; and in every flower there dwelt a little fairy, who sang sweet songs, and in every tuft of grass little elves played to and fro.

In those days there were no cities, roads, or houses; no big human creatures erected big buildings, drained rivers, or built railroads; everything was peaceful and quiet; wild animals lived happily in the forests, for the little fairies never dreamt of hunting or killing them for mere sport, and the fairy flowers grew in luxurious splendour, for the wild beasts did not pluck or cast them away.

In those days, somewhere in the world – I don't think I can tell you exactly where, for it is such a very long time ago – there stood in the midst of the forest a most beautiful lake, surrounded on all sides by graceful rushes, and covered with water-lilies and lotus. This lake was so clear and beautiful that all the little fairies who dwelt in the rushes and grasses round the lake used to come every morning and sit on the water-lilies, while they looked at themselves in the waters of the lake, which reflected their dainty little forms like a mirror.

It was a very truthful mirror too, for the little goldfishes, who dwelt in the lake, gave their opinion very impartially as to the beauty of the various little faces that peeped down at them from above. Sometimes they would argue down below as to the merits of one or the other beauty; then there was great splashing and disturbance in the waters, which amused the little fairies very much, and they would all shout as loudly as possible:

"Goldfish, goldfish, living under the lake,
who will the prize for beauty take?"

Of course you may imagine that opinions on this point among the little goldfish differed very much, and yet there were some days when they were absolutely unanimous, and those were the days when the beautiful fairy princess, Narcissa, came to the lake, and kneeling on one of the lily leaves, looked down into the clear waters, while she combed her golden hair and sang in the sweetest of voices:

"Goldfish, goldfish, tell me where
Is the fairest of the fair?"

Then all the little fish and all the little sprites would skip out of the water merrily, and sing with one accord:

"Of beauteous fairies 'neath the skies,
Princess Narcissa takes the prize."

And Narcissa would go home happy and proud, with her head held well erect, for all around her the birds and beasts would do her homage. Wherever she walked the little birds would flutter round her to whisper sweet words of praise in her ears; the little frogs and rabbits would stop in their play to watch her pass; and all the little gnomes and grass elves would march before her in state, as if she were a queen.

Now I am sorry to say all this praise and admiration had a very bad effect on Narcissa. She grew haughtier and more conceited every day, and, in consequence idler and more disagreeable at home, so that her father and mother were made quite unhappy by their daughter's vanity, till at last it became almost unendurable. She used to go out morning, noon, and night, and sit for hours on the water-lily leaves, looking at her own reflection in the water, and hearing the waves, the winds, the flowers, the beasts, all murmur in concert: "Princess Narcissa is the most beautiful of all the fairies in the world!"

One day, when her poor fairy mother was thus left sitting all alone in her beautiful palace among the bulrushes, after seeing her daughter go off on her usual journey, she suddenly caught sight, near the edge of the lake, of a lovely little cluster of forget-me-nots. So sweet and modest did they look, and withal so exquisitely lovely in colour, that she sighed regretfully, and said, "Oh, how I wish I had another, a tiny blue-eyed daughter, modest and sweet, who would be a comfort to me."

Now the Fairy Queen, who always hears the wishes of all her subjects, heard the poor mother's cry, and shortly after presented her with a nice little daughter, with lovely golden curls all round her tiny head, and such beautiful blue eyes that looked so sweetly out into the world, that her mother and father were almost beside themselves for joy, and named her "Forget-me-not," because she resembled those dainty little flowers.

The haughty Princess Narcissa did not take very much notice of her baby sister just at first; she was too much occupied with herself and her own beauty, inventing new garments for her little person, and new jewellery for her hair. She used to tease and torment her occasionally, though, especially when Forget-me-not began to grow up, compelling her to dress her hair, fasten her dress, and altogether using her as a sort of servant to help to administer to her own adornment. But Forget-me-not was so modest and unassuming, and really looked upon her older sister as a creature of such exquisite loveliness that she gladly did all that Narcissa wished, and even tried to invent all sorts of pretty new contrivances to further enhance her beauty.

This went on for some time; Forget-me-not was growing up very rapidly, and every day she seemed to grow in beauty, as well as in goodness; her hair was now long and glistened like gold, her skin was fine and transparent, as only fairy skin can be, and her eyes were tenderer and bluer than the little flowers after whom she was named. Her father and mother were now perfectly happy, for their little daughter was all the comfort in the world to them. When Narcissa had finished her toilet in the morning, and gone off to the enchanted lake, followed by her crowd of admirers, little Forget-me-not would go about the house singing merrily, chatting to her father, and helping her mother to spin and sew.

The little creature had never been outside her father's garden, she had never seen any one, except her father, and mother, and sister, so she really did not know how beautiful she was, for the latter had no eyes for any one save herself, and the former had such a dread and horror of vanity creeping up in their darling's heart, that they were particularly careful never to speak on the subject before her.

One day, when Forget-me-not was running about in the garden, she saw a beautiful bright-eyed butterfly lying on the grass. She drew near on tiptoe to have a better look, when the butterfly spread out his wings and flew off to the other end of the garden. Forget-me-not ran after him, for she had never seen such a lovely creature before – all blue and silver, with great dark spots, like eyes. Hardly had she, however, come near enough to him, when the butterfly again flew off; this time far to the other side of the garden gates. Forget-me-not was tempted to follow him, and so she ran on and on till she saw him apparently settle on a water-lily leaf, and then disappear from her view.

Little Forget-me-not, who had now reached the edge of the lake, was determined to see where the beautiful butterfly had disappeared to, so, treading softly on the lotus and lily leaves, she looked round her, and then into the clear waters of the lake, but no butterfly could she see; only as she was looking a whole crowd of little goldfish and water sprites (things she had never seen in all her life before) rose from out of the water, and, forming a circle round the leaf on which she stood, they bowed low before her, and sang in the sweetest chorus she had ever heard:

"Forget-me-not, lovely blue-eyed Forget-me-not,
Fairest far of all the lot."

She could hardly tear herself away from them, so beautifully did they all sing, till finally a little goldfish swam quite close to her, and asked her if she would honour him by getting on his back, and allowing him to swim with her to shore, which she did, as she did not like to wound his feelings by refusing so courteous an offer, but she felt very frightened at this altogether new mode of locomotion, and also very upset and shy at being suddenly so surrounded and admired by a crowd of unknown beings.

When she got to shore she was still so nervous that she quite forgot to thank the goldfish and water sprites for their lovely music, and ran home as fast as her fairy legs could carry her, and into her mother's arms, who was very much upset when she heard the whole story, for she felt that evil would come of this if Narcissa were to know.

The next day Narcissa got up and dressed, or rather made Forget-me-not dress her as usual; she was not yet tired of all the admiration her beauty always roused wherever she passed, and she still loved as dearly as ever to gaze at her own reflection in the lake, and provoke its inhabitants into songs of praise. On this particular morning she had made herself look lovelier than ever, and she stepped out of her mother's garden, anxiously peering round for the squirrels, who always greeted her approach joyfully, and escorted her to the edge of the lake with many a bow of admiration and envy. However, this morning the squirrels were not to be seen, she could hear them in the distance holding an animated discussion, but not one of the little faces peeped down at her, and Narcissa thought it very strange that they should think other matters more interesting than the sight of her.

She ran down to the lake, and stepped on the broad water-lily leaves, then sitting on one of the pink blossoms the little vain fairy peeped down at her dainty image. How pretty she was! with her fairy figure, her milk-white skin and rosy lips, her graceful arms bent over her head, while she combed her golden hair with a pearl comb, while her garments, made of moon-beams, shone like silver, and made her appear like a bright jewel in the heart of the lotus flower.

Very soon a large crowd of gold and silver fish had gathered round her, and funny round eyes and gaping mouths peered at her from the green depths below. But instead of the usual chorus of admiration with which they usually greeted her, she found herself apparently the object of an extraordinary curiosity. The fishes appeared to be whispering to each other, then looking at her with their funny wise heads held on one side, till Narcissa could bear the suspense no longer, and she sang in her sweetest tones:

"Goldfish, goldfish, tell me where,
Is the fairest of the fair?"

Then, to her horror and dismay, a mischievous-looking little water sprite rose to the surface and said:

"Although Narcissa very beauteous be,
Forget-me-not is fairer far than she."

Then the whole chorus of fishes echoed:

"Yes, Forget-me-not, little blue-eyed Forget-me-not, is fairer far than she."

Narcissa could hardly believe her own ears. Forget-me-not! ugly little Forget-me-not! Why, she had never been outside her mother's garden! The fishes could never have seen her, and if they had, why, surely there was no comparison between the lovely Narcissa, more beautiful than the Fairy Queen herself, and this tiny, unpretentious little sister of hers. And yet the goldfish would keep on singing:

"Have you seen Forget-me-not,
Fairest far of all the lot?"

Narcissa went ashore, and in a rage picked up some pebbles and pelted the fishes and water sprites with them, but they did not care; they dived down to the very bottom of the lake and re-appeared again, still singing:

"Forgot-me-not, lovely Forget-me-not."

The enraged little fairy ran off as fast as she could. As she passed the rushes where all the frogs had congregated she heard them croaking:

"Little Forget-me-not with blue eyes grand – Quack, quack, quack.
Is loveliest in Fairyland – Quack, quack, quack."

Through the woods she ran, where her friends, the squirrels, always used to pay her homage; now they were running up and down the trees in a great state of excitement, and shouting to each other:

"Have you seen Forget-me-not, the loveliest of all the lot?"

This was too much for Narcissa altogether. She rushed through her mother's garden, up the steps, to where little Forget-me-not sat spinning a dress of spiders' webs. She was quite startled when she saw her sister rush in in so frantic a manner. Narcissa took hold of her hand, told her to leave her spinning and come with her.

Little Forget-me-not was so accustomed to do as she was told that she obeyed, and followed her sister, though she felt very frightened. On the two fairies ran, Narcissa dragging her little sister after her, till they came to an old dried-up well, which led down to the centre of the earth.

"Now," said Narcissa, "I have dropped my spindle in this well, and cannot finish my spinning; you must jump down and fetch it for me."

"But," said little Forget-me-not, "the well is so deep; mother says it has no bottom. I should not know where to look for your spindle."

"If you don't jump down immediately and do as you are told I will throw you in, for I am stronger than you," said Narcissa, and her eyes glittered with rage so that she looked quite ugly.

What was poor little Forget-me-not to do? She was all alone with her wicked sister, and no chance for any one to come and help her, so she thought of her dear mother as she stood one moment hesitating on the brink of the well; then, suddenly Narcissa gave her a push, and down she fell – down, down, down. It was pitch dark round her; she seemed to be floating in absolute space, and the last thing she remembered as she lost consciousness in her terror, was, high up above, a little speck of light, and Narcissa's wicked little face peering down at her and laughing triumphantly.

And so she fell lower and lower yet, the darkness grew more and more intense, and then all of a sudden a ray of light began to penetrate from a long way down below; this little thin streak of light encroached more and more upon the darkness. Little Forget-me-not re-opened her eyes, and suddenly found herself in full daylight on the edge of another well, with tall, over-hanging trees round her; she clambered up and looked round, she was in a strange part of the world, that was very evident, curiously shaped trees and plants surrounded her, flowers she had never seen before, but still they were trees and flowers, and as such Forget-me-not was not frightened at them, but still she did not dare venture through the thick masses of undergrowth, through which even her fairy-like little form could not have always found a passage. She felt very lonely and miserable, and longed for her dear mother, and her own familiar flowers; this was a very strange country, where perhaps she never would meet a friend who would be kind to her, and take her home. Poor little fairy, she sat down and cried, till the great sobs shook her little form, and her heart ached as if it would break.

Suddenly she heard a shrill voice quite close to her, calling her by her name,

"Forget-me-not, Forget-me-not, why do you cry?"

The little fairy, looked up in wonder, and there, standing before her, was the funniest little old woman she ever saw, her face was such a mass of wrinkles that you could not see any of the features, the eyes were hidden by deep furrows and ridges, the mouth appeared like a long narrow slit, only the nose, a very big hook nose, was so prominent and long that it quite frightened poor little Forget-me-not.

Her head was very huge, and seemed much too heavy for the small shrivelled body, all bent as if over-weighted with age. She had large bony hands and feet, with long nails like a bird's claws, and there she stood, blinking at the pretty little fairy, like an old hawk staring at a sparrow.

"Why do you cry?" the old woman repeated impatiently, as poor little Forget-me-not seemed unable to answer, but only stared at her in fear and astonishment.

"Oh," sobbed the poor little fairy, "I am so lonely and so miserable; my sister pushed me down a well, and I have fallen so deep down that now I don't the least bit know where I am, and my poor dear mother at home must be crying after me, and wondering where I am, and I don't remember the way I came here, so I cannot go back. Dear, good, kind fairy, if you are a fairy, take me back to my mother, and I will do anything in the world to serve and help you if I can."

"I don't know that I want to take you back to your mother," the old fairy said, "and I am sure you can be of no possible use to me, so I don't see why I should trouble my head about you at all."

"But I can spin and sew for you," Forget-me-not said eagerly, noticing the funny old green rags in which the old woman was clad, "and I can cook most dainty dishes, and scrub the floors, and dress your hair, in fact, I can make myself most useful about a house, and like doing all kinds of work."

"H'm," said the ugly old fairy, "I have been looking out for a young servant for some time, and you do seem pretty active and willing"... "Well," she said, "if you will come with me and be my maid, attend to my household and look after me, I will undertake to help and protect you. Will you agree to that?"

"But," said little Forget-me-not, "that will never do. I have no other wish but to go back to my dear mother, and go on living my own quiet happy life, and if I go to be your servant, what use is all protection in the world to me, while I know my dear ones at home are mourning for me, and think that I am dead?"

"Well, you can please yourself," said the little old woman, "I have told you under what conditions I will help and protect you, if they don't suit you you can leave them alone, or rather, I will leave you alone, for I am busy, and don't mean to stand here talking with you any longer. If you change your mind, clap your hands three times, and you will see me again. Goodbye."

Saying which, the old fairy hobbled off, leaning on her heavy stick, and laughing maliciously at poor little Forget-me-not, who was left more desolate and lonely than before.

Evening was drawing on rapidly, the forest around grew darker and darker, every moment the poor little fairy began to feel very frightened. She heard strange sounds around her, and great luminous eyes seemed to be staring at her from out the darkness. The moon now rose and shed a soft mysterious light on the strange landscape, and curious little beings, grass-elves and wood-nymphs, came out, skipping and dancing merrily round the now terrified little form. She began to feel that if she spent a whole night here by herself she would die with fright. If only her dear mother could hear her and come to her rescue, or even if the malicious old fairy would be here to keep her company. She felt that anything would be better than stay alone a moment longer, so she clapped her little hands three times, and in a moment, as if she had sprung out of the earth, there stood the funny old woman in her green rags, leaning on her stick. "Oh, take me away from here!" poor Forget-me-not cried. "I will be your servant and do anything you like, but I cannot stay here any longer by myself. I should die of fright."

"Very well," said the old fairy; "you must come with me to my palace, but remember, you are to do everything I tell you, and help me to spin, sew, and cook, and to reward you l will help you and give you shelter."

"Well, then, you must help me now to let my mother know that I am quite safe, and will come back to her as soon as I can."

The old fairy waved her stick three times over her head, and a huge frog carne jumping apparently from nowhere, and waited for orders. "Send any message you like," the old fairy said, "and this frog will convey it to your mother before daybreak."

"Please, Mr Frog," said Forget-me-not, "go to my dear mother and tell her that I am still alive. Narcissa pushed me down the well, but a kind fairy has rescued me, and I am going to be her little servant until she releases me."

"Croak, croak," said the frog, and disappeared from view.

"Now," said the old fairy, "you must come home with me at once, and make the beds for the night. My son will be waiting for me, and you must help to make everything comfortable for him at home."

She again waved her stick, and presently two bats came flying along, each carrying a broomstick. The old fairy mounted the one, and told Forget-me-not to get on to the other and follow her.

Away she flew, high up over the trees. Forget-me-not felt very frightened and uncomfortable, as she had never travelled on a broomstick before. However, the journey was not a very long one, and presently the two fairies landed opposite a most gorgeous palace, made entirely of glass. Through the walls one could see the long suites of exquisite rooms, with crystal domes and golden pillars. But not a soul was visible anywhere, neither in the palace nor in the beautiful moonlit grounds, the whole palace glittering in the moonlight, surrounded with gigantic trees and exquisitely-scented flower beds, wore a fearfully deserted look, and Forget-me-not wondered more and more about the curious old fairy who went about in rags, and owned such a magnificent though solitary abode. As she stepped off her broomstick and helped her mistress to alight she caught sight, in one of the gorgeous halls, of a sumptuously-laid-out feast, beautiful gold and silver dishes filled with the rarest fruits, and wine in diamond goblets. And there, alone, having a lonely meal, sat the handsomest fairy prince she could imagine. Little Forget-me-not could not take her eyes off him, he had such a lovely face, though he looked very dejected and melancholy in his loveliness.

"That is my son," said the old fairy. "I am very proud of him, as he is the handsomest prince in all fairyland, but I don't want him to marry, as then, of course, he would have to leave me. That is why I won't allow a living thing to come anywhere near my palace, for fear they should captivate his fancy, and put thoughts of marriage into his head. As for a bird, I won't have one near the place, as they will chirrup of nothing else but love and home. I have had no servant or attendant entirely on that account, and have been obliged to go about in rags, and eat nothing but nuts and fruit, as I had no one to spin, or sew, or cook for me. Bats and frogs are the only creatures I will tolerate, as I don't think there is the faintest chance of my son falling in love with one of them. I have an old bat's skin somewhere up in my room, you will have to wear that all day, while my son is at home, you may only take it off for three hours after midnight, as then he always goes to sleep, and there is no fear of his seeing you."

Little Forget-me-not did not at all relish the idea of going about all day with a horrible old bat's skin on her, but of course she could say nothing, she had to do as her mistress told her.

The old fairy hobbled up the grand glass staircase, and presently returned carrying the skin. She made Forget-me-not put it on, and her own mother would not have recognized in this old grey bat her pretty blue-eyed little daughter.

The old fairy then told her that she might go to bed and rest for the remainder of the night, she would find her room at the top of one of the towers, and little Forget-me-not, now thoroughly tired and worn out, went up a long winding staircase, till she came to a nice little room, with a clean bed of straw, where she lay herself down, and immediately dropped into a long heavy sleep, where she forgot all about the well, the bats, the broomsticks, the little old woman, and even the handsome fairy prince.

The next morning she was up quite early, dressed herself in her bat's skin, and went downstairs. She cooked the breakfast for the prince and his mother, and all day she was kept busy, sewing and spinning new dresses in place of the fairy's old rags. She had to wait at all the meals too, and oh! it made her quite miserable to see the handsome prince sitting at table, looking so dejected and lonely, with no one to talk to, except his ugly old mother; there seemed to be such longing in his eyes when he looked round him, and saw nothing but ugly beings, frogs, bats or spiders; even the new servant was only another old bat, his eyes seemed to quite ache for something beautiful to look at, and his ears for sweet sounds. Forget-me-not quite longed to tell him of all the lovely things in nature, of the birds, the squirrels, and the butterflies, and also of all the beautiful fairies, of which she herself was one, but she was pledged to the old woman, and was never allowed to take off her disfiguring garment, so she was obliged to hold her peace.

Day after day passed off in solitude for little Forget-me-not, her mistress was very kind to her in her old grim way, but watched over all her movements most rigidly, for fear she should ever speak to the prince. At night only, for three hours after midnight, was the little fairy, allowed to wander freely about the castle and the park, unencumbered by the heavy skin, clad in her pretty dress of cobwebs; she would then run down to the edge of a little neighbouring stream, and gather her little namesakes to weave pretty garlands for her hair, then she would sit on the bank and talk to the frogs and bats, who were her only companions; she had taken a great fancy to them, and loved to hear their quaint talk. They all told her how sorry they were for the poor prince, of whom his mother was so jealous, how they had all hoped when she came to be a little servant, that he would see her, fall in love with her, and marry her, and so change this gloomy, solitary place into one of festivities and gaieties; but, of course, with a badly fitting bat's skin on her, the thing was impossible, and the old fairy, was so watchful all day that it was quite impossible for any one to have a few words with the prince, she only relaxed her vigilance when he was asleep, and then she snored herself.

Forget-me-not listened to all this, and felt more miserable than ever to think that the handsome fairy prince, with whom she was now very much in love, should never have a chance of even knowing there was such a thing as love and beauty in the world; she asked her friend, the chief bat of the establishment, if he could not help her in any way, while her old mistress was asleep.

"Well," said the bat, "if you like to get on my back I can take you into the Prince's room one night, but then he is fast asleep, so I don't know of what use that can be to you."

But Forget-me-not was so desirous of seeing the Prince when his mother was not there, that she told the bat she would not mind his being asleep, would he please take her in at his window and let her see him.

The old bat consented. It was too late then, but on the following night he agreed to wait for Forget-me-not under the old cedar tree. The little fairy could hardly contain her impatience all day. When midnight struck, and the old woman and her son had both gone to sleep, she ran up to her little room and took out her pretty fairy dress, then dressed her beautiful golden hair, and having placed a garland of forget-me-nots on her head, she anxiously awaited her friend, the bat, under the cedar tree.

He was punctual to the minute, and Forget-me-not, having mounted on his back, he deposited her on the sill of the Prince's window. She stepped in, and saw the handsome fairy prince lying asleep, looking, oh! so lonely and dissatisfied. She went up to him and kissed him gently, and a tear fell from her eye on to his pillow, where it changed into a brilliant diamond. Near it she laid the wreath of forget-me-nots from her hair, then stole gently out of the room again and regained her own couch without, fortunately, disturbing her old mistress, who was snoring louder than ever.

The next morning the Prince awoke feeling that he had had a most beautiful dream. He dimly remembered seeing a little form of exquisite beauty fly in at his window, come up close to him and kiss him, and then... But surely it was not a dream, for there, on his pillow, was the wreath of forget-me-nots she wore, and near it glittered the bright tear of love and sympathy which her fair eye had let fall on his forehead, and which had changed into a most brilliant diamond. He took both up and fastened them inside his doublet; then, as it was still very early in the morning, he stole on tiptoe down the stairs, out of the palace, and through the park, into the great world, beyond the crystal gates, which he had never dared to cross before. A new feeling which he could not explain seemed to put an altogether different life into him. Everything around him seemed endowed with unwonted beauty; the great trees waved their majestic branches over his head and whispered words he had never understood before, and when he looked up, there among the boughs, he saw two lovely little beings he had never been allowed to see before, sitting quite close together and chirping sweet words to each other. He seemed to know directly what they were saying: "Love and beauty" was what they were talking of, and that was what the fairy prince was now in quest of – "love and beauty." He was determined to wander until he found the owner of the forget-me-not wreath and the diamond tear. He knew she could not be anywhere within his mother's palace or garden, so he had set off, no matter for how long a distance, until he had once more seen the bright blue eyes which had appeared to him in his dream.

On and on he went; he did not know himself how far he had gone, or how long he had been on the road. He felt no fatigue, all the world was so new to him, and so beautiful. In the forest the nimble squirrels and gaily-coloured birds; in the fields the bright-eyed butterflies, in the grass the tiny elves and fairies, in the waters the jewelled fishes, all were a source of wonder and admiration to him, so beautiful were they all, and yet not one so perfect as the little fairy being whom he had only seen in his dream.

At last, one day, after long, long wanderings, he came to the very lake near which Narcissa and her mother and father still dwelt. As he was beginning to feel very tired, he sat down on the reed-covered bank and looked down with delight at a cluster of forget-me-nots close to him, which so strongly reminded him of the bright blue eyes in his dream. He began to fear that he should never see her; that, perhaps, she did not really exist.

Suddenly he looked up, and coming down the path, he saw a lovely little fairy, walking dejectedly along. She was very beautiful, though not quite so beautiful as his dream. She had golden hair also, and blue eyes, but they were not the same blue eyes he had wandered all this long way to see.

Narcissa, for it was she, had never ceased to come to the edge of the lake, and never ceased to look at herself in the waters and ask the goldfish who was the most beautiful fairy in the land, but the goldfish had never ceased to say:

"Although Princess Narcissa very beauteous be,
Little Forget-me-not, far away, is more beautiful than she."

That is why she looked so dejected, for she was still so vain that she hated the idea that Forget-me-not should still be alive and still be thought more beautiful than she. The Prince looked at the fairy figure in admiration as she trod gracefully on the large lily leaves, then, sitting on a pink lotus, began to comb her golden hair.

Presently a whole row of little goldfish and water sprites put their little heads out of the water, and, looking critically at the fairy, began to sing gaily:

"Although Princess Narcissa very beauteous be,
Little Forget-me-not, far away, is more beautiful than she."

Then the Prince knew that they must mean his own little fairy, the lovely being that he had seen once, and immediately learnt to love, and in search of whom he had wandered from the other end of the world.

He heard Narcissa asking eagerly:

"And tell me, Goldfish, where is Forget-me-not, who you say is a thousand times more beautiful than I?"

"She is there, standing near you! Welcome, Forget-me-not, the most beautiful in all fairy-land."

The Prince looked round in amazement, astonished that this lovely being should have been so near him without his knowing it, but he saw no one, only an ugly old bat, whom he dimly recollected having seen a long time ago in his mother's palace.

Poor little Forget-me-not! When she had perceived the consequences of her midnight adventure, and had seen her dear Prince go forth in quest of her, she resolved to follow him wherever he went. On and on she had wandered, always after him, until she felt so tired and footsore she could hardly walk, till at last she also had arrived near the well-known lake, and had seen her sister, Narcissa, and her old friends, the goldfish, and all the old familiar places; yet she had no eyes for all these, she only thought of her dear prince, and longed to throw off her ugly disguise, and tell him that she was his own little fairy, who had kissed him in the night, and taught him the meaning of love and beauty; yet she dared not, she was pledged to the old fairy not to take off her disguise, and was too frightened of her to break her word. Besides, if Narcissa were to see her now, surely she would throw her into the water and kill her. So she had to stand by, and feel that the Prince was looking at her, and did not recognize her. Narcissa did, however, in one moment; the eyes of envy and vanity are so sharp. She looked round when the goldfish had spoken, and immediately, under the bat's skin, she spied her little blue-eyed sister.

Without a moment's hesitation she rushed at her, and giving her a violent push, threw her into the water.

The Prince, who had learnt to love all living creatures, however mean and humble, could not bear to see even an old bat drown, so he snatched hold of one of its wings to help it swim to shore, when lo! the bat's skin came right off, and in its place he was holding the lovely being from his dream, she was again looking at him with those bright blue eyes, he had never since forgotten. He pulled her to shore, and she at last was happy in his arms.

Now, need I tell my little readers any more? Well! Perhaps they might like to hear that the old fairy mother, though at first sorely vexed at her son's conduct, finally was obliged to give her consent to his marriage with Forget-me-not, so there was a grand wedding in the palace of glass, which henceforth became the abode of mirth and gaiety. As for Narcissa, she was Forget-me-not's bridesmaid, and it was a severe punishment to her for all her wickedness, to hear the whole fairy world, yea even the Queen herself, say joyfully:

"Yes, Forget-me-not, little blue-eyed Forget-me-not, is the most beautiful fairy of the lot!"

The Suitors of the Princess Fire-Fly

FAR, VERY FAR AWAY, and long, very long ago, when all the world was inhabited by the fairies, there lived a great and mighty king called Fire-fly. Now do not run away with the idea that this Fire-fly was in any way like the little glowing insects that are read about in Natural History books. True, he had wings like those flies nowadays, and also a body something like theirs, but he was a fairy fly, and wore a most beautiful crown on his head, which at night shone as brilliantly as the stars. Then this Fire-fly had a most gorgeous palace, which lay right in the middle of a wide river. This palace consisted of one magnificent lotus flower, and a more exquisite dwelling-place it would be impossible to see. His dearest and most precious treasure was his daughter, a most lovely princess. The king was so proud and fond of her that he would not allow any one even to look at her, but kept her hidden inside the pink petals of his beautiful lotus palace, and there the princess grew up more and more lovely every day, till her fame spread far and wide, and all the flies and moths and beetles of the neighbouring kingdoms got out their finest wings in order to go to woo and win this incomparable Fire-fly miss.

But the princess was very proud and very vain of her own beauty, and she said to her mother one day: "It is quite useless for either Dragon-fly or Stag-beetle, or, in fact, any of them to try and woo me, for I will not marry any one unless he perform some perilous task which I will impose upon him. Then if he fails, and dies in the attempt, I shall be thankful to have escaped being married to so foolish and careless a being; or if he should not dare to attempt the task, it will be a proof that he values his life higher than his love, and is therefore not worth having."

As this beautiful princess was very much spoilt at home, her mother and father, King and Queen Fire-fly, both acceded to her whim, and the king issued a proclamation, by which he declared that no suitor should have the hand of his lovely daughter unless he performed the task she imposed upon him.

Forthwith did Prince Gold-beetle start from his kingdom of Gladiola over the grass, and placed his heart and hand at Princess Fire-fly's feet. She listened to all he had to say, and smiled very sweetly. "Yes," she said, "all that you say is very pretty indeed, and I am sure your proposal is exceedingly flattering; but you know the condition, without which I cannot possibly marry you."

"Name the condition, lovely princess," said the Gold-beetle; "no task, be it ever so hard, would be too much to undertake for such a prize."

"You most bring me, from anywhere you like," said the beautiful Fire-fly, "one spark of fire!"

"Is that all you wish for?" said the Gold-beetle. "I fly, and before another night has descended and passed by I will lay this spark at your feet." And away he flew, quite confident that he would be able to obtain so simple a thing as a mere little spark of fire, which the moment night came could be found in every house in the neighbourhood. You will hear presently how he fared in his quest.

In the meantime the beautiful Fire-fly had another suitor. Lord Cockchafer appeared upon the scene, and, obtaining entrance into the Lotus Palace, he boldly asked for the honour of becoming the Princess's husband, but she turned away quite disdainfully from him:

"I don't think I should ever care to marry you at all," she said; "but I am so very, very anxious to possess a spark of fire, and I really would like to know if you would be brave enough to undertake a perilous task in order to please me."

"I will travel night and day," said Lord Cockchafer, "till I bring you what you wish."

Away he went, tripping merrily, and blissfully unconscious of the fact that he was not the only one who was bent on this curious errand.

Presently Fire-fly had another suitor – a beautiful suitor he was too, with his shimmering suit of green and gold, my Lord Dragon-fly. He thought to dazzle her by his beauty and make her forget her foolish fancy about this spark of fire. But the princess would not listen even to him; she only smiled, and said:

"I will only marry him who brings me this spark of fire."

And away he had to go. And thus, day after day, there came a regular crowd of suitors round the beautiful princess; but day after day she sent them off in quest of a spark of fire.

Prince Gold-beetle waited till night set in, then flew off gaily to the nearest city. He came up near a lovely little house, standing in a large garden; he looked in at the window, and there he saw a large table laid out with tea and cakes, sweets and fruit, and twelve little girls and boys sitting round, having their tea; on the table a large lamp was burning very brightly.

"Why, this is just what I want," said Prince Gold-beetle; and as the window was open he flew in. The lamp burnt beautifully, it quite fascinated him; he flew quite close, in order to get a better view of the bright flame.

"Oh, what a lovely beetle," he heard one of the little children say, "Mother, do look! What beautiful wings it has!"

"Oh, dear, it is flying so near the lamp I am sure it will burn its wings," said another.

The Gold-beetle took no notice of what they said, but drew nearer and nearer to the coveted prize; there was a spark of lovely fire, how pleased the beautiful princess would be when he brought it home for her. At last he made a bold dash to catch the flame, when lo! alas! he felt his poor wings all singed and burnt; he could not fly any more, but fell fainting on the tablecloth. He heard the little children say to each other:

"Stupid beetle to go flying into the lamp; now it has burnt its lovely wings."

Then somebody else said, "Throw away the nasty thing, or put it out of its misery."

That was the end of poor Prince Gold-beetle's life.

Another suitor of Fire-fly, a Hawk-moth, while fluttering about one evening, wandered into a room where, at first, he could see nothing, it seemed pitch dark; presently he noticed a large luminous object, which turned out to be long blue flames, apparently emerging from a large bowl, filled with plums; all round he saw eager little laughing faces, and every now and then little fingers would boldly make a dash into the bowl and bring out a flaring sugar plum. Hawk-moth watched them for a time, very much interested; you see, they don't play snap-dragon in the Lotus kingdom. Then he suddenly thought this would be a grand opportunity to steal a lovely spark of blue fire, and with it claim the hand of the proud princess. He fluttered round the bowl for some time, but no one paid any attention to him, they were all so merry pulling out the plums and eating them. It seemed so easy that Hawkmoth determined to try his luck, and boldly flew into the flames. Alas! poor fellow, he was burnt to a cinder, you could hardly tell him from a raisin.

One after another the suitors tried, and one after another they failed. There was a Hornbug who actually, one night, saw a green light in a cat's eye; he tried to snatch that, but you may well imagine how pussy, very much annoyed, made a short meal of my lord Horn-bug.

A venturesome Carrion-beetle having drifted towards the sea-shore, late one night, saw some fish lying there apparently all glowing with fire. He picked off one of the glistening scales, and went away proud and happy, quite convinced that the necessary prize – the much-sought-for spark of fire – was at last in his grasp. He was hurrying to get to Lotus land as fast as his legs could carry him, when he met a Stag-beetle, who apparently was also carrying a luminous object in front of him. The fact of the matter was, that Mr Stag-beetle had also fallen madly in love with the beautiful but capricious princess, and had determined to succeed in bringing her a spark of fire, even if it should cost him his wings!

After several unsuccessful attempts he had found at the foot of a large tree, a funny little bit of old wood, which gave out a beautiful little bright blue light. He approached very carefully (as he had been severely burnt several times), and you may be sure he was delighted when he found that it did not give out any heat, so that he was able to carry it off without burning himself. He was hurrying off with his prize to claim the Princess, when he met Mr Carrion-beetle bent on a similar errand.

They both stopped short, and glared at each other. No explanation was necessary. Each knew where the other one was hurrying to, and each was determined to get there first. They could not both marry Princess Fire-fly, that was very evident, so, after talking matters over for a while, they determined to fight it out till one of them remained dead on the battle-field. It was pitch dark, but the fish-scale and the bit of wood were quite enough light to kill one another by, so they each put down their prize, and began boxing in true beetle-like fashion.

As they both were equally tall, and equally strong, the fight lasted a considerable time. When lo! behold! as the first ray of dawn illumined the eastern sky, and the two combatants turned for a rest, previous to renewing hostilities, there, on the ground, instead of the two tiny sparks of blue flame, lay only a nasty fish's scale and an ugly bit of wood. King Phosphorus had vanished with the dawn. Further fighting was useless. Carrion-beetle and Stagbeetle each went his own way to seek fortune elsewhere.

Meanwhile, the Princess, in her beautiful palace, waited in vain for the return of one of her many suitors. When she heard of the sad fate of Prince Gold-beetle, she wept bitterly, for though she was so proud and vain, she was not wholly devoid of feeling, and of the many who had come wooing her she had preferred Prince Gold-beetle. When the Queen saw her tears, she tried to make her forego her purpose; but all her persuasions were of no avail, for the Princess was very obstinate, and would not own to being in the wrong.

Suitor after suitor came, and they were one and all sent off on the same hopeless errand. One day a most beautiful "Red Admiral" was on the point of committing suicide on the thorn of a rosebush, being so fearfully despondent on account of his non-success, when he caught sight of a luminous object underneath the very branch upon which he meant to end his life. His joy was great; what was it? Would it hurt him? He thought not, it looked so beautiful as it lay and sparkled in the sun. All round it was a hoop of gold. He went closer; no, it did not burn. Then came the question, how was he to convey it to the Princess? It was far too heavy for him to carry. Whilst he was considering how he could possibly convey it, he heard footsteps, and in another second a little child's voice exclaim, "Why, look! here is your diamond ring you lost;… how lucky it is I have found it," and the child picked it up and gave it to a grown-up lady who was a little way off. This was the last straw for the beautiful Red Admiral, and in another minute he had committed suicide.

And thus it was with one and all – some were frightened, and never attempted the task, others were badly singed, some died, none succeeded, and even to this day, in far-off lands, where the lotus grows, we always say when we see a crowd of insects fluttering round a flame: "Ah! Princess Fire-fly has many suitors tonight!"

The Three Oranges

THERE WAS ONCE, I don't know where, a king, who had three sons. They had reached a marriageable age, but could not find any one who suited them, or who pleased their father. "Go, my sons, and look round in the world," said the king, "and try to find wives somewhere else."

The three sons went away, and at bed-time they came to a small cottage, in which a very, very old woman lived. She asked them about the object of their journey, which the princes readily communicated to her. The old woman provided them with the necessaries for the journey as well as she could, and before taking leave of her guests, gave them an orange each, with instructions to cut them open only in the neighbourhood of water, else they would suffer great, very great damage. The three princes started on their way again, and the eldest not being able to restrain his curiosity as to what sort of fruit it could be, or to conceive what harm could possibly happen if he cut it open in a place where there was no water near: cut into the orange; and lo! a beautiful girl, such as he had never seen before, came out of it, and exclaimed, "Water! let me have some water, or I shall die on the spot." The prince ran in every direction to get water, but could not find any, and the beautiful girl died in a short time, as the old woman had said. The princes went on, and now the younger one began to be inquisitive as to what could be in his orange.

They had just sat down to luncheon on a plain, under a tall, leafy tree, when it appeared to them that they could see a lake not very far off. "Supposing there is a girl in the fruit, I can fulfil her wish," he thought to himself, and not being able to restrain his curiosity any longer, as to what sort of girl there could be inside, he cut his orange; and lo! a girl, very much more beautiful than the first, stepped out of it, and called out for water, in order to save her life. He had previously sent his brother to what he thought was a lake; and, as he could not wait for his return with the water, he ran off himself, quite out of breath, but the further he ran the further the lake appeared to be off, because it was only a mirage. He rushed back to the tree nearly beside himself, in order to see whether the girl was yet alive, but only found her body lifeless, and quite cold.

The two elder brothers, seeing that they had lost what they had been searching for, and having given up all hope of finding a prettier one, returned in great sorrow to their father's house, and the youngest continued his journey alone. He wandered about until, after much fatigue, he came to the neighbourhood of some town, where he found a well. He had no doubt that there was a girl in his orange also, so he took courage, and cut it; and, indeed, a girl, who was a hundred times prettier than the first two, came out of it. She called out for water, and the prince gave her some at once, and death had no power over her. The prince now hurried into the town to purchase rich dresses for his love; and that no harm might happen to her during his absence, he made her sit up in a tree with dense foliage, the boughs of which overhung the well.

As soon as the prince left, a gypsy woman came to the well for water. She looked into the well, and saw in the water the beautiful face of the girl in the tree. At first she fancied that she saw the image of her own face, and felt very much flattered; but soon found out her mistake, and looking about discovered the pretty girl in the tree. "What are you waiting for, my pretty maid?" inquired the gypsy woman with a cunning face. The girl told her her story, whereupon the gypsy woman, shamming kindness, climbed up the tree, and pushed the pretty girl into the well, taking her place in the tree, when the pretty girl sank. The next moment a beautiful little gold fish appeared swimming in the water; the gypsy woman recognized it as the girl, and, being afraid that it might be dangerous to her, tried to catch it, when suddenly the prince appeared with the costly dresses, so she at once laid her plans to deceive him: the prince immediately noticed the difference between her and the girl he had left; but she succeeded in making him believe that for a time after having left the fairy world, she had to lose her beauty, but that she would recover it the sooner the more he loved her: so the prince was satisfied and went home to his father's house with the woman he found, and actually loved her in hopes of her regaining her former beauty. The good food and happy life, and also the pretty dresses, improved the sunburnt woman's looks a little: the prince imagining that his wife's prediction was going to be fulfilled, felt still more attached to her, and was anxious to carry out all her wishes.

The woman, however, could not forget the little gold fish, and therefore feigned illness, saying that she would not get better till she had eaten of the liver of a gold fish, which was to be found in such and such a well: the prince had the fish caught at once, and the princess having partaken of the liver, got better, and felt more cheerful than before. It happened, however, that one scale of the fish had been cast out in the courtyard with the water, and from it a beautiful tree began to grow; the princess noticed it and found out the reason, how the tree got there, and again fell ill, and said that she could not get better until they burnt the tree, and cooked her something by the flames. This wish also was fulfilled, and she got better; it happened, however that one of the woodcutters took a square piece of the timber home to his wife, who used it as a lid for a milk jug: these people lived not very far from the royal palace, and were poor, the woman herself keeping the house, and doing all servants' work.

One day she left her house very early, without having put anything in order, and without having done her usual household work; when she came home in the evening, she found all clean, and in the best order; she was very much astonished, and could not imagine how it came to pass; and it happened thus on several days, whenever she had not put her house in order before going out. In order to find out how these things were accomplished, one day she purposely left her home in disorder, but did not go far, but remained outside peeping through the keyhole, to see what would happen. As soon as everything became quiet in the house, the woman saw that the lid of the milk jug which was standing in the window, began to move with gentle noise, and in a few moments a beautiful fairy stepped out of it, who first combed her golden tresses, and performed her toilet, and afterwards put the whole house in order. The woman, in order to trap the fairy before she had time to retransform herself, opened the door abruptly. They both seemed astonished, but the kind and encouraging words of the woman soon dispelled the girl's fear, and now she related her whole story, how she came into the world, how she became a gold fish, and then a tree, and how she used to walk out of the wooden lid of the milk jug to tidy the house; she also enlightened the woman as to who the present queen was. The woman listened to all in great astonishment, and in order to prevent the girl from slipping back into the lid, she had previously picked it up, when she entered, and now threw it into the fire. She at once went to the prince, and told him the whole story.

The prince had already grown suspicious about his wife's beauty, which had been very long in returning, and now he was quite sure that she was a cheat: he sent for the girl and recognized her at once as the pretty fairy whom he had left in the tree. The gypsy woman was put into the pillory, and the prince married the pretty girl, and they lived ever after in happiness.

The Invisible Shepherd Lad

THERE WAS ONCE, I don't know where, a poor man who had a very good son who was a shepherd. One day he was tending his sheep in a rocky neighbourhood, and was sending sighs to Heaven as a man whose heart was throbbing with burning wishes. Hearing a noise as of someone approaching he looked round and saw St. Peter standing in front of him in the guise of a very old grey man. "Why are you sighing, my lad?" inquired he, "and what is your wish?" "Nothing else," replied the lad, respectfully, "but to possess a little bag which never gets full, and a fur cloak which makes me invisible when I put it on." His wish was fulfilled and St. Peter vanished. The lad gave up shepherding now and turned to the capital, where he thought he had a chance of making his fortune. A king lived there who had twelve daughters, and eleven of them wanted at least six pairs of shoes each every night. Their father was very angry about this, because it swallowed up a good deal of his income; he suspected that there was something wrong, but couldn't succeed by any traps to get to the bottom of it. At last he promised the youngest princess to him who would unveil the secret.

The promise enticed many adventurous spirits to the capital, but the girls simply laughed at them, and they were obliged to leave in disgrace. The shepherd lad, relying on his fur cloak, reported himself; but the girls measured him, too, with mocking eyes. Night came, and the shepherd, muffling himself in his fur cloak, stood at the bedroom door where they slept, and stole in amongst them when they went to bed. It was midnight and a ghost walked round the beds and woke the girls. There was now great preparation. They dressed and beautified themselves, and filled a travelling bag with shoes. The youngest knew nothing of all this, but on the present occasion the invisible shepherd woke her – whereupon her sisters got frightened; but as she was let into their secret they thought it best to decoy her with them, to which, after a short resistance, the girl consented. All being ready, the ghost placed a small dish on the table. Everyone anointed their shoulders with the contents, and wings grew to them. The shepherd did the same: and when they all flew through the window, he followed them.

After flying for several hours they came to a huge copper forest, and to a well, the railing round which was of copper, and on this stood twelve copper tumblers. The girls drank here, so as to refresh themselves, when the youngest, who was here for the first time, looked round in fear. The lad, too, had something to drink after the girls had left and put a tumbler, together with a twig that he broke off a tree, in his bag; the tree trembled, and the noise was heard all over the forest. The youngest girl noticed it and warned her sisters that someone was after them, but they felt so safe that they only laughed at her. They continued their journey, and after a short time came to a silver forest, and to a silver well. Here again they drank, and the lad again put a tumbler and a silver twig into his bag. In breaking off the twig the tree shook, and the youngest again warned her sisters, but in vain.

They soon came to the end of the forest and arrived at a golden forest, with a gold well and tumblers. Here again they stopped and drank, and the lad again put a gold tumbler and twig in his bag. The youngest once more warned her sisters of the noise the quivering tree made, but in vain. Having arrived at the end of the forest they came to an immense moss-grown rock, whose awe-inspiring lofty peaks soared up to the very heavens. Here they all stopped. The ghost struck the rock with a golden rod, whereupon it opened, and all entered, the shepherd lad with them. Now they came to a gorgeous room from which several halls opened, which were all furnished in a fairy-like manner. From these twelve fairy youths came forth and greeted them, who were all wonderfully handsome. The number of servants increased from minute to minute who were rushing about getting everything ready for a magnificent dance. Soon after strains of enchanting music were heard, and the doors of a vast dancing hall opened and the dancing went on without interruption. At dawn the girls returned – also the lad – in the same way as they had come, and they lay down as if nothing had happened, which, however, was belied by their worn shoes, and the next morning they got up at the usual hour.

The king was impatiently awaiting the news the shepherd was to bring, who came soon after and told him all that had happened. He sent for his daughters, who denied everything, but the tumblers and the twigs bore witness. What the shepherd told the youngest girl also confirmed, whom the shepherd woke for the purpose. The king fulfilled his promise with regard to the youngest princess and the other eleven were burnt for witchcraft.

The Fairies' Well

TALE, TALE, MATE; a black little bird flew on the tree; it broke one of its legs; a new cloak, a shabby old cloak; it put it on.

Well, to commence! There was in the world a king, who was called the "Green King," and who had three daughters. He did not like them at all; he would have very much preferred if they had been boys. He continually scolded and abused them, and one day, in a fit of passion, the words slipped from his lips: "What is the good of all these wenches? I wish the devil would come and fetch them all three!" The devil wasn't slow; he took the king at his word and ran away with all three girls at once. The king's fondest wish was hereafter fulfilled; his wife bore him three sons, and he was very fond of them.

But the king grew old; his hair turned quite grey. So his sons set out for the fairies' well to fetch their father some youth-giving water. They wandered along till they came to a small road-side inn, where they had something to eat and drink, and gave their horses hay and corn. They tippled for some time, until the two elder princes got jolly, and commenced to dance in true style. The youngest one every now and then reminded them that it was time to continue the journey, but they would not listen to him. "Don't talk so much," they said, "if you are so very anxious to be off you had better leave us and go alone."

So the youngest saddled his horse and left his two brothers. He travelled along until all of a sudden he discovered that he had lost his way and found himself in a vast forest. In wandering hither and thither, he came to a small hut in which an old hermit dwelt. He at once went to it, knocked and entered, and greeted the old man, saying, "May the Lord grant you a happy good day, my father."

"The Lord bless you, my son! where are you going?"

"Well, old father, I intend to go to the fairies' well for some youth-giving water, if I can the way thither."

"May the Lord help you, my son! I don't believe that you will be able to get there unaided, because it is a difficult journey. But I will tell you something. I have a piebald horse, that will carry you without mishap to the fairies' well. I will let you have it if you promise to bring me back some youth-giving water."

"I will bring you some with pleasure, old father. You are quite welcome to it."

"Very well, my son! Get on the piebald, and be off in the name of Heaven!"

The piebald horse was led out and saddled, the prince mounted, and in another second they were high up in the air, like birds, because the piebald was a magic horse that at all times grazed on the silken meadow, the meadow of the fairies. On they travelled, till all at once the piebald said:

"I say, dear master, I suppose you know that once you had three sisters, and that all three were carried off by the devil. We will go and pay a visit to the eldest. It is true, your brother-in-law is at this moment out rabbiting, but he will be back soon if I go to fetch him. He will ask you to bring him, also, some youth-giving water. I'll tell you what to do. He has a plaid which has the power of making the wearer invisible. If you put it on, nobody on this earth can see you. If he will give you that plaid you can promise him as much water as he likes; a whole tub full, if he wants it."

When they reached the house, the prince walked in; and the piebald horse immediately hurried off to the fields, and began to drive the devil so that his eyes sparkled. As the devil ran homewards, he passed a pair of gallows with a man hanging upon them; he lifted off the corpse, and ran away with it. Having arrived at home, he called from the yard through the window: "Take this, wife! Half of him roasted, the other half boiled, for my meal. Be sure to have him ready by the time I get inside." Thereupon he pitched the dead man through the window; the meal was ready in a minute and the devil walked in, sat down and ate him. Having finished, he happened to look towards the oven and caught sight of the prince.

"Halloo! is it you, brother-in-law? Why did you not speak? What a pity that I did not notice you sooner? You are just too late; you could have had a bit or two of my bonne-bouche."

"Thank you, brother-in-law. I don't care for your dainties."

"Well, then get him some wine, wife! perhaps he will have some of that?"

The wife brought in the wine and placed it on the table, and the two set to drinking.

"May I ask, what are you looking for in this strange part of the world?" inquired the devil.

"I am going to the fairies' well for some youth-giving water."

"Look here, my good man, I am a bit of a smart fellow myself, something better than you, and still I could not accomplish that journey. I can get to within about fourteen miles of the place, but even there the heat is so great that it shrivels me up like bacon rind."

"Well, I will go all the same, if Heaven will help me!"

"And I will give you as much gold and silver as you can carry, if you will bring me back a gourdful of that water."

"I'll bring you back some, but for nothing less than for the plaid hanging on that peg. If you will give that to me you shall have the water."

At first the devil would not part with the plaid on any account; but the prince begged so hard that the devil at last yielded.

"Well, brother-in-law! This is such a plaid, that if you put it on nobody can see you."

The prince was just going when the devil asked him, "Have you any money for the journey, brother?"

"I had a little, but I have spent it all."

"Then you had better have some more." Whereupon he emptied a whole dishful of copper coins into the prince's bag. The prince went out into the yard and shook the bridle; the piebald horse at once appeared, and the prince mounted. The devil no sooner caught sight of the piebald than he exclaimed, addressing the prince, "Oh, you rascally fellow! Then you travel on that villainous creature – the persecutor and murderer of our kinsfolk? Give me back at once my plaid and my gourd, I don't want any of your youth-giving water!"

But the prince was not such a fool as to give him back the plaid. In a minute the piebald was high up in the air and flew off like a bird. They travelled along until the horse again spoke and said, "Well then, dear master, we will now go and look up your second sister. True, your brother-in-law is out rabbiting, but he will soon be back if I go for him. He, too, will offer you all sorts of things in return for getting him some youth-giving water. Don't ask for anything else but for a ring on the window sill, which has this virtue, that it will squeeze your finger and wake you in case of need."

The prince went into the house and the piebald fetched the devil. Everything happened as at the previous house. The devil had his meal, recognized his brother-in-law, sent for wine, and asked the prince:

"Well, what are you doing in this neighbourhood?"

"I am going to the fairies' well for some youth-giving water."

"You don't mean that! You have undertaken a very difficult task. I am as good a man as a hundred of your stamp put together, and still I can't go there. The heat there is so great that it would shrivel me up like bacon rind at a distance of fourteen miles. They boil lead there as we boil water here."

"Still I intend to go, by the help of Heaven."

"Very well, brother-in-law. I will give you so much treasure that you can fill several wagons with it, if you will bring me a gourd full of that youth-giving water."

"I don't want anything, brother-in-law, but that ring in the window yonder."

"Of what use would it be to you?"

"Oh! I don't know; let me have it."

So after a good deal of pressing the devil gave him the ring and said:

"Well, brother-in-law, this is such a ring that it will squeeze your finger and wake you, no matter how sound you may be asleep."

By this time the prince had already reached the courtyard, and was ready to start, when the devil stopped him and said:

"Stop a bit, brother-in-law, have you any money for the journey?"

"I had a little, but it is all gone," replied the prince.

"Then you had better have some." Whereupon the devil emptied a dishful of silver money into the prince's bag. The prince then shook the bridle and the piebald horse at once appeared, which nearly frightened the devil into a fit.

"Oh, you rascally fellow!" he exclaimed. "Then you are in league with the persecutor of our kinsfolk? Stop! Give me back that ring and gourd at once. I don't want any of your youth-giving water!"

But the Green Prince took no notice of the devil's shouting and flew away on his piebald like a bird. They had been travelling for some distance when the horse said: "We shall now go to see your youngest sister. Her husband, too, is out at present rabbiting, but I shall fetch him in, in no time. He, also, will beseech you to get him some youth-giving water, but don't you yield, no matter how much wealth he promises you, until he gives you his sword that hangs on the wall. It is such a weapon that at your command it will slay the populations of seven countries."

In the meantime they reached the house. The Green Prince walked in and the piebald went to look for the third devil. Everything happened as on the two previous occasions, and the devil asked his wife to send him in three casks of wine, and they commenced drinking. All of a sudden the devil asked, "Where are you going?"

"I am going to the fairies' well for some youth-giving water. My father has grown very old and requires some of the water to give him back his youth."

The devil replied that it was impossible to get there on account of the great heat. To which the prince said, that he was determined to go, no matter what might happen.

"Very well," continued the devil. "I will give you as much gold and silver as your heart can wish or your mouth name if you will bring me back a gourd full of the water."

"The gold is of no use to me; I have plenty of it at home; as much as I need. But if you will give me that sword on the wall, I will bring you some water from the fairies' well, with pleasure."

"Of what use would that sword be to you? You can't do anything with it."

"No matter. Let me have it."

The devil, at first, would not part with the sword; but, at last, he gave in. The Green Prince went into the yard, and was about to start, when the devil asked:

"Brother-in-law, have you any money left for the journey?"

"I had some; but it's nearly gone."

"Then you had better have some." And with this the devil put a plateful of gold coins into the prince's bag. The latter shook the bridle and his piebald appeared. The devil was very much alarmed at the sight, and exclaimed: "You rascal, then you associate with our arch-persecutor. Let me have back my sword and the gourd, I don't want any of your water." But the prince did not listen to him; in fact he had no time to heed the devil's words even if he had any intention of doing so, as he was already high up in the air, and the piebald now questioned him: "How shall we go, dear master? shall we fly as fast as the whirlwind, or like a flash of thought?" "Just as you please, my dear horse."

And the piebald flew away, with the prince on its back, in the direction of the fairies' well. Soon they reached their goal, and alighted on the ground, whereupon the horse said: "Well, my dear master, we have reached our destination. Put on the plaid that the first devil gave you and walk into the fairy queen's palace. The queen has just sat down to supper. Eat, drink, and enjoy yourself. Don't be afraid, nobody will know that you are there. In the meantime I will go into the silken meadow and graze with the horses of the fairy over night. I shall return in the morning and we will then fill our gourd."

And so it happened. The Green Prince put on the plaid and walked into the fairy queen's dining-room, sat down and supped, and for every glass of wine consumed by the fairy he drank two. The supper over they enjoyed themselves. Suddenly the fairy queen felt a sensation as if she were touched by a man, although she could not see anybody. She thereupon exclaimed to her fairies: "Fairies, fairies, keep the bellows going under the boiling lead. Some calamity will befall us tonight."

In the morning the piebald appeared before the castle; the Green Prince was still fast asleep, but luckily the ring squeezed his finger and he awoke and so was saved. He lost no time in going down to his horse.

"I am glad to tell you, my dear master, that all is well. They have not yet been able to see you. Let us go and get the water at once. This is how you must proceed. Stick the gourd on the point of your sword and then dip it under. But, be careful; the gourd must touch the water before my feet get wet, or else we must pay with our lives for our audacity."

The Green Prince did as he was told. He stuck the gourd on the point of the sword and dipped it into the well, before the piebald's hoofs touched the surface of the water.

"Well, my dear master, this has gone off without mishap. Let us at once go and liberate your sisters." First they visited the youngest. The Green Prince put on the plaid, and brought her away unnoticed. Then he rescued the second princess; and at last the eldest, by the aid of his plaid. And their diabolic husbands never noticed that they had been stolen. Having thus liberated his three sisters, he returned without delay to the hermit's hut.

"Well done, my son! Have you brought back any youth-giving water?" exclaimed the hermit, as he saw the prince approaching in the distance.

"To be sure, old father; I have brought plenty."

With these words the Green Prince approached the hermit, and allowed just one drop of the magic water drop on to the old man's hand; and oh, wonder! immediately a change came over him, and the old man instantly became young, and looked like a lad of sixteen.

"Well, my son; you have not made your journey in vain. You have secured the prize that you have striven for; and I shall always be deeply grateful to you until the end of my days. I won't take back the piebald from you, as I have another one exactly like it hidden away somewhere. True, it is only a little foal; but it will grow, and will then be good enough for me."

Then they parted, and the prince bent his way homewards. Having arrived at home he allowed a drop of the magic water drop on to his father's hand, and the old king immediately became a youth of sixteen. And he not only got younger, but also grew handsomer; and a hundred times better looking than he ever was before.

But the Green Prince had been away for such a length of time on his journey to the fairies' well that not even his father could remember him. The king had completely forgotten that the prince was ever born. What was he to do? Nobody knew him at his father's palace, or would recognize him as his father's son; so he conceived the strange idea of accepting a situation as swineherd in his father's service. He found stables for the piebald in a cellar at the end of the town.

While he tended his father's pigs, and went through his duties as swineherd, the fairies travelled all over the world and searched every nook and corner for the father of the child of their queen. Among other places they also came to the town of the Green King, and declared that it was their intention to examine every prince, as the person for whom they searched could only be a prince. The Green King then suddenly remembered that he had once another son but did not know his whereabouts. Something or other, however, recalled to his mind the swineherd, so he at once took pen and paper and wrote a note to the swineherd. The purport of the writing was that the king was the real father of the swineherd, and that the prince should come home with the least possible delay. The Green King sealed the letter and handed it to a gypsy with strict instructions to at once deliver it to the swineherd. The gypsy went, and the swineherd read the note and handed it back to the messenger, saying:

"My good man, take the note back. They have sent you on a fool's errand. I am not the son of the Green King."

The gypsy took the letter back in great anger. The swineherd, again, ran as fast as his legs would carry him to the stables in the cellar at the outskirts of the town, saddled his piebald, and rode ventre à terre to the centre of the town, and pulled up in front of the king's palace. There was such a sight to be seen. A great number of wonderfully pretty fairies had congregated, and were fanning the fire under a huge cauldron of boiling lead, which emitted such a heat that nobody could approach. The eldest prince came out and was about to try his fortune; he was gorgeously dressed, his garments glittering like a mass of gold. As he approached the cauldron full of boiling lead, a pretty fairy called out to him:

"Son of the Green King! are you the father of the child of the queen of fairies?"

"I am."

"Then jump into this seething mass of boiling lead."

He jumped in and was burnt, shrivelling up to the size of a crab-apple.

"You won't do," said the fairy.

Then the second prince stepped forth; his dress, too, was one mass of sparkling gold. As he approached the cauldron a fairy exclaimed:

"Son of the Green King! are you the father of the child of the queen of fairies?"

"I am."

"Then jump into this seething mass of boiling lead."

He jumped in and fared no better than his elder brother.

Now the swineherd rode forth on his piebald horse. His clothes were one mass of dirt and grease. To him, too, the fairy called out:

"Are you the father of the child of the queen of fairies?"

"I am."

"Then jump into this seething mass of boiling lead like the rest."

And, behold! he spurred the piebald horse, pulled tight the bridle, and again slackened it. The piebald shot up into the air like an arrow; and, having reached a good height, it came down with the swineherd on its back in one bold swoop, and jumped into the cauldron full of boiling lead without a single hair of him getting hurt. Seeing this, the fairies at once lifted him out, tore his dirty clothes from him, and dressed him up in garments becoming a king.

He married the queen of fairies and a sumptuous wedding feast was celebrated.

This is the end of my tale.

The Twin Hunchbacks

ONCE UPON A TIME, long, very long ago, in the midst of Fairyland, there stood an extensive forest, so large that it would take many, many days to walk across it; in fact, it was an enchanted forest, for all night it was the haunt of all the little fairies in the neighbourhood. They would skip and dance there all night long, and far into the next day; but the moment the noonday sun streamed down upon them, they would all run away and go to bed inside the water lilies and pink lotus, and leave fairy rings on the grass to mark the place of their nightly revels.

There was a lovely glade in this forest, with a large pond in the middle, and tall dark trees around, which was a specially favoured spot with all the fairies and elves of the forest. Three little fairies particularly there were, who used to come here every morning at sunrise and enjoy themselves to their hearts' content. They were especially fond of a dance they had invented, which consisted in holding hands and twirling round, singing all the while, "Humpty Dumpty! Humpty Dumpty!"

Well, one day a little hunchback woodcutter, who was out very early in the morning gathering chopsticks, suddenly came upon the lovely glade, and there, before him, he saw the three little fairies dancing in a ring, laughing and singing, "Humpty Dumpty! Humpty Dumpty!" so merrily, that he threw down his bundle of faggots, and joined in their dance and their song with great energy. He danced so amazingly, and amused them so much by turning back somersaults, that they thought it the greatest pity in the world that so brisk a little man should be spoilt by having a great hump on his back; so they took some water from the pond in little golden cups, and each fairy emptied her own tiny vessel on the hunchback, singing the while, "Go away, ugly hump!" Then they again joined hands, and danced round him till his hunch had quite disappeared; whereupon he romped more gaily than before, and was so glad and merry he could hardly sing "Humpty Dumpty!" any more for laughing. After that he kissed each of the fairies, and ran home as fast as his little legs would carry him, singing all the way, "Humpty Dumpty! Humpty Dumpty!" springing in the air, and jumping over every obstacle – so glad was he to have got rid of his ugly hump.

Now this little hunchback had a twin brother just as ugly and deformed as he had been himself, and when the now straightened little man came in at the cottage door his brother was very much astonished to see him skipping about without his hunch, and he naturally asked how he had managed to get rid of his ugly deformity.

"Oh," said the woodcutter, "it happened in a very curious way. I was out chopping sticks very early this morning in the woods, when I suddenly saw three dear little fairies before me, dancing in a ring, and singing, 'Humpty Dumpty! Humpty Dumpty!' They were tripping it so merrily that the desire seized me to join in their dance, so I boldly took them by the hand and joined in the ring, singing with them, 'Humpty, Dumpty! Humpty Dumpty!'

"They seemed to like this very much, for when they got tired of dancing they took some water from the pond, and pouring it over my back, they sang, 'Go away, go away, ugly hunch!' and sure enough my ugly hunch has gone."

The twin brother was very much surprised at the strange story he had just heard. Naturally enough he did not quite care about being known as the "hunchback woodcutter" whilst his brother looked so erect and handsome. In fact, he was not only jealous of his brother, but most anxious to be as good looking. He therefore thought the best plan would be to at once seek out the fairies and get them to be as kind and as useful to him as they had been to his brother. He therefore started off at a run for the enchanted glade, determined to get rid of his hump as his brother had done; unfortunately he was so afraid of being too late, that he ran himself quite out of breath, and was tired out by the time he reached the three little fairies, who were dancing and singing as gaily as ever. The poor little fellow could neither sing nor dance, and had not sufficient breath left to cut a caper or turn a back somersault; this disappointed the little fairies very much. Presently they all joined hands, taking the little hunchback with them, and began their special dance, singing, "Humpty Dumpty! Humpty Dumpty!" but he got so confused and giddy from turning round so fast, that instead of singing, "Humpty Dumpty! Humpty Dumpty!" as the little fairies did, he would add – in his efforts to please them – "Humpty Dumpty sat on a wall!" and kept on saying, "Sat on a wall, sat on a wall!" which so annoyed the fairies, that when they took the water out of the pond in their little golden cups, and poured it over his back, instead of singing, "Go away, ugly hump!" they sang, "Hunch, get twice as big as before!" which it did immediately, and was then such a terrible size that it was frightful to look at, and so heavy that he had to crawl on his hands and knees all the way home.

The Wishing Skin

ONCE UPON A TIME, there lived a woodcutter in a little cottage at the foot of an old gigantic oak tree. He had a wife, but no children, and together they lived humbly, but very contentedly; for in front of his cottage he had a nice little garden in which he grew everything that was necessary for their daily food; fine wheat, with which to bake bread, and rich fruit and vegetables; he also had a cow which gave him abundance of milk, and sheep that yielded him soft wool, which his wife wove into garments for themselves.

One day a pedlar had come wandering past the cottage, with pots and pans and other goods for sale; the wife bought a thing or two from him that she needed, and he again went his way. When he had gone, the woodcutter found an old book of tales lying in the road, which the pedlar had evidently dropped; he took it home to his wife, and, in the evening, when she sat at her spinning, he read some of the stories aloud to her. They were a curious lot of tales, all about fairies and magicians that granted people's wishes and changed woodcutters into kings.

That night the little woodcutter could not sleep a wink, he lay awake thinking of the fairies, and picturing himself having one of those godmothers, whose only duty seemed to consist in waving their wands and fulfilling requests. In the morning he went quite dejectedly to his work, quite different to his usual sprightly, little self. He chopped the wood with a heavy heart for a time, finally he threw down his axe in despair and sat down sullenly on the stump of a tree, wishing at least to see a fairy, and persuade her to take an interest in him. His attention was presently attracted by a bright-eyed rabbit which seemed to have suddenly come from nowhere, and sat opposite to him blinking one eye in a knowing way.

So absorbed was the little woodcutter in the castle he was building in the air, that he never started, even when the rabbit suddenly began talking to him.

"Well, Mr Woodcutter, and what can I do for you? You have been wishing to have a fairy godmother ever since last night; now, though I am not your godmother, I know a thing or two, for instance, I know where the wishing skin lies, which the little fairies have been weaving for three hundred years, and which is now completed, any one wearing the same can have every wish fulfilled the moment he formulates it. Of course, as the skin is made of wishes, every time one is fulfilled it evaporates, and the skin becomes that much smaller, but then what does that matter? The little fairies have hidden the skin under a lightning-struck willow tree, but I have burrowed a hole and I know exactly how to get at it. I will show it you, if you like."

Thereupon the little rabbit darted off, and presently returned dragging a large bundle after it, which he spread out before the woodcutter's eager eyes.

"And is this skin really made of wishes? Oh! Mr Rabbit, please let me put it on just for a few minutes, I would like just to make one wish. I promise I will give it you back directly."

The good-natured little rabbit willingly helped the woodcutter to put the magic skin on, which fitted him somewhat tightly, but still it felt pretty comfortable.

"Oh! How I wish this skin were altogether mine," sighed the woodcutter, "and that I never need part with it."

Hardly had he uttered these words when he felt as if the skin fitted him a shade tighter than before.

"Hallo!" said the rabbit, "what have you been wishing for? Certainly you seem to me to have diminished in size. Here, give me the skin, I must put it back where I found it, or the fairies will be after me."

But the woodcutter knew he need not give up his treasure any more, so looking disdainfully at the rabbit he stalked off in the direction of his cottage, his head full of plans for future grandeur. But Mr Bunny, in a great rage, lopped after him, yelling with all his might, till the woodcutter, losing all patience, turned round and screamed at him, "I wish you'd go to Jericho, and leave me alone." When immediately, the rabbit ran away as hard as he could tear, and he felt the skin again tighten round him. He knew that Mr Bunny had gone to Jericho, and would trouble him no more.

When he got home, he told his wife his wonderful adventure, but she only thought he had been drinking, and advised him to go to bed and sleep it off, when, to convince her, he said, "I wish there was a fine supper table laid all ready here, with roast fowls, roast ducks, and roast turkeys, pies and puddings, and four flunkeys to wait on my wife and me."

Hardly were the words out of his mouth when a most gorgeous table appeared in the centre of the room, heavily laden with the most delicious dishes, fruits and wines, while four servants in gold and silver livery stood waiting to serve the supper.

The wife could hardly believe her eyes, and they both sat down and ate and drank and made merry, for they felt that their future was now likely to be a glorious one. Certainly, the little man felt himself a good bit smaller – his feet, when he sat, no longer reached the ground – but what of that, he would become so rich and proud that his stature would not be of the slightest consequence, so lifting a glass of wine high over his head, he said:

"I wish to be a rich lord, with a castle instead of a cottage, and lands and woods all my own; I wish to wear velvet garments, and my wife to go about in nothing but silk dresses, I wish to eat off nothing but gold plates, and use glasses cut of pure diamonds; I wish..."

But his wife checked him just in time, for at every new wish he uttered he diminished an inch before her very eyes, and, lo! the humble cottage had disappeared, and they were sitting in a grand hall, with marble pillars and soft carpets. They looked out of the window, and, though it was evening, they could see distinctly a lovely garden planted with graceful trees and flowers, and fountains in crystal basins, while soft music filled the air.

The woodcutter looked at his wife and she at him. Poor little man, he was only three feet high now, but he was clad in a sumptuous coat and cloak of velvet lined with ermine;

his wife was dressed in a lovely silk gown, with diamonds on her arms and neck. They could hardly contain themselves for joy, and the wife, seizing her little lord in her arms, began dancing round the room to the time of the distant music. The entrance of a number of lackeys and maid-servants asking his lordship for orders for the night, reminded them of the duties of their new position, and they marched off to their bedchamber in solemn state.

The next day they spent in visiting their extensive domains, the stables, coach houses, farms, and dairies, they found that they were indeed considered enormously wealthy, everybody bowed down to them, and listened deferentially to all they had to say. The only thing that was very annoying was that the little lord felt that his three feet of stature were evidently a source of intense amusement to all his retainers and servants.

In the afternoon, they ordered their gilded coach and six white horses to take them to pay calls on their neighbours, whom they hoped to dazzle with their great splendour. They set off in most gorgeous style, with an army of outriders and flunkeys following the carriage; but to their intense astonishment the various neighbouring lords had just as fine houses and gardens as their own, and wore just as fine dresses and magnificent jewels as they did themselves, so they returned home in disgust, Joan especially was intensely annoyed. One lady on whom she called, wore three more bracelets than she did, another had seven more servants, and a third wore a dress embroidered with real pearls, while her own was only embroidered in silver; and one and all had sneered at her diminutive lord, and pointed to their own handsome husbands. She wished she could be richer and grander than they were, so that they should be obliged to bow down before her, even at the cost of another foot off her husband's stature.

So after supper she talked to her lord about her grievances, and pointed out to him, that while he was merely the equal of his neighbours, they would always laugh at him, but once their superiors, say a royal duke or a prince, they would never dare to do so again. At first Jack refused to wish for anything else just yet, he felt himself quite small enough, and did not think that any additional grandeur could compensate him for the loss of another twelve inches. However, at last, his wife prevailed upon him, and just before going to bed he wished to become a royal duke, second only to the king, and equal to any prince in the land; and the next morning Jack and Joan woke to find themselves in a royal palace, with all the servants in royal liveries calling them their Royal Highnesses; and all the lords and ladies in the land came to pay their respects to them. Joan was proud indeed; not one lady wore such fine jewels, or had such a number of servants and palaces as she had, and though her husband was now only two feet high, all the lords stood round him, loudly laughing at his jokes, and the ladies vied with each other as to who should lift him up into his chair. That very day the king was himself coming, with the queen and all his retinue, to pay a visit to the royal duke and duchess, and grand preparations were made for His Majesty's reception.

When the King and Queen arrived, Jack and Joan received them in the grand hall of their palace. Poor little Jack! He felt very nervous when he had to kiss the Queen's hand, Joan had to lift him into a chair, which amused Their Majesties very much, and caused a titter among the other royal dukes, princes and princesses. During the banquet, the diminutive royal duke had to sit on a very tall stool, and had to have his food placed on his plate for him, as he could not reach the dishes; the King was quite convulsed with laughter, and hardly could eat anything; no one else dared to smile, but the Queen made sneering remarks to the duchess about her funny little husband.

That night Joan and Jack had a frightful difference of opinion: she wished to rule supreme over everybody so that even the King and the Queen, who had laughed at them, should have to come and do homage to her and her husband, whatever be his size. In fact she wished to become the greatest empress in the world; whereas Jack felt that another foot off his height would be a trial he could never undergo. However his wife goaded him on till she had gained her point, and before the sun rose next morning, the woodcutter and his wife became the most powerful emperor and empress in the world. There was not a King or a Queen in the world that did not come to do homage before Their Imperial Majesties, no war was declared between any nations or treaty signed without their consent, they exacted tribute from all duchies, principalities, and even kingdoms around; but alas! for the poor little Emperor he was only six inches high, and had to be carried in state on a cushion to all the great functions, and to stand on a gold table when he received the ambassadors from foreign courts. At banquets and state dinners he had to sit on a little golden chair placed on the table, and be fed with a salt spoon out of the Empress's plate.

Very soon he got tired of all this, more especially as, after a little while, Joan, now having reached the height of her ambition, took very little notice of him, she wouldn't allow him to have any voice in any of the affairs of state, and grew tired of seeing her husband carried before her on a cushion. Finally she had a tiny doll's house built in the garden, into which she relegated her lord and master, and only took him out to play with occasionally. Poor little Jack! He thought sorrowfully of the days when he was a fine grown man and cut wood in the forest and was master of his own little home by the old oak tree. He cursed the rabbit, the fairies, the pedlar, and chiefly his own blind stupidity in wishing to change his own contented happy lot, for all this gilded misery.

At last one day, looking out of one of the tiny windows of his doll's house, he saw a woodcutter going along merrily with his bundle of faggots, whistling a lively tune. The poor little Emperor took his jewelled crown, which he always wore, off his head, and throwing it violently on the ground, so that the gems were scattered in all directions, he said, "Oh, how I wish I were a full-grown man, a woodcutter again, with my wife in my own little cottage, not dreaming even of such things as kings and emperors."

When he had spoken, in one moment, the magnificent palace, the exquisite gardens had vanished, and he sat in his big armchair opposite his wife who was knitting, his feet touched the ground, and his arm reached to where Joan was sitting. They fell into each other's arms. Was it all a dream, little readers? I cannot tell you, but all I know is that henceforth Jack and Joan lived humbly in their little cottage contented and happy ever after.

The Kabouters and the Bells

WHEN THE YOUNG QUEEN Wilhelmina visited Brabant and Limburg, they amused her with pageants and plays, in which the little fellows called kabouters, in Dutch, and kobolds in German, played and showed off their tricks. Other small folk, named gnomes, took part in the tableaux. The kabouters are the dark elves, who live in forests and mines. The white elves live in the open fields and the sunshine.

The gnomes do the thinking, but the kabouters carry out the work of mining and gathering the precious stones and minerals. They are short, thick fellows, very strong and are strenuous in digging out coal and iron, copper and gold. When they were first made, they were so ugly, that they had to live where they could not be seen, that is, in the dark places. The grown imps look like old men with beards, but no one ever heard of a kabouter that was taller than a yardstick. As for the babies, they are hardly bigger than a man's thumb. The big boys and girls, in the kabouter kingdom, are not much over a foot high.

What is peculiar about them all is, that they help the good and wise people to do things better; but they love to plague and punish the dull folks, that are stupid, or foolish or naughty. In impish glee, they lure the blockheads, or in Dutch, the 'cheese-heads,' to do worse.

A long time ago, there were no church spires or bells in the land of the Dutch folks, as there are now by the thousands. The good teachers from the South came into the country and taught the people to have better manners, finer clothes and more wholesome food. They also persuaded them to forget their cruel gods and habits of revenge. They told of the Father in Heaven, who loves us all, as his children, and forgives us when we repent of our evil doings.

Now when the chief gnomes and kabouters heard of the newcomers in the land, they held a meeting and said one to the other:

"We shall help all the teachers that are good and kind, but we shall plague and punish the rough fellows among them."

So word was sent to all little people in the mines and hills, instructing them how they were to act and what they were to do.

Some of the new teachers, who were foreigners, and did not know the customs of the country, were very rude and rough. Every day they hurt the feelings of the people. With their axes they cut down the sacred trees. They laughed scornfully at the holy wells and springs of water. They reviled the people, when they prayed to great Woden, with his black ravens that told him everything, or to the gentle Freya, with her white doves, who helped good girls to get kind husbands. They scolded the children at play, and this made their fathers and mothers feel miserable. This is the reason why so many people were angry and sullen, and would not listen to the foreign teachers.

Worse than this, many troubles came to these outsiders. Their bread was sour, when they took it out of the oven. So was the milk, in their pans. Sometimes they found their beds turned upside down. Gravel stones rattled down into their fireplaces. Their hats and shoes were missing. In fact, they had a terrible time generally and wanted to go back home. When the kabouter has a grudge against any one, he knows how to plague him.

But the teachers that were wise and gentle had no trouble. They persuaded the people with kind words, and, just as a baby learns to eat other food at the table, so the people were weaned away from cruel customs and foolish beliefs. Many of the land's folk came to listen to the teachers and helped them gladly to build churches.

More wonderful than this, were the good things that came to these kind teachers, they knew not how. Their bread and milk were always sweet and in plenty. They found their beds made up and their clothes kept clean, gardens planted with blooming flowers, and much hard work done for them. When they would build a church in a village, they wondered how it was that the wood and the nails, the iron necessary to brace the beams, and the copper and brass for the sacred vessels, came so easily and in plenty. When, on some nights, they wondered where they would get food to eat, they found, on waking up in the morning, that there was always something good ready for them. Thus many houses of worship were built, and the more numerous were the churches, the more did farms, cows, grain fields, and happy people multiply.

Now when the gnomes and kabouters, who like to do work for pleasant people, heard that the good teachers wanted church bells, to call the people to worship, they resolved to help the strangers. They would make not only a bell, or a chime, but, actually a carillon, or concert of bells to hang up in the air.

The dark dwarfs did not like to dig metal for swords or spears, or what would hurt people; but the church bells would guide travellers in the forest, and quiet the storms, that destroyed houses and upset boats and killed or drowned people, besides inviting the people to come and pray and sing. They knew that the good teachers were poor and could not buy bells in France or Italy. Even if they had money, they could not get them through the thick forests, or over the stormy seas, for they were too heavy.

When all the kabouters were told of this, they came together to work, night and day, in the mines. With pick and shovel, crowbar and chisel, and hammer and mallet, they broke up the rocks containing copper and tin. Then they built great roaring fires, to smelt the ore into ingots. They would show the teachers that the Dutch kabouters could make bells, as well as the men in the lands of the South. These dwarfish people are jealous of men and very proud of what they can do.

It was the funniest sight to see these short legged fellows, with tiny coats coming just below their thighs, and little red caps, looking like a stocking and ending in a tassel, on their heads, and in shoes that had no laces, but very long points. They flew around as lively as monkeys, and when the fire was hot they threw off everything and worked much harder and longer than men do.

Were they like other fairies? Well, hardly. One must put away all his usual thoughts, when he thinks of kabouters. No filmy wings on their backs! No pretty clothes or gauzy garments, or stars, or crowns, or wands! Instead of these were hammers, pickaxes, and chisels. But how diligent, useful and lively these little folks, in plain, coarse coats and with bare legs, were! In place of things light, clean and easy, the kabouters had furnaces, crucibles and fires of coal and wood.

Sometimes they were grimy, with smoke and coal dust, and the sweat ran down their faces and bodies. Yet there was always plenty of water in the mines, and when hard work was over they washed and looked plain but tidy. Besides their stores of gold, and silver, and precious stones, which they kept ready, to give to good people, they had tools with which to tease or tantalize cruel, mean or lazy folks.

Now when the kabouter daddies began the roaring fires for the making of the bells, the little mothers and the small fry in the kabouter world could not afford to be idle. One and all, they came down from off the earth, and into the mines they went in a crowd. They left off teasing milkmaids, tangling skeins of flax, tearing fishermen's nets, tying knots in cows' tails, tumbling pots, pans and dishes, in the kitchen, or hiding hats, and throwing stones down the chimneys onto the fireplaces. They even ceased their fun of mocking children, who were calling the cows home, by hiding behind the rocks and shouting to them. Instead of these tricks, they saved their breath to blow the fires into a blast. Everybody wondered where the 'kabs' were, for on the farms and in town nothing happened and all was as quiet as when a baby is asleep.

For days and weeks underground, the dwarfs toiled, until their skins, already dark, became as sooty as the rafters in the houses of our ancestors. Finally, when all the labour was over, the chief gnomes were invited down into the mines to inspect the work.

What a sight! There were at least a hundred bells, of all sizes, like as in a family; where there are daddy, mother, grown ups, young sons and daughters, little folk and babies, whether single, twins or triplets. Big bells, that could scarcely be put inside a hogshead, bells that would go into a barrel, bells that filled a bushel, and others a peck, stood in rows. From the middle, and tapering down the row, were scores more, some of them no larger than cow-bells. Others, at the end, were so small, that one had to think of pint and gill measures.

Besides all these, there were stacks of iron rods and bars, bolts, nuts, screws, and wires and yokes on which to hang the bells.

One party of the strongest of the kabouters had been busy in the forest, close to a village, where some men, ordered to do so by a foreign teacher, had begun to cut down some of the finest and most sacred of the grand old trees. They had left their tools in the woods; but the 'kabs,' at night, seized their axes and before morning, without making any noise, they had levelled all but the holy trees. Those they spared. Then, the timber, all cut and squared, ready to hold the bells, was brought to the mouth of the mine.

Now in Dutch, the name for bell is 'klok.' So a wise and grey-bearded gnome was chosen by the high sounding title of klokken-spieler, or bell player, to test the bells for a carillon. They were all hung, for practice, on the big trestles, in a long row. Each one of these frames was called a 'hang,' for they were just like those on which fishermen's nets were laid to dry and be mended.

So when all were ready, washed, and in their clean clothes, every one of the kabouter families, daddies, mothers, and young ones, were ranged in lines and made to sing. The heavy male tenors and baritones, the female sopranos and contraltos, the trebles of the little folks, and the squeaks of the very small children, down to the babies' cooing, were all heard by the gnomes, who were judges. The high and mighty klokken-spieler, or master of the carillon, chose those voices with best tone and quality, from which to set in order and regulate the bells.

It was pitiful to see how mad and jealous some of the kabouters, both male and female, were, when they were not appointed to the first row, in which were some of the biggest of the males, and some of the fattest of the females. Then the line tapered off, to forty or fifty young folks, including urchins of either sex, down to mere babies, that could hardly stand. These had bibs on and had to be held up by their fond mothers. Each one by itself could squeal and squall, coo and crow lustily; but, at a distance, their voices blended and the noise they made sounded like a tinkle.

All being ready, the old gnome bit his tuning fork, hummed a moment, and then started a tune. Along the line, at a signal from the chief gnome, they started a tune.

In the long line, there were, at first, booms and peals, twanging and clanging, jangling and wrangling, making such a clangour that it sounded more like an uproar than an opera. The chief gnome was almost discouraged.

But neither a gnome nor a kabouter ever gives up. The master of the choir tried again and again. He scolded one old daddy, for singing too low. He frowned at a stalwart young fellow, who tried to drown out all the rest with his bull-like bellow. He shook his finger at a kabouter girl, that was flirting with a handsome lad near her. He cheered up the little folks, encouraging them to hold up their voices, until finally he had all in order. Then they practiced, until the master gnome thought he had his scale of notation perfect and gave orders to attune the bells. To the delight of all the gnomes, kabouters and elves, that had been invited to the concert, the rows of bells, a hundred or more, from boomers to tinklers, made harmony. Strung one above the other, they could render merriment, or sadness, in solos, peals, chimes, cascades and carillons, with sweetness and effect. At the low notes the babies called out "cow, cow;" but at the high notes, "bird, bird."

So it happened that, on the very day that the bishop had his great church built, with a splendid bulb spire on the top, and all nicely furnished within, but without one bell to ring in it, that the kabouters planned a great surprise.

It was night. The bishop was packing his saddle bags, ready to take a journey, on horseback, to Rheims. At this city, the great caravans from India and China ended, bringing to the annual fair, rugs, spices, gems, and things Oriental, and the merchants of Rheims rolled in gold. Here the bishop would beg the money, or ask for a bell, or chimes.

Suddenly, in the night, while in his own house, there rang out music in the air, such as the bishop had never heard in Holland, or in any of the seventeen provinces of the Netherlands. Not even in the old lands, France, or Spain, or Italy, where the Christian teachers, builders and singers, and the music of the bells had long been heard, had such a flood of sweet sounds ever fallen on human ears. Here, in these northern regions, rang out, not a solo, nor a peal, nor a chime, nor even a cascade, from one bell, or from many bells; but, a long programme of richest music in the air – something which no other country, however rich or old, possessed. It was a carillon, that is, a continued mass of real music, in which whole tunes, songs, and elaborate pieces of such length, mass and harmony, as only a choir of many voices, a band of music, or an orchestra of many performers could produce.

To get this grand work of hanging in the spire done in one night, and before daylight, also, required a whole regiment of fairy toilers, who must work like bees. For if one ray of sunshine struck any one of the kabouters, he was at once petrified. The light elves lived in the sunshine and thrived on it; but for dark elves, like the kabouters, whose home was underground, sunbeams were as poisoned arrows bringing sure death; for by these they were turned into stone. Happily the task was finished before the eastern sky grew grey, or the cocks crowed. While it was yet dark, the music in the air flooded the earth. The people in their beds listened with rapture.

"Laus Deo" (Praise God), devoutly cried the surprised bishop. "It sounds like a choir of angels. Surely the cherubim and seraphim are here. Now is fulfilled the promise of the Psalmist: 'The players on instruments shall be there.'"

So, from this beginning, so mysterious to the rough, unwise and stupid teachers, but, by degrees, clearer to the tactful ones, who were kind and patient, the carillons spread over all the region between the forests of Ardennes and the island in the North Sea. The Netherlands became the land of melodious symphonies and of tinkling bells. No town, however poor, but in time had its carillon. Every quarter of an hour, the sweet music of hymn or song, made the air vocal, while at the striking of the hours, the pious bowed their heads and the workmen heard the call for rest, or they took cheer, because their day's toil was over. At sunrise, noon, or sunset, the Angelus, and at night the curfew sounded their calls.

It grew into a fashion, that, on stated days, great concerts were given, lasting over an hour, when the grand works of the masters of music were rendered and famous carillon players came from all over the Netherlands, to compete for prizes. The Low Countries became a famous school, in which klokken-spielers (bell players) by scores were trained. Thus no kingdom, however rich or great, ever equalled the Land of the Carillon, in making the air sweet with both melody and harmony.

Nobody ever sees a kabouter nowadays, for in the new world, when the woods are nearly all cut down, the world made by the steam engine, and telegraph, and wireless message, the automobile, aeroplane and submarine, cycle and under-sea boat, the little folks in the mines and forests are forgotten. The chemists, miners, engineers and learned men possess the secrets which were once those of the fairies only. Yet the artists and architects, the clockmakers and bellfounders, who love beauty, remember what their fathers once thought and believed. That is the reason why, on many a famous clock, either in front of the dial or near the pendulum, are figures of the gnomes, who thought, and the kabouters who wrought, to make the carillons. In Teuton lands, where their cousins are named kobolds, and in France where they are called fée, and in England brownies, they have tolling and ringing of bells, with peals, chimes and cascades of sweet sound; but the Netherlands, still, above all others on earth, is the home of the carillon.

The Phantom Vessel

ONCE A SHIP LOADED with pleasure-seekers was sailing from North China to Shanghai. High winds and stormy weather had delayed her, and she was still one week from port when a great plague broke out on board. This plague was of the worst kind. It attacked passengers and sailors alike until there were so few left to sail the vessel that it seemed as if she would soon be left to the mercy of winds and waves.

On all sides lay the dead, and the groans of the dying were most terrible to hear. Of that great company of travellers only one, a little boy named Ying-lo, had escaped. At last the few sailors, who had been trying hard to save their ship, were obliged to lie down upon the deck, a prey to the dreadful sickness, and soon they too were dead.

Ying-lo now found himself alone on the sea. For some reason – he did not know why – the gods or the sea fairies had spared him, but as he looked about in terror at the friends and loved ones who had died, he almost wished that he might join them.

The sails flapped about like great broken wings, while the giant waves dashed higher above the deck, washing many of the bodies overboard and wetting the little boy to the skin. Shivering with cold, he gave himself up for lost and prayed to the gods, whom his mother had often told him about, to take him from this dreadful ship and let him escape the fatal illness.

As he lay there praying he heard a slight noise in the rigging just above his head. Looking up, he saw a ball of fire running along a yardarm near the top of the mast. The sight was so strange that he forgot his prayer and stared with open-mouthed wonder. To his astonishment, the ball grew brighter and brighter, and then suddenly began slipping down the mast, all the time increasing in size. The poor boy did not know what to do or to think. Were the gods, in answer to his prayer, sending fire to burn the vessel? If so, he would soon escape. Anything would be better than to be alone upon the sea.

Nearer and nearer came the fireball. At last, when it reached the deck, to Ying-lo's surprise, something very, very strange happened. Before he had time to feel alarmed, the light vanished, and a funny little man stood in front of him peering anxiously into the child's frightened face.

"Yes, you are the lad I'm looking for," he said at last, speaking in a piping voice that almost made Ying-lo smile. "You are Ying-lo, and you are the only one left of this wretched company." This he said, pointing towards the bodies lying here and there about the deck.

Although he saw that the old man meant him no harm, the child could say nothing, but waited in silence, wondering what would happen next.

By this time the vessel was tossing and pitching so violently that it seemed every minute as if it would upset and go down beneath the foaming waves, never to rise again. Not many miles distant on the right, some jagged rocks stuck out of the water, lifting their cruel heads as if waiting for the helpless ship.

The newcomer walked slowly towards the mast and tapped on it three times with an iron staff he had been using as a cane. Immediately the sails spread, the vessel righted itself and began to glide over the sea so fast that the gulls were soon left far behind, while the threatening rocks upon which the ship had been so nearly dashed seemed like specks in the distance.

"Do you remember me?" said the stranger, suddenly turning and coming up to Ying-lo, but his voice was lost in the whistling of the wind, and the boy knew only by the moving of his lips that the old man was talking. The greybeard bent over until his mouth was at Ying-lo's ear: "Did you ever see me before?"

With a puzzled look, at first the child shook his head. Then as he gazed more closely there seemed to be something that he recognized about the wrinkled face. "Yes, I think so, but I don't know when."

With a tap of his staff the fairy stopped the blowing of the wind, and then spoke once more to his small companion: "One year ago I passed through your village. I was dressed in rags, and was begging my way along the street, trying to find someone who would feel sorry for me. Alas! no one answered my cry for mercy. Not a crust was thrown into my bowl. All the people were deaf, and fierce dogs drove me from door to door. Finally when I was almost dying of hunger, I began to feel that here was a village without one good person in it. Just then you saw my suffering, ran into the house, and brought me out food. Your heartless mother saw you doing this and beat you cruelly. Do you remember now, my child?"

"Yes, I remember," he answered sadly, "and that mother is now lying dead. Alas! all, all are dead, my father and my brothers also. Not one is left of my family."

"Little did you know, my boy, to whom you were giving food that day. You took me for a lowly beggar, but, behold, it was not a poor man that you fed, for I am Iron Staff. You must have heard of me when they were telling of the fairies in the Western Heaven, and of their adventures here on earth."

"Yes, yes," answered Ying-lo, trembling half with fear and half with joy, "indeed I have heard of you many, many times, and all the people love you for your kind deeds of mercy."

"Alas! they did not show their love, my little one. Surely you know that if any one wishes to reward the fairies for their mercies, he must begin to do deeds of the same kind himself.

No one but you in all your village had pity on me in my rags. If they had known that I was Iron Staff, everything would have been different; they would have given me a feast and begged for my protection.

"The only love that loves aright
Is that which loves in every plight.
The beggar in his sad array
Is moulded of the selfsame clay.

"Who knows a man by what he wears,
By what he says or by his prayers?
Hidden beneath that wrinkled skin
A fairy may reside within.

"Then treat with kindness and with love
The lowly man, the god above;
A friendly nod, a welcome smile –
For love is ever worth the while."

Ying-lo listened in wonder to Iron Staff's little poem, and when he had finished, the boy's face was glowing with the love of which the fairy had spoken. "My poor, poor father and mother!" he cried; "they knew nothing of these beautiful things you are telling me. They were brought up in poverty. As they were knocked about in childhood by those around them, so they learned to beat others who begged them for help. Is it strange that they did not have hearts full of pity for you when you looked like a beggar?"

"But what about you, my boy? You were not deaf when I asked you. Have you not been whipped and punished all your life? How then did you learn to look with love at those in tears?"

The child could not answer these questions, but only looked sorrowfully at Iron Staff. "Oh, can you not, good fairy, will you not restore my parents and brothers, and give them another chance to be good and useful people?"

"Listen, Ying-lo; it is impossible – unless you do two things first," he answered, stroking his beard gravely and leaning heavily upon his staff.

"What are they? What must I do to save my family? Anything you ask of me will not be too much to pay for your kindness."

"First you must tell me of some good deed done by these people for whose lives you are asking. Name only one, for that will be enough; but it is against our rules to help those who have done nothing."

Ying-lo was silent, and for a moment his face was clouded. "Yes, I know," he said finally, brightening. "They burned incense once at the temple. That was certainly a deed of virtue."

"But when was it, little one, that they did this?"

"When my big brother was sick, and they were praying for him to get well. The doctors could not save him with boiled turnip juice or with any other of the medicines they used, so my parents begged the gods."

"Selfish, selfish!" muttered Iron Staff. "If their eldest son had not been dying they would have spent no money at the temple. They tried in this way to buy back his health, for they were expecting him to support them in their old age."

Ying-lo's face fell. "You are right," he answered.

"Can you think of nothing else?"

"Yes, oh, yes, last year when the foreigner rode through our village and fell sick in front of our house, they took him in and cared for him."

"How long?" asked the other sharply.

"Until he died the next week."

"And what did they do with the mule he was riding, his bed, and the money in his bag? Did they try to restore them to his people?"

"No, they said they'd keep them to pay for the trouble." Ying-lo's face turned scarlet.

"But try again, dear boy! Is there not one little deed of goodness that was not selfish? Think once more."

For a long time Ying-lo did not reply. At length he spoke in a low voice; "I think of one, but I fear it amounts to nothing."

"No good, my child, is too small to be counted when the gods are weighing a man's heart."

"Last spring the birds were eating in my father's garden. My mother wanted to buy poison from the shop to destroy them, but my father said no, that the little things must live, and he for one was not in favour of killing them."

"At last, Ying-lo, you have named a real deed of mercy, and as he spared the tiny birds from poison, so shall his life and the lives of your mother and brothers be restored from the deadly plague.

"But remember there is one other thing that depends on you."

Ying-lo's eyes glistened gratefully. "Then if it rests with me, and I can do it, you have my promise. No sacrifice should be too great for a son to make for his loved ones even though his life itself is asked in payment."

"Very well, Ying-lo. What I require is that you carry out to the letter my instructions. Now it is time for me to keep my promise to you."

So saying, Iron Staff called on Ying-lo to point out the members of his family, and, approaching them one by one, with the end of his iron stick he touched their foreheads. In an instant each, without a word, arose. Looking round and recognising Ying-lo, they stood back, frightened at seeing him with the fairy. When the last had risen to his feet, Iron Staff beckoned all of them to listen. This they did willingly, too much terrified to speak, for they saw on all sides signs of the plague that had swept over the vessel, and they remembered the frightful agony they had suffered in dying. Each knew that he had been lifted by some magic power from darkness into light.

"My friends," began the fairy, "little did you think when less than a year ago you drove me from your door that soon you yourselves would be in need of mercy. To-day you have had a peep into the awful land of Yama. You have seen the horror of his tortures, have heard the screams of his slaves, and by another night you would have been carried before him to be judged. What power is it that has saved you from his clutches? As you look back through your wicked lives can you think of any reason why you deserved this rescue? No, there is no memory of goodness in your black hearts. Well, I shall tell you: it is this little boy, this Ying-lo, who many times has felt the weight of your wicked hands and has hidden in terror at your coming. To him alone you owe my help."

Father, mother, and brothers all gazed in turn, first at the fairy and then at the timid child whose eyes fell before their looks of gratitude.

"By reason of his goodness this child whom you have scorned is worthy of a place within the Western Heaven. In truth, I came this very day to lead him to that fairyland. For you, however, he wishes to make a sacrifice. With sorrow I am yielding to his wishes. His sacrifice will be that of giving up a place among the fairies and of continuing to live here on this earth with you. He will try to make a change within your household. If at any time you treat him badly and do not heed his wishes – mark you well my words – by the power of this magic staff which I shall place in his hands, he may enter at once into the land of the fairies, leaving you to die in your wickedness. This I command him to do, and he has promised to obey my slightest wish.

"This plague took you off suddenly and ended your wicked lives. Ying-lo has raised you from its grasp and his power can lift you from the bed of sin. No other hand than his can bear the rod which I am leaving. If one of you but touch it, instantly he will fall dead upon the ground.

"And now, my child, the time has come for me to leave you. First, however, I must show you what you are now able to do. Around you lie the corpses of sailors and passengers. Tap three times upon the mast and wish that they shall come to life," So saying he handed Ying-lo the iron staff.

Although the magic rod was heavy, the child lifted it as if it were a fairy's wand. Then, stepping forward to the mast, he rapped three times as he had been commanded. Immediately on all sides arose the bodies, once more full of life and strength.

"Now command the ship to take you back to your home port, for such sinful creatures as these are in no way fit to make a journey among strangers. They must first return and free their homes of sin."

Again rapping on the mast, the child willed the great vessel to take its homeward course. No sooner had he moved the staff than, like a bird wheeling in the heavens, the bark swung round and started on the return journey. Swifter than a flash of lightning flew the boat, for it was now become a fairy vessel. Before the sailors and the travellers could recover from their surprise, land was sighted and they saw that they were indeed entering the harbour.

Just as the ship was darting toward the shore the fairy suddenly, with a parting word to Ying-lo, changed into a flaming ball of fire which rolled along the deck and ascended the spars. Then, as it reached the top of the rigging, it floated off into the blue sky, and all on board, speechless with surprise, watched it until it vanished.

With a cry of thanksgiving, Ying-lo flung his arms about his parents and descended with them to the shore.

Cat-Kin and the Queen Mother

KOREA IS CALLED the Land of the Plum Blossom, but in winter the rivers freeze over. Then the men cut through the ice which is often several feet thick, to catch with their fishing lines and hooks the fish that swim in the water beneath. Yet they are very glad to welcome any sign of the coming spring, and they watch eagerly for the pussy willows to show themselves.

Now there was a farmer who lived in Nai-po, which is the grain garden of the Korean peninsula, who wanted a little daughter, though other parents cared more for sons.

One day farmer Pak, for that was his name, discovered a pussy willow which seemed to him, after the long winter, like a light shining in a dark place. He plucked it and carried proudly home this branch full of fuzzy little buds. This was a sign of his happiness at the return of spring. He was tired of ice and snow and now he knew that soon the gloomy hills would burst into a glory of bright colors from the blooming flowers, and look like an army with flags.

That same day his prayers were answered and a little girl was born into his home. Giving the pussy willow to his wife, he said: "We shall name our baby Cat-kin, that is Little Puss."

Cat-kin never saw a cradle, for the Korean mothers carry their babies on their backs. She was soon out of infancy, and then it was not long before she was standing up and toddling about and playing with her doggie and pet bull. These little pets on four legs usually take the place of kittens in a country home in Korea, for the cats are wild and do not allow children to fondle them.

Long before she was a dozen years old, Cat-kin became very fond of fairy stories, of which Korea has a great many, besides thousands of tales of wonderful people and animals and what happened to them. She often looked up towards the high hills and distant mountains, where she thought the fairies, dragons, ogres and tigers lived. Here also dwelt the sen-nin or mountain spirits, wise and good, of whom the old people talked and the soldiers painted on their banners when they went to war.

When about eight years old, Cat-kin wanted very much to walk up towards the north star, which her father showed her shining in the heavens. He had once traveled up into one of the Northern provinces, where during the daytime he could see afar off the great snow-white mass of the Ever White Mountain rising up to meet the azure sky. There, at the top he had heard, lay the Dragon Prince's Pool, out of which flowed the two rivers that made Korea an island. One was named the Tumen and the other the Yalu, after the beautiful green and blue sheen on the feathers of a drake's back, so richly colored were its shining waters. When her father told of his travels, Cat-kin also longed to go north to get to the very top and touch the sky.

But this she knew she could not do, even if she had had long legs and were as strong as a man, for the tigers were very numerous and always roaming about. These yellow and black striped brutes were man-eaters. They loved nothing better for a good dinner than a young girl.

So as she did not know any way of getting to the top of the Ever White Mountain and of seeing the deep blue waters of the Pool, except by riding on the back of a dragon, which she sometimes dreamed of, she kept waiting and waiting for one of these flying creatures to come, yet it never came.

Cat-kin was bound to have the fairies visit her, if possible. So one day, sitting under a persimmon tree and reading a story, she held the book in one hand, while she struck the ground several times, saying earnestly:

"Earth-spirit, earth-spirit, come to me; come up and see me."

All of a sudden the air seemed heavy with sweet perfume, and a silver mist like a cloud spread over her house and garden. Then a bright dazzling light flooded everything and there stood before her a glistening chariot, made of blue jade with golden wheels. It was drawn by milk-white horses and on a seat of shining silver sat the Western Heavenly Queen Mother herself.

Attendant upon the Mother Queen were thousands of the most beautiful maidens, who were all dressed in resplendent robes. They wore amber ornaments, and silver girdles, and necklaces of precious stones and silken robes with many tassels. Their feet were shod with gold embroidered velvet slippers, and on their heads were caps of gold studded with glittering gems. Cat-kin could hardly count the rich ornaments, necklaces, breast chains and the jade wands, like sceptres, which they held in their hands. These were shaped like lotus flowers. The faces of all these maidens were rosy, their eyes sparkled, and all had small hands and feet.

In a voice of great sweetness that sounded like music the Heavenly Queen Mother looked at Cat-kin and spoke to her, saying:

"Come forward, little maid, fear not. I shall take you with me to my palace, in the Island of Gems and give you all you want, besides showering blessings on your people, if you will come."

Cat-kin did not feel at all timid or frightened, but came boldly forward and knelt at the base of the chariot.

The Mother Queen first touched her with her milk-white jade wand, that was carved like a lotus bud, and made the little girl rise.

In a moment more, a silver chariot, with wheels made of turquoise and drawn by two young milk-white dragons, wheeled up close to her, and the attendant lady in golden robes bade her step in.

The dragons were fierce, powerful, fire-breathing creatures, with wide spreading wings, and their bodies and tails together were of the length of whales, while their eyes darted fire. Yet Cat-kin was not at all afraid, and thought it was great fun. Then up through and far above the clouds the host of bright beings flew. They followed the Queen Mother's chariot until, far away, they poised in mid-sky. Cat-kin was then told to look over the side of the chariot to the earth and ocean, miles and miles below. She was asked if she could recognize her father's cottage, but she could not. The whole village looked only like a grey mass of thatched roofs, and she could pick out only the temple.

There, spread out, was the great sea, as blue as a sapphire, and in places deep green, like an emerald, but she could see no ships nor any coast or shores, nor any ranges of mountains, nor signs of the land of Korea. Nothing but ripples and waves were visible. Yet in the center of the azure sea was an island. The trees were emeralds and the roofs of the houses were of gold, and the windows diamonds. These were so full of light that no lamps were necessary.

Beautiful beings, all maidens, as lovely in garb and face as those who filled the train of the Queen Mother, walked or played, or sang in the gardens. Or swam and sported in the sapphire waves, or rowed and sailed about in boats that seemed as if made of marble, they were so white.

At a signal from the Queen the singing ceased. Then there rose up wave upon wave of sweetest melody from the players on instruments who were in the gardens below.

Cat-kin thought she heard at intervals the chorus, sounding out the words, rising upward like pulses, through the air, "Welcome lovely mortal! Our Queen invites and we greet thee! Manifold be her gifts to thee and thine! Come, thou honored among all Korean maidens! Come to us and join our band and we shall love thee as one of ourselves."

In the wink of a falcon's eye – so short a time it seemed – the Mother Queen and her host descended.

As the chariots touched the island, a bevy of radiant maidens came forward, some to attend the Queen Mother and some to lead Cat-kin into her own room in the palace. There the most gorgeous robes were put on her, beside a cap begemmed with glittering, precious stones of various colors, and a pair of gold-embroidered velvet slippers.

Cat-kin was surprised when one of the shining maidens set a royal tiara adorned with five gems upon her brow.

"For me?" she asked in surprise.

"Yes for you, whom the Heavenly Mother Queen would honor."

"And what do these five gems, jade, crystal, malachite, amber and agate signify?" asked Cat-kin.

"Ah, that is not for us to tell you, but the Queen Mother ordered these. Tomorrow she will explain to you the secret of each gem."

Cat-kin walked about freely, enjoying the lovely sights and sounds. She also ate with keen appetite and to her full of the delicacies set on the table before her. Yet never once did she feel sleepy, nor see any beds, nor hear anyone talk of retiring. She wondered what they meant when they said "tomorrow"; for she could see no sun or moon or twilight. However, she did not think long about such things, and by and by forgot all about them.

When the entire court and all the hosts of the Queen Mother's attendants had assembled, Her Majesty's chamberlain read the proclamation, which declared that the Queen looked with great favor upon the Korean people, and had decided to bestow great gifts upon them. For this purpose, she had selected and brought to her palace the Korean maid named Cat-kin, to endow them through this, their daughter, with five precious traits of disposition and character. In token of gracious thought and tender love, Her Majesty would now present and explain the meaning of the five precious gems. These were jade, crystal, malachite, amber, and agate.

Cat-kin kneeled down before the Queen, who placed in Cat-kin's hands the shining gems, while an attendant fairy took them from her opened palm and placed each one of them on vermilion velvet, edged with gold. Then five maidens stood by, each with a gem laid on a cushion.

After the ceremony of presentation was over, the Queen made a speech, which told the Korean maiden's fortune and her future.

Cat-kin would be sent back over the clouds and ocean to the King's palace in the capital of her home land, and there be made a princess. Many nobles and king's sons from other countries, hearing of her beauty and her wonderful visit to the Island of Gems would come to pay her court as suitors. Many would ask for her hand, to be wedded to her; but she was to marry none but the king's son, a prince of her own people.

"Take these gems, fair maiden, and bestow their virtues and what they mean upon your people," said the Queen. "A thousand years from now – as men count time – we together will visit Korea again."

Then both the Queen and Cat-kin, stepping into the silver chariot, drawn by the fire-breathing dragons, plunged on and mounted up into space. First they sailed above the clouds and then dipped downwards, steering to Korea and over the mountains, bearing their precious charge to the capital. They reached the ground in a cloud and the wheels of the chariot stood still before the palace gate.

Yet before any mortal eyes could see their full forms, the Queen Mother and the dragons had disappeared, and Cat-kin stood alone, a resplendent maiden of dazzling appearance and in the robes given by the Heavenly Queen Mother, which all recognized at once as coming from the Island of Gems.

A throng of court ladies and palace attendants and a long line of nobles and princes were already waiting for the maiden, who they knew came gift-laden from the Queen Mother, of whom all had heard from childhood. The five gems were laid, each in a covered casket of perfumed wood, encrusted with gold on top and inlaid with mother-of-pearl.

Escorted into the throne room by a bevy of princesses, the Heavenly Mother's gifts in the five caskets were reverently placed on silken fans, spread out on a table having on its top the five cushions of crimson velvet.

Then, by lot and word of the diviners, the choice of a first drawing was awarded to a prince of fair face and mien. The other four nobles, one by one and in turn, approached and each was allowed to choose one of the caskets, all of which looked alike, and none was to be opened until the possessor was in his own home.

Now these were the gifts for body and mind, of which the polished gems were the tokens. According as each prince chose and received, so with the trait, which each gem signified, would his children and posterity be endowed. In the course of centuries, these would become the national features, of twenty millions of Koreans.

One by one the caskets were opened by each prince, and therein he discovered what was a trait in the character of the Korean people. These were:

Procrastination – Putting off until tomorrow, or some other time, what ought to be done today, and keeping back not only one person but the whole nation.

Hospitality – Always glad to see friends, to entertain people, even strangers, and to take care of relations, even to the making of one's self poor – a habit carried too far as the years and centuries rolled on.

Inexactness – The habit of not usually thinking clearly, counting correctly, or stating facts precisely, and when telling a story of "blowing a conch;" that is, of exaggerating.

Love of family – How the mothers and fathers in Korea do love their children, their kinsfolk and their relatives!

Sense of humor – A Korean can always see the funny side of things. He loves to joke and he bears his troubles well, because he likes to smile. As for the girls, they laugh as easily as the rain falls, or the flowers bloom.

And what the Queen Mother predicted came true. Just as five fingers make up the hand, so the average people among the Koreans are known by the five traits, for better or for worse.

Tokgabi and His Pranks

TOKGABI IS THE most mischievous sprite in all Korean fairy-land. He does not like the sunshine or outdoors, and no one ever saw him on the streets.

He lives in the sooty flues that run under the floors along the whole length of the house, from the kitchen at one end of it to the chimney hole in the ground at the other end. He delights in the smoke and smut, and does not mind fire or flame, for he likes to be where it is warm. He has no lungs, and his skin and eyes are both fire-proof. He is as black as night and loves nothing that has white in it. He is always afraid of a bit of silver, even if it be only a hairpin.

Tokgabi likes most to play at night in the little loft over the fireplace. To run along the rafters and knock down the dust and cobwebs is his delight. His favorite game is to make the iron rice-pot lid dance up and down, so that it tumbles inside the rice kettle and cannot easily be got out again. Oh, how many times the cook burns, scalds, or steams her fingers in attempting to fish out that pot lid when Tokgabi has pushed it in! How she does bless the sooty imp!

But Tokgabi is not always mischievous, and most of his capers hurt nobody. He is such a merry fellow that he keeps continually busy, whether people cry or laugh. He does not mean to give any one trouble, but he must have fun every minute, especially at night.

When the fire is out, how he does chase the mice up and down the flues under the floor, and up in the garret over the rafters! When the mousies lie dead on their backs, with their toes turned upward, the street boys take them outdoors and throw them up in the air. Before the mice fall to the ground, the hawks swoop down and eat them up. Many a bird of prey gets his breakfast in this way.

Although Tokgabi plays so many pranks, he is kind to the kitchen maids. When after a hard day's work one is so tired out that she falls asleep, he helps her to do her hard tasks.

Tokgabi washes their dishes and cleans their tables for good servants; so when they wake up the girls find their work done for them. Many a fairy tale is told about this jolly sprite's doings – how he gives good things to the really nice people and makes the bad ones mad by spitefully using them. They do say that the king of all the Tokgabis has a museum of curiosities and a storehouse full of gold and gems and fine clothes, and everything sweet to eat for good boys and girls and for old people that are kind to the birds and dumb animals. For bad folks he has all sorts of things that are ugly and troublesome. He punishes stingy people by making them poor and miserable.

The Tokgabi king has also a menagerie of animals. These he sends to do his errands rewarding the good and punishing naughty folks. Every year the little almanac with red and green covers tells in what quarter of the skies the Tokgabi king lives for that year, so that the farmers and country people will keep out of his way and not provoke him. In his menagerie the kind creatures that help human beings are the dragon, bear, tortoise, frog, dog and rabbit. These are all man's friends. The cruel and treacherous creatures in Tokgabi's menagerie are the tiger, wild boar, leopard, serpent, toad and cat. These are the messengers of the Tokgabi king to do his bidding, when he punishes naughty folks.

The common, every-day Tokgabi plays fewer tricks on the men and boys and enjoys himself more in bothering the girls and women. This, I suppose, is because they spend more time in the house than their fathers or brothers. In the Land of Rat-tat-tat, where the sound of beating the washed clothes never ceases, Tokgabi loves to get hold of the women's laundry sticks which are used for pounding and polishing the starched clothes. He hides them so that they cannot be found. Then Daddy makes a fuss because his long white coat has to go without its usual gloss, but it is all Tokgabi's fault.

Tokgabi does not like starch because it is white. He loves to dance on Daddy's big black hat case that hangs on the wall. Sometimes he wiggles the fetich, or household idol, that is suspended from the rafters. But, most of all, he enjoys dancing a jig among the dishes in the closet over the fireplace, making them rattle and often tumble down with a crash.

Tokgabi likes to bother men sometimes too. If Daddy should get his topknot caught in a rat hole, or his head should slip off his wooden pillow at night and he bump his nose, it is all Tokgabi's fault. When anything happens to a boy's long braid of hair, that hangs down his back and makes him look so much like a girl, Tokgabi is blamed for it. It is even said that naughty men make compacts with Tokgabi to do bad things, but the imp only helps the man for the fun of it. Tokgabi cares nothing about what mortal men call right or wrong. He is only after fun and is up to mischief all the time, so one must watch out for him.

The kitchen maids and the men think they know how to circumvent Tokgabi and spoil his tricks. Knowing that the imp does not like red, a young man when betrothed wears clothes of this bright color. Tokgabi is afraid of shining silver, too, so the men fasten their topknots together, and the girls keep their chignons in shape, with silver hairpins. The magistrates and government officers have little storks made of solid silver in their hats, or else these birds are embroidered with silver thread on their dresses. Every one who can afford them uses white metal dishes and dresses in snowy garments. Tokgabi likes nothing white and that is the reason why every Korean likes to put on clothes that are as dazzling as hoar frost. Tons and mountains of starch are consumed in blanching and stiffening coats and skirts, sleeves and stockings. On festival days the people look as if they were dipped in starch and their garments encrusted in rock candy. In this manner they protect themselves from the pranks of Tokgabi.

Old Timber Top

THE FAIRIES IN THE Korean province of Kang Wen, which means River Meadow, were having great fun, when one of their number told how they played a trick on an ox-driver whom they called Old Timber Top. How he got such a strange name this story will tell.

This driver was a rich and stingy fellow who had made a fortune in lumber. He used to buy up all the trees he could. Then he would have them cut down and sawed up into logs and boards. His men would haul them away in their rough carts, drawn by stout bulls, to his lumber yard. In winter time sleds were used, but whether it was the season of snow and ice, or of tree blossoms and flowers, the animal used to draw sleds or carts was always a bull.

For in Korea, horses or donkeys do not know how to pull anything. The ponies and donkeys are too small. Not being used to the work, if harnessed they would kick the wagon all to pieces.

They can carry loads on their backs, but the bulls can do this also, so the creature with horns is considered to be the most valuable of beasts of burden. Besides, he fills the purse and makes good dinners when his owner is through with him.

You can see these patient carriers loaded with brushwood or sticks piled so high they seem to be carrying small mountains of twigs, grass and leaves for kindlings, or with heavy logs of wood for fuel. Yet when the bull is very young, a mere baby, he has a happier time than a colt or little donkey, for he lives in the house and is the children's pet.

Old Timber Top sold his logs and boards at such high prices that the poor suffered. This was because they were cold and could not afford to pay so many strings of cash for fuel. The people used to say that the old fellow would skin a mosquito for his hide and tallow. So sometimes they gave him the nickname of Skin-flay.

Not many of the villagers were able to buy planks of wood thick and heavy and strong enough to keep their pigs from the tigers, which came down from the mountains and prowled about at night in the villages. These long-haired and black-striped beasts got to be so fond of pork, that even in the snow they would, without fearing the cold or the guns of the hunters, claw up the tops of the pens and get down among the squealing prey. They might get a baby pig at once or perhaps drag out and carry off enough of a big pork to feed their cubs for a week. All the stables and cow-houses had to be made very strong, for the tigers, when they had gone a good while without food, seemed to be hungry enough to eat a horse with all his harness on, and even a grown-up cow or ox. Yet as a rule, no tiger cared to taste either beef or horse meat, if he could get young pork or veal.

Old Timber Top was not satisfied to make money at his lumber yard only. It is the custom in Korea to plant the most beautiful trees around tombs or in the cemeteries. When this skinflint heard of a family which had become so poor that they must needs sell the splendid trees which had been planted around their ancestors' graves he sent his agents to buy the timber. These fellows would load up a horse with long ropes, of copper and iron cash, coins that had a square hole in the middle and were strung together with twine made of twisted straw. It was a heavy horse load to carry twenty dollars' worth of coin. Arrived on the spot, after beating the owner down to the lowest price possible, Old Timber Top's men would go out, chop down and saw up the grand trees, leaving only the sawdust on the graves, while the people wept to lose what they loved.

In this way the landscape was spoiled and this made many villagers very angry at such a man, for the Koreans love natural scenery and almost worship fine trees, which had made the country beautiful for centuries.

But what cared Old Timber Top, provided he could pile up his strings of cash and jingle his silver?

In time, this hard old fellow could think of nothing else but how to get richer out of the wants and sufferings of other people. The wealthier he became, the more he wanted. Yet he did not get any happier. Nobody loved him, while many hated him.

At last he thought he would make a trip to Seoul, the great capital city, which every Korean hopes to see sometime. There he expected to receive honor and appointment to rank and office. Timber Top had a relative who was high in the king's service, who, he thought, would assist him; for all Koreans are kind and helpful to each other, especially when they are related.

To be an officer Timber Top knew would permit him, even to wear a gorgeously shining mandarin's hat with wide flaps or wings on it and a long white silk coat with a big square on the breast of velvet or satin, embroidered with storks or dragons, clouds and waves. When he went out on the streets he could strut about, as if he were the lord of the universe; for he would then wear a hat so high and with such a round wide brim, that he would not dare to go out during a high wind, for fear of being blown away, like a ship in a tempest. In such a costume he would be saluted by servants and the common people, who would bow down before him, because they would think him a great man.

But how could he win such a position and gain the glory of it?

He was not a scholar, learned in books, or in law, or a doctor of medicine. Not being a soldier, either, he knew nothing of war. He could not ride on a monocycle, as a general did, drawn or pushed by four men and dressed in a long red coat studded all over with shining metal with a brass helmet on his head, on the top of which was a little dragon. He feared, even if he were appointed, he might fall off the one-wheeled vehicle and show what a fool he was.

Nevertheless this old fellow was so vain and full of conceit that he followed what was once the common custom in Korea. He took his journey to Seoul, leaving his family behind him to live on the cheapest kind of kimchi, with turnips and millet.

Now the Koreans are all famous for giving welcome and showing hospitality to their poor relations, and often they do this even to tramps and lazy people. When a man becomes rich or holds a high office, he usually has around him many hangers on. Some, we should even say, were loafers.

So on arriving in Seoul, Old Timber Top took up his quarters in one part of his relative's big house. There he lived a long time and was treated decently, for he always was saying soft things and making flattering speeches to his host. In fact, he bowed down like a slave when in presence of his august master. Yet, in truth, he was despised even by the servants and work people.

In order not to wear his welcome entirely out he had to make from time to time a handsome present to his patron. This steadily reduced both his income and his fortune, and while these were shrinking his family at home suffered, so that, by and by, he received notice by letter that his business had dried up and soon no more money could be sent to him in Seoul. While he lingered news from home grew worse and worse. His wife was obliged to sell their house to pay debts. The next item was that she and her daughter were living in a wretched shanty at the end of the village and were no longer in society.

All this time those in Seoul who knew that the foolish fellow was as ambitious as ever to wear the fine white clothes of a scholar, or the gay colors of a soldier, declared that Old Timber Top had no brains. They even jested about a pumpkin set on shoulders, or they laughed when they declared that the wood, which he had sold so long, had gone to his head. They debated in the wine shops whether, if his skull were opened, pumpkin seeds or timber would be found inside of it.

So they, also, called him "Old Timber Top," meaning that inside his skull was a wooden head and no better than that of an idol carved out of persimmon wood, such as were so plentiful in the Buddhist temples. Others declared that he had a real head of bone and brains, but "he carried it under his arm pits," as the saying was.

When the fairies heard all this, they unanimously resolved to reform the old fellow, even if they had to make an ox of him.

Timber Top, now poor and bankrupt, knew he must leave Seoul and go home and work for a living. When he made his final call on his rich Seoul relative and told him he must, to his great regret, take his leave and go back to his native village, he was not well received. Being too poor to buy a present to give to his host, on whose bounty he had lived so long, he was answered coldly and told to go and do as he liked.

And this, after years of fawning and gift-making! Not a word of thanks or appreciation! Poor Timber Top was down in the mouth and his heart was cold in his bosom. He knocked on his head with his fists, to find out whether, after all, it had really turned into timber.

On his way back, a big storm came on and when he came to a village inn, cold, wet and hungry, he begged for shelter over night. The woman who kept it was the wife of a butcher, who was then away from home. This was an awful blow to Timber Top's pride, for butchers were held to be the lowest of people, and they were not even allowed to wear hats, like the rest of the men in Korea.

The woman was kind to the traveler. She gave him a hot supper and let him sleep in that room of the house which had the best stone floor, under which the flues from the kitchen fire ran. So he warmed himself and baked his clothes, which were sopping wet, until they were dry. He was so tired that he kept on sleeping till very late next morning, and nearly to the noon hour. He was altogether so comfortable that to him it seemed as if he were a great man in the capital, thus to receive such kind treatment.

Waking up from one of his naps, he heard what he thought was the big butcher, who had come home, asking of his wife in a gruff tone of voice, "Where is that ox? I must sell him this morning, for it is market day," he said.

In less than a minute more, the man and his wife entered the room with four sticks which the fairies had put there, a halter, and a rope, made of twisted rice straw, besides a thick iron ring, such as they put into bulls' noses, to make them obey their masters. Throwing down the iron ring and rope on the floor, in a trice they had thrust the stick under Old Timber Top's back. In a moment more, he felt horns growing out of his head, and his lips becoming thick as sausages. His mouth was as wide as a saucer and had big teeth growing on the upper jaw. A tail sprouted at his other end and the four sticks became four legs.

Before he could quite understand just what was going on, or what the matter could be, Old Timber Top was standing on four legs and the butcher was slipping the ring through his nose. Oh how it did hurt!

It was an awkward job to get the animal out of the room and through the narrow door, and some of the paper on the walls and the furniture suffered. But finally when out in the open air the bull, that was no other than what had been the man Timber Top, went quietly along to the market place. Any attempt to pull his head away, or to stop or run off, or in any way to misbehave, hurt his nose so dreadfully, that he quickly quit. The butcher needed to give only a slight jerk of the rope when the bull changed his gait and was as quiet as a lamb, even though as an animal he was big enough to gore the man and toss him on its horns, or crush him by trampling on him with his hoofs, if once he got angry.

One would have supposed that Timber Top would be a fighting bull, but no! In the market place he stood patiently and quietly for hours, hardly even stamping, when the flies began to bite.

"Oh that I had been as diligent and kept on at my honest occupation in my native village, as that fly!" mused the bull, that still had a man's memory.

At last there came a man with money to buy. He was a drover, who unloaded his pony and paid down many strings, or about twenty pounds, of copper and iron cash. The owner put the halter in the buyer's hand, and the new master then led off Timber Top to be sold to a butcher who lived up in his home town in the north. This fellow intended first to fatten the animal and then turn him into steaks and stewing meat.

But on his way the new owner thought that, because he had made a good bargain, he must stop at a wine shop and have a drink. So he tied Timber Top's nose with the rope to the low wall, which enclosed a turnip field, and went inside the shop.

But while the drover's wine went in his wits went out, and he fell asleep and stayed in the shop a long time. In fact, it was as the old song said:

"First the man takes a dram,
Then the dram takes another dram;
Then the dram takes the man."

Meanwhile Timber Top looked over the low wall, and, yielding to temptation, pulled up with his teeth some of the plants by the roots, first chewing the green leaves and then grinding the turnips and swallowing them.

Presto! The horns drew in and shrivelled up. The ring dropped out of his nose and fell with a crash on the stones of the village path. His two forelegs turned into arms, the hair and hoofs became human legs and Old Timber Top was a man, and himself once again. To make sure of it he felt himself all over; pulled his own nose, felt around his back to see if he had a tail, and rubbed his head for horns. None there! He looked down and found he had only two legs. Then he swung his arms with delight, at being once more a man.

"Well named, Turn-up thou," he mused, "thou green plant with a mustard-like taste. Thou hast turned me inside out. Or, have the fairies been busy?"

He had hardly got these ideas through his half wooden head, that he was on two legs and a man once more and could think like one, than he started on the road home. Just then the drover rushed out of the wine shop and accosted him, saying:

"Have you seen a stray bull anywhere near this place?"

Of course Timber Top using fine language, like a yang ban, said there was no bull in the neighborhood that he could see or knew of, and he had heard none bellowing. Then he gave the drover a look of contempt for being so stupid, and for asking of him, a gentleman, so foolish a question.

Yet after he was out of sight of the drover he slapped his thighs, as Koreans do when they are amused at their own smartness, and went on joyfully. He kept on repeating to himself, "sticks and turnips, turnips and sticks."

Then a big idea struck him, as if it were a tap on a wooden drum, such as one sees in Buddhist temples. It hit his brain so hard and so swelled his head, that his big Korean hat nearly toppled off. Immediately he put this idea into action.

He returned hastily to the inn and into the room in which he had been turned into a bull and stole the butcher's four fairy sticks, which stood in a corner, then he hied at once over the roads towards the capital.

Reaching Seoul, he went to the house of his rich relative, where he had waited ten years for the fortune and the favor which did not come. Going into his host's bedroom, he tapped the high lord of the house with the fairy sticks, not hard, but only lightly.

Forthwith the man's head became horns at the top, with muzzle of thick lips in front. His hands turned into front hoofs and his legs into the hind quarters of a bull. Yet he was not entirely an ox, but only half animal and half man.

Old Timber Top stopped tapping and then went away, to await events, leaving the creature half man and half ox. He knew that soon he would be called in.

When the family of wife, many sons, several daughters, servants, retainers, hangers-on, and what not, saw their master half man and half ox, with horns and hoofs, they were distracted. Each one had his own notion of how to get him back into human form and like his former self. Each one ran all over town and into the adjoining villages to get and call in the mudangs.

These mudangs were the people, mostly women, whose business it was to drive out the imps and bad fairies, such as had, in this case, done the mischief. The kitchen maids stoutly declared that Tokgabi had wrought the change upon their master. They felt quite sure of it; but the men thought that the gods of the mountains were punishing him for his sins. On the other hand, the mudang woman said she would find out and get him back into his human skin, if they paid her enough money.

With drums and dancing and songs, screams, yells, and every sort of noise, the mudangs kept up such a terrible racket that it almost deafened the family. There were several of them called in, and they knew that they would all be well paid.

Meanwhile the doctors also kept on with their awful medicines, besides rubbing, pounding, blowing, and sticking needles into the bull and burning moxa, or little balls of cottony mugwort, on its hide.

Yet not a hoof or horn, not even a hair changed.

The mudangs declared that the imps had got inside the man and they must get them out. One fellow carried a big bottle to trap the imps and cork them in. Another insisted that they would have to use scissors and snip the skin in about a hundred places, thus making small holes to let the evil creatures out. Then they must bottle them up, lest they should get out and overrun the house and infest the whole town.

There seemed not so many chances of getting well as "one hair among nine oxen"; but the wife pleaded that they would put off using the scissors until all other means had failed. She did not want to see her dear husband's skin made into a colander, or sieve, if it could be helped.

At this point, when the din and the despair were worst and had come to a climax, Old Timber Top appeared. As some of the family had collapsed and lay helpless on the floor, and as all were too tired to ask questions, they at once made way for him. After looking at the patient with a face as wise as an owl's, Old Timber Top solemnly announced that only one thing could save him and that was a rare and wonderful drug, of which only he knew the secret, but which he could speedily procure. Of course the wife, sons and daughters instantly promised to give up their all, to see their husband and father himself again.

So while Timber Top went out to get the famous medicine, they all fell asleep, tired out, while the ox-man lay over on his side resting his horns and hoofs on the floor bed; for in Korea they do not have bedsteads, that is, beds raised up from the floor.

As for Old Timber Top, when once out on the street, he immediately began saying to himself, over and over again, "Turnips and sticks, sticks and turnips."

Going to a vegetable shop, he bought a fine large turnip, or turnip-radish, of the kind that grows in Korea, silvery white and about four feet long. He first peeled, then sliced, and finally pounded it into a sauce very fine. Then entering the house in triumph, he woke up the doctors, kicked the servants awake, and announced that the potent drug would soon restore their master. He solemnly bade them all watch and see him do it.

Pulling and hauling all together, five or six fellows were able to get the man-bull on his two hoofs and two feet and then Timber Top put a spoonful of the sauce on the big tongue.

At once a most marvellous change took place!

The horns shortened until they disappeared, the lips thinned, the mouth became smaller. Hoofs, hair, and hide departed into empty air. In the wagging of a dog's tail, the mighty man of the house had become himself again.

All the doctors, jugglers, and mudangs packed up their imp-bottles and medicines, and with their drums, flutes, bags, boxes and wares slunk away, while the family loaded Old Timber Top with grateful thanks and compliments.

As for the master, he declared Timber Top the greatest physician the world ever knew. He invited him to make the house his permanent home and showered upon him many gifts, with plenty to eat, and white clothes starched as white as snow. The hats with which he presented Timber Top were so big around and had a brim so wide, that he used them when covered with oiled paper covers as umbrellas in rainy weather, but he never went out doors when the wind was blowing, for fear he would be whirled down the street. Besides this, he feared there was still much wood in his head, which might turn into a top and spin round, if he were not careful.

Old Timber Top set up a medicine office, practiced among the nobility and became physician to the king. When he visited the palace, he used a red visiting card, a foot long. He had a plastron, or square of velvet embroidery on his breast. He wore a string of amber beads as big as walnuts over his ears. He soon became fat with a double chin and plump fingers, showing that he reeked with prosperity. He lived to a good old age, his family were made comfortable, his sons and daughters married well, and he had seventeen grandchildren before he died.

Yet all the time, the fairies claimed that they did it all. They made the sticks work one way, and the turnips another, and they still play their tricks on the Koreans, especially those with more or less wood in their heads.

The Woodman and the Mountain Fairies

OVER A HALF THOUSAND years ago there lived in a northern village, near Ping Yang, a wood-cutter named Keel Wee.

He owned a sturdy bull that carried on its back the fuel which he daily cut on the mountains and sold on the main street of his village, at the fair, which was held every fifth day. The docile brute could carry a load of faggots and brushwood piled many feet high over his head and tied down with ropes, so that at a distance nothing but his legs were visible. This beast, although so huge, was the gentlest creature imaginable. The children were all very fond of the big fellow and were accustomed to play with him as if he were one of them, or at least like a pet dog. The reason of this was that when but a week old the bull-calf had been taken from his cow-mother and brought up in the family with the girls and boys. Only the puppy dog, that also occupied the house with the young folks, was a great favorite.

On a fine summer morning, Keel Wee, leaving his beast behind, went up on the mountain and cut enough wood to load up and bring down on another day.

His wife, as she shouted good-bye, told him to be sure and be home in time for supper, for their eldest son had gone a-fishing and a good string of perch was expected.

Shouldering his axe, he started up the mountain path. He had to go pretty far, for near towns or cities in Korea all the timber had long since been cut away. Every year the woodmen have to search farther afield to find fuel.

Arriving in the woods where there was a clearing, Keel Wee prepared to wield his trusty axe. He was about to take off his big hat and outer coat and lay about him, when he spied, at some distance off, two fairy-like beings. They had long hair, looked very wise and were dressed in costume of the Chow dynasty of two thousand years ago. They sat on stones and played the game of go-ban.

Coming near, the woodman took a respectful attitude, and, looking on, soon became interested in the moves of the players. So far from being at all disconcerted at the presence of a stranger, the two fairies seemed by eye-winks to invite him to look on. Feeling quite proud to be thus honored, Keel Wee, leaning his chin upon the handle of his axe, became absorbed in the game and by and by grew quite excited. Forgetting himself and his manners, he stretched forth his right hand to move one of the pieces. At once the fairy nearest to him gave him a crack on the fingers for his impudence, and jerked Keel Wee's arm away. Then without saying a word, he took out from his wallet something that looked like a persimmon seed and put in the woodman's mouth. After this all three were perfectly quiet.

Hour after hour the game proceeded and the players grew more intensely interested. As for Keel Wee, his eyes never winked, so hard did he look at the yellow board covered with the black and white pieces. Several times, when he thought he saw how the fairy on his right could beat in the game, or the one on his left make a better move, he felt like telling one or the other so. When, however, he tried to move his tongue, he found he could not speak, or utter a cry. Somehow he felt as if he were in a dream.

Yet all the time he became more and more wrapped up in the game, so that he determined to see the end of it and know which player had beaten. He forgot that with mountain spirits there is no night or morning, or passing of the hours, nor do they care anything about clocks or bells, because in fairy-land there is no time.

All the while Keel Wee was leaning with his chin on the stout axe-handle, holding it with both hands under his neck. He took no note of the sun or stars, daylight or darkness and he felt no hunger.

Suddenly the timber of his axe seemed to turn to dust and his chin fell. The next thing he knew he had lost his support. Down went his head, and forward fell his body as he tumbled over, upsetting the checker-board, breaking up the game and scattering the round pieces hither and yon over the ground.

Awaking as out of a sleep, and thoroughly ashamed of himself for his impoliteness, he tried to pick himself up and humbly apologize for the accident which he had caused by his own rudeness. He expected and was ready for a good scolding. But when he looked up, the fairies were gone. Nothing whatever was seen of them or of the playboard and checkers, nor any signs of their having been there, except that when he put his hand on the flat stones, which they had used as seats, he found them warm to his touch.

But where was his axe-handle and what had happened? When he had left home, he had come straight from the barber shop, with his face smooth and clean shaven. Now he put his hand to his breast and found that he had grown a long white beard. As for the iron axe-head, it was there, but rusty and half buried in the ground. He had worn one of the big farmer's hats, which, when turned upside down, might hold a bushel or two of turnips, and when fastened to his head spread over his shoulders like a roof. Where could it be? He looked about him to find it, but saw only the bits of the slats inside the frame and a few scraps of what remained, for the rest had long ago rotted away. Meanwhile he had discovered that his joints were stiff, and he felt like an old man. His clothes were a mass of rags, his hemp sandals were no more, and, on both fingers and toes, had grown long nails like bird's claws. His hair had burst its topknot string and hung down his back like a woman's, only it was grayish-white.

Wondering what it all meant, Keel Wee hobbled down the mountain and found the road that ran into the main street of his village. Rocks and hills, rivers and rills were there, but what a change! Instead of the two grinning idol posts, of male and female faces, carved out of trunks and trees, with sawed-out teeth painted white, and artificial ear flaps of wood nailed on, such as had stood before every Korean hamlet since the days of Kija, there was a line of high thick poles, with iron wire stretching from one to the other and for miles in the distance. These, he found out afterward, were called "lightning-thread-trees" (telegraph poles). In place of the rambling and sprawling three-sided thatched houses and yards, divided off with mats hung from sticks, there was a well-built but odd-looking office of painted wood, with openings through which he saw Korean young men sitting. They were dressed in strange clothes and were fingering outlandish-looking clicking instruments.

His curiosity prompted him to go up and look more closely, when something bumped against his nose and nearly knocked him over. When he tried again to get closer, his face was flattened, his nose nearly broken, and his lips knocked against his teeth so that they swelled. Feeling with his hands to solve the mystery, he touched something hard, which he could yet see through. Just then he heard a young man inside shout to him in Korean:

"Here, you mountain daddy, let that glass alone."

"Glass? Glass?" thought Keel Wee. "What is that?" Yet he could not speak.

He had hardly drawn a long breath when, looking down along two lines of shining iron in the street, he saw a house on wheels coming right at him. There was no horse, no donkey, no bull, no man pulling or pushing it, but overhead was a long pole, at the end of which, where it touched a string, as he thought, though it was an iron wire, was something that looked like a squirrel. It was going round and round as if turning somersaults and seemed to be pushing the moving house along. Inside, near the same stuff which he had already heard was glass, sat a dozen or so Koreans. The whole thing, wheels and all, nearly ran over him as it thundered by, and his mouth opened in wonder, while a man on the end shouted rudely:

"Hello, old goblin, where did you get your pumpkin mouth? Look out or you'll swallow the moon. Get out of the way of the trolley."

Thus did the man they called conductor, or guard, make fun of the poor old fellow, for indeed he did look like one of the mummers, who on New Year's Eve amuse or scare the children by putting on their shoulders the huge round devil heads and false faces that represent the aborigines of Korea and the goblins that once lived in the mountains. These masks are usually shaped like a melon and are cut with eyes, nose and mouth, like those which American boys have fun with on All Hallow Eve.

This was just the trouble. The woodman in tatters, with no topknot, long hair down his back and a white beard floating over his breast, leaning on a long white stick as he hobbled down the street, looked just like one of the ancient aborigines that had long ago been driven into the mountains. Nurses and old women frightened naughty children by simply mentioning their names. When one of these mountain men, odd creatures that were half savage in dress and ways, came into the town, all the children laughed and the big dogs barked, while the little ones ran away, for the sight was so unusual. Even the bulls bellowed, the donkeys balked, and the pigs squeaked, as Keel Wee came near. No wonder he was taken for a mountain granddaddy, or a bumpkin dressed up like one, for few of the city or village folks had really ever seen one of the mountain aborigines, any more than they had seen tigers, that are plentiful farther away, but which only the hunters ever caught sight of.

More and more bewildered, Keel Wee wended his way further into the town. He saw that the men no longer wore topknots, or chignons, nor did the lads have on the long braid down their back, which showed that they were youths, but not married yet. Just then some rough boys, supposing that maybe some rustic gawk had mistaken the time of year, jeered at him and cried:

"Hello, hermit, do you think it's New Year's Eve?"

Keel Wee thought he had better ask some questions. So catching sight of a dignified looking gentleman, in black broad-brimmed hat and flowing white clothes, who was coming down the street and toward him, Keel Wee bowed his head low, almost to the ground. As he did so, the stone put in his mouth by the fairies dropped out, and his tongue was loosed. He inquired as follows:

"Exalted sir, can you tell me where may be the wretched hut of my miserable wife and children? She was the daughter of Gee Kim, and your contemptible slave is Keel Wee."

The gentleman, whose dress showed that he was a scholar and person of rank, looked long and hard at the questioner, to satisfy himself that he was not being mocked, or imposed upon by a jester, rope-dancer, sorcerer, or some such disreputable person, and then cried:

"Heavens! man, are you a beggar-spirit of the mountains? Your speech sounds like the dialect spoken in these parts five hundred years ago. In that time such a family lived here, but the head of it, a wood-cutter and fuel-seller, is reported to have gone up into the mountains and was eaten up by a tiger. Yonder in the graveyard are buried ten or more generations of his descendants."

"Tell me, kind sir, what has happened here since King Wang died. It was under his reign that I was born and lived in this village."

Still eyeing the questioner, as if expecting to see him jump out of his rags and declare himself a mummer and the whole affair a joke, the kindly gentleman proceeded to give in outline the history of Korea during the previous five hundred years. There had been many kings. The Tartars first, and then the Japanese had invaded the land. A great war between the Mikado's men and the Chinese had taken place. It was just over and now people rode in cars, talked hundreds of miles over wires, and traveled over iron rails as fast as a dragon could fly, drawn by a steel horse that drank water and fed on wood and black stones that burned. In a word, Korea was in an "era of civilization."

This was too much for Keel Wee. He now realized that he had lived ten times longer than the average man. So, hobbling over to the graveyard, he stumbled among the mounds until he found that one of his clan where the bones of his wife and children lay. Next morning, all that was seen of Keel Wee was a mass of dust, rags, some bones, and much long white hair. Yet, when they buried him, there sprang up around and on his grave strange flowers that no one had ever seen in city or village, but which bloomed only on the high mountains.

The Home of the Fairies

IN THE DAYS of King In-jo (1623–1649) there was a student of Confucius who lived in Ka-pyong. He was still a young man and unmarried. His education had not been extensive, for he had read only a little in the way of history and literature. For some reason or other he left his home and went into Kang-won Province. Travelling on horseback, and with a servant, he reached a mountain, where he was overtaken by rain that wet him through.

Mysteriously, from some unknown cause, his servant suddenly died, and the man, in fear and distress, drew the body to the side of the hill, where he left it and went on his way weeping. When he had gone but a short distance, the horse he rode fell under him and died also. Such was his plight: his servant dead, his horse dead, rain falling fast, and the road an unknown one. He did not know what to do or where to go, and reduced thus to walking, he broke down and cried. At this point there met him an old man with very wonderful eyes, and hair as white as snow. He asked the young man why he wept, and the reply was that his servant was dead, his horse was dead, that it was raining, and that he did not know the way. The patriarch, on hearing this, took pity on him, and lifting his staff, pointed, saying, "There is a house yonder, just beyond those pines, follow that stream and it will bring you to where there are people."

The young man looked as directed, and a li or so beyond he saw a clump of trees. He bowed, thanked the stranger, and started on his way. When he had gone a few paces he looked back, but the friend had disappeared. Greatly wondering, he went on toward the place indicated, and as he drew near he saw a grove of pines, huge trees they were, a whole forest of them. Bamboos appeared, too, in countless numbers, with a wide stream of water flowing by. Underneath the water there seemed to be a marble flooring like a great pavement, white and pure. As he went along he saw that the water was all of an even depth, such as one could cross easily. A mile or so farther on he saw a beautifully decorated house. The pillars and entrance approaches were perfect in form. He continued his way, wet as he was, carrying his thorn staff, and entered the gate and sat down to rest. It was paved, too, with marble, and smooth as polished glass. There were no chinks or creases in it, all was of one perfect surface. In the room was a marble table, and on it a copy of the Book of Changes; there was also a brazier of jade just in front. Incense was burning in it, and the fragrance filled the room. Beside these, nothing else was visible. The rain had ceased and all was quiet and clear, with no wind nor anything to disturb. The world of confusion seemed to have receded from him.

While he sat there, looking in astonishment, he suddenly heard the sound of footfalls from the rear of the building. Startled by it, he turned to see, when an old man appeared. He looked as though he might equal the turtle or the crane as to age, and was very dignified. He wore a green dress and carried a jade staff of nine sections. The appearance of the old man was such as to stun any inhabitant of the earth. He recognized him as the master of the place, and so he went forward and made a low obeisance.

The old man received him kindly, and said, "I am the master and have long waited for you." He took him by the hand and led him away. As they went along, the hills grew more and more enchanting, while the soft breezes and the light touched him with mystifying favour. Suddenly, as he looked the man was gone, so he went on by himself, and arrived soon at another palace built likewise of precious stones. It was a great hall, stretching on into the distance as far as the eye could see.

The young man had seen the Royal Palace frequently when in Seoul attending examinations, but compared with this, the Royal Palace was as a mud hut thatched with straw.

As he reached the gate a man in ceremonial robes received him and led him in. He passed two or three pavilions, and at last reached a special one and went up to the upper storey. There, reclining at a table, he saw the ancient sage whom he had met before. Again he bowed.

This young man, brought up poorly in the country, was never accustomed to seeing or dealing with the great. In fear, he did not dare to lift his eyes. The ancient master, however, again welcomed him and asked him to be seated, saying, "This is not the dusty world that you are accustomed to, but the abode of the genii. I knew you were coming, and so was waiting to receive you." He turned and called, saying, "Bring something for the guest to eat."

In a little a servant brought a richly laden table. It was such fare as was never seen on earth, and there was abundance of it. The young man, hungry as he was, ate heartily of these strange viands. Then the dishes were carried away and the old man said, "I have a daughter who has arrived at a marriageable age, and I have been trying to find a son-in-law, but as yet have not succeeded. Your coming accords with this need. Live here, then, and become my son-in-law." The young man, not knowing what to think, bowed and was silent. Then the host turned and gave an order, saying, "Call in the children."

Two boys about twelve or thirteen years of age came running in and sat down beside him. Their faces were so beautifully white they seemed like jewels. The master pointed to them and said to the guest, "These are my sons," and to the sons he said, "This young man is he whom I have chosen for my son-in-law; when should we have the wedding? Choose you a lucky day and let me know."

The two boys reckoned over the days on their fingers, and then together said, "The day after to-morrow is a lucky day."

The old man, turning to the stranger, said, "That decides as to the wedding, and now you must wait in the guest-chamber till the time arrives." He then gave a command to call So and So. In a little an official of the genii came forward, dressed in light and airy garments. His appearance and expression were very beautiful, a man, he seemed, of glad and happy mien.

The master said, "Show this young man the way to his apartments and treat him well till the time of the wedding."

The official then led the way, and the young man bowed as he left the room. When he had passed outside the gate, a red sedan chair was in waiting for him. He was asked to mount. Eight bearers bore him smoothly along. A mile or so distant they reached another palace, equally wonderful, with no speck or flaw of any kind to mar its beauty. In graceful groves of flowers and trees he descended to enter his pavilion. Beautiful garments were taken from jewelled boxes, and a perfumed bath was given him and a change made. Thus he laid aside his weather-beaten clothes and donned the vestments of the genii. The official remained as company for him till the appointed time.

When that day arrived other beautiful robes were brought, and again he bathed and changed. When he was dressed, he mounted the palanquin and rode to the Palace of the master, twenty or more officials accompanying. On arrival, a guide directed them to the special Palace Beautiful. Here he saw preparations for the wedding, and here he made his bow. This finished he moved as directed, further in. The tinkling sound of jade bells and the breath of sweet perfumes filled the air. Thus he made his entry into the inner quarters.

Many beautiful women were in waiting, all gorgeously apparelled, like the women of the gods. Among these he imagined that he would meet the master's daughter. In a little, accompanied by a host of others, she came, shining in jewels and beautiful clothing so that she lighted up the Palace. He took his stand before her, though her face was hidden from him by a fan of pearls. When he saw her at last, so beautiful was she that his eyes were dazzled. The other women, compared with her, were as the magpie to the phœnix. So bewildered was he that he dared not look up. The friend accompanying assisted him to bow and to go through the necessary forms. The ceremony was much the same as that observed among men. When it was over the young man went back to his bridegroom's chamber. There the embroidered curtains, the golden screens, the silken clothing, the jewelled floor, were such as no men of earth ever see.

On the second day his mother-in-law called him to her. Her age would be about thirty, and her face was like a freshly-blown lotus flower. Here a great feast was spread, with many guests invited. The accompaniments thereof in the way of music were sweeter than mortals ever dreamed of. When the feast was over, the women caught up their skirts, and, lifting their sleeves, danced together and sang in sweet accord. The sound of their singing caused even the clouds to stop and listen. When the day was over, and all had well dined, the feast broke up.

A young man, brought up in a country hut, had all of a sudden met the chief of the genii, and had become a sharer in his glory and the accompaniments of his life. His mind was dazed and his thoughts overcame him. Doubts were mixed with fears. He knew not what to do.

A sharer in the joys of the fairies he had actually become, and a year or so passed in such delight as no words can ever describe.

One day his wife said to him, "Would you like to enter into the inner enclosure and see as the fairies see?"

He replied, "Gladly would I."

She then led him into a special park where there were lovely walks, surrounded by green hills. As they advanced there were charming views, with springs of water and sparkling cascades. The scene grew gradually more entrancing, with jewelled flowers and scintillating spray, lovely birds and animals disporting themselves. A man once entering here would never again think of earth as a place to return to.

After seeing this he ascended the highest peak of all, which was like a tower of many stories. Before him lay a wide stretch of sea, with islands of the blessed standing out of the water, and long stretches of pleasant land in view. His wife showed them all to him, pointing out this and that. They seemed filled with golden palaces and surrounded with a halo of light. They were peopled with happy souls, some riding on cranes, some on the phœnix, some on the unicorn; some were sitting on the clouds, some sailing by on the wind, some walking on the air, some gliding gently up the streams, some descending from above, some ascending, some moving west, some north, some gathering in groups. Flutes and harps sounded sweetly. So many and so startling were the things seen that he could never tell the tale of them. After the day had passed they returned.

Thus was their joy unbroken, and when two years had gone by she bore him two sons.

Time moved on, when one day, unexpectedly, as he was seated with his wife, he began to cry and tears soiled his face. She asked in amazement for the cause of it. "I was thinking," said he, "of how a plain countryman living in poverty had thus become the son-in-law of the king of the genii. But in my home is my poor old mother, whom I have not seen for these years; I would so like to see her that my tears flow."

The wife laughed, and said, "Would you really like to see her? Then go, but do not cry." She told her father that her husband would like to go and see his mother. The master called him and gave his permission. The son thought, of course, that he would call many servants and send him in state, but not so. His wife gave him one little bundle and that was all, so he said good-bye to his father-in-law, whose parting word was, "Go now and see your mother, and in a little I shall call for you again."

He sent with him one servant, and so he passed out through the main gateway. There he saw a poor thin horse with a worn rag of a saddle on his back. He looked carefully and found that they were the dead horse and the dead servant, whom he had lost, restored to him. He gave a start, and asked, "How did you come here?"

The servant answered, "I was coming with you on the road when some one caught me away and brought me here. I did not know the reason, but I have been here for a long time."

The man, in great fear, fastened on his bundle and started on his journey. The genie servant brought up the rear, but after a short distance the world of wonder had become transformed into the old weary world again. Here it was with its fogs, and thorn, and precipice. He looked off toward the world of the genii, and it was but a dream. So overcome was he by his feelings that he broke down and cried.

The genie servant said to him when he saw him weeping, "You have been for several years in the abode of the immortals, but you have not yet attained thereto, for you have not yet forgotten the seven things of earth: anger, sorrow, fear, ambition, hate and selfishness. If you once get rid of these there will be no tears for you." On hearing this he stopped his crying, wiped his cheeks, and asked pardon.

When he had gone a mile farther he found himself on the main road. The servant said to him, "You know the way from this point on, so I shall go back," and thus at last the young man reached his home.

He found there an exorcising ceremony in progress. Witches and spirit worshippers had been called and were saying their prayers. The family, seeing the young man come home thus, were all aghast. "It is his ghost," said they. However, they saw in a little that it was really he himself. The mother asked why he had not come home in all that time. She being a very violent woman in disposition, he did not dare to tell her the truth, so he made up something else. The day of his return was the anniversary of his supposed death, and so they had called the witches for a prayer ceremony. Here he opened the bundle that his wife had given him and found four suits of clothes, one for each season.

In about a year after his return home the mother, seeing him alone, made application for the daughter of one of the village literati. The man, being timid by nature and afraid of offending his mother, did not dare to refuse, and was therefore married; but there was no joy in it, and the two never looked at each other.

The young man had a friend whom he had known intimately from childhood. After his return the friend came to see him frequently, and they used to spend the nights talking together. In their talks the friend inquired why in all these years he had never come home. The young man then told him what had befallen him in the land of the genii, and how he had been there and had been married. The friend looked at him in wonder, for he seemed just as he had remembered him except in the matter of clothing. This he found on examination was of very strange material, neither grass cloth, silk nor cotton, but different from them all, and yet warm and comfortable. When spring came the spring clothes sufficed, when summer came those for summer, and for autumn and winter each special suit. They were never washed, and yet never became soiled; they never wore out, and always looked fresh and new. The friend was greatly astonished.

Some three years passed when one day there came once more a servant from the master of the genii, bringing his two sons. There were also letters, saying, "Next year the place where you dwell will be destroyed and all the people will become 'fish and meat' for the enemy, therefore follow this messenger and come, all of you."

He told his friend of this and showed him his two sons. The friend, when he saw these children that looked like silk and jade, confessed the matter to the mother also. She, too, gladly agreed, and so they sold out and had a great feast for all the people of the town, and then bade farewell. This was the year 1635. They left and were never heard of again.

The year following was the Manchu invasion, when the village where the young man had lived was all destroyed. To this day young and old in Ka-pyong tell this story.

The Art of Netting Learned by Kahukura from the Fairies (Ko Te Korero Mo Nga Patupaiarehe)

ONCE UPON A TIME, a man of the name of Kahukura wished to pay a visit to Rangiaowhia, a place lying far to the northward, near the country of the tribe called Te Rarawa. Whilst he lived at his own village, he was continually haunted by a desire to visit that place. At length he started on his journey, and reached Rangiaowhia, and as he was on his road, he passed a place where some people had been cleaning mackerel, and he saw the inside of the fish lying all about the sand on the sea–shore: surprised at this, he looked about at the marks, and said to himself: 'Oh, this must have been done by some of the people of the district.' But when he came to look a little more narrowly at the footmarks, he saw that the people who had been fishing had made them in the night-time, not that morning, nor in the day; and he said to himself: 'These are no mortals who have been fishing here – spirits must have done this; had they been men, some of the reeds and grass which they sat on in their canoe would have been lying about. 'He felt quite sure from several circumstances, that spirits or fairies had been there; and after observing everything well, he returned to the house where he was stopping. He, however, held fast in his heart what he had seen, as something very striking to tell all his friends in every direction, and as likely to be the means of gaining knowledge which might enable him to find out something new.

So that night he returned to the plaee where he had observed all these things, and just as he reached the spot, back had come the fairies too, to haul their net for mackerel; and some of them were shouting out: 'The net here! the net here!' Then a canoe paddled off to fetch the other in which the net was laid, and as they dropped the net into the water, they began to cry out: 'Drop the net in the sea at Rangiaowliia, and haul it at Mamaku.' These words were sung out by the fairies, as an encouragement in their work, and from the joy of their hearts at their sport in fishing.

As the fairies were dragging the net to the shore, Kahukura managed to mix amongst them, and hauled away at the rope; he happened to be a very fair man, so that his skin was almost as white as that of these fairies, and from that cause he was not observed by them.

As the net came close in to the shore, the fairies began to cheer and shout: 'Go out into the sea some of you, in front of the rock, lest the nets should be entangled in Tawatawauia a Teweteweuia ', for that was the name of a rugged rock standing out from the sandy shore; the main body of the fairies kept hauling at the net, and Kahukura pulled away in the midst of them.

When the first fish reached the shore, thrown up in the ripples driven before the net as they hauled it in, the fairies had not yet remarked Kahukura, for he was almost as fair as they were. It was just at the very first peep of dawn that the fish were all landed, and the fairies ran hastily to pick them up from the sand, and to haul the net up on the beach. They did not act with their fish as men do, dividing them into separate loads for each, but every one took up what fish he liked, and ran a twig through their gills, and as they strung the fish, they continued calling out: 'Make haste, run here, all of you, and finish the work before the sun rises.'

Kahukura kept on stringing his fish with the rest of them. He had only a very short string, and, making a slip-knot at the end of it, when he had covered the string with fish, he lifted them up, but had hardly raised them from the ground when the slip-knot gave way from the weight of the fish, and off they fell; then some of the fairies ran good-naturedly to help him to string his fish again, and one of them tied the knot at the end of the string for him, but the fairy had hardty gone after knotting it, before Kahukura had unfastened it, and again tied a slip-knot at the end; then he began stringing his fish again, and when he had got a great many on, up he lifted them, and off they slipped as before. This trick he repeated several times, and delayed the fairies in their work by getting them to knot his string for him, and put his fish on it. At last full daylight broke, so that there was light enough to distinguish a man's face, and the fairies saw that Kahukura was a man; then they dispersed in confusion, leaving their fish and their net, and abandoning their canoes, which were nothing but stems of the flax. In a moment the fairies started for their own abodes; in their hurry, as has just been said, they abandoned their net, which was made of rushes; and off the good people fled as fast as they could go. Now was first discovered the stitch for netting a net, for they left theirs with Kahukura, and it became a pattern for him. He thus taught his children to make nets, and by them the Maori race were made acquainted with that art, which they have now known from very remote times.

Farmer Mybrow and the Fairies

FARMER MYBROW was one day looking about for a suitable piece of land to convert into a field. He wished to grow corn and yams. He discovered a fine spot, close to a great forest – which latter was the home of some fairies. He set to work at once to prepare the field.

Having sharpened his great knife, he began to cut down the bushes. No sooner had he touched one than he heard a voice say, "Who is there, cutting down the bushes?" Mybrow was too much astonished to answer. The question was repeated.

This time the farmer realized that it must be one of the fairies, and so replied, "I am Mybrow, come to prepare a field." Fortunately for him the fairies were in great good humour. He heard one say, "Let us all help Farmer Mybrow to cut down the bushes." The rest agreed. To Mybrow's great delight, the bushes were all rapidly cut down with very little trouble on his part. He returned home, exceedingly well pleased with his day's work, having resolved to keep the field a secret even from his wife.

Early in January, when it was time to burn the dry bush, he set off to his field, one afternoon, with the means of making a fire. Hoping to have the fairies' assistance once more, he intentionally struck the trunk of a tree as he passed. Immediately came the question, "Who is there, striking the stumps?" He promptly replied, "I am Mybrow, come to burn down the bush." Accordingly, the dried bushes were all burned down, and the field left clear in less time that it takes to tell it.

Next day the same thing happened. Mybrow came to chop up the stumps for firewood and clear the field for digging. In a very short time his faggots and firewood were piled ready, while the field was bare.

So it went on. The field was divided into two parts – one for maize and one for yams. In all the preparations – digging, sowing, planting – the fairies gave great assistance. Still, the farmer had managed to keep the whereabouts of his field a secret from his wife and neighbours.

The soil having been so carefully prepared, the crops promised exceedingly well. Mybrow visited them from time to time, and congratulated himself on the splendid harvest he would have.

One day, while maize and yams were still in their green and milky state, Mybrow's wife came to him. She wished to know where his field lay, that she might go and fetch some of the firewood from it. At first he refused to tell her. Being very persistent, however, she finally succeeded in obtaining the information – but on one condition. She must not answer any question that should be asked her. This she readily promised, and set off for the field.

When she arrived there she was utterly amazed at the wealth of the corn and yam. She had never seen such magnificent crops. The maize looked most tempting – being still in the milky state – so she plucked an ear. While doing so she heard a voice say, "Who is there, breaking the corn?" "Who dares ask me such a question?" she replied angrily – quite forgetting her husband's command. Going to the field of yams she plucked one of them also. "Who is there, picking the yams?" came the question again. "It is I, Mybrow's wife. This is my husband's field and I have a right to pick." Out came the fairies. "Let us all help Mybrow's wife to pluck her corn and yams," said they. Before the frightened woman could say a word, the fairies had all set to work with a will, and the corn and yams lay useless on the ground. Being all green and unripe, the harvest was now utterly spoiled. The farmer's wife wept bitterly, but to no purpose. She returned slowly home, not knowing what to say to her husband about such a terrible catastrophe. She decided to keep silence about the matter.

Accordingly, next day the poor man set off gleefully to his field to see how his fine crops were going on. His anger and dismay may be imagined when he saw his field a complete ruin. All his work and foresight had been absolutely ruined through his wife's forgetfulness of her promise.

La Cenorientola

THEY SAY THERE WAS a merchant who had three daughters. When he went out into foreign countries to buy wares he told them he would bring them rare presents, whatever they might ask for. The eldest asked for precious jewels, the second for rich shawls, but the youngest who was always kept out of sight in the kitchen by the others, and made to do the dirty work of the house, asked only for a little bird.

"So you want a little bird, do you? What is the use of a little bird to you?" said the sisters mocking her, and, "Papa will have something else to think of than minding little birds on a long journey."

"But you will bring me a little bird, won't you, Papa?" pleaded the little girl; "and I can tell you that if you don't the boat you are on will stand still, and will neither move backwards nor forwards."

The merchant went away into a far country and bought precious wares, but he forgot all about the little bird. It was only when he had got on board a boat to go down a mighty river on his homeward way, and the captain found the boat would not move by any means, that he remembered what his daughter had said to him. Then while the captain was wondering how it was the boat would not move, he went to him and told him what he had done. But the captain said, "That is easily set right. Here close by is a garden full of thousands of birds; you can easily creep in and carry off one. *One* will never be missed among so many thousands."

The merchant followed his directions and went into the garden where there were so many thousand birds that he easily caught one. The captain gave him a cage, and he brought it safely home and gave it to his daughter.

That night the elder sisters said as usual, "We are going to the ball; you will stay at home and sweep up the place and mind the fire."

Now all the birds in the garden which the captain had pointed out to the merchant were fairies; so when the others were gone to the ball and the youngest daughter went into her room to her bird, she said to it:

Give me splendid raiment,
And I will give you my rags.

Immediately, the bird gave her the most beautiful suit of clothes, with jewels and golden slippers, and a splendid carriage and prancing horses. With these the maiden went to the ball which was at the king's palace. The moment the king saw her he fell in love with her, and would dance with no one else. The sisters were furious with the stranger because the king danced all night with her and not with them, but they had no idea it was their sister.

The second night she did the same, only the bird gave her a yet more beautiful dress, and the king did all he could to find out who she was, but she would not tell him. Then he asked her name and she said,

"They call me *Cenorientola*."

"*Cenorientola*," said the king; "what a pretty name! I never heard it before."

He had also told the servants that they must run after her carriage and see where it went; but though they ran as fast as the wind they could not come near the pace of her horses.

The third night the sisters went to the ball and left her at home, and she stayed at home with her little bird and said to it,

Give me splendid raiment,
And I will give you my rags.

Then the bird gave her a more splendid suit still, and the king paid her as much attention as ever. But to the servants he had said, "If you don't follow fast enough tonight to see where she lives I will have all your heads cut off." So they used such extra diligence that she in her hurry to get away dropped one of her golden slippers; this the servants picked up and brought to the king.

The next day the king sent a servant into every house in the city till he should find her whom the golden slipper fitted, but there was not one; last of all he came to the merchant's house, and he tried it on the two elder daughters and it would fit neither. Then he said,

"There must be some other maiden in this house;" but they only shrugged their shoulders. "It is impossible; another maiden there must be, for every maiden in the city we have seen and the slipper fits none, therefore one there must be here."

Then they said,

"In truth we have a little sister who sits in the kitchen and does the work. She is called *Cenorientola*, because she is always smutty. We are sure she never went to a ball, and it would only soil the beautiful gold slipper to let her put her smutty feet into it."

"It may be so," replied the king's servant, "but we must try, nevertheless."

So they fetched her, and the king's servant found that the shoe fitted her; and they went and told the king all.

The moment the king heard them say *Cenorientola* he said, "That is she! It is the name she gave me."

So he sent a carriage to fetch her in all haste. The bird meantime had given her a more beautiful dress than any she had had before, and priceless jewels, so that when they came to fetch her she looked quite fit to be a queen. Then the king married her; and though her sisters had behaved so ill to her she gave them two fine estates, so that all were content.

The Transformation-Donkey

THERE WAS ONCE a poor chicory-seller: all chicory-sellers are poor, but this was a very poor one, and he had a large family of daughters and two sons. The daughters he left at home with their mother, but the two sons he took with him to gather chicory. While they were out gathering chicory one day, a great bird flew down before them and dropped an egg and then flew away again. The boys picked up the egg and brought it to their father, because there were some figures like strange writing on it which they could not read; but neither could the father read the strange writing, so he took the egg to a farmer. The farmer read the writing, and it said:

"Whoso eats my head, he shall be an emperor."

"Whoso eats my heart, he shall never want for money."

"Ho, ho!" said the farmer to himself, "it won't do to tell the fellow this; I must manage to eat both the head and the heart myself." So he said, "The meaning of it is that whoever eats the bird will make a very good dinner; so tomorrow when the bird comes back, as she doubtless will to lay another egg, have a good stick ready and knock her down; then you can make a fire, and bake it between the stones, and I will come and eat it with you if you like."

The poor chicory-seller thought his fortune was made when a farmer offered to dine with him, and the hours seemed long enough till next morning came.

With next morning, however, came the bird again. The chicory-seller was ready with his stick and knocked her down, and the boys made a fire and cooked the bird. But as they were not very apt at the trussing and cooking, the head dropped into the fire, and the youngest boy said: "This will never do to serve up, all burnt as it is;" so he ate it. The heart also fell into the fire and got burnt, and the eldest boy said: "This will never do to serve up, all burnt as it is;" so he ate that.

By and by the farmer came, and they all sat down on a bank – the farmer quite jovial at the idea of the immense advantage he was going to gain, and the chicory-seller quite elated at the idea of entertaining a farmer.

"Bring forward the roast, boys," said the father; and the boys brought the bird.

"What have you done with the head?" exclaimed the farmer, the moment he saw the bird.

"Oh, it got burnt, and I ate it," said the younger boy.

The merchant ground his teeth and stamped his foot, but he dared not say why he was so angry; so he sat silent while the chicory-seller took out his knife and cut the bird up in portions.

"Give me the piece with the heart, if I may choose," said the merchant; "I'm very fond of birds' hearts."

"Certainly, any part you like," replied the chicory-seller, nervously turning all the pieces over and over again; "but I can't find any heart. Boys, had the bird no heart?"

"Yes, Papa," answered the elder brother, "it had a heart, sure enough; but it tumbled into the fire and got burnt, and so I ate it."

There was no object in disguising his fury any longer, so the farmer exclaimed testily, "Thank you, I'll not have any then; the head and the heart are just the only parts of a bird I care to eat." And so saying he turned on his heel and went away.

"Look, boys, what you've done! You've thrown away the best chance we ever had in our lives!" cried the father in despair. "After the farmer had taken dinner with us he must have asked us to dine with him, and, as one civility always brings another, there is no saying what it might not have led to. However, as you have chosen to throw the chance away, you may go and look out for yourselves. I've done with you." And with a sound cudgelling he drove them away.

The two boys, left to themselves, wandered on till they came to a stable, when they entered the yard and asked to be allowed to do some work or other as a means of subsistence.

"I've nothing for you to do," said the landlord; "but, as it's late, you may sleep on the straw there, on the condition that you go about your business tomorrow first thing."

The boys, glad to get a night's lodging on any condition, went to sleep in the straw. When the elder brother woke in the morning he found a box of sequins under his head.

"How could this have come here," soliloquized the boy, "unless the host had put it there to see if we were honest? Well, thank God, if we're poor there's no danger of either of us taking what doesn't belong to us." So he took the box to the host, and said: "There's your box of sequins quite safe. You needn't have taken the trouble to test our honesty in that way."

The host was very much surprised, but he thought the best way was to take the money and say nothing but "I'm glad to see you're such good boys." So he gave them breakfast and some provisions for the way.

Next night they found themselves still in the open country and no inn near, and they were obliged to be content to sleep on the bare ground. Next morning when they woke the younger boy again found a box of sequins under his head.

"Only think of that host not being satisfied with trying us once, but to come all this way after us to test our honesty again. However, I suppose we must take it back to him."

So they walked all the way back to the host and said: "Here's your box of sequins back; as we didn't steal it the first time it was not likely we should take it the second time."

The host was more and more astonished; but he took the money without saying anything, only he praised the boys for being so good and gave them a hearty meal. And they went their way, taking a new direction.

The next night the younger brother said: "Do you know I've my doubts about the host having put that box of sequins under your head. How could he have done it out in the open country without our seeing him? Tonight I will watch, and if he doesn't come, and in the morning there is another box of sequins, it will be a sign that it is your own."

He did so, and next morning there w as another box of sequins. So they decided it was honestly their own, and they carried it by turns and journeyed on. About noon they came to a great city where the emperor was lately dead, and all the people were in great excitement about choosing another emperor. The population was all divided in factions, each of which had a candidate, and none would let the candidate of the others reign. There was so much fighting and quarrelling in the streets that the brothers got separated, and saw each other no more.

At this time it happened that it was the turn of the younger brother to be carrying the box of sequins. When the sentinels at the gate saw a stranger coming in carrying a box they said, "We must see what this is," and they took him to the minister. When the minister saw his box was full of sequins he said, "This must be our emperor." And all the people said, "Yes, this is our emperor. Long live our emperor!" And thus the boy became an emperor.

But the elder brother had entered unperceived into the town, and went to ask hospitality in a house where was a woman with a beautiful daughter; so they let him stay. That night also there came a box of sequins under his head; so he went out and bought meat and fuel and all manner of provisions, and gave them to the mother, and said, "Because you took me in when I was poor last night, I have brought you all these provisions out of gratitude," and for the beautiful daughter he bought silks and damasks, and ornaments of gold. But the daughter said, "How comes it, tell me, that you, who were a poor footsore wayfarer last night, have now such boundless riches at command?" And because she was beautiful and spoke kindly to him, he suspected no evil, but told her, saying, "Every morning when I wake now, I find a box of sequins under my head."

"And how comes it," said she, "that you find a box of sequins under your head now, and not formerly?" "I do not know," he answered, "unless it be because one day when I was out with Father gathering chicory, a great bird came and dropped an egg with some strange writing on it, which we could not read. But a farmer read it for us; only he would not tell us what it said, but that we should cook the bird and eat it. While we were cooking it the heart fell into the fire and got burnt, and I ate it: and when the farmer heard this he grew very angry. I think, therefore, the writing on the egg said that he who ate the heart of the bird should have many sequins."

After this they spent the day pleasantly together; but the daughter put an emetic in his wine at supper, and so made him bring up the bird's heart, which she kept for herself, and the next morning when he woke there was no box of sequins under his head. When he rose in the morning also the beautiful girl and her mother turned him out of the house, and he wandered forth again.

At last, being weary and full of sorrow, he sat down on the ground by the side of a stream crying. Immediately three fairies appeared to him and asked him why he wept. And when he told them, they said to him: "Weep no more, for instead of the bird's heart we give you this sheepskin jacket, the pockets of which will always be full of sequins. How many soever you may take out they will always remain full." Then they disappeared; but he immediately went back to the house of the beautiful girl, taking her rich and fine presents; but she said to him, "How comes it that you, who had no money left when you went away, have now the means to buy all these fine presents?" Then he told her of the gift of the three fairies, and they let him sleep in the house again, but the daughter called her maid to her and said: "Make a sheepskin jacket exactly like that in the stranger's room." So she made one, and they put it in his room, and took away the one the fairies had given him, and in the morning they drove him from the house again. Then he went and sat down by the stream and wept again; but the fairies came and asked him why he wept; and he told them, saying, "Because they have driven me away from the house where I stayed, and I have no home to go to, and this jacket has no more sequins in the pockets." Then the fairies looked at the jacket, and they said, "This is not the jacket we gave you; it has been changed by fraud:" so they gave him in place of it a wand, and they said, "With this wand strike the table, and whatever you may desire, be it meat or drink or clothes, or whatsoever you may want, it shall come upon the table." The next day he went back to the house of the woman and her daughter, and sat down without saying anything, but he struck the table with his wand, wishing for a great banquet, and immediately it was covered with the choicest dishes. There was no need to ask him questions this time, for they saw in what his gift consisted, and in the night, when he was asleep, they took his wand away. In the morning they drove him forth out of the house, and he went back to the stream and sat down to cry. Again the fairies appeared to him and comforted him; but they said, "This is the last time we may appear to you. Here is a ring; keep it on your hand; for if you lose this gift there is nothing more we may do for you;" and they went away. But he immediately returned to the house of the woman and her beautiful daughter. They let him in, "Because," they said, "doubtless the fairies have given him some other gift of which we may take profit." And as he sat there he said, "All the other gifts of the fairies have I lost, but this one they have given me now I cannot lose, because it is a ring which fits my finger, and no one can take it from my hand."

"And of what use is your ring?" asked the beautiful daughter.

"Its use is that whatever I wish for while I have it on I obtain directly, whatever it may be."

"Then wish," said she, "that we may be both together on the top of that high mountain, and a sumptuous merenda spread out for us."

"To be sure!" he replied, and he repeated her wish. Instantly they found themselves on the top of the high mountain with a plentiful merenda before them; but she had a vial of opium with her, and while his head was turned away she poured the opium into his wine. Presently after this he fell into a sound sleep, so sound that there was no fear of waking him. Immediately she took the ring from his finger and put it on her own; then she wished that she might be replaced at home and that he might be left on the top of the mountain. And so it was done.

In the morning when he woke and found himself all alone on the top of the high mountain and his ring gone, he wept bitter tears, and felt too weary to attempt the descent of the steep mountain side. For three days he remained there weary and weeping, and then, becoming faint from hunger, he took some of the herbs that grew on the mountain top for food. As soon as he had eaten these he was turned into a donkey, but as he retained his human intelligence, he said to himself, this herb has its uses, and he filled one of the panniers on his back with it. Then he came down from the mountain, and when he was at the foot of it, being hungry with the long journey, he ate of the grass that grew there, and, behold! he was transformed back into his natural shape; so he filled the other basket with this kind of grass and went his way.

Having dressed himself like a street seller, he took the basket of the herb which had the property of changing the eater into a donkey, and stood under the window of the house where he had been so evil entreated, and cried, "Fine salad! fine salad! Who will buy my fine salad?"

"What is there so specially good about your salad?" asked the maid, looking out. "My young mistress is particularly fond of salad, so if yours is so very superfine, you had better come up."

He did not wait to be twice told. As soon as he saw the beautiful daughter, he said, "This is fine salad, indeed, the finest of the fine, all fresh gathered, and the first of its kind that ever was sold."

"Very likely it's the first of its kind that ever was sold," said she; "but I don't like to buy things I haven't tried; it may turn out not to be nice."

"Oh, try it, try it freely; don't buy without trying;" and he picked one of the freshest and crispest bunches.

She took one in her hand and bit a few blades, and no sooner had she done so than she too became a donkey. Then he put the panniers on her back and drove her all over the town, constantly cudgelling her till she sank under the blows. Then one who saw him belabour her thus said, "This must not be; you must come and answer before the emperor for thus belabouring the poor brute;" but he refused to go unless he took the donkey with him; so they went to the emperor and said, "Here is one who is belabouring his donkey till she has sunk under his blows, and he refuses to come before the emperor to answer his cruelty unless he bring his donkey with him." And the emperor made answer, "Let him bring the beast with him."

So they brought him and his donkey before the emperor. When he found himself before the emperor he said, "All these must go away; to the emperor alone can I tell why I belabour my donkey." So the emperor commanded all the people to go to a distance while he took him and his donkey apart. As soon as he found himself alone with the emperor he said, "See, it is I, thy brother!" and he embraced him. Then he told him all that had befallen him since they parted. Then said the emperor to the donkey, "Go now with him home, and show him where thou hast laid all the things – the bird's heart, the sheepskin jacket, the wand, and the ring, that he may bring them hither; and if thou deliver them up faithfully I will command that he give thee of that grass to eat which shall give thee back thy natural form."

So they went back to the house and fetched all the things, and the emperor said, "Come thou now and live with me, and give me of thy sequins, and I will share the empire with thee." Thus they reigned together.

But to the donkey they gave of the grass to eat, which restored her natural form, only that her beauty was marred by the cudgelling she had received. And she said, "Had I not been so wilful and malicious I had now been empress."

Scioccolone

ONCE UPON A TIME there were three brothers, who were woodmen; their employment was not one which required great skill, and they were none of them very clever, but the youngest was the least brilliant of all. So simple was he that all the neighbours, and his very brothers – albeit they were not so very superior in intelligence themselves – gave him the nickname of 'Scioccolone,' the great simpleton, and accordingly Scioccolone he was called wherever he went.

Every day these three brothers went out into the woods to their work, and every evening they all came home, each staggering under his load of wood, which he carried to the dealer who paid them for their toil: thus one day of labour passed away just like another in all respects. So it went on for years.

Nevertheless, one day came at last which was not at all like the others, and if all days were like it the world would be quite upside down, or be at least a very different world from what it is. *Oimè!* that such days never occur now at all! *Basta*, this is what happened. It was in the noontide heat of a very hot day, the three simple brothers committed the imprudence of going out of the shelter of the woods into the world beyond, and there, lying on the grass in the severest blaze of the burning sun, they saw three beautiful peasant girls lying fast asleep.

"Only look at those silly girls sleeping in the full blaze of the sun!" cried the eldest brother.

"They'll get bad in their heads in this heat," said the second.

But Scioccolone said: "Shall we not get some sticks and boughs, and make a little shed to shelter them?"

"Just like one of Scioccolone's fine ideas!" laughed the eldest brother scornfully.

"Well done, Scioccolone! That's the best thing you've thought of this long while. And who will build a shed over us while we're building a shed for the girls, I should like to know?" said the second.

But Scioccolone said: "We can't leave them there like that; they will be burnt to death. If you won't help me I must build the shed alone."

"A wise resolve, and worthy of Scioccolone!" scoffed the eldest brother.

"Goodbye, Scioccolone!" cried the second, as the two elder brothers walked away together. "Goodbye for ever! I don't expect ever to see you alive again, of course."

And they never did see him again, but what it was that happened to him you shall hear.

Without waiting to find a retort to his brothers' gibes, Scioccolone set to work to fell four stout young saplings, and to set them up as supports of his shed in four holes he had previously scooped with the aid of his bill-hook; then he rammed them in with wedges, which he also had to cut and shape. After this he cut four large bushy branches, which he tied to the uprights with the cord he used for tying up his fagots of logs; and as the shade of these was scarcely close enough to keep out all the fierce rays of the sun, he went back to the wood and collected all the large broad leaves he could find, and came back and spread them out over his leafy roof. All this was very hard labour indeed when performed under the dreaded sun, and just in the hours when men do no work; yet so beautiful were the three maidens that, when at last he had completed his task, he could not tear himself away from them to go and seek repose in the shade of the wood, but he must needs continue standing in the full sun gazing at them open-mouthed.

At last the three beautiful maidens awoke, and when they saw what a fragrant shade had refreshed their slumbers they began pouring out their gratitude to their devoted benefactor.

Do not run at hasty conclusions, however, and imagine that of course the three beautiful maidens fell in love on the spot with Scioccolone, and he had only to pick and choose which of them he would have to make him happy as his wife. A very proper ending, you say, for a fairy tale. It was not so, however. Scioccolone looked anything but attractive just then. His meaningless features and uncouth, clownish gait were never at any time likely to inspire the fair maidens with sudden affection; but just then, after his running hither and thither, his felling, digging and hammering in the heat of the day, his face had acquired a tint which made it look rougher and redder and more repulsive than anyone ever wore before.

Besides this, the three maidens were fairies, who had taken the form of beautiful peasant girls for some reason of their own.

But neither did they leave his good deed unrewarded. By no means. Each of the three declared she would give him such a precious gift that he should own to his last hour that they were not ungrateful. So they sat and thought what great gift they could think of which should be calculated to make him very happy indeed.

At last the first of the three got up and exclaimed that she had thought of her gift, and she did not think anyone could give him a greater one; for she would promise him he should one day be a king.

Wasn't that a fine gift!

Scioccolone, however, did not think so. The idea of his being a king! Simple as he was, he could see the incongruity of the idea, and the embarrassment of the situation. How should he the poor clown, everybody's laughing-stock, become a king? And if he did, kingship had no attractions for him.

He was too kind-hearted, however, to say anything in disparagement of the well-meant promise, and too straightforward to assume a show of gratitude he did not feel; so after the first little burst of hilarity which he was not sufficiently master of himself to suppress, he remained standing open-mouthed after his awkward manner.

Then the second fairy addressed him and said:

"I see you don't quite like my sister's gift; but you may be sure she would not have promised it if it had not been a good gift, after you have been so kind to us; and when it comes true, it will somehow all turn out very nice and right. But now, meantime, that I may not similarly disappoint you with my gift by choosing it for you, I shall let you choose it for yourself; so say, what shall it be?"

Scioccolone was almost as much embarrassed with the second fairy's permission of choosing for himself as he had been with the first fairy's choice for him. First he grinned, and then he twisted his great awkward mouth about, and then he grinned again, till, at last, ashamed of keeping the fairies waiting so long for his answer, he said, with another grin:

"Well, to tell you what I should *really* like, it would be that when I have finished making up my fagot of logs this evening, instead of having to stagger home carrying it, it should roll along by itself, and then I get astride of it, and that it should carry *me*.

"That *would* be fine!" he added, and he grinned again as he thought of the fun it would be to be carried home by the load of logs instead of carrying the load as he had been wont.

"Certainly! That wish is granted," replied the second fairy readily. "You will find it all happens just as you have described."

Then the third fairy came forward and said:

"And now choose; what shall *my* gift be? You have only to ask for whatever you like and you shall have it."

Such a heap of wishes rose up in Scioccolone's imagination at this announcement that he could not make up his mind which to select; as fast as he fixed on one thing, he remembered it would be incomplete without some other gift, and as he went on trying to find someone wish that should be as comprehensive as possible, he suddenly blurted out:

"Promise me that *whatever* I wish may come true; that'll be the best gift; and so if I forget a thing one moment I can wish for it the next. That'll be the best gift, to be sure!"

"Granted!" said the third fairy. "You have only to wish for anything and you will find you get it immediately, whatever it is."

The fairies then took leave and went their way, and Scioccolone was reminded by the lengthening shades that it was time he betook himself to complete his day's work. Scarcely succeeding in collecting his thoughts, so dazzled and bewildered was he by the late supernatural conversation, he yet found his way back to the spot where he had been felling wood.

"Oh, dear! how tired I am!" he said within himself as he walked along. "How I wish the wood was all felled and the fagots tied up!" and though he said this mechanically as he might have said it any other day of his life, without thinking of the fairy's promise, which was, indeed, too vast for him to put it consciously to such a practical test then, full of astonishment as he was, yet when he got back to his working-place the wood was felled and laid in order, and tied into a fagot in the best manner.

"Well, to be sure!" soliloquized Scioccolone. "The girls have kept their promise indeed! This is just exactly what I wished. And now, let's see what else did I wish? Oh, yes; that if I got astride on the fagot it should roll along by itself and carry me with it; let's see if that'll come true too!"

With that he got astride on the fagot, and sure enough the fagot moved on all by itself, and carried Scioccolone along with it pleasantly enough.

Only there was one thing Scioccolone had forgotten to ask for, and that was power to guide the fagot; and now, though it took a direction quite contrary to that of his homeward way, he had no means of inducing it to change its tack. After some time spent in fruitless efforts in schooling his unruly mount, Scioccolone began to reason with himself.

"After all, it does not much matter about going home. I only get laughed at and called "Scioccolone." Maybe in some other place they may be better, and as the fagot is acting under the orders of my benefactress, it will doubtless all be for the best."

So he committed himself to the fagot to take him wherever it would. On went the fagot surely and steadily, as if quite conscious where it had to go; and thus, before nightfall, it came to a great city where were many people, who all came out to see the wonder of the fagot of logs moving along by itself, and a man riding on it.

In this city was a king, who lived in a palace with an only daughter. Now this daughter had never been known to laugh. What pains soever the king her father took to divert her were all unavailing; nothing brought a smile to her lips.

Now, however, when all the people ran to the windows to see a man riding on a fagot, the king's daughter ran to look out too; and when she saw the fagot moving by itself, and the uncouth figure of Scioccolone sitting on it, and heard all the people laughing at the sight, then the king's daughter laughed too; laughed for the first time in her life.

But Scioccolone, passing under the palace, heard her clear and merry laugh resounding above the laughter of all the people. He looked up and saw her, and when he saw her looking so bright and fair he said within himself:

"Now, if ever the fairy's power of wishing is to be of use to me, I wish that I might have a little son, and that the beautiful princess should be the mother." But he did not think of wishing to stop there that he might look at her, so the fagot carried him past the palace and past all the houses into the outskirts of the city, till he got tired and weary, and just then passing a wood merchant's yard, the thought rose to his lips,

"I wish that wood merchant would buy this fagot of me!"

Immediately the wood merchant came out and offered to buy the fagot, and as it was such a wonderful fagot that he thought Scioccolone would never consent to sell it, he offered him such a high price that Scioccolone had enough to live on like a prince for a year.

After a time there was again a great stir in the city, everyone was abroad in the streets whispering and consulting. To the king's daughter was born a little son, and no one knew who the father was, not even the princess herself. Then the king sent for all the men in the city, and brought them to the infant, and said, "Is this your father?" but the babe said, "No!" to them all.

Last of all, Scioccolone was brought, and when the king took him up to the babe and said, "Is this your father?" the babe rose joyfully from its cradle and said, "Yes; that is my father!" When the king heard this and saw what a rough ugly clown Scioccolone was, he was very angry with his daughter, and said she must marry him and go away for ever from the palace. It was all in vain that the princess protested she had never seen him but for one moment from the top of the palace. The babe protested quite positively that he was his father; so the king had them married, and sent them away from the palace for ever; and the babe was right, for though Scioccolone and the princess had never met, Scioccolone had wished that he might have a son, of whom she should be the mother, and by the power of the spell the child was born.

Scioccolone was only too delighted with the king's angry decree. He felt quite out of place in the palace, and was glad enough to be sent away from it. All he wanted was to have such a beautiful wife, and he willingly obeyed the king's command to take her away, a long, long way off.

The princess, however, was quite of a different mind. She could not cease from crying, because she was given to such an uncouth, clownish husband that no tidy peasant wench would have married.

When, therefore, Scioccolone saw his beautiful bride so unhappy and distressed, he grew distressed himself; and in his distress he remembered once more the promise of the fairy, that whatever he wished he might have, and he began wishing away at once. First he wished for a pleasant villa, prettily laid-out, and planted, and walled; then, a casino in the midst of it, prettily furnished, and having plenty of pastimes and diversions; then for a farm, well-stocked with beasts for all kinds of uses; for carriages and servants, for fruits and flowers, and all that can make life pleasant. And when he found that with all these things the princess did not seem much happier than before, he bethought himself of wishing that he might be furnished with a handsome person, polished manners and an educated mind, altogether such as the princess wished. All his wishes were fulfilled, and the princess now loved him very much, and they lived very happily together.

After they had been living thus some time, it happened one day that the king, going out hunting, observed this pleasant villa on the wold, where heretofore all had been bare, unplanted and unbuilt.

"How is this?" cried the king; and he drew rein, and went into the villa intending to enquire how the change had come about.

Scioccolone came out to meet him, not only so transformed that the king never recognized him, but so distinguished by courtesy and urbanity that the king himself felt ashamed to question him as to how the villa had grown up so suddenly. He accepted his invitation to come and rest in the casino, however; and there they fell to conversing on a variety of subjects, till the king was so struck with the sagacity and prudence of Scioccolone's talk that when he rose to take leave, he said:

"Such a man as you I have long sought to succeed me in the government of the kingdom. I am growing old and have no children, and you are worthy in all ways to wear the crown. Come up, therefore, if you will, to the palace and live with me, and when I die you shall be king."

Scioccolone, now no longer feeling himself so ill-adapted to live in a palace, willingly consented, and a few days after, with his wife and his little son, he went up to the palace to live with the king.

But the king's delight can scarcely be imagined when he found that the wife of the polished stranger was indeed his very own daughter.

After a few years the old king died, and Scioccolone reigned in his stead. And thus the promises of all the three fairies were fulfilled.

The Fairy Nurse

THERE WAS ONCE a little farmer and his wife living near Coolgarrow. They had three children, and my story happened while the youngest was a baby. The wife was a good wife enough, but her mind was all on her family and her farm, and she hardly ever went to her knees without falling asleep, and she thought the time spent in the chapel was twice as long as it need be. So, friends, she let her man and her two children go before her one day to Mass, while she called to consult a fairy man about a disorder one of her cows had. She was late at the chapel, and was sorry all the day after, for her husband was in grief about it, and she was very fond of him.

Late that night he was wakened up by the cries of his children calling out "Mother! Mother!" When he sat up and rubbed his eyes, there was no wife by his side, and when he asked the little ones what was become of their mother, they said they saw the room full of nice little men and women, dressed in white and red and green, and their mother in the middle of them, going out by the door as if she was walking in her sleep. Out he ran, and searched everywhere round the house but, neither tale nor tidings did he get of her for many a day.

Well, the poor man was miserable enough, for he was as fond of his woman as she was of him. It used to bring the salt tears down his cheeks to see his poor children neglected and dirty, as they often were, and they'd be bad enough only for a kind neighbour that used to look in whenever she could spare time. The infant was away with a nurse.

About six weeks after – just as he was going out to his work one morning – a neighbour, that used to mind women when they were ill, came up to him, and kept step by step with him to the field, and this is what she told him.

"Just as I was falling asleep last night, I heard a horse's tramp on the grass and a knock at the door, and there, when I came out, was a fine-looking dark man, mounted on a black horse, and he told me to get ready in all haste, for a lady was in great want of me. As soon as I put on my cloak and things, he took me by the hand, and I was sitting behind him before I felt myself stirring. "Where are we going, sir?" says I. "You'll soon know," says he; and he drew his fingers across my eyes, and not a ray could I see. I kept a tight grip of him, and I little knew whether he was going backwards or forwards, or how long we were about it, till my hand was taken again, and I felt the ground under me. The fingers went the other way across my eyes, and there we were before a castle door, and in we went through a big hall and great rooms all painted in fine green colours, with red and gold bands and ornaments, and the finest carpets and chairs and tables and window curtains, and grand ladies and gentlemen walking about. At last we came to a bedroom, with a beautiful lady in bed, with a fine bouncing boy beside her. The lady clapped her hands, and in came the Dark Man and kissed her and the baby, and praised me, and gave me a bottle of green ointment to rub the child all over.

"Well, the child I rubbed, sure enough; but my right eye began to smart, and I put up my finger and gave it a rub, and then stared, for never in all my life was I so frightened. The beautiful room was a big, rough cave, with water oozing over the edges of the stones and through the clay; and the lady, and the lord, and the child weazened, poverty-bitten creatures – nothing but skin and bone – and the rich dresses were old rags. I didn't let on that I found any difference, and after a bit says the Dark Man, 'Go before me to the hall door, and I will be with you in a few moments, and see you safe home.' Well, just as I turned into the outside cave, who should I see watching near the door but poor Molly. She looked round all terrified, and says she to me in a whisper, 'I'm brought here to nurse the child of the king and queen of the fairies; but there is one chance of saving me. All the court will pass the cross near Templeshambo next Friday night, on a visit to the fairies of Old Ross. If John can catch me by the hand or cloak when I ride by, and has courage not to let go his grip, I'll be safe. Here's the king. Don't open your mouth to answer. I saw what happened with the ointment.'

"The Dark Man didn't once cast his eye towards Molly, and he seemed to have no suspicion of me. When we came out I looked about me, and where do you think we were but in the dyke of the Rath of Cromogue. I was on the horse again, which was nothing but a big rag-weed, and I was in dread every minute I'd fall off; but nothing happened till I found myself in my own cabin. The king slipped five guineas into my hand as soon as I was on the ground, and thanked me, and bade me good night. I hope I'll never see his face again. I got into bed, and couldn't sleep for a long time; and when I examined my five guineas this morning, that I left in the table drawer the last thing, I found five withered leaves of oak – bad luck to the giver!"

Well, you may all think the fright, and the joy, and the grief the poor man was in when the woman finished her story. They talked and they talked, but we needn't mind what they said till Friday night came, when both were standing where the mountain road crosses the one going to Ross.

There they stood, looking towards the bridge of Thuar, in the dead of the night, with a little moonlight shining from over Kilachdiarmid. At last she gave a start, and "By this and by that," says she, "here they come, bridles jingling and feathers tossing!" He looked, but could see nothing; and she stood trembling and her eyes wide open, looking down the way to the ford of Ballinacoola. "I see your wife," says she, "riding on the outside just so as to rub against us. We'll walk on quietly, as if we suspected nothing, and when we are passing I'll give you a shove. If you don't do your duty then, woe be with you!"

Well, they walked on easy, and the poor hearts beating in both their breasts; and though he could see nothing, he heard a faint jingle and trampling and rustling, and at last he got the push that she promised. He spread out his arms, and there was his wife's waist within them, and he could see her plain; but such a hullabulloo rose as if there was an earthquake, and he found himself surrounded by horrible-looking things, roaring at him and striving to pull his wife away. But he made the sign of the cross and bid them begone in God's name, and held his wife as if it was iron his arms were made of. Bedad, in one moment everything was as silent as the grave, and the poor woman lying in a faint in the arms of her husband and her good neighbour.

Well, all in good time she was minding her family and her business again; and I'll go bail, after the fright she got, she spent more time on her knees, and avoided fairy men all the days of the week, and particularly on Sunday.

It is hard to have anything to do with the good people without getting a mark from them. My brave nurse didn't escape no more than another. She was one Thursday at the market of Enniscorthy, when what did she see walking among the tubs of butter but the Dark Man, very hungry-looking, and taking a scoop out of one tub and out of another. "Oh, sir," says she, very foolish, "I hope your lady is well, and the baby."

"Pretty well, thank you," says he, rather frightened like. "How do I look in this new suit?" says he, getting to one side of her.

"I can't see you plain at all, sir," says she.

"Well, now?" says he, getting round her back to the other side.

"Musha, indeed, sir, your coat looks no better than a withered dock-leaf."

"Maybe, then," says he, "it will be different now," and he struck the eye next him with a switch. Friends, she never saw a glimmer after with that one till the day of her death.

The Legend of Knockgrafton

THERE WAS ONCE a poor man who lived in the fertile glen of Aherlow, at the foot of the gloomy Galtee mountains, and he had a great hump on his back: he looked just as if his body had been rolled up and placed upon his shoulders; and his head was pressed down with the weight so much that his chin, when he was sitting, used to rest upon his knees for support. The country people were rather shy of meeting him in any lonesome place, for though, poor creature, he was as harmless and as inoffensive as a new-born infant, yet his deformity was so great that he scarcely appeared to be a human creature, and some ill-minded persons had set strange stories about him afloat. He was said to have a great knowledge of herbs and charms; but certain it was that he had a mighty skilful hand in plaiting straw and rushes into hats and baskets, which was the way he made his livelihood.

Lusmore, for that was the nickname put upon him by reason of his always wearing a sprig of the fairy cap, or lusmore (the foxglove), in his little straw hat, would ever get a higher penny for his plaited work than anyone else, and perhaps that was the reason why someone, out of envy, had circulated the strange stories about him.

Be that as it may, it happened that he was returning one evening from the pretty town of Cahir towards Cappagh, and as little Lusmore walked very slowly, on account of the great hump upon his back, it was quite dark when he came to the old moat of Knockgrafton, which stood on the right-hand side of his road. Tired and weary was he, and noways comfortable in his own mind at thinking how much farther he had to travel, and that he should be walking all the night; so he sat down under the moat to rest himself, and began looking mournfully enough upon the moon.

Presently there rose a wild strain of unearthly melody upon the ear of little Lusmore; he listened, and he thought that he had never heard such ravishing music before. It was like the sound of many voices, each mingling and blending with the other so strangely that they seemed to be one, though all singing different strains, and the words of the song were these – *Da Luan, Da Mort, Da Luan, Da Mort, Da Luan, Da Mort*; when there would be a moment's pause, and then the round of melody went on again.

Lusmore listened attentively, scarcely drawing his breath lest he might lose the slightest note. He now plainly perceived that the singing was within the moat; and though at first it had charmed him so much, he began to get tired of hearing the same round sung over and over so often without any change; so availing himself of the pause when the *Da Luan, Da Mort*, had been sung three times, he took up the tune, and raised it with the words *augus Da Cadine*, and then went on singing with the voices inside of the moat, *Da Luan, Da Mort*, finishing the melody, when the pause again came, with *augus Da Cadine*.

The fairies within Knockgrafton, for the song was a fairy melody, when they heard this addition to the tune, were so much delighted that, with instant resolve, it was determined to bring the mortal among them, whose musical skill so far exceeded theirs, and little Lusmore was conveyed into their company with the eddying speed of a whirlwind.

Glorious to behold was the sight that burst upon him as he came down through the moat, twirling round and round, with the lightness of a straw, to the sweetest music that kept time to his motion. The greatest honour was then paid him, for he was put above all the musicians, and he had servants tending upon him, and everything to his heart's content, and a hearty welcome to all; and, in short, he was made as much of as if he had been the first man in the land.

Presently Lusmore saw a great consultation going forward among the fairies, and, notwithstanding all their civility, he felt very much frightened, until one stepping out from the rest came up to him and said –

"Lusmore! Lusmore!
Doubt not, nor deplore,
For the hump which you bore
On your back is no more;
Look down on the floor,
And view it, Lusmore!"

When these words were said, poor little Lusmore felt himself so light, and so happy, that he thought he could have bounded at one jump over the moon, like the cow in the history of the cat and the fiddle; and he saw, with inexpressible pleasure, his hump tumble down upon the ground from his shoulders. He then tried to lift up his head, and he did so with becoming caution, fearing that he might knock it against the ceiling of the grand hall, where he was; he looked round and round again with greatest wonder and delight upon everything, which appeared more and more beautiful; and, overpowered at beholding such a resplendent scene, his head grew dizzy, and his eyesight became dim. At last he fell into a sound sleep, and when he awoke he found that it was broad daylight, the sun shining brightly, and the birds singing sweetly; and that he was lying just at the foot of the moat of Knockgrafton, with the cows and sheep grazing peacefully round about him. The first thing Lusmore did, after saying his prayers, was to put his hand behind to feel for his hump, but no sign of one was there on his back, and he looked at himself with great pride, for he had now become a well-shaped dapper little fellow, and more than that, found himself in a full suit of new clothes, which he concluded the fairies had made for him.

Towards Cappagh he went, stepping out as lightly, and springing up at every step as if he had been all his life a dancing-master. Not a creature who met Lusmore knew him without his hump, and he had a great work to persuade everyone that he was the same man – in truth he was not, so far as outward appearance went.

Of course it was not long before the story of Lusmore's hump got about, and a great wonder was made of it. Through the country, for miles round, it was the talk of every one, high and low.

One morning, as Lusmore was sitting contented enough, at his cabin door, up came an old woman to him, and asked him if he could direct her to Cappagh.

"I need give you no directions, my good woman," said Lusmore, "for this is Cappagh; and whom may you want here?"

"I have come," said the woman, "out of Decie's country, in the county of Waterford looking after one Lusmore, who, I have heard tell, had his hump taken off by the fairies; for there is a son of a gossip of mine who has got a hump on him that will be his death;

and maybe if he could use the same charm as Lusmore, the hump may be taken off him. And now I have told you the reason of my coming so far: 'tis to find out about this charm, if I can."

Lusmore, who was ever a good-natured little fellow, told the woman all the particulars, how he had raised the tune for the fairies at Knockgrafton, how his hump had been removed from his shoulders, and how he had got a new suit of clothes into the bargain.

The woman thanked him very much, and then went away quite happy and easy in her own mind. When she came back to her gossip's house, in the county of Waterford, she told her everything that Lusmore had said, and they put the little hump-backed man, who was a peevish and cunning creature from his birth, upon a car, and took him all the way across the country. It was a long journey, but they did not care for that, so the hump was taken from off him; and they brought him, just at nightfall, and left him under the old moat of Knockgrafton.

Jack Madden, for that was the humpy man's name, had not been sitting there long when he heard the tune going on within the moat much sweeter than before; for the fairies were singing it the way Lusmore had settled their music for them, and the song was going on; *Da Luan, Da Mort, Da Luan, Da Mort, Da Luan, Da Mort, augus Da Cadine*, without ever stopping. Jack Madden, who was in a great hurry to get quit of his hump, never thought of waiting until the fairies had done, or watching for a fit opportunity to raise the tune higher again than Lusmore had; so having heard them sing it over seven times without stopping, out he bawls, never minding the time or the humour of the tune, or how he could bring his words in properly, *augus Da Cadine, augus Da Hena*, thinking that if one day was good, two were better; and that if Lusmore had one new suit of clothes given him, he should have two.

No sooner had the words passed his lips than he was taken up and whisked into the moat with prodigious force; and the fairies came crowding round about him with great anger, screeching, and screaming, and roaring out, "Who spoiled our tune? Who spoiled our tune?" and one stepped up to him, above all the rest and said:

"Jack Madden! Jack Madden!
Your words came so bad in
The tune we felt glad in; –
This castle you're had in,
That your life we may sadden;
Here's two humps for Jack Madden!"

And twenty of the strongest fairies brought Lusmore's hump and put it down upon poor Jack's back, over his own, where it became fixed as firmly as if it was nailed on with twelve-penny nails, by the best carpenter that ever drove one. Out of their castle they then kicked him; and, in the morning, when Jack Madden's mother and her gossip came to look after their little man, they found him half dead, lying at the foot of the moat, with the other hump upon his back. Well to be sure, how they did look at each other! But they were afraid to say anything, lest a hump might be put upon their own shoulders. Home they brought the unlucky Jack Madden with them, as downcast in their hearts and their looks as ever two gossips were; and what through the weight of his other hump, and the long journey, he died soon after, leaving they say his heavy curse to anyone who would go to listen to fairy tunes again.

How Cormac Mac Art Went to Faery

CORMAC, SON OF ART, son of Conn of the Hundred Battles, was high King of Ireland, and held his Court at Tara. One day he saw a youth upon the green having in his hand a glittering fairy branch with nine apples of red. And whensoever the branch was shaken, wounded men and women enfeebled by illness would be lulled to sleep by the sound of the very sweet fairy music which those apples uttered, nor could anyone upon earth bear in mind any want, woe, or weariness of soul when that branch was shaken for him.

"Is that branch thy own?" said Cormac.

"It is indeed mine."

"Wouldst thou sell it? And what wouldst thou require for it?"

"Will you give me what I ask?" said the youth.

The king promised, and the youth then claimed his wife, his daughter, and his son. Sorrowful of heart was the king, heaviness of heart filled his wife and children when they learned that they must part from him. But Cormac shook the branch amongst them, and when they heard the soft sweet music of the branch they forgot all care and sorrow and went forth to meet the youth, and he and they took their departure and were seen no more. Loud cries of weeping and mourning were made throughout Erin when this was known: but Cormac shook the branch so that there was no longer any grief or heaviness of heart upon anyone.

After a year Cormac said: "It is a year today since my wife, my son, and my daughter were taken from me. I will follow them by the same path that they took."

Cormac went off, and a dark magical mist rose about him, and he chanced to come upon a wonderful marvellous plain. Many horsemen were there, busy thatching a house with the feathers of foreign birds; when one side was thatched they would go and seek more, and when they returned not a feather was on the roof. Cormac gazed at them for a while and then went forward.

Again, he saw a youth dragging up trees to make a fire; but before he could find a second tree the first one would be burnt, and it seemed to Cormac that his labour would never end.

Cormac journeyed onwards until he saw three immense wells on the border of the plain, and on each well was a head. From out the mouth of the first head there flowed two streams, into it there flowed one; the second head had a stream flowing out of and another stream into its mouth, whilst three streams were flowing from the mouth of the third head. Great wonder seized Cormac, and he said: "I will stay and gaze upon these wells, for I should find no man to tell me your story." With that he set onwards till he came to a house in the middle of a field. He entered and greeted the inmates.

There sat within a tall couple clad in many-hued garments, and they greeted the king, and bade him welcome for the night.

Then the wife bade her husband seek food, and he arose and returned with a huge wild boar upon his back and a log in his hand. He cast down the swine and the log upon the floor, and said: "There is meat; cook it for yourselves."

"How can I do that?" said Cormac.

"I will teach you," said the youth. "Split this great log, make four pieces of it, and make four quarters of the hog; put a log under each quarter; tell a true story, and the meat will be cooked."

"Tell the first story yourself," said Cormac.

"Seven pigs I have of the same kind as the one I brought, and I could feed the world with them. For if a pig is killed I have but to put its bones into the stye again, and it will be found alive the next morning."

The story was true, and a quarter of the pig was cooked.

Then Cormac begged the woman of the house to tell a story.

"I have seven white cows, and they fill seven cauldrons with milk every day, and I give my word that they yield as much milk as would satisfy the men of the whole world if they were out on yonder plain drinking it."

That story was true, and a second quarter of the pig was cooked.

Cormac was bidden now to tell a story for his quarter, and he told how he was upon a search for his wife, his son and his daughter that had been borne away from him a year before by a youth with a fairy branch.

"If what thou sayest be true," said the man of the house, "thou art indeed Cormac, son of Art, son of Conn of the Hundred Battles."

"Truly I am," quoth Cormac.

That story was true, and a quarter of the pig was cooked.

"Eat thy meal now," said the man of the house.

"I never ate before," said Cormac, "having only two people in my company."

"Wouldst thou eat it with three others?"

"If they were dear to me, I would," said Cormac.

Then the door opened, and there entered the wife and children of Cormac: great was his joy and his exultation.

Then Manannan mac Lir, lord of the fairy Cavalcade, appeared before him in his own true form, and said thus:

"I it was, Cormac, who bore away these three from thee. I it was who gave thee this branch, all that I might bring thee here. Eat now and drink."

"I would do so," said Cormac, "could I learn the meaning of the wonders I saw today."

"Thou shalt learn them," said Manannan. "The horsemen thatching the roof with feathers are a likeness of people who go forth into the world to seek riches and fortune; when they return their houses are bare, and so they go on for ever. The young man dragging up the trees to make a fire is a likeness of those who labour for others: much trouble they have, but they never warm themselves at the fire. The three heads in the wells are three kinds of men. Some there are who give freely when they get freely; some who give freely though they get little; some who get much and give little, and they are the worst of the three, Cormac," said Manannan.

After that Cormac and his wife and his children sat down, and a table-cloth was spread before them.

"That is a very precious thing before thee," said Manannan, "there is no food however delicate that shall be asked of it but it shall be had without doubt."

"That is well," quoth Cormac.

After that Manannan thrust his hand into his girdle and brought out a goblet and set it upon his palm. "This cup has this virtue," said he, "that when a false story is told before it, it makes four pieces of it, and when a true story is related it is made whole again."

"Those are very precious things you have, Manannan," said the king.

"They shall all be thine," said Manannan, "the goblet, the branch and the tablecloth."

Then they ate their meal, and that meal was good, for they could not think of any meat but they got it upon the table-cloth, nor of any drink but they got it in the cup. Great thanks did they give to Manannan.

When they had eaten their meal a couch was prepared for them and they laid down to slumber and sweet sleep.

Where they rose on the morrow morn was in Tara of the kings, and by their side were tablecloth, cup, and branch.

Thus did Cormac fare at the Court of Manannan, and this is how he got the fairy branch.

The Leprechaun of Ardmore Tower

THE LEPRECHAUN – that flash from elf-land – was perched comfortably upon the west window ledge, high up in Ardmore Tower. Dawn was just beginning to send misty, grey lights over the rolling land. Winds that have blown since the world began were blowing around the old Irish tower. It was the south wind, this morning, that was blowing the strongest – the wind from the good sea that washed the coast of Ardmore and the high-lands of Ireland. The strong, stone tower, tapering skyward, stood, as it stands today, like a silent sentinel on the 'hill of the sheep' – the 'great hill.' Below its conical top, two windows, east and west, looked out, and it's on the ledge of the west one – mind you – that the Leprechaun was sitting. He had been sitting there since sundown. An iron bar, inside the tower, goes from the top of the west window to the top of the east window, and once, no one knows how long ago, seven small bells hung from this bar under the pinnacle. They are gone now, but in the old days they used to ring often.

("That's so," said the Leprechaun. He was always saying "That's so," to agree with himself or other people – himself oftenest.)

This little elf, in red jacket and green breeches who spends most of his days and some of his nights making shoes for the fairy folk, has been working the past night on a pair of riding boots for the fairy prince who wants the boots by sunrise. Tap, tap, tap – goes the Leprechaun's tiny hammer. Whish, whish, go his swift fingers. Hum, hum-m-m-m – goes his little singing tune, for the Leprechaun could no more work without singing than you could sleep without shutting your eyes.

("That's so!" said the Leprechaun.)

He is only six inches high, and harder to catch than a will-o'-the-wisp. If one could ever succeed in catching him, and then could keep looking at him, he might tell – though not a bit willingly – where a wonderful crock of gold is. But do you think you could keep looking at him and at him alone? Why, just as you think you are looking at nothing else, he, somehow, makes you look away from him, and, ochone, he is gone! He's that clever.

("That's so," said the Leprechaun.)

Many an enchantment the Leprechaun can perform, for all he appears so simple as he pegs away at the riding boots. Yes, himself it is that can blight the corn or snip off hair most unexpectedly. When he sits, crosslegged at his work, whether on a cornice of a roof or on a twig of the low bushes, it's just as well not to let him know you are watching him. The Irish fairy folk are all like that, and draw magic out of earth and sea and sky, or else draw it out of nothing at all.

("Do you hear that?" said the Leprechaun.)

Now this misty, windy dawn of a morning, thousands of days and nights ago, as the Leprechaun, up there on the grey, stone tower, tapped, tapped with his hammer, to finish the prince's boots, promised by sunrise, his elfin mind capered around with many thoughts. The mists were beginning to shine in the dim light of early morning, and the Leprechaun's thoughts, freshened by the south wind, were wafted over the whole land of Erin that stretched beyond the bogs and swamps, beyond the mounds and cromlechs, beyond the hills. He could tell you the colours of all the winds of Ireland. This south wind was white; the north wind, full of blackness; the west wind pale yellow, and the east wind was always a stirring, purple wind. The lesser winds, too, had their colours – yellow of furze, red of fire, grey of fog, green of meadow, brown of autumn leaves, and three more colours that mortals could not see. The Leprechaun, whenever he wished, could travel lightly on whatever wind was blowing and sing a tune as loud as any of them. This morning, in the misty dawn, it was his heart that did the travelling and it was his thoughts that sang tunes to match. When his eyes glanced from his work, toward the sea, his thoughts flew to Manannan Mac Lir, the old sea-god, riding along in his chariot, with thousands of his steeds shaking their manes as they galloped with him. For many a century, the great, slender, round tower had watched these steeds and the spirited charioteer. On many a moonlit night, it had seen invading bands crawl quietly to shore and stealthily march right up to the base of the tower with bad plans to surprise the unprotected people. Again and again the men of Ardmore had gathered their families, with provisions, safely, into the tall tower, barring the narrow door that was many feet high above the ground. There the weak ones and the women and children had lived, for days, until the invaders had been driven away. The Leprechaun laughed aloud as he thought of one stormy day when the old sea-god, Manannan Mac Lir, had bidden his horses keep the invaders from reaching the shore and the tower. The lively horses shook their manes and obeyed – ochone, but they obeyed!

Tap, tap, tap! The south wind, thought the Leprechaun, will be a strong one, this day! And the wind will draw music from the harps of all the Little Good Folk throughout Erin. As the Leprechaun, between his taps, looked westward, there was a break in the light morning vapour, like the gay snatch of song a maiden sings in the midst of her work; and, through the break, the elf's long gaze swept across the river Blackwater, and beside Watergrasshill, over the moor-land to the Bochragh Mountains, and even as far as Mt. Mish. There was a tale about Mt. Mish that rushed in now upon his thinking – a tale about his ancestors, the Tuatha-de-Danann, 'the folk of the god whose mother is Dana.'

On a day, in the early age of the world, when grey moor-land and steep mountains began to blaze brilliant with purple heather and yellow furze, the Danaans, covering themselves with a fog, crept along the east coast to possess the country near Mt. Mish. Fiercely they fought with the inhabitants, the Firbolgs, and won. For a thousand years they held sway – these tall, fair-haired men of Greek descent who had come from the North. After the thousand years and one day more, new invaders, the Milesians, entering along the bank of the Inverskena River, swept up into the land, like the knowing conquerors that they were, to overcome the Danaans.

The Leprechaun now sang, with a little humming chant, the words that Amergin, chief druid of the Milesians, sang when he set his right foot on the soil of Erin:

"I am the wind that blows over the sea,
I am the wave of the ocean,
I am the murmur of the billows,
I am the ox of the seven combats,
I am the vulture upon the rock,
I am a ray of the Sun,
I am the fairest of plants."

When the Danaans had been conquered by the Milesians, they promised that they would dwell inside the hills or under the lakes, and that they would be invisible to mortals, except on rare occasions. This promise they had kept.

("That's so," said the Leprechaun.)

The Leprechaun liked what the Danaans, his ancestors, had done next. The chief druid of the Danaans had raised his golden harp in the dazzling sunlight, the other druids had lifted their silver harps in the glittering morning air, and all the druids had played such deliciously enchanting melodies that the Danaans, in a long procession that seemed like a living green, had followed their leaders, laughing as they went, and singing like merry brooks or happy children. Into the mountains they had gone, disappearing before the very eyes of the Milesians. Forever afterwards they lived within the mountains and became the Ever-Living Living Ones in the Land of Youth.

The Leprechaun knew well that he, and all his elf kin, were descendants of those very Danaans, who still lived in their underground palaces that blazed with light and laughter. Hadn't the drean – the wise, small wren – that druid of birds, often told him what was going on down there? Hadn't he himself been below the tower of Ardmore, where, in a glorious hall that belonged to the Ever-Living Living Ones, the Danaans held many a gay carousal? Didn't he hear, at times, their bells ringing under the bog, on a quiet evening? And hadn't he, more times than once, rung the sweet bells of Ardmore – these bells which never had been rung except by one whose real home was in the Land of Youth? In the Land of Youth was the Leprechaun's home. (Ochone, I should say!) There it had been since the day that Oisin, son of Finn, journeyed to that land. For, on the same day, without Oisin's knowledge, the Leprechaun had sped from the green hills of Erin, through a golden haze, to the country of the Ever-Living Living Ones. Oisin was his hero, his great hero, whom he had helped, invisibly, more than he had helped anyone else. The most valiant Danaan of all was Oisin, and Oisin he would follow to the world's end.

("That's so," said the Leprechaun, as he began the fancy stitching on the prince's riding boots.)

Now, for the thousandth time, he told himself the story of Oisin, for he liked this tale best of all: how Oisin, when hunting, met the maiden, Niam of the Golden Hair, riding her snow-white steed; how, after she sang to him a song of the enchanting "land beyond dreams," Oisin had ridden with her to the Land of Youth (and the Leprechaun, in the shape of a butterfly, had perched on the horse's mane); how, in the realm of her father, the king, fearless Oisin had had brave adventures. He rescued a princess from a giant; subdued the three Hounds of Erin (helped by the Leprechaun who confused the hounds), and found the magic harp – a harp next in wonder to the Dagda's harp whose strings, when touched, would sing the story of the one who last touched them. He had even tilted with the king's cupbearer to win a gold-hilted sword, and had done other worthy deeds. No time at all, it seemed to Oisin, that magical time, in the Land of Youth, but, at last, his heart longed to see his old home. So Niam of the Golden Hair gave him her snow-white steed to ride, but charged him three times that, when he should reach the familiar places of Erin, he must not, once, set foot upon the ground or he would never be able to return to the Land of Youth. Oisin bade her farewell and, with the Leprechaun as a butterfly still on the horse's mane, he began his homeward journey.

As he was riding along, once more, through a beautiful vale of Erin, he saw men, much smaller than himself, trying in vain to push aside a huge boulder that had rolled from the hillside down upon their tilled land. In pity for these weaklings, he instantly jumped from his saddle to the ground (not heeding the Leprechaun who, in his own form, clung with all his might, to remind him of Niam's warning) and, with one push, he sent the boulder out of the way. Alas! Even as the men were shouting praises to their god-like helper, it seemed to Oisin that darkness bore him to the earth. When he opened his eyes, lo, he was an old man, feeble, grey-headed, grey-bearded! The men whom he had helped, had with one accord run away; but the Leprechaun, astride a twig close by, whispered words of cheer and sang part of the song of the Danaans when they went into the mountains. Oisin then roused himself and said faintly, "I hear the voice of bells." Then he added in a resolute tone, "Whenever I shall hear sweet bells ring, young will be my heart." Since that day, the Leprechaun had often rung bells, especially the bells of Ardmore Tower, because he knew that Oisin would hear them and feel young again.

Tap, tap, tap – and the Leprechaun's work is done. It's little that anyone can tell about him making shoes, or about Ireland's heroes, or about its grassy mounds of mystery. He stands up now and stretches himself. If he felt like it, he could blow a blast on the tiny, curved horn, hanging at his side, and call, from the Underland, as many merry-hearted Danaans as he chose. He could cast spells, too, on the sea, beyond the ninth wave from shore. Instead, he whisks from the west window into the tower and out again, through the east window. There he stands for a few moments – his feet braced on the highest circular cornice, his back leaning against the sloping roof top – watching the rim of the sun rise over a mountainous cloud. The sky of gold is changing to the pink of a wild rose. The grey mists, over moorland and mound, are scattering as quickly as the men whom Oisin helped.

The Round Tower of Ardmore again greeted the sun, as the Leprechaun, hugging tightly the riding boots promised to the fairy prince at sunrise, swiftly slid down a sunbeam to the top of the oak tree, where the prince was waiting.

"Here they are, Your Highness," said the elf, with a bow.

The prince smiled, as he took the boots, and gave the Leprechaun a piece of gold. "You've kept your promise," he said.

"That's so," answered the Leprechaun. Then he sprang up on the rollicking south wind and flew away.

Sanntraigh

THERE WAS A HERD'S WIFE in the island of Sanntraigh, and she had a kettle. A woman of peace (fairy) would come every day to seek the kettle. She would not say a word when she came, but she would catch hold of the kettle. When she would catch the kettle, the woman of the house would say –

A smith is able to make
Cold iron hot with coal.
The due of a kettle is bones,
And to bring it back again whole.

The woman of peace would come back every day with the kettle and flesh and bones in it. On a day that was there, the housewife was for going over the ferry to Baile a Chaisteil, and she said to her man, "If thou wilt say to the woman of peace as I say, I will go to Baile Castle." "Oo! I will say it. Surely it's I that will say it." He was spinning a heather rope to be set on the house. He saw a woman coming and a shadow from her feet, and he took fear of her. He shut the door. He stopped his work. When she came to the door she did not find the door open, and he did not open it for her. She went above a hole that was in the house. The kettle gave two jumps, and at the third leap it went out at the ridge of the house. The night came, and the kettle came not. The wife came back over the ferry, and she did not see a bit of the kettle within, and she asked, "Where was the kettle?" "Well then I don't care where it is," said the man; "I never took such a fright as I took at it. I shut the door, and she did not come any more with it." "Good-for-nothing wretch, what didst thou do? There are two that will be ill off – thyself and I." "She will come to-morrow with it." "She will not come."

She hasted herself and she went away. She reached the knoll, and there was no man within. It was after dinner, and they were out in the mouth of the night. She went in. She saw the kettle, and she lifted it with her. It was heavy for her with the remnants that they left in it. When the old carle that was within saw her going out, he said,

Silent wife, silent wife,
That came on us from the land of chase,
Thou man on the surface of the "Bruth,"
Loose the black, and slip the Fierce.

The two dogs were let loose; and she was not long away when she heard the clatter of the dogs coming. She kept the remnant that was in the kettle, so that if she could get it with her, well, and if the dogs should come that she might throw it at them. She perceived the dogs coming. She put her hand in the kettle. She took the board out of it, and she threw at them a quarter of what was in it. They noticed it there for a while. She perceived them again, and she threw another piece at them when they closed upon her. She went away walking as well as she might; when she came near the farm, she threw the mouth of the pot downwards, and there she left them all that was in it. The dogs of the town struck (up) a barking when they saw the dogs of peace stopping. The woman of peace never came more to seek the kettle.

Man

THE MANKS FAIRY CREED is the same as elsewhere in Scotland. Such beings are supposed to exist, and are known by the name of Ferish, which a Manksman assured me was a genuine Manks word. If so, fairy may be old Celtic, and derived from the same root as Peri, instead of being derived from it.

The fairies in the Isle of Man are believed to be spirits. They are not supposed to throw arrows as they are said still to do in the Highlands. None of the old peasants seemed to take the least interest in 'elf shots,' the flint arrows, which generally lead to a story when shown elsewhere. One old man said, "The ferish have no body, no bones and scorned the arrow heads. It is stated in Train's history, that no flint-arrow heads have ever been found in the Isle of Man; but as there are numerous barrows, flint weapons may yet be discovered when some one looks for them.

Still these Manks fairies are much the same as their neighbours on the main land. They go into mills at night and grind stolen corn; they steal milk from the cattle; they live in green mounds; in short, they axe like little mortals invested with supernatural power, thus: There was a man who lived not long ago near Port Erin, who had a Lhiannan Rhee. "He was like other people, but he had a fairy sweetheart; but he noticed her, and they do not like being noticed, the fairies, and so he lost his mind. Well, he was quite quiet like other people, but at night he slept in the barn; and they used to hear him talking to his sweetheart, and scolding her sometimes; but if any one made a noise he would be quiet at once."

Now, the truth of this story is clear enough; the man went mad; but this madness took the form of the popular belief, and that again attributed his madness to the fairy mistress. I am convinced that this was believed to be a case of genuine fairy intercourse; and it shows that the fairy creed still survives in the Isle of Man.

Thomas the Rhymer

OF ALL THE YOUNG GALLANTS in Scotland in the thirteenth century, there was none more gracious and debonair than Thomas Learmont, Laird of the Castle of Ercildoune, in Berwickshire.

He loved books, poetry, and music, which were uncommon tastes in those days; and, above all, he loved to study nature, and to watch the habits of the beasts and birds that made their abode in the fields and woods round about his home.

Now it chanced that, one sunny May morning, Thomas left his Tower of Ercildoune, and went wandering into the woods that lay about the Huntly Burn, a little stream that came rushing down from the slopes of the Eildon Hills. It was a lovely morning – fresh, and bright, and warm, and everything was so beautiful that it looked as Paradise might look.

The tender leaves were bursting out of their sheaths, and covering all the trees with a fresh soft mantle of green; and amongst the carpet of moss under the young man's feet, yellow primroses and starry anemones were turning up their faces to the morning sky.

The little birds were singing like to burst their throats, and hundreds of insects were flying backwards and forwards in the sunshine; while down by the burnside the bright-eyed water-rats were poking their noses out of their holes, as if they knew that summer had come, and wanted to have a share in all that was going on.

Thomas felt so happy with the gladness of it all, that he threw himself down at the root of a tree, to watch the living things around him.

As he was lying there, he heard the trampling of a horse's hooves, as it forced its way through the bushes; and, looking up, he saw the most beautiful lady that he had ever seen coming riding towards him on a grey palfrey.

She wore a hunting dress of glistening silk, the colour of the fresh spring grass; and from her shoulders hung a velvet mantle, which matched the riding-skirt exactly. Her yellow hair, like rippling gold, hung loosely round her shoulders, and on her head sparkled a diadem of precious stones, which flashed like fire in the sunlight.

Her saddle was of pure ivory, and her saddle-cloth of blood-red satin, while her saddle girths were of corded silk and her stirrups of cut crystal. Her horse's reins were of beaten gold, all hung with little silver bells, so that, as she rode along, she made a sound like fairy music.

Apparently she was bent on the chase, for she carried a hunting-horn and a sheaf of arrows; and she led seven greyhounds along in a leash, while as many scenting hounds ran loose at her horse's side.

As she rode down the glen, she lilted a bit of an old Scotch song; and she carried herself with such a queenly air, and her dress was so magnificent, that Thomas was like to kneel by the side of the path and worship her, for he thought that it must be the Blessed Virgin herself.

But when the rider came to where he was, and understood his thoughts, she shook her head sadly.

"I am not that Blessed Lady, as thou thinkest," she said. "Men call me Queen, but it is of a far other country; for I am the Queen of Fairy-land, and not the Queen of Heaven."

And certainly it seemed as if what she said were true; for, from that moment, it was as if a spell were cast over Thomas, making him forget prudence, and caution, and common-sense itself.

For he knew that it was dangerous for mortals to meddle with Fairies, yet he was so entranced with the Lady's beauty that he begged her to give him a kiss. This was just what she wanted, for she knew that if she once kissed him she had him in her power.

And, to the young man's horror, as soon as their lips had met, an awful change came over her. For her beautiful mantle and riding-skirt of silk seemed to fade away, leaving her clad in a long grey garment, which was just the colour of ashes. Her beauty seemed to fade away also, and she grew old and wan; and, worst of all, half of her abundant yellow hair went grey before his very eyes. She saw the poor man's astonishment and terror, and she burst into a mocking laugh.

"I am not so fair to look on now as I was at first," she said, "but that matters little, for thou hast sold thyself, Thomas, to be my servant for seven long years. For whoso kisseth the Fairy Queen must e'en go with her to Fairy-land, and serve her there till that time is past."

When he heard these words poor Thomas fell on his knees and begged for mercy. But mercy he could not obtain. The Elfin Queen only laughed in his face, and brought her dapple-grey palfrey close up to where he was standing.

"No, no," she said, in answer to his entreaties. "Thou didst ask the kiss, and now thou must pay the price. So dally no longer, but mount behind me, for it is full time that I was gone."

So Thomas, with many a sigh and groan of terror, mounted behind her; and as soon as he had done so, she shook her bridle rein, and the grey steed galloped off.

On and on they went, going swifter than the wind; till they left the land of the living behind, and came to the edge of a great desert, which stretched before them, dry, and bare, and desolate, to the edge of the far horizon.

At least, so it seemed to the weary eyes of Thomas of Ercildoune, and he wondered if he and his strange companion had to cross this desert; and, if so, if there were any chance of reaching the other side of it alive.

But the Fairy Queen suddenly tightened her rein, and the grey palfrey stopped short in its wild career.

"Now must thou descend to earth, Thomas," said the Lady, glancing over her shoulder at her unhappy captive, "and lout down, and lay thy head on my knee, and I will show thee hidden things, which cannot be seen by mortal eyes."

So Thomas dismounted, and louted down, and rested his head on the Fairy Queen's knee; and lo, as he looked once more over the desert, everything seemed changed. For he saw three roads leading across it now, which he had not noticed before, and each of these three roads was different.

One of them was broad, and level, and even, and it ran straight on across the sand, so that no one who was travelling by it could possibly lose his way.

And the second road was as different from the first as it well could be. It was narrow, and winding, and long; and there was a thorn hedge on one side of it, and a briar hedge on the other; and those hedges grew so high, and their branches were so wild and tangled, that those who were travelling along that road would have some difficulty in persevering on their journey at all.

And the third road was unlike any of the others. It was a bonnie, bonnie road, winding up a hillside among brackens, and heather, and golden-yellow whins, and it looked as if it would be pleasant travelling, to pass that way.

"Now," said the Fairy Queen, "an' thou wilt, I shall tell thee where these three roads lead to. The first road, as thou seest, is broad, and even, and easy, and there be many that choose it to travel on. But though it be a good road, it leadeth to a bad end, and the folk that choose it repent their choice for ever.

"And as for the narrow road, all hampered and hindered by the thorns and the briars, there be few that be troubled to ask where that leadeth to. But did they ask, perchance more of them might be stirred up to set out along it. For that is the Road of Righteousness;

and, although it be hard and irksome, yet it endeth in a glorious City, which is called the City of the Great King.

"And the third road – the bonnie road – that runs up the brae among the ferns, and leadeth no mortal kens whither, but I ken where it leadeth, Thomas – for it leadeth unto fair Elf-land; and that road take we.

"And, mark 'ee, Thomas, if ever thou hopest to see thine own Tower of Ercildoune again, take care of thy tongue when we reach our journey's end, and speak no single word to anyone save me – for the mortal who openeth his lips rashly in Fairy-land must bide there for ever."

Then she bade him mount her palfrey again, and they rode on. The ferny road was not so bonnie all the way as it had been at first, however. For they had not ridden along it very far before it led them into a narrow ravine, which seemed to go right down under the earth, where there was no ray of light to guide them, and where the air was dank and heavy. There was a sound of rushing water everywhere, and at last the grey palfrey plunged right into it; and it crept up, cold and chill, first over Thomas's feet, and then over his knees.

His courage had been slowly ebbing ever since he had been parted from the daylight, but now he gave himself up for lost; for it seemed to him certain that his strange companion and he would never come safe to their journey's end.

He fell forward in a kind of swoon; and, if it had not been that he had tight hold of the Fairy's ash-grey gown, I warrant he had fallen from his seat, and had been drowned.

But all things, be they good or bad, pass in time, and at last the darkness began to lighten, and the light grew stronger, until they were back in broad sunshine.

Then Thomas took courage, and looked up; and lo, they were riding through a beautiful orchard, where apples and pears, dates and figs and wine-berries grew in great abundance. And his tongue was so parched and dry, and he felt so faint, that he longed for some of the fruit to restore him.

He stretched out his hand to pluck some of it; but his companion turned in her saddle and forbade him.

"There is nothing safe for thee to eat here," she said, "save an apple, which I will give thee presently. If thou touch aught else thou art bound to remain in Fairy-land for ever."

So poor Thomas had to restrain himself as best he could; and they rode slowly on, until they came to a tiny tree all covered with red apples. The Fairy Queen bent down and plucked one, and handed it to her companion.

"This I can give thee," she said, "and I do it gladly, for these apples are the Apples of Truth; and whoso eateth them gaineth this reward, that his lips will never more be able to frame a lie."

Thomas took the apple, and ate it; and for evermore the Grace of Truth rested on his lips; and that is why, in after years, men called him 'True Thomas.'

They had only a little way to go after this, before they came in sight of a magnificent Castle standing on a hillside.

"Yonder is my abode," said the Queen, pointing to it proudly. "There dwelleth my Lord and all the Nobles of his court; and, as my Lord hath an uncertain temper and shows no liking for any strange gallant whom he sees in my company, I pray thee, both for thy sake and mine, to utter no word to anyone who speaketh to thee; and, if anyone should ask me who and what thou art, I will tell them that thou art dumb. So wilt thou pass unnoticed in the crowd."

With these words the Lady raised her hunting-horn, and blew a loud and piercing blast; and, as she did so, a marvellous change came over her again; for her ugly ash-covered gown dropped off her, and the grey in her hair vanished, and she appeared once more in her green riding-skirt and mantle, and her face grew young and fair.

And a wonderful change passed over Thomas also; for, as he chanced to glance downwards, he found that his rough country clothes had been transformed into a suit of fine brown cloth, and that on his feet he wore satin shoon.

Immediately the sound of the horn rang out, the doors of the Castle flew open, and the King hurried out to meet the Queen, accompanied by such a number of Knights and Ladies, Minstrels and Page-boys, that Thomas, who had slid from his palfrey, had no difficulty in obeying her wishes and passing into the Castle unobserved.

Everyone seemed very glad to see the Queen back again, and they crowded into the Great Hall in her train, and she spoke to them all graciously, and allowed them to kiss her hand. Then she passed, with her husband, to a dais at the far end of the huge apartment, where two thrones stood, on which the Royal pair seated themselves to watch the revels which now began.

Poor Thomas, meanwhile, stood far away at the other end of the Hall, feeling very lonely, yet fascinated by the extraordinary scene on which he was gazing.

For, although all the fine Ladies, and Courtiers, and Knights were dancing in one part of the Hall, there were huntsmen coming and going in another part, carrying in great antlered deer, which apparently they had killed in the chase, and throwing them down in heaps on the floor. And there were rows of cooks standing beside the dead animals, cutting them up into joints, and bearing away the joints to be cooked.

Altogether it was such a strange, fantastic scene that Thomas took no heed of how the time flew, but stood and gazed, and gazed, never speaking a word to anybody. This went on for three long days, then the Queen rose from her throne, and, stepping from the dais, crossed the Hall to where he was standing.

"'Tis time to mount and ride, Thomas," she said, "if thou wouldst ever see the fair Castle of Ercildoune again."

Thomas looked at her in amazement. "Thou spokest of seven long years, Lady," he exclaimed, "and I have been here but three days."

The Queen smiled. "Time passeth quickly in Fairy-land, my friend," she replied. "Thou thinkest that thou hast been here but three days. 'Tis seven years since we two met. And now it is time for thee to go. I would fain have had thy presence with me longer, but I dare not, for thine own sake. For every seventh year an Evil Spirit cometh from the Regions of Darkness, and carrieth back with him one of our followers, whomsoever he chanceth to choose. And, as thou art a goodly fellow, I fear that he might choose thee.

"So, as I would be loth to let harm befall thee, I will take thee back to thine own country this very night."

Once more the grey palfrey was brought, and Thomas and the Queen mounted it; and, as they had come, so they returned to the Eildon Tree near the Huntly Burn.

Then the Queen bade Thomas farewell; and, as a parting gift, he asked her to give him something that would let people know that he had really been to Fairy-land.

"I have already given thee the Gift of Truth," she replied. "I will now give thee the Gifts of Prophecy and Poesie; so that thou wilt be able to foretell the future, and also to write wondrous verses. And, besides these unseen gifts, here is something that mortals can see with their own eyes – a Harp that was fashioned in Fairy-land. Fare thee well, my friend. Some day, perchance, I will return for thee again."

With these words the Lady vanished, and Thomas was left alone, feeling a little sorry, if the truth must be told, at parting with such a radiant Being and coming back to the ordinary haunts of men.

After this he lived for many a long year in his Castle of Ercildoune, and the fame of his poetry and of his prophecies spread all over the country, so that people named him True Thomas, and Thomas the Rhymer.

I cannot write down for you all the prophecies which Thomas uttered, and which most surely came to pass, but I will tell you one or two.

He foretold the Battle of Bannockburn in these words:

"The Burn of Breid
Shall rin fou reid,"

which came to pass on that terrible day when the waters of the little Bannockburn were reddened by the blood of the defeated English.

He also foretold the Union of the Crowns of England and Scotland, under a Prince who was the son of a French Queen, and who yet bore the blood of Bruce in his veins.

"A French Quen shall bearre the Sonne;
Shall rule all Britainne to the sea,
As neere as is the ninth degree,"

which thing came true in 1603, when King James, son of Mary, Queen of Scots, became Monarch of both countries.

Fourteen long years went by, and people were beginning to forget that Thomas the Rhymer had ever been in Fairy-land; but at last a day came when Scotland was at war with England, and the Scottish army was resting by the banks of the Tweed, not far from the Tower of Ercildoune.

And the Master of the Tower determined to make a feast, and invite all the Nobles and Barons who were leading the army to sup with him.

That feast was long remembered.

For the Laird of Ercildoune took care that everything was as magnificent as it could possibly be; and when the meal was ended he rose in his place, and, taking his Elfin Harp, he sang to his assembled guests song after song of the days of long ago.

The guests listened breathlessly, for they felt that they would never hear such wonderful music again. And so it fell out.

For that very night, after all the Nobles had gone back to their tents, a soldier on guard saw, in the moonlight, a snow-white Hart and Hind moving slowly down the road that ran past the camp.

There was something so unusual about the animals that he called to his officer to come and look at them. And the officer called to his brother officers, and soon there was quite a crowd softly following the dumb creatures, who paced solemnly on, as if they were keeping time to music unheard by mortal ears.

"There is something uncanny about this," said one soldier at last. "Let us send for Thomas of Ercildoune, perchance he may be able to tell us if it be an omen or no."

"Ay, send for Thomas of Ercildoune," cried every one at once. So a little page was sent in haste to the old Tower to rouse the Rhymer from his slumbers.

When he heard the boy's message, the Seer's face grew grave and wrapt.

"'Tis a summons," he said softly, "a summons from the Queen of Fairy-land. I have waited long for it, and it hath come at last."

And when he went out, instead of joining the little company of waiting men, he walked straight up to the snow-white Hart and Hind. As soon as he reached them they paused for a moment as if to greet him. Then all three moved slowly down a steep bank that sloped to the little river Leader, and disappeared in its foaming waters, for the stream was in full flood.

And, although a careful search was made, no trace of Thomas of Ercildoune was found; and to this day the country folk believe that the Hart and the Hind were messengers from the Elfin Queen, and that he went back to Fairy-land with them.

The Page-Boy and the Silver Goblet

THERE WAS ONCE A LITTLE page-boy, who was in service in a stately Castle. He was a very good-natured little fellow, and did his duties so willingly and well that everybody liked him, from the great Earl whom he served every day on bended knee, to the fat old butler whose errands he ran.

Now the Castle stood on the edge of a cliff overlooking the sea, and although the walls at that side were very thick, in them there was a little postern door, which opened on to a narrow flight of steps that led down the face of the cliff to the sea shore, so that anyone who liked could go down there in the pleasant summer mornings and bathe in the shimmering sea.

On the other side of the Castle were gardens and pleasure grounds, opening on to a long stretch of heather-covered moorland, which, at last, met a distant range of hills.

The little page-boy was very fond of going out on this moor when his work was done, for then he could run about as much as he liked, chasing bumble-bees, and catching butterflies, and looking for birds' nests when it was nesting time.

So one night, when everyone else was asleep, he crept out of the Castle by the little postern door, and stole down the stone steps, and along the sea shore, and up on to the moor, and went straight to the Fairy Knowe.

To his delight he found that what everyone said was true. The top of the Knowe was tipped up, and from the opening that was thus made, rays of light came streaming out.

His heart was beating fast with excitement, but, gathering his courage, he stooped down and slipped inside the Knowe.

He found himself in a large room lit by numberless tiny candles, and there, seated round a polished table, were scores of the Tiny Folk, Fairies, and Elves, and Gnomes, dressed in green, and yellow, and pink; blue, and lilac, and scarlet; in all the colours, in fact, that you can think of.

He stood in a dark corner watching the busy scene in wonder, thinking how strange it was that there should be such a number of these tiny beings living their own lives all unknown to men, at such a little distance from them, when suddenly someone – he could not tell who it was – gave an order.

"Fetch the Cup," cried the owner of the unknown voice, and instantly two little Fairy pages, dressed all in scarlet livery, darted from the table to a tiny cupboard in the rock, and returned staggering under the weight of a most beautiful silver cup, richly embossed and lined inside with gold.

He placed it in the middle of the table, and, amid clapping of hands and shouts of joy, all the Fairies began to drink out of it in turn. And the page could see, from where he stood, that no one poured wine into it, and yet it was always full, and that the wine that was in it was not always the same kind, but that each Fairy, when he grasped its stem, wished for the wine that he loved best, and lo! in a moment the cup was full of it.

"'Twould be a fine thing if I could take that cup home with me," thought the page. "No one will believe that I have been here except I have something to show for it." So he bided his time, and watched.

Presently the Fairies noticed him, and, instead of being angry at his boldness in entering their abode, as he expected that they would be, they seemed very pleased to see him, and invited him to a seat at the table. But by and by they grew rude and insolent, and jeered at him for being content to serve mere mortals, telling him that they saw everything that went on at the Castle, and making fun of the old butler, whom the page loved with all his heart. And they laughed at the food he ate, saying that it was only fit for animals; and when any fresh dainty was set on the table by the scarlet-clad pages, they would push the dish across to him, saying: "Taste it, for you will not have the chance of tasting such things at the Castle."

At last he could stand their teasing remarks no longer; besides, he knew that if he wanted to secure the cup he must lose no time in doing so.

So he suddenly stood up, and grasped the stem of it tightly in his hand. "I'll drink to you all in water," he cried, and instantly the ruby wine was turned to clear cold water.

He raised the cup to his lips, but he did not drink from it. With a sudden jerk he threw the water over the candles, and instantly the room was in darkness. Then, clasping the precious cup tightly in his arms, he sprang to the opening of the Knowe, through which he could see the stars glimmering clearly.

He was just in time, for it fell to with a crash behind him; and soon he was speeding along the wet, dew-spangled moor, with the whole troop of Fairies at his heels.

They were wild with rage, and from the shrill shouts of fury which they uttered, the page knew well that, if they overtook him, he need expect no mercy at their hands.

And his heart began to sink, for, fleet of foot though he was, he was no match for the Fairy Folk, who gained on him steadily.

All seemed lost, when a mysterious voice sounded out of the darkness:

"If thou wouldst gain the Castle door,
Keep to the black stones on the shore."

It was the voice of some poor mortal, who, for some reason or other, had been taken prisoner by the Fairies – who were really very malicious Little Folk – and who did not want a like fate to befall the adventurous page-boy; but the little fellow did not know this.

He had once heard that if anyone walked on the wet sands, where the waves had come over them, the Fairies could not touch him, and this mysterious sentence brought the saying into his mind.

So he turned, and dashed panting down to the shore. His feet sank in the dry sand, his breath came in little gasps, and he felt as if he must give up the struggle; but he persevered, and at last, just as the foremost Fairies were about to lay hands on him, he jumped across the water-mark on to the firm, wet sand, from which the waves had just receded, and then he knew that he was safe.

For the Little Folk could go no step further, but stood on the dry sand uttering cries of rage and disappointment, while the triumphant page-boy ran safely along the shore, his precious cup in his arms, and climbed lightly up the steps in the rock and disappeared through the postern. And for many years after, long after the little page-boy had grown up and become a stately butler, who trained other little page-boys to follow in his footsteps, the beautiful cup remained in the Castle as a witness of his adventure.

Farquhar MacNeill

ONCE UPON A TIME there was a young man named Farquhar MacNeill. He had just gone to a new situation, and the very first night after he went to it his mistress asked him if he would go over the hill to the house of a neighbour and borrow a sieve, for her own was all in holes, and she wanted to sift some meal.

Farquhar agreed to do so, for he was a willing lad, and he set out at once upon his errand, after the farmer's wife had pointed out to him the path that he was to follow, and told him that he would have no difficulty in finding the house, even though it was strange to him, for he would be sure to see the light in the window.

He had not gone very far, however, before he saw what he took to be the light from a cottage window on his left hand, some distance from the path, and, forgetting his Mistress's instructions that he was to follow the path right over the hill, he left it, and walked towards the light.

It seemed to him that he had almost reached it when his foot tripped, and he fell down, down, down, into a Fairy Parlour, far under the ground.

It was full of Fairies, who were engaged in different occupations.

Close by the door, or rather the hole down which he had so unceremoniously tumbled, two little elderly women, in black aprons and white mutches, were busily engaged in grinding corn between two flat millstones. Other two Fairies, younger women, in blue print gowns and white kerchiefs, were gathering up the freshly ground meal, and baking it into bannocks, which they were toasting on a girdle over a peat fire, which was burning slowly in a corner.

In the centre of the large apartment a great troop of Fairies, Elves, and Sprites were dancing reels as hard as they could to the music of a tiny set of bagpipes which were being played by a brown-faced Gnome, who sat on a ledge of rock far above their heads.

They all stopped their various employments when Farquhar came suddenly down in their midst, and looked at him in alarm; but when they saw that he was not hurt, they bowed gravely and bade him be seated. Then they went on with their work and with their play as if nothing had happened.

But Farquhar, being very fond of dancing, and being in no wise anxious to be seated, thought that he would like to have a reel first, so he asked the Fairies if he might join them. And they, although they looked surprised at his request, allowed him to do so, and in a few minutes the young man was dancing away as gaily as any of them.

And as he danced a strange change came over him. He forgot his errand, he forgot his home, he forgot everything that had ever happened to him, he only knew that he wanted to remain with the Fairies all the rest of his life.

And he did remain with them – for a magic spell had been cast over him, and he became like one of themselves, and could come and go at nights without being seen, and could sip the dew from the grass and honey from the flowers as daintily and noiselessly as if he had been a Fairy born.

Time passed by, and one night he and a band of merry companions set out for a long journey through the air. They started early, for they intended to pay a visit to the Man in the Moon and be back again before cock-crow.

All would have gone well if Farquhar had only looked where he was going, but he did not, being deeply engaged in making love to a young Fairy Maiden by his side, so he never saw a cottage that was standing right in his way, till he struck against the chimney and stuck fast in the thatch.

His companions sped merrily on, not noticing what had befallen him, and he was left to disentangle himself as best he could.

As he was doing so he chanced to glance down the wide chimney, and in the cottage kitchen he saw a comely young woman dandling a rosy-cheeked baby.

Now, when Farquhar had been in his mortal state, he had been very fond of children, and a word of blessing rose to his lips.

"God shield thee," he said, as he looked at the mother and child, little guessing what the result of his words would be.

For scarce had the Holy Name crossed his lips than the spell which had held him so long was broken, and he became as he had been before.

Instantly his thoughts flew to his friends at home, and to the new Mistress whom he had left waiting for her sieve; for he felt sure that some weeks must have elapsed since he set out to fetch it. So he made haste to go to the farm.

When he arrived in the neighbourhood everything seemed strange. There were woods where no woods used to be, and walls where no walls used to be. To his amazement, he could not find his way to the farm, and, worst of all, in the place where he expected to find his father's house he found nothing but a crop of rank green nettles.

In great distress he looked about for someone to tell him what it all meant, and at last he found an old man thatching the roof of a cottage.

This old man was so thin and grey that at first Farquhar took him for a patch of mist, but as he went nearer he saw that he was a human being, and, going close up to the wall and shouting with all his might, for he felt sure that such an ancient man would be deaf, he asked him if he could tell him where his friends had gone to, and what had happened to his father's dwelling.

The old man listened, then he shook his head. "I never heard of him," he answered slowly; "but perhaps my father might be able to tell you."

"Your father!" said Farquhar, in great surprise. "Is it possible that your father is alive?"

"Aye he is," answered the old man, with a little laugh. "If you go into the house you'll find him sitting in the arm-chair by the fire."

Farquhar did as he was bid, and on entering the cottage found another old man, who was so thin and withered and bent that he looked as if he must at least be a hundred years old. He was feebly twisting ropes to bind the thatch on the roof.

"Can ye tell me aught of my friends, or where my father's cottage is?" asked Farquhar again, hardly expecting that this second old man would be able to answer him.

"I cannot," mumbled this ancient person; "but perhaps my father can tell you."

"Your father!" exclaimed Farquhar, more astonished than ever. "But surely he must be dead long ago."

The old man shook his head with a weird grimace.

"Look there," he said, and pointed with a twisted finger, to a leathern purse, or sporran, which was hanging to one of the posts of a wooden bedstead in the corner.

Farquhar approached it, and was almost frightened out of his wits by seeing a tiny shrivelled face crowned by a red pirnie, looking over the edge of the sporran.

"Tak' him out; he'll no touch ye," chuckled the old man by the fire.

So Farquhar took the little creature out carefully between his finger and thumb, and set him on the palm of his left hand. He was so shrivelled with age that he looked just like a mummy.

"Dost know anything of my friends, or where my father's cottage is gone to?" asked Farquhar for the third time, hardly expecting to get an answer.

"They were all dead long before I was born," piped out the tiny figure. "I never saw any of them, but I have heard my father speak of them."

"Then I must be older than you!" cried Farquhar, in great dismay. And he got such a shock at the thought that his bones suddenly dissolved into dust, and he fell, a heap of grey ashes, on the floor.

The Minister and the Fairy

NOT LONG SINCE, A PIOUS clergyman was returning home, after administering spiritual consolation to a dying member of his flock. It was late of the night, and he had to pass through a good deal of uncanny land. He was, however, a good and a conscientious minister of the Gospel, and feared not all the spirits in the country.

On his reaching the end of a lake which stretched along the roadside for some distance, he was a good deal surprised at hearing the most melodious strains of music. Overcome by pleasure and curiosity, the minister coolly sat down to listen to the harmonious sounds, and try what new discoveries he could make with regard to their nature and source. He had not sat many minutes before he could distinguish the approach of the music, and also observe a light in the direction from whence it proceeded gliding across the lake towards him. Instead of taking to his heels, as any faithless wight would have done, the pastor fearlessly determined to await the issue of the phenomenon. As the light and music drew near, the clergyman could at length distinguish an object resembling a human being walking on the surface of the water, attended by a group of diminutive musicians, some of them bearing lights, and others instruments of music, from which they continued to evoke those melodious strains which first attracted his attention. The leader of the band dismissed his attendants, landed on the beach, and afforded the minister the amplest opportunities of examining his appearance. He was a little primitive-looking grey-headed man, clad in the most grotesque habit the clergyman had ever seen, and such as led him at once to suspect his real character. He walked up to the minister, whom he saluted with great grace, offering an apology for his intrusion. The pastor returned his compliments, and, without further explanation, invited the mysterious stranger to sit down by his side. The invitation was complied with, upon which the minister proposed the following question: – "Who art thou, stranger, and from whence?"

To this question the fairy, with downcast eye, replied that he was one of those sometimes called Doane Shee, or men of peace, or good men, though the reverse of this title was a more fit appellation for them. Originally angelic in his nature and attributes, and once a sharer of the indescribable joys of the regions of light, he was seduced by Satan to join him in his mad conspiracies; and, as a punishment for his transgression, he was cast down from those regions of bliss, and was now doomed, along with millions of fellow-sufferers, to wander through seas and mountains, until the coming of the Great Day.What their fate would be then they could not divine, but they apprehended the worst. "And," continued he, turning to the minister, with great anxiety, "the object of my present intrusion on you is to learn your opinion, as an eminent divine, as to our final condition on that dreadful day." Here the venerable pastor entered upon a long conversation with the fairy, touching the principles of faith and repentance. Receiving rather unsatisfactory answers to his questions, the minister desired the "sheech" to repeat after him the Paternoster, in attempting to do which, it was not a little remarkable that he could not repeat the word "art," but said "wert," in heaven. Inferring from every circumstance that their fate was extremely precarious, the minister resolved not to puff the fairies up with presumptuous, and, perhaps, groundless expectations. Accordingly, addressing himself to the unhappy fairy, who was all anxiety to know the nature of his sentiments, the reverend gentleman told him that he could not take it upon him to give them any hopes of pardon, as their crime was of so deep a hue as scarcely to admit of it. On this the unhappy fairy uttered a shriek of despair, plunged headlong into the loch, and the minister resumed his course to his home.

Habetrot the Spinstress

IN BYGONE DAYS, in an old farmhouse which stood by a river, there lived a beautiful girl called Maisie. She was tall and straight, with auburn hair and blue eyes, and she was the prettiest girl in all the valley. And one would have thought that she would have been the pride of her mother's heart.

But, instead of this, her mother used to sigh and shake her head whenever she looked at her. And why?

Because, in those days, all men were sensible; and instead of looking out for pretty girls to be their wives, they looked out for girls who could cook and spin, and who gave promise of becoming notable housewives.

Maisie's mother had been an industrious spinster; but, alas! to her sore grief and disappointment, her daughter did not take after her.

The girl loved to be out of doors, chasing butterflies and plucking wild flowers, far better than sitting at her spinning-wheel. So when her mother saw one after another of Maisie's companions, who were not nearly so pretty as she was, getting rich husbands, she sighed and said:

"Woe's me, child, for methinks no brave wooer will ever pause at our door while they see thee so idle and thoughtless." But Maisie only laughed.

At last her mother grew really angry, and one bright Spring morning she laid down three heads of lint on the table, saying sharply, "I will have no more of this dallying. People will say that it is my blame that no wooer comes to seek thee. I cannot have thee left on my hands to be laughed at, as the idle maid who would not marry. So now thou must work; and if thou hast not these heads of lint spun into seven hanks of thread in three days, I will e'en speak to the Mother at St Mary's Convent, and thou wilt go there and learn to be a nun."

Now, though Maisie was an idle girl, she had no wish to be shut up in a nunnery; so she tried not to think of the sunshine outside, but sat down soberly with her distaff.

But, alas! she was so little accustomed to work that she made but slow progress; and although she sat at the spinning-wheel all day, and never once went out of doors, she found at night that she had only spun half a hank of yarn.

The next day it was even worse, for her arms ached so much she could only work very slowly. That night she cried herself to sleep; and next morning, seeing that it was quite hopeless to expect to get her task finished, she threw down her distaff in despair, and ran out of doors.

Near the house was a deep dell, through which ran a tiny stream. Maisie loved this dell, the flowers grew so abundantly there.

This morning she ran down to the edge of the stream, and seated herself on a large stone. It was a glorious morning, the hazel trees were newly covered with leaves, and the branches nodded over her head, and showed like delicate tracery against the blue sky. The primroses and sweet-scented violets peeped out from among the grass, and a little water wagtail came and perched on a stone in the middle of the stream, and bobbed up and down, till it seemed as if he were nodding to Maisie, and as if he were trying to say to her, "Never mind, cheer up."

But the poor girl was in no mood that morning to enjoy the flowers and the birds. Instead of watching them, as she generally did, she hid her face in her hands, and wondered what would become of her. She rocked herself to and fro, as she thought how terrible it would be if her mother fulfilled her threat and shut her up in the Convent of St Mary, with the grave, solemn-faced sisters, who seemed as if they had completely forgotten what it was like to be young, and run about in the sunshine, and laugh, and pick the fresh Spring flowers.

"Oh, I could not do it, I could not do it," she cried at last. "It would kill me to be a nun."

"And who wants to make a pretty wench like thee into a nun?" asked a queer, cracked voice quite close to her.

Maisie jumped up, and stood staring in front of her as if she had been moonstruck. For, just across the stream from where she had been sitting, there was a curious boulder, with a round hole in the middle of it – for all the world like a big apple with the core taken out.

Maisie knew it well; she had often sat upon it, and wondered how the funny hole came to be there.

It was no wonder that she stared, for, seated on this stone, was the queerest little old woman that she had ever seen in her life. Indeed, had it not been for her silver hair, and the white mutch with the big frill that she wore on her head, Maisie would have taken her for a little girl, she wore such a very short skirt, only reaching down to her knees.

Her face, inside the frill of her cap, was round, and her cheeks were rosy, and she had little black eyes, which twinkled merrily as she looked at the startled maiden. On her shoulders was a black and white checked shawl, and on her legs, which she dangled over the edge of the boulder, she wore black silk stockings and the neatest little shoes, with great silver buckles.

In fact, she would have been quite a pretty old lady had it not been for her lips, which were very long and very thick, and made her look quite ugly in spite of her rosy cheeks and black eyes. Maisie stood and looked at her for such a long time in silence that she repeated her question.

"And who wants to make a pretty wench like thee into a nun? More likely that some gallant gentleman should want to make a bride of thee."

"Oh, no," answered Maisie, "my mother says no gentleman would look at me because I cannot spin."

"Nonsense," said the tiny woman. "Spinning is all very well for old folks like me – my lips, as thou seest, are long and ugly because I have spun so much, for I always wet my fingers with them, the easier to draw the thread from the distaff. No, no, take care of thy beauty, child; do not waste it over the spinning-wheel, nor yet in a nunnery."

"If my mother only thought as thou dost," replied the girl sadly; and, encouraged by the old woman's kindly face, she told her the whole story.

"Well," said the old Dame, "I do not like to see pretty girls weep; what if I were able to help thee, and spin the lint for thee?"

Maisie thought that this offer was too good to be true; but her new friend bade her run home and fetch the lint; and I need not tell you that she required no second bidding.

When she returned she handed the bundle to the little lady, and was about to ask her where she should meet her in order to get the thread from her when it was spun, when a sudden noise behind her made her look round.

She saw nothing; but what was her horror and surprise when she turned back again, to find that the old woman had vanished entirely, lint and all.

She rubbed her eyes, and looked all round, but she was nowhere to be seen. The girl was utterly bewildered. She wondered if she could have been dreaming, but no that could not be, there were her footprints leading up the bank and down again, where she had gone for the lint, and brought it back, and there was the mark of her foot, wet with dew, on a stone in the middle of the stream, where she had stood when she had handed the lint up to the mysterious little stranger.

What was she to do now? What would her mother say when, in addition to not having finished the task that had been given her, she had to confess to having lost the greater part of the lint also? She ran up and down the little dell, hunting amongst the bushes, and peeping into every nook and cranny of the bank where the little old woman might have hidden herself. It was all in vain; and at last, tired out with the search, she sat down on the stone once more, and presently fell fast asleep.

When she awoke it was evening. The sun had set, and the yellow glow on the western horizon was fast giving place to the silvery light of the moon. She was sitting thinking of the curious events of the day, and gazing at the great boulder opposite, when it seemed to her as if a distant murmur of voices came from it.

With one bound she crossed the stream, and clambered on to the stone. She was right.

Someone was talking underneath it, far down in the ground. She put her ear close to the stone, and listened.

The voice of the queer little old woman came up through the hole. "Ho, ho, my pretty little wench little knows that my name is Habetrot."

Full of curiosity, Maisie put her eye to the opening, and the strangest sight that she had ever seen met her gaze. She seemed to be looking through a telescope into a wonderful little valley. The trees there were brighter and greener than any that she had ever seen before and there were beautiful flowers, quite different from the flowers that grew in her country. The little valley was carpeted with the most exquisite moss, and up and down it walked her tiny friend, busily engaged in spinning.

She was not alone, for round her were a circle of other little old women, who were seated on large white stones, and they were all spinning away as fast as they could.

Occasionally one would look up, and then Maisie saw that they all seemed to have the same long, thick lips that her friend had. She really felt very sorry, as they all looked exceedingly kind, and might have been pretty had it not been for this defect.

One of the Spinstresses sat by herself, and was engaged in winding the thread, which the others had spun, into hanks. Maisie did not think that this little lady looked so nice as the others. She was dressed entirely in grey, and had a big hooked nose, and great horn spectacles. She seemed to be called Slantlie Mab, for Maisie heard Habetrot address her by that name, telling her to make haste and tie up all the thread, for it was getting late, and it was time that the young girl had it to carry home to her mother.

Maisie did not quite know what to do, or how she was to get the thread, for she did not like to shout down the hole in case the queer little old woman should be angry at being watched.

However, Habetrot, as she had called herself, suddenly appeared on the path beside her, with the hanks of thread in her hand.

"Oh, thank you, thank you," cried Maisie. "What can I do to show you how thankful I am?"

"Nothing," answered the Fairy. "For I do not work for reward. Only do not tell your mother who span the thread for thee."

It was now late, and Maisie lost no time in running home with the precious thread upon her shoulder. When she walked into the kitchen she found that her mother had gone to bed. She seemed to have had a busy day, for there, hanging up in the wide chimney, in order to dry, were seven large black puddings.

The fire was low, but bright and clear; and the sight of it and the sight of the puddings suggested to Maisie that she was very hungry, and that fried black puddings were very good.

Flinging the thread down on the table, she hastily pulled off her shoes, so as not to make a noise and awake her mother; and, getting down the frying-pan from the wall, she took one of the black puddings from the chimney, and fried it, and ate it.

Still she felt hungry, so she took another, and then another, till they were all gone. Then she crept upstairs to her little bed and fell fast asleep.

Next morning her mother came downstairs before Maisie was awake. In fact, she had not been able to sleep much for thinking of her daughter's careless ways, and had been sorrowfully making up her mind that she must lose no time in speaking to the Abbess of St Mary's about this idle girl of hers.

What was her surprise to see on the table the seven beautiful hanks of thread, while, on going to the chimney to take down a black pudding to fry for breakfast, she found that every one of them had been eaten. She did not know whether to laugh for joy that her daughter had been so industrious, or to cry for vexation because all her lovely black puddings – which she had expected would last for a week at least – were gone. In her bewilderment she sang out:

"My daughter's spun se'en, se'en, se'en,
My daughter's eaten se'en, se'en, se'en,
And all before daylight."

Now I forgot to tell you that, about half a mile from where the old farmhouse stood, there was a beautiful Castle, where a very rich young nobleman lived. He was both good and brave, as well as rich; and all the mothers who had pretty daughters used to wish that he would come their way, some day, and fall in love with one of them. But he had never done so, and everyone said, "He is too grand to marry any country girl. One day he will go away to London Town and marry a Duke's daughter."

Well, this fine spring morning it chanced that this young nobleman's favourite horse had lost a shoe, and he was so afraid that any of the grooms might ride it along the hard road, and not on the soft grass at the side, that he said that he would take it to the smithy himself.

So it happened that he was riding along by Maisie's garden gate as her mother came into the garden singing these strange lines.

He stopped his horse, and said good-naturedly, "Good day, Madam; and may I ask why you sing such a strange song?"

Maisie's mother made no answer, but turned and walked into the house; and the young nobleman, being very anxious to know what it all meant, hung his bridle over the garden gate, and followed her.

She pointed to the seven hanks of thread lying on the table, and said, "This hath my daughter done before breakfast."

Then the young man asked to see the Maiden who was so industrious, and her mother went and pulled Maisie from behind the door, where she had hidden herself when the stranger came in; for she had come downstairs while her mother was in the garden.

She looked so lovely in her fresh morning gown of blue gingham, with her auburn hair curling softly round her brow, and her face all over blushes at the sight of such a gallant young man, that he quite lost his heart, and fell in love with her on the spot.

"Ah," said he, "my dear mother always told me to try and find a wife who was both pretty and useful, and I have succeeded beyond my expectations. Do not let our marriage, I pray thee, good Dame, be too long deferred."

Maisie's mother was overjoyed, as you may imagine, at this piece of unexpected good fortune, and busied herself in getting everything ready for the wedding; but Maisie herself was a little perplexed.

She was afraid that she would be expected to spin a great deal when she was married and lived at the Castle, and if that were so, her husband was sure to find out that she was not really such a good spinstress as he thought she was.

In her trouble she went down, the night before her wedding, to the great boulder by the stream in the glen, and, climbing up on it, she laid her head against the stone, and called softly down the hole, "Habetrot, dear Habetrot."

The little old woman soon appeared, and, with twinkling eyes, asked her what was troubling her so much just when she should have been so happy. And Maisie told her.

"Trouble not thy pretty head about that," answered the Fairy, "but come here with thy bridegroom next week, when the moon is full, and I warrant that he will never ask thee to sit at a spinning-wheel again."

Accordingly, after all the wedding festivities were over and the couple had settled down at the Castle, on the appointed evening Maisie suggested to her husband that they should take a walk together in the moonlight.

She was very anxious to see what the little Fairy would do to help her; for that very day he had been showing her all over her new home, and he had pointed out to her the beautiful new spinning-wheel made of ebony, which had belonged to his mother, saying proudly, "To-morrow, little one, I shall bring some lint from the town, and then the maids will see what clever little fingers my wife has."

Maisie had blushed as red as a rose as she bent over the lovely wheel, and then felt quite sick, as she wondered whatever she would do if Habetrot did not help her.

So on this particular evening, after they had walked in the garden, she said that she should like to go down to the little dell and see how the stream looked by moonlight. So to the dell they went.

As soon as they came to the boulder Maisie put her head against it and whispered, "Habetrot, dear Habetrot"; and in an instant the little old woman appeared.

She bowed in a stately way, as if they were both strangers to her, and said, "Welcome, Sir and Madam, to the Spinsters' Dell." And then she tapped on the root of a great oak tree with a tiny wand which she held in her hand, and a green door, which Maisie never remembered having noticed before, flew open, and they followed the Fairy through it into the other valley which Maisie had seen through the hole in the great stone.

All the little old women were sitting on their white chucky stones busy at work, only they seemed far uglier than they had seemed at first; and Maisie noticed that the reason for this was, that, instead of wearing red skirts and white mutches as they had done before, they now wore caps and dresses of dull grey, and instead of looking happy, they all seemed to be trying who could look most miserable, and who could push out their long lips furthest, as they wet their fingers to draw the thread from their distaffs.

"Save us and help us! What a lot of hideous old witches," exclaimed her husband. "Whatever could this funny old woman mean by bringing a pretty child like thee to look at them? Thou wilt dream of them for a week and a day. Just look at their lips"; and, pushing Maisie behind him, he went up to one of them and asked her what had made her mouth grow so ugly.

She tried to tell him, but all the sound that he could hear was something that sounded like spin-n-n.

He asked another one, and her answer sounded like this: span-n-n. He tried a third, and hers sounded like spun-n-n.

He seized Maisie by the hand and hurried her through the green door. "By my troth," he said, "my mother's spinning-wheel may turn to gold ere I let thee touch it, if this is what spinning leads to. Rather than that thy pretty face should be spoilt, the linen chests at the Castle may get empty, and remain so for ever!"

So it came to pass that Maisie could be out of doors all day wandering about with her husband, and laughing and singing to her heart's content. And whenever there was lint at the Castle to be spun, it was carried down to the big boulder in the dell and left there, and Habetrot and her companions spun it, and there was no more trouble about the matter.

The Fairy Boy of Leith

"ABOUT FIFTEEN YEARS SINCE, having business that detained me for some time at Leith, which is near Edinburgh, in the kingdom of Scotland, I often met some of my acquaintance at a certain house there, where we used to drink a glass of wine for our refection. The woman which kept the house was of honest reputation among the neighbours, which made me give the more attention to what she told me one day about a fairy boy (as they called him) who lived about that town. She had given me so strange an account of him, that I desired her I might see him the first opportunity, which she promised; and not long after, passing that way, she told me there was the fairy boy, but a little before I came by; and, casting her eye into the street, said, 'Look you, sir, yonder he is, at play with those other boys'; and pointing him out to me, I went, and by smooth words, and a piece of money, got him to come into the house with me; where, in the presence of divers people, I demanded of him several astrological questions, which he answered with great subtlety; and, through all his discourse, carried it with a cunning much above his years, which seemed not to exceed ten or eleven.

"He seemed to make a motion like drumming upon the table with his fingers, upon which I asked him whether he could beat a drum? To which he replied, 'Yes, sir, as well as any man in Scotland; for every Thursday night I beat all points to a sort of people that used to meet under yonder hill' (pointing to the great hill between Edinburgh and Leith). 'How, boy?' quoth I, 'what company have you there?' 'There are, sir,' said he, 'a great company both of men and women, and they are entertained with many sorts of music besides my drum; they have, besides, plenty of variety of meats and wine, and many times we are carried into France or Holland in the night, and return again, and whilst we are there, we enjoy all the pleasures the country doth afford.' I demanded of him how they got under that hill? To which he replied that there was a great pair of gates that opened to them, though they were invisible to others, and that within there were brave large rooms, as well accommodated as most in Scotland. I then asked him how I should know what he said to be true? Upon which he told me he would read my fortune, saying, I should have two wives, and that he saw the forms of them over my shoulders; and both would be very handsome women.

"The woman of the house told me that all the people in Scotland could not keep him from the rendezvous on Thursday night; upon which, by promising him some more money, I got a promise of him to meet me at the same place in the afternoon, the Thursday following, and so dismissed him at that time. The boy came again at the place and time appointed, and I had prevailed with some friends to continue with me (if possible) to prevent his moving that night. He was placed between us, and answered many questions, until, about eleven of the clock, he was got away unperceived by the company; but I, suddenly missing him, hastened to the door, and took hold of him, and so returned him into the same room. We all watched him, and, of a sudden, he was again got out of doors; I followed him close, and he made a noise in the street, as if he had been set upon, and from that time I could never see him."

The Brownie

THE SCOTTISH BROWNIE formed a class of being distinct in habit and disposition from the freakish and mischievous elves. He was meagre, shaggy, and wild in his appearance. In the day-time he lurked in remote recesses of the old houses which he delighted to haunt, and in the night sedulously employed himself in discharging any laborious task which he thought might be acceptable to the family to whose service he had devoted himself. But the Brownie does not drudge from the hope of recompense. On the contrary, so delicate is his attachment that the offer of reward, but particularly of food, infallibly occasions his disappearance for ever.

It is told of a Brownie, who haunted a border family now extinct, that the lady having fallen unexpectedly ill, and the servant, who was ordered to ride to Jedburgh for the *sage-femme*, showing no great alertness in setting out, the familiar spirit slipped on the greatcoat of the lingering domestic, rode to the town on the laird's best horse, and returned with the midwife *en croupe*. During the short space of his absence, the Tweed, which they must necessarily ford, rose to a dangerous height. Brownie, who transported his charge with all the rapidity of the ghostly lover of Lenore, was not to be stopped by the obstacle. He plunged in with the terrified old lady, and landed her in safety where her services were wanted. Having put the horse into the stable (where it was afterwards found in a woeful plight), he proceeded to the room of the servant, whose duty he had discharged, and finding him just in the act of drawing on his boots, he administered to him a most merciless drubbing with his own horsewhip. Such an important service excited the gratitude of the laird, who, understanding that Brownie had been heard to express a wish to have a green coat, ordered a vestment of the colour to be made, and left in his haunts. Brownie took away the green coat, but was never seen more. We may suppose that, tired of his domestic drudgery, he went in his new livery to join the fairies.

The last Brownie known in Ettrick Forest resided in Bodsbeck, a wild and solitary spot, near the head of Moffat Water, where he exercised his functions undisturbed, till the scrupulous devotion of an old lady induced her to "hire him away," as it was termed, by placing in his haunt a porringer of milk and a piece of money. After receiving this hint to depart, he was heard the whole night to howl and cry, "Farewell to bonnie Bodsbeck!" which he was compelled to abandon for ever.

The Smith and the Fairies

YEARS AGO THERE LIVED IN Crossbrig a smith of the name of MacEachern. This man had an only child, a boy of about thirteen or fourteen years of age, cheerful, strong, and healthy. All of a sudden he fell ill; took to his bed and moped whole days away. No one could tell what was the matter with him, and the boy himself could not, or would not, tell how he felt. He was wasting away fast; getting thin, old, and yellow; and his father and all his friends were afraid that he would die.

At last one day, after the boy had been lying in this condition for a long time, getting neither better nor worse, always confined to bed, but with an extraordinary appetite, – one day, while sadly revolving these things, and standing idly at his forge, with no heart to work, the smith was agreeably surprised to see an old man, well known to him for his sagacity and knowledge of out-of-the-way things, walk into his workshop. Forthwith he told him the occurrence which had clouded his life.

The old man looked grave as he listened; and after sitting a long time pondering over all he had heard, gave his opinion thus – "It is not your son you have got. The boy has been carried away by the 'Daoine Sith,' and they have left a Sibhreach in his place." "Alas! and what then am I to do?" said the smith. "How am I ever to see my own son again?" "I will tell you how," answered the old man. "But, first, to make sure that it is not your own son you have got, take as many empty egg shells as you can get, go with them into the room, spread them out carefully before his sight, then proceed to draw water with them, carrying them two and two in your hands as if they were a great weight, and arrange when full, with every sort of earnestness round the fire." The smith accordingly gathered as many broken egg-shells as he could get, went into the room, and proceeded to carry out all his instructions.

He had not been long at work before there arose from the bed a shout of laughter, and the voice of the seeming sick boy exclaimed, "I am now 800 years of age, and I have never seen the like of that before."

The smith returned and told the old man. "Well, now," said the sage to him, "did I not tell you that it was not your son you had: your son is in Brorra-cheill in a digh there (that is, a round green hill frequented by fairies). Get rid as soon as possible of this intruder, and I think I may promise you your son."

"You must light a very large and bright fire before the bed on which this stranger is lying. He will ask you 'What is the use of such a fire as that?' Answer him at once, 'You will see that presently!' and then seize him, and throw him into the middle of it. If it is your own son you have got, he will call out to save him; but if not, this thing will fly through the roof."

The smith again followed the old man's advice, kindled a large fire, answered the question put to him as he had been directed to do, and seizing the child flung him in without hesitation.

The 'Sibhreach' gave an awful yell, and sprung through the roof, where a hole was left to let the smoke out.

On a certain night the old man told him the green round hill, where the fairies kept the boy, would be open. And on that night the smith, having provided himself with a bible, a dirk, and a crowing cock, was to proceed to the hill. He would hear singing and dancing and much merriment going on, but he was to advance boldly; the bible he carried would be a certain safeguard to him against any danger from the fairies. On entering the hill he was to stick the dirk in the threshold, to prevent the hill from closing upon him; "and then," continued the old man, "on entering you will see a spacious apartment before you, beautifully clean, and there, standing far within, working at a forge, you will also see your own son. When you are questioned, say you come to seek him, and will not go without him."

Not long after this, the time came round, and the smith sallied forth, prepared as instructed. Sure enough as he approached the hill, there was a light where light was seldom seen before. Soon after a sound of piping, dancing, and joyous merriment reached the anxious father on the night wind.

Overcoming every impulse to fear, the smith approached the threshold steadily, stuck the dirk into it as directed, and entered. Protected by the bible he carried on his breast, the fairies could not touch him; but they asked him, with a good deal of displeasure, what he wanted there. He answered, "I want my son, whom I see down there, and I will not go without him."

Upon hearing this, the whole company before him gave a loud laugh, which wakened up the cock he carried dozing in his arms, who at once leaped up on his shoulders, clapped his wings lustily, and crowed loud and long.

The fairies, incensed, seized the smith and his son, and throwing them out of the hill, flung the dirk after them, "and in an instant a' was dark."

For a year and a day the boy never did a turn of work, and hardly ever spoke a word; but at last one day, sitting by his father and watching him finishing a sword he was making for some chief, and which he was very particular about, he suddenly exclaimed, "That is not the way to do it;" and taking the tools from his father's hands he set to work himself in his place, and soon fashioned a sword, the like of which was never seen in the country before.

From that day the young man wrought constantly with his father, and became the inventor of a peculiarly fine and well-tempered weapon, the making of which kept the two smiths, father and son, in constant employment, spread their fame far and wide, and gave them the means in abundance, as they before had the disposition to live content with all the world and very happily with one another.

The Fairy Dancers

IT WAS CHRISTMAS EVE and by the Loch Etive sat two farmers, longing for a drink but with an empty barrel between them. And so it was decided, on that icy Christmas Eve, that these two farmers would walk the road to Kingshouse, their nearest inn, and they would buy a barrel of the best whiskey there, a three-gallon jar that would warm them through the frosty months to come.

So they set off along the winding road, and over the hills that glistened with snow, all frosted with ice, and came to the warm wooded inn at Kingshouse. It was there that a cup of tea was shared, and a wee dram or two, and so the two men were quite merry as they set off home again, the three-gallon jar heavy on the back of the youngest man, for they would take turns carrying its weight on the long journey down the winding road and over the hills.

And over the hills they went but they were stopped there, by the need for a taste of that whiskey, and for a smoke. Then the sound of a fantastic reel grew louder and louder, and a light shone brighter over the hills, towards the north.

"Och, it's just a wee star," said one man, ready for his smoke and his tipple.

"Nah, it's a light, and there's a party there to be sure," said the other, who was a great dancer and loved a reel more than any other.

So they crossed the brae to the north, towards the light, and the sound of pipes, which played a fine tune. There in front of them were dancers, women in silk dresses, bowing and twirling, and men in highland dress, with pipes playing an enchanted, fine tune that drew them towards the hill.

The younger man, who carried the jar, went first, and as he entered the great door in the hillside, and joined the merry throng, the door was closed. When the other farmer, slower than the first, reached the site, there was nothing to be found. For his friend had disappeared and there was no trace of him.

It was a cold and lonely walk home, and the farmer puzzled over what had occurred on that moonlit hill, with a magical reel playing from a light that shone in the darkness. He went first to the farm of the other man, and he told his wife what had happened, but as he talked, faces closed, and brows became furrowed, and it was clear that he was not believed, that no man could lose his friend on a hill just a few miles from home.

And so it was that the policemen were called from Inveraray, and they took him away and asked him questions that made his head spin, and caused him to slump over in exhaustion, and he wished more than anything for a drop of the whiskey that was hung on the other man's back. They kept him there, the police, and he was sent to trial, but he told them all the same thing, how a magical reel had played from a light that shone in the darkness, and how his friend had disappeared without trace.

He was sent back to that prison, and when they asked him again, he could only tell the truth of that fateful night, so they asked him no more, and sent him home, for he would not budge from his story, and that story never changed.

And it was near twelve months before this man had cause to travel past that hill again, and with him this time were some lads from the village who had set themselves the task of catching some fish for the Christmas feast. And with a basket full of fish, they stopped on their way back to their homes, with the need for a smoke and a taste of the whiskey that the farmer had tucked in his belt. And there again they heard that fantastic music, and saw the light beaming from the darkness of the hills.

But the lads from the village had heard too much of this madness, and they struggled home with the fish, ahead of the farmer who wanted more than anything to find his friend, and that barrel of whiskey. So the farmer climbed over the hills, towards that light, and he heard there the sound of pipes, which played a fine tune. There in front of him were dancers, women in silk dresses, bowing and twirling, and men in highland dress, with pipes playing an enchanted, fine tune that drew him towards the hill.

And he stuck his fishing hook in the threshold of the door, for no fairy can touch the metal of a mortal man, and he entered the room which spun with the music, and threatened to drag him into its midst. But this farmer never liked a dance, preferring instead a good smoke and a dram of whiskey, and he resisted the calls on his soul, and struggled through the crowd to find his friend the farmer, who danced in the middle of the reel like a man possessed.

"Och, lad, we've only just begun," the dancer protested, as his friend dragged him away.

And since he had danced for near twelve months with that barrel on his back, he carried it home again, along the winding road and over the hills that glistened with snow, all frosted with ice. They came to the farm of the man who'd been dancing, and what a surprise met his poor lonely wife when she opened the door. For there was her husband, just skin and bones to be sure, but there nonetheless with his barrel of whiskey, just twelve months late.

And they sat up that night, the man and his friend, and each of their wives, and what a Christmas Eve they had with that barrel of whiskey, which had mellowed with the warmth of the fairy hill, and they drank it all, just twelve months late.

The Ainsel

DEEP IN THE HEART of the Border country, where the wind howls with cold, lived a wee boy called Parcie. He lived with his mother in a small, snug cottage where the fire burned bright and bathed the stone clad walls in a soft, cosy glow. They lived alone there for his father was long since gone, but they managed with little, living simply and happily among the trees and the wood folk who inhabited them.

Now like most small boys, Parcie plotted all day in order to avoid being sent to bed each night. He longed to sit by the hearth with his mother, watching the burning embers cast intriguing shadows which danced and performed a story that seemed to Parcie like it could go on forever. But each night it was cut short, as was the sound of his mother's mellifluous voice as she sang to him of fairies and sea-folk, and told of stories and legends of long ago. For it was it at this point that Parcie's mother would close up her bag of mending.

'It's time for your bed, Parcie,' she would say, always the same thing, and Parcie would be packed neatly into his tiny box-bed where the fairies had laid a nest of golden slumberdust so potent that his eyes were shut and he was fast asleep as soon as his head touched his soft pillow. And there he'd sleep all the night, until the next morning he struggled to hatch a plan to stay awake all night, to carry on and on the drowsy contentment of the evening.

But one night Parcie's tired mother could argue no further and when the fire began to sink down into black-red embers, and she said,

'It's time for your bed, Parcie' he would not go. And so she picked up her mending, and tidied it away, setting a bowl of cool, fresh cream by the doorstep as she went along the corridor to her own bed.

'I hope to God the old fairy wife does not get to you, lad, but it will be your own fault if she does,' whispered his mother as she disappeared into her room.

And suddenly the warm red room took on a more sinister cast, and the shadows no longer told a story but taunted him, warning him, tempting him until he was a jumble of fear and confusion. And just as he steeled himself to dash to his warm box-bed, filled with golden slumberdust, a tiny brownie leapt from the chimney and landed on his foot.

Now brownies were common in the days when Parcie lived in the stone cottage with his mother, and they came each day to every house that had the courtesy and the foresight to leave a bowl of cool, fresh cream by the doorstep. And if some foolish occupant forgot that cream one night, she would be sure to find a tumultuous mess the next day. For brownies came to tidy everything away, neat and clean, collecting specks of dust and laying things just so, so that in the morning the lucky household gleamed with shining surfaces and possessions all in order.

But Parcie knew nothing of the magic that dropped through the chimney each night and he was surprised and rather pleased to see this tiny fairy. The brownie was not, however, so pleased to see Parcie, for he was an efficient wee brownie and he liked to have his work done quickly, in order to get to the lovely bowl of cool, fresh cream which awaited him by the doorstep.

'What's your name?' asked Parcie, grinning.

'Ainsel (own self),' replied the brownie, smiling back despite himself. 'And you?'

'My Ainsel,' said Parcie, joining in the joke.

And so Parcie and the brownie played a little together, and Parcie watched with interest while the brownie tidied and cleaned their cottage in a whirlwind of activity. And then, as he neared the grate to sweep away some dust that had come loose from the hearth, Parcie took an inopportune moment to poke the fire, and what should fly out upon the poor brownie but a red-hot ember which burnt him so badly that he howled with pain.

And then, into the snuffling silence that followed, a deep frightening voice boomed down the chimney. It was the old fairy wife who Parcie's mother had warned of, and she flew into a rage when she heard her dear brownie's tears.

'Tell me who hurt ye,' she shouted down the chimney, 'I'll get him, so I will.'

And the brownie called out tearfully, 'It was My Ainsel'. Parcie lost no time in hurling himself from the room and into his box-bed where the golden slumberdust did not cast its magic over the terrified boy, for he laid awake and shaking for a long time after his head touched his soft pillow.

But the old fairy wife was not concerned about Parcie, for she called out, 'What's the fuss, if you did it yer ainsel' and muttering she thrust a long brown arm down the chimney and plucked the sniffling brownie from the fireside.

Now what do you think Parcie's mother thought the next morning when she found her cottage spic and span, but the bowl of cream still standing untouched, cool and fresh by the doorstep. How perplexed she was when the brownie stopped visiting her cottage, although she always left a bowl of cream to tempt him. But in the heart of the Border country, where the wind howls with cold, bad is almost always balanced by good, and so it was then when from that night onwards, Parcie's mother never again had to say to him, 'Parcie, it's time for your bed,' for at the first sudden movement of the shadows, when the fire began to sink down into black-red embers, he was sound asleep in his tiny box-bed, deep in the sleep of the golden slumberdust.

The Little Fairy Bell

WHEN TRISTAN HAD COME BACK to Orri's hut, and had loosened his heavy pilgrim's cape, he saw clearly in his heart that it was time to keep his oath to King Mark and to fly the land.

Three days yet he tarried, because he could not drag himself away from that earth, but on the fourth day he thanked the woodman, and said to Gorvenal:

"Master, the hour is come."

And he went into Wales, into the land of the great Duke Gilain, who was young, powerful, and frank in spirit, and welcomed him nobly as a God-sent guest.

And he did everything to give him honour and joy; but he found that neither adventure, nor feast could soothe what Tristan suffered.

One day, as he sat by the young Duke's side, his spirit weighed upon him, so that not knowing it he groaned, and the Duke, to soothe him, ordered into his private room a fairy thing, which pleased his eyes when he was sad and relieved his own heart; it was a dog, and the varlets brought it in to him, and they put it upon a table there. Now this dog was a fairy dog, and came from the Duke of Avalon; for a fairy had given it him as a love-gift, and no one can well describe its kind or beauty. And it bore at its neck, hung to a little chain of gold, a little bell; and that tinkled so gaily, and so clear and so soft, that as Tristan heard it, he was soothed, and his anguish melted away, and he forgot all that he had suffered for the Queen; for such was the virtue of the bell and such its property: that whosoever heard it, he lost all pain. And as Tristan stroked the little fairy thing, the dog that took away his sorrow, he saw how delicate it was and fine, and how it had soft hair like samite, and he thought how good a gift it would make for the Queen. But he dared not ask for it right out since he knew that the Duke loved this dog beyond everything in the world, and would yield it to no prayers, nor to wealth, nor to wile; so one day Tristan having made a plan in his mind said this:

"Lord, what would you give to the man who could rid your land of the hairy giant Urgan, that levies such a toll?"

"Truly, the victor might choose what he would, but none will dare."

Then said Tristan:

"Those are strange words, for good comes to no land save by risk and daring, and not for all the gold of Milan would I renounce my desire to find him in his wood and bring him down."

Then Tristan went out to find Urgan in his lair, and they fought hard and long, till courage conquered strength, and Tristan, having cut off the giant's hand, bore it back to the Duke.

And "Sire," said he, "since I may choose a reward according to your word, give me the little fairy dog. It was for that I conquered Urgan, and your promise stands."

"Friend," said the Duke, "take it, then, but in taking it you take away also all my joy."

Then Tristan took the little fairy dog and gave it in ward to a Welsh harper, who was cunning and who bore it to Cornwall till he came to Tintagel, and having come there put it secretly into Brangien's hands, and the Queen was so pleased that she gave ten marks of gold to the harper, but she put it about that the Queen of Ireland, her mother, had sent the beast. And she had a goldsmith work a little kennel for him, all jewelled, and incrusted with gold and enamel inlaid; and wherever she went she carried the dog with her in memory of her friend, and as she watched it sadness and anguish and regrets melted out of her heart.

At first she did not guess the marvel, but thought her consolation was because the gift was Tristan's, till one day she found that it was fairy, and that it was the little bell that charmed her soul; then she thought: "What have I to do with comfort since he is sorrowing? He could have kept it too and have forgotten his sorrow; but with high courtesy he sent it to me to give me his joy and to take up his pain again. Friend, while you suffer, so long will I suffer also."

And she took the magic bell and shook it just a little, and then by the open window she threw it into the sea.

The Elves

BESIDES THE DWARFS there was another numerous class of tiny creatures called Lios-alfar, light or white elves, who inhabited the realms of air between heaven and earth, and were gently governed by the genial god Frey from his palace in Alfheim. They were lovely, beneficent beings, so pure and innocent that, according to some authorities, their name was derived from the same root as the Latin word 'white' (*albus*), which, in a modified form, was given to the snow-covered Alps, and to Albion (England), because of her white chalk cliffs which could be seen afar.

The elves were so small that they could flit about unseen while they tended the flowers, birds, and butterflies; and as they were passionately fond of dancing, they often glided down to earth on a moonbeam, to dance on the green. Holding one another by the hand, they would dance in circles, thereby making the 'fairy rings,' which were to be discerned by the deeper green and greater luxuriance of the grass which their little feet had pressed.

If any mortal stood in the middle of one of these fairy rings he could, according to popular belief in England, see the fairies and enjoy their favour; but the Scandinavians and Teutons vowed that the unhappy man must die. In illustration of this superstition, a story is told of how Sir Olaf, riding off to his wedding, was enticed by the fairies into their ring. On the morrow, instead of a merry marriage, his friends witnessed a triple funeral, for his mother and bride also died when they beheld his lifeless corpse.

These elves, who in England were called fairies or fays, were also enthusiastic musicians, and delighted especially in a certain air known as the elf-dance, which was so irresistible that no one who heard it could refrain from dancing. If a mortal, overhearing the air, ventured to reproduce it, he suddenly found himself incapable of stopping and was forced to play on and on until he died of exhaustion, unless he were deft enough to play the tune backwards, or some one charitably cut the strings of his violin. His hearers, who were forced to dance as long as the tones continued, could only stop when they ceased.

In medieval times, the will-o'-the-wisps were known in the North as elf lights, for these tiny sprites were supposed to mislead travellers; and popular superstition held that the Jack-o'-lanterns were the restless spirits of murderers forced against their will to return to the scene of their crimes. As they nightly walked thither, it is said that they doggedly repeated with every step, "It is right;" but as they returned they sadly reiterated, "It is wrong."

In Scandinavia and Germany sacrifices were offered to the elves to make them propitious. These sacrifices consisted of some small animal, or of a bowl of honey and milk, and were known as Alf-blot. They were quite common until the missionaries taught the people that the elves were mere demons, when they were transferred to the angels, who were long entreated to befriend mortals, and propitiated by the same gifts.

Many of the elves were supposed to live and die with the trees and plants which they tended, but these moss, wood, or tree maidens, while remarkably beautiful when seen in front, were hollow like a trough when viewed from behind. They appear in many of the popular tales, but almost always as benevolent and helpful spirits, for they were anxious to do good to mortals and to cultivate friendly relations with them.

No discussion of the elves is complete without a few words about Oberon. There are stories told far and wide of the fairy king Oberon, and his delicate queen Titiania. Oberon was so exquisitely handsome, that mortals were drawn into his fairy world after just one glance at his elegant profile. In every country across the world, there was a sense of unease on the eve of Midsummer, for this is when the fairies congregate around Oberon and Titiana and dance. Fairy dances are a magical thing, and their music is so compelling that all who hear it find it irresistible. But once a human, or indeed a god, succumbs to the fairy music, and begins to dance, he will be damned to do so until the end of his days, when he will die of an exhaustion like none other.

Oberon was also very powerful, and his tricks above ground became legend throughout many lands. With the passing of the dwarfs, humankind had no help with their work, and the little folk were no longer considered to be a blessed addition to a household. Many believe that Oberon harnessed the powers of Frey when he fell, and used them beneath the earth to set up a kingdom of fairies which was a complex and commanding as Asgard had once been. With his strength, and his overwhelming beauty, he was considered by man to be nothing more than a demon.

In Scandinavia the elves, both light and dark, were worshipped as household divinities, and their images were carved on the doorposts. The Norsemen, who were driven from home by the tyranny of Harald Harfager in 874, took their carved doorposts with them upon their ships. Similar carvings, including images of the gods and heroes, decorated the pillars of their high seats which they also carried away. The exiles showed their trust in their gods by throwing these wooden images overboard when they neared the Icelandic shores and settling where the waves carried the posts, even if the spot scarcely seemed the most desirable. 'Thus they carried with them the religion, the poetry, and the laws of their race, and on this desolate volcanic island they kept these records unchanged for hundreds of years, while other Teutonic nations gradually became affected by their intercourse with Roman and Byzantine Christianity.' These records, carefully collected by Saemund the learned, form the Elder Edda, the most precious relic of ancient Northern literature, without which we should know comparatively little of the religion of our forefathers.

The sagas relate that the first settlements in Greenland and Vinland were made in the same way, – the Norsemen piously landing wherever their household gods drifted ashore.

Monsters, Deities & Legendary Figures

Introduction

THE TUATHA DÉ DANANN were deities till, defeated by the invading Milesians – invading mortals, the first of the Irish Gaels – they were relegated to the rank of fairies. Still supernatural, but no longer super-powerful, they made mischief for the Irish around their homes. Rather than spanning the skies now, their domains were highly localized: they had a home in this hump, reigned in this hollow, patrolled this wood, danced in that field. However reduced they were from their former glory, the Tuatha Dé Danann still brought a touch of enchantment to a dull, damp countryside. Greek nymphs were goddesses at a human scale, like the nature sprites of Dutch and Hungarian tradition and the Mountain Fairies of the Korean tale. All did their bit to animate the landscape, jolt the everyday out of what might otherwise have been a drearily monotonous routine. Making a journey in the opposite direction, Lu-San in the Chinese story starts out a poor fisherman's daughter and transforms her fortunes – and those of her family – by her upbeat attitude. She ends up being deified, borne aloft by doves, to reign in Heaven, 'a star within the azure realms above'.

The River Fairy

A VERY LONG TIME AGO a dreadful plague swept through Uganda, whole provinces were laid waste and returned to jungle, for those who had possessed the land had died, and there were none to inherit the villages and gardens. In one village every one died except one little girl, and she wandered away down the road till she came to the river Nile. She had a very, very, very long name, which means "Glory." She sat down by the river very lonely and miserable, and while she was wondering what to do a fisher- man came past. The child told him her story and he was sorry for her, and took her home with him, and his wife was kind to her, and for a little while they lived happily together.

But the dreadful plague swept on and killed the fisherman and his wife, and again the little girl sat desolate and hungry by the river Nile. Suddenly she saw the tail of a great fish as it turned in the water. Glory was a little frightened, for she had never seen such a huge fish in the river before. To her surprise, as it came nearer, she saw that it had a woman's head and that half its body was that of a woman. The fish spoke to her:

"Do not be afraid, little girl; I have seen you here very often, and I want to be your friend. Tell me your sorrow."

Glory did not feel frightened any more; she said:

"I am all alone, every one I know has died of the plague. I cannot dig and plant a garden all by myself, and I cannot live all by myself, and I don't know what to do." And she began to cry.

The fish-woman came nearer and pulled her- self up on a rock, and Glory stopped crying to look at the beautiful tail covered with golden- brown scales which flashed in the sunlight as the drops of water ran off it:

"What a beautiful tail you have!" she said. "I am the Fairy of the river Nile," said the fish-woman, "and we all have beautiful tails in my country."

"Where is your country?" asked Glory.

The River Fairy pulled herself into a more comfortable position on the rock and began:

"You see the Great Lake which stretches away above the Ripon Falls? When you look at it you see only the top of a wonderful land. Under those blue waters, far, far down lies a beautiful country. It is not like the country you know, but it has fields of soft green seaweed, forests of great sea-palms, sea-flowers of every colour and shade. In the middle of this country is the Lake City where the King of the Fish- people lives, a wonderful city of caves cut in the rocks. There are long streets full of blue water, and the caves are the homes of the fish- people. There is one cave larger and more beautiful than the others, and that is the King's Palace. All the fish-people are his servants, we each have our own work, and we all obey his orders. My work is to watch the entrance of the river Nile. All day I live in my cave under the Falls, and at sunset I swim by a passage through the rock into the Great Lake above, and go to give my day's report to the King of the Lake City. Very early in the morning I come back, and at dawn I am in my cave again at work. There are other fairies who guard the entrance of rivers which flow into the Great Lake, but mine is the only river which flows out of it. My river dashes over the Falls and hurries away to the Rapids, and on and on, through deserts and plains till it reaches another Great Sea."

"I should like to see your cave and your Lake City," said Glory.

"Can you swim?" asked the River Fairy. "No," said Glory, "but I could sit on your back."

The River Fairy laughed. "I am afraid that would not do, for we should have to swim under the water, and you would lose your hold and be drowned. Unless you consent to become a fish-maiden you can never see the Lake City, and my cave under the Falls."

"How can I become a fish-maiden?" asked Glory.

"It needs a great deal of courage for a mortal to join us. I should have to cut off your feet, and from them a tail would grow."

Glory looked down at her little brown feet and dug her toes in and out of the soft sand, and said:

"I *don't* want my feet cut off."

"I must not stay any longer now," said the River Fairy. "I will be here again at daybreak." And she slipped off her rock into the foaming water and disappeared under the Falls.

When Glory was left alone she felt very unhappy and longed for the River Fairy to come back. She was very hungry too, and went to look for some food; but the gardens were empty and over-grown, and she could hardly find any fruit. Every now and then she looked down at her little brown toes, and said to herself:

"I don't want my feet cut off."

She watched the big red sun drop down behind the hills, and quickly the darkness fell round her. She crept into her cold, empty hut, and shut the reed door, and tried to get warm under the barkcloths; but the night was damp and foggy, and she shivered all alone. She heard the owls hooting to each other, outside, and the bats squeal as they hung on to the porch of the hut for a minute or two on their way to hunt, and poor little Glory sobbed bitterly, worn out with cold and hunger and loneliness. Suddenly she sat up.

"I will give up my little brown feet and go and live with my kind friend the River Fairy," she said to herself. She drew aside the reed door, and the frightened bats fled squeaking away into the shadows. She huddled her little barkcloth round her and crept down the path to the river, but just as she was reaching the bank a huge form loomed out of the mist and a cow-hippo came puffing and blowing and snorting up the path. Glory hid behind a bush and did not dare to move until she saw the dawn begin to break. Streaks of light flashed quickly across the sky, the bats darted back- wards and forwards, the birds began to twitter and wake, and suddenly the sun rose. Glory hurried down to the river, and there sat her friend the fish-woman on the same rock, her golden-brown tail catching the rays of the rising sun.

"Oh, dear River Fairy," she cried, "I have changed my mind! I want to come and live in your cave and be your little girl."

Then she gave such a start that she nearly fell into the river, for she heard the same puffing and blowing and snorting coming down the path.

"It is only my great friend the cow-hippo," said the River Fairy.

The huge hippopotamus stopped and looked at the child:

"I thought all the mortals had died," she said.

"Only this little girl is left," said the River Fairy," and she wants to become a fish-maiden and live with me."

"Very wise of her," said the cow-hippo; "but she looks very hungry."

Poor little Glory was quite worn out with cold and hunger and the long hours spent on the river bank, and when she tried to get up she fainted.

The River Fairy and the cow-hippo did everything they could, for they were much distressed, they laid her in the warm sunshine on the soft sand and rubbed her hands and feet. "We must get her some food," they said to each other.

"I have only raw sweet potatoes," said the cow-hippo, "and she can't eat them uncooked, for I have often seen the fires which mortals make. If we could get some sweet bananas she might eat those."

By this time the sun was well up and the whole world was awaking to the life of a new day. A cheeky-looking monkey swung himself down by a branch and screamed:

"How have you slept? How have you slept, Hippo and Fish-People."

"Come here at once," commanded the cow- hippo; and the monkey turned a somersault and landed on the ground.

"Do you know the golden sweet bananas that mortals eat?" asked the cow-hippo.

"Of course I do," said the monkey, "I have eaten bunches of them myself."

"Then go and fetch a bunch *at once*," said the cow-hippo.

The monkey scratched his head, then he looked up at the sun and blinked his eyes, then he scratched his shoulders and said meekly:

"Did you ask me to do anything?"

"Now, listen to me," said the cow-hippo firmly, "you are to go *very quickly*, and fetch a bunch of golden sweet bananas."

"Where from?" asked the monkey.

"From where they grow," said the cow- hippo.

A flight of grey parrots had come over from the nearer islands in search of food, and as they rested for a moment on a tree near, they heard the conversation. One of them flew down and said to the cow-hippo:

"It is absolutely useless to send the monkey on any errand alone, he will simply forget what he has set out to do. We will go with him and see that he brings the bananas."

"I don't want you," said the monkey sulkily; but in a minute he began to laugh and jump about and dance and forgot that he was offended. All the animals know how silly the monkeys are in this way, but they forgive them many things because they are so funny. The monkey went off with the parrots and every time he stopped to play they shrieked at him:

"Remember the bananas." And at last they brought him back safely with a big bunch of ripe golden fruit, and Glory ate them until she was hungry no more. Then she cuddled down in a nook in the river bank and went fast asleep. While she slept, the cow-hippo and the River Fairy watched over her, and when she woke they asked her:

"Do you still want to be a fish-maiden? "And Glory looked at her little brown feet and replied:

"Yes; today I will come to you. I cannot go back to my cold hut any more."

Then the River Fairy gave her some sea- weed to eat. It tasted very bitter, but as soon as she had eaten it she fell asleep, and while she slept the River Fairy bound her legs together with broad bands of seaweed and cut off her little brown feet with a sharp shell, and at once a little tail appeared growing from them. Then she slipped into the water and carried Glory to her cave under the Falls, and laid her on a lovely soft bed of seaweed. There she slept for a whole week and every day her tail grew more beautiful, and when she woke it looked like mother o' pearl. She was very hungry when she woke after her long sleep, and the River Fairy gave her seaweed and sea-fruit to eat, and now it did not taste bitter, for she had become a fish-maiden and could open her eyes under water and swim about and turn her tail in the white foam. Then the River Fairy took Glory to the Lake City and presented her to the King of the Fish-People. They swam down the blue streets bordered by caves and sea-palms; beautiful sea-plants and flowers were on every hand, and then they reached the King's Palace, and bowed before the King. The King was an old, old man who had ruled the Fish-People for hundreds of years. He looked earnestly at the little girl and spoke:

"Little Fish-maiden, you are to live with the River Fairy and guard the Falls of the Nile. You are to learn her work so that in years to come you too may help us in keeping our beauti-ful Lake Country pure and clean, that the water which dashes over the Falls may carry greetings from the Great Lake to the Great Sea which lies far away to the North."

And now in Uganda, when the sun has set and the fires are lighted in the fishermen's huts near the river Nile, and the people have eaten their evening meal and gather round the fire, they tell stories; perhaps a fisherman will say:

"Once I saw a big fish near the Falls, as big as a woman, with a head and shoulders and arms like a woman."

And the others will say:

"How wonderful! How wonderful!" But in their hearts they think:

"He is lying, he did not see this fish."

But the fisherman is not lying, for he has seen Glory, the Fish-maiden, who is now the River Fairy and guards the Ripon Falls. Here the Great Lake sends its blue waters over the rocks, and they hurry away foaming towards the Rapids, and on and on over the deserts and plains until they reach the Great Sea which lies far away to the North.

Lu-San, Daughter of Heaven

LU-SAN WENT TO BED without any supper, but her little heart was hungry for something more than food. She nestled up close beside her sleeping brothers, but even in their slumber they seemed to deny her that love which she craved. The gentle lapping of the water against the sides of the houseboat, music which had so often lulled her into dreamland, could not quiet her now. Scorned and treated badly by the entire family, her short life had been full of grief and shame.

Lu-san's father was a fisherman. His life had been one long fight against poverty. He was ignorant and wicked. He had no more feeling of love for his wife and five children than for the street dogs of his native city. Over and over he had threatened to drown them one and all, and had been prevented from doing so only by fear of the new mandarin. His wife did not try to stop her husband when he sometimes beat the children until they fell half dead upon the deck. In fact, she herself was cruel to them, and often gave the last blow to Lu-san, her only daughter. Not on one day in the little girl's memory had she escaped this daily whipping, not once had her parents pitied her.

On the night with which this story opens, not knowing that Lu-san was listening, her father and mother were planning how to get rid of her.

"The mandarin cares only about boys," said he roughly. "A man might kill a dozen girls and he wouldn't say a word."

"Lu-san's no good anyway," added the mother. "Our boat is small, and she's always in the wrong place."

"Yes, and it takes as much to feed her as if she were a boy. If you say so, I'll do it this very night."

"All right," she answered, "but you'd better wait till the moon has set."

"Very well, wife, we'll let the moon go down first, and then the girl."

No wonder Lu-san's little heart beat fast with terror, for there could be no doubt as to the meaning of her parents' words.

At last when she heard them snoring and knew they were both sound asleep, she got up silently, dressed herself, and climbed the ladder leading to the deck. Only one thought was in her heart, to save herself by instant flight. There were no extra clothes, not a bite of food to take with her. Besides the rags on her back there was only one thing she could call her own, a tiny soapstone image of the goddess Kwan-yin, which she had found one day while walking in the sand. This was the only treasure and plaything of her childhood, and if she had not watched carefully, her mother would have taken even this away from her. Oh, how she had nursed this idol, and how closely she had listened to the stories an old priest had told about Kwan-yin the Goddess of Mercy, the best friend of women and children, to whom they might always pray in time of trouble.

It was very dark when Lu-san raised the trapdoor leading to the outer air, and looked out into the night. The moon had just gone down, and frogs were croaking along the shore. Slowly and carefully she pushed against the door, for she was afraid that the wind coming in suddenly might awaken the sleepers or, worse still, cause her to let the trap fall with a bang. At last, however, she stood on the deck, alone and ready to go out into the big world. As she stepped to the side of the boat the black water did not make her feel afraid, and she went ashore without the slightest tremble.

Now she ran quickly along the bank, shrinking back into the shadows whenever she heard the noise of footsteps, and thus hiding from the passers-by. Only once did her heart quake, full of fear. A huge boat dog ran out at her barking furiously. The snarling beast, however, was not dangerous, and when he saw this trembling little girl of ten he sniffed in disgust at having noticed any one so small, and returned to watch his gate.

Lu-san had made no plans. She thought that if she could escape the death her parents had talked about, they would be delighted at her leaving them and would not look for her. It was not, then, her own people that she feared as she passed the rows of dark houses lining the shore. She had often heard her father tell of the dreadful deeds done in many of these houseboats. The darkest memory of her childhood was of the night when he had almost decided to sell her as a slave to the owner of a boat like these she was now passing. Her mother had suggested that they should wait until Lu-san was a little older, for she would then be worth more money. So her father had not sold her. Lately, perhaps, he had tried and failed.

That was why she hated the river dwellers and was eager to get past their houses. On and on she sped as fast as her little legs could carry her. She would flee far away from the dark water, for she loved the bright sunshine and the land.

As Lu-san ran past the last houseboat she breathed a sigh of relief and a minute later fell in a little heap upon the sand. Not until now had she noticed how lonely it was. Over there was the great city with its thousands of sleepers. Not one of them was her friend. She knew nothing of friendship, for she had had no playmates. Beyond lay the open fields, the sleeping villages, the unknown world. Ah, how tired she was! How far she had run! Soon, holding the precious image tightly in her little hand and whispering a childish prayer to Kwan-yin, she fell asleep.

When Lu-san awoke, a cold chill ran through her body, for bending over her stood a strange person. Soon she saw to her wonder that it was a woman dressed in beautiful clothes like those worn by a princess. The child had never seen such perfect features or so fair a face. At first, conscious of her own filthy rags, she shrank back fearfully, wondering what would happen if this beautiful being should chance to touch her and thus soil those slender white fingers. As the child lay there trembling on the ground, she felt as if she would like to spring into the fairy creature's arms and beg for mercy. Only the fear that the lovely one would vanish kept her from so doing. Finally, unable to hold back any longer, the little girl, bending forward, stretched out her hand to the woman, saying, "Oh, you are so beautiful! Take this, for it must be you who lost it in the sand."

The princess took the soapstone figure, eyed it curiously, and then with a start of surprise said, "And do you know, my little creature, to whom you are thus giving your treasure?"

"No," answered the child simply, "but it is the only thing I have in all the world, and you are so lovely that I know it belongs to you. I found it on the river bank."

Then a strange thing happened. The graceful, queenly woman bent over, and held out her arms to the ragged, dirty child. With a cry of joy the little one sprang forward; she had found the love for which she had been looking so long.

"My precious child, this little stone which you have kept so lovingly, and which without a thought of self you have given to me – do you know of whom it is the image?"

"Yes," answered Lu-san, the colour coming to her cheeks again as she snuggled up contentedly in her new friend's warm embrace, "it is the dear goddess Kwan-yin, she who makes the children happy."

"And has this gracious goddess brought sunshine into your life, my pretty one?" said the other, a slight flush covering her fair cheeks at the poor child's innocent words.

"Oh, yes indeed; if it had not been for her I should not have escaped tonight. My father would have killed me, but the good lady of heaven listened to my prayer and bade me stay awake. She told me to wait until he was sleeping, then to arise and leave the houseboat."

"And where are you going, Lu-san, now that you have left your father? Are you not afraid to be alone here at night on the bank of this great river?"

"No, oh no! for the blessed mother will shield me. She has heard my prayers, and I know she will show me where to go."

The lady clasped Lu-san still more tightly, and something glistened in her radiant eye. A tear-drop rolled down her cheek and fell upon the child's head, but Lu-san did not see it, for she had fallen fast asleep in her protector's arms.

When Lu-san awoke, she was lying all alone on her bed in the houseboat, but, strange to say, she was not frightened at finding herself once more near her parents. A ray of sunlight came in, lighting up the child's face and telling her that a new day had dawned. At last she heard the sound of low voices, but she did not know who were the speakers. Then as the tones grew louder she knew that her parents were talking. Their speech, however, seemed to be less harsh than usual, as if they were near the bed of some sleeper whom they did not wish to wake.

"Why," said her father, "when I bent over to lift her from the bed, there was a strange light about her face. I touched her on the arm, and at once my hand hung limp as if it had been shot. Then I heard a voice whispering in my ears, 'What! would you lay your wicked hands on one who made the tears of Kwan-yin flow? Do you not know that when she cries the gods themselves are weeping?'"

"I too heard that voice," said the mother, her voice trembling; "I heard it, and it seemed as if a hundred wicked imps pricked me with spears, at every prick repeating these terrible words, 'And would you kill a daughter of the gods?'"

"It is strange," he added, "to think how we had begun to hate this child, when all the time she belonged to another world than ours. How wicked we must be since we could not see her goodness."

"Yes, and no doubt for every time we have struck her, a thousand blows will be given us by Yama, for our insults to the gods."

Lu-san waited no longer, but rose to dress herself. Her heart was burning with love for everything around her. She would tell her parents that she forgave them, tell them how she loved them still in spite of all their wickedness. To her surprise the ragged clothes were nowhere to be seen. In place of them she found on one side of the bed the most beautiful garments. The softest of silks, bright with flowers – so lovely that she fancied they must have been taken from the garden of the gods – were ready to slip on her little body. As she dressed herself she saw with surprise that her fingers were shapely, that her skin was soft and smooth. Only the day before, her hands had been rough and cracked by hard work and the cold of winter. More and more amazed, she stooped to put on her shoes. Instead of the worn-out soiled shoes of yesterday, the prettiest little satin slippers were there all ready for her tiny feet.

Finally she climbed the rude ladder, and lo, everything she touched seemed to be changed as if by magic, like her gown. The narrow rounds of the ladder had become broad steps of polished wood, and it seemed as if she was mounting the polished stairway of some fairy-built pagoda. When she reached the deck everything was changed. The ragged patchwork which had served so long as a sail had become a beautiful sheet of canvas that rolled and floated proudly in the river breeze. Below were the dirty fishing smacks which Lu-san was used to, but here was a stately ship, larger and fairer than any she had ever dreamed of, a ship which had sprung into being as if at the touch of her feet.

After searching several minutes for her parents she found them trembling in a corner, with a look of great fear on their faces. They were clad in rags, as usual, and in no way changed except that their savage faces seemed to have become a trifle softened. Lu-san drew near the wretched group and bowed low before them.

Her mother tried to speak; her lips moved, but made no sound: she had been struck dumb with fear.

"A goddess, a goddess!" murmured the father, bending forward three times and knocking his head on the deck. As for the brothers, they hid their faces in their hands as if dazzled by a sudden burst of sunlight.

For a moment Lu-san paused. Then, stretching out her hand, she touched her father on the shoulder. "Do you not know me, father? It is Lu-san, your little daughter."

The man looked at her in wonder. His whole body shook, his lips trembled, his hard brutish face had on it a strange light. Suddenly he bent far over and touched his forehead to her feet. Mother and sons followed his example. Then all gazed at her as if waiting for her command.

"Speak, father," said Lu-san. "Tell me that you love me, say that you will not kill your child."

"Daughter of the gods, and not of mine," he mumbled, and then paused as if afraid to continue.

"What is it, father? Have no fear."

"First, tell me that you forgive me."

The child put her left hand upon her father's forehead and held the right above the heads of the others, "As the Goddess of Mercy has given me her favour, so I in her name bestow on you the love of heaven. Live in peace, my parents. Brothers, speak no angry words. Oh, my dear ones, let joy be yours for ever. When only love shall rule your lives, this ship is yours and all that is in it."

Thus did Lu-san change her loved ones. The miserable family which had lived in poverty now found itself enjoying peace and happiness. At first they did not know how to live as Lu-san had directed. The father sometimes lost his temper and the mother spoke spiteful words; but as they grew in wisdom and courage they soon began to see that only love must rule.

All this time the great boat was moving up and down the river. Its company of sailors obeyed Lu-san's slightest wish. When their nets were cast overboard they were always drawn back full of the largest, choicest fish. These fish were sold at the city markets, and soon people began to say that Lu-san was the richest person in the whole country.

One beautiful day during the Second Moon, the family had just returned from the temple. It was Kwan-yin's birthday, and, led by Lu-san, they had gone gladly to do the goddess honour. They had just mounted to the vessel's deck when Lu-san's father, who had been looking off towards the west, suddenly called the family to his side. "See!" he exclaimed. "What kind of bird is that yonder in the sky?"

As they looked, they saw that the strange object was coming nearer and nearer, and directly towards the ship. Everyone was excited except Lu-san. She was calm, as if waiting for something she had long expected.

"It is a flight of doves," cried the father in astonishment, "and they seem to be drawing something through the air."

At last, as the birds flew right over the vessel, the surprised onlookers saw that floating beneath their wings was a wonderful chair, all white and gold, more dazzling even than the one they had dreamed the Emperor himself sat in on the Dragon Throne. Around each snow-white neck was fastened a long streamer of pure gold, and these silken ribbons were tied to the chair in such a manner as to hold it floating wherever its light-winged coursers chose to fly.

Down, down, over the magic vessel came the empty chair, and as it descended, a shower of pure white lilies fell about the feet of Lu-san, until she, the queen of all the flowers, was almost buried. The doves hovered above her head for an instant, and then gently lowered their burden until it was just in front of her.

With a farewell wave to her father and mother, Lu-san stepped into the fairy car. As the birds began to rise, a voice from the clouds spoke in tones of softest music: "Thus Kwan-yin, Mother of Mercies, rewards Lu-san, daughter of the earth. Out of the dust spring the flowers; out of the soil comes goodness. Lu-san! that tear which you drew from Kwan-yin's eye fell upon the dry ground and softened it; it touched the hearts of those who loved you not. Daughter of earth no longer, rise into the Western Heaven, there to take your place among the fairies, there to be a star within the azure realms above."

As Lu-san's doves disappeared in the distant skies, a rosy light surrounded her flying car. It seemed to those who gazed in wonder that heaven's gates were opening to receive her. At last when she was gone beyond their sight, suddenly it grew dark upon the earth, and the eyes of all that looked were wet with tears.

Sam-Chung and the Water Demon

SAM-CHUNG WAS ONE of the most famous men in the history of the Buddhist Church, and had distinguished himself by the earnestness and self-denial with which he had entered on the pursuit of eternal life. His mind had been greatly exercised and distressed at the pains and sorrows which mankind were apparently doomed to endure. Even those, however, terrible as they were, he could have managed to tolerate had they not ended, in the case of every human being, in the crowning calamity which comes upon all at the close of life.

Death was the great mystery which cast its shadow on every human being. It invaded every home. The sage whose virtues and teachings were the means of uplifting countless generations of men came under its great law. Men of infamous and abandoned character seemed often to outlive the more virtuous of their fellow-beings; but they too, when the gods saw fit, were hurried off without any ceremony. Even the little ones, who had never violated any of the laws of Heaven, came under this universal scourge; and many of them, who had only just commenced to live were driven out into the Land of Shadows by this mysterious force which dominates all human life.

Accordingly Sam-Chung wanted to be freed from the power of death, so that its shadow should never darken his life in the years to come.

After careful enquiry, and through friendly hints from men who, he had reason to believe, were fairies in disguise and had been sent by the Goddess of Mercy to help those who aspired after a higher life, he learned that it was possible by the constant pursuit of virtue to arrive at that stage of existence in which death would lose all its power to injure, and men should become immortal. This boon of eternal life could be won by every man or woman who was willing to pay the price for so precious a gift. It could be gained by great self-denial, by willingness to suffer, and especially by the exhibition of profound love and sympathy for those who were in sorrow of any kind. It appeared, indeed, that the one thing most imperatively demanded by the gods from those who aspired to enter their ranks was that they should be possessed of a divine compassion, and that their supreme object should be the succouring of distressed humanity. Without this compassion any personal sacrifice that might be made in the search for immortality would be absolutely useless.

Sam-Chung was already conscious that he was a favourite of the gods, for they had given him two companions, both with supernatural powers, to enable him to contend against the cunning schemes of the evil spirits, who are ever planning how to thwart and destroy those whose hearts are set upon higher things.

One day, accompanied by Chiau and Chu, the two attendants commissioned by the Goddess of Mercy to attend upon him, Sam-Chung started on his long journey for the famous Tien-ho river, to cross which is the ambition of every pilgrim on his way to the land of the Immortals. They endured many weeks of painful travelling over high mountains and through deep valleys which lay in constant shadow, and across sandy deserts where men perished of thirst or were struck down by the scorching heat of the sun, before they met any of the infernal foes that they expected to be lying in wait for them.

Weary and footsore, they at last arrived one evening on the shores of the mighty Tien-ho, just as the sun was setting. The glory of the clouds in the west streamed on to the waters of the river, and made them sparkle with a beauty which seemed to our wearied travellers to transform them into something more than earthly. The river here was so wide that it looked like an inland sea. There was no sign of land on the distant horizon, nothing but one interminable vista of waters, stretching away as far as the eye could reach.

One thing, however, greatly disappointed Sam-Chung and his companions, and that was the absence of boats. They had planned to engage one, and by travelling across the river during the night, they hoped to hurry on their way and at the same time to rest and refresh themselves after the fatigues they had been compelled to endure on their long land journey.

It now became a very serious question with them where they were to spend the night. There was no sign of any human habitation round about. There was the sandy beach along which they were walking, and there was the wide expanse of the river, on which the evening mists were slowly gathering; but no appearance of life. Just as they were wondering what course they should pursue, the faint sound of some musical instruments came floating on the air and caught their ear. Hastening forward in the direction from which the music came, they ascended a piece of rising ground, from the top of which they were delighted to see a village nestling on the hillside, and a small temple standing on the very margin of the river.

With hearts overjoyed at the prospect of gaining some place where they could lodge for the night, they hurried forward to the hamlet in front of them. As they drew nearer, the sounds of music became louder and more distinct. They concluded that some festival was being observed, or that some happy gathering amongst the people had thrown them all into a holiday mood. Entering the village, they made their way to a house which stood out prominently from the rest, and which was better built than any others they could see. Besides, it was the one from which the music issued, and around its doors was gathered a number of people who had evidently been attending some feast inside.

As the three travellers came up to the door, a venerable-looking old man came out to meet them. Seeing that they were strangers, he courteously invited them to enter; and on Sam-Chung asking whether they could be entertained for the night, he assured them that there was ample room for them in the house, and that he gladly welcomed them to be his guests for as long as it was their pleasure to remain.

"In the meanwhile you must come in," he said, "and have some food, for you must be tired and hungry after travelling so far, and the tables are still covered with the good things which were prepared for the feast to-day."

After they had finished their meal, they began to talk to the old gentleman who was so kindly entertaining them. They were greatly pleased with his courtesy and with the hearty hospitality which he had pressed upon them. They noticed, however, that he was very absent-minded, and looked as if some unpleasant thought lay heavy on his heart.

"May I ask," said Sam-Chung, "what was the reason for the great gathering here to-day? There is no festival in the Chinese calendar falling on this date, so I thought I would take the liberty of enquiring what occasion you were really commemorating."

"We were not commemorating anything," the old man replied with a grave face. "It was really a funeral service for two of my grand-children, who, though they are not yet dead, will certainly disappear out of this life before many hours have passed."

"But how can such a ceremony be performed over persons who are still alive?" asked Sam-Chung with a look of wonder in his face.

"When I have explained the circumstances to you, you will then be no longer surprised at this unusual service," replied the old man.

"You must know," he continued, "that this region is under the control of a Demon of a most cruel and bloodthirsty disposition. He is not like the ordinary spirits, whose images are enshrined in our temples, and whose main aim is to protect and guard their worshippers. This one has no love for mankind, but on the contrary the bitterest hatred, and his whole life seems to be occupied in scheming how he may inflict sorrow and disaster on them. His greatest cruelty is to insist that every year just about this time two children, one a boy and the other a girl, shall be conveyed to his temple by the river side to be devoured by him. Many attempts have been made to resist this barbarous demand, but they have only resulted in increased suffering to those who have dared to oppose him. The consequence is that the people submit to this cruel murder of their children, though many a heart is broken at the loss of those dearest to them."

"But is there any system by which the unfortunate people may get to know when this terrible sacrifice is going to be demanded from them?" asked Sam-Chung.

"Oh yes," replied the man. "The families are taken in rotation, and when each one's turn comes round, their children are prepared for the sacrifice. Moreover, that there may be no mistake, the Demon himself appears in the home a few days before, and gives a threatening command to have the victims ready on such a date. Only the day before yesterday, this summons came to us to have our children ready by tomorrow morning at break of day. That is why we had a feast to-day, and performed the funeral rites for the dead, so that their spirits may not be held under the control of this merciless Damon, but may in time be permitted to issue from the Land of Shadows, and be born again under happier circumstances into this world, which they are leaving under such tragic circumstances."

"But what is the Demon like?" enquired Sam-Chung.

"Oh, no one can ever tell what he is like," said the man. "He has no bodily form that one can look upon. His presence is known by a strong blast of wind which fills the place with a peculiar odour, and with an influence so subtle that you feel yourself within the grip of a powerful force, and instinctively bow your head as though you were in the presence of a being who could destroy you in a moment were he so disposed."

"One more question and I have finished," said Sam-Chung. "Where did this Demon come from, and how is it that he has acquired such an overmastering supremacy over the lives of men, that he seems able to defy even Heaven itself, and all the great hosts of kindly gods who are working for the salvation of mankind?"

"This Demon," the man replied, "was once an inhabitant of the Western Heaven, and under the direct control of the Goddess of Mercy. He must, however, have been filled with evil devices and fiendish instincts from the very beginning, for he seized the first opportunity to escape to earth, and to take up his residence in the grottoes and caverns that lie deep down beneath the waters of the Tien-ho. Other spirits almost as bad as himself have also taken up their abode there, and they combine their forces to bring calamity and disaster upon the people of this region."

Sam-Chung, whose heart was filled with the tenderest feelings of compassion for all living things, so much so that his name was a familiar one even amongst the Immortals in the far-off Western Heaven, felt himself stirred by a mighty indignation when he thought of how innocent childhood had been sacrificed to minister to the unnatural passion of this depraved Demon. Chiau and Chu were as profoundly indignant as he, and a serious consultation ensued as to the best methods to be adopted to save the little ones who were doomed to destruction on the morrow, and at the same time to break the monster's rule so that it should cease for ever.

Chiau, who was the more daring of the two whom I the goddess had deputed to protect Sam-Chung, at length cried out with flashing eyes, "I will personate the boy, Chu shall act the girl, and together we will fight the Demon and overthrow and kill him, and so deliver the people from his dreadful tyranny."

Turning to the old man, he said, "Bring the children here so that we may see them, and make our plans so perfect that the Demon with all his cunning will not be able to detect or frustrate them."

In a few moments the little ones were led in by their grandfather. The boy was seven and the girl was one year older. They were both of them nervous and shy, and clung timidly to the old man as if for protection.

They were very interesting-looking children. The boy was a proud, brave-spirited little fellow, as one could see by the poise of his head as he gazed at the strangers. If anything could be predicted from his looks, he would one day turn out to be a man of great power, for he had in his youthful face all the signs which promise a life out of the common. The girl was a shy little thing, with her hair done up in a childlike fashion that well became her. She was a dainty little mortal. Her eyes were almond-shaped, and with the coyness of her sex she kept shooting out glances from the corners of them at the three men who were looking at her. Her cheeks were pale, with just a suspicion of colour painted into them by the deft hand of nature; whilst her lips had been touched with the faintest dash of carmine, evidently just a moment ago, before she left her mother's side.

"Now, my boy," said Chiau to the little fellow, "keep your eyes fixed on me, and never take them from me for a moment; and you, little sister," addressing the girl, "do the same to the man next to me, and you will see something that will make you both laugh."

The eyes of them both were at once riveted on the two men, and a look of amazement slowly crept into their faces. And no wonder, for as they gazed they saw the two men rapidly changing, and becoming smaller and smaller, until they were the exact size and image of themselves. In their features and dress, and in every minute detail they were the precise pattern of the children, who with staring eyes were held spellbound by the magic change which had taken place in front of them.

"Now," said Chiau to the old gentleman, "the transformation is complete. Take the children away and hide them in the remotest and most inaccessible room that you have in your house. Let them be seen by no chattering woman or servant who might divulge our secret, so that in some way or other it might reach the ears of the Demon, and put him on his guard. Remember that from this moment these little ones are not supposed to exist, but that we are your grand-children who are to be taken to the temple tomorrow morning at break of day."

Just as the eastern sky showed the first touch of colour, two sedan-chairs were brought up to the door to carry the two victims away to be devoured by the Demon. A few frightened-looking neighbours peered through the gloom to catch a last glimpse of the children, but not one of them had the least suspicion that the boy and girl were really fairies who were about to wage a deadly battle with the Demon in order to deliver them from the curse under which they lived.

No sooner had the children been put into the temple, where a dim rush-light did but serve to disclose the gloom, and the doors had been closed with a bang, than the chair-bearers rushed away in fear for their very lives.

An instant afterwards a hideous, gigantic form emerged from an inner room and advanced towards the children. The Demon was surprised, however, to find that on this occasion the little victims did not exhibit any signs of alarm, as had always been the case hitherto, but seemed to be calmly awaiting his approach. There was no symptom of fear about them, and not a cry of terror broke from their lips; but with a fearless and composed mien they gazed upon him as he advanced.

Hesitating for a moment, as if to measure the foe which he began to fear might lie concealed beneath the figures of the boy and girl before him, the Demon's great fiery eyes began to flash with deadly passion as he saw the two little ones gradually expand in size, until they were transformed into beings as powerful and as mighty as himself. He knew at once that he had been outwitted, and that he must now battle for his very life; so, drawing a sword which had always stood him in good stead, he rushed upon the two who faced him so calmly and with such apparent confidence in themselves.

Chiau and Chu were all ready for the fray, and with weapons firmly gripped and with hearts made strong by the consciousness of the justice of their cause, they awaited the onslaught of the Demon.

And what a battle it was that then ensued in the dim and shadowy temple! It was a conflict of great and deadly significance, waged on one side for the deliverance of helpless childhood, and on the other for the basest schemes that the spirits of evil could devise. It was a battle royal, in which no quarter was either asked or given. The clash of weapons, and sounds unfamiliar to the human ear, and groans and cries which seemed to come from a lost soul, filled the temple with their hideous uproar.

At last the Demon, who seemed to have been grievously wounded, though by his magic art he had caused his wounds to be instantly healed, began to see that the day was going against him. One more mighty lunge with his broadsword, and one more furious onset, and his craven heart failed him. With a cry of despair he fled from the temple, and plunged headlong into the river flowing by its walls.

Great were the rejoicings when Chiau and Chu returned to report to Sam-Chung the glorious victory they had gained over the Demon. Laughter and rejoicing were heard in every home, and men and women assembled in front of their doors and at the corners of the narrow alley-ways to congratulate each other on the great deliverance which that day had come to them and to their children. The dread of the Demon had already vanished, and a feeling of freedom so inspired the men of the village that as if by a common impulse, they rushed impetuously down to where the temple stood, and in the course of a few hours every vestige of it had disappeared beneath the waters into which the Demon had plunged.

After his great defeat the baffled spirit made his way to the grotto beneath the waters, where he and the other demons had taken up their abode. A general council was called to devise plans to wipe out the disgrace which had been sustained, and to regain the power that had slipped from the Demon's grasp. They wished also to visit Sam-Chung with condign punishment which would render him helpless for the future.

"We must capture him," said one wicked-looking imp, who always acted as counsellor to the rest. "I have been told that to devour some of his flesh would ensure the prolongation of life for more than a thousand years."

The suggestion to seize Sam-Chung was unanimously accepted as a very inspiration of genius, and the precise measures which were to be adopted in order to capture him were agreed to after a long discussion.

On the very next morning, a most violent snowstorm set in, so that the face of the river and the hills all round about, and the very heavens themselves were lost in the blinding snow-drifts that flew before the gale. Gradually the cold became so intense that the Ice King laid his grip upon the waters of the Tien-ho, and turned the flowing stream into a crystal highway, along which men might travel with ease and safety. Such a sight had never been seen before by any of the people who lived upon its banks, and many were the speculations as to what such a phenomenon might mean to the welfare of the people of the region. It never occurred to any one that this great snow-storm which had turned into ice a river that had never been known to freeze before, was all the work of demons determined on the destruction of Sam-Chung.

Next day the storm had passed, but the river was one mass of ice which gleamed and glistened in the morning rays. Much to the astonishment of Sam-Chung and his two companions, they caught sight of a number of people, who appeared to be merchants, moving about on the bank of the river, together with several mules laden with merchandise. The whole party seemed intent on their preparations for crossing the river, which they were observed to test in various places to make sure that it was strong enough to bear their weight. This they seemed satisfied about, for in a short time the men and animals set forward on their journey across the ice.

Sam-Chung immediately insisted upon following their example, though the plan was vigorously opposed by the villagers, who predicted all kinds of dangers if he entered on such an uncertain and hazardous enterprise. Being exceedingly anxious to proceed on his journey, however, and seeing no prospect of doing so if he did not take advantage of the present remarkable condition of the river, he hastened to follow in the footsteps of the merchants, who by this time had already advanced some distance on the ice.

He would have been less anxious to enter on this perilous course, had he known that the innocent-looking traders who preceded him were every one of them demons who had changed themselves into the semblance of men in order to lure him to his destruction.

Sam-Chung and his companions had not proceeded more than five or six miles, when ominous symptoms of coming disaster began to manifest themselves. The extreme cold in the air suddenly ceased, and a warm south wind began to blow. The surface of the ice lost its hardness. Streamlets of water trickled here and there, forming great pools which made walking exceedingly difficult.

Chiau, whose mind was a very acute and intelligent one, became terrified at these alarming symptoms of danger, especially as the ice began to crack, and loud and prolonged reports reached them from every direction. Another most suspicious thing was the sudden disappearance of the company of merchants, whom they had all along kept well in sight. There was something wrong, he was fully convinced, and so with all his wits about him, he kept himself alert for any contingency. It was well that he did this, for before they had proceeded another mile, the ice began to grow thinner, and before they could retreat there was a sudden crash and all three were precipitated into the water.

Hardly had Chiau's feet touched the river, than with a superhuman effort he made a spring into the air, and was soon flying with incredible speed in the direction of the Western Heaven, to invoke the aid of the Goddess of Mercy to deliver Sam-Chung from the hands of an enemy who would show him no quarter.

In the meanwhile Sam-Chung and Chu were borne swiftly by the demons, who were eagerly awaiting their immersion in the water, to the great cave that lay deep down at the bottom of the mighty river. Chu, being an immortal and a special messenger of the Goddess, defied all the arts of the evil spirits to injure him, so that all they could do was to imprison him in one of the inner grottoes and station a guard over him to prevent his escape. Sam-Chung, however, was doomed to death, and the Demon, in revenge for the disgrace he had brought upon him, and in the hope of prolonging his own life by a thousand years, decided that on the morrow he would feast upon his flesh. But he made his plans without taking into consideration the fact that Sam-Chung was an especial favourite with the Goddess.

During the night a tremendous commotion occurred. The waters of the river fled in every direction as before the blast of a hurricane, and the caverns where the demons were assembled were illuminated with a light so brilliant that their eyes became dazzled, and for a time were blinded by the sudden blaze that flashed from every corner. Screaming with terror, they fled in all directions. Only one remained, and that was the fierce spirit who had wrought such sorrow amongst the people of the land near by. He too would have disappeared with the rest, had not some supernatural power chained him to the spot where he stood.

Soon the noble figure of the Goddess of Mercy appeared, accompanied by a splendid train of Fairies who hovered round her to do her bidding. Her first act was to release Sam-Chung, who lay bound ready for his death, which but for her interposition would have taken place within a few hours. He and his two companions were entrusted to the care of a chosen number of her followers, and conveyed with all speed across the river.

The Goddess then gave a command to some who stood near her person, and in a moment, as if by a flash of lightning, the cowering, terrified Demon had vanished, carried away to be confined in one of the dungeons where persistent haters of mankind are kept imprisoned, until their hearts are changed by some noble sentiment of compassion and the Goddess sees that they are once more fit for liberty.

And then the lights died out, and the sounds of fairy voices ceased. The waters of the river, which had been under a divine spell, returned to their course, and the Goddess with her magnificent train of beneficent spirits departed to her kingdom in the far-off Western Heaven.

The Princess Kwan-Yin

ONCE UPON A TIME in China there lived a certain king who had three daughters. The fairest and best of these was Kwan-yin, the youngest. The old king was justly proud of this daughter, for of all the women who had ever lived in the palace she was by far the most attractive. It did not take him long, therefore, to decide that she should be the heir to his throne, and her husband ruler of his kingdom. But, strange to say, Kwan-yin was not pleased at this good fortune. She cared little for the pomp and splendour of court life. She foresaw no pleasure for herself in ruling as a queen, but even feared that in so high a station she might feel out of place and unhappy.

Every day she went to her room to read and study. As a result of this daily labour she soon went far beyond her sisters along the paths of knowledge, and her name was known in the farthest corner of the kingdom as "Kwan-yin, the wise princess." Besides being very fond of books, Kwan-yin was thoughtful of her friends. She was careful about her behaviour both in public and in private. Her warm heart was open at all times to the cries of those in trouble. She was kind to the poor and suffering. She won the love of the lower classes, and was to them a sort of goddess to whom they could appeal whenever they were hungry and in need. Some people even believed that she was a fairy who had come to earth from her home within the Western Heaven, while others said that once, long years before, she had lived in the world as a prince instead of a princess. However this may be, one thing is certain – Kwan-yin was pure and good, and well deserved the praises that were showered upon her.

One day the king called this favourite daughter to the royal bedside, for he felt that the hour of death was drawing near. Kwan-yin kowtowed before her royal father, kneeling and touching her forehead on the floor in sign of deepest reverence. The old man bade her rise and come closer. Taking her hand tenderly in his own, he said, "Daughter, you know well how I love you. Your modesty and virtue, your talent and your love of knowledge, have made you first in my heart. As you know already, I chose you as heir to my kingdom long ago. I promised that your husband should be made ruler in my stead. The time is almost ripe for me to ascend upon the dragon and become a guest on high. It is necessary that you be given at once in marriage."

"But, most exalted father," faltered the princess, "I am not ready to be married."

"Not ready, child! Why, are you not eighteen? Are not the daughters of our nation often wedded long before they reach that age? Because of your desire for learning I have spared you thus far from any thought of a husband, but now we can wait no longer."

"Royal father, hear your child, and do not compel her to give up her dearest pleasures. Let her go into a quiet convent where she may lead a life of study!"

The king sighed deeply at hearing these words. He loved his daughter and did not wish to wound her. "Kwan-yin," he continued, "do you wish to pass by the green spring of youth, to give up this mighty kingdom? Do you wish to enter the doors of a convent where women say farewell to life and all its pleasures? No! your father will not permit this. It grieves me sorely to disappoint you, but one month from this very day you shall be married. I have chosen for your royal partner a man of many noble parts. You know him by name already, although you have not seen him. Remember that, of the hundred virtues filial conduct is the chief, and that you owe more to me than to all else on earth."

Kwan-yin turned pale. Trembling, she would have sunk to the floor, but her mother and sisters supported her, and by their tender care brought her back to consciousness.

Every day of the month that followed, Kwan-yin's relatives begged her to give up what they called her foolish notion. Her sisters had long since given up hope of becoming queen. They were amazed at her stupidity. The very thought of any one's choosing a convent instead of a throne was to them a sure sign of madness. Over and over again they asked her reason for making so strange a choice. To every question, she shook her head, replying, "A voice from the heavens speaks to me, and I must obey it."

On the eve of the wedding day Kwan-yin slipped out of the palace, and, after a weary journey, arrived at a convent called, "The Cloister of the White Sparrow." She was dressed as a poor maiden. She said she wished to become a nun. The abbess, not knowing who she was, did not receive her kindly. Indeed, she told Kwan-yin that they could not receive her into the sisterhood, that the building was full. Finally, after Kwan-yin had shed many tears, the abbess let her enter, but only as a sort of servant, who might be cast out for the slightest fault.

Now that Kwan-yin found herself in the life which she had long dreamt of leading, she tried to be satisfied. But the nuns seemed to wish to make her stay among them most miserable. They gave her the hardest tasks to do, and it was seldom that she had a minute to rest. All day long she was busy, carrying water from a well at the foot of the convent hill or gathering wood from a neighbouring forest. At night when her back was almost breaking, she was given many extra tasks, enough to have crushed the spirit of any other woman than this brave daughter of a king. Forgetting her grief, and trying to hide the lines of pain that sometimes wrinkled her fair forehead, she tried to make these hard-hearted women love her. In return for their rough words, she spoke to them kindly, and never did she give way to anger.

One day while poor Kwan-yin was picking up brushwood in the forest she heard a tiger making his way through the bushes. Having no means of defending herself, she breathed a silent prayer to the gods for help, and calmly awaited the coming of the great beast. To her surprise, when the bloodthirsty animal appeared, instead of bounding up to tear her in pieces, he began to make a soft purring noise. He did not try to hurt Kwan-yin, but rubbed against her in a friendly manner, and let her pat him on the head.

The next day the princess went back to the same spot. There she found no fewer than a dozen savage beasts working under the command of the friendly tiger, gathering wood for her. In a short time enough brush and firewood had been piled up to last the convent for six months. Thus, even the wild animals of the forest were better able to judge of her goodness than the women of the sisterhood.

At another time when Kwan-yin was toiling up the hill for the twentieth time, carrying two great pails of water on a pole, an enormous dragon faced her in the road. Now, in China, the dragon is sacred, and Kwan-yin was not at all frightened, for she knew that she had done no wrong.

The animal looked at her for a moment, switched its horrid tail, and shot out fire from its nostrils. Then, dashing the burden from the startled maiden's shoulder, it vanished. Full of fear, Kwan-yin hurried up the hill to the nunnery. As she drew near the inner court, she was amazed to see in the centre of the open space a new building of solid stone. It had sprung up by magic since her last journey down the hill. On going forward, she saw that there were four arched doorways to the fairy house. Above the door facing west was a tablet with these words written on it: "In honour of Kwan-yin, the faithful princess." Inside was a well of the purest water, while, for drawing this water, there a strange machine, the like of which neither Kwan-yin nor the nuns had ever seen.

The sisters knew that this magic well was a monument to Kwan-yin's goodness. For a few days they treated her much better. "Since the gods have dug a well at our very gate," they said, "this girl will no longer need to bear water from the foot of the hill. For what strange reason, however, did the gods write this beggar's name on the stone?"

Kwan-yin heard their unkind remarks in silence. She could have explained the meaning of the dragon's gift, but she chose to let her companions remain in ignorance. At last the selfish nuns began to grow careless again, and treated her even worse than before. They could not bear to see the poor girl enjoy a moment's idleness.

"This is a place for work," they told her. "All of us have laboured hard to win our present station. You must do likewise." So they robbed her of every chance for study and prayer, and gave her no credit for the magic well.

One night the sisters were awakened from their sleep by strange noises, and soon they heard outside the walls of the compound the blare of a trumpet. A great army had been sent by Kwan-yin's father to attack the convent, for his spies had at last been able to trace the runaway princess to this holy retreat.

"Oh, who has brought this woe upon us?" exclaimed all the women, looking at each other in great fear. "Who has done this great evil? There is one among us who has sinned most terribly, and now the gods are about to destroy us." They gazed at one another, but no one thought of Kwan-yin, for they did not believe her of enough importance to attract the anger of heaven, even though she might have done the most shocking of deeds. Then, too, she had been so meek and lowly while in their holy order that they did not once dream of charging her with any crime.

The threatening sounds outside grew louder and louder. All at once a fearful cry arose among the women: "They are about to burn our sacred dwelling." Smoke was rising just beyond the enclosure where the soldiers were kindling a great fire, the heat of which would soon be great enough to make the convent walls crumble into dust.

Suddenly a voice was heard above the tumult of the weeping sisters: "Alas! I am the cause of all this trouble."

The nuns, turning in amazement, saw that it was Kwan-yin who was speaking. "You?" they exclaimed, astounded.

"Yes, I, for I am indeed the daughter of a king. My father did not wish me to take the vows of this holy order. I fled from the palace. He has sent his army here to burn these buildings and to drag me back a prisoner."

"Then, see what you have brought upon us, miserable girl!" exclaimed the abbess. "See how you have repaid our kindness! Our buildings will be burned above our heads! How wretched you have made us! May heaven's curses rest upon you!"

"No, no!" exclaimed Kwan-yin, springing up, and trying to keep the abbess from speaking these frightful words. "You have no right to say that, for I am innocent of evil. But, wait! You shall soon see whose prayers the gods will answer, yours or mine!" So saying, she pressed her forehead to the floor, praying the almighty powers to save the convent and the sisters.

Outside the crackling of the greedy flames could already be heard. The fire king would soon destroy every building on that hill-top. Mad with terror, the sisters prepared to leave the compound and give up all their belongings to the cruel flames and still more cruel soldiers. Kwan-yin alone remained in the room, praying earnestly for help.

Suddenly a soft breeze sprang up from the neighbouring forest, dark clouds gathered overhead, and, although it was the dry season a drenching shower descended on the flames. Within five minutes the fire was put out and the convent was saved. Just as the shivering nuns were thanking Kwan-yin for the divine help she had brought them, two soldiers who had scaled the outer wall of the compound came in and roughly asked for the princess.

The trembling girl, knowing that these men were obeying her father's orders, poured out a prayer to the gods, and straightway made herself known. They dragged her from the presence of the nuns who had just begun to love her. Thus disgraced before her father's army, she was taken to the capital.

On the morrow, she was led before the old king. The father gazed sadly at his daughter, and then the stern look of a judge hardened his face as he beckoned the guards to bring her forward.

From a neighbouring room came the sounds of sweet music. A feast was being served there amid great splendour. The loud laughter of the guests reached the ears of the young girl as she bowed in disgrace before her father's throne. She knew that this feast had been prepared for her, and that her father was willing to give her one more chance.

"Girl," said the king, at last regaining his voice, "in leaving the royal palace on the eve of your wedding day, not only did you insult your father, but your king. For this act you deserve to die. However, because of the excellent record you had made for yourself before you ran away, I have decided to give you one more chance to redeem yourself. Refuse me, and the penalty is death: obey me, and all may yet be well – the kingdom that you spurned is still yours for the asking. All that I require is your marriage to the man whom I have chosen."

"And when, most august King, would you have me decide?" asked Kwan-yin earnestly.

"This very day, this very hour, this very moment," he answered sternly. "What! would you hesitate between love upon a throne and death? Speak, my daughter, tell me that you love me and will do my bidding!"

It was now all that Kwan-yin could do to keep from throwing herself at her father's feet and yielding to his wishes, not because he offered her a kingdom, but because she loved him and would gladly have made him happy. But her strong will kept her from relenting. No power on earth could have stayed her from doing what she thought her duty.

"Beloved father," she answered sadly, and her voice was full of tenderness, "it is not a question of my love for you – of that there is no question, for all my life I have shown it in every action. Believe me, if I were free to do your bidding, gladly would I make you happy, but a voice from the gods has spoken, has commanded that I remain a virgin, that I devote my life to deeds of mercy. When heaven itself has commanded, what can even a princess do but listen to that power which rules the earth?"

The old king was far from satisfied with Kwan-yin's answer. He grew furious, his thin wrinkled skin turned purple as the hot blood rose to his head. "Then you refuse to do my bidding! Take her, men! Give to her the death that is due to a traitor to the king!" As they bore Kwan-yin away from his presence the white-haired monarch fell, swooning, from his chair.

That night, when Kwan-yin was put to death, she descended into the lower world of torture. No sooner had she set foot in that dark country of the dead than the vast region of endless punishment suddenly blossomed forth and became like the gardens of Paradise. Pure white lilies sprang up on every side, and the odour of a million flowers filled all the rooms and corridors. King Yama, ruler of the dominion, rushed forth to learn the cause of this wonderful change. No sooner did his eyes rest upon the fair young face of Kwan-yin than he saw in her the emblem of a purity which deserved no home but heaven.

"Beautiful virgin, doer of many mercies," he began, after addressing her by her title, "I beg you in the name of justice to depart from this bloody kingdom. It is not right that the fairest flower of heaven should enter and shed her fragrance in these halls. Guilt must suffer here, and sin find no reward. Depart thou, then, from my dominion. The peach of immortal life shall be bestowed upon you, and heaven alone shall be your dwelling place."

Thus Kwan-yin became the Goddess of Mercy; thus she entered into that glad abode, surpassing all earthly kings and queens. And ever since that time, on account of her exceeding goodness, thousands of poor people breathe out to her each year their prayers for mercy. There is no fear in their gaze as they look at her beautiful image, for their eyes are filled with tears of love.

The War Between the Gods of Fire and Water

FOR A GREAT MANY YEARS after Nu Wa had created human beings, the earth remained a peaceful and joyous place and it was not until the final years of the Goddess's reign that mankind first encountered pain and suffering. For Nu Wa was extremely protective of the race she had created and considered it her supreme duty to shelter it from all harm and evil. People depended on Nu Wa for her guardianship and she, in turn, enabled them to live in comfort and security.

One day, however, two of the Gods who dwelt in the heavens, known as Gong Gong and Zhurong, became entangled in a fierce and bitter dispute. No one knew precisely why the two Gods began to shout and threaten one another, but before long they were resolved to do battle against each other and to remain fighting to the bitter end. Gong Gong, who was the God of Water, was well known as a violent and ambitious character and his bright red wavy hair perfectly mirrored his fiery and riotous spirit. Zhurong, the God of Fire, was equally belligerent when provoked and his great height and bulk rendered him no less terrifying in appearance.

Several days of fierce fighting ensued between the two of them during which the skies buckled and shifted under the strain of the combat. An end to this savage battle seemed to be nowhere in sight, as each God thrust and lunged with increasing fury and rage, determined to prove himself more powerful than the other. But on the fourth day, Gong Gong began to weary and Zhurong gained the upper hand, felling his opponent to the ground and causing him to tumble right out of the heavens.

Crashing to the earth with a loud bang, Gong Gong soon became acutely aware of the shame and disgrace of his defeat and decided that he would never again have the courage to face any of his fellow Gods. He was now resolved to end his own life and looked around him for some means by which he might perform this task honourably and successfully. And seeing a large mountain range in the distance rising in the shape of a giant pillar to the skies, Gong Gong ran towards it with all the speed he could muster and rammed his head violently against its base.

As soon as he had done this, a terrifying noise erupted from within the mountain, and gazing upwards, Gong Gong saw that a great wedge of rock had broken away from the peak, leaving behind a large gaping hole in the sky. Without the support of the mountain, the sky began to collapse and plummet towards the earth's surface, causing great crevasses to appear on impact. Many of these crevasses released intensely hot flames which instantly engulfed the earth's vegetation, while others spouted streams of filthy water which merged to form a great ocean. And as the flood and destruction spread throughout the entire world, Nu Wa's people no longer knew where to turn to for help. Thousands of them drowned, while others wandered the earth in terror and fear, their homes consumed by the raging flames and their crops destroyed by the swift-flowing water.

Nu Wa witnessed all of this in great distress and could not bear to see the race she had created suffer such appalling misery and deprivation. Though she was now old and looking forward to her time of rest, she decided that she must quickly take action to save her people, and it seemed that the only way for her to do this was to repair the heavens as soon as she possibly could with her very own hands.

Nu Wa Repairs the Sky

Nu Wa rapidly set about gathering the materials she needed to mend the great hole in the sky. One of the first places she visited in her search was the river Yangtze where she stooped down and gathered up as many pebbles as she could hold in both arms. These were carefully chosen in a variety of colours and carried to a forge in the heavens where they were melted down into a thick, gravel-like paste. Once she had returned to earth, Nu Wa began to repair the damage, anxiously filling the gaping hole with the paste and smoothing whatever remained of it into the surrounding cracks in the firmament. Then she hurried once more to the river bank and, collecting together the tallest reeds, she built a large, smouldering fire and burnt the reeds until they formed a huge mound of ashes. With these ashes Nu Wa sealed the crevasses of the earth, so that water no longer gushed out from beneath its surface and the swollen rivers gradually began to subside.

After she had done this, Nu Wa surveyed her work, yet she was still not convinced that she had done enough to prevent the heavens collapsing again in the future. So she went out and captured one of the giant immortal tortoises which were known to swim among the jagged rocks at the deepest point of the ocean and brought it ashore to slaughter it. And when she had killed the creature, she chopped off its four sturdy legs and stood them upright at the four points of the compass as extra support for the heavens. Only now was the Goddess satisfied and she began to gather round her some of her frightened people in an attempt to reassure them that order had finally been restored.

To help them forget the terrible experiences they had been put through, Nu Wa made a flute for them out of thirteen sticks of bamboo and with it she began to play the sweetest, most soothing music. All who heard it grew calmer almost at once and the earth slowly began to emerge from the chaos and destruction to which it had been subjected. From that day forth, Nu Wa's people honoured her by calling her 'Goddess of music' and many among them took great pride in learning the instrument she had introduced them to.

But even though the heavens had been repaired, the earth was never quite the same again. Gong Gong's damage to the mountain had caused the skies to tilt permanently towards the north-west so that the Pole Star, around which the heavens revolved, was dislodged from its position directly overhead. The sun and the moon were also tilted, this time in the direction of the west, leaving a great depression in the south-east. And not only that, but the peak of the mountain which had crashed to the earth had left a huge hollow where it landed in the east into which the rivers and streams of the world flowed incessantly.

Nu Wa had done all she could to salvage the earth and shortly afterwards, she died. Her body was transformed into a thousand fairies who watched over the human race on her behalf. Her people believe that the reason China's rivers flow eastwards was because of Gong Gong's foolish collision with the mountain, a belief that is still shared by their ancestors today.

The Ape Sun Wu King

FAR, FAR AWAY to the east, in the midst of the Great Sea there is an island called the Mountain of Flowers and Fruits. And on this mountain there is a high rock. Now this rock, from the very beginning of the world, had absorbed all the hidden seed power of heaven and earth and sun and moon, which endowed it with supernatural creative gifts. One day the rock burst, and out came an egg of stone. And out of this stone egg a stone ape was hatched by magic power. When he broke the shell he bowed to all sides. Then he gradually learned to walk and to leap, and two streams of golden radiance broke from his eyes which shot up to the highest of the castles of heaven, so that the Lord of the Heavens was frightened. So he sent out the two gods, Thousandmile-Eye and Fine-Ear, to find out what had happened. The two gods came back and reported: "The rays shine from the eyes of the stone ape who was hatched out of the egg which came from the magic rock. There is no reason for uneasiness."

Little by little the ape grew up, ran and leaped about, drank from the springs in the valleys, ate the flowers and fruits, and time went by in unconstrained play.

One day, during the summer, when he was seeking coolness, together with the other apes on the island, they went to the valley to bathe. There they saw a waterfall which plunged down a high cliff. Said the apes to each other: "Whoever can force his way through the waterfall, without suffering injury, shall be our king." The stone ape at once leaped into the air with joy and cried: "I will pass through!" Then he closed his eyes, bent down low and leaped through the roar and foam of the waters. When he opened his eyes once more he saw an iron bridge, which was shut off from the outer world by the waterfall as though by a curtain.

At its entrance stood a tablet of stone on which were graven the words: "This is the heavenly cave behind the water-curtain on the Blessed Island of Flowers and Fruits." Filled with joy, the stone ape leaped out again through the waterfall and told the other apes what he had found. They received the news with great content, and begged the stone ape to take them there. So the tribe of apes leaped through the water on the iron bridge, and then crowded into the cave castle where they found a hearth with a profusion of pots, cups and platters. But all were made of stone. Then the apes paid homage to the stone ape as their king, and he was given the name of Handsome King of the Apes. He appointed long-tailed, ring-tailed and other monkeys to be his officials and counsellors, servants and retainers, and they led a blissful life on the mountain, sleeping by night in their cave castle, keeping away from birds and beasts, and their king enjoyed untroubled happiness. In this way some three hundred years went by.

One day, when the King of the Apes sat with his subjects at a merry meal, he suddenly began to weep. Frightened, the apes asked him why he so suddenly grew sad amid all his bliss. Said the King: "It is true that we are not subject to the law and rule of man, that birds and beasts do not dare attack us, yet little by little we grow old and weak, and some day the hour will strike when Death, the Ancient, will drag us off! Then we are gone in a moment, and can no longer dwell upon earth!" When the apes heard these words, they hid their faces and sobbed. But an old ape, whose arms were connected in such a way that he could add the length of one to that of the other, stepped forth from the ranks. In a loud tone of voice he said: "That you have hit upon this thought, O King, shows the desire to search for truth has awakened you! Among all living creatures, there are but three kinds who are exempt from Death's power: the Buddhas, the blessed spirits and the gods. Whoever attains one of these three grades escapes the rod of re-birth, and lives as long as the Heavens themselves."

The King of the Apes said: "Where do these three kinds of beings live?" And the old ape replied: "They live in caves and on holy mountains in the great world of mortals." The King was pleased when he heard this, and told his apes that he was going to seek out gods and sainted spirits in order to learn the road to immortality from them. The apes dragged up peaches and other fruits and sweet wine to celebrate the parting banquet, and all made merry together.

On the following morning the Handsome King of the Apes rose very early, built him a raft of old pine trees and took a bamboo staff for a pole. Then he climbed on the raft, quite alone, and poled his way through the Great Sea. Wind and waves were favourable and he reached Asia. There he went ashore. On the strand he met a fisherman. He at once stepped up to him, knocked him down, tore off his clothes and put them on himself. Then he wandered around and visited all famous spots, went into the market-places, the densely populated cities, learned how to conduct himself properly, and how to speak and act like a well-bred human being. Yet his heart was set on learning the teaching of the Buddhas, the blessed spirits and the holy gods. But the people of the country in which he was were only concerned with honours and wealth. Not one of them seemed to care for life. Thus he went about until nine years had passed by unnoticed. Then he came to the strand of the Western Sea and it occurred to him: "No doubt there are gods and saints on the other side of the sea!" So he built another raft, floated it over the Western Sea and reached the land of the west. There he let his raft drift, and went ashore. After he had searched for many days, he suddenly saw a high mountain with deep, quiet valleys. As the Ape King went toward it, he heard a man singing in the woods, and the song sounded like one the blessed spirits might sing. So he hastily entered the wood to see who might be singing. There he met a wood-chopper at work. The Ape King bowed to him and said: "Venerable, divine master, I fall down and worship at your feet!"

Said the wood-chopper: "I am only a workman; why do you call me divine master?"

"Then, if you are no blessed god, how comes it you sing that divine song?" The wood-chopper laughed and said: "You are at home in music. The song I was singing was really taught me by a saint."

"If you are acquainted with a saint," said the Ape King, "he surely cannot live far from here. I beg of you to show me the way to his dwelling."

The wood-chopper replied: "It is not far from here. This mountain is known as the Mountain of the Heart. In it is a cave where dwells a saint who is called 'The Discerner.' The number of his disciples who have attained blessedness is countless. He still has some thirty to forty disciples gathered about him. You need only follow this path which leads to the south, and you cannot miss his dwelling." The Ape King thanked the wood-chopper and, sure enough, he came to the cave which the latter had described to him. The gate was locked and he did not venture to knock. So he leaped up into a pine tree, picked pine-cones and devoured the seed.

Before long one of the saint's disciples came and opened the door and said: "What sort of a beast is it that is making such a noise?" The Ape King leaped down from his tree, bowed, and said: "I have come in search of truth. I did not venture to knock." Then the disciple had to laugh and said: "Our master was seated lost in meditation, when he told me to lead in the seeker after truth who stood without the gate, and here you really are. Well, you may come along with me!" The Ape King smoothed his clothes, put his hat on straight, and stepped in. A long passage led past magnificent buildings and quiet hidden huts to the place where the master was sitting upright on a seat of white marble. At his right and left stood his disciples, ready to serve him. The Ape King flung himself down on the ground and greeted the master humbly. In answer to his questions he told him how he had found his way to him. And when he was asked his name, he said: "I have no name. I am the ape who came out of the stone." So the master said: "Then I will give you a name. I name you Sun Wu Kung." The Ape King thanked him, full of joy, and thereafter he was called Sun Wu Kung. The master ordered his oldest disciple to instruct Sun Wu Kung in sweeping and cleaning, in going in and out, in good manners, how to labour in the field and how to water the gardens. In the course of time he learned to write, to burn incense and read the sutras. And in this way some six or seven years went by.

One day the master ascended the seat from which he taught, and began to speak regarding the great truth. Sun Wu Kung understood the hidden meaning of his words, and commenced to jerk about and dance in his joy. The master reproved him: "Sun Wu Kung, you have still not laid aside your wild nature! What do you mean by carrying on in such an unfitting manner?" Sun Wu Kung bowed and answered: "I was listening attentively to you when the meaning of your words was disclosed to my heart, and without thinking I began to dance for joy. I was not giving way to my wild nature." Said the master: "If your spirit has really awakened, then I will announce the great truth to you. But there are three hundred and sixty ways by means of which one may reach this truth. Which way shall I teach you?" Said Sun Wu Kung: "Whichever you will, O Master!" Then the Master asked: "Shall I teach you the way of magic?" Said Sun Wu Kung: "What does magic teach one?" The Master replied: "It teaches one to raise up spirits, to question oracles, and to foretell fortune and misfortune."

"Can one secure eternal life by means of it?" inquired Sun Wu Kung.

"No," was the answer.

"Then I will not learn it."

"Shall I teach you the sciences?"

"What are the sciences?"

"They are the nine schools of the three faiths. You learn how to read the holy books, pronounce incantations, commune with the gods, and call the saints to you."

"Can one gain eternal life by means of them?"

"No."

"Then I will not learn them."

"The way of repose is a very good way."

"What is the way of repose?"

"It teaches how to live without nourishment, how to remain quiescent in silent purity, and sit lost in meditation."

"Can one gain eternal life in this way?"

"No."

"Then I will not learn it."

"The way of deeds is also a good way."

"What does that teach?"

"It teaches one to equalize the vital powers, to practise bodily exercise, to prepare the elixir of life and to hold one's breath."

"Will it give one eternal life?"

"Not so."

"Then I will not learn it! I will not learn it!"

Thereupon the Master pretended to be angry, leaped down from his stand, took his cane and scolded: "What an ape! This he will not learn, and that he will not learn! What are you waiting to learn, then?" With that he gave him three blows across the head, retired to his inner chamber, and closed the great door after him.

The disciples were greatly excited, and overwhelmed Sun Wu Kung with reproaches. Yet the latter paid no attention to them, but smiled quietly to himself, for he had understood the riddle which the Master had given him to solve. And in his heart he thought: "His striking me over the head three times meant that I was to be ready at the third watch of the night. His withdrawing to his inner chamber and closing the great door after him, meant that I was to go in to him by the back door, and that he would make clear the great truth to me in secret." Accordingly he waited until evening, and made a pretense of lying down to sleep with the other disciples. But when the third watch of the night had come he rose softly and crept to the back door. Sure enough it stood ajar. He slipped in and stepped before the Master's bed. The Master was sleeping with his face turned toward the wall, and the ape did not venture to wake him, but knelt down in front of the bed. After a time the Master turned around and hummed a stanza to himself:

"A hard, hard grind,Truth's lesson to expound.One talks oneself deaf, dumb and blind,Unless the right man's found."

Then Sun Wu Kung replied: "I am waiting here reverentially!"

The Master flung on his clothes, sat up in bed and said harshly: "Accursed ape! Why are you not asleep? What are you doing here?"

Sun Wu Kung answered: "Yet you pointed out to me yesterday that I was to come to you at the third watch of the night, by the back door, in order to be instructed in the truth. Therefore I have ventured to come. If you will teach me in the fulness of your grace, I will be eternally grateful to you."

Thought the Master to himself: "There is real intelligence in this ape's head, to have made him understand me so well." Then he replied: "Sun Wu Kung, it shall be granted you! I will speak freely with you. Come quite close to me, and then I will show you the way to eternal life."

With that he murmured into his ear a divine, magical incantation to further the concentration of his vital powers, and explained the hidden knowledge word for word. Sun Wu Kung listened to him eagerly, and in a short time had learned it by heart. Then he thanked his teacher, went out again and lay down to sleep. From that time forward he practised the right mode of breathing, kept guard over his soul and spirit, and tamed the natural instincts of his heart. And while he did so three more years passed by. Then the task was completed.

One day the Master said to him: "Three great dangers still threaten you. Everyone who wishes to accomplish something out of the ordinary is exposed to them, for he is pursued by the envy of demons and spirits. And only those who can overcome these three great dangers live as long as the heavens."

Then Sun Wu Kung was frightened and asked: "Is there any means of protection against these dangers?"

Then the Master again murmured a secret incantation into his ear, by means of which he gained the power to transform himself seventy-two times.

And when no more than a few days had passed Sun Wu Kung had learned the art.

One day the Master was walking before the cave in the company of his disciples. He called Sun Wu Kung up to him and asked: "What progress have you made with your art? Can you fly already?"

"Yes, indeed," said the ape.

"Then let me see you do so."

The ape leaped into the air to a distance of five or six feet from the ground. Clouds formed beneath his feet, and he was able to walk on them for several hundred yards. Then he was forced to drop down to earth again.

The Master said with a smile: "I call that crawling around on the clouds, not floating on them, as do the gods and saints who fly over the whole world in a single day. I will teach you the magic incantation for turning somersaults on the clouds. If you turn one of those somersaults you advance eighteen thousand miles at a clip."

Sun Wu Kung thanked him, full of joy, and from that time on he was able to move without limitation of space in any direction.

One day Sun Wu Kung was sitting together with the other disciples under the pine-tree by the gate, discussing the secrets of their teachings. Finally they asked him to show them some of his transforming arts. Sun Wu Kung could not keep his secret to himself, and agreed to do so.

With a smile he said: "Just set me a task! What do you wish me to change myself into?"

They said: "Turn yourself into a pine-tree."

So Sun Wu Kung murmured a magic incantation, turned around – and there stood a pine-tree before their very eyes. At this they all broke out into a horse-laugh. The Master heard the noise and came out of the gate, dragging his cane behind him.

"Why are you making such a noise?" he called out to them harshly.

Said they: "Sun Wu Kung has turned himself into a pine-tree, and this made us laugh."

"Sun Wu Kung, come here!" said the Master. "Now just tell me what tricks you are up to? Why do you have to turn yourself into a pine-tree? All the work you have done means nothing more to you than a chance to make magic for your companions to wonder at. That shows that your heart is not yet under control."

Humbly Sun Wu Kung begged his forgiveness.

But the Master said: "I bear you no ill will, but you must go away."

With tears in his eyes Sun Wu Kung asked him: "But where shall I go?"

"You must go back again whence you came," said the Master. And when Sun Wu Kung sadly bade him farewell, he threatened him: "Your savage nature is sure to bring down evil upon you some time. You must tell no one that you are my pupil. If you so much as breathe a word about it, I will fetch your soul and lock it up in the nethermost hell, so that you cannot escape for a thousand eternities."

Sun Wu Kung replied: "I will not say a word! I will not say a word!"

Then he once more thanked him for all the kindness shown him, turned a somersault and climbed up to the clouds.

Within the hour he had passed the seas, and saw the Mountain of Flowers and Fruits lying before him. Then he felt happy and at home again, let his cloud sink down to earth and cried: "Here I am back again, children!" And at once, from the valley, from behind the rocks, out of the grass and from amid the trees came his apes. They came running up by thousands, surrounded and greeted him, and inquired as to his adventures. Sun Wu Kung said: "I have now found the way to eternal life, and need fear Death the Ancient no longer." Then all the apes were overjoyed, and competed with each other in bringing flowers and fruits, peaches and wine, to welcome him. And again they honoured Sun Wu Kung as the Handsome Ape King.

Sun Wu Kung now gathered the apes about him and questioned them as to how they had fared during his absence.

Said they: "It is well that you have come back again, great king! Not long ago a devil came here who wanted to take possession of our cave by force. We fought with him, but he dragged away many of your children and will probably soon return."

Sun Wu Kung grew very angry and said: "What sort of a devil is this who dares be so impudent?"

The apes answered: "He is the Devil-King of Chaos. He lives in the north, who knows how many miles away. We only saw him come and go amid clouds and mist."

Sun Wu Kung said: "Wait, and I will see to him!" With that he turned a somersault and disappeared without a trace.

In the furthest north rises a high mountain, upon whose slope is a cave above which is the inscription: 'The Cave of the Kidneys.' Before the door little devils were dancing. Sun Wu Kung called harshly to them: "Tell your Devil-King quickly that he had better give me my children back again!" The little devils were frightened, and delivered the message in the cave. Then the Devil-King reached for his sword and came out. But he was so large and broad that he could not even see Sun Wu Kung. He was clad from head to foot in black armour, and his face was as black as the bottom of a kettle. Sun Wu Kung shouted at him: "Accursed devil, where are your eyes, that you cannot see the venerable Sun?" Then the devil looked to the ground and saw a stone ape standing before him, bare-headed, dressed in red, with a yellow girdle and black boots. So the Devil-King laughed and said: "You are not even four feet high, less than thirty years of age, and weaponless, and yet you venture to make such a commotion." Said Sun Wu Kung: "I am not too small for you; and I can make myself large at will. You scorn me because I am without a weapon, but my two fists can thresh to the very skies." With that he stooped, clenched his fists and began to give the devil a beating.

The devil was large and clumsy, but Sun Wu Kung leaped about nimbly. He struck him between the ribs and between the wind and his blows fell ever more fast and furious. In his despair the devil raised his great knife and aimed a blow at Sun Wu Kung's head. But the latter avoided the blow, and fell back on his magic powers of transformation. He pulled out a hair, put it in his mouth, chewed it, spat it out into the air and said: "Transform yourself!" And at once it turned into many hundreds of little apes who began to attack the devil. Sun Wu Kung, be it said, had eighty-four thousand hairs on his body, every single one of which he could transform. The little apes with their sharp eyes, leaped around with the greatest rapidity. They surrounded the Devil-King on all sides, tore at his clothes, and pulled at his legs, until he finally measured his length on the ground. Then Sun Wu Kung stepped up, tore his knife from his hand, and put an end to him. After that he entered the cave and released his captive children, the apes. The transformed hairs he drew to him again, and making a fire, he burned the evil cave to the ground. Then he gathered up those he had released, and flew back with them like a storm-wind to his cavern on the Mountain of Flowers and Fruits, joyfully greeted by all the apes.

After Sun Wu Kung had obtained possession of the Devil-King's great knife, he exercised his apes every day. They had wooden swords and lances of bamboo, and played their martial music on reed pipes. He had them build a camp so that they would be prepared for all dangers. Suddenly the thought came to Sun Wu Kung: "If we go on this way, perhaps we may incite some human or animal king to fight with us, and then we would not be able to withstand him with our wooden swords and bamboo lances!" And to his apes he said: "What should be done?" Four baboons stepped forward and said: "In the capital city of the Aulai empire there are warriors without number. And there coppersmiths and steelsmiths are also to be found. How would it be if we were to buy steel and iron and have those smiths weld weapons for us?"

A somersault and Sun Wu Kung was standing before the city moat. Said he to himself: "To first buy the weapons would take a great deal of time. I would rather make magic and take some." So he blew on the ground. Then a tremendous storm-wind arose which drove sand and stones before it, and caused all the soldiers in the city to run away in terror. Then Sun Wu Kung went to the armoury, pulled out one of his hairs, turned it into thousands of little apes, cleared out the whole supply of weapons, and flew back home on a cloud.

Then he gathered his people about him and counted them. In all they numbered seventy-seven thousand. They held the whole mountain in terror, and all the magic beasts and spirit princes who dwelt on it. And these came forth from seventy-two caves and honoured Sun Wu Kung as their head.

One day the Ape King said: "Now you all have weapons; but this knife which I took from the Devil-King is too light, and no longer suits me. What should be done?"

Then the four baboons stepped forward and said: "In view of your spirit powers, O king, you will find no weapon fit for your use on all the earth! Is it possible for you to walk through the water?"

The Ape King answered: "All the elements are subject to me and there is no place where I cannot go."

Then the baboons said: "The water at our cave here flows into the Great Sea, to the castle of the Dragon-King of the Eastern Sea. If your magic power makes it possible, you could go to the Dragon-King and let him give you a weapon."

This suited the Ape King. He leaped on the iron bridge and murmured an incantation. Then he flung himself into the waves, which parted before him and ran on till he came to the palace of water-crystal. There he met a Triton who asked who he was. He mentioned his name and said: "I am the Dragon-King's nearest neighbour, and have come to visit him." The Triton took the message to the castle, and the Dragon-King of the Eastern Sea came out hastily to receive him. He bade him be seated and served him with tea.

Sun Wu Kung said: "I have learned the hidden knowledge and gained the powers of immortality. I have drilled my apes in the art of warfare in order to protect our mountain; but I have no weapon I can use, and have therefore come to you to borrow one."

The Dragon-King now had General Flounder bring him a great spear. But Sun Wu Kung was not satisfied with it. Then he ordered Field-Marshal Eel to fetch in a nine-tined fork, which weighed three thousand six hundred pounds. But Sun Wu Kung balanced it in his hand and said: "Too light! Too light! Too light!"

Then the Dragon-King was frightened, and had the heaviest weapon in his armoury brought in. It weighed seven thousand two hundred pounds. But this was still too light for Sun Wu Kung. The Dragon-King assured him that he had nothing heavier, but Sun Wu Kung would not give in and said: "Just look around!"

Finally the Dragon-Queen and her daughter came out, and said to the Dragon-King: "This saint is an unpleasant customer with whom to deal. The great iron bar is still lying here in our sea; and not so long ago it shone with a red glow, which is probably a sign it is time for it to be taken away."

Said the Dragon-King: "But that is the rod which the Great Yu used when he ordered the waters, and determined the depth of the seas and rivers. It cannot be taken away."

The Dragon-Queen replied: "Just let him see it! What he then does with it is no concern of ours."

So the Dragon-King led Sun Wu Kung to the measuring rod. The golden radiance that came from it could be seen some distance off. It was an enormous iron bar, with golden clamps on either side.

Sun Wu Kung raised it with the exertion of all his strength, and then said: "It is too heavy, and ought to be somewhat shorter and thinner!"

No sooner had he said this than the iron rod grew less. He tried it again, and then he noticed that it grew larger or smaller at command. It could be made to shrink to the size of a pin. Sun Wu Kung was overjoyed and beat about in the sea with the rod, which he had let grow large again, till the waves spurted mountain-high and the dragon-castle rocked on its foundations. The Dragon-King trembled with fright, and all his tortoises, fishes and crabs drew in their heads.

Sun Wu Kung laughed, and said: "Many thanks for the handsome present!" Then he continued: "Now I have a weapon, it is true, but as yet I have no armour. Rather than hunt up two or three other households, I think you will be willing to provide me with a suit of mail."

The Dragon-King told him that he had no armour to give him.

Then the ape said: "I will not leave until you have obtained one for me." And once more he began to swing his rod.

"Do not harm me!" said the terrified Dragon-King, "I will ask my brothers."

And he had them beat the iron drum and strike the golden gong, and in a moment's time all the Dragon-King's brothers came from all the other seas. The Dragon-King talked to them in private and said: "This is a terrible fellow, and we must not rouse his anger! First he took the rod with the golden clamps from me, and now he also insists on having a suit of armour. The best thing to do would be to satisfy him at once, and complain of him to the Lord of the Heavens later."

So the brothers brought a magic suit of golden mail, magic boots and a magic helmet.

Then Sun Wu Kung thanked them and returned to his cave. Radiantly he greeted his children, who had come to meet him, and showed them the rod with the golden clamps.

They all crowded up and wished to pick it up from the ground, if only a single time; but it was just as though a dragon-fly had attempted to overthrow a stone column, or an ant were trying to carry a great mountain. It would not move a hair's breadth. Then the apes opened their mouths and stuck out their tongues, and said: "Father, how is it possible for you to carry that heavy thing?" So he told them the secret of the rod and showed them its effects. Then he set his empire in order, and appointed the four baboons field-marshals; and the seven beast-spirits, the ox-spirit, the dragon-spirit, the bird-spirit, the lion-spirit and the rest also joined him.

One day he took a nap after dinner. Before he did so he had let the bar shrink, and had stuck it in his ear. While he was sleeping he saw two men come along in his dream, who had a card on which was written 'Sun Wu Kung.' They would not allow him to resist, but fettered him and led his spirit away. And when they reached a great city the Ape King gradually came to himself. Over the city gate he saw a tablet of iron on which was engraved in large letters: 'The Nether World.'

Then all was suddenly clear to him and he said: "Why, this must be the dwelling-place of Death! But I have long since escaped from his power, and how dare he have me dragged here!" The more he reflected the wilder he grew. He drew out the golden rod from his ear, swung it and let it grow large. Then he crushed the two constables to mush, burst his fetters, and rolled his bar before him into the city. The ten Princes of the Dead were frightened, bowed before him and asked: "Who are you?"

Sun Wu Kung answered: "If you do not know me then why did you send for me and have me dragged to this place? I am the heaven-born saint Sun Wu Kung of the Mountain of Flowers and Fruits. And now, who are you? Tell me your names quickly or I will strike you!"

The ten Princes of the Dead humbly gave him their names.

Sun Wu Kung said: "I, the Venerable Sun, have gained the power of eternal life! You have nothing to say to me! Quick, let me have the Book of Life!"

They did not dare defy him, and had the scribe bring in the book. Sun Wu Kung opened it. Under the head of 'Apes,' No. 1350, he read: "Sun Wu Kung, the heaven-born stone ape. His years shall be three hundred and twenty-four. Then he shall die without illness."

Sun Wu Kung took the brush from the table and struck out the whole ape family from the Book of Life, threw the book down and said: "Now we are even! From this day on I will suffer no impertinences from you!"

With that he cleared a way for himself out of the Nether World by means of his rod, and the ten Princes of the Dead did not venture to stay him, but only complained of him afterward to the Lord of the Heavens.

When Sun Wu Kung had left the city he slipped and fell to the ground. This caused him to wake, and he noticed he had been dreaming. He called his four baboons to him and said: "Splendid, splendid! I was dragged to Death's castle and I caused considerable uproar there. I had them give me the Book of Life, and I struck out the mortal hour of all the apes!" And after that time the apes on the mountain no longer died, because their names had been stricken out in the Nether World.

But the Lord of the Heavens sat in his castle, and had all his servants assembled about him. And a saint stepped forward and presented the complaint of the Dragon-King of the Eastern Sea. And another stepped forward and presented the complaint of the ten Princes of the Dead. The Lord of the Heavens glanced through the two memorials. Both told of the wild, unmannerly conduct of Sun Wu Kung. So the Lord of the Heavens ordered a god to descend to earth and take him prisoner. The Evening Star came forward, however, and said: "This ape was born of the purest powers of heaven and earth and sun and moon. He has gained the hidden knowledge and has become an immortal. Recall, O Lord, your great love for all that which has life, and forgive him his sin! Issue an order that he be called up to the heavens, and be given a charge here, so that he may come to his senses. Then, if he again oversteps your commands, let him be punished without mercy." The Lord of the Heavens was agreeable, had the order issued, and told the Evening Star to take it to Sun Wu Kung. The Evening Star mounted a coloured cloud and descended on the Mountain of Flowers and Fruits.

He greeted Sun Wu Kung and said to him: "The Lord had heard of your actions and meant to punish you. I am the Evening Star of the Western Skies, and I spoke for you. Therefore he has commissioned me to take you to the skies, so that you may be given a charge there."

Sun Wu Kung was overjoyed and answered: "I had just been thinking I ought to pay Heaven a visit some time, and sure enough, Old Star, here you have come to fetch me!"

Then he had his four baboons come and said to them impressively: "See that you take good care of our mountain! I am going up to the heavens to look around there a little!"

Then he mounted a cloud together with the Evening Star and floated up. But he kept turning his somersaults, and advanced so quickly that the Evening Star on his cloud was left behind. Before he knew it he had reached the Southern Gate of Heaven and was about to step carelessly through. The gate-keeper did not wish to let him enter, but he did not let this stop him. In the midst of their dispute the Evening Star came up and explained matters, and then he was allowed to enter the heavenly gate. When he came to the castle of the Lord of the Heavens, he stood upright before it, without bowing his head.

The Lord of the Heavens asked: "Then this hairy face with the pointed lips is Sun Wu Kung?"

He replied: "Yes, I am the Venerable Sun!"

All the servants of the Lord of the Heavens were shocked and said: "This wild ape does not even bow, and goes so far as to call himself the Venerable Sun. His crime deserves a thousand deaths!"

But the Lord said: "He has come up from the earth below, and is not as yet used to our rules. We will forgive him."

Then he gave orders that a charge be found for him. The marshal of the heavenly court reported: "There is no charge vacant anywhere, but an official is needed in the heavenly stables." Thereupon the Lord made him stablemaster of the heavenly steeds. Then the servants of the Lord of the Heavens told him he should give thanks for the grace bestowed on him. Sun Wu Kung called out aloud: "Thanks to command!" took possession of his certificate of appointment, and went to the stables in order to enter upon his new office.

Sun Wu Kung attended to his duties with great zeal. The heavenly steeds grew sleek and fat, and the stables were filled with young foals. Before he knew it half a month had gone by. Then his heavenly friends prepared a banquet for him.

While they were at table Sun Wu Kung asked accidentally: "Stablemaster? What sort of a title is that?"

"Why, that is an official title," was the reply.

"What rank has this office?"

"It has no rank at all," was the answer.

"Ah," said the ape, "is it so high that it outranks all other dignities?"

"No, it is not high, it is not high at all," answered his friends. "It is not even set down in the official roster, but is quite a subordinate position. All you have to do is to attend to the steeds. If you see to it that they grow fat, you get a good mark; but if they grow thin or ill, or fall down, your punishment will be right at hand."

Then the Ape King grew angry: "What, they treat me, the Venerable Sun, in such a shameful way!" and he started up. "On my mountain I was a king, I was a father! What need was there for him to lure me into his heaven to feed horses? I'll do it no longer! I'll do it no longer!"

Hola, and he had already overturned the table, drawn the rod with the golden clamps from his ear, let it grow large and beat a way out for himself to the Southern gate of Heaven. And no one dared stop him.

Already he was back in his island mountain and his people surrounded him and said: "You have been gone for more than ten years, great king! How is it you do not return to us until now?"

The Ape King said: "I did not spend more than about ten days in Heaven. This Lord of the Heavens does not know how to treat his people. He made me his stablemaster, and I had to feed his horses. I am so ashamed that I am ready to die. But I did not put up with it, and now I am here once more!"

His apes eagerly prepared a banquet to comfort him. While they sat at table two horned devil-kings came and brought him a yellow imperial robe as a present. Filled with joy he slipped into it, and appointed the two devil-kings leaders of the vanguard. They thanked him and began to flatter him: "With your power and wisdom, great king, why should you have to serve the Lord of the Heavens? To call you the Great Saint who is Heaven's Equal would be quite in order."

The ape was pleased with this speech and said: "Good, good!" Then he ordered his four baboons to have a flag made quickly, on which was to be inscribed: 'The Great Saint Who Is Heaven's Equal.' And from that time on he had himself called by that title.

When the Lord of the Heavens learned of the flight of the ape, he ordered Li Dsing, the pagoda-bearing god, and his third son, Notscha, to take the Ape King prisoner. They sallied forth at the head of a heavenly warrior host, laid out a camp before his cave, and sent a brave warrior to challenge him to single combat. But he was easily beaten by Sun Wu Kung and obliged to flee, and Sun Wu Kung even shouted after him, laughing: "What a bag of wind! And he calls himself a heavenly warrior! I'll not slay you. Run along quickly and send me a better man!"

When Notscha saw this he himself hurried up to do battle.

Said Sun Wu Kung to him: "To whom do you belong, little one? You must not play around here, for something might happen to you!"

But Notscha cried out in a loud voice: "Accursed ape! I am Prince Notscha, and have been ordered to take you prisoner!" And with that he swung his sword in the direction of Sun Wu Kung.

"Very well," said the latter, "I will stand here and never move."

Then Notscha grew very angry, and turned into a three-headed god with six arms, in which he held six different weapons. Thus he rushed on to the attack.

Sun Wu Kung laughed. "The little fellow knows the trick of it! But easy, wait a bit! I will change shape, too!"

And he also turned himself into a figure with three heads and with six arms, and swung three gold-clamp rods. And thus they began to fight. Their blows rained down with such rapidity that it seemed as though thousands of weapons were flying through the air. After thirty rounds the combat had not yet been decided. Then Sun Wu Kung hit upon an idea. He secretly pulled out one of his hairs, turned it into his own shape, and let it continue the fight with Notscha. He himself, however, slipped behind Notscha, and gave him such a blow on the left arm with his rod that his knees gave way beneath him with pain, and he had to withdraw in defeat.

So Notscha told his father Li Dsing: "This devil-ape is altogether too powerful! I cannot get the better of him!" There was nothing left to do but to return to the Heavens and admit their overthrow. The Lord of the Heavens bowed his head, and tried to think of some other hero whom he might send out.

Then the Evening Star once more came forward and said: "This ape is so strong and so courageous, that probably not one of us here is a match for him. He revolted because the office of stablemaster appeared too lowly for him. The best thing would be to temper justice with mercy, let him have his way, and appoint him Great Saint Who Is Heaven's Equal. It will only be necessary to give him the empty title, without combining a charge with it, and then the matter would be settled."

The Lord of the Heavens was satisfied with this suggestion, and once more sent the Evening Star to summon the new saint. When Sun Wu Kung heard that he had arrived, he said: "The old Evening Star is a good fellow!" and he had his army draw up in line to give him a festive reception. He himself donned his robes of ceremony and politely went out to meet him.

Then the Evening Star told him what had taken place in the Heavens, and that he had his appointment as Great Saint Who Is Heaven's Equal with him.

Thereupon the Great Saint laughed and said: "You also spoke in my behalf before, Old Star! And now you have again taken my part. Many thanks! Many thanks!"

Then when they appeared together in the presence of the Lord of the Heavens the latter said: "The rank of Great Saint Who Is Heaven's Equal is very high. But now you must not cut any further capers."

The Great Saint expressed his thanks, and the Lord of the Heavens ordered two skilled architects to build a castle for him east of the peach-garden of the Queen-Mother of the West. And he was led into it with all possible honours.

Now the Saint was in his element. He had all that heart could wish for, and was untroubled by any work. He took his ease, walked about in the Heavens as he chose, and paid visits to the gods. The Three Pure Ones and the Four Rulers he treated with some little respect; but the planetary gods and the lords of the twenty-eight houses of the moon, and of the twelve zodiac signs, and the other stars he addressed familiarly with a "Hey, you!" Thus he idled day by day, without occupation among the clouds of the Heavens. On one occasion one of the wise said to the Lord of the Heavens: "The holy Sun is idle while day follows day. It is to be feared that some mischievous thoughts may occur to him, and it might be better to give him some charge."

So the Lord of the Heavens summoned the Great Saint and said to him: "The life-giving peaches in the garden of the Queen-Mother will soon be ripe. I give you the charge of watching over them. Do your duty conscientiously!"

This pleased the Saint and he expressed his thanks. Then he went to the garden, where the caretakers and gardeners received him on their knees.

He asked them: "How many trees in all are there in the garden?"

"Three thousand six hundred," replied the gardener. "There are twelve-hundred trees in the foremost row. They have red blossoms and bear small fruit, which ripens every three thousand years. Whoever eats it grows bright and healthy. The twelve hundred trees in the middle row have double blossoms and bear sweet fruit, which ripens every six thousand years. Whoever eats of it is able to float in the rose-dawn without aging. The twelve hundred trees in the last row bear red-striped fruit with small pits. They ripen every nine thousand years. Whoever eats their fruit lives eternally, as long as the Heavens themselves, and remains untouched for thousands of eons."

The Saint heard all this with pleasure. He checked up the lists and from that time on appeared every day or so to see to things. The greater part of the peaches in the last row were already ripe. When he came to the garden, he would on each occasion send away the caretakers and gardeners under some pretext, leap up into the trees, and gorge himself to his heart's content with the peaches.

At that time the Queen-Mother of the West was preparing the great peach banquet to which she was accustomed to invite all the gods of the Heavens. She sent out the fairies in their garments of seven colours with baskets, that they might pick the peaches. The caretaker said to them: "The garden has now been entrusted to the guardianship of the Great Saint Who is Heaven's Equal, so you will first have to announce yourselves to him." With that he led the seven fairies into the garden. There they looked everywhere for the Great Saint, but could not find him. So the fairies said: "We have our orders and must not be late. We will begin picking the peaches in the meantime!" So they picked several baskets full from the foremost row. In the second row the peaches were already scarcer. And in the last row there hung only a single half-ripe peach. They bent down the bough and picked it, and then allowed it to fly up again.

Now it happened that the Great Saint, who had turned himself into a peach-worm, had just been taking his noon-day nap on this bough. When he was so rudely awakened, he appeared in his true form, seized his rod and was about to strike the fairies.

But the fairies said: "We have been sent here by the Queen-Mother. Do not be angry, Great Saint!"

Said the Great Saint: "And who are all those whom the Queen-Mother has invited?"

They answered: "All the gods and saints in the Heavens, on the earth and under the earth."

"Has she also invited me?" said the Saint.

"Not that we know of," said the fairies.

Then the Saint grew angry, murmured a magic incantation and said: "Stay! Stay! Stay!"

With that the seven fairies were banned to the spot. The Saint then took a cloud and sailed away on it to the palace of the Queen-Mother.

On the way he met the Bare-Foot God and asked him: "Where are you going?"

"To the peach banquet," was the answer.

Then the Saint lied to him, saying: "I have been commanded by the Lord of the Heavens to tell all the gods and saints that they are first to come to the Hall of Purity, in order to practise the rites, and then go together to the Queen-Mother."

Then the Great Saint changed himself into the semblance of the Bare-Foot God and sailed to the palace of the Queen-Mother. There he let his cloud sink down and entered quite unconcerned. The meal was ready, yet none of the gods had as yet appeared. Suddenly the Great Saint caught the aroma of wine, and saw well-nigh a hundred barrels of the precious nectar standing in a room to one side. His mouth watered. He tore a few hairs out and turned them into sleep-worms. These worms crept into the nostrils of the cup-bearers so that they all fell asleep. Thereupon he enjoyed the delicious viands to the full, opened the barrels and drank until he was nearly stupefied. Then he said to himself: "This whole affair is beginning to make me feel creepy. I had better go home first of all and sleep a bit." And he stumbled out of the garden with uncertain steps. Sure enough, he missed his way, and came to the dwelling of Laotzse. There he regained consciousness. He arranged his clothing and went in. There was no one to be seen in the place, for at the moment Laotzse was at the God of Light's abode, talking to him, and with him were all his servants, listening. Since he found no one at home the Great Saint went as far as the inner chamber, where Laotzse was in the habit of brewing the elixir of life. Beside the stove stood five gourd containers full of the pills of life which had already been rolled. Said the Great Saint: "I had long since intended to prepare a couple of these pills. So it suits me very well to find them here." He poured out the contents of the gourds, and ate up all the pills of life. Since he had now had enough to eat and drink he thought to himself: "Bad, bad! The mischief I have done cannot well be repaired. If they catch me my life will be in danger. I think I had better go down to earth again and remain a king!" With that he made himself invisible, went out at the Western Gate of Heaven, and returned to the Mountain of Flowers and Fruits, where he told his people who received him the story of his adventures.

When he spoke of the wine-nectar of the peach garden, his apes said: "Can't you go back once more and steal a few bottles of the wine, so that we too may taste of it and gain eternal life?"

The Ape King was willing, turned a somersault, crept into the garden unobserved, and picked up four more barrels. Two of them he took under his arms and two he held in his hands. Then he disappeared with them without leaving a trace and brought them to his cave, where he enjoyed them together with his apes.

In the meantime the seven fairies, whom the Great Saint had banned to the spot, had regained their freedom after a night and a day. They picked up their baskets and told the Queen-Mother what had happened to them. And the cup-bearers, too, came hurrying up and reported the destruction which someone unknown had caused among the eatables and drinkables. The Queen-Mother went to the Lord of the Heavens to complain. Shortly afterward Laotzse also came to him to tell about the theft of the pills of life. And the Bare-Foot God came along and reported that he had been deceived by the Great Saint Who Is Heaven's Equal; and from the Great Saint's palace the servants came running and said that the Saint had disappeared and was nowhere to be found. Then the Lord of the Heavens was frightened, and said: "This whole mess is undoubtedly the work of that devilish ape!"

Now the whole host of Heaven, together with all the star-gods, the time-gods and the mountain-gods was called out in order to catch the ape. Li Dsing once more was its commander-in-chief. He invested the entire mountain, and spread out the sky-net and the earth-net, so that no one could escape. Then he sent his bravest heroes into battle. Courageously the ape withstood all attacks from early morn till sundown. But by that time his most faithful followers had been captured. That was too much for him. He pulled out a hair and turned it into thousands of Ape-Kings, who all hewed about them with golden-clamped iron rods. The heavenly host was vanquished, and the ape withdrew to his cave to rest.

Now it happened that Guan Yin had also gone to the peach banquet in the garden, and had found out what Sun Wu Kung had done. When she went to visit the Lord of the Heavens, Li Dsing was just coming in, to report the great defeat which he had suffered on the Mountain of Flowers and Fruits. Then Guan Yin said to the Lord of the Heavens: "I can recommend a hero to you who will surely get the better of the ape. It is your grandson Yang Oerlang. He has conquered all the beast and bird spirits, and overthrown the elves in the grass and the brush. He knows what has to be done to get the better of such devils."

So Yang Oerlang was brought in, and Li Dsing led him to his camp. Li Dsing asked Yang Oerlang how he would go about getting the better of the ape.

Yang Oerlang laughed and said: "I think I will have to go him one better when it comes to changing shapes. It would be best for you to take away the sky-net so that our combat is not disturbed." Then he requested Li Dsing to post himself in the upper air with the magic spirit mirror in his hand, so that when the ape made himself invisible, he might be found again by means of the mirror. When all this had been arranged, Yang Oerlang went out in front of the cave with his spirits to give battle.

The ape leaped out, and when he saw the powerful hero with the three-tined sword standing before him he asked: "And who may you be?"

The other said: "I am Yang Oerlang, the grandson of the Lord of the Heavens!"

Then the ape laughed and said: "Oh yes, I remember! His daughter ran away with a certain Sir Yang, to whom heaven gave a son. You must be that son!"

Yang Oerlang grew furious, and advanced upon him with his spear. Then a hot battle began. For three hundred rounds they fought without decisive results. Then Yang Oerlang turned himself into a giant with a black face and red hair.

"Not bad," said the ape, "but I can do that too!"

So they continued to fight in that form. But the ape's baboons were much frightened. The beast and planet spirits of Yang Oerlang pressed the apes hard. They slew most of them and the others hid away. When the ape saw this his heart grew uneasy. He drew the magic giant-likeness in again, took his rod and fled. But Yang Oerlang followed hard on his heels. In his urgent need the ape thrust the rod, which he had turned into a needle, into his ear, turned into a sparrow, and flew up into the crest of a tree. Yang Oerlang who was following in his tracks, suddenly lost sight of him. But his keen eyes soon recognized that he had turned himself into a sparrow. So he flung away spear and crossbow, turned himself into a sparrow-hawk, and darted down on the sparrow. But the latter soared high into the air as a cormorant. Yang Oerlang shook his plumage, turned into a great sea-crane, and shot up into the clouds to seize the cormorant. The latter dropped, flew into a valley and dove beneath the waters of a brook in the guise of a fish. When Yang Oerlang reached the edge of the valley, and had lost his trail he said to himself: "This ape has surely turned himself into a fish or a crab! I will change my form as well in order to catch him." So he turned into a fish-hawk and floated above the surface of the water. When the ape in the water caught sight of the fish-hawk, he saw that he was Yang Oerlang. He swiftly swung around and fled, Yang Oerlang in pursuit. When the latter was no further away than the length of a beak, the ape turned, crept ashore as a water-snake and hid in the grass. Yang Oerlang, when he saw the water-snake creep from the water, turned into an eagle and spread his claws to seize the snake. But the water-snake sprang up and turned into the lowest of all birds, a speckled buzzard, and perched on the steep edge of a cliff. When Yang Oerlang saw that the ape had turned himself into so contemptible a creature as a buzzard, he would no longer play the game of changing form with him. He reappeared in his original form, took up his crossbow and shot at the bird. The buzzard slipped and fell down the side of the cliff. At its foot the ape turned himself into the chapel of a field-god. He opened his mouth for a gate, his teeth became the two wings of the door, his tongue the image of the god, and his eyes the windows. His tail was the only thing he did not know what to do with. So he let it stand up stiffly behind him in the shape of a flagpole. When Yang Oerlang reached the foot of the hill he saw the chapel, whose flagpole stood in the rear. Then he laughed and said: "That ape is really a devil of an ape! He wants to lure me into the chapel in order to bite me. But I will not go in. First I will break his windows for him, and then I will stamp down the wings of his door!" When the ape heard this he was much frightened. He made a bound like a tiger, and disappeared without a trace in the air. With a single somersault he reached Yang Oerlang's own temple. There he assumed Yang Oerlang's own form and stepped in. The spirits who were on guard were unable to recognize him. They received him on their knees. So the ape then seated himself on the god's throne, and had the prayers which had come in submitted to him.

When Yang Oerlang no longer saw the ape, he rose in the air to Li Dsing and said: "I was vying with the ape in changing shape. Suddenly I could no longer find him. Take a look in the mirror!" Li Dsing took a look in the magic spirit mirror and then he laughed and said: "The ape has turned himself into your likeness, is sitting in your temple quite at home there, and making mischief." When Yang Oerlang heard this he took his three-tined spear, and hastened to his temple. The door-spirits were frightened and said: "But father came in only this very minute! How is it that another one comes now?" Yang Oerlang, without paying attention to them, entered the temple and aimed his spear at Sun Wu Kung. The latter resumed his own shape, laughed and said: "Young sir, you must not be angry! The god of this place is now Sun Wu Kung." Without uttering a word Yang Oerlang assailed him. Sun Wu Kung took up his rod and returned the blows. Thus they crowded out of the temple together, fighting, and wrapped in mists and clouds once more gained the Mountain of Flowers and Fruits.

In the meantime Guan Yin was sitting with Laotzse, the Lord of the Heavens and the Queen-Mother in the great hall of Heaven, waiting for news. When none came she said: "I will go with Laotzse to the Southern Gate of Heaven and see how matters stand." And when they saw that the struggle had still not come to an end she said to Laotzse: "How would it be if we helped Yang Oerlang a little? I will shut up Sun Wu Kung in my vase."

But Laotzse said: "Your vase is made of porcelain. Sun Wu Kung could smash it with his iron rod. But I have a circlet of diamonds which can enclose all living creatures. That we can use!" So he flung his circlet through the air from the heavenly gate, and struck Sun Wu Kung on the head with it. Since he had his hands full fighting, the latter could not guard himself against it, and the blow on the forehead caused him to slip. Yet he rose again and tried to escape. But the heavenly hound of Yang Oerlang bit his leg until he fell to the ground. Then Yang Oerlang and his followers came up and tied him with thongs, and thrust a hook through his collar-bone so that he could no longer transform himself. And Laotzse took possession of his diamond circlet again, and returned with Guan Yin to the hall of Heaven. Sun Wu Kung was now brought in in triumph, and was condemned to be beheaded. He was then taken to the place of execution and bound to a post. But all efforts to kill him by means of ax and sword, thunder and lightning were vain. Nothing so much as hurt a hair on his head.

Said Laotzse: "It is not surprising. This ape has eaten the peaches, has drunk the nectar and also swallowed the pills of life. Nothing can harm him. The best thing would be for me to take him along and thrust him into my stove in order to melt the elixir of life out of him again. Then he will fall into dust and ashes."

So Sun Wu Kung's fetters were loosed, and Laotzse took him with him, thrust him into his oven, and ordered the boy to keep up a hot fire.

But along the edge of the oven were graven the signs of the eight elemental forces. And when the ape was thrust into the oven he took refuge beneath the sign of the wind, so that the fire could not injure him; and the smoke only made his eyes smart. He remained in the oven seven times seven days. Then Laotzse had it opened to take a look. As soon as Sun Wu Kung saw the light shine in, he could no longer bear to be shut up, but leaped out and upset the magic oven. The guards and attendants he threw to the ground and Laotzse himself, who tried to seize him, received such a push that he stuck his legs up in the air like an onion turned upside down. Then Sun Wu Kung took his rod out of his ear, and without looking where he struck, hewed everything to bits, so that the star-gods closed their doors and the guardians of the Heavens ran away. He came to the castle of the Lord of the Heavens, and the guardian of the gate with his steel whip was only just in time to hold him back. Then the thirty-six thunder gods were set at him, and surrounded him, though they could not seize him.

The Lord of the Heavens said: "Buddha will know what is to be done. Send for him quickly!"

So Buddha came up out of the west with Ananada and Kashiapa, his disciples. When he saw the turmoil he said: "First of all, let weapons be laid aside and lead out the Saint. I wish to speak with him!" The gods withdrew. Sun Wu Kung snorted and said: "Who are you, who dare to speak to me?" Buddha smiled and replied: "I have come out of the blessed west, Shakiamuni Amitofu. I have heard of the revolt you have raised, and am come to tame you!"

Said Sun Wu Kung: "I am the stone ape who has gained the hidden knowledge. I am master of seventy-two transformations, and will live as long as Heaven itself. What has the Lord of the Heavens accomplished that entitles him to remain eternally on his throne? Let him make way for me, and I will be satisfied!"

Buddha replied with a smile: "You are a beast which has gained magic powers. How can you expect to rule here as Lord of the Heavens? Be it known to you that the Lord of the Heavens has toiled for eons in perfecting his virtues. How many years would you have to pass before you could attain the dignity he has gained? And then I must ask you whether there is anything else you can do, aside from playing your tricks of transformation?"

Said Sun Wu Kung: "I can turn cloud somersaults. Each one carries me eighteen thousand miles ahead. Surely that is enough to entitle me to be the Lord of the Heavens?"

Buddha answered with a smile: "Let us make a wager. If you can so much as leave my hand with one of your somersaults, then I will beg the Lord of the Heavens to make way for you. But if you are not able to leave my hand, then you must yield yourself to my fetters."

Sun Wu Kung suppressed his laughter, for he thought: "This Buddha is a crazy fellow! His hand is not a foot long; how could I help but leap out of it?" So he opened his mouth wide and said: "Agreed!"

Buddha then stretched out his right hand. It resembled a small lotus-leaf. Sun Wu Kung leaped up into it with one bound. Then he said: "Go!" And with that he turned one somersault after another, so that he flew along like a whirlwind. And while he was flying along he saw five tall, reddish columns towering to the skies. Then he thought: "That is the end of the world! Now I will turn back and become Lord of the Heavens. But first I will write down my name to prove that I was there." He pulled out a hair, turned it into a brush, and wrote with great letters on the middle column: 'The Great Saint Who Is Heaven's Equal.' Then he turned his somersaults again until he had reached the place whence he had come. He leaped down from the Buddha's hand laughing and cried: "Now hurry, and see to it that the Lord of the Heavens clears his heavenly castle for me! I have been at the end of the world and have left a sign there!"

Buddha scolded: "Infamous ape! How dare you claim that you have left my hand? Take a look and see whether or not 'The Great Saint Who Is Heaven's Equal,' is written on my middle finger!"

Sun Wu Kung was terribly frightened, for at the first glance he saw that this was the truth. Yet outwardly he pretended that he was not convinced, said he would take another look, and tried to make use of the opportunity to escape. But Buddha covered him with his hand, shoved him out of the gate of Heaven, and formed a mountain of water, fire, wood, earth and metal, which he softly set down on him to hold him fast. A magic incantation pasted on the mountain prevented his escape.

Here he was obliged to lie for hundreds of years, until he finally reformed and was released, in order to help the Monk of the Yangtze-kiang fetch the holy writings from out of the west. He honoured the Monk as his master, and thenceforward was known as the Wanderer. Guan Yin, who had released him, gave the Monk a golden circlet. Sun Wu Kung was induced to put it on, and it at once grew into his flesh so that he could not remove it. And Guan Yin gave the Monk a magic formula by means of which the ring could be tightened, should the ape grow disobedient. But from that time on he was always polite and well-mannered.

The Birth of Karna

KING PANDU became a mighty monarch, and was renowned as a warrior and a just ruler of his kingdom. He married two wives: Pritha, who was chief rani, and Madri, whom he loved best.

Now Pritha was of celestial origin, for her mother was a nymph; her father was a holy Brahman, and her brother, Vasudeva, was the father of Krishna. As a baby she had been adopted by the King of Shurasena, whose kingdom was among the Vindhya mountains. She was of pious heart, and ever showed reverence towards holy men. Once the great Rishi Durvasas came to the palace, and she ministered to him faithfully by serving food at any hour he desired, and by kindling the sacred fire in the sacrificial chamber. After his stay of a full year, Durvasas, in reward for her services, imparted to Pritha a powerful charm, by virtue of which she could compel the love of a celestial being. One day she had a vision of Surya, god of the sun; she muttered the charm, and received him when he came near in the attire of a king, wearing the celestial earrings. In secret she became in time the mother of his son, Karna, who was equipped at birth with celestial earrings and an invulnerable coat of mail, which had power to grow as the wearer increased in stature. The child had the eyes of a lion and the shoulders of a bull.

In her maidenly shame Pritha resolved to conceal her newborn babe. So she wrapped him in soft sheets and, laying his head on a pillow, placed him in a wicker basket which she had smeared over with wax. Then, weeping bitterly, she set the basket afloat on the river, saying: "My babe, be you protected by all who are on land, and in the water, and in the sky, and in the celestial regions! May all who see you love you! May Varuna, god of the waters, shield you from harm. May your father, the sun, give you warmth!... I shall know you in days to come, wherever you may be, by your coat of golden mail.... She who will find you and adopt you will be surely blessed.... Oh my son, she who will cherish you will behold you in youthful prime like to a maned lion in Himalayan forests."

The basket drifted down the River Aswa until it was no longer seen by that lotus-eyed damsel, and after some time it reached the Jumna; the Jumna gave it to the Ganges, and by that great and holy river it was carried to the country of Anga.... The child, lying in soft slumber, was kept alive because of the virtues possessed by the celestial armour and the earrings.

Now there was a woman of Anga whose name was Radha, and she had peerless beauty. Her husband was Shatananda, the charioteer. Both husband and wife had long wished for a son of their own. One day, however, their wish was granted. It happened that Radha went down to the river bank, and she saw the basket drifting on the waves. She brought it ashore; and when it was uncovered, she gazed with wonder at a sleeping babe who was as fair as the morning sun. Her heart was immediately filled with happiness, and she cried out: "The gods have heard me at last, and they have sent me a son." So she adopted the babe and cherished him. And the years went past, and Karna grew up and became a powerful youth and a mighty bowman.

Giants and Doliones

THE ARGONAUTS NOW PURSUED their voyage, till contrary winds drove them towards an island, inhabited by the Doliones, whose king Cyzicus received them with great kindness and hospitality. The Doliones were descendants of Poseidon, who protected them against the frequent attacks of their fierce and formidable neighbours, the earth-born Giants—monsters with six arms.

Whilst his companions were attending a banquet given by king Cyzicus, Heracles, who, as usual, had remained behind to guard the ship, observed that these Giants were busy blocking up the harbour with huge rocks. He at once realized the danger, and, attacking them with his arrows, succeeded in considerably thinning their numbers; then, assisted by the heroes, who at length came to his aid, he effectually destroyed the remainder.

The Argo now steered out of the harbour and set sail; but in consequence of a severe storm which arose at night, was driven back once more to the shores of the kindly Doliones. Unfortunately, however, owing to the darkness of the night, the inhabitants failed to recognize their former guests, and, mistaking them for enemies, commenced to attack them. Those who had so recently parted as friends were now engaged in mortal combat, and in the battle which ensued, Jason himself pierced to the heart his friend king Cyzicus; whereupon the Doliones, being deprived of their leader, fled to their city and closed the gates. When morning dawned, and both sides perceived their error, they were filled with the deepest sorrow and remorse; and for three days the heroes remained with the Doliones, celebrating the funereal rites of the slain, with every demonstration of mourning and solemnity.

The Argonauts once more set sail, and after a stormy voyage arrived at Mysia, where they were hospitably received by the inhabitants, who spread before them plentiful banquets and sumptuously regaled them.

While his friends were feasting, Heracles, who had declined to join them, went into the forest to seek a fir-tree which he required for an oar, and was missed by his adopted son Hylas, who set out to seek him. When the youth arrived at a spring, in the most secluded part of the forest, the nymph of the fountain was so struck by his beauty that she drew him down beneath the waters, and he was seen no more. Polyphemus, one of the heroes, who happened to be also in the forest, heard his cry for help, and on meeting Heracles informed him of the circumstance. They at once set out in search of the missing youth, no traces of whom were to be found, and whilst they were engaged looking for him, the Argo set sail and left them behind.

The ship had proceeded some distance before the absence of Heracles was observed. Some of the heroes were in favour of returning for him, others wished to proceed on their journey, when, in the midst of the dispute, the sea-god Glaucus arose from the waves, and informed them that it was the will of Zeus that Heracles, having another mission to perform, should remain behind. The Argonauts continued their voyage without their companions; Heracles returned to Argos, whilst Polyphemus remained with the Mysians, where he founded a city and became its king.

Next morning the Argo touched at the country of the Bebrycians, whose king Amycus was a famous pugilist, and permitted no strangers to leave his shores without matching their strength with his. When the heroes, therefore, demanded permission to land, they were informed that they could only do so provided that one of their number should engage in a boxing-match with the king. Pollux, who was the best pugilist in Greece, was selected as their champion, and a contest took place, which, after a tremendous struggle, proved fatal to Amycus, who had hitherto been victorious in all similar encounters.

The Gorgon's Head

PERSEUS WAS THE SON OF DANAE, who was the daughter of a king. And when Perseus was a very little boy, some wicked people put his mother and himself into a chest, and set them afloat upon the sea. The wind blew freshly, and drove the chest away from the shore, and the uneasy billows tossed it up and down; while Danae clasped her child closely to her bosom, and dreaded that some big wave would dash its foamy crest over them both. The chest sailed on, however, and neither sank nor was upset; until, when night was coming, it floated so near an island that it got entangled in a fisherman's nets, and was drawn out high and dry upon the sand. The island was called Seriphus, and it was reigned over by King Polydectes, who happened to be the fisherman's brother.

This fisherman, I am glad to tell you, was an exceedingly humane and upright man. He showed great kindness to Danae and her little boy; and continued to befriend them, until Perseus had grown to be a handsome youth, very strong and active, and skilful in the use of arms. Long before this time, King Polydectes had seen the two strangers – the mother and her child – who had come to his dominions in a floating chest. As he was not good and kind, like his brother the fisherman, but extremely wicked, he resolved to send Perseus on a dangerous enterprise, in which he would probably be killed, and then to do some great mischief to Danae herself. So this bad-hearted king spent a long while in considering what was the most dangerous thing that a young man could possibly undertake to perform. At last, having hit upon an enterprise that promised to turn out as fatally as he desired, he sent for the youthful Perseus.

The young man came to the palace, and found the king sitting upon his throne.

"Perseus," said King Polydectes, smiling craftily upon him, "you are grown up a fine young man. You and your good mother have received a great deal of kindness from myself, as well as from my worthy brother the fisherman, and I suppose you would not be sorry to repay some of it."

"Please your Majesty," answered Perseus, "I would willingly risk my life to do so."

"Well, then," continued the king, still with a curving smile on his lips, "I have a little adventure to propose to you; and, as you are a brave and enterprising youth, you will doubtless look upon it as a great piece of good luck to have so rare an opportunity of distinguishing yourself. You must know, my good Perseus, I think of getting married to the beautiful Princess Hippodamia; and it is customary, on these occasions, to make the bride a present of some far-fetched and elegant curiosity. I have been a little perplexed, I must honestly confess, where to obtain anything likely to please a princess of her exquisite taste. But, this morning, I flatter myself, I have thought of precisely the article."

"And can I assist your Majesty in obtaining it?" cried Perseus, eagerly.

"You can, if you are as brave a youth as I believe you to be," replied King Polydectes, with the utmost graciousness of manner. "The bridal gift which I have set my heart on presenting to the beautiful Hippodamia is the head of the Gorgon Medusa, with the snaky locks; and I depend on you, my dear Perseus, to bring it to me. So, as I am anxious to settle affairs with the princess, the sooner you go in quest of the Gorgon, the better I shall be pleased."

"I will set out to-morrow morning," answered Perseus.

"Pray do so, my gallant youth," rejoined the king. "And, Perseus, in cutting off the Gorgon's head, be careful to make a clean stroke, so as not to injure its appearance. You must bring it home in the very best condition, in order to suit the exquisite taste of the beautiful Princess Hippodamia."

Perseus left the palace, but was scarcely out of hearing before Polydectes burst into a laugh; being greatly amused, wicked king that he was, to find how readily the young man fell into the snare. The news quickly spread abroad, that Perseus had undertaken to cut off the head of Medusa with the snaky locks. Everybody was rejoiced; for most of the inhabitants of the island were as wicked as the king himself, and would have liked nothing better than to see some enormous mischief happen to Danae and her son. The only good man in this unfortunate island of Seriphus appears to have been the fisherman. As Perseus walked along, therefore, the people pointed after him, and made mouths, and winked to one another, and ridiculed him as loudly as they dared.

"Ho, ho!" cried they; "Medusa's snakes will sting him soundly!"

Now, there were three Gorgons alive, at that period; and they were the most strange and terrible monsters that had ever been since the world was made, or that have been seen in after days, or that are likely to be seen in all time to come. I hardly know what sort of creature or hobgoblin to call them. They were three sisters, and seem to have borne some distant resemblance to women, but were really a very frightful and mischievous species of dragon. It is, indeed, difficult to imagine what hideous beings these three sisters were. Why, instead of locks of hair, if you can believe me, they had each of them a hundred enormous snakes growing on their heads, all alive, twisting, wriggling, curling, and thrusting out their venomous' tongues, with forked stings at the end! The teeth of the Gorgons were terribly long tusks; their hands were made of brass; and their bodies were all over scales, which, if not iron, were something as hard and impenetrable. They had wings, too, and exceedingly splendid ones, I can assure you; for every feather in them was pure, bright, glittering, burnished gold, and they looked very dazzlingly, no doubt, when the Gorgons were flying about in the sunshine.

But when people happened to catch a glimpse of their glittering brightness, aloft in the air, they seldom stopped to gaze, but ran and hid themselves as speedily as they could. You will think, perhaps, that they were afraid of being stung by the serpents that served the Gorgons instead of hair – or of having their heads bitten off by their ugly tusks – or of being torn all to pieces by their brazen claws. Well, to be sure, these were some of the dangers, but by no means the greatest, nor the most difficult to avoid. For the worst thing about these abominable Gorgons was, that, if once a poor mortal fixed his eyes full upon one of their faces, he was certain, that very instant, to be changed from warm flesh and blood into cold and lifeless stone!

Thus, as you will easily perceive, it was a very dangerous adventure that the wicked King Polydectes had contrived for this innocent young man. Perseus himself, when he had thought over the matter, could not help seeing that he had very little chance of coming safely through it, and that he was far more likely to become a stone image than to bring back the head of Medusa with the snaky locks. For, not to speak of other difficulties, there was one which it would have puzzled an older man than Perseus to get over. Not only must he fight with and slay this golden-winged, iron-scaled, long-tusked, brazen-clawed, snaky-haired monster, but he must do it with his eyes shut, or, at least, without so much as a glance at the enemy with whom he was contending. Else, while his arm was lifted to strike, he would stiffen into stone, and stand with that uplifted arm for centuries, until time, and the wind and weather, should crumble him quite away. This would be a very sad thing to befall a young man who wanted to perform a great many brave deeds, and to enjoy a great deal of happiness, in this bright and beautiful world.

So disconsolate did these thoughts make him, that Perseus could not bear to tell his mother what he had undertaken to do. He therefore took his shield, girded on his sword, and crossed over from the island to the mainland, where he sat down in a solitary place, and hardly refrained from shedding tears.

But, while he was in this sorrowful mood, he heard a voice close beside him.

"Perseus," said the voice, "why are you sad?"

He lifted his head from his hands, in which he had hidden it, and, behold! all alone as Perseus had supposed himself to be, there was a stranger in the solitary place. It was a brisk, intelligent, and remarkably shrewd-looking young man, with a cloak over his shoulders, an odd sort of cap on his head, a strangely twisted staff in his hand, and a short and very crooked sword hanging by his side. He was exceedingly light and active in his figure, like a person much accustomed to gymnastic exercises, and well able to leap or run. Above all, the stranger had such a cheerful, knowing, and helpful aspect (though it was certainly a little mischievous, into the bargain), that Perseus could not help feeling his spirits grow livelier, as he gazed at him. Besides, being really a courageous youth, he felt greatly ashamed that anybody should have found him with tears in his eyes, like a timid little school-boy, when, after all, there might be no occasion for despair. So Perseus wiped his eyes, and answered the stranger pretty briskly, putting on as brave a look as he could.

"I am not so very sad," said he; "only thoughtful about an adventure that I have undertaken."

"Oho!" answered the stranger. "Well, tell me all about it, and possibly I may be of service to you. I have helped a good many young men through adventures that looked difficult enough beforehand. Perhaps you may have heard of me. I have more names than one; but the name of Quicksilver suits me as well as any other. Tell me what your trouble is, and we will talk the matter over, and see what can be done."

The stranger's words and manner put Perseus into quite a different mood from his former one. He resolved to tell Quicksilver all his difficulties, since he could not easily be worse off than he already was, and, very possibly, his new friend might give him some advice that would turn out well in the end. So he let the stranger know, in few words, precisely what the case was – how that King Polydectes wanted the head of Medusa with the snaky locks as a bridal gift for the beautiful Princess Hippodamia, and how that he had undertaken to get it for him, but was afraid of being turned into stone.

"And that would be a great pity," said Quicksilver, with his mischievous smile. "You would make a very handsome marble statue, it is true, and it would be a considerable number of centuries before you crumbled away; but, on the whole, one would rather be a young man for a few years, than a stone image for a great many."

"O, far rather!" exclaimed Perseus, with the tears again standing in his eyes. "And, besides, what would my dear mother do, if her beloved son were turned into a stone?"

"Well, well; let us hope that the affair will not turn out so very badly," replied Quicksilver, in an encouraging tone. "I am the very person to help you, if anybody can. My sister and myself will do our utmost to bring you safe through the adventure, ugly as it now looks."

"Your sister?" repeated Perseus.

"Yes, my sister," said the stranger. "She is very wise, I promise you; and as for myself, I generally have all my wits about me, such as they are. If you show yourself bold and cautious, and follow our advice, you need not fear being a stone image yet awhile. But, first of all, you must polish your shield, till you can see your face in it as distinctly as in a mirror."

This seemed to Perseus rather an odd beginning of the adventure; for he thought it of far more consequence that the shield should be strong enough to defend him from the Gorgon's brazen claws, than that it should be bright enough to show him the reflection of his face. However, concluding that Quicksilver knew better than himself, he immediately set to work, and scrubbed the shield with so much diligence and good-will, that it very quickly shone like the moon at harvest-time. Quicksilver looked at it with a smile, and nodded his approbation. Then, taking off his own short and crooked sword, he girded it about Perseus, instead of the one which he had before worn.

"No sword but mine will answer your purpose," observed he; "the blade has a most excellent temper, and will cut through iron and brass as easily as through the slenderest twig. And now we will set out. The next thing is to find the Three Grey Women, who will tell us where to find the Nymphs."

"The Three Grey Women!" cried Perseus, to whom this seemed only a new difficulty in the path of his adventure; "pray, who may the Three Grey Women be? I never heard of them before."

"They are three very strange old ladies," said Quicksilver, laughing. "They have but one eye among them, and only one tooth. Moreover, you must find them out by starlight, or in the dusk of the evening; for they never show themselves by the light either of the sun or moon."

"But," said Perseus, "why should I waste my time with these Three Grey Women? Would it not be better to set out at once in search of the terrible Gorgons?"

"No, no," answered his friend. "There are other things to be done, before you can find your way to the Gorgons. There is nothing for it but to hunt up these old ladies; and when we meet with them, you may be sure that the Gorgons are not a great way off. Come, let us be stirring!"

Perseus, by this time, felt so much confidence in his companion's sagacity, that he made no more objections, and professed himself ready to begin the adventure immediately. They accordingly set out, and walked at a pretty brisk pace; so brisk, indeed, that Perseus found it rather difficult to keep up with his nimble friend Quicksilver. To say the truth, he had a singular idea that Quicksilver was furnished with a pair of winged shoes, which, of course, helped him along marvellously. And then, too, when Perseus looked sideways at him, out of the corner of his eye, he seemed to see wings on the side of his head; although, if he turned a full gaze, there were no such things to be perceived, but only an odd kind of cap. But, at all events, the twisted staff was evidently a great convenience to Quicksilver, and enabled him to proceed so fast, that Perseus, though a remarkably active young man, began to be out of breath.

"Here!" cried Quicksilver, at last – for he knew well enough, rogue that he was, how hard Perseus found it to keep pace with him – "take you the staff, for you need it a great deal more than I. Are there no better walkers than yourself, in the island of Seriphus?"

"I could walk pretty well," said Perseus, glancing slyly at his companion's feet, "if I had only a pair of winged shoes."

"We must see about getting you a pair," answered Quicksilver.

But the staff helped Perseus along so bravely, that he no longer felt the slightest weariness. In fact, the stick seemed to be alive in his hand, and to lend some of its life to Perseus. He and Quicksilver now walked onward at their ease, talking very sociably together; and Quicksilver told so many pleasant stories about his former adventures, and how well his wits had served him on various occasions, that Perseus began to think him a very wonderful person. He evidently knew the world; and nobody is so charming to a young man as a friend who has that kind of knowledge. Perseus listened the more eagerly, in the hope of brightening his own wits by what he heard.

At last, he happened to recollect that Quicksilver had spoken of a sister, who was to lend her assistance in the adventure which they were now bound upon.

"Where is she?" he inquired. "Shall we not meet her soon?"

"All at the proper time," said his companion. "But this sister of mine, you must understand, is quite a different sort of character from myself. She is very grave and prudent, seldom smiles, never laughs, and makes it a rule not to utter a word unless she has something particularly profound to say. Neither will she listen to any but the wisest conversation."

"Dear me!" ejaculated Perseus; "I shall be afraid to say a syllable."

"She is a very accomplished person, I assure you," continued Quicksilver, "and has all the arts and sciences at her fingers' ends. In short, she is so immoderately wise, that many people call her wisdom personified. But, to tell you the truth, she has hardly vivacity enough for my taste; and I think you would scarcely find her so pleasant a travelling companion as myself. She has her good points, nevertheless; and you will find the benefit of them, in your encounter with the Gorgons."

By this time it had grown quite dusk. They were now come to a very wild and desert place, overgrown with shaggy bushes, and so silent and solitary that nobody seemed ever to have dwelt or journeyed there. All was waste and desolate, in the grey twilight, which grew every moment more obscure. Perseus looked about him, rather disconsolately, and asked Quicksilver whether they had a great deal farther to go.

"Hist! Hist!" whispered his companion. "Make no noise! This is just the time and place to meet the Three Grey Women. Be careful that they do not see you before you see them; for, though they have but a single eye among the three, it is as sharp-sighted as half a dozen common eyes."

"But what must I do," asked Perseus, "when we meet them?"

Quicksilver explained to Perseus how the Three Grey Women managed with their one eye. They were in the habit, it seems, of changing it from one to another, as if it had been a pair of spectacles, or – which would have suited them better – quizzing-glass. When one of the three had kept the eye a certain time, she took it out of the socket and passed it to one of her sisters, whose turn it might happen to be, and who immediately clapped it into her own head, and enjoyed a peep at the visible world. Thus it will easily be understood that only one of the Three Grey Women could see, while the other two were in utter darkness; and, moreover, at the instant when the eye was passing from hand to hand, neither of the poor old ladies was able to see a wink. I have heard of a great many strange things, in my day, and have witnessed not a few; but none, it seems to me, that can compare with the oddity of these Three Grey Women, all peeping through a single eye.

So thought Perseus, likewise, and was so astonished that he almost fancied his companion was joking with him, and that there were no such old women in the world.

"You will soon find whether I tell the truth or no," observed Quicksilver. "Hark! Hush! Hist! Hist! There they come, now!"

Perseus looked earnestly through the dusk of the evening, and there, sure enough, at no great distance off, he descried the Three Grey Women. The light being so faint, he could not well make out what sort of figures they were; only he discovered that they had long grey hair; and, as they came nearer, he saw that two of them had but the empty socket of an eye, in the middle of their foreheads. But, in the middle of the third sister's forehead, there was a very large, bright, and piercing eye, which sparkled like a great diamond in a ring; and so penetrating did it seem to be, that Perseus could not help thinking it must possess the gift of seeing in the darkest midnight just as perfectly as at noonday. The sight of three persons' eyes was melted and collected into that single one.

Thus the three old dames got along about as comfortably, upon the whole, as if they could all see at once. She who chanced to have the eye in her forehead led the other two by the hands, peeping sharply about her, all the while; insomuch that Perseus dreaded lest she should see right through the thick clump of bushes behind which he and Quicksilver had hidden themselves. My stars! it was positively terrible to be within reach of so very sharp an eye!

But, before they reached the clump of bushes, one of the Three Grey Women spoke.

"Sister! Sister Scarecrow!" cried she, "you have had the eye long enough. It is my turn now!"

"Let me keep it a moment longer, Sister Nightmare," answered Scarecrow. "I thought I had a glimpse of something behind that thick bush."

"Well, and what of that?" retorted Nightmare, peevishly. "Can't I see into a thick bush as easily as yourself? The eye is mine, as well as yours; and I know the use of it as well as you, or may be a little better. I insist upon taking a peep immediately!"

But here the third sister, whose name was Shakejoint, began to complain, and said that it was her turn to have the eye, and that Scarecrow and Nightmare wanted to keep it all to themselves. To end the dispute, old Dame Scarecrow took the eye out of her forehead, and held it forth in her hand.

"Take it, one of you," cried she, "and quit this foolish quarrelling. For my part, I shall be glad of a little thick darkness. Take it quickly, however, or I must clap it into my own head again!"

Accordingly, both Nightmare and Shakejoint stretched out their hands, groping eagerly to snatch the eye out of the hand of Scarecrow. But, being both alike blind, they could not easily find where Scarecrow's hand was; and Scarecrow, being now just as much in the dark as Shakejoint and Nightmare, could not at once meet either of their hands, in order to put the eye into it. Thus (as you will see, with half an eye, my wise little auditors), these good old dames had fallen into a strange perplexity. For, though the eye shone and glistened like a star, as Scarecrow held it out, yet the Grey Women caught not the least glimpse of its light, and were all three in utter darkness, from too impatient a desire to see.

Quicksilver was so much tickled at beholding Shakejoint and Nightmare both groping for the eye, and each finding fault with Scarecrow and one another, that he could scarcely help laughing aloud.

"Now is your time!" he whispered to Perseus.

"Quick, quick! before they can clap the eye into either of their heads. Rush out upon the old ladies, and snatch it from Scarecrow's hand!"

In an instant, while the Three Grey Women were still scolding each other, Perseus leaped front behind the clump of bushes, and made himself master of the prize. The marvellous eye, as he held it in his hand, shone very brightly, and seemed to look up into his face with a knowing air, and an expression as if it would have winked, had it been provided with a pair of eyelids for that purpose. But the Grey Women knew nothing of what had happened; and, each supposing that one of her sisters was in possession of the eye, they began their quarrel anew. At last, as Perseus did not wish to put these respectable dames to greater inconvenience than was really necessary, he thought it right to explain the matter. "My good ladies," said he, "pray do not be angry with one another. If anybody is in fault, it is myself; for I have the honour to hold your very brilliant and excellent eye in my own hand!"

"You! you have our eye! And who are you?" screamed the Three Grey Women, all in a breath; for they were terribly frightened, of course, at hearing a strange voice, and discovering that their eyesight had got into the hands of they could not guess whom. "O, what shall we do, sisters? what shall we do? We are all in the dark! Give us our eye! Give us our one, precious, solitary eye! You have two of your own! Give us our eye!"

"Tell them," whispered Quicksilver to Perseus, "that they shall have back the eye as soon as they direct you where to find the Nymphs who have the flying slippers, the magic wallet, and the helmet of darkness."

"My dear, good, admirable old ladies," said Perseus, addressing the Grey Women, "there is no occasion for putting yourselves into such a fright. I am by no means a bad young man. You shall have back your eye, safe and sound, and as bright as ever, the moment you tell me where to find the Nymphs."

"The Nymphs! Goodness me! sisters, what Nymphs does he mean?" screamed Scarecrow. "There are a great many Nymphs, people say; some that go a hunting in the woods, and some that live inside of trees, and some that have a comfortable home in fountains of water. We know nothing at all about them. We are three unfortunate old souls, that go wandering about in the dusk, and never had but one eye amongst us, and that one you have stolen away. O, give it back, good stranger! – whoever you are, give it back!"

All this while the Three Grey Women were groping with their outstretched hands, and trying their utmost to get hold of Perseus. But he took good care to keep out of their reach.

"My respectable dames," said he – for his mother had taught him always to use the greatest civility – "I hold your eye fast in my hand, and shall keep it safely for you, until you please to tell me where to find these Nymphs. The Nymphs, I mean, who keep the enchanted wallet, the flying slippers, and the what is it? – the helmet of invisibility."

"Mercy on us, sisters! what is the young man talking about?" exclaimed Scarecrow, Nightmare, and Shakejoint, one to another, with great appearance of astonishment. "A pair of flying slippers, quoth he! His heels would quickly fly higher than his head, if he were silly enough to put them on. And a helmet of invisibility! How could a helmet make him invisible, unless it were big enough for him to hide under it? And an enchanted wallet! What sort of a contrivance may that be, I wonder? No, no, good stranger! we can tell you nothing of these marvellous things. You have two eyes of your own, and we have but a single one amongst us three. You can find out such wonders better than three blind old creatures, like us."

Perseus, hearing them talk in this way, began really to think that the Grey Women knew nothing of the matter; and, as it grieved him to have put them to so much trouble, he was just on the point of restoring their eye and asking pardon for his rudeness in snatching it away. But Quicksilver caught his hand.

"Don't let them make a fool of you!" said he. "These Three Grey Women are the only persons in the world that can tell you where to find the Nymphs; and, unless you get that information, you will never succeed in cutting off the head of Medusa with the snaky locks. Keep fast hold of the eye, and all will go well."

As it turned out, Quicksilver was in the right. There are but few things that people prize so much as they do their eyesight; and the Grey Women valued their single eye as highly as if it had been half a dozen, which was the number they ought to have had. Finding that there was no other way of recovering it, they at last told Perseus what he wanted to know. No sooner had they done so, than he immediately, and with the utmost respect, clapped the eye into the vacant socket in one of their foreheads, thanked them for their kindness, and bade them farewell. Before the young man was out of hearing, however, they had got into a new dispute, because he happened to have given the eye to Scarecrow, who had already taken her turn of it when their trouble with Perseus commenced.

It is greatly to be feared that the Three Grey Women were very much in the habit of disturbing their mutual harmony by bickerings of this sort; which was the more pity, as they could not conveniently do without one another, and were evidently intended to be inseparable companions. As a general rule, I would advise all people, whether sisters or brothers, old or young, who chance to have but one eye amongst them, to cultivate forbearance, and not all insist upon peeping through it at once.

Quicksilver and Perseus, in the mean time, were making the best of their way in quest of the Nymphs. The old dames had given them such particular directions, that they were not long in finding them out. They proved to be very different persons from Nightmare, Shakejoint, and Scarecrow; for, instead of being old, they were young and beautiful; and instead of one eye amongst the sisterhood, each Nymph had two exceedingly bright eyes of her own, with which she looked very kindly at Perseus. They seemed to be acquainted with Quicksilver; and when he told them the adventure which Perseus had undertaken, they made no difficulty about giving him the valuable articles that were in their custody. In the first place, they brought out what appeared to be a small purse, made of deer-skin, and curiously embroidered, and bade him be sure and keep it safe. This was the magic wallet. The Nymphs next produced a pair of shoes, or slippers, or sandals, with a nice little pair of wings at the heel of each.

"Put them on, Perseus," said Quicksilver. "You will find yourself as light-heeled as you can desire, for the remainder of our journey."

So Perseus proceeded to put one of the slippers on, while he laid the other on the ground by his side. Unexpectedly, however, this other slipper spread its wings, fluttered up off the ground, and would probably have flown away, if Quicksilver had not made a leap, and luckily caught it in the air.

"Be more careful," said he, as he gave it back to Perseus. "It would frighten the birds, up aloft, if they should see a flying slipper amongst them."

When Perseus had got on both of these wonderful slippers, he was altogether too buoyant to tread on earth. Making a step or two, lo and behold! upward he popt into the air, high above the heads of Quicksilver and the Nymphs, and found it very difficult to clamber down again. Winged slippers, and all such high-flying contrivances, are seldom quite easy to manage, until one grows a little accustomed to them. Quicksilver laughed at his companion's involuntary activity, and told him that he must not be in so desperate a hurry, but must wait for the invisible helmet.

The good-natured Nymphs had the helmet, with its dark tuft of waving plumes, all in readiness to put upon his head. And now there happened about as wonderful an incident as anything that I have yet told you. The instant before the helmet was put on, there stood Perseus, a beautiful young man, with golden ringlets and rosy cheeks, the crooked sword by his side, and the brightly polished shield upon his arm – a figure that seemed all made up of courage, sprightliness, and glorious light. But when the helmet had descended over his white brow, there was no longer any Perseus to be seen! Nothing but empty air! Even the helmet, that covered him with its invisibility, had vanished!

"Where are you, Perseus?" asked Quicksilver.

"Why, here, to be sure!" answered Perseus, very quietly, although his voice seemed to come out of the transparent atmosphere. "Just where I was a moment ago. Don't you see me?"

"No, indeed!" answered his friend. "You are hidden under the helmet. But, if I cannot see you, neither can the Gorgons. Follow me, therefore, and we will try your dexterity in using the winged slippers."

With these words, Quicksilver's cap spread its wings, as if his head were about to fly away from his shoulders; but his whole figure rose lightly into the air, and Perseus followed. By the time they had ascended a few hundred feet, the young man began to feel what a delightful thing it was to leave the dull earth so far beneath him, and to be able to flit about like a bird.

It was now deep night. Perseus looked upward, and saw the round, bright, silvery moon, and thought that he should desire nothing better than to soar up thither, and spend his life there. Then he looked downward again, and saw the earth, with its seas, and lakes, and the silver courses of its rivers, and its snowy mountain-peaks, and the breadth of its fields, and the dark cluster of its woods, and its cities of white marble; and, with the moonshine sleeping over the whole scene, it was as beautiful as the moon or any star could be. And, among other objects, he saw the island of Seriplius, where his dear mother was. Sometimes, he and Quicksilver approached a cloud, that, at a distance, looked as if it were made of fleecy silver; although, when they plunged into it, they found themselves chilled and moistened with grey mist. So swift was their flight, however, that, in an instant, they emerged from the cloud into the moonlight again. Once, a high-soaring eagle flew right against the invisible Perseus. The bravest sights were the meteors, that gleamed suddenly out, as if a bonfire had been kindled in the sky, and made the moonshine pale for as much as a hundred miles around them.

As the two companions flew onward, Perseus fancied that he could hear the rustle of a garment close by his side; and it was on the side opposite to the one where he beheld Quicksilver, yet only Quicksilver was visible.

"Whose garment is this," inquired Perseus, "that keeps rustling close beside me, in the breeze?"

"O, it is my sister's!" answered Quicksilver. "She is coming along with us, as I told you she would. We could do nothing without the help of my sister. You have no idea how wise she is. She has such eyes, too! Why, she can see you, at this moment, just as distinctly as if you were not invisible; and I'll venture to say, she will be the first to discover the Gorgons."

By this time, in their swift voyage through the air, they had come within sight of the great ocean, and were soon flying over it. Far beneath them, the waves tossed themselves tumultuously in mid-sea, or rolled a white surf-line upon the long beaches, or foamed against the rocky cliffs, with a roar that was thunderous, in the lower world; although it became a gentle murmur, like the voice of a baby half asleep, before it reached the ears of Perseus. Just then a voice spoke in the air close by him. It seemed to be a woman's voice, and was melodious, though not exactly what might be called sweet, but grave and mild.

"Perseus," said the voice, "there are the Gorgons."

"Where?" exclaimed Perseus. "I cannot see them."

"On the shore of that island beneath you," replied the voice. "A pebble, dropped from your hand, would strike in the midst of them."

"I told you she would be the first to discover them," said Quicksilver to Perseus. "And there they are!"

Straight downward, two or three thousand feet below him, Perseus perceived a small island, with the sea breaking into white foam all around its rocky shore, except on one side, where there was a beach of snowy sand. He descended towards it, and, looking earnestly at a cluster or heap of brightness, at the foot of a precipice of black rocks, behold, there were the terrible Gorgons! They lay fast asleep, soothed by the thunder of the sea; for it required a tumult that would have deafened everybody else to lull such fierce creatures into slumber. The moonlight glistened on their steely scales, and on their golden wings, which drooped idly over the sand. Their brazen claws, horrible to look at, were thrust out, and clutched the wave-beaten fragments of rock, while the sleeping Gorgons dreamed of tearing some poor mortal all to pieces. The snakes that served them instead of hair seemed likewise to be asleep; although, now and then, one would writhe, and lift its head, and thrust out its forked tongue, emitting a drowsy hiss, and then let itself subside among its sister snakes.

The Gorgons were more like an awful, gigantic kind of insect – immense, golden-winged beetles, or dragon-flies, or things of that sort –at once ugly and beautiful – than like anything else; only that they were a thousand and a million times as big. And, with all this, there was something partly human about them, too. Luckily for Perseus, their faces were completely hidden from him by the posture in which they lay; for, had he but looked one instant at them, he would have fallen heavily out of the air, an image of senseless stone.

"Now," whispered Quicksilver, as he hovered by the side of Perseus – "now is your time to do the deed! Be quick; for, if one of the Gorgons should awake, you are too late!"

"Which shall I strike at?" asked Perseus, drawing his sword and descending a little lower. "They all three look alike. All three have snaky locks. Which of the three is Medusa?"

It must be understood that Medusa was the only one of these dragon-monsters whose head Perseus could possibly cut off. As for the other two, let him have the sharpest sword that ever was forged, and he might have hacked away by the hour together, without doing there the least harm.

"Be cautious," said the calm voice which had before spoken to him. "One of the Gorgons is stirring in her sleep, and is just about to turn over. That is Medusa. Do not look at her! The sight would turn you to stone! Look at the reflection of her face and figure in the bright mirror of your shield."

Perseus now understood Quicksilver's motive for so earnestly exhorting him to polish his shield. In its surface he could safely look at the reflection of the Gorgon's face. And there it was – that terrible countenance – mirrored in the brightness of the shield, with the moonlight falling over it, and displaying all its horror. The snakes, whose venomous natures could not altogether sleep, kept twisting themselves over the forehead. It was the fiercest and most horrible face that ever was seen or imagined, and yet with a strange, fearful, and savage kind of beauty in it. The eyes were closed, and the Gorgon was still in a deep slumber; but there was an unquiet expression disturbing her features, as if the monster was troubled with an ugly dream. She gnashed her white tusks, and dug into the sand with her brazen claws.

The snakes, too, seemed to feel Medusa's dream, and to be made more restless by it. They twined themselves into tumultuous knots, writhed fiercely, and uplifted a hundred hissing heads, without opening their eyes.

"Now, now!" whispered Quicksilver, who was growing impatient. "Make a dash at the monster!"

"But be calm," said the grave, melodious voice, at the young man's side. "Look in your shield, as you fly downward, and take care that you do not miss your first stroke."

Perseus flew cautiously downward, still keeping his eyes on Medusa's face, as reflected in his shield. The nearer he came, the more terrible did the snaky visage and metallic body of the monster grow. At last, when he found himself hovering over her within arm's length, Perseus uplifted his sword, while, at the same instant, each separate snake upon the Gorgon's head stretched threateningly upward, and Medusa unclosed her eyes. But she awoke too late. The sword was sharp; the stroke fell like a lightning-flash; and the head of the wicked Medusa tumbled from her body!

"Admirably done!" cried Quicksilver. "Make haste, and clap the head into your magic wallet."

To the astonishment of Perseus, the small, embroidered wallet, which he had hung about his neck, and which had hitherto been no bigger than a purse, grew all at once large enough to contain Medusa's head. As quick as thought, he snatched it up, with the snakes still writhing upon it, and thrust it in.

"Your task is done," said the calm voice. "Now fly; for the other Gorgons will do their utmost to take vengeance for Medusa's death."

It was, indeed, necessary to take flight; for Perseus had not done the deed so quietly, but that the clash of his sword, and the hissing of the snakes, and the thump of Medusa's head as it tumbled upon the sea-beaten sand, awoke the other two monsters. There they sat, for an instant, sleepily rubbing their eyes with their brazen fingers, while all the snakes on their heads reared themselves on end with surprise, and with venomous malice against they knew not what. But when the Gorgons saw the scaly carcass of Medusa, headless, and her golden wings all ruffled, and half spread out on the sand, it was really awful to hear what yells and screeches they set up. And then the snakes! They sent forth a hundred-fold hiss, with one consent, and Medusa's snakes answered them out of the magic wallet.

No sooner were the Gorgons broad awake, than they hurtled upward into the air, brandishing their brass talons, gnashing their horrible tusks, and flapping their huge wings so wildly, that some of the golden feathers were shaken out, and floated down upon the shore. And there, perhaps, those very feathers he scattered, till this day. Up rose the Gorgons, as I tell you, staring horribly about, in hopes of turning somebody to stone. Had Perseus looked them in the face, or had he fallen into their clutches, his poor mother would never have kissed her boy again! But he took good care to turn his eyes another way; and, as he wore the helmet of invisibility, the Gorgons knew not in what direction to follow him; nor did he fail to make the best use of the winged slippers, by soaring upward a perpendicular mile or so. At that height, when the screams of those abominable creatures sounded faintly beneath him, he made a straight course for the island of Seriphus, in order to carry Medusa's head to King Polydectes.

I have no time to tell you of several marvellous things that befell Perseus, on his way homeward; such as his killing a hideous sea-monster, just as it was on the point of devouring a beautiful maiden; nor how he changed an enormous giant into a mountain of stone, merely by showing him the head of the Gorgon. If you doubt this latter story, you may make a voyage to Africa, some day or other, and see the very mountain, which is still known by the ancient giant's name.

Finally, our brave Perseus arrived at the island, where he expected to see his dear mother. But, during his absence, the wicked king had treated Danae so very ill, that she was compelled to make her escape, and had taken refuge in a temple, where some good old priests were extremely kind to her. These praiseworthy priests, and the kind-hearted fisherman, who had first shown hospitality to Danae and little Perseus when he found them afloat in the chest, seem to have been the only persons on the island who cared about doing right. All the rest of the people, as well as King Polydectes himself, were remarkably ill-behaved, and deserved no better destiny than that which was now to happen.

Not finding his mother at home, Perseus went straight to the palace and was immediately ushered into the presence of the king. Polydectes was by no means rejoiced to see him; for he had felt almost certain, in his own evil mind, that the Gorgons would have torn the poor young man to pieces, and have eaten him up, out of the way. However, seeing him safely returned, he put the best face he could upon the matter and asked Perseus how he had succeeded.

"Have you performed your promise?" inquired he. "Have you brought me the head of Medusa with the snaky locks? If not, young man, it will cost you dear; for I must have a bridal present for the beautiful Princess Hippodamia, and there is nothing else that she would admire so much."

"Yes, please your Majesty," answered Perseus, in a quiet way, as if it were no very wonderful deed for such a young man as he to perform. "I have brought you the Gorgon's head, snaky locks and all!"

"Indeed! Pray let me see it," quoth King Polydectes. "It must be a very curious spectacle, if all that travellers tell about it be true!"

"Your Majesty is in the right," replied Perseus. "It is really an object that will be pretty certain to fix the regards of all who look at it. And, if your Majesty think fit, I would suggest that a holiday be proclaimed, and that all your Majesty's subjects be summoned to behold this wonderful curiosity. Few of them, I imagine, have seen a Gorgon's head before, and perhaps never may again!"

The king well knew that his subjects were an idle set of reprobates, and very fond of sight-seeing, as idle persons usually are. So he took the young man's advice, and sent out heralds and messengers, in all directions, to blow the trumpet at the street-corners, and in the market-places, and wherever two roads met, and summon everybody to court. Thither, accordingly, came a great multitude of good-for-nothing vagabonds, all of whom, out of pure love of mischief, would have been glad if Perseus had met with some ill-hap, in his encounter with the Gorgons. If there were any better people in the island (as I really hope there may have been, although the story tells nothing about any such), they stayed quietly at home, minding their own business, and taking care of their little children. Most of the inhabitants, at all events, ran as fast as they could to the palace, and shoved, and pushed, and elbowed one another, in their eagerness to get near a balcony, on which Perseus showed himself, holding the embroidered wallet in his hand.

On a platform, within full view of the balcony, sat the mighty King Polydectes, amid his evil counsellors, and with his flattering courtiers in a semicircle round about him. Monarch, counsellors, courtiers, and subjects, all gazed eagerly towards Perseus.

"Show us the head! Show us the head!" shouted the people; and there was a fierceness in their cry as if they would tear Perseus to pieces, unless he should satisfy them with what he had to show. "Show us the head of Medusa with the snaky locks!"

A feeling of sorrow and pity came over the youthful Perseus.

"O King Polydectes," cried he, "and ye many people, I am very loath to show you the Gorgon's head!"

"Ah, the villain and coward!" yelled the people, more fiercely than before. "He is making game of us! He has no Gorgon's head! Show us the head, if you have it, or we will take your own head for a football!"

The evil counsellors whispered bad advice in the king's ear; the courtiers murmured, with one consent, that Perseus had shown disrespect to their royal lord and master; and the great King Polydectes himself waved his hand, and ordered him, with the stern, deep voice of authority, on his peril, to produce the bead.

"Show me the Gorgon's head, or I will cut off your own!"

And Perseus sighed.

"This instant," repeated Polydectes, "or you die!"

"Behold it, then!" cried Perseus, in a voice like the blast of a trumpet.

And, suddenly holding up the head, not an eyelid had time to wink before the wicked King Polydectes, his evil counsellors, and all his fierce subjects were no longer anything but the mere images of a monarch and his people. They were all fixed, forever, in the look and attitude of that moment! At the first glimpse of the terrible head of Medusa, they whitened into marble! And Perseus thrust the head back into his wallet, and went to tell his dear mother that she need no longer be afraid of the wicked King Polydectes.

How the Centaur Trained the Heroes on Pelion

HERE FOLLOWS a tale of heroes who sailed away into a distant land, to win themselves renown forever, in the adventure of the Golden Fleece.

And what was that first Golden Fleece? The old Hellens said that it hung in Colchis, which we call the Circassian coast, nailed to a beech-tree in the war-God's wood; and that it was the fleece of the wondrous ram who bore Phrixus and Helle across the Euxine sea. For Phrixus and Helle were the children of the cloud-nymph, and of Athamas the Minuan king. And when a famine came upon the land, their cruel step-mother Ino wished to kill them, that her own children might reign, and said that they must be sacrificed on an altar, to turn away the anger of the Gods. So the poor children were brought to the altar, and the priest stood ready with his knife, when out of the clouds came the Golden Ram, and took them on his back, and vanished. Then madness came upon that foolish king, Athamas, and ruin upon Ino and her children. For Athamas killed one of them in his fury, and Ino fled from him with the other in her arms, and leaped from a cliff into the sea, and was changed into a dolphin, such as you have seen, which wanders over the waves for ever sighing, with its little one clasped to its breast.

But the people drove out King Athamas, because he had killed his child; and he roamed about in his misery, till he came to the Oracle in Delphi. And the Oracle told him that he must wander for his sin, till the wild beasts should feast him as their guest. So he went on in hunger and sorrow for many a weary day, till he saw a pack of wolves. The wolves were tearing a sheep; but when they saw Athamas they fled, and left the sheep for him, and he ate of it; and then he knew that the oracle was fulfilled at last. So he wandered no more; but settled, and built a town, and became a king again.

But the ram carried the two children far away over land and sea, till he came to the Thracian Chersonese, and there Helle fell into the sea. So those narrow straits are called 'Hellespont,' after her; and they bear that name until this day.

Then the ram flew on with Phrixus to the north-east across the sea which we call the Black Sea now; but the Hellens call it Euxine. And at last, they say, he stopped at Colchis, on the steep Circassian coast; and there Phrixus married Chalciope, the daughter of Aeetes the king; and offered the ram in sacrifice; and Aeetes nailed the ram's fleece to a beech, in the grove of Ares the war-God.

And after awhile Phrixus died, and was buried, but his spirit had no rest; for he was buried far from his native land, and the pleasant hills of Hellas. So he came in dreams to the heroes of the Minuai, and called sadly by their beds, "Come and set my spirit free, that I may go home to my fathers and to my kinsfolk, and the pleasant Minuan land."

And they asked, "How shall we set your spirit free?"

"You must sail over the sea to Colchis, and bring home the golden fleece; and then my spirit will come back with it, and I shall sleep with my fathers and have rest."

He came thus, and called to them often; but when they woke they looked at each other, and said, "Who dare sail to Colchis, or bring home the golden fleece?"

And in all the country none was brave enough to try it; for the man and the time were not come.

Phrixus had a cousin called Aeson, who was king in Iolcos by the sea. There he ruled over the rich Minuan heroes, as Athamas his uncle ruled in Boeotia; and, like Athamas, he was an unhappy man. For he had a step-brother named Pelias, of whom some said that he was a nymph's son, and there were dark and sad tales about his birth. When he was a babe he was cast out on the mountains, and a wild mare came by and kicked him. But a shepherd passing found the baby, with its face all blackened by the blow; and took him home, and called him Pelias, because his face was bruised and black. And he grew up fierce and lawless, and did many a fearful deed; and at last he drove out Aeson his step-brother, and then his own brother Neleus, and took the kingdom to himself, and ruled over the rich Minuan heroes, in Iolcos by the sea.

And Aeson, when he was driven out, went sadly away out of the town, leading his little son by the hand; and he said to himself, "I must hide the child in the mountains; or Pelias will surely kill him, because he is the heir."

So he went up from the sea across the valley, through the vineyards and the olive groves, and across the torrent of Anauros, toward Pelion the ancient mountain, whose brows are white with snow.

He went up and up into the mountain, over marsh, and crag, and down, till the boy was tired and footsore, and Aeson had to bear him in his arms, till he came to the mouth of a lonely cave, at the foot of a mighty cliff.

Above the cliff the snow-wreaths hung, dripping and cracking in the sun; but at its foot around the cave's mouth grew all fair flowers and herbs, as if in a garden, ranged in order, each sort by itself. There they grew gaily in the sunshine, and the spray of the torrent from above; while from the cave came the sound of music, and a man's voice singing to the harp.

Then Aeson put down the lad, and whispered:

"Fear not, but go in, and whomsoever you shall find, lay your hands upon his knees, and say, 'In the name of Zeus, the father of Gods and men, I am your guest from this day forth.'"

Then the lad went in without trembling, for he too was a hero's son; but when he was within, he stopped in wonder to listen to that magic song.

And there he saw the singer lying upon bear-skins and fragrant boughs: Cheiron, the ancient centaur, the wisest of all things beneath the sky. Down to the waist he was a man, but below he was a noble horse; his white hair rolled down over his broad shoulders, and his white beard over his broad brown chest; and his eyes were wise and mild, and his forehead like a mountain-wall.

And in his hands he held a harp of gold, and struck it with a golden key; and as he struck, he sang till his eyes glittered, and filled all the cave with light.

And he sang of the birth of Time, and of the heavens and the dancing stars; and of the ocean, and the ether, and the fire, and the shaping of the wondrous earth. And he sang of the treasures of the hills, and the hidden jewels of the mine, and the veins of fire and metal, and the virtues of all healing herbs, and of the speech of birds, and of prophecy, and of hidden things to come.

Then he sang of health, and strength, and manhood, and a valiant heart; and of music, and hunting, and wrestling, and all the games which heroes love: and of travel, and wars, and sieges, and a noble death in fight; and then he sang of peace and plenty, and of equal justice in the land; and as he sang the boy listened wide-eyed, and forgot his errand in the song.

And at the last old Cheiron was silent, and called the lad with a soft voice.

And the lad ran trembling to him, and would have laid his hands upon his knees; but Cheiron smiled, and said, "Call hither your father Aeson, for I know you, and all that has befallen, and saw you both afar in the valley, even before you left the town."

Then Aeson came in sadly, and Cheiron asked him, "Why camest you not yourself to me, Aeson the Aeolid?"

And Aeson said:

"I thought, Cheiron will pity the lad if he sees him come alone; and I wished to try whether he was fearless, and dare venture like a hero's son. But now I entreat you by Father Zeus, let the boy be your guest till better times, and train him among the sons of the heroes, that he may avenge his father's house."

Then Cheiron smiled, and drew the lad to him, and laid his hand upon his golden locks, and said, "Are you afraid of my horse's hoofs, fair boy, or will you be my pupil from this day?"

"I would gladly have horse's hoofs like you, if I could sing such songs as yours."

And Cheiron laughed, and said, "Sit here by me till sundown, when your playfellows will come home, and you shall learn like them to be a king, worthy to rule over gallant men."

Then he turned to Aeson, and said, "Go back in peace, and bend before the storm like a prudent man. This boy shall not cross the Anauros again, till he has become a glory to you and to the house of Aeolus."

And Aeson wept over his son and went away; but the boy did not weep, so full was his fancy of that strange cave, and the centaur, and his song, and the playfellows whom he was to see.

Then Cheiron put the lyre into his hands, and taught him how to play it, till the sun sank low behind the cliff, and a shout was heard outside.

And then in came the sons of the heroes, Aeneas, and Heracles, and Peleus, and many another mighty name.

And great Cheiron leapt up joyfully, and his hoofs made the cave resound, as they shouted, "Come out, Father Cheiron; come out and see our game."

And one cried, "I have killed two deer;" and another, "I took a wild cat among the crags;" and Heracles dragged a wild goat after him by its horns, for he was as huge as a mountain crag; and Coeneus carried a bear-cub under each arm, and laughed when they scratched and bit, for neither tooth nor steel could wound him.

And Cheiron praised them all, each according to his deserts.

Only one walked apart and silent, Asclepius, the too-wise child, with his bosom full of herbs and flowers, and round his wrist a spotted snake; he came with downcast eyes to Cheiron, and whispered how he had watched the snake cast its old skin, and grow young again before his eyes, and how he had gone down into a village in the vale, and cured a dying man with a herb which he had seen a sick goat eat.

And Cheiron smiled, and said, "To each Athene and Apollo give some gift, and each is worthy in his place; but to this child they have given an honour beyond all honours, to cure while others kill."

Then the lads brought in wood, and split it, and lighted a blazing fire; and others skinned the deer and quartered them, and set them to roast before the fire; and while the venison was cooking they bathed in the snow-torrent, and washed away the dust and sweat.

And then all ate till they could eat no more (for they had tasted nothing since the dawn), and drank of the clear spring water, for wine is not fit for growing lads. And when the remnants were put away, they all lay down upon the skins and leaves about the fire, and each took the lyre in turn, and sang and played with all his heart.

And after a while they all went out to a plot of grass at the cave's mouth, and there they boxed, and ran, and wrestled, and laughed till the stones fell from the cliffs.

Then Cheiron took his lyre, and all the lads joined hands; and as be played, they danced to his measure, in and out, and round and round. There they danced hand in hand, till the night fell over land and sea, while the black glen shone with their broad white limbs and the gleam of their golden hair.

And the lad danced with them, delighted, and then slept a wholesome sleep, upon fragrant leaves of bay, and myrtle, and marjoram, and flowers of thyme; and rose at the dawn, and bathed in the torrent, and became a schoolfellow to the heroes' sons, and forgot Iolcos, and his father, and all his former life. But he grew strong, and brave and cunning, upon the pleasant downs of Pelion, in the keen hungry mountain air. And he learnt to wrestle, and to box, and to hunt, and to play upon the harp; and next he learnt to ride, for old Cheiron used to mount him on his back; and he learnt the virtues of all herbs and how to cure all wounds; and Cheiron called him Jason the healer, and that is his name until this day.

How Perseus Slew the Gorgon

SO PERSEUS STARTED on his journey, going dry-shod over land and sea; and his heart was high and joyful, for the winged sandals bore him each day a seven days' journey.

And he went by Cythnus, and by Ceos, and the pleasant Cyclades to Attica; and past Athens and Thebes, and the Copaic lake, and up the vale of Cephissus, and past the peaks of Oeta and Pindus, and over the rich Thessalian plains, till the sunny hills of Greece were behind him, and before him were the wilds of the north. Then he passed the Thracian mountains, and many a barbarous tribe, Paeons and Dardans and Triballi, till he came to the Ister stream, and the dreary Scythian plains. And he walked across the Ister dry-shod, and away through the moors and fens, day and night toward the bleak north-west, turning neither to the right hand nor the left, till he came to the Unshapen Land, and the place which has no name.

And seven days he walked through it, on a path which few can tell; for those who have trodden it like least to speak of it, and those who go there again in dreams are glad enough when they awake; till he came to the edge of the everlasting night, where the air was full of feathers, and the soil was hard with ice; and there at last he found the three Grey Sisters, by the shore of the freezing sea, nodding upon a white log of drift-wood, beneath the cold white winter moon; and they chanted a low song together, 'Why the old times were better than the new.'

There was no living thing around them, not a fly, not a moss upon the rocks. Neither seal nor sea-gull dare come near, lest the ice should clutch them in its claws. The surge broke up in foam, but it fell again in flakes of snow; and it frosted the hair of the three Grey Sisters, and the bones in the ice-cliff above their heads. They passed the eye from one to the other, but for all that they could not see; and they passed the tooth from one to the other, but for all that they could not eat; and they sat in the full glare of the moon, but they were none the warmer for her beams. And Perseus pitied the three Grey Sisters; but they did not pity themselves.

So he said, "Oh, venerable mothers, wisdom is the daughter of old age. You therefore should know many things. Tell me, if you can, the path to the Gorgon."

Then one cried, "Who is this who reproaches us with old age?" And another, "This is the voice of one of the children of men."

And he, "I do not reproach, but honour your old age, and I am one of the sons of men and of the heroes. The rulers of Olympus have sent me to you to ask the way to the Gorgon."

Then one, "There are new rulers in Olympus, and all new things are bad." And another, "We hate your rulers, and the heroes, and all the children of men. We are the kindred of the Titans, and the Giants, and the Gorgons, and the ancient monsters of the deep." And another, "Who is this rash and insolent man who pushes unbidden into our world?" And the first, "There never was such a world as ours, nor will be; if we let him see it, he will spoil it all."

Then one cried, "Give me the eye, that I may see him;" and another, "Give me the tooth, that I may bite him."

But Perseus, when he saw that they were foolish and proud, and did not love the children of men, left off pitying them, and said to himself, "Hungry men must needs be hasty; if I stay making many words here, I shall be starved." Then he stepped close to them, and watched till they passed the eye from hand to hand. And as they groped about between themselves, he held out his own hand gently, till one of them put the eye into it, fancying that it was the hand of her sister. Then he sprang back, and laughed, and cried:

"Cruel and proud old women, I have your eye; and I will throw it into the sea, unless you tell me the path to the Gorgon, and swear to me that you tell me right."

Then they wept, and chattered, and scolded; but in vain. They were forced to tell the truth, though, when they told it, Perseus could hardly make out the road.

"You must go," they said, "foolish boy, to the southward, into the ugly glare of the sun, till you come to Atlas the Giant, who holds the heaven and the earth apart. And you must ask his daughters, the Hesperides, who are young and foolish like yourself. And now give us back our eye, for we have forgotten all the rest."

So Perseus gave them back their eye; but instead of using it, they nodded and fell fast asleep, and were turned into blocks of ice, till the tide came up and washed them all away. And now they float up and down like icebergs for ever, weeping whenever they meet the sunshine, and the fruitful summer and the warm south wind, which fill young hearts with joy.

But Perseus leaped away to the southward, leaving the snow and the ice behind: past the isle of the Hyperboreans, and the tin isles, and the long Iberian shore, while the sun rose higher day by day upon a bright blue summer sea. And the terns and the sea-gulls swept laughing round his head, and called to him to stop and play, and the dolphins gambolled up as he passed, and offered to carry him on their backs. And all night long the sea-nymphs sang sweetly, and the Tritons blew upon their conchs, as they played round Galataea their queen, in her car of pearled shells. Day by day the sun rose higher, and leaped more swiftly into the sea at night, and more swiftly out of the sea at dawn; while Perseus skimmed over the billows like a sea-gull, and his feet were never wetted; and leapt on from wave to wave, and his limbs were never weary, till he saw far away a mighty mountain, all rose-red in the setting sun. Its feet were wrapped in forests, and its head in wreaths of cloud; and Perseus knew that it was Atlas, who holds the heavens and the earth apart.

He came to the mountain, and leapt on shore, and wandered upward, among pleasant valleys and waterfalls, and tall trees and strange ferns and flowers; but there was no smoke rising from any glen, nor house, nor sign of man.

At last he heard sweet voices singing; and he guessed that he was come to the garden of the Nymphs, the daughters of the Evening Star.

They sang like nightingales among the thickets, and Perseus stopped to hear their song; but the words which they spoke he could not understand; no, nor no man after him for many a hundred years. So he stepped forward and saw them dancing, hand in hand around the charmed tree, which bent under its golden fruit; and round the tree-foot was coiled the dragon, old Ladon the sleepless snake, who lies there for ever, listening to the song of the maidens, blinking and watching with dry bright eyes.

Then Perseus stopped, not because he feared the dragon, but because he was bashful before those fair maids; but when they saw him, they too stopped, and called to him with trembling voices:

"Who are you? Are you Heracles the mighty, who will come to rob our garden, and carry off our golden fruit?"

And he answered, "I am not Heracles the mighty, and I want none of your golden fruit. Tell me, fair Nymphs, the way which leads to the Gorgon, that I may go on my way and slay her."

"Not yet, not yet, fair boy; come dance with us around the tree in the garden which knows no winter, the home of the south wind and the sun. Come hither and play with us awhile; we have danced alone here for a thousand years, and our hearts are weary with longing for a playfellow. So come, come, come!"

"I cannot dance with you, fair maidens; for I must do the errand of the Immortals. So tell me the way to the Gorgon, lest I wander and perish in the waves."

Then they sighed and wept; and answered: "The Gorgon! She will freeze you into stone."

"It is better to die like a hero than to live like an ox in a stall. The Immortals have lent me weapons, and they will give me wit to use them."

Then they sighed again and answered, "Fair boy, if you are bent on your own ruin, be it so. We know not the way to the Gorgon; but we will ask the giant Atlas, above upon the mountain peak, the brother of our father, the silver Evening Star. He sits aloft and sees across the ocean, and far away into the Unshapen Land."

So they went up the mountain to Atlas their uncle, and Perseus went up with them. And they found the giant kneeling, as he held the heavens and the earth apart.

They asked him, and he answered mildly, pointing to the sea-board with his mighty hand, "I can see the Gorgons lying on an island far away, but this youth can never come near them, unless he has the hat of darkness, which whosoever wears cannot be seen."

Then cried Perseus, "Where is that hat, that I may find it?"

But the giant smiled. "No living mortal can find that hat, for it lies in the depths of Hades, in the regions of the dead. But my nieces are immortal, and they shall fetch it for you, if you will promise me one thing and keep your faith."

Then Perseus promised; and the giant said, "When you come back with the head of Medusa, you shall show me the beautiful horror, that I may lose my feeling and my breathing, and become a stone for ever; for it is weary labour for me to hold the heavens and the earth apart."

Then Perseus promised, and the eldest of the Nymphs went down, and into a dark cavern among the cliffs, out of which came smoke and thunder, for it was one of the mouths of Hell.

And Perseus and the Nymphs sat down seven days, and waited trembling, till the Nymph came up again; and her face was pale, and her eyes dazzled with the light, for she had been long in the dreary darkness; but in her hand was the magic hat.

Then all the Nymphs kissed Perseus, and wept over him a long while; but he was only impatient to be gone. And at last they put the hat upon his head, and he vanished out of their sight.

But Perseus went on boldly, past many an ugly sight, far away into the heart of the Unshapen Land, beyond the streams of Ocean, to the isles where no ship cruises, where is neither night nor day, where nothing is in its right place, and nothing has a name; till he heard the rustle of the Gorgons' wings and saw the glitter of their brazen talons; and then he knew that it was time to halt, lest Medusa should freeze him into stone.

He thought awhile with himself, and remembered Athene's words. He rose aloft into the air, and held the mirror of the shield above his head, and looked up into it that he might see all that was below him.

And he saw the three Gorgons sleeping as huge as elephants. He knew that they could not see him, because the hat of darkness hid him; and yet he trembled as he sank down near them, so terrible were those brazen claws.

Two of the Gorgons were foul as swine, and lay sleeping heavily, as swine sleep, with their mighty wings outspread; but Medusa tossed to and fro restlessly, and as she tossed Perseus pitied her, she looked so fair and sad. Her plumage was like the rainbow, and her face was like the face of a nymph, only her eyebrows were knit, and her lips clenched, with everlasting care and pain; and her long neck gleamed so white in the mirror that Perseus had not the heart to strike, and said, "Ah, that it had been either of her sisters!"

But as he looked, from among her tresses the vipers' heads awoke, and peeped up with their bright dry eyes, and showed their fangs, and hissed; and Medusa, as she tossed, threw back her wings and showed her brazen claws; and Perseus saw that, for all her beauty, she was as foul and venomous as the rest.

Then he came down and stepped to her boldly, and looked steadfastly on his mirror, and struck with Herpé stoutly once; and he did not need to strike again.

Then he wrapped the head in the goat-skin, turning away his eyes, and sprang into the air aloft, faster than he ever sprang before.

For Medusa's wings and talons rattled as she sank dead upon the rocks; and her two foul sisters woke, and saw her lying dead.

Into the air they sprang yelling and looked for him who had done the deed. Thrice they swung round and round, like hawks who beat for a partridge; and thrice they snuffed round and round, like hounds who draw upon a deer. At last they struck upon the scent of the blood, and they checked for a moment to make sure; and then on they rushed with a fearful howl, while the wind rattled hoarse in their wings.

On they rushed, sweeping and flapping, like eagles after a hare; and Perseus' blood ran cold, for all his courage, as he saw them come howling on his track; and he cried, "Bear me well now, brave sandals, for the hounds of Death are at my heels!"

And well the brave sandals bore him, aloft through cloud and sunshine, across the shoreless sea; and fast followed the hounds of Death, as the roar of their wings came down the wind. But the roar came down fainter and fainter, and the howl of their voices died away; for the sandals were too swift, even for Gorgons, and by nightfall they were far behind, two black specks in the southern sky, till the sun sank and he saw them no more.

Then he came again to Atlas, and the garden of the Nymphs; and when the giant heard him coming he groaned, and said, "Fulfil thy promise to me."

Then Perseus held up to him the Gorgon's head, and he had rest from all his toil; for he became a crag of stone, which sleeps for ever far above the clouds.

Then he thanked the Nymphs, and asked them, "By what road shall I go homeward again, for I wandered far round in coming hither?"

And they wept and cried, "Go home no more, but stay and play with us, the lonely maidens, who dwell for ever far away from Gods and men."

But he refused, and they told him his road, and said, "Take with you this magic fruit, which, if you eat once, you will not hunger for seven days. For you must go eastward and eastward ever, over the doleful Lybian shore, which Poseidon gave to Father Zeus, when he burst open the Bosphorus and the Hellespont, and drowned the fair Lectonian land. And Zeus took that land in exchange, a fair bargain, much bad ground for a little good, and to this day it lies waste and desert with shingle, and rock, and sand."

Then they kissed Perseus, and wept over him, and he leapt down the mountain, and went on, lessening and lessening like a sea-gull, away and out to sea.

Athena and Arachne

IN THIS STORY from the ancient Roman poet Ovid's *Metamorphoses*, Arachne, vainglorious of her ingenuity, challenges Minerva (the Roman equivalent of Athena) to a contest of skill in her art. The Goddess accepts the challenge, and, being enraged to see herself outdone, strikes her rival with her shuttle; upon which, Arachne, in her distress, hangs herself. Minerva, touched with compassion, transforms her into a spider:

Tritonia (an epithet of Athena) turns her mind to the fate of the Mæonian Arachne; who, as she had heard, did not yield to her in the praises of the art of working in wool. She was renowned not for the place of her birth, nor for the origin of her family, but for her skill alone. Idmon, of Colophon, her father, used to dye the soaking wool in Phocæan purple. Her mother was dead; but she, too, was of the lower rank, and of the same condition with her husband. Yet Arachne, by her skill, had acquired a memorable name throughout the cities of Lydia; although, born of a humble family, she used to live in the little town of Hypæpæ. Often did the Nymphs desert the vineyards of their own Tymolus, that they might look at her admirable workmanship; often did the Nymphs of the river Pactolus forsake their streams. And not only did it give them pleasure to look at the garments when made, but even, too, while they were being made, so much grace was there in her working. Whether it was that she was rolling the rough wool into its first balls, or whether she was unravelling the work with her fingers, and was softening the fleeces worked over again with long drawings out, equalling the mists in their fineness; or whether she was moving the smooth round spindle with her nimble thumb, or was embroidering with the needle, you might perceive that she had been instructed by Pallas (another epithet of Athena).

This, however, she used to deny; and, being displeased with a mistress so famed, she said, "Let her contend with me. There is nothing which, if conquered, I should refuse to endure." Pallas impersonates an old woman; she both places false gray hair on her temples, and supports as well her infirm limbs by a staff. Then thus she begins to speak: "Old age has not everything which we should avoid; experience comes from lengthened years. Do not despise my advice; let the greatest fame for working wool be sought by thee among mortals. But yield to the Goddess, and, rash woman, ask pardon for thy speeches with suppliant voice. She will grant pardon at my entreaty." The other beholds her with scowling eyes, and leaves the threads she has begun; and scarcely restraining her hand, and discovering her anger by her looks, with such words as these does she reply to the disguised Pallas: "Thou comest here bereft of thy understanding, and worn out with prolonged old age; and it is thy misfortune to have lived too long. If thou hast any daughter-in-law, if thou hast any daughter of thy own, let her listen to these remarks. I have sufficient knowledge for myself in myself, and do not imagine that thou hast availed anything by thy advice; my opinion is still the same. Why does not she come herself? why does she decline this contest?"

Then the Goddess says, "Lo! she is come;" and she casts aside the figure of an old woman, and shows herself as Pallas. The Nymphs and the Mygdonian matrons venerate the Goddess.

The virgin alone is not daunted. But still she blushes, and a sudden flush marks her reluctant features, and again it vanishes; just as the sky is wont to become tinted with purple, when Aurora is first stirring, and after a short time to grow white from the influence of the Sun. She persists in her determination, and, from a desire for a foolish victory, she rushes upon her own destruction. Nor, indeed, does the daughter of Jupiter decline it, or advise her any further, nor does she now put off the contest. There is no delay; they both take their stand in different places, and stretch out two webs on the loom with a fine warp. The web is tied around the beam; the sley separates the warp; the woof is inserted in the middle with sharp shuttles, which the fingers hurry along, and being drawn within the warp, the teeth notched in the moving sley strike it. Both hasten on, and girding up their garments to their breasts, they move their skilful arms, their eagerness beguiling their fatigue. There both the purple is being woven, which is subjected to the Tyrian brazen vessel, and fine shades of minute difference; just as the rainbow, with its mighty arch, is wont to tint a long tract of the sky by means of the rays reflected by the shower: in which, though a thousand different colors are shining, yet the very transition eludes the eyes that look upon it; to such a degree is that which is adjacent the same; and yet the extremes are different. There, too, the pliant gold is mixed with the threads, and ancient subjects are represented on the webs.

Pallas embroiders the rock of Mars in Athens, the citadel of Cecrops, and the old dispute about the name of the country. Twice six celestial Gods are sitting on lofty seats in august state, with Jupiter in the midst. His own proper likeness distinguishes each of the Gods. The form of Jupiter is that of a monarch. She makes the God of the sea to be standing there, and to be striking the rugged rocks with his long trident, and a wild horse to be springing forth out of the midst of the opening of the rock; by which pledge of his favor he lays claim to the city. But to herself she gives the shield, she gives the lance with its sharp point; she gives the helmet to her head, and her breast is protected by the Ægis. She there represents, too, the earth struck by her spear, producing a shoot of pale olive with its berries, and the Gods admiring it. Victory is the end of her work. But that the rival of her fame may learn from precedents what reward to expect for an attempt so mad, she adds, in four different parts, four contests bright in their coloring, and distinguished by diminutive figures. One corner contains Thracian Rhodope and Hæmus, now cold mountains, formerly human bodies, who assumed to themselves the names of the supreme Gods. Another part contains the wretched fate of the Pygmæan matron. Her, overcome in a contest, Juno commanded to be a crane, and to wage war against her own people. She depicts, too, Antigone, who once dared to contend with the wife of the great Jupiter; and whom the royal Juno changed into a bird; nor did Ilion protect her, or her father Laomedon, from assuming wings, and as a white crane, from commending herself with her chattering beak. The only corner that remains, represents the bereft Cinyras; and he, embracing the steps of a temple, once the limbs of his own daughters, and lying upon the stone, appears to be weeping. She surrounds the exterior borders with peaceful olive. That is the close; and with her own tree she puts an end to the work.

The Mæonian Nymph delineates Europa, deceived by the form of the bull; and you would think it a real bull, and real sea. She herself seems to be looking upon the land which she has left, and to be crying out to her companions, and to be in dread of the touch of the dashing waters, and to be drawing up her timid feet. She drew also Asterie, seized by the struggling eagle; and made Leda, reclining beneath the wings of the swan. She added, how Jupiter, concealed under the form of a Satyr, impregnated Antiope, the beauteous daughter of Nycteus, with a twin offspring; how he was Amphitryon, when he beguiled thee, Tirynthian dame; how, turned to gold, he deceived Danaë; how, changed into fire, the daughter of Asopus; how, as a shepherd, Mnemosyne; and as a speckled serpent, Deois. She depicted thee too, Neptune, changed into a fierce bull, with the virgin daughter of Æolus. Thou, seeming to be Enipeus, didst beget the Aloïdæ; as a ram, thou didst delude Theophane, the daughter of Bisaltis. Thee too the most bounteous mother of corn, with her yellow hair, experienced as a steed; thee, the mother of the winged horse, with her snaky locks, received as a bird; Melantho, as a dolphin. To all these did she give their own likeness, and the real appearance of the various localities. There was Phœbus, under the form of a rustic; and how, besides, he was wearing the wings of a hawk at one time, at another the skin of a lion; how, too, as a shepherd, he deceived Isse, the daughter of Macareus. How Liber deceived Erigone, in a fictitious bunch of grapes; and how Saturn begot the two-formed Chiron, in the form of a horse. The extreme part of the web, being enclosed in a fine border, had flowers interwoven with the twining ivy.

Pallas could not blame that work, nor could Envy censure it. The yellow-haired Virgin grieved at her success, and tore the web embroidered with the criminal acts of the Gods of heaven. And as she was holding her shuttle made of boxwood from Mount Cytorus, three or four times did she strike the forehead of Arachne, the daughter of Idmon. The unhappy creature could not endure it; and being of a high spirit, she tied up her throat in a halter. Pallas, taking compassion, bore her up as she hung; and thus she said: "Live on indeed, wicked one, but still hang; and let the same decree of punishment be pronounced against thy race, and against thy latest posterity, that thou mayst not be free from care in time to come." After that, as she departed, she sprinkled her with the juices of an Hecatean herb; and immediately her hair, touched by the noxious drug, fell off, and together with it her nose and ears. The head of herself, now small as well throughout her whole body, becomes very small. Her slender fingers cleave to her sides as legs; her belly takes possession of the rest of her; but out of this she gives forth a thread; and as a spider, she works at her web as formerly.

Calypso's Island

ODYSSEUS COULD SEE LAND and in the distance a beautiful nymph, the most beautiful woman on whom he had ever laid eyes. Her milk-white skin was gleaming in the moonlight, and the wrathful winds tossed her silken hair. Her voice was soft, inviting above the raging storms.

'Come to me, Odysseus,' she whispered. 'Here you will find love, and eternal life.'

Odysseus struggled for breath, filled with longing and wonder. She reached a slender hand towards him, across the expanse of water, and lifted him from its depths, the strength of her grip, the length of her reach inhuman. He shuddered at her touch.

'You have come to join me,' she said calmly, as Odysseus laid restless and dripping beneath her.

Odysseus nodded, his passion spent. He was alive. The others had been clutched by the revengeful Poseidon. He was grateful to this nymph. He would plan his escape later.

'I have asked for you, and you have come,' she intoned quietly, settling herself at his side. Odysseus felt the first stirring of fear, but dismissed it as the lovely maiden smiled down on him.

She was Calypso, the lovely daughter of Thetis, and like Circe she was an enchantress. She lived alone on the island, in a comfortable cavern overhung by vines and fragrant foliage. She was gentle, and quiet, tending to Odysseus's every need, feeding him with morsels of delicious foods, warming him with handspun garments which clung to his body like a new skin, and she welcomed him in her bed, running his body over with hot hands that explored and relaxed the beaten hero until he grew to love her, and to build his life with her on the idyllic island.

For seven years he lived with Calypso, drunk with luxury and love. She was more beautiful than any he had seen before, and her island was dripping with pleasures. And as his happiness grew deeper, his fire and fervour spent to become a peaceful equilibrium, he felt the jab of conscience, of something untoward eating at the corners of his idyll, and he realized that he was living in a numb oblivion, that his passion to return home, to see his family, to take up the responsibilities of his leadership, were as strong in him as they had ever been and that he must allow them to surge forth, to fill him again with fiery ambition.

And in that seventh year he spent more and more time seated on the banks of the island, gazing towards his own land where time did not stand still and where his wife's suitors were threatening to take over his country, his rule. He came eventually to the notice of Athene, whose favour he had kept despite the outrage of the other gods, and she went at once to Zeus on his behalf. Zeus was fair and kind, and he balanced the sins of Odysseus against his innate good will, and the struggles to keep in check his unruly crews, all of which were lost to him now. Poseidon was away from Olympus and the time seemed right to set Odysseus free, for he had lived long enough in an enchanted purgatory.

Calypso reluctantly agreed to allow him his freedom, and she provided him with the tools to create a sturdy boat, and with provisions of food and drink enough to last the entire journey. She bathed him, dressed him in fine silks and jewels, as befitted a returning warrior, and kissing him gently but with all the fire of her love for him, she bade him go, with a tear-stained farewell. She had provided him with instructions which would see him round the dangers, across the perils that could beset him. He set sail for Ithaca.

Scylla and Charybdis

CIRCE HAD WARNED ODYSSEUS of the dangers that would beset him and his crew should they choose to ignore the words of wise Tiresias. The next part of their journey would take them though a narrow strait, peopled by some of the most fearsome monsters in all the lands. Odysseus was to guide the ship through the narrow passage, through fierce and rolling waters, looking neither up nor down, embodying all humility.

But the pride of Odysseus was more deeply rooted than his fear, and ignoring Circe's words, he took a stand on the prow of his ship, heavily armoured and emboldened by the support of his men. Here he stood as they passed the rocks of Charybdis, the hateful daughter of Poseidon, who came to the surface three times each day in order to belch out a powerful whirlpool, drawing into her frothing gut all that came back with it. There was no sign of her now, the waters suspiciously stilled. Ahead lay an island, drenched in warm sunlight, beckoning to the weary sailors. They must just make it through.

Odysseus had kept the details of this fearsome strait from his men. They had been weakened by battle, and by the horrific sights which had met their eyes since leaving Troy. They were so close to Ithaca, he dared not cast their hopes and anticipation into shadow. And so it was that only Odysseus knew of the next monster who was to be thrust upon them in that dangerous channel, only Odysseus who knew that she was capable of tasks more gruesome than any of them had seen in all their travels.

For Scylla was a gluttonous and evil creature that haunted the strait, making her home in a gore-splattered den where she feasted on the remains of luckless sailors. She was, they said, a nymph who had been the object of Glaucus's attentions. Glaucus was a sea-god who had been turned into a merman by a strange herb he had unwittingly swallowed. And as much as he adored Scylla, so he was loved by Circe who, in a jealous rage, had turned Scylla into a terrible sea-monster with six dog's heads around her waist. She lived there in the cliff face in the straits of Messina, and devoured sailors who passed. She moved silently. Odysseus was loath to admit it, but the silent danger she represented placed more fear in his heart than the bravest of enemies.

Odysseus and his men passed further into the quiet strait, their mouths dry with fear. A silence hung over them like a shroud. And then it was broken by a tiny splash, and tinkle of water dripping, and up, with a mighty roar, came Scylla, the mouths on each head gaping open, their lethal jaws sprung for one purpose alone. Smoothly she leaned forward and in a flash of colour, of torn clothing and hellish screams, six of his best men were plucked from their posts aboard ship and drawn into the mouth of her cave. Their cries rent at the heart, at the conscience of Odysseus, and he turned helplessly to his remaining crew who looked at him with genuine fear, distrust and anger. A mutinous fever bubbled at the edges of their loyalty, and Odysseus knew he had lost them. He looked back at the cave where Scylla had silenced his hapless men, and signalled the others to row faster. A repeat of her attack would leave him with too few men to carry on. They rowed towards the shores of the great three-cornered island, Thrinacie, where the herds of the Sun-god Helios grazed peacefully on the hilltops.

The Golden Fleece

ATHAMAS, KING OF BOEOTIA, had married Nephele, a cloud-nymph, and their children were Helle and Phryxus. The restless and wandering nature of Nephele, however, soon wearied her husband, who, being a mortal, had little sympathy with his ethereal consort; so he divorced her, and married the beautiful but wicked Ino (sister of Semele), who hated her step-children, and even planned their destruction. But the watchful Nephele contrived to circumvent her cruel designs, and succeeded in getting the children out of the palace. She then placed them both on the back of a winged ram, with a fleece of pure gold, which had been given to her by Hermes; and on this wonderful animal brother and sister rode through the air over land and sea; but on the way Helle, becoming seized with giddiness, fell into the sea (called after her the Hellespont) and was drowned.

Phryxus arrived safely at Colchis, where he was hospitably received by king Aëtes, who gave him one of his daughters in marriage. In gratitude to Zeus for the protection accorded him during his flight, Phryxus sacrificed to him the golden ram, whilst the fleece he presented to Aëtes, who nailed it up in the Grove of Ares, and dedicated it to the god of War. An oracle having declared that the life of Aëtes depended on the safe-keeping of the fleece, he carefully guarded the entrance to the grove by placing before it an immense dragon, which never slept.

The Birth of Oisín

ONE DAY as Finn and his companions and dogs were returning from the chase to their Dún on the Hill of Allen, a beautiful fawn started up on their path and the chase swept after her, she taking the way which led to their home. Soon, all the pursuers were left far behind save only Finn himself and his two hounds Bran and Sceolaun. Now these hounds were of strange breed, for Tyren, sister to Murna, the mother of Finn, had been changed into a hound by the enchantment of a woman of the Fairy Folk, who loved Tyren's husband Ullan; and the two hounds of Finn were the children of Tyren, born to her in that shape. Of all hounds in Ireland they were the best, and Finn loved them much, so that it was said he wept but twice in his life, and once was for the death of Bran.

At last, as the chase went on down a valley side, Finn saw the fawn stop and lie down, while the two hounds began to play round her and to lick her face and limbs. So he gave commandment that none should hurt her, and she followed them to the Dún of Allen, playing with the hounds as she went.

The same night Finn awoke and saw standing by his bed the fairest woman his eyes had ever beheld.

"I am Saba, O Finn," she said, "and I was the fawn ye chased today. Because I would not give my love to the Druid of the Fairy Folk, who is named the Dark, he put that shape upon me by his sorceries, and I have borne it these three years. But a slave of his, pitying me, once revealed to me that if I could win to thy great Dún of Allen, O Finn, I should be safe from all enchantments and my natural shape would come to me again. But I feared to be torn in pieces by thy dogs, or wounded by thy hunters, till at last I let myself be overtaken by thee alone and by Bran and Sceolaun, who have the nature of man and would do me no hurt."

"Have no fear, maiden," said Finn, "we the Fianna, are free and our guest-friends are free; there is none who shall put compulsion on you here."

So Saba dwelt with Finn, and he made her his wife; and so deep was his love for her that neither the battle nor the chase had any delight for him, and for months he never left her side. She also loved him as deeply, and their joy in each other was like that of the Immortals in the Land of Youth. But at last word came to Finn that the warships of the Northmen were in the bay of Dublin, and he summoned his heroes to the fight, "for," said he to Saba, "the men of Erinn give us tribute and hospitality to defend them from the foreigner, and it were shame to take it from them and not to give that to which we, on our side, are pledged." And he called to mind that great saying of Goll mac Morna when they were once sore bested by a mighty host – "a man," said Goll, "lives after his life but not after his honour."

Seven days was Finn absent, and he drove the Northmen from the shores of Erinn. But on the eighth day he returned, and when he entered his Dún he saw trouble in the eyes of his men and of their fair womenfolk, and Saba was not on the rampart expecting his return. So he bade them tell him what had chanced, and they said –

"Whilst thou, our father and lord, wert afar off smiting the foreigner, and Saba looking ever down the pass for thy return, we saw one day as it were the likeness of thee approaching, and Bran and Sceolaun at thy heels. And we seemed also to hear the notes of the Fian hunting call blown on the wind. Then Saba hastened to the great gate, and we could not stay her, so eager was she to rush to the phantom. But when she came near, she halted and gave a loud and bitter cry, and the shape of thee smote her with a hazel wand, and lo, there was no woman there anymore, but a deer. Then those hounds chased it, and ever as it strove to reach again the gate of the Dún they turned it back. We all now seized what arms we could and ran out to drive away the enchanter, but when we reached the place there was nothing to be seen, only still we heard the rushing of flying feet and the baying of dogs, and one thought it came from here, and another from there, till at last the uproar died away and all was still. What we could do, O Finn, we did; Saba is gone."

Finn then struck his hand on his breast but spoke no word, and he went to his own chamber. No man saw him for the rest of that day, nor for the day after. Then he came forth, and ordered the matters of the Fianna as of old, but for seven years thereafter he went searching for Saba through every remote glen and dark forest and cavern of Ireland, and he would take no hounds with him save Bran and Sceolaun. But at last he renounced all hope of finding her again, and went hunting as of old. One day as he was following the chase on Ben Gulban in Sligo, he heard the musical bay of the dogs change of a sudden to a fierce growling and yelping as though they were in combat with some beast, and running hastily up he and his men beheld, under a great tree, a naked boy with long hair, and around him the hounds struggling to seize him, but Bran and Sceolaun fighting with them and keeping them off. And the lad was tall and shapely, and as the heroes gathered round he gazed undauntedly on them, never heeding the rout of dogs at his feet. The Fians beat off the dogs and brought the lad home with them, and Finn was very silent and continually searched the lad's countenance with his eyes. In time, the use of speech came to him, and the story that he told was this:

He had known no father, and no mother save a gentle hind with whom he lived in a most green and pleasant valley shut in on every side by towering cliffs that could not be scaled, or by deep chasms in the earth. In the summer he lived on fruits and such-like, and in the winter, store of provisions was laid for him in a cave. And there came to them sometimes a tall dark-visaged man, who spoke to his mother, now tenderly, and now in loud menace, but she always shrunk away in fear, and the man departed in anger. At last there came a day when the Dark Man spoke very long with his mother in all tones of entreaty and of tenderness and of rage, but she would still keep aloof and give no sign save of fear and abhorrence. Then at length the Dark Man drew near and smote her with a hazel wand; and with that he turned and went his way, but she, this time, followed him, still looking back at her son and piteously complaining. And he, when he strove to follow, found himself unable to move a limb; and crying out with rage and desolation he fell to the earth and his senses left him. When he came to himself he was on the mountain side, on Ben Gulban, where he remained some days, searching for that green and hidden valley, which he never found again. And after a while the dogs found him; but of the hind his mother and of the Dark Druid, there is no man knows the end.

Finn called his name Oisín, and he became a warrior of fame, but far more famous for the songs and tales that he made; so that of all things to this day that are told of the Fianna of Erinn, men are wont to say, "So sang the bard, Oisín, son of Finn."

The Dwarfie Stone

FAR UP IN A GREEN valley in the Island of Hoy stands an immense boulder. It is hollow inside, and the natives of these northern islands call it the Dwarfie Stone, because long centuries ago, so the legend has it, Snorro the Dwarf lived there.

Nobody knew where Snorro came from, or how long he had dwelt in the dark chamber inside the Dwarfie Stone. All that they knew about him was that he was a little man, with a queer, twisted, deformed body and a face of marvellous beauty, which never seemed to look any older, but was always smiling and young.

Men said that this was because Snorro's father had been a Fairy, and not a denizen of earth, who had bequeathed to his son the gift of perpetual youth, but nobody knew whether this were true or not, for the Dwarf had inhabited the Dwarfie Stone long before the oldest man or woman in Hoy had been born.

One thing was certain, however: he had inherited from his mother, whom all men agreed had been mortal, the dangerous qualities of vanity and ambition. And the longer he lived the more vain and ambitious did he become, until at last he always carried a mirror of polished steel round his neck, into which he constantly looked in order to see the reflection of his handsome face.

And he would not attend to the country people who came to seek his help, unless they bowed themselves humbly before him and spoke to him as if he were a King.

I say that the country people sought his help, for he spent his time, or appeared to spend it, in collecting herbs and simples on the hillsides, which he carried home with him to his dark abode, and distilled medicines and potions from them, which he sold to his neighbours at wondrous high prices.

He was also the possessor of a wonderful leathern-covered book, clasped with clasps of brass, over which he would pore for hours together, and out of which he would tell the simple Islanders their fortunes, if they would.

For they feared the book almost as much as they feared Snorro himself, for it was whispered that it had once belonged to Odin, and they crossed themselves for protection as they named the mighty Enchanter.

But all the time they never guessed the real reason why Snorro chose to live in the Dwarfie Stone.

I will tell you why he did so. Not very far from the Stone there was a curious hill, shaped exactly like a wart. It was known as the Wart Hill of Hoy, and men said that somewhere in the side of it was hidden a wonderful carbuncle, which, when it was found, would bestow on its finder marvellous magic gifts – Health, Wealth, and Happiness. Everything, in fact, that a human being could desire.

And the curious thing about this carbuncle was, that it was said that it could be seen at certain times, if only the people who were looking for it were at the right spot at the right moment.

Now Snorro had made up his mind that he would find this wonderful stone, so, while he pretended to spend all his time in reading his great book or distilling medicines from his herbs, he was really keeping a keen look-out during his wanderings, noting every tuft of grass or piece of rock under which it might be hidden. And at night, when everyone else was asleep, he would creep out, with pickaxe and spade, to turn over the rocks or dig over the turf, in the hope of finding the long-sought-for treasure underneath them.

He was always accompanied on these occasions by an enormous grey-headed Raven, who lived in the cave along with him, and who was his bosom friend and companion. The Islanders feared this bird of ill omen as much, perhaps, as they feared its Master; for, although they went to consult Snorro in all their difficulties and perplexities, and bought medicines and love-potions from him, they always looked upon him with a certain dread, feeling that there was something weird and uncanny about him.

Now, at the time we are speaking of, Orkney was governed by two Earls, who were half-brothers. Paul, the elder, was a tall, handsome man, with dark hair, and eyes like sloes. All the country people loved him, for he was so skilled in knightly exercises, and had such a sweet and loving nature, that no one could help being fond of him. Old people's eyes would brighten at the sight of him, and the little children would run out to greet him as he rode by their mothers' doors.

And this was the more remarkable because, with all his winning manner, he had such a lack of conversation that men called him Paul the Silent, or Paul the Taciturn.

Harold, on the other hand, was as different from his brother as night is from day. He was fair-haired and blue-eyed, and he had gained for himself the name of Harold the Orator, because he was always free of speech and ready with his tongue.

But for all this he was not a favourite. For he was haughty, and jealous, and quick-tempered, and the old folks' eyes did not brighten at the sight of him, and the babes, instead of toddling out to greet him, hid their faces in their mothers' skirts when they saw him coming.

Harold could not help knowing that the people liked his silent brother best, and the knowledge made him jealous of him, so a coldness sprang up between them.

Now it chanced, one summer, that Earl Harold went on a visit to the King of Scotland, accompanied by his mother, the Countess Helga, and her sister, the Countess Fraukirk.

And while he was at Court he met a charming young Irish lady, the Lady Morna, who had come from Ireland to Scotland to attend upon the Scottish Queen. She was so sweet, and good, and gentle that Earl Harold's heart was won, and he made up his mind that she, and only she, should be his bride.

But although he had paid her much attention, Lady Morna had sometimes caught glimpses of his jealous temper; she had seen an evil expression in his eyes, and had heard him speak sharply to his servants, and she had no wish to marry him. So, to his great amazement, she refused the honour which he offered her, and told him that she would prefer to remain as she was.

Earl Harold ground his teeth in silent rage, but he saw that it was no use pressing his suit at that moment. So what he could not obtain by his own merits he determined to obtain by guile.

Accordingly he begged his mother to persuade the Lady Morna to go back with them on a visit, hoping that when she was alone with him in Orkney, he would be able to overcome her prejudice against him, and induce her to become his wife. And all the while he never remembered his brother Paul; or, if he did, he never thought it possible that he could be his rival.

But that was just the very thing that happened. The Lady Morna, thinking no evil, accepted the Countess Helga's invitation, and no sooner had the party arrived back in Orkney than Paul, charmed with the grace and beauty of the fair Irish Maiden, fell head over ears in love with her. And the Lady Morna, from the very first hour that she saw him, returned his love.

Of course this state of things could not long go on hidden, and when Harold realised what had happened his anger and jealousy knew no bounds. Seizing a dagger, he rushed up to the turret where his brother was sitting in his private apartments, and threatened to stab him to the heart if he did not promise to give up all thoughts of winning the lovely stranger.

But Paul met him with pleasant words.

"Calm thyself, Brother," he said. "It is true that I love the lady, but that is no proof that I shall win her. Is it likely that she will choose me, whom all men name Paul the Silent, when she hath the chance of marrying you, whose tongue moves so swiftly that to you is given the proud title of Harold the Orator?"

At these words Harold's vanity was flattered, and he thought that, after all, his step-brother was right, and that he had a very small chance, with his meagre gift of speech, of being successful in his suit. So he threw down his dagger, and, shaking hands with him, begged him to pardon his unkind thoughts, and went down the winding stair again in high good-humour with himself and all the world.

By this time it was coming near to the Feast of Yule, and at that Festival it was the custom for the Earl and his Court to leave Kirkwall for some weeks, and go to the great Palace of Orphir, nine miles distant. And in order to see that everything was ready, Earl Paul took his departure some days before the others.

The evening before he left he chanced to find the Lady Morna sitting alone in one of the deep windows of the great hall. She had been weeping, for she was full of sadness at the thought of his departure; and at the sight of her distress the kind-hearted young Earl could no longer contain himself, but, folding her in his arms, he whispered to her how much he loved her, and begged her to promise to be his wife.

She agreed willingly. Hiding her rosy face on his shoulder, she confessed that she had loved him from the very first day that she had seen him; and ever since that moment she had determined that, if she could not wed him, she would wed no other man.

For a little time they sat together, rejoicing in their new-found happiness. Then Earl Paul sprang to his feet.

"Let us go and tell the good news to my mother and my brother," he said. "Harold may be disappointed at first, for I know, Sweetheart, he would fain have had thee for his own. But his good heart will soon overcome all that, and he will rejoice with us also."

But the Lady Morna shook her head. She knew, better than her lover, what Earl Harold's feeling would be; and she would fain put off the evil hour.

"Let us hold our peace till after Yule," she pleaded. "It will be a joy to keep our secret to ourselves for a little space; there will be time enough then to let all the world know."

Rather reluctantly, Earl Paul agreed; and next day he set off for the Palace at Orphir, leaving his lady-love behind him.

Little he guessed the danger he was in! For, all unknown to him, his step-aunt, Countess Fraukirk, had chanced to be in the hall, the evening before, hidden behind a curtain, and she had overheard every word that Morna and he had spoken, and her heart was filled with black rage.

For she was a hard, ambitious woman, and she had always hated the young Earl, who was no blood-relation to her, and who stood in the way of his brother, her own nephew; for, if Paul were only dead, Harold would be the sole Earl of Orkney.

And now that he had stolen the heart of the Lady Morna, whom her own nephew loved, her hate and anger knew no bounds. She had hastened off to her sister's chamber as soon as the lovers had parted; and there the two women had remained talking together till the chilly dawn broke in the sky.

Next day a boat went speeding over the narrow channel of water that separates Pomona (on the mainland) from Hoy. In it sat a woman, but who she was, or what she was like, no one could say, for she was covered from head to foot with a black cloak, and her face was hidden behind a thick, dark veil.

Snorro the Dwarf knew her, even before she laid aside her trappings, for Countess Fraukirk was no stranger to him. In the course of her long life she had often had occasion to seek his aid to help her in her evil deeds, and she had always paid him well for his services in yellow gold. He therefore welcomed her gladly; but when he had heard the nature of her errand his smiling face grew grave again, and he shook his head.

"I have served thee well, Lady, in the past," he said, "but methinks that this thing goeth beyond my courage. For to compass an Earl's death is a weighty matter, especially when he is so well beloved as is the Earl Paul.

"Thou knowest why I have taken up my abode in this lonely spot – how I hope some day to light upon the magic carbuncle. Thou knowest also how the people fear me, and hate me too, forsooth. And if the young Earl died, and suspicion fell on me, I must needs fly the Island, for my life would not be worth a grain of sand. Then my chance of success would be gone. Nay! I cannot do it, Lady; I cannot do it."

But the wily Countess offered him much gold, and bribed him higher and higher, first with wealth, then with success, and lastly she promised to obtain for him a high post at the Court of the King of Scotland; and at that his ambition stirred within him, his determination gave way, and he consented to do what she asked.

"I will summon my magic loom," he said, "and weave a piece of cloth of finest texture and of marvellous beauty; and before I weave it I will so poison the thread with a magic potion that, when it is fashioned into a garment, whoever puts it on will die ere he hath worn it many minutes."

"Thou art a clever knave," answered the Countess, a cruel smile lighting up her evil face, "and thou shalt be rewarded. Let me have a couple of yards of this wonderful web, and I will make a bonnie waistcoat for my fine young Earl and give it to him as a Yuletide gift. Then I reckon that he will not see the year out."

"That will he not," said Dwarf Snorro, with a malicious grin; and the two parted, after arranging that the piece of cloth should be delivered at the Palace of Orphir on the day before Christmas Eve.

Now, when the Countess Fraukirk had been away upon her wicked errand, strange things were happening at the Castle at Kirkwall. For Harold, encouraged by his brother's absence, offered his heart and hand once more to the Lady Morna. Once more she refused him, and in order to make sure that the scene should not be repeated, she told him that she had plighted her troth to his brother. When he heard that this was so, rage and fury were like to devour him. Mad with anger, he rushed from her presence, flung himself upon his horse, and rode away in the direction of the sea shore.

While he was galloping wildly along, his eyes fell on the snow-clad hills of Hoy rising up across the strip of sea that divided the one island from the other. And his thoughts flew at once to Snorro the Dwarf, who he had had occasion, as well as his step-aunt, to visit in bygone days.

"I have it," he cried. "Stupid fool that I was not to think of it at once. I will go to Snorro, and buy from him a love-potion, which will make my Lady Morna hate my precious brother and turn her thoughts kindly towards me."

So he made haste to hire a boat, and soon he was speeding over the tossing waters on his way to the Island of Hoy. When he arrived there he hurried up the lonely valley to where the Dwarfie Stone stood, and he had no difficulty in finding its uncanny occupant, for Snorro was standing at the hole that served as a door, his raven on his shoulder, gazing placidly at the setting sun.

A curious smile crossed his face when, hearing the sound of approaching footsteps, he turned round and his eyes fell on the young noble.

"What bringeth thee here, Sir Earl?" he asked gaily, for he scented more gold.

"I come for a love-potion," said Harold; and without more ado he told the whole story to the Wizard. "I will pay thee for it," he added, "if thou wilt give it to me quickly."

Snorro looked at him from head to foot. "Blind must the maiden be, Sir Orator," he said, "who needeth a love-potion to make her fancy so gallant a Knight."

Earl Harold laughed angrily. "It is easier to catch a sunbeam than a woman's roving fancy," he replied. "I have no time for jesting. For, hearken, old man, there is a proverb that saith, 'Time and tide wait for no man,' so I need not expect the tide to wait for me. The potion I must have, and that instantly."

Snorro saw that he was in earnest, so without a word he entered his dwelling, and in a few minutes returned with a small phial in his hand, which was full of a rosy liquid.

"Pour the contents of this into the Lady Morna's wine-cup," he said, "and I warrant thee that before four-and-twenty hours have passed she will love thee better than thou lovest her now."

Then he waved his hand, as if to dismiss his visitor, and disappeared into his dwelling-place.

Earl Harold made all speed back to the Castle; but it was not until one or two days had elapsed that he found a chance to pour the love-potion into the Lady Morna's wine-cup. But at last, one night at supper, he found an opportunity of doing so, and, waving away the little page-boy, he handed it to her himself.

She raised it to her lips, but she only made a pretence at drinking, for she had seen the hated Earl fingering the cup, and she feared some deed of treachery. When he had gone back to his seat she managed to pour the whole of the wine on the floor, and smiled to herself at the look of satisfaction that came over Harold's face as she put down the empty cup.

His satisfaction increased, for from that moment she felt so afraid of him that she treated him with great kindness, hoping that by doing so she would keep in his good graces until the Court moved to Orphir, and her own true love could protect her.

Harold, on his side, was delighted with her graciousness, for he felt certain that the charm was beginning to work, and that his hopes would soon be fulfilled.

A week later the Court removed to the Royal Palace at Orphir, where Earl Paul had everything in readiness for the reception of his guests.

Of course he was overjoyed to meet Lady Morna again, and she was overjoyed to meet him, for she felt that she was now safe from the unwelcome attentions of Earl Harold.

But to Earl Harold the sight of their joy was as gall and bitterness, and he could scarcely contain himself, although he still trusted in the efficacy of Snorro the Dwarf's love-potion.

As for Countess Fraukirk and Countess Helga, they looked forward eagerly to the time when the magic web would arrive, out of which they hoped to fashion a fatal gift for Earl Paul.

At last, the day before Christmas Eve, the two wicked women were sitting in the Countess Helga's chamber talking of the time when Earl Harold would rule alone in Orkney, when a tap came to the window, and on looking round they saw Dwarf Snorro's grey-headed Raven perched on the sill, a sealed packet in its beak.

They opened the casement, and with a hoarse croak the creature let the packet drop on to the floor; then it flapped its great wings and rose slowly into the air again its head turned in the direction of Hoy.

With fingers that trembled with excitement they broke the seals and undid the packet. It contained a piece of the most beautiful material that anyone could possibly imagine, woven in all the colours of the rainbow, and sparkling with gold and jewels.

"'Twill make a bonnie waistcoat," exclaimed Countess Fraukirk, with an unholy laugh. "The Silent Earl will be a braw man when he gets it on."

Then, without more ado, they set to work to cut out and sew the garment. All that night they worked, and all next day, till, late in the afternoon, when they were putting in the last stitches, hurried footsteps were heard ascending the winding staircase, and Earl Harold burst open the door.

His cheeks were red with passion, and his eyes were bright, for he could not but notice that, now that she was safe at Orphir under her true love's protection, the Lady Morna's manner had grown cold and distant again, and he was beginning to lose faith in Snorro's charm.

Angry and disappointed, he had sought his mother's room to pour out his story of vexation to her.

He stopped short, however, when he saw the wonderful waistcoat lying on the table, all gold and silver and shining colours. It was like a fairy garment, and its beauty took his breath away.

"For whom hast thou purchased that?" he asked, hoping to hear that it was intended for him.

"'Tis a Christmas gift for thy brother Paul," answered his mother, and she would have gone on to tell him how deadly a thing it was, had he given her time to speak. But her words fanned his fury into madness, for it seemed to him that this hated brother of his was claiming everything.

"Everything is for Paul! I am sick of his very name," he cried. "By my troth, he shall not have this!" and he snatched the vest from the table.

It was in vain that his mother and his aunt threw themselves at his feet, begging him to lay it down, and warning him that there was not a thread in it which was not poisoned. He paid no heed to their words, but rushed from the room, and, drawing it on, ran downstairs with a reckless laugh, to show the Lady Morna how fine he was.

Alas! alas! Scarce had he gained the hall than he fell to the ground in great pain.

Everyone crowded round him, and the two Countesses, terrified now by what they had done, tried in vain to tear the magic vest from his body. But he felt that it was too late, the deadly poison had done its work, and, waving them aside, he turned to his brother, who, in great distress, had knelt down and taken him tenderly in his arms.

"I wronged thee, Paul," he gasped. "For thou hast ever been true and kind. Forgive me in thy thoughts, and," he added, gathering up his strength for one last effort, and pointing to the two wretched women who had wrought all this misery, "beware of those two women, for they seek to take thy life." Then his head sank back on his brother's shoulder, and, with one long sigh, he died.

When he learned what had happened, and understood where the waistcoat came from, and for what purpose it had been intended, the anger of the Silent Earl knew no bounds. He swore a great oath that he would be avenged, not only on Snorro the Dwarf, but also on his wicked step-mother and her cruel sister.

His vengeance was baulked, however, for in the panic and confusion that followed Harold's death, the two Countesses slipped out of the Palace and fled to the coast, and took boat in haste to Scotland, where they had great possessions, and where they were much looked up to, and where no one would believe a word against them.

But retribution fell on them in the end, as it always does fall, sooner or later, on everyone who is wicked, or selfish, or cruel; for the Norsemen invaded the land, and their Castle was set on fire, and they perished miserably in the flames.

When Earl Paul found that they had escaped, he set out in hot haste for the Island of Hoy, for he was determined that the Dwarf, at least, should not escape. But when he came to the Dwarfie Stone he found it silent and deserted, all trace of its uncanny occupants having disappeared.

No one knew what had become of them; a few people were inclined to think that the Dwarf and his Raven had accompanied the Countess Fraukirk and the Countess Helga on their flight, but the greater part of the Islanders held to the belief, which I think was the true one, that the Powers of the Air spirited Snorro away, and shut him up in some unknown place as a punishment for his wickedness, and that his Raven accompanied him.

At any rate, he was never seen again by any living person, and wherever he went, he lost all chance of finding the magic carbuncle.

As for the Silent Earl and his Irish Sweetheart, they were married as soon as Earl Harold's funeral was over; and for hundreds of years afterwards, when the inhabitants of the Orkney Isles wanted to express great happiness, they said, "As happy as Earl Paul and the Countess Morna."

Luran

THERE ONCE WAS A CROFTER and his wife, and they lived in a glen far from the prying eyes of neighbours. They were quiet folk, but they lived well, with a herd of cattle to be envied, and a good bit of land. Their house was snug and warm in the coldest months, they had cream and milk and butter, and they wanted for nothing, in that glen, far from the prying eyes of neighbours.

Now that crofter was a healthy man, and he liked nothing more than a good meal, particularly if it was a feast of his favourite oakcakes, smeared with butter and dipped again in cream. And he partook of this kind of meal on most days so he grew rather heavy and clumsy. But their house was safe from any kind of danger, being far from the prying eyes of neighbours, and he grew perhaps a little too satisfied, and a little too complacent in his happy home.

For it was a cold Hallowe'en evening that strange things began to happen on the land of that satisfied crofter, and although everyone living near the fairy folk knows that Hallowe'en evening is their time for mischief, the crofter had not had cause to worry before this particular Hallowe'en night.

It was just as he was settling himself and his wife into their beds that they heard the howling of their guard dog, and a rumpus going on in the henhouse. And then they heard the cattle lowing, and everyone knows that cattle never low in the dead of night, so the crofter and his wife grew alarmed. Then he put back on his outdoor clothes, and he lit a lantern and headed towards the barnyard.

There, an astonishing sight met his eyes, for the barnyard was empty, his cattle gone, his pig sty clean, his henhouse bare. And the crofter sat down and held his head in his hands, and he asked himself how such a thing could happen to a house tucked so neatly in the glen, far from the prying eyes of neighbours. And then he started, for there was the sound of a lowing cow just over the knoll, and when he looked more closely there were tracks heading there too.

And so it was that the crofter plucked up his courage that Hallowe'en night, and went over that knoll, into the realm of the fairies. He crept there silently, until he heard voices. Then he stopped and he listened.

'Luran didn't run,' came a voice.

'Didn't run at all,' said another.

'Couldn't run at all,' giggled the first, and then there was a great deal of scuffling and laughter.

'If only his bread were not so hard,' said the other, 'but if Luran were fed on porridge, Luran would outrun the deer.'

And the crofter heard this conversation, and filled with fear (for everyone knows that fairies who speak English are the most dangerous of all) he peeked over the hilltop. There sat two smug fairies and just beyond them were his cattle, and all the livestock of the barnyard. He sat back again, Luran the satisfied crofter, and he began to think.

And when he returned home to greet his anxious wife, he was still thinking, and again in the morning when she offered him his favourite meal of oatcakes, smeared in butter and dipped again in cream. And so it was that Luran held up his hand and said to his wife, 'You'll have to give me porridge and milk every day.'

As the days shortened and then lengthened again, Luran grew long and lean, and a fine, fit sight of a man he was. He worked on his farm and he raised more cattle, and on that house in the glen, far from the prying eyes of neighbours, Luran plotted his revenge.

It was twelve months now, and Luran was ready. Hallowe'en night found the crofter hidden in the stable of cattle, peering restlessly across their troughs. He was soon rewarded, for in popped the same two fairies who had visited there before, and as they led the first cattle away from his barn, Luran leapt up and chased those fairies over the knoll. And when he caught them, not far from the top, they gazed at him in surprise, and danced a fairy dance of approval.

So the crofter returned to his cosy house, leading his cattle back to the stable. And never again did those fairies trouble that house, tucked in the glen, far from the prying eyes of neighbours, for the master of that house ate nothing but porridge and milk, as all good men should.

Reygoch

I

ONCE UPON A BEAUTIFUL SUMMER NIGHT, the men were watching their horses in the meadow. And as they watched, they fell asleep. And as they slept, the fairies flew out of the clouds to have some sport with the horses, as is the fairies' way. Each fairy caught a horse, mounted it, and then whipped it with her golden hair, urging it round and round the dewy meadow.

Among the fairies there was one quite young and tiny, called Curlylocks, who had come down to earth from the clouds for the first time that night.

Curlylocks thought it lovely to ride through the night like a whirlwind. And it so happened that she had got hold of the most spirited horse of all – a Black – small, but fierce as fire. The Black galloped round and round with the other horses, but he was the swiftest of all. Soon he was all in a lather of foam.

But Curlylocks wanted to ride faster still. She bent down and pinched the Black's right ear. The horse started, reared, and then bolted straight ahead, leaving behind the rest of the horses, the meadow and all, as he flew away like the wind with Curlylocks into the wide, wide world.

Curlylocks thoroughly enjoyed her lightning ride. The Black went like the wind, by field and by river, by meadow and mountain, over dale and hill. "Good gracious! what a lot of things there are in the world!" thought Curlylocks, full of delight as she looked at all the pretty sights. But what pleased her best was when they came through a country where there were mountains all covered with glorious forests, and at the foot of the mountains two golden fields like two great gold kerchiefs, and in the midst of them two white villages, like two white doves, and a little further on a great sheet of water.

But the Black would not stop, neither there nor anywhere, but rushed on and on as if he were possessed.

So the Black carried Curlylocks far and far away till at last they came to a great plain, with a cold wind blowing over it. The Black galloped into the plain, and there was nothing there but yellow sand, neither trees nor grass, and the further they went into that great waste, the colder it grew. But how large that plain is, I cannot tell you, for the good reason that the man does not live who could cross it.

The Black ran on with Curlylocks for seven days and seven nights. The seventh day, just before sunrise, they reached the centre of the plain, and in the centre of the plain they found the ruinous walls of the terribly great city of Frosten, and there it is always bitterly cold.

As the Black raced up to the ancient gates of Frosten, Curlylocks threw her magic veil on the wall, and so caught hold of the wall. The Black galloped away from under her, and so continued his wild career up to his old age to and fro between the huge walls of Frosten, till at last he found the northern gate and galloped out again into the plain – God knows whither!

But Curlylocks came down from the wall and began to walk about the city, and it was cold as cold! Her magic veil, without which she could not fly among the clouds, she wound about her shoulders, for she took great care of it. And so Curlylocks walked and walked about the city of Frosten, and all the time she felt as if she must come upon something very wonderful in this city, which was so marvellous and so great. However, nothing did she see but only great crumbling walls, and nothing did she hear but now and again a stone cracking with the cold.

Suddenly, just as Curlylocks had turned the corner of the very biggest wall, she saw, fast asleep at the foot of the wall, a huge man, bigger than the biggest oak in the biggest forest. The man was dressed in a huge cloak of coarse linen, and the strap he wore for a belt was five fathoms long. His head was as big as the biggest barrel, and his beard was like a shock of corn. He was so big, that man, you might have thought there was a church tower fallen down beside the wall!

This giant was called Reygoch, and he lived at Frosten. All he did was count the stones of the city of Frosten. He could never have finished counting them but for that huge head of his, as big as a barrel. But he counted and counted – he had counted for a thousand years and had already counted thirty walls and five gates of the city.

When Curlylocks spied Reygoch, she clasped her hands and wondered. She never thought there could be such an immense creature in the world.

So Curlylocks sat down by Reygoch's ear (and Reygoch's ear was as big as the whole of Curlylocks), and called down his ear, "Aren't you cold, daddy?"

Reygoch woke up, laughed, and looked at Curlylocks. "Cold? I should think I was cold," answered Reygoch, and his voice was as deep as distant thunder. Reygoch's big nose was all red with the cold, and his hair and beard were all thick with hoar-frost.

"Dear me!" said Curlylocks, "you're such a big man, and you aren't going to build yourself a roof to keep out of the cold?"

"Why should I?" said Reygoch, and he laughed again. "The sun will be out presently."

Reygoch heaved himself up so as to sit. He sat up. He clapped his left shoulder with his right hand, and his right shoulder he clapped with the left hand, so as to beat out the hoar-frost; and the hoar-frost came off each shoulder as if it were snow slipping off a roof!

"Look out! look out, daddy! you'll smother me!" cried Curlylocks. But Reygoch could scarcely hear her, because it was a long way from Curlylocks to his ear, so big was he when he sat up.

So Reygoch lifted Curlylocks onto his shoulder, told her his name and his business, and she told him how she had come.

"And here comes the sun," said Reygoch, and he pointed for Curlylocks to see.

Curlylocks looked, and there was the sun rising, but so pale and feeble, as if there were no one for him to warm.

"Well, you are silly, Reygoch!" said Curlylocks. "`you are really silly to live here and spend your life counting these tiresome stones of Frosten. Come along, Reygoch, and see how beautiful the world is, and find something more sensible to do."

Now it had never occurred to Reygoch to want a finer home for himself than Frosten city, nor had he ever thought that there might be better work than his in the world. Reygoch always thought, "I was meant to count the stones of Frosten," and had never asked for anything better.

Curlylocks, however, gave him no peace, but persuaded him to come out and see the world with her.

"I'll take you to a lovely country," said Curlylocks, "where there is an ancient forest, and beside the forest two golden fields."

Curlylocks talked for a long time. And old Reygoch had never had anybody to talk to, and so he couldn't resist persuasion.

"Well, let's go!" said he.

Curlylocks was mightily pleased with this.

But now they had to contrive something, so that Reygoch could carry Curlylocks, because Reygoch himself had nothing.

So Curlylocks drew out from her bosom a little bag of pearls. It was her mother who had given Curlylocks these pearls before allowing her to go down to earth, and she had told her, "If you ever should need anything, just throw down a pearl, and it will turn into whatever you want. Be very careful of those pearls, because there are so many things in the world that you will want more and more as you go on."

Curlylocks took out a tiny seed-pearl, threw it down, and lo, before their eyes there grew a little basket, just as big as Curlylocks, and the basket had a loop attached, just big enough to fit Reygoch's ear.

Curlylocks jumped into the basket; and Reygoch picked up the basket and hung it on his ear like an earring!

Whenever Reygoch laughed, whenever he sneezed or shook his head, Curlylocks rocked as if she were in a swing; and she thought it a capital way of travelling.

So Reygoch started to walk, and had already taken a ten-yard stride, when Curlylocks stopped him and begged, "Couldn't we go underground, perhaps, Reygoch dear, so that I might see what there is under the earth?"

"Why not?" answered Reygoch; for he could break into the earth as easy as fun, only it had never entered his head to look what might be underground.

But Curlylocks wanted to know everything about everything, and so they agreed to travel underground until they should arrive under the forest by the golden fields, and there they would come up.

When they had settled that, Reygoch began to break up the earth. He lifted up his great feet and stamped for the first time, and at that the whole of the great city of Frosten shook and a great many walls tumbled down. Reygoch raised his feet a second time and stamped again, and the whole plain quaked. Reygoch raised his feet a third time and stamped, and lo, half the world trembled, the solid earth gaped under Reygoch, and Reygoch and Curlylocks fell into the hole and down under the earth.

When they got there, they found the earth all honeycombed with pillars and passages on every side, and heaven alone knew where they all led to. And they could hear waters rushing and the moaning of the winds.

They followed one of the passages, and for a while they had light from the hole through which they had fallen. But as they went on it grew darker and darker – black darkness, such as there is nowhere save in the bowels of the earth.

Reygoch tramped calmly on in the dark. With his great hands he felt his way from pillar to pillar.

But Curlylocks was frightened by the great darkness.

She clung to Reygoch's ear and cried, "It's dark, Reygoch dear!"

"Well, and why not?" returned Reygoch. "The dark didn't come to us. It's we have come to it."

Then Curlylocks got cross, because Reygoch never minded anything and she had expected great things from so huge a man.

"I should be in a nice fix with you but for my pearls," said Curlylocks quite angrily.

Then she threw down another pearl, and a tiny lantern grew in her hand, bright as if it were lit with gold. The darkness crept back deeper into the earth, and the light shone far through the underground passages.

Curlylocks was delighted with her lantern, because it showed up all the marvels which had been swallowed by the earth in days of old. In one place she saw lordly castles, with doors and windows all fretted with gold and framed in red marble. In another place were warriors' weapons, slender-barrelled muskets and heavy scimitars studded with gems and precious stones. In a third place she saw long-buried treasures, golden dishes and silver goblets full of gold ducats, and the Emperor's very crown of gold three times refined. All these treasures had been swallowed up by God's will, and it is God's secret why so much treasure should lie there undisturbed.

But Curlylocks was quite dazzled with all these marvels; and instead of going straight ahead by the way they had settled upon, she begged Reygoch to put her down so that she might play about a little and admire all the strange things and gaze upon the wonders of God's secret.

So Reygoch set Curlylocks down, and Curlylocks took her little lantern and ran to the castles, and to the weapons, and to the treasure-hoards. And lest she might lose her little bag of pearls while she was playing, she laid it down beside a pillar.

As for Reygoch, he sat down to rest not far off.

Curlylocks began to play with the treasures; she looked at the beautiful things and rummaged among them. With her tiny hands she scattered the golden ducats, examined the goblets chased in silver, and put upon her head the crown of gold three times refined. She played about, looked round and admired, and at last caught sight of a very slender little ivory staff propped up against a mighty pillar.

But it was just that slender staff that kept the mighty pillar from collapsing, because the pillar was already completely hollowed out by the water. And therefore God had caused that little staff to fall down there, and the staff held up the pillar under the earth.

But Curlylocks wondered, "Why is that little staff just there?" And she went and picked up the staff to look at it.

But no sooner had Curlylocks taken the staff and moved it than the subterranean passages re-echoed with a terrible rumbling noise. The great pillar trembled, swayed and crashed down amid a whole mountain of falling earth, closing and blocking up the path between Reygoch and Curlylocks. They could neither see nor hear one another, nor could they reach one another...

There was the poor little fairy Curlylocks caught in the bowels of the earth! She was buried alive in that vast grave, and perhaps would never again see those golden fields for which she had set out, and all because she would not go straight on by the way they had intended, but would loiter and turn aside to the right and to the left to pry into God's secrets!

Curlylocks wept and cried, and tried to get to Reygoch. But she found that there was no way through, and that her plight was hopeless; and as for the bag of pearls, which might have helped her, it was buried under the landslide.

When Curlylocks realised this she stopped crying, for she was proud, and she thought, "There is no help for it, and I must die. Reygoch won't come to my rescue, because his wits are too slow even to help himself, let alone to make him remember to help me. So there is nothing for it, and I must die."

So Curlylocks prepared for death. But in case folk should ever find her in her grave she wanted them to know that she came of royal blood. So she set the crown of gold three times refined upon her head, took the ivory staff in her hand, and lay down to die. There was no one beside Curlylocks except her little lantern, burning as if it were lit with gold; and as Curlylocks began to grow cold and stiff, so the lantern burned low and dim.

Reygoch was really an old simpleton. When the pillar crashed down and there was the big landslide between him and Curlylocks he never moved, but sat still in the dark. Thus he sat for quite a long time, before it occurred to him to go and find out what had happened.

He felt his way in the dark to the spot where Curlylocks had been, groped about, and realised that the earth had subsided there and that the passage was indeed blocked.

"Eh, but that way is choked up now," considered Reygoch. And nothing else could he think of, but turned round, left the mound of fallen earth and Curlylocks beyond it, and went back by the road they had travelled from Frosten city.

* * *

Thus old Reygoch went his way, pillar by pillar. He had already gone a goodish bit; but there was all the time something worrying him. Reygoch himself couldn't imagine what it was that worried him.

He arranged the strap around his waist – perhaps it had been too tight; and then he stretched his arm – perhaps his arm had gone to sleep. Yet it was neither the one nor the other, but something else that worried him. Reygoch wondered what in the world it could be. He wondered, and as he wondered he shook his head.

And as Reygoch shook his head, the little basket swung at his ear. And when Reygoch felt how light the basket was, and that there was no Curlylocks inside, a bitter pang shot through his heart and breast, and – simpleton though he was – he knew well enough that he was grieved because he missed Curlylocks, and he realised also that he ought to save her.

It had taken Reygoch a lot of trouble to think out all that; but once he had thought it out, he turned like the wind and flew back to the place where the landslide was, to find Curlylocks behind the heap of earth. He flew, and he arrived just in time. Reygoch burrowed away with both hands, and in a little while he had burrowed a big hole, so that he could see Curlylocks lying there, the crown of fine gold on her head. She was already growing cold and rigid, with her little lantern beside her, and the flame of it as feeble as the tiniest little glow-worm.

If Reygoch had cried out in his grief the earth would have rocked, and the little lantern would have gone out altogether – even the little glow-worm light by the side of Curlylocks would have died away.

But Reygoch's throat was all tight with pain, so that he could not cry out. He put out his great big hand and gently picked up poor Curlylocks, who was already quite cold, and warmed her between the hollowed palms of his huge hands as you would warm a starved dicky-bird in winter. And lo! in a little while Curlylocks moved her little head, and at once the lantern burned a little brighter; and then Curlylocks moved her arm, and the lantern burned brighter still. At last Curlylocks opened her eyes, and the lantern burned as brightly as if its flame were pure gold!

Then Curlylocks jumped to her feet, caught hold of Reygoch's beard, and they both of them cried for pure joy. Reygoch's tears were as big as pears and Curlylocks' as tiny as millet-seed, but except for size they were both the same sort; and from that moment these two were mightily fond of one another.

When they had finished their cry, Curlylocks found her pearls, and then they went on. But they touched no more of the things they saw underground, neither the sunken ships with their hoards of treasure, which had worked their way down from the bottom of the sea, nor the red coral, nor the yellow amber which twined round the underground pillars. They touched nothing, but went straight along by the way that would take them to the golden fields.

When they had gone on thus for a long time, Curlylocks asked Reygoch to hold her up; and when he did so, Curlylocks took a handful of earth from above her head.

She took the earth, looked at her hand, and there, among the soil, she found leaves and fibres.

"Here we are, daddy, under the forest beside the golden fields," said Curlylocks. "Let's hurry up and get out."

So Reygoch stretched himself and began to break through the earth with his head.

II

And indeed they were under the forest, just underneath a wooded glen between the two villages and the two counties. No one ever came to this glen but the herd boys and girls from both villages and both counties.

Now there was bitter strife between the two villages – strife over the threshing-floors, and the pastures, and the mills, and the timber-felling, and most of all over the staff of headmanship, which one of the villages had long claimed as belonging to it by rights, and the other would not give up. And so these two villages were at enmity with one another.

But the herd boys and girls of both villages were just simple young folk, who understood nothing about the rights of their elders, and cared less, but met every day on the boundary between the two villages and the two counties. Their flocks mingled and fed together, while the boys played games, and over their games would often be late in bringing the sheep home of an evening.

For this the poor boys and girls would be soundly rated and scolded in both villages. But in one of the villages there was a great-grandfather and a great-grandmother who could remember all that had ever happened in either village, and they said, "Leave the children alone. A better harvest will spring from their childish games than ever from your wheat in the fields."

So the shepherds kept on coming, as before, with their sheep to the glen, and in time the parents stopped bothering about what the children did.

And so it was on the day when Reygoch broke through the earth at that very spot. The boys and girls happened to be all gathered together under the biggest oak, getting ready to go home. One was tying up his shoes, another fixing a thong to a stick, and the girls were collecting the sheep. All of a sudden they heard a dreadful thumping in the earth right underneath their feet! There was a thud, then a second, and at the third thud the earth gaped, and up there came, right in the midst of the shepherds, a fearsome large head as big as a barrel, with a beard like a shock of corn, and the beard still bristling with hoar-frost from Frosten city!

The boys and girls all screamed with fright and fell down in a dead faint – not so much because of the head as big as a barrel, but because of the beard, that looked for all the world like a shock of corn!

So the shepherds fainted away – all but young Lilio, who was the handsomest and cleverest among the lads of both villages and both counties.

Lilio kept his feet and went close up to see what sort of monster it might be.

"Don't be afraid, children," said Lilio to the shepherds. "The Lord never created that monstrous giant for evil, else he would have killed half the world by now."

So Lilio walked boldly up to Reygoch, and Reygoch lifted the basket with Curlylocks down from his ear and set it on the ground.

"Come – oh come quickly, boys!" cried Lilio. "There is a little girl with him, little and lovely as a star!"

The herd boys and girls got up and began to peep from behind each other at Curlylocks; and those who had at first been the most frightened were now the foremost in coming up to Curlylocks, because, you see, they were always quickest in everything.

No sooner had the herd boys and girls seen dear little Curlylocks than they loved her. They helped her out of her basket, led her to where the turf was softest, and fell to admiring her lovely robes, which were light as gossamer and blue as the sky, and her hair, which was shining and soft as the morning light; but most of all they admired her fairy veil, for she would wave it just for a moment, and then rise from the grass and float in the air.

The herd boys and girls and Curlylocks danced in a ring together, and played all kinds of games. Curlylocks's little feet twinkled for pure joy, her eyes laughed, and so did her lips, because she had found companions who liked the same things as she did.

Then Curlylocks brought out her little bag of pearls to give presents and pleasure to her new friends. She threw down a pearl, and a little tree grew up in their midst, all decked with coloured ribbons, silk kerchiefs and red necklaces for the girls. She threw down a second pearl, and from all parts of the forest came forth haughty peacocks; they stalked and strutted, they flew up and away, shedding their glorious feathers all over the turf, so that the grass fairly sparkled with them. And the herd boys stuck the feathers in their caps and doublets. Yet another pearl did Curlylocks throw out, and from a lofty branch there dropped a golden swing with silken ropes; and when the boys and girls got on the swing, it swooped and stooped as light as a swallow, and as gently as the grand barge of the Duke of Venice.

The children shouted for joy, and Curlylocks threw out all the pearls in her bag one after another, never thinking that she ought to save them; because Curlylocks liked nothing in the world better than lovely games and pretty songs. And so she spent her pearls down to the last little seed pearl, though heaven alone knew how badly she would need them soon, both she and her new friends.

"I shall never leave you anymore," cried Curlylocks merrily. And the herd boys and girls clapped their hands and threw up their caps for joy over her words.

Only Lilio had not joined in their games, because he was rather sad and worried that day. He stayed near Reygoch, and from there he watched Curlylocks in all her loveliness, and all the pretty magic she made there in the forest.

Meantime Reygoch had come out of his hole. Out he came and stood up among the trees of the forest, and as he stood there his head rose above the hundred-year-old forest, so terribly big was Reygoch.

Over the forest looked Reygoch, and out into the plain.

The sun had already set, and the sky was all crimson. In the plain you could see the two golden fields spread out like two gold kerchiefs, and in the midst of the fields two villages like two white doves. A little way beyond the two villages flowed the mighty River Banewater, and all along the river rose great grass-grown dykes; and on the dykes you could see herds and their keepers moving.

"Well, well!" said Reygoch. "And to think that I have spent a thousand years in Frosten city, in that desert, when there is so much beauty in the world!" And Reygoch was so delighted with looking into the plain that he just stood there with his great head as big as a barrel turning from right to left, like a huge scarecrow nodding above the tree-tops.

Presently Lilio called to him, "Sit down, daddy, for fear the elders of the villages should see you."

Reygoch sat down, and the two started talking, and Lilio told Reygoch why he was so sad that day.

"A very wicked thing is going to happen today," said Lilio. "I overheard the elders of our village talking last night, and this is what they said: 'Let us pierce the dyke along the River Banewater. The river will widen the hole, the dyke will fall, and the water will flood the enemy village; it will drown men and women, flood the graveyard and the fields, till the water will be level above them, and nothing but a lake to show where the enemy village has been. But our fields are higher, and our village lies on a height, and so no harm will come to us.' And then they really went out with a great ram to pierce the dyke secretly and at dead of night. But, daddy," continued Lilio, "I know that our fields are not so high, and I know that the water will overflow them too, and before the night is over there will be a lake where our two villages used to be. And that is why I am so sad."

They were still talking when a terrible noise and clamour arose from the plain.

"There!" cried Lilio, "the dreadful thing has happened!"

Reygoch drew himself up, picked up Lilio, and the two looked out over the plain. It was a sad sight to see! The dyke was crumbling, and the mighty Black Banewater rolling in two arms across the beautiful fields. One arm rolled towards the one village, and the second arm towards the other village. Animals were drowning, the golden fields disappeared below the flood. Above the graves the crosses were afloat, and both villages rang with cries and shouting. For in both villages the elders had gone out to the threshing-floors with cymbals, drums and fifes, and there they were drumming and piping away each to spite the other village, so crazed were they with malice, while over and above that din the village dogs howled dismally, and the women and children wept and wailed.

"Daddy," cried Lilio, "why have I not your hands to stop the water?"

Terrified and bewildered by the dreadful clamour in the plain, the herd boys and girls crowded round Reygoch and Lilio.

When Curlylocks heard what was the matter, she called out quick and sprightly, as befits a little fairy, "Come on, Reygoch – come on and stop the water!"

"Yes, yes, let's go!" cried the herd boys of both villages and both counties, as they wept and sobbed without stopping. "Come on, Reygoch, and take us along too!"

Reygoch stooped, gathered up Lilio and Curlylocks (who was still carrying her lantern) in his right hand, and all the rest of the herd boys and girls in his left, and then Reygoch raced with ten-fathom strides through the forest clearing and down into the plain. Behind him ran the sheep, bleating with terror. And so they reached the plain.

Through fog and twilight ran Reygoch with the children in his arms and the terrified flocks at his heels in frantic flight – all running towards the dyke. And out to meet them flowed the Black Banewater, killing and drowning as it flowed. It is terribly strong, is that water. Stronger than Reygoch? Who knows? Will it sweep away Reygoch, too? Will it drown those poor herd boys and girls also, and must the dear little Fairy Curlylocks die – and she as lovely as a star?

So Reygoch ran on across the meadow, which was still dry, and came all breathless to the dyke, where there was a great breach, through which the river was pouring with frightful force.

"Stop it up, Reygoch – stop it up!" wailed the boys and girls.

Not far from the dyke there was a little mound in the plain.

"Put us on that mound," cried Curlylocks briskly.

Reygoch set down Lilio and Curlylocks and the herd boys and girls on the hillock, and the sheep and lambs crowded round them. Already the hillock was just an island in the middle of the water.

But Reygoch took one mighty stride into the water and then lay down facing the dyke, stopping up the breach with his enormous chest. For a little while the water ceased to flow; but it was so terribly strong that nothing on earth could stop it. The water pressed forward; it eddied round Reygoch's shoulders; it broke through under him, over him, about him – everywhere – and rolled on again over the plain. Reygoch stretched out both arms and piled up the earth in great handfuls; but as fast as he piled it up, the water carried it away.

And in the plain the water kept on rising higher and higher; fields, villages, cattle, threshing-floors, not one of them could be seen anymore. Of both villages, the roofs and church steeples were all that showed above the flood.

Even around the hillock where the herd boys and girls were standing with Lilio and Curlylocks the flood was rising higher and higher. The poor young things were weeping and crying, some for their mothers, others for their brothers and sisters, and some for their homes and gardens; because they saw that both villages had perished, and not a soul saved – and the water rising about them, too!

So they crowded up higher and higher upon the hillock; they huddled together around Lilio and Curlylocks, who were standing side by side in the midst of their friends.

Lilio stood still and white as marble; but Curlylocks's eyes shone, and she held up her lantern towards Reygoch to give him light for his work. Curlylocks's veil rose and fluttered in the night wind and hovered above the water, as though the little fairy were about to fly away and vanish from among all these terrors.

"Curlylocks! Curlylocks! Don't go! Don't leave us!" wailed the herd boys, to whom it seemed as if there were an angel with them while they could look upon Curlylocks.

"I'm not going – I'm not going away!" cried Curlylocks. But her veil fluttered, as if it would carry her away of its own accord, over the water and up into the clouds.

Suddenly they heard a scream. The water had risen and caught one of the girls by the hem of her skirt and was washing her away. Lilio stooped just in time, seized the girl, and pulled her back onto the hillock.

"We must tie ourselves together," cried the herd boys. "We must be tied each to the other, or we shall perish."

"Here, children – here!" cried Curlylocks, who had a kind and pitiful heart.

Quickly she stripped her magic veil off her shoulders and gave it to the herd girls. They tore the veil into strips, knotted the strips into long ropes, and bound themselves together, each to other, round Lilio and Curlylocks. And round the shepherds bleated the poor sheep in terror of being drowned.

But Curlylocks was now among these poor castaways, no better off than the rest of them. Her pearls she had wasted on toys, and her magic veil she had given away and torn up out of the goodness of her heart, and now she could no longer fly, nor save herself out of this misery.

But Lilio loved Curlylocks better than anything else in the world, and when the water was already up to his feet he called, "Don't be afraid, Curlylocks! I will save you and hold you up!" And he held up Curlylocks in his arms.

With one hand Curlylocks clung round Lilio's neck, and with the other she held up her little lantern aloft towards Reygoch.

And Reygoch, lying on his chest in the water, was all the time steadily fighting the flood. Right and left of Reygoch rose the ruins of the dyke like two great horns. Reygoch's beard was tousled, his shoulders were bleeding. Yet he could not stop the Banewater, and the flood round the hillock was rising and rising to drown the poor remnant there. And now it was night – yea, midnight.

All of a sudden a thought flashed through Curlylocks, and through all the sobbing and crying she laughed aloud as she called to Reygoch, "Reygoch, you old simpleton! why don't you sit between these two horns of the dyke? Why don't you dam the flood with your shoulders?"

The herd boys and girls stopped wailing at once. So dumbfounded were they at the idea that not one of them had thought of that before!

"Uhuhu!" was all you could hear, and that was Reygoch laughing. And when Reygoch laughs, mind you, it's no joke! All the water round him boiled and bubbled as he shook with laughter over his own stupidity!

Then Reygoch stood up, faced about, and – in a twinkling – he sat down between those two horns!

And then happened the most wonderful thing of all! For the Black Banewater stood as though you had rolled a wall into the breach! It stood, and could not rise above Reygoch's shoulders, but followed its usual course, as before, the whole current behind Reygoch's back. And surely that was a most marvellous rescue!

The boys and girls were saved from the worst of the danger; and Reygoch, sitting comfortably, took up earth in handfuls and all slow-and-surely rebuilt the dyke under himself and on either hand. He began in the middle of the night, and when the dawn broke, the job was finished. And just as the sun rose, Reygoch got up from the dyke with his work done, and started combing his beard, which was all caked with mud, twigs, and little fishes.

But the poor boys and girls were not yet done with their troubles; for where were they to go, and how were they to get there? There they stood on the top of the hillock. All around them was a waste of water. Nothing was to be seen of the two villages but just a few roofs – and not a soul alive in either. To be sure, the villagers might have saved themselves if they had taken refuge in their attics. But in both villages everybody had gone to the threshing-floor with cymbals and fifes to make merry, so that each could watch the destruction of the other. And when the water was up to their waists, they were still clanging their cymbals; and when it was up to their necks, they still blew their fifes for gratified spite. And so they were drowned, one and all, with their fifes and cymbals – and serve them right for their malice and uncharitableness!

So the poor children were left without a soul to cherish or protect them, all houseless and homeless.

"We're not sparrows, to live on the housetops," said the boys sadly, as they saw only the roofs sticking out of the water, "and we're not foxes, to live in burrows in the hills. If someone could clear our villages of the water, we might make shift to get along somehow, but as it is, we might as well jump into the water with our flocks and be drowned like the rest, for we have nowhere and no one to turn to."

That was a sad plight indeed, and Reygoch himself was dreadfully sorry for them. But here was an evil he could in no wise remedy. He looked out over the water and said, "There's too much water here for me to bale out or to drink up so as to clear your villages. Eh, children, what shall I do for you?"

But then up and spoke Lilio, that was the wisest lad in these parts: "Reygoch, daddy, if you cannot drink so much water, the Earth can. Break a hole in the ground, daddy, and drain off the water into the earth."

Dearie me! and wasn't that great wisdom in a lad no bigger than Reygoch's finger?

Forthwith Reygoch stamped on the ground and broke a hole; and the Earth, like a thirsty dragon, began to drink and to drink, and swallow, and suck down into herself all that mighty water from off the whole plain. Before long the Earth had gulped down all the water; villages, fields, and meadows reappeared, ravaged and mud-covered, to be sure, but with everything in its right place.

The young castaways cheered up at the sight, but none was so glad as Curlylocks. She clapped her hands and cried, "Oh, won't it be lovely when the fields all grow golden again and the meadows green!"

But hereupon the herd boys and girls were all downcast once more, and Lilio said, "Who will show us how to till the ground now that not one of our parents is left alive?"

And indeed, far and wide, there was not a soul alive older than that company of helpless young things in the midst of the ravaged plain, and none with them but Reygoch, who was so big and clumsy and simple that he could not turn his head inside one of their houses, nor did he know anything about ploughing or husbandry.

So they were all in the dumps once more, and most of all Reygoch, who was so fond of pretty Curlylocks, and now he could do nothing for her nor her friends!

And, worst of all, Reygoch was getting horribly homesick for his desolate city of Frosten. This night he had swallowed mud enough to last him a thousand years, and had seen more than enough of trouble. And so he was just dying to be back in his vast, empty city, where he had counted the stones in peace for so many hundred years.

So the herd boys were very crestfallen, and Lilio was crestfallen, and Reygoch the most crestfallen of all. And really it was sad to look upon all these poor boys and girls, doomed to perish without their parents and wither like a flower cut off from its root.

Only Curlylocks looked gaily about her, right and left, for nothing could damp her good spirits.

Suddenly Curlylocks cried out, "Look – oh look! What are those people? Oh dear, but they must have seen sights and wonders!"

All looked towards the village, and there, at one of the windows, appeared the heads of an aged couple – an old man and an old woman. They waved their kerchiefs, they called the young people by name, and laughed till their wrinkled faces all shone with joy. They were great-grandfather and great-grandmother, who had been the only sensible people in the two villages, and had saved themselves by taking refuge in the attic!

Oh dear! If the children had seen the sun at his rising and the morning star at that attic window, they would not have shouted so for joy. The very heavens rang again as they called out, "Granny! Grandad!"

They raced to the village like young whippets, Curlylocks in front, with her golden hair streaming in the wind, and after them the ewes and lambs. They never stopped till they reached the village, and there grandfather and grandmother were waiting for them at the gate. They welcomed them, hugged them, and none of them could find words to thank God enough for His mercy in giving grandad and grandma so much wisdom as to make them take refuge in the attic! And that was really a very good thing, because these were only quite simple villages, where there were no books nor written records; and who would have reminded the herd boys and girls of the consequences of wickedness if grandad and grandma had not been spared?

When they had done hugging each other, they remembered Reygoch. They looked round the plain, but there was no Reygoch. He was gone – gone all of a sudden, the dear huge thing – gone like a mouse down its hole.

And Reygoch had indeed gone like a mouse down its hole. For when grandpa and grandma appeared at the attic window, Reygoch got a fright such as he had never yet had in his life. He was terrified at the sight of their furrowed, wrinkled, withered old faces.

"Oh dear! oh dear! what a lot of trouble these old people must have been through in these parts to have come to look like that!" thought Reygoch; and in his terror he that very instant jumped down into the hole through which the Black Banewater had sunk down, and so ran away back to his desolate Frosten city.

* * *

All went well in the village. Grandad and Grandma taught the young folk, and the young folk ploughed and sowed. Upon the grandparents' advice they built just one village, one threshing-floor, one church, and one graveyard, so that there should be no more jealousy nor trouble.

All went well; but the best of all was that in the heart of the village stood a beautiful tower of mountain marble, and on the top of it they had made a garden, where blossomed oranges and wild olive. There lived Curlylocks, the lovely fairy, and looked down upon the land that had been so dear to her from the moment when she first came to earth.

And of an evening, when the field work was done, Lilio would lead the herd boys and girls to the tower, and they would sing songs and dance in a ring in the garden with Curlylocks, always lovely, gentle, and joyous.

But under the earth Reygoch once more fell in with the Black Banewater as it roared and burbled underneath, while he wrestled with it till he forced it deeper and deeper into the earth, and right down to the bottom of the Pit, so that it might never again serve the spite and envy of man. And then Reygoch went on to Frosten city. There he is sitting to this very day, counting the stones and praying the Lord never again to tempt him away from that vast and desolate spot, which is the very place for one so big and so simple.

Frey

FREY, OR FRO, as he was called in Germany, was the son of Niord and Nerthus, or of Niord and Skadi, and was born in Vanaheim. He therefore belonged to the race of the Vanas, the divinities of water and air, but was warmly welcomed in Asgard when he came thither as hostage with his father. As it was customary among the Northern nations to bestow some valuable gift upon a child when he cut his first tooth, the Aesir gave the infant Frey the beautiful realm of Alfheim or Fairyland, the home of the Light Elves.

Here Frey, the god of the golden sunshine and the warm summer showers, took up his abode, charmed with the society of the elves and fairies, who implicitly obeyed his every order, and at a sign from him flitted to and fro, doing all the good in their power, for they were pre-eminently beneficent spirits.

Frey also received from the gods a marvellous sword (an emblem of the sunbeams), which had the power of fighting successfully, and of its own accord, as soon as it was drawn from its sheath. Frey wielded this principally against the frost giants, whom he hated almost as much as did Thor, and because he carried this glittering weapon, he has sometimes been confounded with the sword-god Tyr or Saxnot.

The dwarfs from Svartalfaheim gave Frey the golden-bristled boar Gullin-bursti (the golden-bristled), a personification of the sun. The radiant bristles of this animal were considered symbolical either of the solar rays, of the golden grain, which at his bidding waved over the harvest fields of Midgard, or of agriculture; for the boar (by tearing up the ground with his sharp tusk) was supposed to have first taught mankind how to plough.

Frey sometimes rode astride of this marvellous boar, whose speed was very great, and at other times harnessed him to his golden chariot, which was said to contain the fruits and flowers which he lavishly scattered abroad over the face of the earth.

Frey was, moreover, the proud possessor not only of the dauntless steed Blodug-hofi, which would dash through fire and water at his command, but also of the magic ship Skidbladnir, a personification of the clouds. This vessel, sailing over land and sea, was always wafted along by favourable winds, and was so elastic that, while it could assume large enough proportions to carry the gods, their steeds, and all their equipments, it could also be folded up like a napkin and thrust into a pocket.

It is related in one of the lays of the Edda that Frey once ventured to ascend Odin's throne Hlidskialf, from which exalted seat his gaze ranged over the wide earth. Looking towards the frozen North, he saw a beautiful young maiden enter the house of the frost giant Gymir, and as she raised her hand to lift the latch her radiant beauty illuminated sea and sky.

A moment later, this lovely creature, whose name was Gerda, and who is considered as a personification of the flashing Northern lights, vanished within her father's house, and Frey pensively wended his way back to Alfheim, his heart oppressed with longing to make this fair maiden his wife. Being deeply in love, he was melancholy and absent-minded in the extreme, and began to behave so strangely that his father, Niord, became greatly alarmed about his health, and bade his favourite servant, Skirnir, discover the cause of this sudden change. After much persuasion, Skirnir finally won from Frey an account of his ascent of Hlidskialf, and of the fair vision he had seen. He confessed his love and also his utter despair, for as Gerda was the daughter of Gymir and Angur-boda, and a relative of the murdered giant Thiassi, he feared she would never view his suit with favour.

Skirnir, however, replied consolingly that he could see no reason why his master should take a despondent view of the case, and he offered to go and woo the maiden in his name, providing Frey would lend him his steed for the journey, and give him his glittering sword for reward.

Overjoyed at the prospect of winning the beautiful Gerda, Frey willingly handed Skirnir the flashing sword, and gave him permission to use his horse. But he quickly relapsed into the state of reverie which had become usual with him since falling in love, and thus he did not notice that Skirnir was still hovering near him, nor did he perceive him cunningly steal the reflection of his face from the surface of the brook near which he was seated, and imprison it in his drinking horn, with intent "to pour it out in Gerda's cup, and by its beauty win the heart of the giantess for the lord" for whom he was about to go a-wooing. Provided with this portrait, with eleven golden apples, and with the magic ring Draupnir, Skirnir now rode off to Jotunheim, to fulfil his embassy. As he came near Gymir's dwelling he heard the loud and persistent howling of his watch-dogs, which were personifications of the wintry winds. A shepherd, guarding his flock in the vicinity, told him, in answer to his inquiry, that it would be impossible to approach the house, on account of the flaming barrier which surrounded it; but Skirnir, knowing that Blodug-hofi would dash through any fire, merely set spurs to his steed, and, riding up unscathed to the giant's door, was soon ushered into the presence of the lovely Gerda.

To induce the fair maiden to lend a favourable ear to his master's proposals, Skirnir showed her the stolen portrait, and proffered the golden apples and magic ring, which, however, she haughtily refused to accept, declaring that her father had gold enough and to spare.

Indignant at her scorn, Skirnir now threatened to decapitate her with his magic sword, but as this did not in the least frighten the maiden, and she calmly defied him, he had recourse to magic arts. Cutting runes in his stick, he told her that unless she yielded ere the spell was ended, she would be condemned either to eternal celibacy, or to marry some aged frost giant whom she could never love.

Terrified into submission by the frightful description of her cheerless future in case she persisted in her refusal, Gerda finally consented to become Frey's wife, and dismissed Skirnir, promising to meet her future spouse on the ninth night, in the land of Buri, the green grove, where she would dispel his sadness and make him happy.

Delighted with his success, Skirnir hurried back to Alfheim, where Frey came eagerly to learn the result of his journey. When he learned that Gerda had consented to become his wife, his face grew radiant with joy; but when Skirnir informed him that he would have to wait nine nights ere he could behold his promised bride, he turned sadly away, declaring the time would appear interminable.

In spite of this loverlike despondency, however, the time of waiting came to an end, and Frey joyfully hastened to the green grove, where, true to her appointment, he found Gerda, and she became his happy wife, and proudly sat upon his throne beside him.

According to some mythologists, Gerda is not a personification of the aurora borealis, but of the earth, which, hard, cold, and unyielding, resists the spring-god's proffers of adornment and fruitfulness (the apples and ring), defies the flashing sunbeams (Frey's sword), and only consents to receive his kiss when it learns that it will else be doomed to perpetual barrenness, or given over entirely into the power of the giants (ice and snow). The nine nights of waiting are typical of the nine winter months, at the end of which the earth becomes the bride of the sun, in the groves where the trees are budding forth into leaf and blossom.

Frey and Gerda, we are told, became the parents of a son called Fiolnir, whose birth consoled Gerda for the loss of her brother Beli. The latter had attacked Frey and had been slain by him, although the sun-god, deprived of his matchless sword, had been obliged to defend himself with a stag horn which he hastily snatched from the wall of his dwelling.

Besides the faithful Skirnir, Frey had two other attendants, a married couple, Beyggvir and Beyla, the personifications of mill refuse and manure, which two ingredients, being used in agriculture for fertilising purposes, were therefore considered Frey's faithful servants, in spite of their unpleasant qualities..

Magic, Adventure & Quests

Introduction

"Tell your honourable master … that, try us as he will, he will not be disappointed," says one of the entertainers in the Chinese tale 'The Two Jugglers'.

> *"Tell him that we come from the unknown land of dreams and visions, that we can turn rocks into mountains, rivers into oceans, mice into elephants, in short, that there is nothing in magic too difficult for us to do."*

The same might be said of the stories in this book and the tricks they play with the reader's imagination. One Roman tale turns a poor tripe-seller into a queen – at least her courtiers, tiring of her tantrums, install her there, handing their king's consort over to the tripe-man in her place. It's no surprise to find the tripe-seller making a more convincing queen, naturally calm and magnanimous as a monarch should be. Others have to travel far to find their destiny, like Jason the Greek hero, forced to cross the Aegean to find the Golden Fleece. A yet longer voyage awaits the Maori as they make their way to a new home in what is now New Zealand. A heroic story certainly, but a tale too of treachery and conflict – as perhaps any journey through this earthly life must be.

The Goblin City

LONG, LONG AGO, in the island of Ceylon, there was a large city full of nothing but goblins. They were all She-goblins, too; and if they wanted husbands, they used to get hold of travellers and force them to marry; and afterwards, when they were tired of their husbands, they gobbled them up.

One day a ship was wrecked upon the coast near the goblin city, and five hundred sailors were cast ashore. The She-goblins came down to the seashore, and brought food and dry clothes for the sailors, and invited them to come into the city. There was nobody else there at all; but for fear that the sailors should be frightened away, the goblins, by their magic power, made shapes of people appear all around, so that there seemed to be men ploughing in the fields, or shepherds tending their sheep, and huntsmen with hounds, and all the sights of the quiet country life. So, when the sailors looked round, and saw everything as usual, they felt quite secure; although, as you know, it was all a sham.

The end of it was, that they persuaded the sailors to marry them, telling them that their own husbands had gone to sea in a ship, and had been gone these three years, so that they must be drowned and lost for ever. But really, as you know, they had served others in just the same way, and their last batch of husbands were then in prison, waiting to be eaten.

In the middle of the night, when the men were all asleep, the She-goblins rose up, put on their hats, and hurried down to the prison; there they killed a few men, and gnawed their flesh, and ate them up; and after this orgie they went home again. It so happened that the captain of the sailors woke up before his wife came home, and not seeing her there, he watched. By-and-by in she came; he pretended to be asleep, and looked out of the tail of his eye. She was still munching and crunching, and as she munched she muttered:

"Man's meat, man's meat,
That's what goblins like to eat!"

She said it over and over again, then lay down; and soon she was snoring loudly.

The captain was horribly frightened to find he had married a goblin. What was he to do? They could not fight with goblins, and they were in the goblins' power. If they had a ship they might have sailed away, because goblins hate the water worse than a cat; but their ship was gone. He could think of nothing.

However, next morning, he found a chance of telling his mates what he had discovered. Some of them believed him, and some said he must have been dreaming; they were sure their wives would not do such a thing. Those who believed him agreed that they would look out for a chance of escape.

But there was a kind fairy who hated those goblins; and she determined to save the men. So she told her flying horse to go and carry them away. And accordingly, as the men were out for a walk next day, the captain saw in the air a beautiful horse with large white and gold wings. The horse fluttered down, and hovered just above them, crying out, in a human voice:

"Who wants to go home? who wants to go home? who wants to go home?"

"I do, I do!" called out the sailors.

"Climb up, then!" said the horse, dropping within reach. So one climbed up, and then another, and another; and, although the horse looked no bigger than any other horse, there was room for everybody on his back. I think that somehow, when they got up, the fairy made them shrink small, till they were no bigger than so many ants, and thus there was plenty of room for all. When all who wanted to go had got up on his back, away flew the beautiful horse and took them safely home.

As for those who remained behind, that very night the goblins set upon them and mangled them, and munched them to mincemeat.

Tales of Heaven

IN THAT FAIR DOMAIN it is neither too hot nor too cold. Life there is devoid of sorrow; age does not bring frailties, and no one is ever hungry or thirsty; it is without wretchedness, or fatigue, or evil feelings. Everything, whether celestial or human, that the heart seeks after is found there. Sweet are the juicy fruits, delicious the fragrance of flowers and tree blossoms, and waters are there, both cold and hot, to give refreshment and comfort. Nymphs dance and sing to the piping of celestial elves, and merry laughter always blends with the strains of alluring music.

The Assembly House of Yama, which was made by Twashtri, has splendour equal to the sun; it shines like burnished gold. There the servants of the Lord of Justice measure out the allotted days of mortals. Great rishis and ancestors wait on Yama, King of the Pitris (fathers), and adore him. Sanctified by holiness, their shining bodies are dressed in swan-white garments, and decked with many-coloured bracelets and golden earrings. Sweet sounds, alluring perfumes, and brilliant flower garlands make that building eternally pleasant and supremely blessed. Hundreds of thousands of saintly beings worship the illustrious King of the Pitris.

The heaven of Indra was constructed by the great artisan-god himself. Like a chariot it can be moved anywhere at will. The Assembly House has many rooms and seats, and is adorned by celestial trees. Indra sits there with his beautiful queen, wearing his crown, with gleaming bracelets on his upper arms; he is decked with flowers, and dressed in white garments. He is waited on by brilliant Maruts, and all the gods and the rishis and saints, whose sins have been washed off their pure souls, which are as resplendent as fire. There is no sorrow, or fear, or suffering in Indra's home, which is inhabited by the spirits of wind and thunder, fire and water, plants and clouds, and planets and stars, and also the spirits of Prosperity, Religion, Joy, Faith, and Intelligence. Fairies and elves (Apsaras and Gandharvas) dance and sing to sweet music; feats of skill are performed by celestial battle heroes; auspicious rites are also practised. Divine messengers come and go in celestial chariots, looking as bright as Soma himself.

The heaven of Varuna was built by Vishwakarman (Twashtri) within the sea. Its walls and arches are pure white, and they are surrounded by celestial trees, made of sparkling jewels, which always blossom and always bear fruit. In the many-coloured bowers beautiful and variegated birds sing delightful melodies. In the Assembly House, which is also pure white, there are many rooms and many seats. Varuna, richly decked with jewels and golden ornaments and flowers, is throned there with his queen. Adityas wait on the lord of the waters, as also do hooded snakes (Nagas) with human heads and arms, and Daityas and Danavas (giants and demons) who have taken vows and have been rewarded with immortality. All the holy spirits of rivers and oceans are there, and the holy spirits of lakes and springs and pools, and the personified forms of the points of the heavens, the ends of the earth, and the great mountains. Music and dances provide entertainment, while sacred hymns are sung in praise of Varuna.

The Voyage to New Zealand

WHEN THE CANOES were built and ready for sea, they were dragged afloat, the separate lading of each canoe was collected and put on board, with all the crews. Tama-te-kapua then remembered that he had no skilful priest on board his canoe, and he thought the best thing he could do was to outwit Ngatoro-i-rangi, the chief who had com–mand of the Tainui. So just as his canoe shoved off, he called out to Ngatoro: 'I say, Ngatoro, just come on board my canoe, and perform the necessary religious rites for me.' Then the priest Ngatoro came on board, and Tama-te-kapua said to him: 'You had better also call your wife, Kearoa on board, that she may make the canoe clean or common, with an offering of sea-weed to be laid in the canoe instead of an offering of fish, for you know the second fish caught in a canoe, or seaweed, or some substitute, ought to be offered for the females, the first for the males; then my canoe will be quite common, for all the ceremonies will have been observed, which should be followed with canoes made by priests.' Ngatoro assented to all this, and called his wife, and they both go into Tama's canoe. The very moment they were on board, Tama' called out to the men on board his canoe: 'Heave up the anchors and make sail '; and he carried off with him Ngatoro and his wife, that he might have a priest and wise man on board his canoe. Then they up with the fore-sail, the main-sail, and the mizen, and away shot the canoe. Up then came Ngatoro from below, and said:

'Shorten sail, that we may go more slowly, lest I miss my own canoe.' And Tama' replied: 'Oh, no, no; wait a little, and your canoe will follow after us.' For a short time it kept near them, but soon dropped more and more astern, and when darkness overtook them, on they sailed, each canoe proceeding on its own course.

Two thefts were upon this occasion perpetrated by Tama-te-kapua; he carried off the wife of Ruaeo, and Ngatoro and his wife, on board the Arawa. He made a fool of Ruaeo too, for he said to him: 'Oh, Rua', you, like a good fellow, just run back to the village and fetch me my axe Tutauru, I pushed it in under the sill of the window of my house.' And Rua' was foolish enough to run back to the house. Then off went Tama' with the canoe, and when Rua' came back again, the canoe was so far off that its sails did not look much bigger than little flies. So he fell to weeping for all his goods on board the canoe, and for his wife Whakaoti-rangi, whom Tama-te-kapua had carried off as a wife for himself. Tama-te-kapua committed these two great thefts when he sailed for these islands. Hence this proverb: 'A descendant of Tama-te-kapua will steal anything he can'.

When evening came on, Rua' threw himself into the water, as a preparation for his incantations to recover his wife, and he then changed the stars of evening into the stars of morning, and those of the morning into the stars of the evening, and this was accomplished. In the meantime the Arawa scudded away far out on the ocean, and Ngatoro thought to himself: 'What a rate this canoe goes at – what a vast space we have already traversed. I know what I'll do, I'll climb up upon the roof of the house which is built on the platform joining the two canoes, and try to get a glimpse of the land in the horizon, and ascertain whether we are near it, or very far off.' But in the first place he felt some suspicions about his wife, lest Tama-te-kapua should steal her too, for he had found out what a treacherous person he was. So ho took a string and tied one end of it to his wife's hair, and kept the other end of the string in his hand, and then he climbed up on the roof. He had hardly got on the top of the roof when Tama' laid hold of his wife, and he cunningly untied the end of the string which Ngatoro had fastened to her hair, and made it fast to one of the beams of the canoe, and Ngatoro feeling it tight thought his wife had not moved, and that it was still fast to her. At last Ngatoro came down again, and Tama-te-kapua heard the noise of his steps as he was coming, but he had not time to get the string tied fast to the hair of Kearoa's head again, but he jumped as fast as he could into his own berth, which was next to that of Ngatoro, and Ngatoro, to his surprise, found one end of the string tied fast to the beam of the canoe.

Then he knew that his wife had been disturbed by Tama', and he asked her, saying: 'Oh, wife, has not some one disturbed you?' Then his wife replied to him: 'Cannot you tell that from the string being fastened to the beam of the canoe?' And then he asked her: 'Who was it?' And she said: 'Who was it, indeed? Could it be any one else but Tama-te-kapua?' Then her husband said to her: 'You are a noble woman indeed thus to confess this; you have gladdened my heart by this confession; I thought after Tama' had carried us both off in this way, that he would have acted generously, and not loosely in this manner; but, since he has dealt in this way, I will now have my revenge on him.'

Then that priest again went forth upon the roof of the house and stood there, and he called aloud to the heavens, in the same way that Rua' did, and he changed the stars of the evening into those of morn–ing, and he raised the winds that they should blow upon the prow of the canoe, and drive it astern, and the crew of the canoe were at their wits' end, and quite forgot their skill as seamen, and the canoe drew straight into the whirlpool, called 'The throat of Te Parata' , and dashed right into that whirlpool.

The canoe became engulphed by the whirlpool, and its prow disappeared in it. In a moment the waters reached the first bailing place in the bows, in another second they reached the second bailing place in the centre, and the canoe now appeared to be going down into the whirlpool head foremost; then up started Hei, but before he could rise they had already sunk far into the whirlpool. Next the rush of waters was heard by Ihenga, who slept forward, and he shouted out: 'Oh, Ngatoro, oh, we are settling down head first. The pillow of your wife Kearoa has already fallen from under her head!' Ngatoro sat astern listening; the same cries of distress reached him a second time. Then up sprang Tama-te-kapua, and he in despair shouted out: 'Oh, Ngatoro, Ngatoro, aloft there! Do you hear?' The canoe is gone down so much by the bow, that Kearoa' s pillow has rolled from under her head.' The priest heard them, but neither moved nor answered until he heard the goods rolling from the decks and splashing into the water; the crew meanwhile held on to the canoe with their hands with great difficulty, some of them having already fallen into the sea.

When these things all took place, the heart of Ngatoro was moved with pity, for he heard, too, the shrieks and cries of the men, and the weeping of the women and children. Then up stood that mighty man again, and by his incantations changed the aspect of the heavens, so that the storm ceased, and he repeated another incantation to draw the canoe back out of the whirlpool, that is, to lift it up again.

Lo, the canoe rose up from the whirlpool, floating rightly; but, although the canoe itself thus floated out of the whirlpool, a great part of its lading had been thrown out into the water, a few things only were saved, and remained in the canoe. A great part of their provisions were lost as the canoe was sinking into the whirlpool. Thence comes the native proverb, if they can give a stranger but little food, or only make a present of a small basket of food: 'Oh, it is the half-filled basket of Whakaoti-rangi, for she only managed to save a very small part of her provisions '. Then they sailed on, and landed at Whanga-Paraoa, in Aotea here. As they drew near to land, they saw with surprise some pohutu–kawa trees of the sea-coast, covered with beautiful red flowers, and the still water reflected back the redness of the trees.

Then one of the chiefs of the canoe cried out to his messmates: 'See there, red ornaments for the head are much more plentiful in this country than in Hawaiki, so I'll throw my red head ornaments into the water '; and, so saying, he threw them into the sea. The name of that man was Tauninihi; the name of the red head ornament he threw into the sea was Taiwhakaea. The moment they got on shore they run to gather the pohutukawa flowers, but no sooner did they touch them than the flowers fell to pieces; then they found out that these red head ornaments were nothing but flowers. All the chiefs on board the Arawa were then troubled that they should have been so foolish as to throw away their red head ornaments into the sea. Very shortly afterwards the ornaments of Tauninihi were found by Mahina on the beach of Mabiti. As soon as Tauninihi heard they had been picked up, he ran to Mahina to get them again, but Mahina would not give them up to him; thence this proverb for anything which has been lost and is found by another person: 'I will not give it up, 'tis the red head ornament which Mahina found'.

As soon as the party landed at Whanga-Paraoa, they planted sweet potatoes, that they might grow there; and they are still to be found growing on the cliffs at that place.

Then the crew, wearied from the voyage, wandered idly along the shore, and there they found the fresh carcase of a sperm whale stranded upon the beach. The Tainui had already arrived in the same neigh–bourhood, although they did not at first see that canoe nor the people who had come in it; when, however, they met, they began to dispute as to who had landed first and first found the dead whale, and as to which canoe it consequently belonged; so, to settle the question, they agreed to examine the sacred place which each party had set up to return thanks in to the gods for their safe arrival, that they might see which had been longest built; and, doing so, they found that the posts of the sacred place put up by the Arawa were quite green, whilst the posts of the sacred place set up by the Tainui had evidently been carefully dried over the fire before they had been fixed in the ground. The people who had come in the Tainui also showed part of a rope which they had made fast to its jawbone. When these things were seen, it was admitted that the whale belonged to the people who came in the Tainui, and it was surrendered to them. And the people in the Arawa, determining to separate from those in the Tainui, selected some of their crew to explore the country in a north-west direction, following the coast line. The canoe then coasted along, the land party following it along the shore; this was made up of 140 men, whose chief was Taikehu, and these gave to a place the name of Te Ranga of Taikehu.

The Tainui left Whanga-Paraoa shortly after the Arawa, and, proceeding nearly in the same direction as the Arawa, made the Gulf of Hauraki, and then coasted along to Rakau-mangamanga, or Cape Brett, and to the island with an arched passage through it, called Motukokako, which lies off the cape; thence they ran along the coast to Whiwhia, and to Te Aukanapanapa, and to Muri-whenua, or the country near the North Cape. Finding that the land ended there, they returned again along the coast until they reached the Tamaki, and landed there, and after–wards proceeded up the creek to Tau-oma, or the portage, where they were surprised to see flocks of sea-gulls and oyster-catchers passing over from the westward; so they went off to explore the country in that direction, and to their great surprise found a large sheet of water lying immediately behind them, so they determined to drag their canoes over the portage at a place they named Otahuhu, and to launch them again on the vast sheet of salt-water which they had found.

The first canoe which they hauled across was the Toko-maru – that they got across without difficulty. They next began to drag the Tainui over the isthmus; they hauled away at it in vain, they could not stir it; for one of the wives of Hoturoa, named Marama-kiko-hura, who was unwilling that the tired crews should proceed further on this new expedition, had by her enchantments fixed it so firmly to the earth that no human strength could stir it; so they hauled, they hauled, they excited themselves with cries and cheers, but they hauled in vain, they cried aloud in vain, they could not move it. When their strength was quite exhausted by these efforts, then another of the wives of Hoturoa, more learned in magic and incantations than Marama-kiko-hura, grieved at seeing the exhaustion and distress of her people, rose up, and chanted forth an incantation far more powerful than that of Marama-kiko-hura; then at once the canoe glided easily over the carefully-laid skids, and it soon floated securely upon the harbour of Manuka. The willing crews urged on the canoes with their paddles; they soon discovered the mouth of the harbour upon the west coast, and passed out through it into the open sea; they coasted along the western coast to the southwards, and discovering the small port of Kawhia, they entered it, and, hauling up their canoe, fixed themselves there for the time, whilst the Arawa was left at Maketu.

We now return to the Arawa. We left the people of it at Tauranga. That canoe next floated at Motiti; they named that place after a spot in Ha–waiki (because there was no firewood there). Next Tia, to commemorate his name, called the place now known by the name of Rangiuru, Takapu-o-tapui-ika-nui-a-Tia. Then Hei stood up and called out: 'I name that place Takapu-o-wai-tahanui-a-Hei'; the name of that place is now Otawa. Then stood up Tama-te-kapua, and pointing to the place now called the Heads of Maketu, he called out: 'I name that place Te Kuraetanga-o-te-ihu-o-Tama-te-kapua.' Next Kahu called a place, after his name, Motiti-nui-a-Kahu.

Ruaeo, who had already arrived at Maketu, started up. He was the first to arrive there in his canoe – the Pukeatea-wai-nui – for he had been left behind by the Arawa, and his wife Whakaoti-rangi had been carried off by Tama-te-kapua, and after the Arawa had left he had sailed in his own canoe for these islands, and landed at Maketu, and his canoe reached land the first; well, he started up, cast his line into the sea, with the hooks attached to it, and they got fast in one of the beams of the Arawa, and it was pulled ashore by him (whilst the crew were asleep), and the hundred and forty men who had accompanied him stood upon the beach of Maketu, with skids all ready laid, and the Arawa was by them dragged upon the shore in the night, and left there; and Ruaeo seated himself under the side of the Arawa, and played upon his flute, and the music woke his wife, and she said: 'Dear me, that's Rua'!' – and when she looked, there he was sitting under the side of the canoe, and they passed the night together.

At last Rua' said: 'O mother of my children, go back now to your new husband, and presently I'll play upon the flute and putorino, so that both you and Tama-te-kapua may hear. Then do you say to Tama-te-kapua ' O! la, I had a dream in the night that I heard Rua playing a tune upon his flute' , and that will make him so jealous that he will give you a blow, and then you can run away from him again, as if you were in a rage and hurt, and you can come to me.'

Then Whakaoti-rangi returned, and lay down by Tama-te-kapua, and she did everything exactly as Rua' had told her, and Tama' began to beat her (and she ran away from him). Early in the morning Rua' performed incantations, by which he kept all the people in the canoe in a profound sleep, and whilst they still slept from his enchantments, the sun rose, and mounted high up in the heavens. In the forenoon, Rua' gave the canoe a heavy blow with his club; they all started up; it was almost noon, and when they looked down over the edge of their canoe, there were the hundred and forty men of Rua' sitting under them, all beautifully dressed with feathers, as if they had been living on the Gannet Island, in the channel of Karewa, where feathers are so abundant; and when the crew of the Arawa heard this, they all rushed upon deck, and saw Rua' standing in the midst of his one hundred and forty warriors.

Then Rua' shouted out as he stood: 'Come here, Tama-te-kapua; let us two fight the battle, you and I alone. If you are stronger than I am, well and good, let it be so; if I am stronger than you are, I'll dash you to the earth.'

Up sprang then the hero Tama-te-kapua; he held a carved two-handed sword, a sword the handle of which was decked with red feathers. Rua' held a similar weapon. Tama' first struck a fierce blow at Rua'. Rua' parried it, and it glanced harmlessly off; then Rua' threw away his sword, and seized both the arms of Tama-te-kapua; he held his arms and his sword, and dashed him to the earth. Tama' half rose, and was again dashed down; once more he almost rose, and was thrown again. Still Tama' fiercely struggled to rise and renew the fight. For the fourth time he almost rose up, then Rua', overcome with rage, took a heap of vermin (this he had prepared for the purpose, to cover Tama' with insult and shame), and rubbed them on Tama-te–kapua's head and ear, and they adhered so fast that Tama' tried in vain to get them out.

Then Rua' said: 'There, I've beaten you; now keep the woman, as a payment for the insults I've heaped upon you, and for having been beaten by me.' But Tama' did not hear a word he said; he was almost driven mad with the pain and itching, and could do nothing but stand scratching and rubbing his head; whilst Rua' departed with his hundred and forty men to seek some other dweling-place for themselves; if they had turned against Tama' and his people to fight against them, they would have slain them all.

These men were giants – Tama-te-kapua was nine feet high, Rua' was eleven feet high; there have been no men since that time so tall as those heroes.

The only man of these later times who was as tall as these was Tu-hou-rangi: he was nine feet high; he was six feet up to the armpits. This generation have seen his bones, they used to be always set up by the priests in the sacred places when they were made high places for the sacred sacrifices of the natives, at the times the potatoes and sweet potatoes were dug up, and when the fishing season commenced, and when they attacked an enemy; then might be seen the people collecting, in their best garments, and with their ornaments, on the days when the priests exposed Tu-hou-rangi's bones to their view. At the time that the island Mokoia, in the lake of Roto-rua, was stormed and taken by the Nga-Puhi, they probably carried those bones off, for they have not since been seen.

After the dispute between Tama-te-kapua and Rua' took place, Tama' and his party dwelt at Maketu, and their descendants after a little time spread to other places. Ngatoro-i-rangi went, however, about the country, and where he found dry valleys, stamped on the earth, and brought forth springs of water; he also visited the mountains, and placed Patupaiarehe, or fairies, there, and then returned to Maketu and dwelt there.

After this a dispute arose between Tama-te-kapua and Kahu-mata-momoe, and in consequence of that disturbance, Tama' and Ngatoro removed to Tauranga, and found Taikehu living there, and collecting food for them (by fishing), and that place was called by them Te Bang a-a-Taikehu; it lies beyond Motu-hoa; then they departed from Tauranga, and stopped at Kati-kati, where they ate food. Tama's men devoured the food very fast, whilst he kept on only nibbling his, therefore they applied this circumstance as a name for the place, and called it: 'Kati-kati-o-Tama-te-kapua ', the nibbling of Tama-te kapua; then they halted at Whakahau, so called because they here ordered food to be cooked, which they did not stop to eat, but went right on with Ngatoro, and this circumstance gave its name to the place; and they went on from place to place till they arrived at Whitianga, which they so called from their crossing the river there, and they continued going from one place to another till they came to Tangiaro, and Ngatoro stuck up a stone and left it there, and they dwelt in Moehau and Hau-raki.

They occupied those places as a permanent residence, and Tama-te-kapua died, and was buried there. When he was dying, he ordered his children to return to Maketu, to visit his relations; and they assented, and went back. If the children of Tama-te-kapua had remained at Hau-raki, that place would now have been left to them as a possession.

Tama-te-kapua, when dying, told his children where the precious ear-drop Kaukau-matua was, which he had hidden under the window of his house; and his children returned with Ngatoro to Maketu, and dwelt there; and as soon as Ngatoro arrived, he went to the waters to bathe himself, as he had come there in a state of tapu, upon account of his having buried Tama-te-kapua, and having bathed, he then became free from the tapu and clean.

Ngatoro then took the daughter of Ihenga to wife, and he went and searched for the precious ear-drop Kaukau-matua, and found it, as Tama-te-kapua had told him. After this the wife of Kahu-mata-momoe conceived a child.

At this time Ihenga, taking some dogs with him to catch kiwis with, went to Paritangi by way of Hakomiti, and kiwi was chased by one of his dogs, and caught in a lake, and the dog ate some of the fish and shellfish in the lake, after diving in the water to get them, and returned to its master carrying the captured kiwi in its mouth, and on reaching its master, it dropped the kiwi, and vomited up the raw fish and shell-fish which it had eaten.

When Ihenga saw his dog wet all over, and the fish it had vomited up, he knew there was a lake there, and was extremely glad, and returned joyfully to Maketu, and there he had the usual religious ceremonies which follow the birth of a child performed over his wife and the child she had given birth to; and when this had been done, he went to explore the coimtry which he had previously visited with his dog.

To his great surprise he discovered a lake; it was Lake Roto-iti; he left a mark there to show that he claimed it as his own. He went farther and discovered Lake Roto-rua; he saw that its waters were running; he left there also a mark to show that he claimed the lake as his own. As he went along the side of the lake; he found a man occupying the ground; then he thought to himself that he would endeavour to gain possession of it by craft, so he looked out for a spot fit for a sacred place, where men could offer up their prayers, and for another spot fit for a sacred place, where nets could be hung up, and he found fit spots; then he took suitable stones to surround the sacred place with, and old pieces of seaweed, looking as if they had years ago been employed as offerings, and he went into the middle of the shrubbery, thick with boughs of the taha shrub, of the koromuka, and of the karamu; there he stuck up the posts of the sacred place in the midst of the shrubs, and tied bunches of fiax-leaves on the posts, and having done this, he went to visit the village of the people who lived there.

They saw someone approaching and cried out:

'A stranger, a stranger, is coming here!' As soon as Ihenga heard these cries, he sat down upon the ground, and then, without waiting for the people of the place to begin the speeches, he jumped up, and commenced to speak thus: 'What theft is this, what theft is this of the people here, that they are taking away my land?' – for he saw that they had their store-houses full of prepared fern-roots and of dried fish, and shell-fish, and their heaps of fishing-nets, so as he spoke, he appeared to swell with rage, and his throat appeared to grow large from passion as he talked: 'Who authorized you to come here, and take possession of my place? Be off, be off, be off! leave alone the place of the man who speaks to you, to whom it has belonged for a very long time, for a very long time indeed.'

Then Maru-punga-nui, the son of Tua-Roto-rua, the man to whom the place really belonged, said to Ihenga: 'It is not your place, it belongs to me; if it belongs to you, where is your village, where is your sacred place, where is your net, where are your cultivations and gardens?'

Ihenga answered him: 'Come here and see them.' So they went together, and ascended a hill, and Ihenga said: 'See there, there is my net hanging up against the ricks'; but it was no such thing, it was only a mark like a net hanging up, caused by part of a cliff having slipped away; and there are the posts of the pine round my village' ; but there was really nothing but some old stumps of trees; look there too at my sacred place a little beyond yours; and now come with me, and see my sacred place, if you are quite sure you see my village, and my fishing-net – come along.' So they went together, and there he saw the sacred place standing in the shrubbery, until at last he believed Ihenga, and the place was all given up to Ihenga, and he took possession of it and lived there, and the descendants of Tua-Roto-rua departed from that place, and a portion of them, under the chiefs Kawa-arero and Mata-aho, occupied the island of Mokoia, in Lake Roto-rua.

At this time Ngatoro again went to stamp on the earth, and to bring forth springs in places where there was no water, and came out on the great central plains which surround Lake Taupo, where a piece of large cloak made of kiekie-leaves was stripped off by the bushes, and the strips took root, and became large trees, nearly as large as the Kahikatea tree (they are called Painanga, and many of them are growing there still).

Whenever he ascended a hill, he left marks there, to show that he claimed it; the marks he left were fairies. Some of the generation now living have seen these spirits; they are malicious spirits. If you take embers from an oven in which food has been cooked, and use them for a fire in a house, these spirits become offended; although there be many people sleeping in that house, not one of them could escape (the fairies would, whilst they slept, press the whole of them to death).

Ngatoro went straight on and rested at Taupo, and he beheld that the summit of Mount Tongariro was covered with snow, and he was seized with a longing to ascend it, and he climbed up, saying to his companions who remained below at their encampment: 'Remember now, do not you, who I am going to leave behind, taste food from the time I leave you until I return, when we will all feast together.' Then he began to ascend the mountain, but he had not quite got to the summit when those he had left behind began to eat food, and he therefore found the greatest difficulty in reacliing the summit of the mountain, and the hero nearly perished in the attempt.

At last he gathered strength, and thought he could save himself, if he prayed aloud to the gods of Hawaiki to send fire to him, and to produce a volcano upon the mountain; (and his prayer was answered,) and fire was given to him, and the mountain became a volcano, and it came by the way of Whakaari, or White Island, of Mau-tohora, of Okakaru, of Roto-ehu, of Roto-iti, of Roto-rua, of Tara-wera, of Pae-roa, of Orakeikorako, and of Taupo; it came right underneath the earth, spouting up at all the above-mentioned places, and ascended right up Tongariro, to him who was sitting upon the top of the mountain, and thence the hero was revived again, and descended, and returned to Maketu, and dwelt there.

The Arawa had been laid up by its crew at Maketu, where they landed, and the people who had arrived with the party in the Arawa spread themselves over the country, examining it, some penetrating to Roto-rua, some to Taupo, some to Whanganui, some to Ruatahuna, and no one was left at Maketu but Hei' and his son, and Tia and his son, and the usual place of residence of Ngatoro-i-rangi was on the island of Motiti. The people who came with the Tainui were still in Kawhia, where they had landed.

One of their chiefs, named Raumati, heard that the Arawa was laid up at Maketu, so he started with all his own immediate dependants, and reaching Tauranga, halted there, and in the evening again pressed on towards Maketu, and reached the bank of the river, opposite that on which the Arawa was lying, thatched over with reeds and dried branches and leaves; then he slung a dart, the point of which was bound round with combustible materials, over to the other side of the river; the point of the dart was lighted, and it stuck right in the dry thatch of the roof over the Arawa, and the shed of dry stuff taking fire, the canoe was entirely destroyed.

On the night that the Arawa was burnt by Raumati, there was not a person left at Maketu; they wore all scattered in the forests, at Tapu-ika, and at Waitaha, and Ngatoro-i-rangi was at that moment at his residence on the island of Motiti. The pa, or fortified village at Maketu, was left quite empty, without a soul in it. The canoe was lying alone, with none to watch it; they had all gone to collect food of different kinds

– it happened to be a season in which food was very abundant, and from that cause the people were all scattered in small parties about the country, fishing, fowling, and collecting food.

As soon as the next morning dawned, Raumati could see that the fortified village of Maketu was empty, and not a person left in it, so he and his armed followers at once passed over the river and entered the village, which they found entirely deserted.

At night, as the Arawa burnt, the people, who were scattered about in the various parts of the country, saw the fire, for the bright glare of the gleaming flames was reflected in the sky, lighting up the heavens, and they all thought that it was the village at Maketu that had been burnt; but those persons who were near Waitaha and close to the sea-shore near where the Arawa was, at once said: 'That must be the Arawa which is burning; it must have been accidentally set on fire by some of our friends who have come to visit us.' The next day they went to see what had taken place, and when they reached the place where the Arawa had been lying, they found it had been burnt by an enemy, and that nothing but the ashes of it were left them. Then a messenger started to all th© places where the people were scattered about, to warn them of what had taken place, and they then first heard the bad news.

The children of Hou, as they discussed in their house of assembly the burning of the Arawa, remembered the proverb of their father, which he spake to them as they were on the point of leaving Hawaiki, and when he bid them farewell.

He then said to them: 'my children, Mako, O Tia, O Hei, hearken to these my words: There was but one great chief in Hawaiki, and that was Whakatauihu. Now do you, my dear children, depart in peace, and when you reach the place you are going to, do not follow after the deeds of Tu, the god of war; if you do you will perish, as if swept off by the winds, but rather follow quiet and useful occupations, then you will die tranquilly a natural death. Depart, and dwell in peace with all, leave war and strife behind you here. Depart, and dwell in peace. It is war and its evils which are driving you from hence; dwell in peace where you are going, conduct yourselves like men, let there be no quarrelling amongst you, but build up a great people.'

These were the last words which Houmai-ta-whiti addressed to his children, and they ever kept these sayings of their father firmly fixed in their hearts. 'Depart in peace to explore new homes for yourselves.'

Uenuku perhaps gave no such parting words of advice to his children, when they left him for this country, because they brought war and its evils with them from the other side of the ocean to New Zealand. But, of course, when Raumati burnt the Arawa, the descendants of Houmai-ta-whiti could not help continually considering what they ought to do, whether they should declare war upon account of the destruction of their canoe, or whether they should let this act pass by without notice. They kept these thoughts always close in mind, and impatient feelings kept ever rising up in their hearts. They could not help saying to one another: 'It was upon account of war and its consequences, that we deserted our own country, that we left our fathers, our homes, and our people, and war and evil are following after us here. Yet we cannot remain patient under such an injury, every feeling urges us to revenge this wrong.'

At last they made an end of deliberation, and unanimously agreed that they would declare war, to obtain compensation for the evil act of Raumati in burning the Arawa; and then commenced the great war which was waged between those who arrived in the Arawa and those who arrived in the Tainui.

The Two Jugglers

ONE BEAUTIFUL SPRING DAY two men strolled into the public square of a well-known Chinese city. They were plainly dressed and looked like ordinary countrymen who had come in to see the sights. Judging by their faces, they were father and son. The elder, a wrinkled man of perhaps fifty, wore a scant grey beard. The younger had a small box on his shoulder.

At the hour when these strangers entered the public square, a large crowd had gathered, for it was a feast day, and everyone was bent on having a good time. All the people seemed very happy. Some, seated in little open-air booths, were eating, drinking, and smoking. Others were buying odds and ends from the street-vendors, tossing coins, and playing various games of chance.

The two men walked about aimlessly. They seemed to have no friends among the pleasure-seekers. At last, however, as they stood reading a public notice posted at the entrance of the town-hall or yamen, a bystander asked them who they were.

"Oh, we are jugglers from a distant province," said the elder, smiling and pointing towards the box. "We can do many tricks for the amusement of the people."

Soon it was spread about among the crowd that two famous jugglers had just arrived from the capital, and that they were able to perform many wonderful deeds. Now it happened that the mandarin or mayor of the city, at that very moment was entertaining a number of guests in the yamen. They had just finished eating, and the host was wondering what he should do to amuse his friends, when a servant told him of the jugglers.

"Ask them what they can do," said the mandarin eagerly. "I will pay them well if they can really amuse us, but I want something more than the old tricks of knife-throwing and balancing. They must show us something new."

The servant went outside and spoke to the jugglers: "The great man bids you tell him what you can do. If you can amuse his visitors he will bring them out to the private grand stand, and let you perform before them and the people who are gathered together."

"Tell your honourable master," said the elder, whom we shall call Chang, "that, try us as he will, he will not be disappointed. Tell him that we come from the unknown land of dreams and visions, that we can turn rocks into mountains, rivers into oceans, mice into elephants, in short, that there is nothing in magic too difficult for us to do."

The official was delighted when he heard the report of his servant. "Now we may have a little fun," he said to his guests, "for there are jugglers outside who will perform their wonderful tricks before us."

The guests filed out on to the grand stand at one side of the public square. The mandarin commanded that a rope should be stretched across so as to leave an open space in full view of the crowd, where the two Changs might give their exhibition.

For a time the two strangers entertained the people with some of the simpler tricks, such as spinning plates in the air, tossing bowls up and catching them on chopsticks, making flowers grow from empty pots, and transforming one object into another. At last, however, the mandarin cried out: "These tricks are very good of their kind, but how about those idle boasts of changing rivers into oceans and mice into elephants? Did you not say that you came from the land of dreams? These tricks you have done are stale and shopworn. Have you nothing new with which to regale my guests on this holiday?"

"Most certainly, your excellency. But surely you would not have a labourer do more than his employer requires? Would that not be quite contrary to the teachings of our fathers? Be assured, sir, anything that you demand I can do for you. Only say the word."

The mandarin laughed outright at this boasting language. "Take care, my man! Do not go too far with your promises. There are too many impostors around for me to believe every stranger. Hark you! no lying, for if you lie in the presence of my guests, I shall take great pleasure in having you beaten."

"My words are quite true, your excellency," repeated Chang earnestly. "What have we to gain by deceit, we who have performed our miracles before the countless hosts of yonder Western Heaven?"

"Ha, ha! hear the braggarts!" shouted the guests. "What shall we command them to do?"

For a moment they consulted together, whispering and laughing.

"I have it," cried the host finally. "Our feast was short of fruit, since this is the off season. Suppose we let this fellow supply us. Here, fellow, produce us a peach, and be quick about it. We have no time for fooling."

"What, masters, a peach?" exclaimed the elder Chang in mock dismay. "Surely at this season you do not expect a peach."

"Caught at his own game," laughed the guests, and the people began to hoot derisively.

"But, father, you promised to do anything he required," urged the son. "If he asks even a peach, how can you refuse and at the same time save your face?"

"Hear the boy talk," mumbled the father, "and yet, perhaps he's right. Very well, masters," turning to the crowd, "if it's a peach you want, why, a peach you shall have, even though I must send into the garden of the Western Heaven for the fruit."

The people became silent and the mandarin's guests forgot to laugh. The old man, still muttering, opened the box from which he had been taking the magic bowls, plates, and other articles. "To think of people wanting peaches at this season! What is the world coming to?"

After fumbling in the box for some moments he drew out a skein of golden thread, fine spun and as light as gossamer. No sooner had he unwound a portion of this thread than a sudden gust of wind carried it up into the air above the heads of the onlookers. Faster and faster the old man paid out the magic coil, higher and higher the free end rose into the heavens, until, strain his eyes as he would, no one present could see into what far-region it had vanished.

"Wonderful, wonderful!" shouted the people with one voice, "the old man is a fairy."

For a moment they forgot all about the mandarin, the jugglers, and the peach, so amazed were they at beholding the flight of the magic thread.

At last the old man seemed satisfied with the distance to which his cord had sailed, and, with a bow to the spectators, he tied the end to a large wooden pillar which helped to support the roof of the grand stand. For a moment the structure trembled and swayed as if it too would be carried off into the blue ether, the guests turned pale and clutched their chairs for support, but not even the mandarin dared to speak, so sure were they now that they were in the presence of fairies.

"Everything is ready for the journey," said old Chang calmly.

"What! shall you leave us?" asked the mayor, finding his voice again.

"I? Oh, no, my old bones are not spry enough for quick climbing. My son here will bring us the magic peach. He is handsome and active enough to enter that heavenly garden. Graceful, oh graceful is that peach tree – of course, you remember the line from the poem – and a graceful man must pluck the fruit."

The mandarin was still more surprised at the juggler's knowledge of a famous poem from the classics. It made him and his friends all the more certain that the newcomers were indeed fairies.

The young man at a sign from his father tightened his belt and the bands about his ankles, and then, with a graceful gesture to the astonished people, sprang upon the magic string, balanced himself for a moment on the steep incline, and then ran as nimbly up as a sailor would have mounted a rope ladder. Higher and higher he climbed till he seemed no bigger than a lark ascending into the blue sky, and then, like some tiny speck, far, far away, on the western horizon.

The people gazed in open-mouthed wonder. They were struck dumb and filled with some nameless fear; they hardly dared to look at the enchanter who stood calmly in their midst, smoking his long-stemmed pipe.

The mandarin, ashamed of having laughed at and threatened this man who was clearly a fairy, did not know what to say. He snapped his long finger nails and looked at his guests in mute astonishment. The visitors silently drank their tea, and the crowd of sightseers craned their necks in a vain effort to catch sight of the vanished fairy. Only one in all that assembly, a bright-eyed little boy of eight, dared to break the silence, and he caused a hearty burst of merriment by crying out, "Oh, daddy, will the bad young man fly off into the sky and leave his poor father all alone?"

The greybeard laughed loudly with the others, and tossed the lad a copper. "Ah, the good boy," he said smiling, "he has been well trained to love his father; no fear of foreign ways spoiling his filial piety."

After a few moments of waiting, old Chang laid aside his pipe and fixed his eyes once more on the western sky. "It is coming," he said quietly. "The peach will soon be here."

Suddenly he held out his hand as if to catch some falling object, but, look as they would, the people could see nothing. Swish! thud! it came like a streak of light, and, lo, there in the magician's fingers was a peach, the most beautiful specimen the people had ever seen, large and rosy. "Straight from the garden of the gods," said Chang, handing the fruit to the mandarin, "a peach in the Second Moon, and the snow hardly off the ground."

Trembling with excitement, the official took the peach and cut it open. It was large enough for all his guests to have a taste, and such a taste it was! They smacked their lips and wished for more, secretly thinking that never again would ordinary fruit be worth the eating.

But all this time the old juggler, magician, fairy or whatever you choose to call him, was looking anxiously into the sky. The result of this trick was more than he had bargained for. True, he had been able to produce the magic peach which the mandarin had called for, but his son, where was his son? He shaded his eyes and looked far up into the blue heavens, and so did the people, but no one could catch a glimpse of the departed youth.

"Oh, my son, my son," cried the old man in despair, "how cruel is the fate that has robbed me of you, the only prop of my declining years! Oh, my boy, my boy, would that

I had not sent you on so perilous a journey! Who now will look after my grave when I am gone?"

Suddenly the silken cord on which the young man had sped so daringly into the sky, gave a quick jerk which almost toppled over the post to which it was tied, and there, before the very eyes of the people, it fell from the lofty height, a silken pile on the ground in front of them.

The greybeard uttered a loud cry and covered his face with his hands. "Alas! the whole story is plain enough," he sobbed. "My boy was caught in the act of plucking the magic peach from the garden of the gods, and they have thrown him into prison. Woe is me! Ah! woe is me!"

The mandarin and his friends were deeply touched by the old man's grief, and tried in vain to comfort him. "Perhaps he will return," they said. "Have courage!"

"Yes, but in what a shape?" replied the magician. "See! even now they are restoring him to his father."

The people looked, and they saw twirling and twisting through the air the young man's arm. It fell upon the ground in front of them at the fairy's feet. Next came the head, a leg, the body. One by one before the gasping, shuddering people, the parts of the unfortunate young man were restored to his father.

After the first outburst of wild, frantic grief the old man by a great effort gained control of his feelings, and began to gather up these parts, putting them tenderly into the wooden box.

By this time many of the spectators were weeping at the sight of the father's affliction. "Come," said the mandarin at last, deeply moved, "let us present the old man with sufficient money to give his boy a decent burial."

All present agreed willingly, for there is no sight in China that causes greater pity than that of an aged parent robbed by death of an only son. The copper cash fell in a shower at the juggler's feet, and soon tears of gratitude were mingled with those of sorrow. He gathered up the money and tied it in a large black cloth. Then a wonderful change came over his face. He seemed all of a sudden to forget his grief. Turning to the box, he raised the lid. The people heard him say: "Come, my son; the crowd is waiting for you to thank them. Hurry up! They have been very kind to us."

In an instant the box was thrown open with a bang, and before the mandarin and his friends, before the eyes of all the sightseers the young man, strong and whole once more, stepped forth and bowed, clasping his hands and giving the national salute.

For a moment all were silent. Then, as the wonder of the whole thing dawned upon them, the people broke forth into a tumult of shouts, laughter, and compliments. "The fairies have surely come to visit us!" they shouted. "The city will be blessed with good fortune! Perhaps it is Fairy Old Boy himself who is among us!"

The mandarin rose and addressed the jugglers, thanking them in the name of the city for their visit and for the taste they had given to him and his guests of the peach from the heavenly orchard.

Even as he spoke, the magic box opened again; the two fairies disappeared inside, the lid closed, and the chest rose from the ground above the heads of the people. For a moment it floated round in a circle like some homing pigeon trying to find its bearings before starting on a return journey. Then, with a sudden burst of speed, it shot off into the heavens and vanished from the sight of those below, and not a thing remained as proof of the strange visitors except the magic peach seed that lay beside the teacups on the mandarin's table.

According to the most ancient writings there is now nothing left to tell of this story. It has been declared, however, by later scholars that the official and his friends who had eaten the magic peach, at once began to feel a change in their lives. While, before the coming of the fairies, they had lived unfairly, accepting bribes and taking part in many shameful practices, now, after tasting of the heavenly fruit, they began to grow better. The people soon began to honour and love them, saying, "Surely these great men are not like others of their kind, for these men are just and honest in their dealings with us. They seem not to be ruling for their own reward!"

However this may be, we do know that before many years their city became the centre of the greatest peach-growing section of China, and even yet when strangers walk in the orchards and look up admiringly at the beautiful sweet-smelling fruit, the natives sometimes ask proudly, "And have you never heard about the wonderful peach which was the beginning of all our orchards, the magic peach the fairies brought us from the Western Heaven?"

The Kindly Magician

ONCE UPON A TIME there was a man named Du Dsi Tschun. In his youth he was a spendthrift and paid no heed to his property. He was given to drink and idling. When he had run through all his money, his relatives cast him out. One winter day he was walking barefoot about the city, with an empty stomach and torn clothes. Evening came on and still he had not found any food. Without end or aim he wandered about the market place. He was hungry, and the cold seemed well nigh unendurable. So he turned his eyes upward and began to lament aloud.

Suddenly an ancient man stood before him, leaning on a staff, who said: "What do you lack since you complain so?"

"I am dying of hunger," replied Du Dsi Tschun, "and not a soul will take pity on me!"

The ancient man said: "How much money would you need in order to live in all comfort?"

"If I had fifty thousand pieces of copper it would answer my purpose," replied Du Dsi Tschun.

The ancient said: "That would not answer."

"Well, then, a million!"

"That is still too little!"

"Well, then, three million!"

The ancient man said: "That is well spoken!" He fetched a thousand pieces of copper out of his sleeve and said: "That is for this evening. Expect me tomorrow by noon, at the Persian Bazaar!"

At the time set Du Dsi Tschun went there, and, sure enough, there was the ancient, who gave him three million pieces of copper. Then he disappeared, without giving his name.

When Du Dsi Tschun held the money in his hand, his love for prodigality once more awoke. He rode pampered steeds, clothed himself in the finest furs, went back to his wine, and led such an extravagant life that the money gradually came to an end. Instead of wearing brocade he had to wear cotton, and instead of riding horseback he went to the dogs. Finally he was again running about barefoot and in rags as before, and did not know how to satisfy his hunger. Once more he stood in the market-place and sighed. But the ancient was already there, took him by the hand and said: "Are you back already to where you were? That is strange! However, I will aid you once more!"

But Du Dsi Tschun was ashamed and did not want to accept his help. Yet the ancient insisted, and led him along to the Persian Bazaar. This time he gave him ten million pieces of copper, and Du Dsi Tschun thanked him with shame in his heart.

With money in hand, he tried to give time to adding to it, and saving in order to gain great wealth. But, as is always the case, it is hard to overcome ingrown faults. Gradually he began to fling his money away again, and gave free rein to all his desires. And once more his purse grew empty. In a couple of years he was as poor as ever he had been.

Then he met the ancient the third time, but was so ashamed of himself that he hid his face when he passed him.

The ancient seized his arm and said: "Where are you going? I will help you once more. I will give you thirty million. But if then you do not improve you are past all aid!"

Full of gratitude, Du Dsi Tschun bowed before him and said: "In the days of my poverty my wealthy relatives did not seek me out. You alone have thrice aided me. The money you give me to-day shall not be squandered, that I swear; but I will devote it to good works in order to repay your great kindness. And when I have done this I will follow you, if needs be through fire and through water."

The ancient replied: "That is right! When you have ordered these things ask for me in the temple of Laotsze beneath the two mulberry trees!"

Du Dsi Tschun took the money and went to Yangdschou. There he bought a hundred acres of the best land, and built a lofty house with many hundreds of rooms on the highway. And there he allowed widows and orphans to live. Then he bought a burial-place for his ancestors, and supported his needy relations. Countless people were indebted to him for their livelihood.

When all was finished, he went to inquire after the ancient in the temple of Laotsze. The ancient was sitting in the shade of the mulberry trees blowing the flute. He took Du Dsi Tschun along with him to the cloudy peaks of the holy mountains of the West. When they had gone some forty miles into the mountains, he saw a dwelling, fair and clean. It was surrounded by many-colored clouds, and peacocks and cranes were flying about it. Within the house was a herb-oven nine feet high. The fire burned with a purple flame, and its glow leaped along the walls. Nine fairies stood at the oven, and a green dragon and a white tiger crouched beside it. Evening came. The ancient was no longer clad like an ordinary man; but wore a yellow cap and wide, flowing garments. He took three pellets of the White Stone, put them into a flagon of wine, and gave them to Du Dsi Tschun to drink. He spread out a tiger-skin against the western wall of the inner chamber, and bade Du Dsi Tschun sit down on it, with his face turned toward the East. Then he said to him: "Now beware of speaking a single word – no matter what happens to you, whether you encounter powerful gods or terrible demons, wild beasts or ogres, or all the tortures of the nether world, or even if you see your own relatives suffer – for all these things are only deceitful images! They cannot harm you. Think only of what I have said, and let your soul be at rest!" And when he had said this the ancient disappeared.

Then Du Dsi Tschun saw only a large stone jug full of clear water standing before him. Fairies, dragon and tiger had all vanished. Suddenly he heard a tremendous crash, which made heaven and earth tremble. A man towering more than ten feet in height appeared.

He called himself the great captain, and he and his horse were covered with golden armor. He was surrounded by more than a hundred soldiers, who drew their bows and swung their swords, and halted in the courtyard.

The giant called out harshly: "Who are you? Get out of my way!"

Du Dsi Tschun did not move. And he returned no answer to his questions.

Then the giant flew into a passion and cried with a thundering voice: "Chop off his head!"

But Du Dsi Tschun remained unmoved, so the giant went off raging.

Then a furious tiger and a poisonous serpent came up roaring and hissing. They made as though to bite him and leaped over him. But Du Dsi Tschun remained unperturbed in spirit, and after a time they dissolved and vanished.

Suddenly a great rain began to fall in streams. It thundered and lightninged incessantly, so that his ears rang and his eyes were blinded. It seemed as though the house would fall. The water rose to a flood in a few moments' time, and streamed up to the place where he was sitting. But Du Dsi Tschun remained motionless and paid no attention to it. And after a time the water receded.

Then came a great demon with the head of an ox. He set up a kettle in the middle of the courtyard, in which bubbled boiling oil. He caught Du Dsi Tschun by the neck with an iron fork and said: "If you will tell me who you are I will let you go!"

Du Dsi Tschun shut his eyes and kept silent. Then the demon picked him up with the fork and flung him into the kettle. He withstood the pain, and the boiling oil did not harm him. Finally the demon dragged him out again, and drew him down the steps of the house before a man with red hair and a blue face, who looked like the prince of the nether world. The latter cried: "Drag in his wife!"

After a time Du Dsi Tschun's wife was brought on in chains. Her hair was torn and she wept bitterly.

The demon pointed to Du Dsi Tschun and said: "If you will speak your name we will let her go!"

But he answered not a word.

Then the prince of evil had the woman tormented in all sorts of ways. And she pleaded with Du Dsi Tschun: "I have been your wife now for ten years. Will you not speak one little word to save me? I can endure no more!" And the tears ran in streams from her eyes. She screamed and scolded. Yet he spoke not a word.

Thereupon the prince of evil shouted: "Chop her into bits!" And there, before his eyes, it seemed as though she were really being chopped to pieces. But Du Dsi Tschun did not move.

"The scoundrel's measure is full!" cried the prince of evil. "He shall dwell no longer among the living! Off with his head!" And so they killed him, and it seemed to him that his soul fled his body. The ox-headed demon dragged him down into the nether regions, where he tasted all the tortures in turn. But Du Dsi Tschun remembered the words of the ancient. And the tortures, too, seemed bearable. So he did not scream and said not a word.

Now he was once more dragged before the prince of evil. The latter said: "As punishment for his obstinacy this man shall come to earth again in the shape of a woman!"

The demon dragged him to the wheel of life and he returned to earth in the shape of a girl. He was often ill, had to take medicine continually, and was pricked and burned with hot needles. Yet he never uttered a sound. Gradually he grew into a beautiful maiden. But since he never spoke, he was known as the dumb maid. A scholar finally took him for his bride, and they lived in peace and good fellowship. And a son came to them who, in the course of two years was already beyond measure wise and intelligent. One day the father was carrying the son on his arm. He spoke jestingly to his wife and said: "When I look at you it seems to me that you are not really dumb. Won't you say one little word to me? How delightful it would be if you were to become my speaking rose!"

The woman remained silent. No matter how he might coax and try to make her smile, she would return no answer.

Then his features changed: "If you will not speak to me, it is a sign that you scorn me; and in that case your son is nothing to me, either!" And with that he seized the boy and flung him against the wall.

But since Du Dsi Tschun loved this little boy so dearly, he forgot the ancient's warning, and cried out: "Oh, oh!"

And before the cry had died away Du Dsi Tschun awoke as though from a dream and found himself seated in his former place. The ancient was there as well. It must have been about the fifth hour of the night. Purple flames rose wildly from the oven, and flared up to the sky. The whole house caught fire and burned like a torch.

"You have deceived me!" cried the ancient. Then he seized him by the hair and thrust him into the jug of water. And in a minute the fire went out. The ancient spoke: "You overcame joy and rage, grief and fear, hate and desire, it is true; but love you had not driven from your soul. Had you not cried out when the child was flung against the wall, then my elixir would have taken shape and you would have attained immortality. But in the last moment you failed me. Now it is too late. Now I can begin brewing my elixir of life once more from the beginning and you will remain a mere mortal man!"

Du Dsi Tschun saw that the oven had burst, and that instead of the philosopher's stone it held only a lump of iron. The ancient man cast aside his garments and chopped it up with a magic knife. Du Dsi Tschun took leave of him and returned to Yangdschou, where he lived in great affluence. In his old age he regretted that he had not completed his task. He once more went to the mountain to look for the ancient. But the ancient had vanished without leaving a trace.

The Dream of the King's Son

THERE WAS ONCE a king who had three sons. One evening, when the young princes were going to sleep, the king ordered them to take good note of their dreams and come and tell them to him next morning.

So the next day the princes went to their father as soon as they awoke, and the moment the king saw them he asked of the eldest, "Well, what have you dreamt?"

The prince answered, "I dreamt that I should be the heir to your throne."

And the second said, "And I dreamt that I should be the first subject in the kingdom."

Then the youngest said, "I dreamt that I was going to wash my hands, and that the princes, my brothers, held the basin, whilst the queen, my mother, held fine towels for me to dry my hands with, and Your Majesty's self poured water over them from a golden ewer."

The king, hearing this last dream, became very angry, and exclaimed, "What! I – the king – pour water over the hands of my own son! Go away this instant out of my palace, and out of my kingdom! You are no longer my son."

The poor young prince tried hard to make his peace with his father, saying that he was really not to be blamed for what he had only dreamed, but the king grew more and more furious, and at last actually thrust the prince out of the palace.

So the young prince was obliged to wander up and down in different countries, until one day, being in a large forest, he saw a cave, and entered it to rest. There, to his great surprise and joy, he found a large kettle full of Indian corn boiling over a fire and, being exceedingly hungry, began to help himself to the corn. In this way he went on until he was shocked to see he had eaten up nearly all the maize, and then, being afraid some mischief would come of it, he looked about for a place in which to hide himself. At this moment, however, a great noise was heard at the cave mouth, and he had only time to hide himself in a dark corner before a blind old man entered, riding on a great goat and driving a number of goats before him.

The old man rode straight up to the kettle, but as soon as he found that the corn was nearly all gone, he began to suspect someone was there, and groped about the cave until he caught hold of the prince.

"Who are you?" asked he sharply. And the prince answered, "I am a poor, homeless wanderer about the world, and have come now to beg you to be good enough to receive me."

"Well," said the old man, "why not? I shall at least have someone to mind my corn whilst I am out with my goats in the forest."

So they lived together for some time; the prince remained in the cave to boil the maize, whilst the old man drove out his goats every morning into the forest.

One day, however, the old man said to the prince, "I think you shall take out the goats today, and I will stay at home to mind the corn."

This the prince consented to very gladly, as he was tired of living so long quietly in the cave. But the old man added, "Mind only one thing! There are nine different mountains, and you can let the goats go freely over eight of them, but you must on no account go on the ninth. The Vilas (fairies) live there, and they will certainly put out your eyes as they have put out mine, if you venture on their mountain."

The prince thanked the old man for his warning, and then, mounting the great goat, drove the rest of the goats before him out of the cave.

Following the goats, he had passed over all the mountains to the eighth, and from this he could see the ninth mountain, and could not resist the temptation he felt to go upon it. So he said to himself, "I will venture up, whatever happens!"

Hardly had he stepped on the ninth mountain before the fairies surrounded him, and prepared to put out his eyes. But happily a thought came into his head, and he exclaimed quickly, "Dear Vilas, why take this sin on your heads? Better let us make a bargain, that if you spring over a tree that I will place ready to jump over, you shall put out my eyes, and I will not blame you!"

So the Vilas consented to this, and the prince went and brought a large tree, which he cleft down the middle almost to the root. This done, he placed a wedge to keep the two halves of the trunk open a little.

When it was fixed upright, he himself first jumped over it, and then he said to the Vilas, "Now it is your turn. Let us see if you can spring over the tree!"

One Vila attempted to spring over, but at the same moment the prince knocked the wedge out, and the trunk closing, at once held the Vila fast. Then all the other fairies were alarmed, and begged him to open the trunk and let their sister free, promising, in return, to give him anything he might ask. The prince said, "I want nothing except to keep my own eyes, and to restore eyesight to that poor old man." So the fairies gave him a certain herb, and told him to lay it over the old man's eyes, and then he would recover his sight. The prince took the herb, opened the tree a little so as to let the fairy free, and then rode back on the goat to the cave, driving the other goats before him. When he arrived there, he placed at once the herb on the old man's eyes, and in a moment his eyesight came back, to his exceeding surprise and joy.

Next morning the old man, before he drove out his goats, gave the prince the keys of eight closets in the cave, but warned him on no account to open the ninth closet, although the key hung directly over the door. Then he went out, telling the prince to take good care that the corn was ready for their suppers.

Left alone in the cave, the young man began to wonder what might be in the ninth closet, and at last he could not resist the temptation to take down the key and open the door to look in.

What was his surprise to see there a golden horse, with a golden greyhound beside him, and near them a golden hen and golden chickens were busy picking up golden millet seeds.

The young prince gazed at them for some time, admiring their beauty, and then he spoke to the golden horse: "Friend, I think we had better leave this place before the old man comes back again."

"Very well," answered the golden horse, "I am quite willing to go away, only you must take heed to what I am going to tell. Go and find linen cloth enough to spread over the stones at the mouth of the cave, for if the old man hears the ring of my hoofs he will be certain to kill you. Then you must take with you a little stone, a drop of water, and a pair of scissors, and the moment I tell you to throw them down you must obey me quickly, or you are lost."

The prince did everything that the golden horse had ordered him, and then, taking up the golden hen with her chickens in a bag, he placed it under his arm, and mounted the horse and rode quickly out of the cave, leading with him, in a leash, the golden greyhound. But the moment they were in the open air, the old man, although he was very far off tending his goats on a distant mountain, heard the clang of the golden hoofs, and cried to his great goat, "They have run away. Let us follow them at once."

In a wonderfully short time, the old man on his great goat came so near the prince on his golden horse that the latter shouted, "Throw now the little stone!"

The moment the prince had thrown it down, a high rocky mountain rose up between him and the old man, and before the goat had climbed over it, the golden horse had gained much ground. Very soon, however, the old man was so nearly catching them that the horse shouted, "Throw now the drop of water!" The prince obeyed instantly, and immediately saw a broad river flowing between him and his pursuer.

It took the old man on his goat so long to cross the river that the prince on his golden horse was far away before them. But for all that, it was not very long before the horse heard the goat so near behind him that he shouted, "Throw the scissors!" The prince threw them, and the goat, running over them, injured one of his forelegs very badly. When the old man saw this, he exclaimed, "Now I see I cannot catch you, so you may keep what you have taken. But you will do wisely to listen to my counsel. People will be sure to kill you for the sake of your golden horse, so you had better buy at once a donkey, and take the hide to cover your horse. And do the same with your golden greyhound."

Having said this, the old man turned and rode back to his cave. And the prince lost no time in attending to his advice, and covered with donkey hide his golden horse and his golden hound.

After travelling a long time, the prince came unawares to the kingdom of his father. There he heard that the king had had a ditch dug – three hundred yards wide and four hundred yards deep – and had proclaimed that whosoever should leap his horse over it should have the princess, his daughter, for wife.

Almost a whole year had elapsed since the proclamation was issued, but as yet no one had dared to risk the leap. When the prince heard this, he said, "I will leap over it with my donkey and my dog!" And he leapt over it.

But the king was very angry when he heard that a poorly dressed man on a donkey had dared to leap over the great ditch which had frightened back his bravest knights. So he had the disguised prince thrown into one of his deepest dungeons, together with his donkey and his dog.

Next morning the king sent some of his servants to see if the man was still living, and these soon ran back to him, full of wonder, and told him that they had found in the dungeon, instead of a poor man and his donkey, a young man, beautifully dressed, a golden horse, a golden greyhound, and a golden hen, surrounded by golden chickens, which were picking up golden millet seeds from the ground.

Then the king said, "That must be some powerful prince." So he ordered the queen, and the princes, his sons, to prepare all things for the stranger to wash his hands. Then he went down himself into the dungeon, and led the prince up with much courtesy, desiring thus to make amends for the past ill-treatment.

The king himself took a golden ewer full of water, and poured some over the prince's hands, whilst the two princes held the basin under them, and the queen held out fine towels to dry them on.

This done, the young prince exclaimed, "Now, my dream is fulfilled." And they all at once recognized him, and were very glad to see him once again amongst them.

The Three Brothers

I

THERE WAS ONCE upon a time an old man whose family consisted of his wife and three sons. They were exceedingly poor, and finding that they could not possibly all live at home, the three sons went out into the world in different directions to find some means of living. Thus the old man and his wife remained alone.

Having neither horses nor oxen, the old man was obliged to go every day to the forest for fuel, and carry home the firewood on his back.

On one occasion it was nearly evening when he started to go to the forest, and his wife, who was afraid to remain alone in the house, begged very hard to be permitted to go with him. He objected very much at first, but as she persisted in her entreaties, he at length consented to her following him, first bidding her, however, take good care to make the house door safe, lest someone should break into the house.

The old woman thought the door would be safest if she took it off its hinges, and carried it away on her back. So she took it off and followed her husband as fast as she was able. The old man, however, was not angry when he saw how she had mistaken his words, and the manner she had chosen to make sure of the door; for, he reflected, there was little or nothing at all in the house for anyone to steal.

When they had reached the forest, the husband began to cut wood, and his wife gathered the branches together in a heap. Meanwhile it had got very late, and they were anxious as to how they should pass the night, seeing their own house was so far off that they would be unable to reach it before morning, and there were no houses in the neighbourhood where they could sleep. At last they observed a very tall and widely spreading pine tree, and they resolved to climb up and pass the night on one of its branches.

The man got up first, and his wife followed him, drawing, with great difficulty, the door after her. Her husband advised her to leave the door on the ground under the tree, but she would not listen to him, and could not be persuaded to remain in the tree without her house door. Hardly had they settled themselves on a branch, the old woman holding fast her door, before they heard a great noise, which came nearer and nearer.

They were excessively frightened at the noise, and dared neither speak nor move.

In a short time they saw a captain of robbers, followed by twelve of his men, approach the tree. The robbers were dressed all alike, in gold and silver, and one of them carried a sheep killed and ready for roasting. When the old man and woman saw the band of robbers come and settle under the pine tree in which they had themselves taken refuge, they thought their time was come, and gave themselves up for lost.

As soon as the robbers had settled themselves, the youngest of them made a fire and put the sheep down to roast, whilst the captain conversed with the others. The sheep was already roasted and cut up, and the robbers had begun with great gaiety to eat it, when the old woman told her husband that she could not possibly hold the door any longer, but must let it fall. The old man begged her piteously not to let it go, but to hold it fast and keep quiet, lest the robbers should discover and kill them. The old woman said, however, that she was so exceedingly tired she could no longer by any possibility hold it. The old man, seeing it was no good talking about it, declared that, as he could not hold his corner of the door any longer when she had let go her corner, it was not worthwhile to complain. "Since," as he said, "what must be must be, and it is no use to be sorry for anything in this world." Thereupon they both loosened their holds of the door at once, and it fell down, making a great noise – especially with its iron lock – as it fell from branch to branch.

The door made so much noise in falling that the whole forest echoed with the sound.

The robbers, greatly astonished at the noise, and too frightened by the unexpected clashing above their heads to see what was the cause, took to their heels, without once thinking of the roast sheep they left behind, or of any of the treasures which they had brought with them. One of them alone did not run away far from the spot, but hid himself behind a tree, and waited to see what might come of so much noise.

The old couple, seeing the robbers did not return, came down from the tree, and, being exceedingly hungry, began to eat heartily, the old man all the time praising the wisdom of his wife in throwing down the door.

The robber who had hidden himself, seeing only the old people near the fire, came up to them, and begged to be allowed to share their meal, as he had not eaten anything for the last twenty-four hours. This they permitted, and spoke of all kinds of things, until the old man exclaimed suddenly to the robber, "Take care! you have a hair on your tongue! Do not choke yourself, for I have no means to bury you here!"

The brigand took this joke in earnest, and begged the old man to take the hair out of his mouth, and he would in return show him a cave wherein a great treasure was hidden. As he was describing the great heaps of gold ducats, thalers, shillings, and other coins which he said were in the cave, the old woman interrupted him, saying, "I will take the hair out of your mouth, without pay! Only put your tongue out and shut your eyes!" The robber very gladly did as she told him, and she caught up a knife, and in a moment cut off a piece of his tongue. Then she said, "Well, now! I have taken the hair out!" When the robber felt what had been done to him, he jumped up and down in pain, and at length ran away without hat or coat in the same direction as his companions had gone, shouting all the time, "Help! help! give me some plaster!" His companions, hearing imperfectly these words, misunderstood him, and thought he cried to them, "Help yourselves; here is the police-master!" especially as he ran as if the captain of police with a large force was at his heels. Accordingly, the robbers themselves ran faster and farther away.

Meanwhile the old couple thought it no longer safe to stay under the pine tree, so they gathered up quickly all the money, whether gold or silver, that they could carry, and hurried back to their home. When they got there, they found the hens of the neighbours had pulled off the thatch of their house. They were, however, the less sorry for this, since they had now money enough to build another and a better home. And this they did, and continued to live in their fine new house without once remembering their sons, who had been wandering about the world already some nine long years.

II

In the meantime, the sons had been working each in a different part of the world. When, however, they had been away from their home nine years, they all, as if by common consent, conceived an ardent desire to go back once more to their father's house. So they took the whole of the savings which they had laid up in their nine years' service, and commenced their journeys homeward.

On his travels the eldest brother met with three gypsies, who were teaching a young bear to dance by putting him on a red-hot plate of iron. He felt compassion for the creature in its sufferings, and asked the gypsies why they were thus tormenting the animal. "Better," he said, "let me have it, and I will give you three pieces of silver for it!" The gypsies accepted the offer eagerly, took the three pieces of silver, and gave him the bear. Travelling farther on, he met with some huntsmen who had caught a young wolf, which they were about to kill. He offered them also three pieces of silver for the animal, and they, pleased to get so much, readily sold it. A little further still, he met some shepherds, who were about to hang a little dog. He was sorry for the poor brute, and offered to give them two pieces of silver if they would give the dog to him, and this they very gladly agreed to.

So he travelled on homeward, attended by the young bear, the wolf-cub, and the little dog. As all his nine years' savings had amounted only to nine pieces of silver, he had now but a single piece left.

Before he reached his father's house, he met some boys who were about to drown a cat. He offered them his last piece of money if they would give him the cat, and they were content with the bargain and gave it up to him. So, at last he arrived at his home without any money, but with a bear, a wolf, a dog, and a cat.

Just so, it had happened with the other two brothers. By their nine years' work they had only saved nine pieces of silver, and on their way home they had spent them in ransoming animals, exactly as the eldest brother had done.

Soon after they had returned, the old father died. Then the three brothers consulted together, and decided to invest part of the money, which their father and mother had got from the robbers, in the purchase of four horses and one grass field.

A few days later, they all went into the fields to bring in the hay which the two elder ones had mown. They found, however, hardly the third part of the hay which they had left. At this they wondered greatly, and looked about to see who had stolen it, but, finding no one, after a little while they took up what was left and returned home.

At length the year, on which all this had happened, passed away. The next year, however, they dared not leave their mown grass unwatched. So they discussed which of them should first keep guard. Each of them offered to do it, but at last they agreed that the youngest brother should begin to watch. So he prepared himself, and at night went out into the field. Having come there, he climbed up into a tree and resolved to remain there until daybreak. About midnight, he heard a great noise and shouting, which frightened him so much that he dared not stir at all. Some creatures came into the field and ate up most of the hay, and what they did not eat they tossed about and spoiled, so that it was fit for nothing. When daylight came, the youngest brother came down from the tree and went home to tell what he had seen.

So that year they had no hay.

Next year, when hay harvest came, the three brothers took counsel together how to preserve their hay. The second brother now volunteered to watch in the field, and seemed quite sure he would be able to save the hay. Accordingly he went, and climbed into the tree, just as his brother had done the previous year. About midnight, three winged horses came into the field with a company of fairies. The winged horses began to eat the newly mown hay, and the fairies danced over it. After the greater part of the hay had been eaten by the horses and all the rest had been spoiled by the dancing of the fairies, the whole company left the field just as day began to dawn. The watcher in the tree had witnessed all this; he was, however, too frightened to do anything – indeed, he hardly dared to move. When he went home, he told his brothers all that he had seen, at which they were sad, since this year again they would have no hay.

However, the time passed, and the third summer came on. Again the three brothers cut the grass in their meadow, and consulted together anxiously how they should manage to keep their new hay.

At length it was settled that it was now the turn of the eldest brother to keep watch. If he also failed to save the hay, it was agreed that they should divide amongst them the little property which they had left, and go out again, separately, to seek their fortunes in the world, seeing they had no luck in their own country.

As had been agreed upon, the eldest brother now went out into the field at night; but, instead of going up into the tree as his brothers had done, he lay quietly down on a heap of hay, and waited to see what would happen. About midnight, he heard a great noise afar off and, by-and-by, a troop of fairies, with three winged horses, came straight towards the place where he lay. Having got there, the fairies began to dance, and the horses to eat the hay and canter about. The eldest brother looked on and, at first, felt much afraid, and wished heartily the whole company would go away without seeing him. As, however, they seemed in no hurry to do this, he considered what he should do and, at length, decided that it would be worthwhile to try to catch one of the three horses. So when they came near him, he jumped on the back of one of them, and clung fast to it. The other two horses instantly ran away, and the fairies with them.

The horse that the eldest brother had caught tried all sorts of tricks to throw off his unwelcome rider, but he could not succeed. Finding all his attempts to free himself quite useless, at last he said, "Let me go, my good man, and I will be of use to you some other time." The man answered, "I will set you free on one condition; that is, you must promise never more to come in this field, and you must give me some pledge that you will keep your promise."

The horse gladly agreed to this condition, and gave the man a hair from his tail, saying, "Whenever you happen to be in need, hold this hair to a fire, and I will instantly be at your service."

Thereupon the horse went off, and the eldest brother returned home. His brothers had waited impatiently for his return and, when they saw him, pressed him immediately to tell them all that had happened. So he told everything, except that he had got a hair from the horse's tail, because he did not believe that the horse would keep his promise and come to him in his need. The two younger brothers, however, had no confidence that the fairies and winged horses would fulfil their promise and never come again to ruin their hayfield, so they proposed that the property should be at once divided, and that they should separate. The eldest brother tried to persuade them to remain at least one other year longer, to see what would happen; he was not able, however, to succeed in this. Accordingly they divided the remnant of their property, took each their animals, that is, each his bear, his wolf, his dog, and his cat, and left their home for the second time to seek their fortunes in the world.

The first day they travelled together, but the second day they were obliged to separate because, having come to a crossway, and trying to keep on the same path, they found they could not take a step forward so long as they were together. They therefore left that path and tried another. It was, however, of no use, for they could not move a step forward as long as they were together. And when they tried the third path, the same happened there also. So they tried if two of them could go on in one road if one of them went before and the other behind. But this also they were unable to do; they could not get on one step, try as hard as they would, so nothing was left them but to separate and each of them to go alone by a different road. They were exceedingly sorry to part, but could not help themselves.

Before the brothers separated, the eldest brother said, "Now, brothers, before we part, let us stick our knives in this oak tree; as long as we live, our knives will remain where we stick them; when one of us dies, his knife will fall out. Let us, then, come here every third year to see if the knives are still in their places. Thus we shall know something, at least, about each other." The other two agreed to this, and, having stuck their knives in the oak tree and kissed each other, went, each one his own way, taking his animals with him.

III

Let us first follow the youngest brother in his wanderings. He travelled, with his attendant animals, all that day and the following night without stopping, and the next day saw before him a king's palace, and went straight towards it. Having been taken into the presence of the king, he begged His Majesty to employ him in watching his goats. The king consented to take him as goatherd, and from that day he had the charge of the king's goats and lived on thus quietly for a long time.

One day the new goatherd chanced to drive his flock to a high hill, not far from the king's palace. On the summit of the hill there was a very tall pine tree, and the instant he saw it he resolved to climb up and look about from its top on the surrounding country. Accordingly, he climbed up, and enjoyed exceedingly the extensive and beautiful prospect. As he looked in one direction he saw, a long way off, a great smoke arising from a mountain. The moment he saw the smoke he fancied that one of his brothers must be there, as he thought it unlikely that anyone else would be in such a wilderness. So he resolved at once to give up his place of goatherd, and travel to the mountain which he had seen in the distance. Coming down from the tree, therefore, he immediately collected his goats, which was a very easy task for him to do, since he had such good help from his bear, his wolf, his dog, and his cat.

No sooner had he reached the palace than he went straight to the king and said, "Sir, I can no longer be Your Majesty's goatherd. I must go away, for I saw today a smoking mountain, and I believe that one of my brothers is there, and I wish to go and see if this be so. I therefore beg Your Majesty to pay me what you owe me, and to let me go!" All this time he thought the king knew nothing about the smoking mountain.

When he had said this, however, the king immediately began to advise him on no account to go to the mountain – for, as he assured him, whoever went there never came back again. He told him that all who had gone thither seemed at once to have sunk into the earth, for no one ever heard anything more about them. All the king's warnings and counsels, however, availed nothing; the goatherd was bent on going to the smoking mountain, and looking after his two brothers.

After he had made all preparations for the journey, he set out, accompanied, as usual, by his four animals. He went straight to the mountain, but, having got there, he could not at first find the fire. Indeed, he had trouble enough before he discovered it. At length, however, he found a large fire burning under a beech tree, and went near it to warm himself. At the same time, he looked about on all sides to see who had made the fire. After looking about some time, he heard a woman's voice, and upon his looking up to see whence the sound came, he saw an old woman sitting on one of the branches above his head. She sat huddled together all of a heap and shaking with cold.

No sooner had he discovered her than the old woman begged him to allow her to come down to the fire and warm herself a little. So he told her she might come down and warm herself as soon as she pleased. She answered, however, "Oh, my son, I dare not come down because of your company. I am afraid of the animals you have with you – your bear, and wolf, and dog, and cat."

At this he tried to reassure her and said, "Don't be afraid! They will do you no harm." However, she would not trust them, so she plucked a hair from her head, and threw it down, saying, "Put that hair on their necks and then I shall not be afraid to come down."

Accordingly the man took the hair and threw it over his animals, and in a moment the hair was turned into an iron chain which kept his four-footed followers bound fast together.

When the old woman saw that he had done as she desired, she came down from the tree and took her place by the fire. She seemed at first a very little woman; as she sat by the fire, however, she began to grow larger. When he saw this, he was greatly astonished, and said to her, "But, my old woman, it seems to me that you grow bigger and bigger!" Thereupon she answered, shivering, "Ha! ha! no, no, my son! I am only warming myself!" But, nevertheless, she continued to grow taller and taller, and had already grown half as tall as the beech tree. The goatherd watched her growing with wide-open eyes, and, beginning to get frightened, said again, "But really you are getting a fearful size, and are growing taller and taller every moment."

"Ha, ha, my son," she coughed and shivered, "I am only warming myself!" Seeing, however, that she was now as tall as the tallest beech tree, and, fearing that his life was in danger, he called anxiously to his companions, "Hold her fast, my bear! Hold her fast, my wolf! Hold her fast, my dog! Hold her fast, my cat!" But it was all in vain that he called to them; none of them could move a step from his place. When he saw that, he endeavoured to run away, but found that he could no more move from his place than if he were fast chained to it. Then the old woman, seeing everything had gone on just as she wished, bent down a little, and, touching him with her little finger, said, "Go, you have lost your head!" And the self-same moment he turned to ashes. After that, she touched, with the little toe of her left foot, all his animals, one after the other, and they also turned at once to ashes as their master had done.

Having collected all the ashes, she buried them under an oak tree. Then as soon as she took the iron chain in her hand, it turned again into a hair, which she put back into its place on her head.

She had before done with many young and noble knights just as she had now done with this poor goatherd.

The second brother, after serving a long time in a strange place, was seized with a great desire to go to the oak tree at the crossroads, where he had parted with his brothers, in order to see if their knives were still sticking in the tree. When he got there, he found the knife of his eldest brother still firmly fixed in the trunk of the oak, but his youngest brother's knife had fallen to the ground. Then he knew that his younger brother was dead, or in great danger of death, and he resolved at once to follow the way he had gone and try to discover what had become of him. Going then along the same road which his younger brother had travelled, he came, on the third day, to the king's palace, and went in and begged the king to take him into his service. Whereupon the king took him as goatherd, exactly as he had taken before the youngest brother.

When the second brother had tended the king's goats a long time, he one day drove them up a high hill, and, finding there a very tall pine tree, resolved at once to climb up to its top and look about to see what kind of a country lay on the other side of the hill. When he had looked round a while from the tree, he noticed a great volume of smoke rising from a mountain afar off, and the thought came at once to his mind that his brothers might be there. Accordingly, he came down quickly, collected his goats, and went back to the king's palace, followed by his four companions – that is to say, by his bear, his wolf, his dog, and his cat. When he had reached the palace, he went straight to the king, and begged him to pay him his wages at once, and to let him go to look after his brothers, for he had seen a smoke upon a mountain, and he believed they were there. The king tried in vain to dissuade him by telling him that none who went there ever came back. But all His Majesty's words availed nothing. Thereupon, seeing he was decided on going, the king paid him what he owed him and let him go.

He at once set out and went straight to the mountain. But, when he got there, it was a long time before he could find any fire. At last, however, he found one burning under a beech tree, and he went up to it to warm himself, wondering all the time who had made it, since he saw no one near. As he warmed himself, he heard a woman's voice in the tree above his head and, looking up, saw there an old woman huddled up on a branch and shaking with cold.

As soon as he saw her, the old woman asked him to let her come down and warm herself by the fire, and he told her she might come and warm herself as long as she liked.

She said, however, "I am afraid of the company which you have with you. Take this hair and lay it over your bear, and wolf, and dog, and cat, and then I shall be able to come down."

So saying, she pulled a hair out of her head and threw it down. He laughed at her fears, and assured her that his companions would not hurt her. Finding, however, notwithstanding all he said, that she was still afraid to come down from the tree, he at last took the hair and laid it on the beasts as she had directed. In an instant the hair turned into an iron chain and bound the four animals fast together. Then the old woman came down and took a place by the fire to warm herself. As the second brother watched her warming herself, he saw her grow bigger and bigger, until she had grown half as tall as the beech tree.

Wondering greatly, he exclaimed, "Old woman, you are growing bigger and bigger." "Hy, hy! my son," said she, coughing and shivering, "I am only warming myself." But when he saw that she was already as tall as the beech tree, he became frightened, and called to his companions, "Hold her, my bear! Hold her, my wolf! Hold her, my dog! Hold her, my cat!" They were none of them, however, able to move, so fast were they held together by the iron chain.

Seeing that, the old woman stooped down and touched him with her little finger, and he fell immediately into ashes. Then she touched the four animals, one after the other, with the little toe of her left foot, and they also crumbled to ashes.

No sooner had the old woman done this than she collected all the ashes in a heap and buried them under an oak tree. As she had before done with the ashes of many a youthful knight and gentleman, so she did now with those of this poor simple man. Pity, if they were to die, that some more worthy means than one hair from the head of a miserable old woman had not brought about their deaths!

A very long time had passed, and yet the eldest brother never once thought of going back to the crossroads where he had parted with his brothers. He was engaged in the service of a good and honest master, and, finding himself so well off, fancied that his brothers were the same. His master was an innkeeper, and the whole work of the servant was to prepare, morning and evening, the beds of the guests. He did his duty so well that his master thought of adopting him for his son, as he himself was childless.

One day a gentleman of great distinction came to pass the night at the inn, and the servant thought that the stranger looked remarkably like his youngest brother. He wished to ask him his name, but could not for shame, partly because he feared his brother would reproach him for having forgotten to go to the crossroads; partly because the guest's manners were so polished and his clothes were of fine silk and velvet, whereas he had left his brother very poorly clad, and of rustic manners.

As he thought of the likeness which the guest bore to his youngest brother, he considered that, in his travels about the world, his brother might have found wisdom, and by his wisdom might have succeeded in some way of business, and by his business might have gained money; and then, having got money, that it would be easy for him to get as fine clothes as the stranger wore. Reasoning thus, he took courage at last to ask the gentleman about his family, and at length grew bold enough to ask him plainly if he was not his brother.

This, however, the stranger quickly and positively denied, and asked, in return, about the servant's family. To all the particulars which the servant gave him he listened with a smile.

Next morning, the guest left the inn very early. And when the servant went to arrange the bed in which he had slept, he found, under the pillow, a little stone.

He thought the stone must be valuable, having been in the possession of so rich a man, and yet he considered its loss could hardly be felt by one who went clothed in silks and velvets. He lifted it to his lips to kiss it, before putting it in his pocket. But the moment his lips touched it, two men started out and asked him, "What are your orders, sir?" He was frightened by the suddenness of their appearance, and answered, "I do not order anything." Then the men disappeared, and he put the stone in his pocket.

The more he thought of this, the more he marvelled at the wonderful stone, and considered what he should do with it. By-and-by, in order to find out what the two men could do, he took the stone out of his pocket and raised it again to his lips. The moment he did so, the men reappeared and asked him again, "What do you demand, sir?" He replied quickly, "I desire to have the finest clothes prepared for me, of which no two pieces must be made from the same kind of stuff." In a very few moments the men brought him the most beautiful clothes possible; so fine indeed were they all, that he could not decide which piece was the most beautiful. Then, dismissing the men, who disappeared in the stone, he dressed himself. He was admiring the fine fit of his clothes, when his master came to the door of his room, and, seeing a stranger in such an exceedingly rich dress, said humbly, "Excuse me, sir, where do you come from?"

"From not far off," the servant answered.

"Wait a moment, sir," said the innkeeper. "I will call my servant to take your orders." And, going outside, he called loudly for his servant.

Meanwhile, the servant quickly threw off his fine clothes and gave them back to the two men. Dressing himself hurriedly in his old clothes, he rushed out of his room. Then, finding the pantry open, he began to arrange the things.

His master found him employed in this way, and ordered him at once to leave that business, and to go into the house to make coffee for a distinguished guest who had that moment arrived.

The strange guest, however, was nowhere to be found. The innkeeper looked, with his servant, into all the rooms, but there was no sign of a guest anywhere. Then the master, greatly astonished, thought that some thieves had been playing him a trick, and bid the servant in future to look more sharply who came in and who went out of the inn. The servant listened quietly to his master. But, having once remembered his brothers, he had now an irresistible desire to look after them, and so he told the innkeeper that he had resolved to go away, and desired that he might be paid his wages.

The innkeeper was very sad at hearing this, and offered to raise his wages, and tried all means to keep him, but it was of no use. Seeing that the servant was resolved to go away, the master then paid him, and let him leave the inn. Then the eldest brother took with him his four animals – his bear, wolf, dog, and cat – and went away.

After travelling a very long time, his good fortune brought him to the crossroads where he had parted with his brothers. Instantly he rushed to the oak to see if the knives were still sticking in it, but his own knife alone stood in the tree. The two others had fallen out, and he was much grieved at this, believing that his brothers were dead or that they were in great danger. In his trouble he had quite forgotten the wonderful hair and stone which he possessed. He resolved to go and search after his brothers, and therefore went along the same road his youngest brother had taken when they parted.

As he travelled he remembered the hair which the winged horse had given him, and the stone which he had found at the inn. But these did not much console him, he was so exceedingly sorry for his brothers. After travelling some time, he found himself before a large palace, the doorkeeper of which asked him if he would take charge of the king's goats. He said he would, if the king could only tell him something about his two brothers, who had travelled that way with a similar company to that which he had. The king said that no men with such a company had passed that way during his reign. And this was quite true, inasmuch as he had only recently mounted the throne, the old king, under whom the two brothers had served, having lately died. However, though the eldest brother could learn nothing of his two younger brothers, he decided to stay some time there, and so engaged himself to the king as goat-keeper.

As he drove the goats out, day by day, he looked about on all sides for some trace of his brothers; for, although their knives had fallen out of the oak tree, he tried to believe that they were not dead.

One day, as he thus wandered about with his goats, he met an old man, who was going to the forest, with his axe on his shoulder, to cut wood.

So he asked him if he had seen anything of his two brothers. The old man answered, "Who knows? Perhaps they have been lost on that mountain where so many other men have lost their lives. Drive your goats up that high hill. From its top you will see a much higher mountain, which smokes, and never ceases to smoke. On that mountain many people have been lost. Perhaps your brothers also have perished there. I will, however, give you one piece of good advice: do not go, for anything in the world, to the place where it smokes. I am now an old man, but I never remember to have seen one man return who went there. Therefore, if your life is dear to you, do not go up that mountain." So saying, the old man went off.

The goat-keeper drove his goats up the hill, and from its top he saw, as he had been told, a very high mountain which smoked. He tried to discover if any living creature was thereon, but he could not see the traces of a single one there. He considered within himself whether he should go there or not, and, after revolving it over in his mind, he at length determined to go.

In the evening, when he drove the goats home, he told the king of his intention. The king tried hard to dissuade him, and promised to raise his wages if he would stay with him. However, nothing could turn him from his resolution. So the king paid him, and he went away.

Having come to the mountain, he found the fire, and wondered who lit it. As he thought over this, he heard a woman's voice, saying, "Hy, hy!" So he looked up, and was astonished at seeing, in the branches of the beech tree over his head, an old woman huddled there. Her hair was longer than her body, and as white as snow. When he looked up, she said to him, "My son, I am so cold. I should like to warm myself, but I am afraid of your beasts. I made that fire myself, but, seeing you coming with your animals, I was frightened, and got up here to save myself."

"Well, you can now come down again, and warm yourself as much as you please," said he. However, she protested, "I dare not – your beasts would bite me. But I will throw you a hair, and you shall bind them with it. Then I can come down." The eldest brother thought to himself that the hair must be a very singular hair indeed, if it could bind his bear, his wolf, his dog, and his cat. So, instead of throwing it over the animals, he threw it into the fire. Meanwhile the old woman came down from the tree, and they both sat by the fire. But he never moved his eyes from her.

Very soon she began to grow, and grow, and in a short time she was ten yards high. Then he remembered the words of the old woodcutter, and trembled. However, he only said to her, "How you are growing, auntie." "Oh, no, my son," she answered, "I am only warming myself." She still grew taller and taller, and had grown as tall as the beech tree, when he again exclaimed, "But how you are growing, old woman!"

"Oh, no, my son. I am only warming myself," she repeated as before.

But he saw that she meant him mischief, so he shouted to his companions, "Hold her, my dog! Hold her, my little bear! Hold her, my little wolf! Hold her, my pussy!" Thereupon they all jumped on the old woman and began to tear her. Seeing she was unable to help herself, she begged him to save her from her furious enemies, and promised she would give him whatever he asked. "Well," said he, "I demand that you bring back to life my two brothers, with their companions, and all those you have destroyed. Besides that, I demand ten loads of ducats. If you will not comply with these demands, I shall leave you to be torn to pieces by my animals." The old woman agreed to do all this, only she begged hard that one man should not be brought back to life, because she had said, when she had turned him to ashes, "When you arise, may I lie down in your place!" And, therefore, she was afraid she should be turned to ashes herself if he came back to life.

As the eldest brother, however, thought that she was trying to cheat him, he would not comply with her request.

Finding that she could not otherwise help herself, she at length said to him, "Take some ashes from that heap under the tree, and throw them over yourself and your company, and whilst you do so, say, 'Arise up, dust and ashes – what I am now may you also be!'"

Wonder of wonders! The moment he did as she told him, there arose up crowds of men – more than ten thousand of them. On seeing such a multitude of people coming from under the tree, he was almost struck senseless with astonishment. But he explained to them briefly what had happened. Most of them thanked him heartily. Some, however, would not believe him, and said with anger, "We would rather you had not awakened us." Then they went away in crowds; some took one way, some another, until they were all dispersed. Only his two brothers remained behind, though they, too, for some time could not believe that he was their brother. However, when they saw that their animals recognized his, they remembered that no one but themselves had had such a strange company of beasts. Having recognized each other, the brothers fell into each other's arms and embraced affectionately. Then they divided the ducats which the old woman had given to the eldest, loaded their animals with their treasures, and went straight away towards the place where they were born, and where their parents had died.

As for the old woman, when the last man arose from the ashes under the oak tree, she herself crumbled into ashes under it.

IV

The three brothers built three fine palaces for themselves, and lived therein some time unmarried. At length, however, they began to think what would become of all their property after their deaths, and said to each other that it would be a pity for them to die without heirs. So they resolved to marry, that their wealth might be left to their sons and daughters.

The eldest brother said, "Let me go and find the best wives I can for all three of us; meantime you two will remain here, and take care of our property." The others gladly agreed to this, as the eldest brother had given proofs enough that he was by far the wisest of the three, and they felt sure that he would be able also to bring this important business to a successful issue. So he made the needful preparations, and started on his journey to look out for three wives for himself and the two younger brothers who remained at home.

After long travelling, he arrived at a large city, and resolved to remain there all night, and to continue his journey in the morning.

It happened that the king of that place had just arranged a horserace, and promised his only daughter as the prize, and, with her, ten loads of treasure to the winner.

The very evening the eldest brother arrived, he heard the public bell-man proclaiming aloud through the streets that everyone who had a horse should come tomorrow to the royal field, and whoever should spring first over the ditch should be rewarded with the king's daughter, and should receive, with her, ten loads of gold.

He listened to the proclamation without saying anything. Next morning he went out into the king's field in order to see the racing, and found there already innumerable horses of all kinds.

A little later came also the princess, the king's daughter, and behind her were brought ten loads of treasures.

When he saw the king's daughter, he thought her so exceedingly beautiful that he went instantly a little aside from the crowd to get a better sight of her. He then remembered his wonderful stone. Taking it out, he now lifted it to his lips, and immediately the two men appeared and said, "Master, what do you command?" He replied, "Bring me clothes of silk and velvet, together with precious stones, and ten good horses! And bring them as soon as possible!" He had not winked twice before the men had placed before him everything which he had demanded. Then he took out the hair, and, striking fire with a flint, held the hair near it. The moment he did this, the same cream-coloured horse that had given him the hair stood beside him and asked, "Master, what do you command?" He answered, "I wish that today we leave all the other horses behind us in the race, so that I may gain the king's daughter. Therefore prepare yourself, and let us go at once, as the other horses are now ready for starting."

The instant he had spoken these words, the cream-coloured horse stood, pawing the earth, ready and eager to begin the race. The man then mounted it, and off they went. The other racers, having started a few moments before, were already pretty far from the starting point. In an instant, however, he had reached them, and in another had passed and left them far behind. When he reached the ditch – which was a hundred and five yards deep, and a hundred yards wide – the horse made so great a spring that it touched ground some fifty yards beyond the ditch, broad as it was.

Then he rode back and took the maiden, the king's daughter, and, placing her behind him on his horse, carried her off, together with the loads of gold. All the people, seeing this, wondered greatly who the strange knight could be who had left all the best horses so far behind in the race, and had won the beautiful princess, with all her rich treasures.

He rode along until he came to a wood pretty far from the city, and there he let his wonderful horse go until he should want him again. He then took off all his beautiful clothes, and put on his old dress, and in this manner went on with the maiden and the loads of gold.

About evening he arrived at a strange city, and decided to remain there. After he had rested a little while, the people in the inn told him that all day long the city bell-man had proclaimed that whoever had a good horse should go tomorrow to the horserace, for the king of the palace had offered his only daughter as a prize, together with a hundredweight of gold and jewels; but that there was a ditch to be sprung over, which was three hundred and fifty yards deep and a hundred and fifty yards wide. When he heard this, he was greatly pleased, for he was quite sure that he should win this race also.

Next morning, by the help of the little stone and the wonderful hair, he was again dressed in the finest clothes, and mounted on his cream-coloured horse, and so took his place amongst the racers.

Everyone wondered from what country this knight came, and were delighted at his rich dress; as for the horse, the people were never tired of admiring it. When the racehorses were arranged for the start, he remained purposely behind. He knew well enough that this was of no consequence to him, as in one moment he could reach and pass them all. At length he started, and in a moment distanced the fleetest horse, arriving at the ditch, and leaping over it as if it were nothing. Then, without waiting a minute, he took possession of the king's daughter and her treasures, and went straight to the city where he had left the first king's daughter and her loads of gold.

Taking the two princesses and all the wealth with him, he now thought that it was time for him to go back home. On his way, however, he had the great good luck to come again to a large city, where he resolved to remain during the night. There, also, the public crier had been proclaiming all day long that the king had determined to give his only daughter and fifteen hundredweight of gold to whoever should win the race which was to be run on the morrow. In this instance, however, the horses would have to leap over a ditch one thousand yards deep and four hundred and fifty yards wide. On hearing this proclamation, the eldest brother became very joyful, for he knew that no racer had any chance of beating his wonderful horse.

On the morrow, therefore, by means of his little stone and the hair, he ordered fifteen horses to be ready, to carry away the treasures he felt sure of winning, and, at the same time, directed the two men to bring him his fairy courser and dresses so splendid that not even a king could buy them.

Richly dressed in this way, and mounted, as he was, on his marvellous horse, all the world, who had gathered to see the great race, could look at nothing except at him.

When all the racers were arranged for the start, he lingered behind and let them all speed off like falcons. He wished everyone to see that he was the last to start, that they might not charge him afterwards with having in any way cheated. When they had already gone pretty far, he started himself, and in a moment he had reached them, passed them, and left them all a long, long distance behind. How could it be otherwise? When did the crow outfly the falcon?

Coming to the ditch, he touched the bridle a little, and, in an instant, his horse had leaped over the ditch, and they were safe on the other side. So, without any delay, he took away the maiden, together with all the gold, and went back to the city. Having collected his immense treasures, he now took with him the three princesses and went straight home.

As he travelled along with his company, everyone who met him asked him, "Where are you going?" For you see the princesses were exceedingly beautiful.

But beyond all others, his two brothers, when he reached home, wondered and were delighted at the sight of the three beautiful princesses. They did not rejoice half so much over the great riches he had gained for them as over the marvellous fairness of the king's daughters whom he had brought to be their wives.

Thus each of the three brothers married a beautiful princess. The eldest brother, however, who had shown himself so much the bravest and wisest of them, married the youngest and most beautiful of the three.

Fisherman Plunk and His Wife

I

FISHERMAN PLUNK WAS SICK AND TIRED of his miserable life. He lived alone by the desolate sea-shore, and every day he caught fish with a bone hook, because they didn't know about nets in those parts at that time. And how much fish can you catch with a hook, anyhow?

"What a dog's life it is, to be sure!" cried Plunk to himself. "What I catch in the morning I eat up at night, and there's no joy for me in this world at all, at all."

And then Plunk heard that there were also rich sheriffs in the land, and men of great power and might, who lived in luxury and comfort, lapped in gold and fed on truffles. Then Plunk fell a-thinking how he too might come to look upon such riches and live in the midst of them. So he made up his mind that for three whole days he would sit still in his boat on the sea and not take any fish at all, but see if that spell would help him.

So Plunk sat for three days and nights in his boat on the face of the sea – three days he sat there, three days he fasted, and for three days he caught no fish. When the third day began to dawn, lo and behold, a silver boat arose from the sea – a silver boat with golden oars – and in the boat, fair as a king's daughter, stood the Pale Dawn-Maiden.

"For three days you have spared my little fishes' lives," said the Dawn-Maiden, "and now tell me what you would like me to do for you?"

"Help me out of this miserable and dreary life. Here am I all day long slaving away in this desolate place. What I catch during the day I eat up at night, and there is no joy for me in the world at all, at all," said Plunk.

"Go home," said the Dawn-Maiden, "and you will find what you need." And as she spoke, she sank in the sea, silver boat and all.

Plunk hurried back to the shore and then home. When he came to the house, a poor orphan girl came out to meet him, all weary with the long tramp across the hills. The girl said, "My mother is dead, and I am all alone in the world. Take me for your wife, Plunk."

Plunk hardly knew what to do. "Is this the good fortune which the Dawn-Maiden has sent me?" Plunk could see that the girl was just a poor body like himself; on the other hand, he was afraid of making a mistake and turning away his luck. So he consented, and took the poor girl to be his wife; and she, being very tired, lay down and slept till the morning.

Plunk could scarcely await the next day for wondering how his good fortune would show itself. But nothing happened that day except that Plunk took his hook and went out fishing, and the woman went up the hill to gather wild spinach. Plunk came home at night, and so did the woman, and they supped upon fish and wild spinach. "Eh, if that is all the good luck there is to it, I could just as well have done without," thought Plunk.

As the evening wore on, the woman sat down beside Plunk to tell him stories, to wile away the time for him. She told him about nabobs and kings' castles, about dragons that watch treasure-hoards, and kings' daughters who sow their gardens with pearls and reap gems. Plunk listened, and his heart within him began to sing for joy. Plunk forgot that he was poor; he could have sat and listened to her for three years together. But Plunk was still better pleased when he considered: "She is a fairy wife. She can show me the way to the dragons' hoards or the kings' gardens. I need only be patient and not make her angry."

So Plunk waited; and day after day went by, a year went by, two years passed. A little son was born to them; they called him little Winpeace. Yet all went on as usual. Plunk caught fish, and his wife gathered wild spinach in the mountains. In the evening she cooked the supper, and after supper she rocked the baby and told Plunk stories. Her stories grew prettier and prettier, and Plunk found it harder and harder to wait, till at last, one evening, he had had enough of it; and just as his wife was telling him about the immense treasures of the Sea King, Plunk jumped up in a rage, shook her by the arm and cried, "I tell you I'll wait no longer. Tomorrow in the morning you shall take me down to the Sea King's Castle!"

The woman was quite frightened when Plunk jumped up like that. She told him that she did not know where the Sea King had his Castle, but Plunk began to beat his poor wife most unmercifully, and threatened to kill her unless she told him her fairy secret.

Then the poor girl understood that Plunk had taken her for a fairy. She burst into tears and cried, "Truly I am no fairy, but a poor orphan girl who knows no spells nor magic. And for the tales I have told you, I had them from my own heart to beguile your weariness."

Now this only put Plunk all the more in a rage, because he had lived in a fool's paradise for over two years; and he angrily bade the woman go away next morning ere dawn with the child, along the sea-shore to the right-hand side, and he, Plunk, would go to the left, and she was not to come back again till she had found the way to the Sea King's Castle.

When the dawn came, the woman wept and begged Plunk not to send her away. "Who knows where one of us may be destroyed on this desolate sea-shore?" said she. But Plunk fell upon her again, so that she took up her child and went away crying whither her husband had bidden her. And Plunk went off in the opposite direction.

So the woman went on with her baby, little Winpeace. She went on for a week; she went on for a fortnight, and nowhere did she find the way to the Sea King. She grew so terribly tired that one day she fell asleep on a stone beside the sea. When she woke up, her baby was gone – her little Winpeace.

Her grief was so great that the tears froze fast in her heart, and not a word could she speak for sorrow, but became dumb from that hour.

So the poor dumb creature wandered back along the sea-shore and home. And next day Plunk came home, too. He had not found the way to the Sea King, and he came back disappointed and cross.

When he got home, there was no baby Winpeace, and his wife had gone dumb. She could not tell him what had happened, but was all haggard with the great trouble.

And so it was with them from that day forward. The woman neither wept nor complained, but did her housework and waited upon Plunk in silence; and the house was still and quiet as the grave. For some time Plunk stood it, but in the end he got thoroughly weary. He had just felt almost sure of the Sea King's treasure, and lo! all this trouble and worry had come upon him.

So Plunk made up his mind to try his sea-spell once more. Again for three whole days he sat in his boat on the sea, for three days he fasted, for three days he caught no fish. At the third day, at daybreak, the Dawn-Maiden arose before him.

Plunk told her what had happened, and complained bitterly.

"I'm worse off than ever before. The baby is gone, the wife is dumb, and my house dreary as the grave, and I'm just about bursting with trouble."

To this the Dawn-Maiden said never a word, but just asked Plunk a question: "What do you want? I will help you just this once more."

But Plunk was such a zany that he couldn't think of anything else but just this, that he was set on seeing and enjoying the Sea King's treasure; and so he didn't wish for his child back again, or that his wife should regain the power of speech, but he begged the Dawn-Maiden: "Fair Dawn-Maiden," said he, "show me the way to the Sea King."

And again the Dawn-Maiden said nothing, but very kindly set Plunk on his way. "When day dawns at the next New Moon, get into your boat, wait for the wind, and then drift eastward with the wind. The wind will carry you to the Isle Bountiful, to the stone Gold-a-Fire. And there I shall be waiting for you to show you the way to the Sea King."

Plunk went joyfully home.

When it was about the New Moon (but he never told his wife anything) he went out at the streak of dawn, got into his boat, waited for the wind, and let the wind carry him away toward the east.

The wind caught the boat and carried it along to the Unknown Sea, to the Isle Bountiful. Like a green garden the fruitful island floats upon the sea. The grass grows rank, and the meadows lush, the vines are full of grapes and the almond trees pink with blossom. In the midst of the island there is precious stone, the white blazing stone Gold-a-Fire. One half of the stone sheds its glow upon the island, and the other half lights up the sea under the island. And there on the Isle Bountiful, on the stone Gold-a-Fire, sits the Dawn-Maiden.

Very kindly did the Dawn-Maiden receive Plunk, and very kindly did she set him on his way. She showed him a mill-wheel drifting on the sea towards the island, and the mermaids dancing in a ring around the wheel. Then she told him – always very kindly – how he must ask the mill-wheel politely to take him down to the Sea King and not let the Dark Deeps of the Sea swallow him.

Last of all the Dawn-Maiden said, "Great store of gold and treasure will you enjoy in the Sea King's domain. But mark – to earth you cannot return, for three terrible watchers bar the way. One troubles the waves, the second raises the storm, and the third wields the lightning."

But Plunk was happy as a grig in his boat as he paddled towards the mill-wheel, and thought to himself, "It's easy to see, fair Dawn-Maiden, that you've never known want in this world. I shan't hanker back after this earth, where I'm leaving nothing but ill-luck behind!"

So he paddled up to the mill-wheel, where round the mill-wheel the mermaids were playing their foolish games. They dived and chased each other through the water; their long hair floated on the waves, their silver fins glittered, and their red lips smiled. And they sat on the mill-wheel and made the sea all foamy around it.

The boat reached the mill-wheel, and Plunk did as the Dawn-Maiden had told him. He held his paddle aloft so that the Dark Deeps should not swallow him, and he politely asked the mill-wheel, "Round wheel giddy-go-round, please take me down, either to the Dead Dark Deep or to the Sea King's Palace."

As Plunk said this, the mermaids came swishing along like so many silver fish, swarmed round the mill-wheel, seized the spokes in their snowy hands, and began to turn the wheel – swiftly, giddily.

An eddy formed in the sea – a fierce eddy, a terrible whirlpool. The whirlpool caught Plunk; it swept him round like a twig and sucked him down to the Sea King's fastness.

Plunk's ears were still ringing with the swirl of the sea and the mermaids' silly laughter when he suddenly found himself sitting on beautiful sand – fine sand of pure gold.

Plunk looked round and cried out, "Ho, there's a wonder for you! A whole field of golden sand."

Now what Plunk had taken to be a big field was only the great Hall of the Sea King. Round the Hall stood the sea like a marble wall, and above the Hall hung the sea, like a glass dome. Down from the stone Gold-a-Fire streamed a bluish glare, livid and pale as moonlight. From the ceiling hung festoons of pearls, and on the floor below stood tables of coral.

And at the end – the far end, where slender pipes were piping and tiny bells tinkling – there lazed and lounged the Sea King himself; he stretched his limbs on the golden sand, raising only his great bullock's head, beside him a coral table, and behind him a golden hedge.

What with the quick, shrill music of the pipes, the tinkling of the bells, and the sheen and glimmer all around him, Plunk wouldn't have believed there could be so much pleasure or wealth in the world!

Plunk went clean mad for pure joy – joy went to his head like strong wine; his heart sang; he clapped his hands; he skipped about the golden sand like a frolicsome child; he turned head over heels once, twice, and again – just like a jolly boy.

Now this amused the Sea King vastly. For the Sea King's feet are heavy – far too heavy – and his great bullock's head is heavier still. The Sea King guffawed as he lounged on the golden sand; he laughed so heartily that the golden sand blew up all round him.

"You're fine and light on your feet, my boy," said the Sea King, and he reached up and pulled down a branch of pearls and gave it to Plunk. And then the Sea King ordered the Under Seas Fairies to bring choice viands and honeyed drink in golden vessels. And Plunk had leave to sit beside the Sea King at the coral table, and surely that was a great honour!

When Plunk had dined, the Sea King asked him:

"Is there anything else you would like, my man?"

Now what should a poor man ask for, who had never known what it is to have a good time? But Plunk was hungry from his long journey, and he had made but a poor meal of it off the choice viands and the honeyed drinks. So he said to the Sea King, "Just as you were saying that, O King of the Sea, I was wishing that I had a good helping of boiled wild spinach."

The Sea King was rather surprised, but he recovered himself quickly, laughed and said to Plunk, "Eh, brother of mine, wild spinach is very dear down here, dearer than pearls and mother-o'-pearl, because it's a long way from here to the place where it grows. But since you have just asked for it, I will send a Foam Fairy to bring you some from the land where the wild spinach grows. But you must turn three more coach-wheels for me."

As Plunk was already in the best of humours, he didn't find that hard either. Lightly he leapt to his feet, and quickly they all flocked round him, the mermaids and the tiny folk in the Palace, and all for to see that wonder!

Plunk took a run over the golden sand, turned a beautiful coach-wheel, then a second and a third, light as a squirrel, and the Sea King and all the tiny folk rocked with laughter at such cunning.

But heartiest of all laughed a little baby, and that was the little King whom the mermaids themselves had crowned King for fun and idle sport. The wee baby was sitting up in a golden cradle. His little shirt was of silk, the cradle was hung with tiny bells of pearl, and in his hands the child held a golden apple.

While Plunk was turning coach-wheels and the little King laughed so heartily, Plunk looked round at him. He looked at the little King, and then – Plunk started. It was his own baby boy, little Winpeace.

Well, Plunk was suddenly disgusted. He would never have guessed that he would grow sick of it so soon.

Plunk frowned; he was angry, and when he had got over his shock a bit he thought, "Look at him, the urchin, how he's got on, lording it here in idleness and sport, and his mother at home gone dumb with grieving!"

Plunk was vexed; he hated seeing himself or the child in this Palace, yet he dared not say a word lest they should part him from the boy. So he made himself the servant of his son, of little Winpeace, and thought to himself, "Perhaps I shall be left alone with him sometimes. Then I will remind the boy of his father and mother; I will run away with him; I will carry off the little brat and go back with him to his mother."

So thought Plunk, and one fine day, when he happened to be alone with the little King, he whispered to the child, "Come along, my boy, let's run away with father."

But Winpeace was only a baby, and what with living so long under the sea, he had quite forgotten his father. He laughed; the little King laughed. He thought, "Plunk is making fun," and he kicked Plunk with his little foot.

"You are not my father; you are the silly-billy who turns head-over-heels before the Sea King."

That stung Plunk to the heart, so that he well-nigh died with the pain of it. He went out and wept for sheer bitter sorrow. All the Sea King's attendants gathered round him and said one to the other, "Well, well, he must have been a great lord on earth, to weep amid such splendours."

"Upon my soul," cried Plunk wrathfully, "I was the same as your Sea King here. I had a son who tugged my beard, a wife who showed me marvels, and wild spinach, brothers, as much as you want – and no need to turn coach-wheels before anybody either."

The sea-folk marvelled at such magnificence, and left Plunk to mourn his lost greatness. But Plunk went on serving the little King. He did all he could to please the boy, thinking, "I shall get him somehow to run away with me." But the little King grew sillier and more wayward every day; the days passed, and every day the child only thought Plunk more than ever a zany.

II

Now all this time Plunk's wife was at home, all alone and grieving. The first evening she made up the fire and kept the supper hot for Plunk; but when she gave up expecting Plunk, she let the fire go out, nor did she kindle it again.

So the poor dumb soul sat on her threshold. She neither worked, nor tidied, nor wept, nor lamented, but just pined away with grief and sorrow. She could not take counsel with anyone, because she was dumb; nor could she cross the sea after Plunk, because she was all broken up with grieving.

Where could she go, poor soul! but back one day to the far hills, where her mother lay buried. And as she stood by her mother's grave, a beautiful Hind up came to her.

And as the dumb animals speak, so the Hind spoke to the Woman: "You must not sit there and pine away, my daughter, for else your heart will break and your house will perish. But every evening you must get Plunk's supper ready for him, and after supper you must unpick some fine hemp. If Plunk does not come home, then you must take his supper in the morning and the fine hemp as well, and also the slender twin pipes, and go up into the rocky mountain. Play upon the twin pipes; the snakes and their young will come and eat up the supper, and the sea-fowl will line their nests with the hemp."

Full well the daughter understood all that her mother said, and as she was bid so did she do. Every evening she cooked supper, and after supper she unpicked hemp. Plunk did not come back; and so the woman took her little twin pipes in the morning, and carried both supper and hemp to the rocky mountain. And as she played on her little pipes, played softly on the right-hand pipe, lo, snakes and baby snakes came out of the rocks. They ate up the supper and thanked the woman in the dumb speech. And when she played on the left-hand pipe, lo, gulls great and small came flying, carried off the hemp to their nests, and thanked the woman.

For three months the woman went on in this way; thrice the moon waxed and waned, and still Plunk had not come home.

Again grief overcame the poor dumb soul, so that she went again to her mother's grave.

The Hind came up, and in dumb speech the woman said to her, "Well, Mother, I have done all you told me, and Plunk has not come back. I am weary of waiting. Shall I throw myself into the sea, or fling myself down from the cliffs?"

"Daughter of mine," said the Hind, "you must not fail in your trust. Your Plunk is in grievous trouble. Now listen and hear how you may help him. In the Unknown Sea there is a Big Bass, and that Bass has a golden fin, and on that fin grows a golden apple. If you catch that Bass by moonlight you will deliver your dear Plunk from his trouble. But on the road to the Unknown Sea you will have to pass three caverns of cloud. In the first there is a monstrous Snake, the Mother of All Snakes – it is she who troubles the sea and stirs up the waves; in the second there is a monstrous Bird, the Mother of All Birds – it is she who raises the storm; and in the third there is a Golden Bee – it is she who flashes and wields the lightning. Go, daughter dear, to the Unknown Sea, and take nothing with you but your bone hook and slender twin pipes, and if you should find yourself in great trouble, rip open your right-hand sleeve, all white and unhemmed."

The daughter gave good heed. Next day she took out the boat and put off to sea, taking nothing with her but her hook and the slender twin pipes.

She drifted and sailed on the face of the sea till the waters bore her to a far-off place, and there on the sea, lo, three terrible caverns of lowering cloud!

From the entrance of the first cavern peered the head of a fearsome Snake, the Mother of All Snakes. Her grisly head blocked up all the entrance, her body lay coiled along the cave, and with her monstrous tail she lashed the sea, troubling the waters and stirring up the waves.

The woman did not dare go near the terrible sight, but remembered her little pipes, and began to play upon the right-hand pipe. And as she played, there came from the far-off, rock-bound lands snakes and baby snakes galore swimming over the sea. Great coloured snakes and tiny little snakes all came hurrying up and scurrying up and begged the fearsome Snake –

"Let the woman take her boat through your cavern, Mother dear! She has done us a great good turn and fed us every day in the morning."

"Through my cavern I may not let her pass," answered the fearsome Snake, "for today I must stir up the waves of the sea. But if she did you such a good turn, I will repay it with another. Would she rather have a bar of gold or six strings of pearls?"

But a true wife is not to be beguiled with gold or pearls, and so the woman answered in dumb speech, "'Tis only for a small matter I have come here – for the Bass that lives in the Unknown Sea. If I have done you a good turn, let me pass through your cavern, fearsome Snake."

"Let her pass, Mother dear," said the snakes and baby snakes again. "Here are many of us whom she has fed – full many to whom she gave meat. You just lie down, Mother dear, and take a nap, and we'll stir up the waters for you."

Now the Snake couldn't very well disoblige such a big family, and she had been longing for sleep for a thousand years. So she let the woman through the cavern, and then curled up on the floor of the cavern and fell into a fearsome sleep. But before she fell asleep she reminded the snakes and baby snakes once more: "Now, stir me up the waters right properly, children dear, while I rest a little."

So the woman passed through the cavern, and the snakes and their young stayed in the cavern; but instead of stirring up the sea they soothed it and made it calm.

The woman sailed on, and came to the second cavern. And in the second cavern there was a monstrous Bird, the Mother of All Birds. She craned her frightful head through the opening, her iron beak gaped wide; she spread her vast wings in the cavern and flapped them, and whenever she flapped her wings she raised a storm.

The woman took up her twin pipes and sweetly played upon the left-hand pipe. And from the far shore came flying gulls great and small, and begged the monstrous bird to let the woman pass with her boat through her cavern, for that she had been a good friend to them and unpicked hemp for them every day.

"I can't let her pass through my cavern, for today I must raise a mighty storm. But if she was so kind to you, I will repay her with even greater kindness. From my iron beak I will give her of the Water of Life, so that the power of speech shall be restored to her."

Well, and wasn't it a sore temptation for the poor dumb creature who desired above all things that the power of speech should return to her? But she remained steadfast, and this is what she answered the Bird: "'Tis not for my own good that I came, but for a small matter – for the Bass that lives in the Unknown Sea. If I have done you a good turn, let me pass through your cavern."

Then the grey gulls all entreated the Mother Bird and also advised her to take a little nap, and they would meanwhile raise the storm for her. The Mother Bird listened to her children's entreaty, clung to the wall of the cavern with her iron talons, and went to sleep.

But the gulls great and small, instead of raising the storm, calmed the wild winds and soothed them.

So the dumb woman sailed through the second cavern and came to the third.

In the third cavern she found the Golden Bee. The Golden Bee buzzed in the entrance; she wielded the fiery lightning and the rolling thunder. Sea and cavern resounded; lightnings flashed from the clouds.

Fear seized upon the woman when she found herself all alone with these terrors. But she remembered her right sleeve; she ripped it off, her sleeve all white and unhemmed, flung it over the Golden Bee and caught her in the sleeve!

The thunder and lightning were stilled at once, and the Golden Bee began to coax the woman: "Set me free, O woman! and in return I will show you something. Look out over the wide waters, and it's a joyful sight you will see."

The woman looked out over the wide waters. The sun was just on the horizon. The sky grew pink overhead, the sea grew crimson from the east, and from the sea arose a silver boat. And in the boat sat the Dawn-Maiden, pale and fair as a king's daughter, and beside her a little child in a silken shirt and with a golden apple in his hand. It was the Dawn-Maiden taking the little King for his morning sail on the sea.

The woman recognized her lost baby.

Now isn't that a wonder of wonders, that the sea should be so wide that a mother cannot encompass it, and the sun so high that a mother should not be able to reach it?

Her joy took hold of her like terror. She trembled like the slender aspen. Should she stretch out her hand to the child? Or call to him tenderly? Or should she just stand and look at him for ever and ever?

The silver boat glided over the crimson sea. It faded away in the distance; the boat sank under the waves, and the mother roused herself with a start.

"I will show you," said the Golden Bee to the woman, "how to get to the little King, your son, and live with him in joy and happiness. But first set me free, that I may wield the lightnings in the cavern – and through my cavern I cannot let you pass!"

A fierce pang overcame the poor mother, overwhelmed, and shook her. She had seen her darling; her eyes had beheld her heart's desire; she had seen and beheld him, but not hugged him, not kissed him! The pang shook her from head to foot. Should she be true to Plunk or no? Should she let the Bee go and win to her child, or pass through the cavern to the Unknown Sea for the sake of the Big Bass?

But even as the pang shot through the woman, the tears gushed forth from her heart; the power of speech returned to her, and 'twas in living words that she answered the Golden Bee: "Don't sting me, O Golden Bee! I shall not let you go, because I must pass through your cavern. I have wept for my child and buried him in my heart. I have not come here for my own happiness, but for a small matter – for the Big Bass that lives in the Unknown Sea."

Thus said the woman, and passed into the cavern. She rested in the cavern; she took her ease in the boat, and there she waited for nightfall and moonrise.

Eh, my dearie, but the sea was quiet that day, with the winds at rest in the sky, and the fearsome Snake asleep in the first cavern, and the monstrous Bird asleep in the second, and the wearied woman in the third!

So the day went quietly by; evening came, and the moon rose. When the moon rode high in the heavens, the woman sailed out upon the Unknown Sea at midnight, and in the midst of the Sea she let down her little bone hook.

III

That very evening the little King bade Plunk knit him a nice set of silken reins. "First thing tomorrow morning I shall harness you to my little carriage, and you shall give me a ride on the golden sands."

Dearie me, considered poor Plunk, and where was he to hide from the Dawn-Maiden when she would go down into the sea in the morning and behold him thus tomorrow harnessed to a cart by his own son?

All the Sea King's court slept. The Sea King slept. The wilful little King slept – only Plunk was awake and knitting away at the reins. He knitted fiercely, like one who is thinking hard. When it seemed to him that the strings were strong enough, Plunk said to himself, "I never asked anyone's counsel when I was making a fool of myself, nor shall I do so now that I have come to my senses."

And as he said this he went softly up to the cradle where his son lay fast asleep, wound the reins round and round the rockers of the cradle, lashed the cradle to his own back, and started to run away with his son.

Softly Plunk strode over the golden sand – strode through the mighty Hall, spacious as a wide meadow; slipped through the golden hedge, parting the branches of pearls; and when he came to where the sea stood up like a wall, nothing daunted, Plunk dived into the water with his boy.

But it is far – terribly far – from the Sea King's fastness to the world of day above! Plunk swam and swam; but how was a poor fisherman to swim when he was weighed down by the little King – golden cradle, golden apple and all – on his back?

Plunk felt as if the sea was piling itself up above him, higher and higher, and heavier and heavier!

And just as Plunk was at the last gasp, he felt something scrape along the golden cradle, something that caught in the rocker of the cradle; and when it had caught fast, it began to haul them along apace!

"Now it's all up with me!" said poor Plunk to himself. "Here's a sea-monster carrying me away on his tusk."

But it wasn't the tusk of a sea-monster; it was a bone fishhook, the very hook that Plunk's wife had let down.

When the woman felt that her hook had caught, she joyfully summoned all her strength, pulling and hauling with all her might, for fear of losing the great Big Bass.

As she began to haul in her catch the golden rocker began to show above the water. The woman could not distinguish it rightly by moonlight, but thought, "It is the golden fin of the Bass."

Next came up the child with the golden apple. Again the woman thought, "It is the golden apple on the fish's fin." And when at last Plunk's head came up, the woman cried out joyfully, "And here is the head of the great Big Bass."

And as she cried out she hauled in her catch, and when she had hauled it close alongside – why, dearie mine, how am I to tell you rightly how overjoyed were those three when they met again in the boat, all in the moonlight, in the middle of the Unknown Sea?

But they dare not lose any time. They had to pass through the three caverns ere the monstrous watchers should awaken. So they took out the oars and rowed with all their might and main.

But oh dear! the bad luck they had! When the little King awoke and saw his mummy, he remembered her at once. He threw both his little arms round his mummy's neck – and the golden apple fell out of his hand. Down fell the apple into the sea, down to the very bottom and into the Sea King's Castle, and hit the Sea King right on his shoulder!

The Sea King woke up and bellowed with rage. All the court jumped to their feet. They saw at once that the little King and his servant were missing!

They gave chase. The mermaids swam out under the moonlight; the light foam fairies flew out over the water; runners were sent out to rouse the watchers in the caverns.

But the boat had already passed through the caverns, and so they had to pursue it farther on. Plunk and the woman were rowing – rowing for dear life, their pursuers close in their wake. The mermaids whipped up the waters, the swift foam fairies darted after the boat, the angry waves rose up in wrath behind them, and the wind howled from the clouds. Nearer and nearer came the pursuers. The finest ship afloat would not have had a chance, and how could a tiny two-oared boat? For hours and hours the boat flew on before the tempest, and just as the day began to break, lo, terror gathered from all sides around the boat.

For the hurricane beat upon the boat, the crested billows towered above it, and the mermaids joined in a ring around it. The ring heaved and swayed around the boat, the mermaids raised their linked hands high to let the mountainous waves pass through, but never let the little craft escape the waves. Sea and storm whistled and roared.

The fear of death was upon Plunk, and in his dire need he cried out, "Oh, fair Dawn-Maiden, help!"

The Dawn-Maiden arose from the sea. She saw Plunk but never looked at him. She looked at the little King, but no gift had she for him; but to the faithful wife she swiftly gave her gift – a broidered kerchief and a pin.

Quickly they hoisted the kerchief, and it became a white sail, and the pin turned into a rudder. The wind filled the sail, so that it bulged like a ripe apple, and the woman gripped the rudder with a strong hand. The mermaids' ring round the boat was broken; the boat rode upon the azure sea like a star across the blue heavens! A wonder of wonders, it flew over the sea before its terrible pursuers; the fiercer the pursuit, the greater help it was to them; for the swifter the wind blew, the more swiftly yet flew the boat before the wind, and the swifter the sea, the more swiftly rode the boat upon the sea.

Already the rock-bound shore loomed afar, and upon the shore Plunk's little cottage and the bar of white sand before it.

As soon as the land hove in sight, the pursuit slackened. The foam fairies fear the shore; the mermaids keep away from the coast. Wind and waves stayed on the high seas, and only the boat flew straight ahead to land like a child to its mother's lap.

The boat flew to land over the white sand bar and struck on a rock. The boat split on the rock. Down went sail and rudder, down went the golden cradle, away flew the Golden-winged Bee, and Plunk and his wife and child were left alone on the beach outside their cottage.

When they sat down that night to their supper of wild spinach, they had clean forgotten all that had happened. And but for those twin pipes, there's not a soul would remember it now. But whoever starts to play on the pipes, the fat pipe at once begins to drone out about Plunk:

Harum-scarum Plunk would go
Where the pearls and corals grow;
There he found but grief and woe.

And then the little pipe reminds us of the woman:

Rise, O Dawn, in loveliness!
Here is new-born happiness;
Were it three times drown'd in ill.
Faith and Love would save it still!

And that is the twin pipes' message to the wide, wide world.

The Good Ferryman and the Water Nymphs

THERE WAS ONCE AN OLD MAN, very poor, with three sons. They lived chiefly by ferrying people over a river; but he had had nothing but ill-luck all his life. And to crown all, on the night he died, there was a great storm, and in it the crazy old ferry-boat, on which his sons depended for a living, was sunk.

As they were lamenting both their father and their poverty, an old man came by, and learning the reason of their sorrow said, "Never mind; all will come right in time. Look! there is your boat as good as new."

And there was a fine new ferry-boat on the water, in place of the old one, and a number of people waiting to be ferried over.

The three brothers arranged to take turns with the boat and divide the fares they took.

They were, however, very different in disposition. The two elder brothers were greedy and avaricious, and would never take anyone over the river without being handsomely paid for it.

But the youngest brother took over poor people, who had no money, for nothing; and moreover, he frequently relieved their wants out of his own pocket.

One day at sunset, when the eldest brother was at the ferry, the same old man, who had visited them on the night their father died, came and asked for a passage.

"I have nothing to pay you with but this empty purse," he said.

"Go and get something to put in it then first," replied the ferryman, "and be off with you now!"

Next day it was the second brother's turn; and the same old man came and offered his empty purse as his fare. But he met with a like reply.

The third day it was the youngest brother's turn; and when the old man arrived and asked to be ferried over for charity, he answered, "Yes, get in, old man."

"And what is the fare?" asked the old man.

"That depends upon whether you can pay or not," was the reply, "but if you cannot, it is all the same to me."

"A good deed is never without its reward," said the old man, "but in the meantime take this empty purse; though it is very worn and looks worth nothing. But if you shake it, and say:

'For his sake who gave it, this purse I hold,
I wish may always be full of gold;'

it will always afford you as much gold as you wish for."

The youngest brother came home, and his brothers, who were sitting over a good supper, laughed at him, because he had taken only a few copper coins that day, and they told him he should have no supper. But when he began to shake his purse and scatter gold coins all about, they jumped up from the table and began picking them up eagerly.

And as it was share and share alike, they all grew rich very quickly. The youngest brother made good use of his riches, for he gave away money freely to the poor. But the greedy elder brothers envied him the possession of the wonderful purse, and contrived to steal it from him. Then they left their old home; and the one bought a ship, laded it with all sorts of merchandize, for a trading voyage. But the ship ran upon a rock, and everyone on board was drowned. The second brother was no more fortunate, for as he was travelling through a forest with an enormous treasure of precious stones, in which he had laid out his wealth, to sell at a profit, he was waylaid by robbers, who murdered him and shared the spoil among them.

The youngest brother, who remained at home, having lost his purse, became as poor as before. But he still did as formerly, took pay from passengers who could afford it, ferried over poor folks for nothing, and helped those who were poorer than himself so far as he could.

One day the same old man with the long white beard came by; the ferryman welcomed him as an old friend, and while rowing him over the river, told him all that had happened since he last saw him.

"Your brothers did very wrong, and they have paid for it," said the old man, "but you were in fault yourself. Still, I will give you one more chance. Take this hook and line; and whatever you catch, mind you hold fast, and not let it escape you, or you will bitterly repent it."

The old man then disappeared, and the ferryman looked in wonder at his new fishing-tackle – a diamond hook, a silver line, and a golden rod.

All at once the hook sprang of itself into the water; the line lengthened out along the river current, and there came a strong pull upon it. The fisherman drew it in, and beheld a most lovely creature, upwards from the waist a woman, but with a fish's tail.

"Good ferryman, let me go," she said. "Take your hook out of my hair! The sun is setting, and after sunset I can no longer be a water-nymph again."

But without answering, the ferryman only held her fast and covered her over with his coat, to prevent her escaping. Then the sun set, and she lost her fish-tail.

"Now," she said, "I am yours; so let us go to the nearest church and get married."

She was already dressed as a bride, with a myrtle garland on her head, in a white dress, with a rainbow-coloured girdle, and rich jewels in her hair and on her neck. And she held in her hand the wonderful purse that was always full of gold.

They found the priest and all ready at the church, were married in a few minutes, and then came home to their wedding-feast, to which all the neighbours were invited. They were royally entertained, and when they were about to leave, the bride shook the wonderful purse and sent a shower of gold pieces flying among the guests; so they all went home very well pleased.

The good ferryman and his marvellous wife lived most happily together; they never wanted for anything, and gave freely to all who came. He continued to ply his ferry-boat; but he now took all passengers over for nothing, and gave them each a piece of gold into the bargain.

Now there was a king over that country, who a year ago had just succeeded to his elder brother. He had heard of the ferryman, who was so marvellously rich, and wishing to ascertain the truth of the story he had heard, came on purpose to see for himself. But when he saw the ferryman's beautiful young wife, he resolved to have her for himself, and determined to get rid of her husband somehow.

At that time there was an eclipse of the sun; and the king sent for the ferryman, and told him he must find out the cause of this eclipse, or be put to death.

He came home in great distress to his wife; but she replied, "Never mind, my dear. I will tell you what to do, and how to gratify the king's curiosity."

So she gave him a wonderful ball of thread, which he was to throw before him, and follow the thread as it kept unwinding – towards the East.

He went on a long way, over high mountains, deep rivers, and wide regions. At last he came to a ruined city, where a number of corpses were lying about unburied, tainting the air with pestilence.

The good man was sorry to see this, and took the pains to summon men from the neighbouring cities, and get the bodies properly buried. He then resumed his journey.

He came at last to the ends of the earth. Here he found a magnificent golden palace, with an amber roof, and diamond doors and windows.

The ball of thread went straight into the palace, and the ferryman found himself in a vast apartment, where sat a very dignified old lady, spinning from a golden distaff.

"Wretched man! what are you here for?" she exclaimed, when she saw him. "My son will come back presently and burn you up."

He explained to her how he had been forced to come out of sheer necessity.

"Well, I must help you," replied the old lady, who was no less than the Mother of the Sun, "because you did Sol that good turn some days ago, in burying the inhabitants of that town, when they were killed by a dragon. He journeys every day across the wide arch of heaven, in a diamond car drawn by twelve grey horses with golden manes, giving heat and light to the whole world. He will soon be back here, to rest for the night…But…here he comes; hide yourself, and take care to observe what follows."

So saying, she changed her visitor into a lady-bird, and let him fly to the window.

Then the neighing of the wonderful horses and the rattling of chariot wheels were heard, and the bright Sun himself presently came in and, stretching himself upon a coral bed, remarked to his mother, "I smell a human being here!"

"What nonsense you talk!" replied his mother. "How could any human being come here? You know it is impossible."

The Sun, as if he did not quite believe her, began to peer anxiously about the room.

"Don't be so restless," said the old lady, "but tell me why you suffered eclipse a month or two ago."

"How could I help it?" answered the Sun. "When the dragon from the deep abyss attacked me, and I had to fight him? Perhaps I should have been fighting with the monster till now, if a wonderful mermaid had not come to help me. When she began to sing, and looked at the dragon with her beautiful eyes, all his rage softened at once; he was absorbed in gazing upon her beauty, and I meanwhile burnt him to ashes, and threw them into the sea."

The Sun then went to sleep, and his mother again touched the ferryman with her spindle; he then returned to his natural shape, and slipped out of the palace. Following the ball of thread, he reached home at last, and next day went to the king and told him all.

But the king was so enchanted at the description of the beautiful sea-maiden that he ordered the ferryman to go and bring her to him, on pain of death.

He went home very sad to his wife, but she told him she would manage this also. So saying, she gave him another ball of thread to show him which way to go, and she also gave him a carriage-load of costly lady's apparel, jewels, and ornaments – told him what he was to do, and they took leave of one another.

On the way the ferryman met a youth riding on a fine grey horse, who asked, "What have you got there, man?"

"A woman's wearing apparel, most costly and beautiful." He had several dresses, not simply one.

"I say, give me some of those as a present for my intended, whom I am going to see. I can be of use to you, for I am the Storm-wind. I will come, whenever you call upon me thus:

'Storm-wind! Storm-wind! come with speed!
Help me in my sudden need!'"

The ferryman gave him some of the most beautiful things he had, and the Storm-wind passed.

A little further on he met an old man, grey-haired, but strong and vigorous-looking, who also said, "What have you got there?"

"Women's garments costly and beautiful."

"I am going to my daughter's wedding; she is to marry the Storm-wind; give me something as a wedding present for her, and I will be of use to you. I am the Frost; if you need me call upon me thus:

'Frost, I call thee; come with speed;
Help me in my sudden need!'"

The ferryman let him take all he wanted and went on.

And now he came to the sea-coast; here the ball of thread stopped, and would go no further.

The ferryman waded up to his waist into the sea, and set up two high poles, with cross-bars between them, upon which he hung dresses of various colours, scarves, ribbons, gold chains, diamond earrings and pins, shoes, and looking-glasses, and then hid himself, with his wonderful hook and line ready.

As soon as the morning rose from the sea, there appeared far away on the smooth waters a silvery boat, in which stood a beautiful maiden with a golden oar in one hand, while with the other she gathered together her long golden hair, all the while singing so beautifully to the rising sun, that, if the ferryman had not quickly stopped his ears, he would have fallen into a delicious reverie, and then asleep.

She sailed along a long time in her silver boat, and round her leaped and played golden fishes with rainbow wings and diamond eyes. But all at once she perceived the rich clothes and ornaments hung up on the poles, and as she came nearer, the ferryman called out:

"Storm-wind! Storm-wind! come with speed!
Help me in my sudden need!"

"What do you want?" asked the Storm-wind.

The ferryman without answering him, called out:

"Frost, I call thee; come with speed,
Help me in my sudden need!"

"What do you want?" asked the Frost.

"I want to capture the sea-maiden."

Then the wind blew and blew, so that the silver boat was capsized, and the frost breathed on the sea till it was frozen over.

Then the ferryman rushed up to the sea-maiden, entangling his hook in her golden hair, lifted her on his horse, and rode off as swift as the wind after his wonderful ball of thread.

She kept weeping and lamenting all the way. But as soon as they reached the ferryman's home, and saw his wife, all her sorrow changed into joy; she laughed with delight, and threw herself into her arms.

And then it turned out that the two were sisters.

Next morning the ferryman went to court with both his wife and sister-in-law, and the king was so delighted with the beauty of the latter that he at once offered to marry her. But she could give him no answer until he had the Self-playing Guitar.

So the king ordered the ferryman to procure him this wonderful guitar, or be put to death.

His wife told him what to do, and gave him a handkerchief of hers, embroidered with gold, telling him to use this in case of need.

Following the ball of thread, he came at last to a great lake, in the midst of which was a green island.

He began to wonder how he was to get there, when he saw a boat approaching, in which was an old man with a long white beard, and he recognized him with delight as his former benefactor.

"How are you, ferryman?" he asked. "Where are you going?"

"I am going wherever the ball of thread leads me, for I must fetch the Self-playing Guitar."

"This guitar," said the old man, "belongs to Goldmore, the lord of that island. It is a difficult matter to have to do with him; but perhaps you may succeed. You have often ferried me over the water; I will ferry you now."

The old man pushed off, and they reached the island.

On arriving the ball of thread went straight into a palace, where Goldmore came out to meet the traveller, and asked him where he was going and what he wanted.

He explained, "I am come for the Self-playing Guitar."

"I will only let you have it on condition that you do not go to sleep for three days and nights. And if you do, you will not only lose all chance of the Self-playing Guitar, but you must die."

What could the poor man do but agree to this?

So Goldmore conducted him to a great room and locked him in. The floor was strewn with sleepy-grass, so he fell asleep directly.

Next morning in came Goldmore, and on waking him up said, "So you went to sleep! Very well, you shall die!"

And he touched a spring in the floor, and the unhappy ferryman fell down into an apartment beneath, where the walls were of looking-glass, and there were great heaps of gold and precious stones lying about.

For three days and nights he lay there; he was fearfully hungry. And then it dawned upon him that he was to be starved to death!

He called out, and entreated in vain. Nobody answered, and though he had piles of gold and jewels about him, they could not purchase him a morsel of food.

He sought in vain for any means of exit. There was a window of clearest crystal, but it was barred by a heavy iron grating. But the window looked into a garden whence he could hear nightingales singing, doves cooing, and the murmur of a brook. But inside he saw only heaps of useless gold and jewels, and his own face, worn and haggard, reflected a thousand times.

He could now only pray for a speedy death, and took out a little iron cross, which he had kept by him since his boyhood. But in doing so he also drew out the gold-embroidered handkerchief, given him by his wife, and which he had quite forgotten till now.

Goldmore had been looking on, as he often did, from an opening in the ceiling to enjoy the sight of his prisoner's sufferings. All at once he recognized the handkerchief as belonging to his own sister, the ferryman's wife.

He at once changed his treatment of his brother-in-law, as he had discovered him to be, took him out of prison, led him to his own apartments, gave him food and drink, and the Self-playing Guitar into the bargain.

Coming home, the ferryman met his wife half-way.

"The ball of thread came home alone," she explained, "so I judged that some misfortune had befallen you, and I was coming to help you."

He told her all his adventures, and they returned home together.

The king was all eagerness to see and hear the Self-playing Guitar; so he ordered the ferryman, his wife, and her sister to come with it to the palace at once.

Now the property of this Self-playing Guitar was such that wherever its music was heard, the sick became well, those who were sad merry, ugly folks became handsome, sorceries were dissolved, and those who had been murdered rose from the dead and slew their murderers.

So when the king, having been told the charm to set the guitar playing, said the words, all the court began to be merry and dance – except the king himself! For all at once the door opened, the music ceased, and the figure of the late king stood up in his shroud, and said, "I was the rightful possessor of the throne! And you, wicked brother, who caused me to be murdered, shall now reap your reward!"

So saying, he breathed upon him, and the king fell dead – on which the phantom vanished.

But as soon as they recovered from their fright, all the nobility who were present acclaimed the ferryman as their king.

The next day, after the burial of the late king, the beautiful sea-maiden, the beloved of the Sun, went back to the sea, to float about in her silvery canoe, in the company of the rainbow fishes, and to rejoice in the sunbeams.

But the good ferryman and his wife lived happily ever after as king and queen. And they gave a grand ball to the nobility and to the people. The Self-playing Guitar furnished the music, the wonderful purse scattered gold all the time, and the king entertained all the guests right royally.

The Three Princes, the Three Dragons, and the Woman with the Iron Nose

ON THE SHORES OF THE BLUE SEA there was a land in which dragons grew. This land had a king whose court was draped in black, and whose eye never ceased to weep, because every Friday he had to send ninety-nine men to the dragons, who were the pest of the place, and who slew and devoured the ninety-nine human beings sent to them. The king had three sons, each of whom was handsomer and more clever than the other. The king was very fond of his sons, and guarded them most carefully. The eldest was called Andrew, the next Emerich, and the youngest Ambrose. There were no other lads left in the land, for the dragons fed on lads' flesh only.

One day Andrew and Emerich went to their father and begged him to allow them to go and fight the dragons, as they were sure they could conquer them, and that the dragons would not want any more human flesh after they had been there. But the father would not even listen to his sons' request. As for Ambrose, he did not even dare so much as to submit such a request to his father. Andrew and Emerich, at length, by dint of much talking, prevailed upon their father to allow them to go and fight the dragons. Now, there were only three dragons left in the land: one had seven heads, another eight, and the third nine; and these three had devoured all the other dragons, when they found that there were no more lads to be had. Andrew and Emerich joyfully galloped off towards the copper, silver, and golden bridges in the neighbourhood of which the dragons lived, and Ambrose was left alone to console his royal father, who bewailed his other sons.

Ambrose's godmother was a fairy, and as it is the custom for godmothers to give presents to their godchildren, Ambrose received a present from his fairy godmother, which consisted of a black egg with five corners, which she placed under Ambrose's left armpit. Ambrose carried his egg about with him under his left armpit for seven winters and seven summers, and on Ash Wednesday, in the eighth year, a horse with five legs and three heads jumped out of the egg; this horse was a Táltos and could speak.

At the time when the brothers went out to fight the dragons, Ambrose was thirteen years and thirteen days old, and his horse was exactly five years old. The two elder brothers had been gone some time, when he went into the stable to his little horse, and, laying his head upon its neck, began to weep bitterly. The little horse neighed loudly and said, "Why are you crying, my dear master?" "Because," replied Ambrose, "I dare not ask my father to let me go away, although I should like to do so very much." "Go to your royal father, my dear master, for he has a very bad attack of toothache just now, and tell him that the king of herbs sends word to him through the Táltos-horse with three heads, that his toothache will not cease until he gives you permission to go and fight the dragons; and you can also tell him that if you go, there will be no more dragons left on this earth; but if you do not go his two elder boys will perish in the stomachs of the dragons. Tell him, also, that I have assured you that you will be able to make the dragons vomit out, at once, all the lads whomsoever they have swallowed; and that his land will become so powerful when the lads, who have grown strong in the stomachs of the dragons, return, that, while the world lasts, no nation will ever be able to vanquish him." Thus spoke the Táltos colt, and neighed so loudly that the whole world rang with the sound. The little boy told his father what the Táltos colt had told him; but the king objected for a long time, and no wonder, as he was afraid lest evil might happen to his only son: but at last his sufferings got the better of him, and, after objecting for three hours, he promised his son that if the Táltos were able to carry out its promise he would give him permission to go and fight the dragons.

As soon as he had uttered these words his toothache left him. The little lad ran off and told the message to his little horse, which capered and neighed with delight. "I heard you when you were bargaining," said the horse to its little master, who in his delight didn't know what to do with himself, "and I should have heard you even if you had been a hundred miles away. Don't fear anything, my little master; our ride, it is true, will be a long one, but in the end it will turn out a lucky one. Go, my great-great-grandmother's great-great-grandmother's saddle is there on that crooked willow; put it on me, it will fit me exactly!"

The prince ran, in fact he rushed like a madman, fetched the ragged old saddle, put it on his horse, and tied it to a gate-post. Before leaving his father's home, the little horse asked its little master to plug up one of its nostrils; the prince did so, and the little horse blew upon him with the other nostril which he had left open, when, oh, horror! the little boy became mangy like a diseased sucking pig. The little horse, however, turned into a horse with golden hair, and glistened like a mirror. When the little boy caught sight of his ugly face amidst the hair of his shining horse, he became very sad. "Plug up my other nostril, too!" said the horse with the golden hair. At first the little master would not do it, until the horse neighed very loudly and bade him do it at once, as it was very unwise to delay obeying the commands of a Táltos. So what could the poor lad do but plug up the other nostril of the horse. The horse then opened wide its mouth, and breathed upon the lad, who at once became a most handsome prince, worthy to be a fairy king. "Now sit on my back, my little master, my great king, we are worthy of each other; and there is no thing in the world that we cannot overcome. Rejoice! You will conquer the dragons, and restore the young men to your father's realm; only do as I bid you, and listen to no one else."

In an hour's time they arrived on the shore of the Red Sea, which flows into the Blue Sea. There they found an inn, and close to the inn, within earshot, stood the copper bridge, on the other side of which the dragon with seven heads roamed about. Andrew and Emerich were already at the inn, and as they were very tired, they sat down and began to eat and drink: when the new guest arrived the knives and forks dropped from the two princes' hands; but when they learned that he, too, had come to fight the dragons they made friends with him. They could not, however, recognize him for all the world. Night set in, and Andrew and Emerich had eaten and drunk too much, and became decidedly drunk, and so slept very deeply. Ambrose ate little, drank nothing, and slept lightly. At dawn the Táltos horse pulled his master's hair, in order to wake him; because it knew that the dragon had least strength at dawn, and that the sun increased his strength. Ambrose at once jumped on horseback and arrived at the copper bridge: the dragon heard the clattering of the horse's hooves, and at once flew to meet him. "Pooh!" cried the dragon and snorted, "I smell a strange smell! Ambrose, is it you? I know you; may you perish, you and your horse! Come on!" They fought for one hour and three quarters. Ambrose, with two strokes, slashed six of the dragon's heads off, but could not, for a long time succeed in cutting off the seventh, for in it lay the dragon's magic power. But, at last, the seventh head came off too.

The dragon had seven horses, these Ambrose fastened together, and took them to the inn, where he tied them by the side of Emerich's horse. Andrew and Emerich did not awake till nine o'clock, when Emerich asked Andrew if he had killed the dragon, and Andrew asked Emerich if he had done so; at last Ambrose told them that he had killed the dragon with seven heads and taken away his seven horses, which he gave to Emerich, who thanked him for them. The three then continued their journey together as far as the silver bridge: here again they found an inn, which stood close to the bridge. Emerich and Andrew ate and drank and went to sleep as before; the Táltos horse, as soon as day began to break, awoke his master, who cheerfully jumped up, dressed neatly, and left the princes asleep. The Táltos scented the dragon quite ten miles off, and growled like a dog, and the dragon in his rage began to throw his sparks at them when four German miles off; they rushed upon each other and met with a tremendous clash on the bridge; it was a very difficult task for Ambrose to conquer this huge monster, but at last, through the skilful manœuvring of his horse, he deprived the dragon of all his eight heads: the eight horses belonging to the dragon he tied to a post near the head of the eldest prince, Andrew. Andrew and Emerich did not awake till noon, and were astonished at the sight of the splendid horses, questioning each other as to who could have brought them there at such an early hour, and then came to the conclusion that the prince must have killed the dragon, and that these horses had belonged to the monster, for no such horses ever neighed under a man before. Ambrose again confessed that he had killed the dragon, and brought away his horses for them. He also urged his two companions to hurry on to kill the third dragon, or they would be too late. They all got on horseback, but in their joy two of them had had to eat and drink, till they had more than enough, but Ambrose, according to his custom, took but little; the two elder brothers again went to sleep and slept like tops; but again the little Táltos pulled Ambrose's hair, so soon as the morning star began to glimmer.

Ambrose got up at once, and dressed even more quickly than before; for the journey he took a small flask of wine, which he secured upon his saddle. The horse warned its master to approach the dragon with great caution, because it was a very excitable one, and if he got frightened the least it would be very difficult to conquer the monster. Soon the monster with nine heads arrived, thumped once on the golden bridge, so that it trembled under the thump; Ambrose dashed at the dragon and fought with it, but they could not conquer each other, although they fought fiercely and long. At the last hug, especially, Ambrose grew so weak that, if he had not taken a long draught from his flask he would have been done for on the spot; the draught, however, renewed his strength, and they dashed at each other again, but still neither could conquer the other.

So the dragon asked Ambrose to change himself into a steel hoop and he, the dragon, would become a flint hoop, and that they should both climb to the top of yon rock, which was so high that the sun was only a good span above it; and that they should roll down together, and if, while running, the flint hoop left the rut, and, striking the steel hoop, drew sparks therefrom, that Ambrose's head should fall off; but if on the other hand, the steel hoop left the rut and struck the flint hoop so as to draw sparks, then all the dragon's heads should fall off. But they were both wise and stuck to their own ruts, rolling down in a straight course till they reached the foot of the mountain without touching each other, and lay down when they got to the bottom. As they could not manage in this way, the dragon proposed: "I will become a red flame and you will become a white one, and which ever flame reaches highest he shall be victor." Ambrose agreed to this also; while they were contending, they both noticed an old crow, which croaked at them from a hollow tree; the dragon was an old acquaintance of the aged crow, and requested it to bring in its beak as much water as would extinguish the white flame, and promised that if he won, he would give his foe's flesh to the crow, every bit of it.

Ambrose asked for a single drop of water, and promised the crow all the flesh of the big-bodied dragon. The crow helped Ambrose: it soaked its crop full of water and spat it over the red flame; thus Ambrose conquered his last foe. He got on his horse, tied together the nine horses of the dragon with nine heads and took them to his brothers, who were still snoring loudly, although the sun had reached its zenith and was hot enough to make a roast. At last the two lazy people got up, and Ambrose divided the nine horses between them and took leave of them, saying, "Go in peace, I myself am obliged to run wherever my eyes can see." The two good-for-nothing brothers were secretly delighted, and galloped off homewards. Ambrose turned himself into a small rabbit, and as it ran over hill and dale it ran into a small hut where the three wives of the three dragons were seated. The wife of the dragon with seven heads took it into her lap and stroked it for a long time, and thus addressed it: "I don't know whether Ambrose has killed my husband; if he has, there will be a plague in the world, because I will turn into a great pear tree, and the odour of its fruit will be smelt seven miles off, and will be sweet to the taste but deadly poison. The tree which thus grows from me will not dry up till Ambrose plunge his sword into its root, then both it and myself will die." Then the wife of the dragon with eight heads also took the little rabbit in her lap, and spoke thus: "If Ambrose has killed my husband there will be a plague in the world, I can tell you! because in my sorrow I will change into a spring; there will be eight streams flowing out of this spring, each one of which will run eight miles, where it again will subdivide into eight more branches. And whoever drinks of the water will die; but if Ambrose wash his sword in my blood – which is the water of the spring – all the water will at once dry up and I shall die." Then the wife of the dragon with nine heads spoke to the rabbit, saying, "If Ambrose has killed my husband, in my sorrow I will change into a huge bramble, and will stretch all over the world, all along the highroads. And whoever trips over me, will die; but if Ambrose cut my stalk in two anywhere the bramble will dry up everywhere and I shall die."

Having listened to all this, the little rabbit scampered off out of the hut; but an old woman with an iron nose, the mother of the three dragons, chased him, and chased him over hill and dale: he ran, and rushed about, till at length he overtook his brothers; jumping on his little horse's back, he continued his journey at his leisure. As they travelled on, his eldest brother longed for some good fruit; just then they saw a fine pear tree, whereupon Ambrose jumped from his horse, and plunged his sword into the roots of the tree, and drew blood, and a moaning voice was heard. They travelled on for a few miles, when Emerich all of a sudden became very thirsty: he discovered a spring, and jumped off his horse in order to drink, but Ambrose was first to arrive at the water; when, plunging his sword into it, it became blood, and fearful screams were heard, and in one moment the whole of the water dried up. From this point Ambrose galloped on in front till he left his brothers two miles behind, because he knew that the bramble was stretching far along the country road; he cut it in two, blood oozed out, and the bramble at once dried up. Having thus cleared away all dangers from his brothers' way, he blest them and separated from them.

The brothers went home, but the old woman with the iron nose persecuted Ambrose more than ever, being in a great rage at his having killed her sons and her daughters-in-law. Ambrose ran as hard as he could, for he had left his horse with his brothers; but when he was quite exhausted and had lost all confidence in himself, he ran into a smithy, and promised the smith that he would serve him for two years for nothing if he would hide him safely and well. The bargain was soon struck, and no sooner had the smith hidden him than the old woman appeared on the spot and inquired after a youth: she described his figure, the shape of his eyes and mouth, height, colour of his moustache and hair, dress, and general appearance. But the smith was not such a fool as to betray the lad who had engaged to work at his anvil for him for two years for nothing. So the old witch with the iron nose got to know nothing and left the place growling. One day Ambrose was perspiring heavily by the side of the anvil, so at eventide he went for a short walk in the road in order to get a mouthful of fresh air. When he had nearly reached the edge of the wood, which was only at a dog's trot from the smithy, he met a very old woman with wizened face, whose carriage was drawn by two small cats: the old woman began to ogle little Ambrose, making sheep's eyes at him, like fast young women do. "May hell swallow you, you old hag," said Ambrose to her angrily, "I see you have still such foolish ideas in your head, although you have grown so old!" Having said this he gave the carriage in which the witch sat, a kick, but poor Ambrose's right foot stuck fast to the axle, and the two cats scampered off over hill and dale with him until he suddenly discovered that he was trotting in hell, and saw old Pilate staring at him. The old witch with the iron nose – because it was she who had the carriage and pair of cats – fell over head and ears in love with the young lad, and at once asked him to marry her.

Ambrose shuddered when he heard this repulsive, unnatural request. "Very well," said the woman with the iron nose, "as you don't intend to marry me, into jail you go! Twelve hundredweight of iron on your feet!" Nine black servants seized hold of poor Ambrose, at once, and took him nine miles down into the bowels of the earth, and fastened a piece of iron weighing twelve hundredweight on his feet and secured it with a lock. The poor lad wept and groaned, but no one had admission to where he was, with the exception of the old witch and one of her maids. The maid of the witch with the iron nose was not quite such an ugly fright as her wizened old mistress, in fact she was such a pretty girl that one would have to search far for a prettier lass. She commenced to visit Ambrose in his prison rather often, sometimes even when the old witch did not dream of it – to tell the truth, she fell head over ears in love with the lad, nor did Ambrose dislike the pretty girl; on the contrary, he promised to marry her if she were able to effect his escape from his deep prison. The girl did not require any further coaxing, but commenced plotting at once. At last she hit upon a scheme, and thus spoke to her darling Ambrose: "You cannot get out of this place, unless you marry the old woman with the iron nose. She having once become your wife will reveal to you all her secrets; she will also tell you how she manages to keep alive so long, and by what ways and means she may be got rid of." Ambrose followed her instructions and was married to the old witch by a clergyman – there are clergy even in hell, as many as you want. The first night Ambrose, after having for a long time been kissing and making love to the old iron nose, asked her: "What keeps you alive for so long, and when do you think you will die? I don't ask these questions, my dearest love," he added, flatteringly, "as if I wished for your death, but because I should like to use those means myself which prolong your life and keep away everything from me which would shorten life, and thus preserve me, living long and happily with you." The old woman at first was half inclined to believe his words, but while meditating over what she had just heard, she suddenly kicked out in bed, and Ambrose flew three miles into hell in his fright.

But the result of all the questioning and flattering in the end was that the old woman confessed. She confided to him that she kept a wild boar in the silken meadow, and if it were killed, they would find a hare inside, inside the hare a pigeon, inside the pigeon a small box, inside the little box one black and one shining beetle: the shining beetle held her life, the black one her power; if those two beetles died then her life would come to an end, too. As soon as the old woman went out for a drive – which she had to do every day – Ambrose killed the wild boar, took out the hare, from the hare the pigeon, from the pigeon the box, and from the box the two beetles: he killed the black one at once, but kept the shining one alive. The old witch's power left her immediately. When she returned home her bed had to be made for her. Ambrose sat by her bedside and looked very sad, and asked her with tears if she, who was the other half of his soul, died what would become of him, who was a man from earth and a good soul, who had no business there. "In case I die, my dear husband," said the doomed woman, in a mild voice, "open with the key which I keep in my bosom yon black closet in the wall. But you can't remove the key from my bosom until I am dead. In the closet you will find a small golden rod; with this rod you must strike the side of the castle in which we are, and it will become a golden apple. You, then, can get into the upper world by harnessing my two cats in my carriage, and by whipping them with the golden rod." Hereupon Ambrose killed the shining beetle too, and her pára (animal soul) left the old witch at once.

He then struck the castle side with the golden rod, and it turned into an apple; having harnessed the two cats and patted them with the golden rod, he bade the maid sit by him, and in a wink they reached the upper world. The maid had been kidnapped by the old witch with the iron nose from the king of the country in the upper world, in whose land the mouth of hell was situated. Ambrose placed the golden apple in the prettiest part of the country and tapped its side with the rod and it became a beautiful castle of gold, in which he married his sweetheart and lived with her happily. Some time after he returned to his father's land, where an immense number of strong soldiers had grown up since Ambrose had killed the dragons. The old king distributed his realm among his three sons, giving the most beautiful empires to Ambrose, who took his father to him and kept him in great honour. His wife bore pretty children who rode out every day on the Táltos.

The Elves and Their Antics

THE ELVES ARE THE LITTLE WHITE CREATURES that live between heaven and earth. They are not in the clouds, nor down in the caves and mines, like the kabouters. They are bright and fair, dwelling in the air, and in the world of light. The direct heat of the sun is usually too much for them, so they are not often seen during the day, except towards sunset. They love the silvery moonlight. There used to be many folks, who thought they had seen the beautiful creatures, full of fun and joy, dancing hand in hand, in a circle.

In these old days, long since gone by, there were more people than there are now, who were sure they had many times enjoyed the sight of the elves. Some places in Holland show, by their names, where this kind of fairies used to live. These little creatures, that looked as thin as gauze, were very lively and mischievous, though they often helped honest and hard working people in their tasks, as we shall see. But first and most of all, they were fond of fun. They loved to vex cross people and to please those who were bonnie and blithe. They hated misers, but they loved the kind and generous. These little folks usually took their pleasure in the grassy meadows, among the flowers and butterflies. On bright nights they played among the moonbeams.

There were certain times when the elves were busy, in such a way as to make men and girls think about them. Then their tricks were generally in the stable, or in the field among the cows. Sometimes, in the kitchen or dairy, among the dishes or milk-pans, they made an awful mess for the maids to clean up. They tumbled over the churns, upset the milk jugs, and played hoops with the round cheeses. In a bedroom they made things look as if the pigs had run over them.

When a farmer found his horse's mane twisted into knots, or two cows with their tails tied together, he said at once, "That's the work of elves." If the mares did not feel well, or looked untidy, their owners were sure the elves had taken the animals out and had been riding them all night. If a cow was sick, or fell down on the grass, it was believed that the elves had shot an arrow into its body. The inquest, held on many a dead calf or its mother, was, that it died from an "elf-shot." They were so sure of this, that even when a stone arrow head – such as our far-off ancestors used in hunting, when they were cave men – was picked up off the ground, it was called an 'elf bolt,' or 'elf-arrow.'

Near a certain village named Elf-berg or Elf Hill, because there were so many of the little people in that neighbourhood, there was one very old elf, named Styf, which means Stiff, because though so old he stood up straight as a lance. Even more than the young elves, he was famous for his pranks. Sometimes he was nicknamed Haan-e'-kam or Cock's Comb. He got this name, because he loved to mock the roosters, when they crowed, early in the morning. With his red cap on, he did look like a rooster. Sometimes he fooled the hens, that heard him crowing. Old Styf loved nothing better than to go to a house where was a party indoors. All the wooden shoes of the twenty or thirty people within, men and women, girls and boys, would be left outside the door. All good Dutch folks step out of their heavy timber shoes, or klomps, before they enter a house. It is always a curious sight, at a country church, or gathering of people at a party, to see the klomps, big and little, belonging to baby boys and girls, and to the big men, who wear a number thirteen shoe of wood. One wonders how each one of the owners knows his own, but he does. Each pair is put in its own place, but Old Styf would come and mix them all up together, and then leave them in a pile. So when the people came out to go home, they had a terrible time in finding and sorting out their shoes. Often they scolded each other; or, some innocent boy was blamed for the mischief. Some did not find out, till the next day, that they had on one foot their own, and on another foot, their neighbour's shoe. It usually took a week to get the klomps sorted out, exchanged, and the proper feet into the right shoes. In this way, which was a special trick with him, this naughty elf, Styf, spoiled the temper of many people.

Beside the meadow elves, there were other kinds in Elfin Land; some living in the woods, some in the sand-dunes, but those called Staalkaars, or elves of the stall, were Old Styf's particular friends. These lived in stables and among the cows. The Moss Maidens, that could do anything with leaves, even turning them into money, helped Styf, for they too liked mischief. They teased men-folks, and enjoyed nothing better than misleading the stupid fellows that fuddled their brains with too much liquor.

Styf's especially famous trick was played on misers. It was this. When he heard of any old fellow, who wanted to save the cost of candles, he would get a kabouter to lead him off in the swamps, where the sooty elves come out, on dark nights, to dance. Hoping to catch these lights and use them for candles, the mean fellow would find himself in a swamp, full of water and chilled to the marrow. Then the kabouters would laugh loudly.

Old Styf had the most fun with another stingy fellow, who always scolded children when he found them spending a penny. If he saw a girl buying flowers, or a boy giving a copper coin for a waffle, he talked roughly to them for wasting money. Meeting this miser one day, as he was walking along the brick road, leading from the village, Styf offered to pay the old man a thousand guilders, in exchange for four striped tulips, that grew in his garden. The miser, thinking it real silver, eagerly took the money and put it away in his iron strong box. The next night, when he went, as he did three times a week, to count, and feel, and rub, and gloat, over his cash, there was nothing but leaves in a round form. These, at his touch, crumbled to pieces. The Moss Maidens laughed uproariously, when the mean old fellow was mad about it.

But let no one suppose that the elves, because they were smarter than stupid human beings, were always in mischief. No, no! They did, indeed, have far more intelligence than dull grown folks, lazy boys, or careless girls; but many good things they did. They sewed shoes for poor cobblers, when they were sick, and made clothes for children, when the mother was tired. When they were around, the butter came quick in the churn.

When the blue flower of the flax bloomed in Holland, the earth, in spring time, seemed like the sky. Old Styf then saw his opportunity to do a good thing. Men thought it a great affair to have even coarse linen tow for clothes. No longer need they hunt the wolf and deer in the forest, for their garments. By degrees, they learned to make finer stuff, both linen for clothes and sails for ships, and this fabric they spread out on the grass until the cloth was well bleached. When taken up, it was white as the summer clouds that sailed in the blue sky. All the world admired the product, and soon the word 'Holland' was less the name of a country, than of a dainty fabric, so snow white, that it was fit to robe a queen. The world wanted more and more of it, and the Dutch linen weaver grew rich. Yet still there was more to come.

Now, on one moonlight night in summer, the lady elves, beautiful creatures, dressed in gauze and film, with wings to fly and with feet that made no sound, came down into the meadows for their fairy dances. But when, instead of green grass, they saw a white landscape, they wondered, Was it winter?

Surely not, for the air was warm. No one shivered, or was cold. Yet there were whole acres as white as snow, while all the old fairy rings, grass and flowers were hidden.

They found that the meadows had become bleaching grounds, so that the cows had to go elsewhere to get their dinner, and that this white area was all linen. However, they quickly got over their surprise, for elves are very quick to notice things. But now that men had stolen a march on them, they asked whether, after all, these human beings had more intelligence than elves. Not one of these fairies but believed that men and women were the inferiors of elves.

So, then and there, began a battle of wits.

"They have spoiled our dancing floor with their new invention; so we shall have to find another," said the elfin queen, who led the party.

"They are very proud of their linen, these men are; but, without the spider to teach them, what could they have done? Even a wild boar can instruct these human beings. Let us show them, that we, also, can do even more. I'll get Old Styf to put on his thinking cap. He'll add something new that will make them prouder yet."

"But we shall get the glory of it," the elves shouted in chorus. Then they left off talking and began their dances, floating in the air, until they looked, from a distance, like a wreath of stars.

The next day, a procession of lovely elf maidens and mothers waited on Styf and asked him to devise something that would excel the invention of linen; which, after all, men had learned from the spider.

"Yes, and they would not have any grain fields, if they had not learned from the wild boar," added the elf queen.

Old Styf answered "yes" at once to their request, and put on his red thinking cap. Then some of the girl elves giggled, for they saw that he did, really, look like a cock's comb. "No wonder they called him Haan-e'-kam," said one elf girl to the other.

Now Old Styf enjoyed fooling, just for the fun of it, and he taught all the younger elves that those who did the most work with their hands and head, would have the most fun when they were old.

First of all, he went at once to see Fro, the spirit of the golden sunshine and the warm summer showers, who owned two of the most wonderful things in the world. One was his sword, which, as soon as it was drawn out of its sheath, against wicked enemies, fought of its own accord and won every battle. Fro's chief enemies were the frost giants, who wilted the flowers and blasted the plants useful to man. Fro was absent, when Styf came, but his wife promised he would come next day, which he did. He was happy to meet all the elves and fairies, and they, in turn, joyfully did whatever he told them. Fro knew all the secrets of the grain fields, for he could see what was in every kernel of both the stalks and the ripe ears. He arrived, in a golden chariot, drawn by his wild boar which served him instead of a horse. Both chariot and boar drove over the tops of the ears of wheat, and faster than the wind.

The Boar was named Gullin, or Golden Bristles because of its sunshiny colour and splendour. In this chariot, Fro had specimens of all the grains, fruits, and vegetables known to man, from which Styf could choose, for these he was accustomed to scatter over the earth.

When Styf told him just what he wanted to do, Fro picked out a sheaf of wheat and whispered a secret in his ear. Then he drove away, in a burst of golden glory, which dazzled even the elves, that loved the bright sunshine. These elves were always glad to see the golden chariot coming or passing by.

Styf also summoned to his aid the kabouters, and, from these ugly little fellows, got some useful hints; for they, dwelling in the dark caverns, know many secrets which men used to name alchemy, and which they now call chemistry.

Then Styf fenced himself off from all intruders, on the top of a bright, sunny hilltop, with his thinking cap on and made experiments for seven days. No elves, except his servants, were allowed to see him. At the end of a week, still keeping his secret and having instructed a dozen or so of the elf girls in his new art, he invited all the elves in the Low Countries to come to a great exhibition, which he intended to give.

What a funny show it was! On one long bench, were half a dozen washtubs; and on a table, near by, were a dozen more washtubs; and on a longer table not far away were six ironing boards, with smoothing irons. A stove, made hot with a peat fire, was to heat the irons. Behind the tubs and tables, stood the twelve elf maidens, all arrayed in shining white garments and caps, as spotless as snow. One might almost think they were white elves of the meadow and not kabouters of the mines. The wonder was that their linen clothes were not only as dainty as stars, but that they glistened, as if they had laid on the ground during a hoar frost.

Yet it was still warm summer. Nothing had frozen, or melted, and the rosy-faced elf-maidens were as dry as an ivory fan. Yet they resembled the lilies of the garden when pearly with dew-drops.

When all were gathered together, Old Styf called for some of the company, who had come from afar, to take off their dusty and travel-stained linen garments and give them to him. These were passed over to the trained girls waiting to receive them. In a jiffy, they were washed, wrung out, rinsed and dried. It was noticed that those elf-maidens, who were standing at the last tub, were intently expecting to do something great, while those five elf maids at the table took off the hot irons from the stove. They touched the bottom of the flat-irons with a drop of water to see if it rolled off hissing. They kept their eyes fixed on Styf, who now came forward before all and said, in a loud voice:

"Elves and fairies, moss maidens and stall sprites, one and all, behold our invention, which our great friend Fro and our no less helpful friends, the kabouters, have helped me to produce. Now watch me prove its virtues."

Forthwith he produced before all a glistening substance, partly in powder, and partly in square lumps, as white as chalk. He easily broke up a handful under his fingers, and flung it into the fifth tub, which had hot water in it. After dipping the washed garments in the white gummy mass, he took them up, wrung them out, dried them with his breath, and then handed them to the elf ironers. In a few moments, these held up, before the company, what a few minutes before had been only dusty and stained clothes. Now, they were white and resplendent. No fuller's earth could have bleached them thus, nor added so glistening a surface.

It was starch, a new thing for clothes. The fairies, one and all, clapped their hands in delight.

"What shall we name it?" modestly asked Styf of the oldest gnome present.

"Hereafter, we shall call you Styf Sterk, Stiff Starch." They all laughed.

Very quickly did the Dutch folks, men and women, hear and make use of the elves' invention. Their linen closets now looked like piles of snow. All over the Low Countries, women made caps, in new fashions, of lace or plain linen, with horns and wings, flaps and crimps, with quilling and with whirligigs. Soon, in every town, one could read the sign 'Hier mangled men' (Here we do ironing).

In time, kings, queens and nobles made huge ruffs, often so big that their necks were invisible, and their heads nearly lost from sight, in rings of quilled linen, or of lace, that stuck out a foot or so. Worldly people dyed their starch yellow; zealous folk made it blue; but moderate people kept it snowy white.

Starch added money and riches to the nation. Kings' treasuries became fat with money gained by taxes laid on ruffs, and on the cargoes of starch, which was now imported by the shipload, or made on the spot, in many countries. So, out of the ancient grain came a new spirit that worked for sweetness and beauty, cleanliness, and health. From a useful substance, as old as Egypt, was born a fine art, that added to the sum of the world's wealth and pleasure.

Helga

AN OLD MAN and his wife once lived in a cottage beside the sea, far away from any other habitations. They had three daughters; the eldest was called Fredegond, the second Olga, and the youngest Helga.

Now, although the parents were not rich, owning only a few acres of land, which they tilled themselves, Fredegond and Olga were treated as if they were princesses. They never did any work, but sat all day amusing themselves and decking themselves in any finery their father brought them home from the neighbouring town, whilst Helga, who was far more beautiful and clever than either of her sisters, was always kept in the background. She never shared in any pleasures that her elder sisters often enjoyed; no presents were ever brought home for her; but all day long, from early morning till late at night, poor Helga had to work and toil for the whole family, receiving nothing but sour looks, often accompanied by blows, from the elder sisters.

Now, it happened one day that the fire on their hearth had been allowed to go out. Helga was busy working in the fields, and as they had to send a long way to fetch fresh fire, the old man told Fredegond she must go for it

At first Fredegond grumbled, for she was trying to dress her hair in a new way; but then she thought a walk through the woods might be pleasant, so she started.

After she had gone some little distance, she came to a hillock, and heard a deep voice saying, "Would you rather have me with you or against you?"

Fredegond, thinking it was some labourer or woodcutter, said she did not care in the least, and that it was very impertinent of him to address her, and went on to the cave whence they fetched their fire.

When she got there, to her great surprise she saw a big cauldron, filled with meat, boiling on the fire, and beside it stood a pan, filled with dough, waiting to be made into cakes, but not a creature in sight.

Fredegond, being very hungry after her long walk, stirred up the fire beneath the cauldron, to make the meat boil quickly, and then began baking some cakes. But although she made one specially nice for herself, she let all the others burn, so that they were quite uneatable. Then as soon as the meat was cooked she took a bowl from a shelf, filled it with all the best bits, and sat down and made a good meal, finishing up with the cake.

Just as she had finished, a big black dog ran up to her, and began wagging his tail and begging for some food. But Fredegond angrily gave him a slap, and chased him away. Then the dog grew angry, and, jumping upon her, bit one of her hands.

Screaming with fright and pain, Fredegond jumped up, and, in her hurry to get away, forgot all about the fire she was to bring, and ran home to tell her parents what had happened.

They were very sorry, both for her sore hand, which they bathed and bandaged, and the lack of the fire. It was really very unfortunate, for that cave was the nearest place where they could procure some fire, as it was generally used by charcoal-burners. So, though very unwilling to send Olga, who was their pet and favourite, she had to go, for they all feared that if Helga were sent, she might run away and never come back again. And then there would be no one on whom to vent their bad tempers, or to do the work of the whole household – for did she not wait on father and mother and both her sisters? So it was decided that Olga should go.

But, alas! Olga fared even worse than her sister. She was so spoilt, that she thought she ought always to have the best of everything. So, when she reached the cave, she too helped herself to all the best bits of meat, and, making a nice cake for herself, threw the rest of the dough on the fire.

Then when the dog came up to her and wagged his tail and sat up and begged for some food, Olga took up some of the boiling broth and threw it on him. This made the dog so angry that he jumped up and bit off the point of her nose; and Olga ran home crying and screaming, with only half a nose and no fire.

This time the parents were quite beside themselves with anger, and decided that Helga must go and fetch the fire. If she succeeded, well and good; and if not, why, the dog might eat her, for all they cared. It would be a good riddance.

So, taking up the big fire-shovel, Helga went on her way to the cave. As she passed the hillock, she too heard a voice, saying, "Would you rather I was with you than against you?"

To this question she answered, "A well-known proverb says, 'There is nothing so bad that it is not better to have it on your side than against you;' so, as I do not know who you are who ask me this question, I would rather that you were with me than against me."

And hearing nothing further and seeing no one, Helga continued her way till she reached the cave. Here she found everything the same as her sisters had done. The cauldron was on the fire, and the dough was ready for baking, but, instead of thinking only of herself, Helga looked after the meat, and saw that it was nicely cooked; then, with great care, she made up the dough into cakes, and never thought of taking anything for herself, although she was very hungry, for she had had nothing for her breakfast but some hard, dry crusts, and a glass of cold water. Neither would she now help herself to any of the fire without asking leave from the owner of the cave.

Feeling very tired after her long walk, Helga sat down on a bench to rest. But she had hardly done so, when she heard a loud rumbling noise; the ground began to tremble; and Helga, fearful that the cave might fall in, rose hastily from her seat. But as she turned to run out, she saw a big, three-headed giant standing at the entrance of the cave, followed by a large black dog.

Helga was terribly frightened; but being fond of animals, she held out her hand and patted the dog, and she quite regained courage when the giant, in a kind voice, said, "You have done the work well, which you found waiting here. It is only right, therefore, that you should get your share. Sit down, therefore, on that bench, and share my dinner; afterwards you can take home some of the fire you have come for."

The giant then got a bowl from the shelf and helped Helga to some broth out of the big cauldron, carefully giving her the tenderest bits of meat. As he did so, the ground again began to shake and tremble, and fearful noises, like claps of thunder, frightened Helga greatly.

But the giant in a gentle voice bade her sit down beside him, and she finished her broth.

Then the giant got up and gave her one of the cakes she had baked; but no sooner had she finished it, than the ground again began to shake and tremble, the thunder pealed, and flash after flash of lightning lit up the inside of the cave. Helga got so terrified that she ran up to the giant for protection, and as she clung to his arm the noises ceased, and as the darkness passed away Helga saw that the giant had disappeared, and that she was holding on to the arm of a handsome young prince.

"Nay, do not be frightened," he said; "I can never thank you enough, dear Helga, for you have rescued me from the horrible enchantment the wicked fairy Gondomar pronounced on me at my birth. I am Torquil, the son of King Osbert, who reigns in the neighbouring island; but because my father refused to marry Gondomar, and chose my mother instead, the wicked fairy condemned me to go through life a three-headed monster, until some young girl should, despite my frightful appearance, place full trust and confidence in me."

As Prince Torquil said these words, he seated himself beside Helga on a stone, thickly covered with soft green moss. Then Helga told him her history, and why she came to the cave, and also the fate of her sisters who had gone to the cave on the same errand, adding that she must hasten back with the fire, else her father and mother would scold and beat her.

"You shall not be ill treated any more," replied Torquil; and he went to the back of the cave, and presently returned, carrying a casket and a small bundle in his hands.

"See, this casket contains gold, and pearls, and precious stones," he said. "You can give some of these to your sisters; but this," and he placed the bundle on a stool, "you must wear under your own dress, when you get home, and be very careful that no one sees it."

So saying, he undid the bundle, and unfolded a beautiful dress of cloth of gold, all worked with silver and precious stones.

Helga could not repress a cry of admiration when she saw the lovely gown, and warmly thanked the prince for all his beautiful gifts.

Torquil then filled her fire-shovel with burning coals, and carried it for her some part of the way home; but ere they came in sight of the cottage he stopped, and, taking her hand, placed a heavy gold ring on her finger.

"Keep this ring, dear Helga," he said, "and let no one take it from you. It will not be long ere I come to claim my bride, but I must first return to my parents and tell them the joyful news that the wicked charm is broken at last." With these words he took a loving farewell of Helga, and started her on her homeward journey.

When she reached the cottage, and her parents saw that she had succeeded in bringing back the fire, Helga, for once in her life, received a kind word of welcome; but when she showed them the casket and was about to give her sisters some of the jewels, they seized upon it, and dividing the contents among themselves, returned Helga the empty casket. They might also have taken away her beautiful dress, but, after Torquil left her, she had taken the precaution to slip it on under her old gown, so no one knew anything about it.

And thus some days passed on. Matters relapsed into their former way. Fredegond and Olga did nothing all day but deck themselves with the jewels out of the casket, quarrelling and fighting over them and Helga, as before, had to do the work for the whole family, when one day the mother, who had been to the higher meadow for some herbs she wanted, came back and said that she had seen a beautiful big ship lying at anchor on the shore below their cottage.

The old man hastened down to the strand to find out who the owner of the fine vessel might be, and seeing a boat pulling off from it, he waited till the stranger, who was a handsome young man, had landed, and then entered into conversation with him. But though he plied him with many questions, he could not find out his name.

Then the young man in his turn began to question him, and asked him how many children he had.

"Only two daughters," replied the old man, "and such good and beautiful girls they are too," he added.

"I should much like to see them," said the stranger.

The old man, greatly delighted, led the way back to his cottage, where his two eldest daughters had hurried on their best frocks and decked themselves with all the jewels out of Helga's casket.

The stranger expressed himself as being very pleased with the girls.

"But," he asked, "why has one of your daughters got her hand tied up with a cloth, and the other one a handkerchief fastened across her nose?"

At first the father said they had met with an accident, and slipped down the cliffs; but when the stranger pressed for further particulars, the story of the dogs and the cave had to be told.

"But surely you have another daughter?" said the stranger; "one who, I know, is always kind to all animals."

At first the old man and his wife both declared they only had those two daughters; but when the stranger kept on urging him, he at last admitted that he had another girl. "But she is so ugly, lazy, and wicked," he added, "that she is more like some wild animal than a human being."

But the stranger said he did not mind that at all, and that he must see her. So the old man was obliged at last to call Helga.

The poor girl came out from the kitchen dressed just as she was, in her shabby old dress, when the young man went up to her; and as he took her hand the ragged old gown slipped from her shoulders, and there, to the astonishment and rage of her sisters, stood Helga, arrayed in the beautiful garment the prince had given her.

Prince Torquil rated the old man and the two wicked sisters soundly for all their unkindness to Helga. He also made the sisters give up all the jewels they had taken from her. But Helga begged that they might be allowed to keep a few; and the prince consenting, she gave each of them two chains, two brooches, two bracelets, and two pairs of ear-rings. Then Torquil led Helga down to the shore and took her on board his beautiful ship, where his sister gave her a kindly welcome; and when they reached his own country, King Osbert and his queen prepared a great wedding-feast, and Torquil and Helga were married, and lived long and happily together.

Filagranata

ONCE UPON A TIME there was a poor woman who had a great fancy for eating parsley. To her it was the greatest luxury, and as she had no garden of her own, and no money to spend on anything not an absolute necessity of life, she had to go about poaching in other people's gardens to satisfy her fancy.

Near her cottage was the garden of a great palace, and in this garden grew plenty of fine parsley; but the garden was surrounded by a wall, and to get at it she had to carry a ladder with her to get up by, and, as soon as she had reached the top of the wall, to let it down on the other side to get down to the parsley-bed. There was such a quantity of parsley growing here that she thought it would never be missed, and this made her bold, so that she went over every day and took as much as ever she liked.

But the garden belonged to a witch, who lived in the palace, and, though she did not often walk in this part of the garden, she knew by her supernatural powers that someone was eating her parsley; so she came near the place one day, and lay in wait till the poor woman came. As soon, therefore, as she came, and began eating the parsley, the witch at once pounced down, and asked her, in her gruff voice, what she was doing there. Though dreadfully frightened, the poor woman thought it best to own the whole truth; so she confessed that she came down by the ladder, adding that she had not taken anything except the parsley, and begged forgiveness.

"I know nothing about forgiveness," replied the witch. "You have eaten my parsley, and must take the consequences; and the consequences are these: I must be godmother to your first child, be it boy or girl; and as soon as it is grown to be of an age to dress itself without help, it must belong to me."

When, accordingly, the poor woman's first child was born, the witch came, as she had declared she would, to be its godmother. It was a fine little girl, and she gave it the name of Filagranata; after that she went away again, and the poor woman saw her no more till her little girl was grown up old enough to dress herself, and then she came and fetched her away inexorably; nor could the poor mother, with all her tears and entreaties, prevail on her to make any exchange for her child.

So Filagranata was taken to the witch's palace to live, and was put in a room in a little tower by herself, where she had to feed the pigeons. Filagranata grew fond of her pigeons, and did not at all complain of her work, yet, without knowing why, she began to grow quite sad and melancholy as time went by; it was because she had no one to play with, no one to talk to, except the witch, who was no very delightful companion. The witch came every day, once in the day, to see that she was attending properly to her work, and as there was no door or staircase to the tower – this was on purpose that she might not escape – the witch used to say when she came under the tower:

Filagranata, so fair, so fair,
Unloose thy tresses of golden hair:
I, thy old godmother, am here;

and as she said these words, Filagranata had to let down her beautiful long hair through the window, and by it the witch climbed up into her chamber to her. This she did every day.

Now, it happened that about this time a king's son was travelling that way searching for a beautiful wife; for you know it is the custom for princes to go searching all over the world to find a maiden fit to be a prince's wife; at least they say so.

Well, this prince, travelling along, came by the witch's palace where Filagranata was lodged. And it happened that he came that way just as the witch was singing her ditty. If he was horrified at the sight of the witch, he was in proportion enchanted when Filagranata came to the window. So struck was he with the sight of her beauty, and modesty, and gentleness, that he stopped his horse that he might watch her as long as she stayed at the window, and thus became a spectator of the witch's wonderful way of getting into the tower.

The prince's mind was soon made up to gain a nearer view of Filagranata, and with this purpose he rode round and round the tower seeking some mode of ingress in vain, till at last, driven to desperation, he made up his mind that he must enter by the same strange means as the witch herself. Thinking that the old creature had her abode there, and that she would probably go out for some business in the morning, and return at about the same hour as on the present occasion, he rode away, commanding his impatience as well as he could, and came back the next day a little earlier.

Though he could hardly hope quite to imitate the hag's rough and tremulous voice so as to deceive Filagranata into thinking it was really the witch, he yet made the attempt and repeated the words he had heard:

Filagranata, thou maiden fair,
Loose thy tresses of golden hair:
I, thy old godmother, am here.

Filagranata, surprised at the soft modulation of voice, such as she had never heard before, ran quickly to the window with a look of pleasure and astonishment which gave her face a more winning expression than ever.

The prince looked up, all admiration and expectation; and the thought quickly ran through Filagranata's head: "I have been taught to loose my hair whenever those words are said; why should not I loose it to draw up such a pleasant-looking cavalier, as well as for the ugly old hag?" And, without waiting for a second thought, she untied the ribbon that bound her tresses and let them fall upon the prince. The prince was equally quick in taking advantage of the occasion, and, pressing his knees firmly into his horse's flanks, so that it might not remain below to betray him, drew himself up, together with his steed, just as he had seen the witch do.

Filagranata, half frightened at what she had done the moment the deed was accomplished, had not a word to say, but blushed and hung her head. The prince, on the other hand, had so many words to pour out, expressive of his admiration for her, his indignation at her captivity, and his desire to be allowed to be her deliverer, that the moments flew quickly by, and it was only when Filagranata found herself drawn to the window by the power of the witch's magic words that they remembered the dangerous situation in which they stood.

Another might have increased the peril by cries of despair, or lost precious time in useless lamentations; but Filagranata showed a presence of mind worthy of a prince's wife by catching up a wand of the witch, with which she had seen her do wonderful things. With this she gave the prince a little tap, which immediately changed him into a pomegranate, and then another to the horse, which transformed him into an orange. These she set by on the shelf, and then proceeded to draw up the witch after the usual manner.

The old hag was not slow in perceiving there was something unusual in Filagranata's room.

"What a stink of Christians! What a stink of Christians!" she kept exclaiming, as she poked her nose into every hole and corner. Yet she failed to find anything to reprehend; for as for the beautiful ripe pomegranate and the golden orange on the shelf, the Devil himself could not have thought there was anything wrong with them. Thus baffled, she was obliged to finish her inspection of the state of the pigeons, and end her visit in the usual way.

As soon as she was gone Filagranata knew she was free till the next day, and so once more, with a tap of the wand, restored the horse and his rider to their natural shapes.

"And this is how your life passes every day! Is it possible?" exclaimed the prince. "No, I cannot leave you here. You may be sure my good horse will be proud to bear your little weight; you have only to mount behind me, and I will take you home to my kingdom, and you shall live in the palace with my mother, and be my queen."

It is not to be supposed but that Filagranata very much preferred the idea of going with the handsome young prince who had shown so devoted an appreciation of her, and being his queen, to remaining shut up in the doorless tower and being the witch's menial; so she offered no opposition, and the prince put her on to his good horse behind him, and away they rode.

On, on, on, they rode for a long, long way, until they came at last to a wood; but for all the good horse's speed, the witch, who was not long in perceiving their escape and setting out in pursuit, was well nigh overtaking them. Just then they saw a little old woman standing by the way, making signs and calling to them to arrest their course. How great soever was their anxiety to get on, so urgent was her appeal to them to stop and listen to her that they yielded to her entreaties. Nor were they losers by their kindness, for the little old woman was a fairy, and she had stopped them, not on her own account, but to give them the means of escaping from the witch.

To the prince she said: "Take these three gifts, and when the witch comes very near throw down first the mason's trowel; and when she nearly overtakes you again throw down the comb; and when she nearly comes upon you again after that, throw down this jar of oil. After that she won't trouble you anymore." And to Filagranata she whispered some words, and then let them go.

But the witch was now close behind, and the prince made haste to throw down the mason's trowel. Instantly there rose up a high stone wall between them, which it took the witch some time to climb over. Nevertheless, by her supernatural powers she was not long in making up for the lost time, and had soon overtaken the best speed of the good horse. Then the prince threw down the comb, and immediately there rose up between them a strong hedge of thorns, which it took the witch some time to make her way through, and that only with her body bleeding all over from the thorns. Nevertheless, by her supernatural powers she was not long in making up for the lost time, and had soon overtaken the best speed of the good horse. Then the prince threw down the jar of oil, and the oil spread and spread till it had overflowed the whole countryside; and as wherever you step in a pool of oil the foot only slides back, the witch could never get out of that, so the prince and Filagranata rode on in all safety towards the prince's palace.

"And now tell me what it was the old woman in the wood whispered to you," said the prince, as soon as they saw their safety sufficiently secured to breathe freely.

"It was this," answered Filagranata; "that I was to tell you that when you arrive at your own home you must kiss no one – no one at all, not your father, or mother, or sisters, or anyone – till after our marriage. Because if you do you will forget all about your love for me, and all you have told me you think of me, and all the faithfulness you have promised me, and we shall become as strangers again to each other."

"How dreadful!" said the prince. "Oh, you may be sure I will kiss no one if that is to be the consequence; so be quite easy. It will be rather odd, to be sure, to return from such a long journey and kiss none of them at home, not even my own mother; but I suppose if I tell them how it is they won't mind. So be quite easy about that."

Thus they rode on in love and confidence, and the good horse soon brought them home.

On the steps of the palace the chancellor of the kingdom came out to meet them, and saluted Filagranata as the chosen bride the prince was to bring home; he informed him that the king his father had died during his absence, and that he was now sovereign of the realm. Then he led him in to the queen-mother, to whom he told all his adventures, and explained why he must not kiss her till after his marriage.

The queen-mother was so pleased with the beauty, and modesty, and gentleness of Filagranata, that she gave up her son's kiss without repining, and before they retired to rest that night it was announced to the people that the prince had returned home to be their king, and the day was proclaimed when the feast for his marriage was to take place.

Then all in the palace went to their sleeping-chambers. But the prince, as it had been his wont from his childhood upwards, went into his mother's room to kiss her after she was asleep, and when he saw her placid brow on the pillow, with the soft white hair parted on either side of it, and the eyes which were wont to gaze on him with so much love, resting in sleep, he could not forbear from pressing his lips on her forehead and giving the wonted kiss.

Instantly there passed from his mind all that had taken place since he last stood there to take leave of the queen-mother before he started on his journey. His visit to the witch's palace, his flight from it, the life-perils by the way, and, what is more, the image of Filagranata herself – all passed from his mind like a vision of the night, and when he woke up and they told him he was king, it was as if he heard it for the first time, and when they brought Filagranata to him it was as though he knew her not nor saw her.

"But," he said, "if I am king there must be a queen to share my throne;" and as a reigning sovereign could not go over the world to seek a wife, he sent and fetched him a princess meet to be the king's wife, and appointed the betrothal. The queen-mother, who loved Filagranata, was sad, and yet nothing that she could say could bring back to his mind the least remembrance of all he had promised her and felt towards her.

But Filagranata knew that the prince had kissed his mother, and this was why the spell was on him; so she said to her mother-in-law: "You get me much fine-sifted flour and a large bag of sweetmeats, and I will try if I cannot yet set this matter straight." So the queen-mother ordered that there should be placed in her room much sifted flour and a large bag of sweetmeats. And Filagranata, when she had shut close the door, set to work and made paste of the flour, and of the paste she moulded two pigeons, and filled them inside with the comfits.

Then at the banquet of the betrothal she asked the queen-mother to have her two pigeons placed on the table; and she did so, one at each end. But as soon as all the company were seated, before anyone was helped, the two pigeons which Filagranata had made began to talk to each other across the whole length of the table: and everybody stood still with wonder to listen to what the pigeons of paste said to each other.

"Do you remember," said the first pigeon, "or is it possible that you have really forgotten, when I was in that doorless tower of the witch's palace, and you came under the window and imitated her voice, saying,

Filagranata, thou maiden fair,
Loose thy tresses of golden hair:
I, thy old godmother, am here,

till I drew you up?"

And the other pigeon answered:

"Si, signora, I remember it now."

And as the young king heard the second pigeon say "Si, signora, I remember it now," he, too, remembered having been in a doorless tower, and having sung such a verse.

"Do you remember," continued the first pigeon, "how happy we were together after I drew you up into that little room where I was confined, and you swore if I would come with you we should always be together and never be separated from each other anymore at all?"

And the second pigeon replied:

"Ah yes! I remember it now."

And as the second pigeon said, "Ah yes! I remember it now," there rose up in the young king's mind the memory of a fair sweet face on which he had once gazed with loving eyes, and of a maiden to whom he had sworn lifelong devotion.

But the first pigeon continued:

"Do you remember, or have you quite forgotten, how we fled away together, and how frightened we were when the witch pursued us, and how we clung to each other, and vowed, if she overtook us to kill us, we would die in each other's arms, till a fairy met us and gave us the means to escape, and forbade you to kiss anyone, even your own mother, till after our marriage?"

And the second pigeon answered:

"Yes, ah yes! I remember it now."

And when the second pigeon said, "Yes, ah yes! I remember it now," the whole of the past came back to his mind, and with it all his love for Filagranata. So he rose up and would have stroked the pigeons which had brought it all to his mind, but when he touched them they melted away, and the sweetmeats were scattered all over the table, and the guests picked them up. But the prince ran in haste to fetch Filagranata, and he brought her and placed her by his side in the banquet-hall. But the second bride was sent back, with presents, to her own people.

"And so it all came right at last," pursued the narrator. "Lackaday! that there are no fairies now to make things all happen right. There are plenty of people who seem to have the devil in them for doing you a mischief, but there are no fairies to set things straight again, alas."

The Queen and the Tripe-Seller

THEY SAY THERE WAS a queen who had such a bad temper that she made everybody about her miserable. Whatever her husband might do to please her, she was always discontented, and as for her maids she was always slapping their faces.

There was a fairy who saw all this, and she said to herself, "This must not be allowed to go on;" so she went and called another fairy, and said, "What shall we do to teach this naughty queen to behave herself?" and they could not imagine what to do with her; so they agreed to think it over, and meet again another day.

When they met again, the first fairy said to the other, "Well, have you found any plan for correcting this naughty queen?"

"Yes," replied the second fairy; "I have found an excellent plan. I have been up and all over the whole town, and in a dirty little back lane I have found a tripe-seller as like to this queen as two peas."

"Excellent!" exclaimed the first fairy. "I see what you mean to do. One of us will take some of the queen's clothes and dress up the tripe-seller, and the other will take some of the tripe-seller's clothes and dress up the queen in them, and then we will exchange them till the queen learns better manners."

"That's the plan," replied the second fairy. "You have said it exactly. When shall we begin?"

"This very night," said the first fairy.

"Agreed!" said the second fairy; and that very night, while everyone else was gone quietly to bed they went, one into the palace and fetched some of the queen's clothes, and, bringing them to the tripe-seller's room, placed them by the side of her bed; and the other went to the tripe-seller's room and fetched her clothes, and took them and put them by the side of the queen's bed. They also woke them very early, and when each got up she put on the things that were by the side of the bed, thinking they were the things she had left there the night before. Thus the queen was dressed like a tripe-seller, and the tripe-seller like a queen.

Then one fairy took the queen, dressed like a tripe-seller, and put her down in the tripe-seller's shop, and the other fairy took the tripe-seller, dressed like a queen, and placed her in the palace, and both of them did their work so swiftly that neither the queen nor the tripe-seller perceived the flight at all.

The queen was very much astonished at finding herself in a tripe-shop, and began staring about, wondering how she got there.

"Here! Don't stand gaping about like that!" cried the tripe-man, who was a very hot-tempered fellow; "Why, you haven't boiled the coffee!"

"Boiled the coffee!" repeated the queen, hardly apprehending what he meant.

"Yes; you haven't boiled the coffee!" said the tripe-man. "Don't repeat my words, but do your work!" and he took her by the shoulders, put the coffee-pot in her hand, and stood over her looking so fierce that she was frightened into doing what she had never done or seen done in all her life before.

Presently the coffee began to boil over.

"There! Don't waste all the coffee like that!" cried the tripe-man, and he got up and gave her a slap, which made the tears come in her eyes.

"Don't blubber!" said the tripe-man; "but bring the coffee here and pour it out."

The queen did as she was told; but when she began to drink it, though she had made it herself, it was so nasty she didn't know how to drink it. It was very different stuff from what she got at the palace; but the tripe-man had his eye on her, and she didn't dare not to drink it.

"A halfp'th of cat's-meat!" sang out a small boy in the shop.

"Why don't you go and serve the customer?" said the tripe-man, knocking the cup out of the queen's hand.

Fearing another slap, she rose hastily to give the boy what he wanted, but not knowing one thing in the shop from another, she gave him a large piece of the best tripe fit for a prince.

"Oh, what fine tripe today!" cried the small boy, and ran away as fast as he could.

It was in vain the tripe-man halloed after him, he was in too great a hurry to secure his prize to think of returning.

"Look what you've done!" cried the tripe-man, giving the queen another slap; "you've given that boy for a penny a bunch of tripe worth a shilling." Luckily, other customers came in and diverted the man's attention.

Presently all the tripe hanging up had been sold, and more customers kept coming in.

"What has come to you today?" roared the tripe-man, as the queen stood not knowing what to do with herself. "Do you mean to say you haven't washed that other lot of tripe?" And this time he gave her a kick.

To escape his fury, the queen turned to do her best with washing the other tripe, but she did it so awkwardly that she got a volley of abuse and blows too.

Then came dinnertime, and nothing prepared, or even bought to prepare, for dinner. Another stormy scene ensued at the discovery, and the tripe-man went to dine at the inn, leaving her to go without any dinner at all, in punishment for having neglected to prepare it.

While he was gone she helped all the customers to the wrong things, and, when he came home, got another scolding and more blows for her stupidity. And all through the afternoon it was the same story.

But the tripe-seller, when she found herself all in a palace, with half a dozen maids waiting to attend her, was equally bewildered. When they kept asking her if there was nothing she pleased to want, she kept answering, "No thank you," in such a gentle tone, the maids began to think that a reign of peace had come to them at last.

By and by, when the ladies came, instead of saying, as the queen had been wont, "What an ugly dress you have got; go and take it off!" she said, "How nice you look; how tasteful your dress is!"

Afterwards the king came in, bringing her a rare nosegay. Instead of throwing it on one side to vex him, as the queen had been wont, she showed so much delight, and expressed her thanks so many times, that he was quite overcome.

The change that had come over the queen soon became the talk of the whole palace, and everyone congratulated himself on an improvement which made them all happy. The king was no less pleased than all the rest, and for the first time for many years he said he would drive out with the queen; for on account of her bad temper he had long given up driving with her. So the carriage came round with four prancing horses, and an escort of cavalry to ride before and behind it. The tripe-seller hardly could believe she was to drive in this splendid carriage, but the king handed her in before she knew where she was. Then, as he was so pleased with her gentle and grateful ways, he further asked her to say which way she would like to drive.

The tripe-seller, partly because she was too much frightened to think of any other place, and partly because she thought it would be nice to drive in state through her own neighbourhood, named the broader street out of which turned the lane in which she lived, for the royal carriage could hardly have turned down the lane itself. The king repeated the order, and away drove the royal cortège.

The circumstance of the king and queen driving out together was sufficient to excite the attention of the whole population, and wherever they passed the people crowded into the streets; thus a volley of shouts and comments ran before the carriage towards the lane of the tripe-man. The tripe-man was at the moment engaged in administering a severe chastisement to the queen for her latest mistake, and the roar of the people's voices afforded a happy pretext for breaking away from him.

She ran with the rest to the opening of the lane just as the royal carriage was passing.

"My husband! my husband!" she screamed as the king drove by, and plaintive as was her voice, and different from her usual imperious tone, he heard it and turned his head towards her.

"My husband! my royal husband!" pleaded the humbled queen.

The king, in amazement, stopped the carriage and gazed from the queen in the gutter to the tripe-seller in royal array by his side, unable to solve the problem.

"This is certainly my wife!" he said at last, as he extended his hand to the queen. "Who then can you be?" he added, addressing the tripe-seller.

"I will tell the truth," replied the good tripe-seller. "I am no queen; I am the poor wife of the tripe-seller down the lane there; but how I came into the palace is more than I can say."

"And how come you here?" said the king, addressing the real queen.

"That, neither can I tell; I thought you had sent me hither to punish me for my bad temper; but if you will only take me back I will never be bad-tempered again; only take me away from this dreadful tripe-man, who has been beating me all day."

Then the king made answer: "Of course you must come back with me, for you are my wife. But," he said to the tripe-seller; "what shall I do with you? After you have been living in luxury in the palace, you will feel it hard to go back to sell tripe."

"It's true I have not many luxuries at home," answered the tripe-seller; "but yet I had rather be with my husband than in any palace in the world;" and she descended from the carriage, while the queen got in.

"Stop!" said the king. "This day's transformation, howsoever it was brought about, has been a good day, and you have been so well behaved, and so truth-spoken, I don't like your going back to be beaten by the tripe-man."

"Oh, never mind that," said the good wife; "he never beats me unless I do something very stupid. And, after all, he's my husband, and that's enough for me."

"Well, if you're satisfied, I won't interfere any further," said the king; "except to give you some mark of my royal favour."

So he bestowed on the tripe-man and his wife a beautiful villa, with a nice casino outside the gates, on condition that he never beat her anymore.

The tripe-man was so pleased with the gifts which had come to him through his wife's good conduct that he kept his word, and was always thereafter very kind to her. And the queen was so frightened at the thought that she might find herself suddenly transformed into a tripe-seller again that she kept a strict guard over her temper, and became the delight of her husband and the whole court.

The Wanderings

THE FIRST STOP ON JASON'S VOYAGE was the island of Lemnos, off the coast of Asia Minor. Lemnos was an island blighted by the gods. Aphrodite, annoyed by the womenfolk's lack of veneration, punished them by imbuing their bodies with a nauseating smell that repelled their husbands. The Lemnian men therefore started to turn to other women, stoking the fury of their neglected wives. Maddened with yearning and anger, the women of Lemnos killed all the male inhabitants of the islands, and lived on under the rule of their queen, Hypsipyle.

The Argonauts' stay at Lemnos would not be a short one. In return for the right to land, Hypsipyle made Jason promise that they would stay for some duration before departing. In the end, Lemnos was home to the warrior crew for a full year – all except Heracles and a small contingent of more disciplined men, who stayed on the Argo. The women, grateful for the male company, lauded the men with pageant and dance, fragrant sacrifices and exquisite foods. Days rolled into weeks, and weeks into months. Some of the warriors even had children with these women; Jason himself had two children with the queen. The Argo sat listlessly at its anchorage under an impassive sun, until Heracles expressed his wrath, and awakened the sense of purpose once more. Jason made his farewells to Hypsipyle, and soon the Argo was on its way east once more.

The experience on Lemnos had lapped at the Argonauts' moral strength. A test of physical and martial strength would face them at their next port of call, the Cyzicus peninsula. Here King Cyzicus of the Doliones welcomed them enthusiastically, but with his own hidden purpose. The Doliones were being terrorized by a tribe of fearsome six-armed giants, the Gegeines, who lived in the land beyond Bear Mountain. King Cyzicus evoked the physical delights of this land, while omitting to mention its earth-shaking inhabitants. Meanwhile, the Gegeines themselves – spurred by greed – had spotted the Argo at anchorage and plotted to raid her. At the moment when most of the crew were ashore, the Gegeines rushed down from the hillside, expecting easy plunder. What they found was the iron resistance and swift muscle of Heracles and a small group of other warriors, who fought the giants with no thought of the struggle being unequal. The Gegeines suffered grievously, many of them killed before the return of the rest of the Argo's crew put the survivors into rout.

Tragedy followed, however. Once the celebrations of victory had died down, Jason put his ship to sea once more, but night-time, smarting rain and capricious winds drove them back to Cyzicus. As they landed, the Doliones confused them with Pelasgian raiders, and fierce battle ensued. Their eyes seeing only a muted world of half shapes, Jason and the king fought a battle, in which Cyzicus was slain. When morning revealed a horror of sword-hewn bodies, and a dead king, the lamentations were compounded by the suicide of the king's daughter, who hanged herself in grief.

Angry storms kept the Argo at anchor until the gods were appeased, then the ship set sail once again, still far from Colchis. Fate then dealt another adverse hand, when Heracles broke an oar, his muscles greater in strength than the oak he gripped. The ship landed at Cius to find a replacement. Heracles' beloved servant Hylas here wandered off on his own, hoping to find water for the evening meal. He happened upon a pool which gave up no reflection when he faced its haunting surface. Instead, he saw the sensuous, floating grace of the water nymphs, creatures with a magnetizing beauty, bodies curving ceaselessly and effortlessly in the water. Hylas was never seen again, drawn down into the nymph's depthless world. Heracles, when he discovered the loss, was distraught, and left the Argo for good to search for Hylas. Jason had lost one of his stalwart warriors.

The events of the recent past focused Jason's thoughts on what might be to come. Thus he took the ship to Salmydessus in Thrace, seeking out the counsel of Phineus, king of Thrace and a seer of unmatched vision. Phineus had been blinded by an offended Zeus, and his misery was multiplied tenfold by the shrill visitations of the Harpies, winged monsters with the head of a haggard woman and the body of a decrepit, razor-clawed bird. Sickening, stinking creatures, the Harpies would prey on Phineus every time he tried to eat, snatching or defiling his food. Half-starved, Phineus pleaded with the Argonauts to help, and they succeeding in freeing him from this torture. Phineus, in his gratitude, told Jason how to pass through the Symplegades ('Clashing Rocks').

The Symplegades were, since the foundation of the Earth, granite guardians at the entrance to the Black Sea. To prevent passage through the straits, these towering rocks, opposing one another, would snap shut in a split second rush, accompanied by a sonorous crack and a tsunami-like displacement of water. Even swift-swimming sea creatures such as dolphins could not always escape the vice-like rocks, and many ships were splintered to destruction. Phineus suggested that Jason release a dove as he approached the rocks; the Symplegades would snap shut on the bird, then the Argo could pass through as they reopened.

It remained to be seen whether Phineus's vision would work in practice. The crew sat in cold fear under the shadow of the rocks as the dove was released. With explosive force, the Symplegades smashed their faces together, just nipping out the tail feathers of the dove as it passed through. Now was the Argo's chance, yet the swelling waves pushed the ship back, delaying its movement forward for crucial seconds. As the Argo moved into the kill zone, the Symplegades towered above them like hammers of death, and a rumbling signalled their imminent crushing movement. Seeing disaster unfold, the goddess Athene herself intervened, holding back one of the rocks with her left hand, while pushing the Argo through the straits. Even the strength of a goddess eventually gave way to the clashing rocks; they smashed together with a roar that seemed to shatter heaven, clipping off the tip of the Argo's stern – but the ship was safe.

The now-weary crew pushed on towards Colchis, enduring further challenges. On the way, their spirits were chilled by the screams of Prometheus, the Titan sentenced to punishment by Zeus. His agony was to be tied to a rock, and each day a mighty eagle would swoop in to tear open his belly and feast on his liver. Prometheus, body arched in torment, back scraped on the sun-bleached coastal rock, did not die; his liver reformed after each ordeal, only to be gouged from him again the next day, and every day thereafter. Near the Caucasian mountains, the Argonauts saw the rush of wind from the eagle's wings billow the sails, and heard its wing beat disturb the air above the clouds. Then came the dire screams of Prometheus, as he experienced his daily torture. Slowly the cries faded into the distance, and the Argo eventually came to its destination. Colchis drew into view and the anchor thumped into the still coastal waters. The Golden Fleece was now the goal.

The Yellow Dwarf

ONCE UPON A TIME there lived a queen who had been the mother of a great many children, and of them all only one daughter was left. But then she was worth at least a thousand.

Her mother, who, since the death of the King, her father, had nothing in the world she cared for so much as this little princess, was so terribly afraid of losing her that she quite spoiled her, and never tried to correct any of her faults. The consequence was that this little person, who was as pretty as possible, and was one day to wear a crown, grew up so proud and so much in love with her own beauty that she despised everyone else in the world.

The Queen, her mother, by her caresses and flatteries, helped to make her believe that there was nothing too good for her. She was dressed almost always in the prettiest frocks, as a fairy, or as a queen going out to hunt, and the ladies of the court followed her dressed as forest-fairies.

And to make her more vain than ever the Queen caused her portrait to be taken by the cleverest painters and sent it to several neighbouring kings with whom she was very friendly.

When they saw this portrait they fell in love with the Princess – every one of them, but upon each it had a different effect. One fell ill, one went quite crazy, and a few of the luckiest set off to see her as soon as possible; but these poor princes became her slaves the moment they set eyes on her.

Never has there been a gayer court. Twenty delightful kings did everything they could think of to make themselves agreeable, and after having spent ever so much money in giving a single entertainment thought themselves very lucky if the Princess said "That's pretty."

All this admiration vastly pleased the Queen. Not a day passed but she received seven or eight thousand sonnets, and as many elegies, madrigals, and songs, which were sent her by all the poets in the world. All the prose and the poetry that was written just then was about Bellissima – for that was the Princess's name – and all the bonfires that they had were made of these verses, which crackled and sparkled better than any other sort of wood.

Bellissima was already fifteen years old, and every one of the princes wished to marry her, but not one dared to say so. How could they when they knew that any of them might have cut off his head five or six times a day just to please her, and she would have thought it a mere trifle, so little did she care? You may imagine how hard-hearted her lovers thought her; and the Queen, who wished to see her married, did not know how to persuade her to think of it seriously.

"Bellissima," she said, "I do wish you would not be so proud. What makes you despise all these nice kings? I wish you to marry one of them, and you do not try to please me."

"I am so happy," Bellissima answered: "do leave me in peace, madam. I don't want to care for anyone."

"But you would be very happy with any of these princes," said the Queen, "and I shall be very angry if you fall in love with anyone who is not worthy of you."

But the Princess thought so much of herself that she did not consider any one of her lovers clever or handsome enough for her; and her mother, who was getting really angry at her determination not to be married, began to wish that she had not allowed her to have her own way so much.

At last, not knowing what else to do, she resolved to consult a certain witch who was called 'The Fairy of the Desert.' Now this was very difficult to do, as she was guarded by some terrible lions; but happily the Queen had heard a long time before that whoever wanted to pass these lions safely must throw to them a cake made of millet flour, sugar-candy, and crocodile's eggs. This cake she prepared with her own hands, and putting it in a little basket, she set out to seek the Fairy. But as she was not used to walking far, she soon felt very tired and sat down at the foot of a tree to rest, and presently fell fast asleep. When she awoke she was dismayed to find her basket empty. The cake was all gone! and, to make matters worse, at that moment she heard the roaring of the great lions, who had found out that she was near and were coming to look for her.

"What shall I do?" she cried; "I shall be eaten up," and being too much frightened to run a single step, she began to cry, and leant against the tree under which she had been asleep. Just then she heard some one say: "H'm, h'm!"

She looked all round her, and then up at the tree, and there she saw a little tiny man, who was eating oranges.

"Oh! Queen," said he, "I know you very well, and I know how much afraid you are of the lions; and you are quite right too, for they have eaten many other people: and what can you expect, as you have not any cake to give them?"

"I must make up my mind to die," said the poor Queen. "Alas! I should not care so much if only my dear daughter were married."

"Oh! you have a daughter," cried the Yellow Dwarf (who was so called because he was a dwarf and had such a yellow face, and lived in the orange tree). "I'm really glad to hear that, for I've been looking for a wife all over the world. Now, if you will promise that she shall marry me, not one of the lions, tigers, or bears shall touch you."

The Queen looked at him and was almost as much afraid of his ugly little face as she had been of the lions before, so that she could not speak a word.

"What! you hesitate, madam," cried the Dwarf. "You must be very fond of being eaten up alive."

And, as he spoke, the Queen saw the lions, which were running down a hill towards them.

Each one had two heads, eight feet, and four rows of teeth, and their skins were as hard as turtle shells, and were bright red.

At this dreadful sight, the poor Queen, who was trembling like a dove when it sees a hawk, cried out as loud as she could, "Oh! dear Mr. Dwarf, Bellissima shall marry you."

"Oh, indeed!" said he disdainfully. "Bellissima is pretty enough, but I don't particularly want to marry her – you can keep her."

"Oh! noble sir," said the Queen in great distress, "do not refuse her. She is the most charming Princess in the world."

"Oh! well," he replied, "out of charity I will take her; but be sure you don't forget that she is mine."

As he spoke a little door opened in the trunk of the orange tree, in rushed the Queen, only just in time, and the door shut with a bang in the faces of the lions.

The Queen was so confused that at first she did not notice another little door in the orange tree, but presently it opened and she found herself in a field of thistles and nettles. It was encircled by a muddy ditch, and a little further on was a tiny thatched cottage, out of which came the Yellow Dwarf with a very jaunty air. He wore wooden shoes and a little yellow coat, and as he had no hair and very long ears he looked altogether a shocking little object.

"I am delighted," said he to the Queen, "that, as you are to be my mother-in-law, you should see the little house in which your Bellissima will live with me. With these thistles and nettles she can feed a donkey which she can ride whenever she likes; under this humble roof no weather can hurt her; she will drink the water of this brook, and eat frogs – which grow very fat about here; and then she will have me always with her, handsome, agreeable, and gay as you see me now. For if her shadow stays by her more closely than I do I shall be surprised."

The unhappy Queen, seeing all at once what a miserable life her daughter would have with this Dwarf, could not bear the idea, and fell down insensible without saying a word

When she revived she found to her great surprise that she was lying in her own bed at home, and, what was more, that she had on the loveliest lace nightcap that she had ever seen in her life. At first she thought that all her adventures, the terrible lions, and her promise to the Yellow Dwarf that he should marry Bellissima must have been a dream, but there was the new cap with its beautiful ribbon and lace to remind her that it was all true, which made her so unhappy that she could neither eat, drink, nor sleep for thinking of it.

The Princess, who, in spite of her wilfulness, really loved her mother with all her heart, was much grieved when she saw her looking so sad, and often asked her what was the matter; but the Queen, who didn't want her to find out the truth, only said that she was ill, or that one of her neighbours was threatening to make war against her. Bellissima knew quite well that something was being hidden from her – and that neither of these was the real reason of the Queen's uneasiness. So she made up her mind that she would go and consult the Fairy of the Desert about it, especially as she had often heard how wise she was, and she thought that at the same time she might ask her advice as to whether it would be as well to be married, or not.

So, with great care, she made some of the proper cake to pacify the lions, and one night went up to her room very early, pretending that she was going to bed; but, instead of that, she wrapped herself up in a long white veil, and went down a secret staircase, and set off, all by herself, to find the Witch.

But when she got as far as the same fatal orange tree, and saw it covered with flowers and fruit, she stopped and began to gather some of the oranges – and then, putting down her basket, she sat down to eat them. But when it was time to go on again the basket had disappeared, and, though she looked everywhere, not a trace of it could she find. The more she hunted for it the more frightened she got, and at last she began to cry. Then all at once she saw before her the Yellow Dwarf.

"What's the matter with you, my pretty one?" said he. "What are you crying about?"

"Alas!" she answered; "no wonder that I am crying, seeing that I have lost the basket of cake that was to help me to get safely to the cave of the Fairy of the Desert."

"And what do you want with her, pretty one?" said the little monster, "for I am a friend of hers, and, for the matter of that, I am quite as clever as she is."

"The Queen, my mother," replied the Princess, "has lately fallen into such deep sadness that I fear that she will die; and I am afraid that perhaps I am the cause of it, for she very much wishes me to be married, and I must tell you truly that as yet I have not found anyone I consider worthy to be my husband. So for all these reasons I wished to talk to the Fairy."

"Do not give yourself any further trouble, Princess," answered the Dwarf. "I can tell you all you want to know better than she could. The Queen, your mother, has promised you in marriage—"

"Has promised me!" interrupted the Princess. "Oh! no. I'm sure she has not. She would have told me if she had. I am too much interested in the matter for her to promise anything without my consent – you must be mistaken."

"Beautiful Princess," cried the Dwarf suddenly, throwing himself on his knees before her, "I flatter myself that you will not be displeased at her choice when I tell you that it is to me she has promised the happiness of marrying you."

"You!" cried Bellissima, starting back. "My mother wishes me to marry you! How can you be so silly as to think of such a thing?"

"Oh! it isn't that I care much to have that honour," cried the Dwarf angrily; "but here are the lions coming; they'll eat you up in three mouthfuls, and there will be an end of you and your pride."

And, indeed, at that moment the poor Princess heard their dreadful howls coming nearer and nearer.

"What shall I do?" she cried. "Must all my happy days come to an end like this?"

The malicious Dwarf looked at her and began to laugh spitefully. "At least," said he, "you have the satisfaction of dying unmarried. A lovely princess like you must surely prefer to die rather than be the wife of a poor little dwarf like myself."

"Oh! don't be angry with me," cried the Princess, clasping her hands. "I'd rather marry all the dwarfs in the world than die in this horrible way."

"Look at me well, Princess, before you give me your word," said he. "I don't want you to promise me in a hurry."

"Oh!" cried she, "the lions are coming. I have looked at you enough. I am so frightened. Save me this minute, or I shall die of terror."

Indeed, as she spoke she fell down insensible, and when she recovered she found herself in her own little bed at home; how she got there she could not tell, but she was dressed in the most beautiful lace and ribbons, and on her finger was a little ring, made of a single red hair, which fitted so tightly that, try as she might, she could not get it off.

When the Princess saw all these things, and remembered what had happened, she, too, fell into the deepest sadness, which surprised and alarmed the whole court, and the Queen more than anyone else. A hundred times she asked Bellissima if anything was the matter with her; but she always said that there was nothing.

At last the chief men of the kingdom, anxious to see their Princess married, sent to the Queen to beg her to choose a husband for her as soon as possible. She replied that nothing would please her better, but that her daughter seemed so unwilling to marry, and she recommended them to go and talk to the Princess about it themselves; so this they at once did. Now Bellissima was much less proud since her adventure with the Yellow Dwarf, and she could not think of a better way of getting rid of the little monster than to marry some powerful king, therefore she replied to their request much more favourably than they had hoped, saying that, though she was very happy as she was, still, to please them, she would consent to marry the King of the Gold Mines. Now he was a very handsome and powerful Prince, who had been in love with the Princess for years, but had not thought that she would ever care about him at all. You can easily imagine how delighted he was when he heard the news, and how angry it made all the other kings to lose for ever the hope of marrying the Princess; but after all Bellissima could not have married twenty kings – indeed, she had found it quite difficult enough to choose one, for her vanity made her believe that there was nobody in the world who was worthy of her.

Preparations were begun at once for the grandest wedding that had ever been held at the palace. The King of the Gold Mines sent such immense sums of money that the whole sea was covered with the ships that brought it. Messengers were sent to all the gayest and most refined courts, particularly to the Court of France, to seek out everything rare and precious to adorn the Princess, although her beauty was so perfect that nothing she wore could make her look prettier. At least that is what the King of the Gold Mines thought, and he was never happy unless he was with her.

As for the Princess, the more she saw of the King the more she liked him; he was so generous, so handsome and clever, that at last she was almost as much in love with him as he was with her. How happy they were as they wandered about in the beautiful gardens together, sometimes listening to sweet music! and the King used to write songs for Bellissima. This is one that she liked very much:

In the forest all is gay
When my Princess walks that way.
All the blossoms then are found
Downward fluttering to the ground,
Hoping she may tread on them.
And bright flowers on slender stem
Gaze up at her as she passes,
Brushing lightly through the grasses.
Oh! my Princess, birds above
Echo back our songs of love,
As through this enchanted land
Blithe we wander, hand in hand.

They really were as happy as the day was long. All the King's unsuccessful rivals had gone home in despair. They said good-bye to the Princess so sadly that she could not help being sorry for them.

"Ah! madam," the King of the Gold Mines said to her, "how is this? Why do you waste your pity on these princes, who love you so much that all their trouble would be well repaid by a single smile from you?"

"I should be sorry," answered Bellissima, "if you had not noticed how much I pitied these princes who were leaving me for ever; but for you, sire, it is very different: you have every reason to be pleased with me, but they are going sorrowfully away, so you must not grudge them my compassion."

The King of the Gold Mines was quite overcome by the Princess's good-natured way of taking his interference, and, throwing himself at her feet, he kissed her hand a thousand times and begged her to forgive him.

At last the happy day came. Everything was ready for Bellissima's wedding. The trumpets sounded, all the streets of the town were hung with flags and strewn with flowers, and the people ran in crowds to the great square before the palace. The Queen was so over-joyed that she had hardly been able to sleep at all, and she got up before it was light to give the necessary orders and to choose the jewels that the Princess was to wear. These were nothing less than diamonds, even to her shoes, which were covered with them, and her dress of silver brocade was embroidered with a dozen of the sun's rays. You may imagine how much these had cost; but then nothing could have been more brilliant, except the beauty of the Princess! Upon her head she wore a splendid crown, her lovely hair waved nearly to her feet, and her stately figure could easily be distinguished among all the ladies who attended her.

The King of the Gold Mines was not less noble and splendid; it was easy to see by his face how happy he was, and everyone who went near him returned loaded with presents, for all round the great banqueting hall had been arranged a thousand barrels full of gold, and numberless bags made of velvet embroidered with pearls and filled with money, each one containing at least a hundred thousand gold pieces, which were given away to everyone who liked to hold out his hand, which numbers of people hastened to do, you may be sure – indeed, some found this by far the most amusing part of the wedding festivities.

The Queen and the Princess were just ready to set out with the King when they saw, advancing towards them from the end of the long gallery, two great basilisks, dragging after them a very badly made box; behind them came a tall old woman, whose ugliness was even more surprising than her extreme old age. She wore a ruff of black taffeta, a red velvet hood, and a farthingale all in rags, and she leaned heavily upon a crutch. This strange old woman, without saying a single word, hobbled three times round the gallery, followed by the basilisks, then stopping in the middle, and brandishing her crutch threateningly, she cried:

"Ho, ho, Queen! Ho, ho, Princess! Do you think you are going to break with impunity the promise that you made to my friend the Yellow Dwarf? I am the Fairy of the Desert; without the Yellow Dwarf and his orange tree my great lions would soon have eaten you up, I can tell you, and in Fairyland we do not suffer ourselves to be insulted like this. Make up your minds at once what you will do, for I vow that you shall marry the Yellow Dwarf. If you don't, may I burn my crutch!"

"Ah! Princess," said the Queen, weeping, "what is this that I hear? What have you promised?"

"Ah! my mother," replied Bellissima sadly, "what did you promise, yourself?"

The King of the Gold Mines, indignant at being kept from his happiness by this wicked old woman, went up to her, and threatening her with his sword, said:

"Get away out of my country at once, and for ever, miserable creature, lest I take your life, and so rid myself of your malice."

He had hardly spoken these words when the lid of the box fell back on the floor with a terrible noise, and to their horror out sprang the Yellow Dwarf, mounted upon a great Spanish cat. "Rash youth!" he cried, rushing between the Fairy of the Desert and the King. "Dare to lay a finger upon this illustrious Fairy! Your quarrel is with me only. I am your enemy and your rival. That faithless Princess who would have married you is promised to me. See if she has not upon her finger a ring made of one of my hairs. Just try to take it off, and you will soon find out that I am more powerful than you are!"

"Wretched little monster!" said the King; "do you dare to call yourself the Princess's lover, and to lay claim to such a treasure? Do you know that you are a dwarf – that you are so ugly that one cannot bear to look at you – and that I should have killed you myself long before this if you had been worthy of such a glorious death?"

The Yellow Dwarf, deeply enraged at these words, set spurs to his cat, which yelled horribly, and leapt hither and thither – terrifying everybody except the brave King, who pursued the Dwarf closely, till he, drawing a great knife with which he was armed, challenged the King to meet him in single combat, and rushed down into the courtyard of the palace with a terrible clatter. The King, quite provoked, followed him hastily, but they had hardly taken their places facing one another, and the whole court had only just had time to rush out upon the balconies to watch what was going on, when suddenly the sun became as red as blood, and it was so dark that they could scarcely see at all. The thunder crashed, and the lightning seemed as if it must burn up everything; the two basilisks appeared, one on each side of the bad Dwarf, like giants, mountains high, and fire flew from their mouths and ears, until they looked like flaming furnaces. None of these things could terrify the noble young King, and the boldness of his looks and actions reassured those who were looking on, and perhaps even embarrassed the Yellow Dwarf himself; but even his courage gave way when he saw what was happening to his beloved Princess. For the Fairy of the Desert, looking more terrible than before, mounted upon a winged griffin, and with long snakes coiled round her neck, had given her such a blow with the lance she carried that Bellissima fell into the Queen's arms bleeding and senseless. Her fond mother, feeling as much hurt by the blow as the Princess herself, uttered such piercing cries and lamentations that the King, hearing them, entirely lost his courage and presence of mind. Giving up the combat, he flew towards the Princess, to rescue or to die with her; but the Yellow Dwarf was too quick for him. Leaping with his Spanish cat upon the balcony, he snatched Bellissima from the Queen's arms, and before any of the ladies of the court could stop him he had sprung upon the roof of the palace and disappeared with his prize.

The King, motionless with horror, looked on despairingly at this dreadful occurrence, which he was quite powerless to prevent, and to make matters worse his sight failed him, everything became dark, and he felt himself carried along through the air by a strong hand.

This new misfortune was the work of the wicked Fairy of the Desert, who had come with the Yellow Dwarf to help him carry off the Princess, and had fallen in love with the handsome young King of the Gold Mines directly she saw him. She thought that if she carried him off to some frightful cavern and chained him to a rock, then the fear of death would make him forget Bellissima and become her slave. So, as soon as they reached the place, she gave him back his sight, but without releasing him from his chains, and by her magic power she appeared before him as a young and beautiful fairy, and pretended to have come there quite by chance.

"What do I see?" she cried. "Is it you, dear Prince? What misfortune has brought you to this dismal place?"

The King, who was quite deceived by her altered appearance, replied:

"Alas! beautiful Fairy, the fairy who brought me here first took away my sight, but by her voice I recognized her as the Fairy of the Desert, though what she should have carried me off for I cannot tell you."

"Ah!' cried the pretended Fairy, "if you have fallen into her hands, you won't get away until you have married her. She has carried off more than one Prince like this, and she will certainly have anything she takes a fancy to." While she was thus pretending to be sorry for the King, he suddenly noticed her feet, which were like those of a griffin, and knew in a moment that this must be the Fairy of the Desert, for her feet were the one thing she could not change, however pretty she might make her face.

Without seeming to have noticed anything, he said, in a confidential way:

"Not that I have any dislike to the Fairy of the Desert, but I really cannot endure the way in which she protects the Yellow Dwarf and keeps me chained here like a criminal. It is true that I love a charming princess, but if the Fairy should set me free my gratitude would oblige me to love her only."

"Do you really mean what you say, Prince?" said the Fairy, quite deceived.

"Surely," replied the Prince; "how could I deceive you? You see it is so much more flattering to my vanity to be loved by a fairy than by a simple princess. But, even if I am dying of love for her, I shall pretend to hate her until I am set free."

The Fairy of the Desert, quite taken in by these words, resolved at once to transport the Prince to a pleasanter place. So, making him mount her chariot, to which she had harnessed swans instead of the bats which generally drew it, away she flew with him. But imagine the distress of the Prince when, from the giddy height at which they were rushing through the air, he saw his beloved Princess in a castle built of polished steel, the walls of which reflected the sun's rays so hotly that no one could approach it without being burnt to a cinder! Bellissima was sitting in a little thicket by a brook, leaning her head upon her hand and weeping bitterly, but just as they passed she looked up and saw the King and the Fairy of the Desert. Now, the Fairy was so clever that she could not only seem beautiful to the King, but even the poor Princess thought her the most lovely being she had ever seen.

"What!" she cried; "was I not unhappy enough in this lonely castle to which that frightful Yellow Dwarf brought me? Must I also be made to know that the King of the Gold Mines ceased to love me as soon as he lost sight of me? But who can my rival be, whose fatal beauty is greater than mine?"

While she was saying this, the King, who really loved her as much as ever, was feeling terribly sad at being so rapidly torn away from his beloved Princess, but he knew too well how powerful the Fairy was to have any hope of escaping from her except by great patience and cunning.

The Fairy of the Desert had also seen Bellissima, and she tried to read in the King's eyes the effect that this unexpected sight had had upon him.

"No one can tell you what you wish to know better than I can," said he. "This chance meeting with an unhappy princess for whom I once had a passing fancy, before I was lucky enough to meet you, has affected me a little, I admit, but you are so much more to me than she is that I would rather die than leave you."

"Ah! Prince," she said, "can I believe that you really love me so much?"

"Time will show, madam," replied the King; "but if you wish to convince me that you have some regard for me, do not, I beg of you, refuse to aid Bellissima."

"Do you know what you are asking?" said the Fairy of the Desert, frowning, and looking at him suspiciously. "Do you want me to employ my art against the Yellow Dwarf, who is my best friend, and take away from him a proud princess whom I can but look upon as my rival?"

The King sighed, but made no answer – indeed, what was there to be said to such a clear-sighted person? At last they reached a vast meadow, gay with all sorts of flowers; a deep river surrounded it, and many little brooks murmured softly under the shady trees, where it was always cool and fresh. A little way off stood a splendid palace, the walls of which were of transparent emeralds. As soon as the swans which drew the Fairy's chariot had alighted under a porch, which was paved with diamonds and had arches of rubies, they were greeted on all sides by thousands of beautiful beings, who came to meet them joyfully, singing these words:

"When Love within a heart would reign,
Useless to strive against him 'tis.
The proud but feel a sharper pain,
And make a greater triumph his."

The Fairy of the Desert was delighted to hear them sing of her triumphs; she led the King into the most splendid room that can be imagined, and left him alone for a little while, just that he might not feel that he was a prisoner; but he felt sure that she had not really gone quite away, but was watching him from some hiding-place. So walking up to a great mirror, he said to it, "Trusty counsellor, let me see what I can do to make myself agreeable to the charming Fairy of the Desert; for I can think of nothing but how to please her."

And he at once set to work to curl his hair, and, seeing upon a table a grander coat than his own, he put it on carefully. The Fairy came back so delighted that she could not conceal her joy.

"I am quite aware of the trouble you have taken to please me," said she, "and I must tell you that you have succeeded perfectly already. You see it is not difficult to do if you really care for me."

The King, who had his own reasons for wishing to keep the old Fairy in a good humour, did not spare pretty speeches, and after a time he was allowed to walk by himself upon the sea-shore. The Fairy of the Desert had by her enchantments raised such a terrible storm that the boldest pilot would not venture out in it, so she was not afraid of her prisoner's being able to escape; and he found it some relief to think sadly over his terrible situation without being interrupted by his cruel captor.

Presently, after walking wildly up and down, he wrote these verses upon the sand with his stick:

At last may I upon this shore
Lighten my sorrow with soft tears.
Alas! alas! I see no more
My Love, who yet my sadness cheers.
And thou, O raging, stormy Sea,
Stirred by wild winds, from depth to height,
Thou hold'st my loved one far from me,
And I am captive to thy might.
My heart is still more wild than thine,
For Fate is cruel unto me.
Why must I thus in exile pine?
Why is my Princess snatched from me?
O! lovely Nymphs, from ocean caves,
Who know how sweet true love may be,
Come up and calm the furious waves
And set a desperate lover free!

While he was still writing he heard a voice which attracted his attention in spite of himself. Seeing that the waves were rolling in higher than ever, he looked all round him, and presently saw a lovely lady floating gently towards him upon the crest of a huge pillow, her long hair spread all about her; in one hand she held a mirror, and in the other a comb, and instead of feet she had a beautiful tail like a fish, with which she swam.

The King was struck dumb with astonishment at this unexpected sight; but as soon as she came within speaking distance, she said to him, "I know how sad you are at losing your Princess and being kept a prisoner by the Fairy of the Desert; if you like I will help you to escape from this fatal place, where you may otherwise have to drag on a weary existence for thirty years or more."

The King of the Gold Mines hardly knew what answer to make to this proposal. Not because he did not wish very much to escape, but he was afraid that this might be only another device by which the Fairy of the Desert was trying to deceive him. As he hesitated the Mermaid, who guessed his thoughts, said to him:

"You may trust me: I am not trying to entrap you. I am so angry with the Yellow Dwarf and the Fairy of the Desert that I am not likely to wish to help them, especially since I constantly see your poor Princess, whose beauty and goodness make me pity her so much: and I tell you that if you will have confidence in me I will help you to escape."

"I trust you absolutely," cried the King, "and I will do whatever you tell me; but if you have seen my Princess I beg of you to tell me how she is and what is happening to her."

"We must not waste time in talking," said she. "Come with me and I will carry you to the Castle of Steel, and we will leave upon this shore a figure so like you that even the Fairy herself will be deceived by it."

So saying she quickly collected a bundle of sea-weed, and, blowing it three times, she said:

"My friendly sea-weeds, I order you to stay here stretched upon the sand until the Fairy of the Desert comes to take you away." And at once the sea-weeds became like the King, who stood looking at them in great astonishment, for they were even dressed in a coat like his, but they lay there pale and still as the King himself might have lain if one of the great waves had overtaken him and thrown him senseless upon the shore. And then the Mermaid caught up the King, and away they swam joyfully together.

"Now," said she, "I have time to tell you about the Princess. In spite of the blow which the Fairy of the Desert gave her, the Yellow Dwarf compelled her to mount behind him upon his terrible Spanish cat; but she soon fainted away with pain and terror, and did not recover till they were within the walls of his frightful Castle of Steel. Here she was received by the prettiest girls it was possible to find, who had been carried there by the Yellow Dwarf, who hastened to wait upon her and showed her every possible attention. She was laid upon a couch covered with cloth of gold, embroidered with pearls as big as nuts."

"Ah!" interrupted the King of the Gold Mines; "if Bellissima forgets me, and consents to marry him, I shall break my heart."

"You need not be afraid of that," answered the Mermaid; "the Princess thinks of no one but you, and the frightful Dwarf cannot persuade her to look at him."

"Pray go on with your story," said the King.

"What more is there to tell you?" replied the Mermaid. "Bellissima was sitting in the wood when you passed, and saw you with the Fairy of the Desert, who was so cleverly disguised that the Princess took her to be prettier than herself; you may imagine her despair, for she thought that you had fallen in love with her."

"She believes that I love her!" cried the King. "What a fatal mistake! What is to be done to undeceive her?"

"You know best," answered the Mermaid, smiling kindly at him. "When people are as much in love with one another as you two are, they don't need advice from anyone else."

As she spoke they reached the Castle of Steel, the side next the sea being the only one which the Yellow Dwarf had left unprotected by the dreadful burning walls.

"I know quite well," said the Mermaid, "that the Princess is sitting by the brook-side, just where you saw her as you passed, but as you will have many enemies to fight with before you can reach her, take this sword; armed with it you may dare any danger, and overcome the greatest difficulties, only beware of one thing – that is, never to let it fall from your hand. Farewell; now I will wait by that rock, and if you need my help in carrying off your beloved Princess I will not fail you, for the Queen, her mother, is my best friend, and it was for her sake that I went to rescue you."

So saying, she gave to the King a sword made from a single diamond, which was more brilliant than the sun. He could not find words to express his gratitude, but he begged her to believe that he fully appreciated the importance of her gift, and would never forget her help and kindness.

We must now go back to the Fairy of the Desert. When she found that the King did not return, she hastened out to look for him, and reached the shore, with a hundred of the ladies of her train, loaded with splendid presents for him. Some carried baskets full of diamonds, others golden cups of wonderful workmanship, and amber, coral, and pearls, others, again, balanced upon their heads bales of the richest and most beautiful stuffs, while the rest brought fruit and flowers, and even birds. But what was the horror of the Fairy, who followed this gay troop, when she saw, stretched upon the sands, the image of the King which the Mermaid had made with the sea-weeds. Struck with astonishment and sorrow, she uttered a terrible cry, and threw herself down beside the pretended King, weeping, and howling, and calling upon her eleven sisters, who were also fairies, and who came to her assistance. But they were all taken in by the image of the King, for, clever as they were, the Mermaid was still cleverer, and all they could do was to help the Fairy of the Desert to make a wonderful monument over what they thought was the grave of the King of the Gold Mines. But while they were collecting jasper and porphyry, agate and marble, gold and bronze, statues and devices, to immortalise the King's memory, he was thanking the good Mermaid and begging her still to help him, which she graciously promised to do as she disappeared; and then he set out for the Castle of Steel. He walked fast, looking anxiously round him, and longing once more to see his darling Bellissima, but he had not gone far before he was surrounded by four terrible sphinxes who would very soon have torn him to pieces with their sharp talons if it had not been for the Mermaid's diamond sword. For, no sooner had he flashed it before their eyes than down they fell at his feet quite helpless, and he killed them with one blow. But he had hardly turned to continue his search when he met six dragons covered with scales that were harder than iron. Frightful as this encounter was the King's courage was unshaken, and by the aid of his wonderful sword he cut them in pieces one after the other. Now he hoped his difficulties were over, but at the next turning he was met by one which he did not know how to overcome. Four-and-twenty pretty and graceful nymphs advanced towards him, holding garlands of flowers, with which they barred the way.

"Where are you going, Prince?" they said; "it is our duty to guard this place, and if we let you pass great misfortunes will happen to you and to us. We beg you not to insist upon going on. Do you want to kill four-and-twenty girls who have never displeased you in any way?"

The King did not know what to do or to say. It went against all his ideas as a knight to do anything a lady begged him not to do; but, as he hesitated, a voice in his ear said:

"Strike! strike! and do not spare, or your Princess is lost for ever!"

So, without replying to the nymphs, he rushed forward instantly, breaking their garlands, and scattering them in all directions; and then went on without further hindrance to the little wood where he had seen Bellissima. She was seated by the brook looking pale and weary when he reached her, and he would have thrown himself down at her feet, but she drew herself away from him with as much indignation as if he had been the Yellow Dwarf.

"Ah! Princess," he cried, "do not be angry with me. Let me explain everything. I am not faithless or to blame for what has happened. I am a miserable wretch who has displeased you without being able to help himself."

"Ah!" cried Bellissima, "did I not see you flying through the air with the loveliest being imaginable? Was that against your will?"

"Indeed it was, Princess," he answered; "the wicked Fairy of the Desert, not content with chaining me to a rock, carried me off in her chariot to the other end of the earth, where I should even now be a captive but for the unexpected help of a friendly mermaid, who brought me here to rescue you, my Princess, from the unworthy hands that hold you. Do not refuse the aid of your most faithful lover." So saying, he threw himself at her feet and held her by her robe. But, alas! in so doing he let fall the magic sword, and the Yellow Dwarf, who was crouching behind a lettuce, no sooner saw it than he sprang out and seized it, well knowing its wonderful power.

The Princess gave a cry of terror on seeing the Dwarf, but this only irritated the little monster; muttering a few magical words he summoned two giants, who bound the King with great chains of iron.

"Now," said the Dwarf, "I am master of my rival's fate, but I will give him his life and permission to depart unharmed if you, Princess, will consent to marry me."

"Let me die a thousand times rather," cried the unhappy King.

"Alas!" cried the Princess, "must you die? Could anything be more terrible?"

"That you should marry that little wretch would be far more terrible," answered the King.

"At least," continued she, "let us die together."

"Let me have the satisfaction of dying for you, my Princess," said he.

"Oh, no, no!" she cried, turning to the Dwarf; "rather than that I will do as you wish."

"Cruel Princess!" said the King, "would you make my life horrible to me by marrying another before my eyes?"

"Not so," replied the Yellow Dwarf; "you are a rival of whom I am too much afraid: you shall not see our marriage." So saying, in spite of Bellissima's tears and cries, he stabbed the King to the heart with the diamond sword.

The poor Princess, seeing her lover lying dead at her feet, could no longer live without him; she sank down by him and died of a broken heart.

So ended these unfortunate lovers, whom not even the Mermaid could help, because all the magic power had been lost with the diamond sword.

As to the wicked Dwarf, he preferred to see the Princess dead rather than married to the King of the Gold Mines; and the Fairy of the Desert, when she heard of the King's adventures, pulled down the grand monument which she had built, and was so angry at the trick that had been played her that she hated him as much as she had loved him before.

The kind Mermaid, grieved at the sad fate of the lovers, caused them to be changed into two tall palm trees, which stand always side by side, whispering together of their faithful love and caressing one another with their interlacing branches.

The Cauldron

THE LITTLE ISLAND OF SANDRAY juts firmly through the waves of the Atlantic Ocean, which spits and surges around it. No human lives there, although sheep graze calmly on the succulent green grass, freshened by the moist salt air, and kept company by the fairy folk who live in a verdant knoll. But once upon a time there were men and women on the island of Sandray, and one was a herder's wife, called Mairearad, who kept a tiny cottage on the northernmost tip.

She had in her possession a large copper cauldron, blackened with age and with use. One day, as she wiped it clean of the evening meal, she was visited by a Woman of Peace, a fairy woman who tiptoed quietly into the cottage and asked to take away the cauldron for a short time. Now this was an older fairy, with a nature that was gentle and kind, and she presented little danger to Mairearad. She had a wizened fairy face, and features as tiny as the markings of a butterfly, and she moved swiftly and silently, advising no one of her coming or going. Mairearad passed her the cauldron, and as the Woman of Peace retreated down the cottage path, towards the twin hills that marked the fairy's Land of Light, she said to the fairy,

A smith is able to make
Cold iron hot with a coal;
The due of the kettle is bones,
And to bring it back again whole.

And so it was that the cauldron was returned that evening, left quietly on the cottage doorstop, filled with juicy bones.

The Woman of Peace came again, later that day, and without saying a word, indicated the cauldron. And as days turned into years, an unspoken relationship developed between the two women, fairy and mortal. Mairearad would loan her cauldron, and in exchange she would have it filled with delicious bones. She never forgot to whisper, as the fairy drew out of sight,

A smith is able to make
Cold iron hot with a coal;
The due of the kettle is bones,
And to bring it back again whole.

Then one day, Mairearad had to leave her cottage for a day, to travel to Castlebay, across the sea on Barra.

She said to her husband before she left, 'When the Woman of Peace comes to the doorstep, you must let her take the cauldron, but do not forget to say to her what I always say.'

And so her husband worked his field, as he always did, and as he returned for his midday meal he met with a curious sight, for scurrying along the path in front of him was a wee woman, her face gnarled with age, her eyes bright and shrewd. Suddenly he felt an inexplicable fear, for most men have had fed to them as bairns the tales of fairies and the cruel tricks they play, their enchantments and their evil spells. He remembered them all now in a rush of tortuous thought, and pushed past the fairy woman to slam the cottage door. She knocked firmly, but he refused to answer, panting with terror on the other side of the door.

At last there was silence, and then, a weird howl echoed around the cottage walls and there was a scrambling on the roof. Through the chimney was thrust the long brown arm of the fairy woman, and she reached straight down to the fire upon which the cauldron sat, and pulled it with a rush of air, through the cottage roof.

Mairearad's husband was still pressed against the door when she returned that evening, and she looked curiously at the empty hearth, remarking, 'The Woman of Peace always returns the cauldron before darkness falls.'

Then her husband hung his head in shame and told her how he'd barred the door, and when the fairy had taken the cauldron, he'd forgotten to ask for its return. Well Mairearad scolded her husband, and putting on her overcoat and boots, she left the cottage, lantern in hand.

Darkness can play tricks as devilish as those of the fairies themselves, and it was not long before the dancing shadows, and whispering trees sent a shiver along the spine of the fierce wife Mairearad, but still she pressed on, safe in the knowledge that the Woman of Peace was her friend. She reached the threshold of the Land of Light and saw on a fire, just inside the door, her cauldron, filled as usual with tender bones. And so she grabbed it, and half-fearing where she was, began to ran, exciting the attention of the black fairy dogs that slept beside an old man who guarded the entrance.

Up they jumped, and woke the old man, who cried out,

Silent woman, dumb woman,
Who has come to us from the Land of the Dead
Since you have not blessed the brugh –
Unleash Black and let go Fierce.

And he let the dogs free to chase the terrified woman right back to the door of her cottage, baying and howling, spitting with determination and hunger. As she ran she dropped the tasty bones, buying herself a moment or two's respite from the snarling dogs. For fairy dogs are faster than any dogs on earth, and will devour all human flesh that comes across their paths. Mairearad fled down the path, finally reaching her door and slamming it shut behind her. There she told her breathless story to her husband, and they held one another's ears against the painful wailing of the hounds. Finally there was silence.

Never again did the fairy Woman of Peace come to Mairearad's cottage, nor did she borrow the cauldron. Mairearad and her husband missed the succulent bones, but never again did they trouble the fairy folk. They are long dead now, buried on the grassy verge on the island of Sandray, where the sheep graze calmly on the succulent green grass, freshened by the moist salt air, kept company by the fairy folk who live in a verdant knoll.

The Quest of the Children of Tuirenn

INUADA OF THE SILVER HAND rose to become King of the Tuatha De Danann during the most savage days of the early invasions. The Fomorians, a repulsive band of sea-pirates, were the fiercest of opponents who swept through the country destroying cattle and property and imposing tribute on the people of the land. Every man of the Tuatha De Danann, no matter how rich or poor, was required to pay one ounce of gold to the Fomorians and those who neglected to pay this tax at the annual assembly on the Hill of Uisneach were maimed or murdered without compassion. Balor of the Evil Eye was leader of these brutal invaders, and it was well known that when he turned his one glaring eyeball on his foes they immediately fell dead as if struck by a thunderbolt. Everyone lived in mortal fear of Balor, for no weapon had yet been discovered that could slay or even injure him. Times were bleak for the Tuatha De Danann and the people had little faith in King Nuada who appeared powerless to resist Balor's tyranny and oppression. As the days passed by, they yearned for a courageous leader who would rescue them from their life of wretched servitude.

The appalling misery of the Tuatha De Danann became known far and wide and, after a time, it reached the ears of Lugh of the Long Arm of the fairymounds, whose father was Cian, son of Cainte. As soon as he had grown to manhood, Lugh had proven his reputation as one of the most fearless warriors and was so revered by the elders of Fairyland that they had placed in his charge the wondrous magical gifts of Manannan the sea-god which had protected their people for countless generations. Lugh rode the magnificent white steed of Manannan, known as Aenbarr, a horse as fleet of foot as the wailing gusts of winter whose charm was such that no rider was ever wounded while seated astride her. He had the boat of Manannan, which could read a man's thoughts and travel in whatever direction its keeper demanded. He also wore Manannan's breast-plate and body armour which no weapon could ever pierce, and he carried the mighty sword known as 'The Retaliator' that could cut through any battle shield.

The day approached once more for the People of Dana to pay their annual taxes to the Fomorians and they gathered together, as was customary, on the Hill of Uisneach to await the arrival of Balor's men. As they stood fearful and terrified in the chill morning air, several among them noticed a strange cavalry coming over the plain from the east towards them. At the head of this impressive group, seated high in command above the rest, was Lugh of the Long Arm, whose proud and noble countenance mirrored the splendour of the rising sun. The King was summoned to witness the spectacle and he rode forth to salute the leader of the strange army. The two had just begun to converse amiably when they were interrupted by the approach of a grimy-looking band of men, instantly known to all as Fomorian tax-collectors. King Nuada bowed respectfully towards them and instructed his subjects to deliver their tributes without delay. Such a sad sight angered and humiliated Lugh of the Long Arm and he drew the King aside and began to reproach him:

'Why do your subjects bow before such an evil-eyed brood,' he demanded, 'when they do not show you any mark of respect in return?'

'We are obliged to do this,' replied Nuada. 'If we refuse we would be killed instantly and our land has witnessed more than enough bloodshed at the hands of the Fomorians.'

'Then it is time for the Tuatha De Danann to avenge this great injustice,' replied Lugh, and with that, he began slaughtering Balor's emissaries single-handedly until all but one lay dead at his feet. Dragging the surviving creature before him, Lugh ordered him to deliver a stern warning to Balor:

'Return to your leader,' he thundered, 'and inform him that he no longer has any power over the People of Dana. Lugh of the Long Arm, the greatest of warriors, is more than eager to enter into combat with him if he possesses enough courage to meet the challenge.'

Knowing that these words would not fail to enrage Balor, Lugh lost little time preparing himself for battle. He enlisted the King's help in assembling the strongest men in the kingdom to add to his own powerful army. Shining new weapons of steel were provided and three thousand of the swiftest white horses were made ready for his men. A magnificent fleet of ships, designed to withstand the most venomous ocean waves, remained moored at port, awaiting the moment when Balor and his malicious crew would appear on the horizon.

The time finally arrived when the King received word that Balor's fierce army had landed at Eas Dara on the northwest coast of Connacht. Within hours, the Fomorians had pillaged the lands of Bodb the Red and plundered the homes of noblemen throughout the province. Hearing of this wanton destruction, Lugh of the Long Arm was more determined than ever to secure victory for the Tuatha De Danann. He rode across the plains of Erin back to his home to enlist the help of Cian, his father, who controlled all the armies of the fairymounds. His two uncles, Cu and Cethen, also offered their support and the three brothers set off in different directions to round up the remaining warriors of Fairyland.

Cian journeyed northwards and he did not rest until he reached Mag Muirthemne on the outskirts of Dundalk. As he crossed the plain, he observed three men, armed and mailed, riding towards him. At first he did not recognize them, but as they drew closer, he knew them to be the sons of Tuirenn whose names were Brian, Iucharba and Iuchar. A long-standing feud had existed for years between the sons of Cainte and the sons of Tuirenn and the hatred and enmity they felt towards each other was certain to provoke a deadly contest. Wishing to avoid an unequal clash of arms, Cian glanced around him for a place to hide and noticed a large herd of swine grazing nearby. He struck himself with a druidic wand and changed himself into a pig. Then he trotted off to join the herd and began to root up the ground like the rest of them.

The sons of Tuirenn were not slow to notice that the warrior who had been riding towards them had suddenly vanished into thin air. At first, they all appeared puzzled by his disappearance, but then Brian, the eldest of the three, began to question his younger brothers knowingly:

'Surely brothers you also saw the warrior on horseback,' he said to them. 'Have you no idea what became of him?'

'We do not know,' they replied.

'Then you are not fit to call yourselves warriors,' chided Brian, 'for that horseman can be no friend of ours if he is cowardly enough to change himself into one of these swine. The instruction you received in the City of Learning has been wasted on you if you cannot even tell an enchanted beast from a natural one.'

And as he was saying this, he struck Iucharba and Iuchar with his own druidic wand, transforming them into two sprightly hounds that howled and yelped impatiently to follow the trail of the enchanted pig.

Before long, the pig had been hunted down and driven into a small wood where Brian cast his spear at it, driving it clean through the animal's chest. Screaming in pain, the injured pig began to speak in a human voice and begged his captors for mercy:

'Allow me a dignified death,' the animal pleaded. 'I am originally a human being, so grant me permission to pass into my own shape before I die.'

'I will allow this,' answered Brian, 'since I am often less reluctant to kill a man than a pig.'

Then Cian, son of Cainte, stood before them with blood trickling down his cloak from the gaping wound in his chest.

'I have outwitted you,' he cried, 'for if you had killed me as a pig you would only be sentenced for killing an animal, but now you must kill me in my own human shape. And I must warn you that the penalty you will pay for this crime is far greater than any ever paid before on the death of a nobleman, for the weapons you shall use will cry out in anguish, proclaiming your wicked deed to my son, Lugh of the Long Arm'.

'We will not slay you with any weapons in that case,' replied Brian triumphantly, 'but with the stones that lie on the ground around us.' And the three brothers began to pelt Cian with jagged rocks and stones until his body was a mass of wounds and he fell to the earth battered and lifeless. The sons of Tuirenn then buried him where he had fallen in an unmarked grave and hurried off to join the war against the Fomorians.

With the great armies of Fairyland and the noble cavalcade of King Nuada at his side, Lugh of the Long Arm won battle after battle against Balor and his men. Spears shot savagely through the air and scabbards clashed furiously until at last, the Fomorians could hold out no longer. Retreating to the coast, the terrified survivors and their leader boarded their vessels and sailed as fast as the winds could carry them back through the northern mists towards their own depraved land. Lugh of the Long Arm became the hero of his people and they presented him with the finest trophies of valour the kingdom had to offer, including a golden war chariot, studded with precious jewels which was driven by four of the brawniest milk-white steeds.

When the festivities had died down somewhat, and the Tuatha De Danann had begun to lead normal lives once more, Lugh began to grow anxious for news of his father. He called several of his companions to him and appealed to them for information, but none among them had received tidings of Cian since the morning he had set off towards the north to muster the armies of the fairymounds.

'I know that he is no longer alive,' said Lugh, 'and I give you my word that I will not rest again, or allow food or drink to pass my lips, until I have knowledge of what happened to him.'

And so Lugh, together with a number of his kinsmen, rode forth to the place where he and his father had parted company. From here, the horse of Manannan guided him to the Plain of Muirthemne where Cian had met his tragic death. As soon as he entered the shaded wood, the stones of the ground began to cry out in despair and they told Lugh of how the sons of Tuirenn had murdered his father and buried him in the earth. Lugh wept bitterly when he heard this tale and implored his men to help him dig up the grave so that he might discover in what cruel manner Cian had been slain. The body was raised from the ground and the litter of wounds on his father's cold flesh was revealed to him. Lugh rose gravely to his feet and swore angry vengeance on the sons of Tuirenn:

'This death has so exhausted my spirit that I cannot hear through my ears, and I cannot see anything with my eyes, and there is not one pulse beating in my heart for grief of my father. Sorrow and destruction will fall on those that committed this crime and they shall suffer long when they are brought to justice.'

The body was returned to the ground and Lugh carved a headstone and placed it on the grave. Then, after a long period of mournful silence, he mounted his horse and headed back towards Tara where the last of the victory celebrations were taking place at the palace.

Lugh of the Long Arm sat calmly and nobly next to King Nuada at the banqueting table and looked around him until he caught sight of the three sons of Tuirenn. As soon as he had fixed his eye on them, he stood up and ordered the Chain of Attention of the Court to be shaken so that everyone present would fall silent and listen to what he had to say.

'I put to you all a question,' said Lugh. 'I ask each of you what punishment you would inflict upon the man that had murdered your father?'

The King and his warriors were astonished at these words, but finally Nuada spoke up and enquired whether it was Lugh's own father that had been killed.

'It is indeed my own father who lies slain,' replied Lugh 'and I see before me in this very room the men who carried out the foul deed.'

'Then it would be far too lenient a punishment to strike them down directly,' said the King. 'I myself would ensure that they died a lingering death and I would cut off a single limb each day until they fell down before me writhing in agony.'

Those who were assembled agreed with the King's verdict and even the sons of Tuirenn nodded their heads in approval. But Lugh declared that he did not wish to kill any of the Tuatha De Danann, since they were his own people. Instead, he would insist that the perpetrators pay a heavy fine, and as he spoke he stared accusingly towards Brian, Iuchar and Iucharba, so that the identity of the murderers was clearly exposed to all. Overcome with guilt and shame, the sons of Tuirenn could not bring themselves to deny their crime, but bowed their heads and stood prepared for the sentence Lugh was about to deliver.

'This is what I demand of you,' he announced.

Three ripened apples
The skin of a pig
A pointed spear
Two steeds and a chariot
Seven pigs
A whelping pup
A cooking spit
Three shouts on a hill.

'And,' Lugh added, 'if you think this fine too harsh, I will now reduce part of it. But if you think it acceptable, you must pay it in full, without variation, and pledge your loyalty to me before the royal guests gathered here.'

'We do not think it too great a fine,' said Brian, 'nor would it be too large a compensation if you multiplied it a hundredfold. Therefore, we will go out in search of all these things you have described and remain faithful to you until we have brought back every last one of these objects.'

'Well, now,' said Lugh, 'since you have bound yourselves before the court to the quest assigned you, perhaps you would like to learn more detail of what lies in store,' And he began to elaborate on the tasks that lay before the sons of Tuirenn.

'The apples I have requested of you,' Lugh continued, 'are the three apples of the Hesperides growing in the gardens of the Eastern World. They are the colour of burnished gold and have the power to cure the bloodiest wound or the most horrifying illness. To retrieve these apples, you will need great courage, for the people of the east have been forewarned that three young warriors will one day attempt to deprive them of their most cherished possessions.

'And the pig's skin I have asked you to bring me will not be easy to obtain either, for it belongs to the King of Greece who values it above everything else. It too has the power to heal all wounds and diseases.

'The spear I have demanded of you is the poisoned spear kept by Pisar, King of Persia. This spear is so keen to do battle that its blade must always be kept in a cauldron of freezing water to prevent its fiery heat melting the city in which it is kept.

'And do you know who keeps the chariot and the two steeds I wish to receive from you?' Lugh continued.

'We do not know,' answered the sons of Tuirenn.

'They belong to Dobar, King of Sicily,' said Lugh, 'and such is their unique charm that they are equally happy to ride over sea or land, and the chariot they pull is unrivalled in beauty and strength.

'And the seven pigs you must gather together are the pigs of Asal, King of the Golden Pillars. Every night they are slaughtered, but every morning they are found alive again, and any person who eats part of them is protected from ill-health for the rest of his life.

'Three further things I have demanded of you,' Lugh went on. 'The whelping hound you must bring me guards the palace of the King of Iruad. Failinis is her name and all the wild beasts of the world fall down in terror before her, for she is stronger and more splendid than any other creature known to man.

'The cooking-spit I have called for is housed in the kitchen of the fairywomen on Inis Findcuire, an island surrounded by the most perilous waters that no man has ever safely reached.

'Finally, you must give the three shouts requested of you on the Hill of Midcain where it is prohibited for any man other than the sons of Midcain to cry aloud. It was here that my father received his warrior training and here that his death will be hardest felt. Even if I should one day forgive you of my father's murder, it is certain that the sons of Midcain will not.'

As Lugh finished speaking, the children of Tuirenn were struck dumb by the terrifying prospect of all that had to be achieved by them and they went at once to where their father lived and told him of the dreadful sentence that had been pronounced on them.

'It is indeed a harsh fine,' said Tuirenn, 'but one that must be paid if you are guilty, though it may end tragically for all three of you.' Then he advised his sons to return to Lugh to beg the loan of the boat of Manannan that would carry them swiftly over the seas on their difficult quest. Lugh kindly agreed to give them the boat and they made their way towards the port accompanied by their father. With heavy hearts, they exchanged a sad farewell and wearily set sail on the first of many arduous journeys.

'We shall go in search of the apples to begin with,' said Brian, and his command was answered immediately by the boat of Manannan which steered a course towards the Eastern World and sailed without stopping until it came to rest in a sheltered harbour in the lands of the Hesperides. The brothers then considered how best they might remove the apples from the garden in which they were growing, and it was eventually decided among them that they should transform themselves into three screeching hawks.

'The tree is well guarded,' Brian declared, 'but we shall circle it, carefully avoiding the arrows that will be hurled at us until they have all been spent. Then we will swoop on the apples and carry them off in our beaks.'

The three performed this task without suffering the slightest injury and headed back towards the boat with the stolen fruit. The news of the theft had soon spread throughout the kingdom, however, and the king's three daughters quickly changed themselves into three-taloned ospreys and pursued the hawks over the sea. Shafts of lightning lit up the skies around them and struck the wings of the hawks, scorching their feathers and causing them to plummet towards the waters below. But Brian managed to take hold of his druidic wand and he transformed himself and his brothers into swans that darted below the waves until the ospreys had given up the chase and it was safe for them to return to the boat.

After they had rested awhile, it was decided that they should travel on to Greece in search of the skin of the pig.

'Let us visit this land in the shape of three bards of Erin,' said Brian, 'for if we appear as such, we will be honoured and respected as men of wit and wisdom.'

They dressed themselves appropriately and set sail for Greece composing some flattering verses in honour of King Tuis as they journeyed along. As soon as they had landed, they made their way to the palace and were enthusiastically welcomed as dedicated men of poetry who had travelled far in search of a worthy patron. An evening of drinking and merry-making followed; verses were read aloud by the King's poets and many ballads were sung by the court musicians. At length, Brian rose to his feet and began to recite the poem he had written for King Tuis. The King smiled rapturously to hear himself described as 'the oak among kings' and encouraged Brian to accept some reward for his pleasing composition.

'I will happily accept from you the pig's skin you possess,' said Brian, 'for I have heard that it can cure all wounds.'

'I would not give this most precious object to the finest poet in the world,' replied the King, 'but I shall fill the skin three times over with red gold, one skin for each of you, which you may take away with you as the price of your poem.'

The brothers agreed to this and the King's attendants escorted them to the treasure-house where the gold was to be measured out. They were about to weigh the very last share when Brian suddenly snatched the pig's skin and raced from the room, striking down several of the guards as he ran. He had just found his way to the outer courtyard when King Tuis appeared before him, his sword drawn in readiness to win back his most prized possession. Many bitter blows were exchanged and many deep wounds were inflicted by each man on the other until, at last, Brian dealt the King a fatal stroke and he fell to the ground never to rise again.

Armed with the pig's skin that could cure their battle wounds, and the apples that could restore them to health, the sons of Tuirenn grew more confident that they would succeed in their quest. They were determined to move on as quickly as possible to the next task Lugh had set them and instructed the boat of Manannan to take them to the land of Persia, to the court of King Pisar, where they appeared once more in the guise of poets. Here they were also made welcome and were treated with honour and distinction. After a time, Brian was called upon to deliver his poem and, as before, he recited some verses in praise of the King which won the approval of all who were gathered. Again, he was persuaded to accept some small reward for his poem and, on this occasion, he requested the magic spear of Persia. But the King grew very angry at this request and the benevolent attitude he had previously displayed soon turned to open hostility:

'It was most unwise of you to demand my beloved spear as a gift,' bellowed the King, 'the only reward you may expect now is to escape death for having made so insolent a request.'

When Brian heard these words he too was incensed and grabbing one of the three golden apples, he flung it at the King's head, dashing out his brains. Then the three brothers rushed from the court, slaughtering all they encountered along the way, and hurried towards the stables where the spear of Pisar lay resting in a cauldron of water. They quickly seized the spear and headed for the boat of Manannan, shouting out their next destination as they ran, so that the boat made itself ready and turned around in the direction of Sicily and the kingdom of Dobar.

'Let us strike up a friendship with the King,' said Brian, 'by offering him our services as soldiers of Erin.'

And when they arrived at Dobar's court they were well received and admitted at once to the King's great army where they won the admiration of all as the most valiant defenders of the realm. The brothers remained in the King's service for a month and two weeks, but during all this time they never once caught a glimpse of the two steeds and the chariot Lugh of the Long Arm had spoken of.

'We have waited long enough,' Brian announced impatiently. 'Let us go to the King and inform him that we will quit his service unless he shows us his famous steeds and his chariot.'

So they went before King Dobar who was not pleased to receive news of their departure, for he had grown to rely on the three brave warriors. He immediately sent for his steeds and ordered the chariot to be yoked to them and they were paraded before the sons of Tuirenn. Brian watched carefully as the charioteer drove the steeds around in a circle and as they came towards him a second time he sprung onto the nearest saddle and seized the reins. His two brothers fought a fierce battle against those who tried to prevent them escaping, but it was not long before they were at Brian's side, riding furiously through the palace gates, eager to pursue their fifth quest.

They sailed onwards without incident until they reached the land of King Asal of the Pillars of Gold. But their high spirits were quickly vanquished by the sight of a large army guarding the harbour in anticipation of their arrival. For the fame of the sons of

Tuirenn was widespread by this time, and their success in carrying away with them the most coveted treasures of the world was well known to all. King Asal himself now came forward to greet them and demanded to know why they had pillaged the lands of other kings and murdered so many in their travels. Then Brian told King Asal of the sentence Lugh of the Long Arm had pronounced upon them and of the many hardships they had already suffered as a result.

'And what have you come here for?' the King enquired.

'We have come for the seven pigs which Lugh has also demanded as part of that compensation,' answered Brian, 'and it would be far better for all of us if you deliver them to us in good will.'

When the King heard these words, he took counsel with his people, and it was wisely decided that the seven pigs should be handed over peacefully, without bloodshed. The sons of Tuirenn expressed their gratitude to King Asal and pledged their services to him in all future battles. Then Asal questioned them on their next adventure, and when he discovered that they were journeying onwards to the land of Iruad in search of a puppy hound, he made the following request of them:

'Take me along with you,' he said 'for my daughter is married to the King of Iruad and I am desperate, for love of her, to persuade him to surrender what you desire of him without a show of arms.'

Brian and his brothers readily agreed to this and the boats were made ready for them to sail together for the land of Iruad.

When they reached the shores of the kingdom, Asal went ahead in search of his son-in-law and told him the tale of the sons of Tuirenn from beginning to end and of how he had rescued his people from a potentially bloody war. But Iruad was not disposed to listen to the King's advice and adamantly refused to give up his hound without a fight. Seizing his weapon, he gave the order for his men to begin their attack and went himself in search of Brian in order to challenge him to single combat. A furious contest ensued between the two and they struck each other viciously and angrily. Eventually, however, Brian succeeded in overpowering King Iruad and he hauled him before Asal, bound and gagged like a criminal.

'I have spared his life,' said Brian, 'perhaps he will now hand over the hound in recognition of my clemency.'

The King was untied and the hound was duly presented to the sons of Tuirenn who were more than pleased that the battle had come to a swift end. And there was no longer any bitterness between Iruad and the three brothers, for Iruad had been honestly defeated and had come to admire his opponents. They bid each other a friendly farewell and the sons of Tuirenn took their leave of the land of the Golden Pillars and set out to sea once again.

Far across the ocean in the land of Erin, Lugh of the Long Arm had made certain that news of every success achieved by the sons of Tuirenn had been brought to his attention. He was fully aware that the quest he had set them was almost drawing to a close and became increasingly anxious at the thought. But he desired above everything else to take possession of the valuable objects that had already been recovered, for Balor of the Evil Eye had again reared his ugly head and the threat of another Fomorian invasion was imminent. Seeking to lure the sons of Tuirenn back to Erin, Lugh sent a druidical spell after the brothers, causing them to forget that their sentence had not yet been fully completed. Under its influence, the sons of Tuirenn entertained visions of the heroic reception that awaited them on the shores of the Boyne and their hearts were filled with joy to think that they would soon be reunited with their father.

Within days, their feet had touched on Erin's soil again and they hastened to Tara to the Annual Assembly, presided over by the High King of Erin. Here, they were heartily welcomed by the royal family and the Tuatha De Danann who rejoiced alongside them and praised them for their great courage and valour. And it was agreed that they should submit the tokens of their quest to the High King himself who undertook to examine them and to inform Lugh of the triumphant return of the sons of Tuirenn. A messenger was despatched to Lugh's household and within an hour he had arrived at the palace of Tara, anxious to confront the men he still regarded as his enemies.

'We have paid the fine on your father's life,' said Brian, as he pointed towards the array of objects awaiting Lugh's inspection.

'This is indeed an impressive sight,' replied Lugh of the Long Arm, 'and would suffice as payment for any other murder. But you bound yourselves before the court to deliver everything asked for and I see that you have not done so. Where is the cooking-spit I was promised? And what is to be done about the three shouts on the hill which you have not yet given?'

When the sons of Tuirenn heard this, they realized that they had been deceived and they collapsed exhausted to the floor. Gloom and despair fell upon them as they faced once more the reality of long years of searching and wandering. Leaving behind the treasures that had hitherto protected them, they made their way wearily towards their ship which carried them swiftly away over the storm-tossed seas.

They had spent three months at sea and still they could not discover the smallest trace of the island known as Inis Findcurie. But when their hopes had almost faded, Brian suggested that they make one final search beneath the ocean waves and he put on his magical water-dress and dived over the side of the boat. After two long weeks of swimming in the salt water, he at last happened upon the island, tucked away in a dark hollow of the ocean bed. He immediately went in search of the court and found it occupied by a large group of women, their heads bent in concentration, as they each embroidered a cloth of gold. The women appeared not to notice Brian and he seized this opportunity to move forward to where the cooking-spit rested in a corner of the room. He had just lifted it from the hearth when the women broke into peals of laughter and they laughed long and heartily until finally the eldest of them condescended to address him:

'Take the spit with you, as a reward for your heroism,' she said mockingly, 'but even if your two brothers had attended you here, the weakest of us would have had little trouble preventing you from removing what you came for.'

And Brian took his leave of them knowing they had succeeded in humiliating him, yet he was grateful, nonetheless, that only one task remained to be completed.

They lost no time in directing the boat of Manannan towards their final destination and had reached the Hill of Midcain shortly afterwards, on whose summit they had pledged themselves to give three shouts. But as soon as they had begun to ascend to the top, the guardian of the hill, none other than Midcain himself, came forward to challenge the sons of Tuirenn:

'What is your business in my territory,' demanded Midcain.

'We have come to give three shouts on this hill,' said Brian, 'in fulfilment of the quest we have been forced to pursue in the name of Lugh of the Long Arm.'

'I knew his father well,' replied Midcain, 'and I am under oath not to permit anyone to cry aloud on my hill.'

'Then we have no option but to fight for that permission,' declared Brian, and he rushed at his opponent with his sword before Midcain had the opportunity to draw his own, killing him with a single thrust of his blade through the heart.

Then the three sons of Midcain came out to fight the sons of Tuirenn and the conflict that followed was one of the bitterest and bloodiest ever before fought by any group of warriors. They battled with the strength of wild bears and the ruthlessness of starving lions until they had carved each other to pieces and the grass beneath their feet ran crimson with blood. In the end, however, it was the sons of Tuirenn who were victorious, but their wounds were so deep that they fell to the ground one after the other and waited forlornly for death to come, wishing in vain that they still had the pig skin to cure them.

They had rested a long time before Brian had the strength to speak, and he reminded his brothers that they had not yet given the three shouts on the Hill of Midcain that Lugh had demanded of them. Then slowly they raised themselves up off the ground and did as they had been requested, satisfied at last that they had entirely fulfilled their quest. And after this, Brian lifted his wounded brothers into the boat, promising them a final glimpse of Erin if they would only struggle against death a brief while longer.

And on this occasion the boat of Manannan did not come to a halt on the shores of the Boyne, but moved speedily overland until it reached Dun Tuirenn where the dying brothers were delivered into their father's care. Then Brian, who knew that the end of his life was fast approaching, pleaded fretfully with Tuirenn:

'Go, beloved father,' he urged, 'and deliver this cooking-spit to Lugh, informing him that we have completed all the tasks assigned us. And beg him to allow us to cure our wounds with the pig skin he possesses, for we have suffered long and hard in the struggle to pay the fine on Cian's murder.'

Then Tuirenn rode towards Tara in all haste, fearful that his sons might pass away before his return. And he demanded an audience with Lugh of the Long Arm who came out to meet him at once and graciously received the cooking-spit presented to him.

'My sons are gravely ill and close to death,' Tuirenn exclaimed piteously. 'I beg you to part with the healing pig skin they brought you for one single night, so that I may place it upon their battle wounds and witness it restore them to full health.'

But Lugh of the Long Arm fell silent at this request and stared coldly into the distance towards the Plain of Muirthemne where his father had fallen. When at length he was ready to give Tuirenn his answer, the expression he wore was cruel and menacing and the tone of his voice was severe and merciless:

'I would rather give you the expanse of the earth in gold,' said Lugh, 'than hand over any object that would save the lives of your sons. Let them die in the knowledge that they have achieved something good because of me, and let them thank me for bringing them renown and glory through such a valorous death.'

On hearing these words, Tuirenn hung his head in defeat and accepted that it was useless to bargain with Lugh of the Long Arm. He made his way back despondently to where his sons lay dying and gave them his sad news. The brothers were overcome with grief and despair and were so utterly devastated by Lugh's decision that not one of them lived to see the sun set in the evening sky. Tuirenn's heart was broken in two and after he had placed the last of his sons in the earth, all life departed from him and he fell dead over the bodies of Brian, Iucharba and Iuchar. The Tuatha De Danann witnessed the souls of all four rise towards the heavens and the tragic tale of the sons of Tuirenn was recounted from that day onwards throughout the land, becoming known as one of the Three Sorrows of Story-Telling.

The Fairies and the Blacksmith

THERE ONCE WAS A BLACKSMITH by the name of Alasdair MacEachern, and he lived in a cottage on the Isle of Islay with his son Neil. They lived alone for the blacksmith's poor wife had breathed no more than once or twice when Neil was born to them, but Alasdair MacEachern, or Alasdair of the Strong Arm, as he came to be known, found great comfort in his son and they lived contentedly, with familiar habits and routines that brought them much happiness.

Neil was a slim youth, with unruly hair and eyes that shone with dreams. He was quiet, but easy, and his slight, pale frame gave him the countenance of one weaker than he was. When Neil was but a child the neighbours of Alasdair MacEachern had warned the blacksmith of the fairies who lived just over the knoll, the fairies who would find one so slight and dreamy a perfect prize for their Land of Light. And so it was that each night Alasdair MacEachern hung above the door to his cottage a branch of rowan, a charm against the fairies who might come to steal away his son.

They lived many years this way, until the day came when Alasdair MacEachern had to travel some distance, sleeping the night away from his cottage and his son. Before he left, he warned his son about the rowan branch, and Neil agreed to put it in its place above the door that night. Neil loved the green grass of the hills, and to breathe in the crisp, sunlit air of the banks of the streams that trickled through their land, but he loved more his life with his father and his work on the forge. He had no wish for a life of dancing and eternal merriment in the Land of Light.

And so it was that Neil wished his father a fond farewell, swept the cottage, tended to the goats and to the chickens, and made himself a feast of corn-bread and oatcakes, and goat's cheese and milk, and took himself to the soft green grass of the hills, and walked there by the sunlit banks of the streams until dark fell upon him. And then Neil returned to his cottage next to the forge, and he swept the crumbs from his pockets, and tended to the goats and to the chickens, and laid himself in his tiny box-bed in the corner of the room, by the roaring hearth, and fell fast asleep. Not once had the thought of the branch of rowan crept across his sleepy mind.

It was late in the afternoon when Alasdair of the Strong Arm returned to his cottage, and he found the hearth quite cold, and the floor unswept, and the goats and the chickens untended. His son was there, for he answered his fa-ther's call, but there was no movement from his box-bed in the corner and Alasdair crossed the room with great concern.

'I am ill, Father,' said a small, weak voice, and there laid the body of Neil, yellowed and shrunk, hardly denting his meagre mattress.

'But how ... how could, in just one day ...' Alasdair stared with shock at his son, for he smelled old, of decay, and his skin was like charred paper, folded and crisp and creased. But it was his son, no doubt, for the shape and the face were the same. And Neil laid like this for days on end, changing little, but eating steadily, his appetite strange and fathomless. And it was because of this strange illness that Alasdair MacEachern paid a visit to a wiseman, who came at once to the bedside of Neil, for he was a boy well regarded by his neighbours.

The wiseman looked only once at Neil, and drew the unhappy blacksmith outside the cottage. He asked many questions and then he was quiet. When he finally spoke his words were measured, and his tone quite fearful. The blood of Alasdair MacEachern ran cold.

'This is not your son Neil,' said the man of knowledge. 'He has been carried off by the Little People and they have left a changeling in his place.'

'Alas, then, what can I do?' The great blacksmith was visibly trembling now, for Neil was as central to his life as the fiery heat of the forge itself. And then the wiseman spoke, and he told Alasdair MacEachern how to proceed.

'You must first be sure that is a changeling lying in the bed of Neil, and you must go back to the cottage and collect as many egg shells as you can, filling them with water and carrying them as if they weighed more than ten tons of iron and bricks. And then, arrange them round the side of the fire where the changeling can see you. His words will give him away.'

So Alasdair MacEachern gathered together the shells of twenty eggs and did as he was bidden, and soon a thin voice called out from his son's bed, 'In all of my eight hundred years I have never seen such a sight.' And with a hoot and a cackle, the changeling sank back into the bed.

Alasdair returned to the wiseman and confirmed what had taken place. The old man nodded his head.

'It is indeed a changeling and he must be disposed of, before you can bring back your son. You must follow these steps: light a large, hot fire in the centre of the cottage, where it can be easily seen by the changeling. And then, when he asks you "What's the use of that", you must grab him by the shirtfront, and thrust him deep into the fire. Then he'll fly through the roof of the cottage.'

Alasdair of the Strong Arm did as requested, certain now that that wizened, strange creature was not his son, and as the fire began to roar, the voice called out, reedy and slim, 'What's the use of that?' at which the brave blacksmith seized the body that lay in Neil's bed and placed it firmly in the flames. There was a terrible scream, and the changeling flew straight through the roof, a sour yellow smoke all that remained of him.

And so Alasdair MacEachern cleared away the traces of the fire, and returned once more to the man of knowledge, for it was time to find his son, and he could delay no longer.

The wiseman bade him go to fetch three things: a Bible, a sword, and a crow-ing cock. He was to follow the stream that trickled through their land to the grassy green knoll where the fairies danced and played eternally. On the night of the next full moon, that hill would open, and it was through this door that Alasdair must go to seek his son.

It was many days before the moon had waned, and then waxed again, but it stood, a gleaming beacon in the sky at last, and Alasdair MacEachern col-lected together his sword and his Bible and his crowing cock and set out for the green knoll where the fairies danced. And as the moon rose high in the sky, and lit the shadowy land, a door burst open in the hill, spilling out laugh-ter and song and a bright light that blazed like the fire in the hearth of the blacksmith's cottage. And it was into that light and sound that the courageous Alasdair MacEachern stepped, firmly thrusting his sword into the frame of the door to stop it closing, for no fairy can touch the sword of a mortal man.

There, at a steaming forge, stood his son, as small and as wild-looking as the little folk themselves. He worked silently, absorbed in his labours, and started only when he heard the voice of his father.

'Release my son from this enchantment,' shouted Alasdair MacEachern, hold-ing the Bible high in the air, for fairies have no power over mortals who hold the good Lord's book, and they stood back now, cross and foiled.

'Return him to me, to his own land,' bawled the blacksmith, but the fairies be-gan to smirk, and they slowly crept around him in a circle, taunting him, pok-ing at him with blades of honed green grass. They began to dance, a slow and wiry gyration, moving to a weird song that tugged at the mind of the black-smith, that threatened to overcome him. He struggled to stay upright, and as he stabbed his arms out in front of him, he dropped his cock, who woke with a howl and gave one mighty crow that sent the little fairies shrieking from the doorway to the other side, sent them howling away from the cock and the blacksmith and his son, who they pushed now towards him, sending them all slipping towards the threshold of their world. For daylight was the curfew of the fairies, and it was with true fear that the crow of the red-combed cock was heard, for little people may never see the light of day per chance they turn at once to stone.

They struggled now, prodding the mortals from their world, and begging in an awkward chant for Alasdair MacEachern to release his dirk from their door. And as he drew it from the threshold, and stood once more in the land of mortals with his son, a small and crafty fairy thrust his face from the hill-side, and called out a curse that fell upon the son of the hapless blacksmith like the mist of a foggy night.

'May your son not speak until the day he breaks the curse.' The head popped back, and the fairy was gone, never to be seen again.

And so it was that Alasdair MacEachern and his son Neil went to live again in their familiar, cosy cottage next to the forge, and took up their work, their habits and their routines in place once more. Neil's tongue was frozen by the curse of the fairies, but his manner was unchanged, and this father and his son lived contentedly, for speech is not always necessary to those who live simply, with things and people to which they have grown accustomed.

One day, a year and a week from the fairy's fateful full moon, Alasdair set his son the task of forging the new claymore for the Chief of his clan. As his silent son held the metal to the fire, he started, and looked for one instant as wild as he had in the Land of the Light, for suddenly Neil had remembered, and in that flash of memory he recalled the intricate forging of the fairies' swords, how he'd learned to temper the blades of their glowing weapons with words of wisdom and charms, with magic and spells as well as with fire. Now he leapt into action, and worked with a ferocity and speed that set his father, Alasdair of the Strong Arm, reeling with shock and with fear.

And then the motion stopped, and holding up a sword that gleamed like the light of the full moon, he said quietly, 'There is a sword that will never fail the man who grasps it by the hilt.'

From that time onwards Neil spoke again, for unwittingly he had removed the curse of the fairies by fashioning a fairy sword to sever a fairy spell. Never again did he remember his days in the fairy kingdom, never again could he forge a fairy sword, but the Chief of his clan never lost a battle from that day, and the sword remained the greatest of his possessions.

Neil and his father, Alasdair MacEachern, returned to their cottage, the finest blacksmiths in all the land, their forge casting a glow that could be seen from hills all round, almost as far as the Land of Light, where the fairies kick up their heels in fury at the thought of that blacksmith and his clever son.

The Fairy Changeling

THERE ONCE WAS A WOMAN who lived on the sea, where the winds blew cold and damp. By day she combed the sands for seaweed, and by night she lay alone in her bed, weak and lonely, for her husband was a fisherman and by the light of the moon he trawled the rocky coasts, eking a cruel living, but one which kept them fed and warm in a cosy cottage.

The woman longed for a child, but it was many years before she was granted her wish, and when her baby finally came he was small and feeble. Her neighbours said he would die, or worse, be snatched by the fairies who loved a child so fair of complexion, so slight of build. He would be taken, they said, to the Land of Light where the fairies danced and sang and played all day, where they set traps and tricks for mortal folk who crossed their merry paths.

The fisherman's poor wife could not help but think that a life of laughter would bring roses to the cheeks of her white child, and she wished with all her being that he would be stolen by the fairies, and taken to a land where he could become strong. And so it was that the fisherman's wife set her child out on the rocks, on the edge of her land, and watched and waited. She slept for a few moments, but otherwise moved not, and still her baby lay there, swad-dled and spiritless, an invitation to the little folk which was not accepted.

At length she berated herself for the foolhardy actions, and brought her baby into the cottage once more. And there he surprised her by pulling himself up and demanding food, attaching himself to her teat with such relish that she drew back. He suckled the woman dry, and then demanded porridge, but still he lay small and wizened, more yellow than before, but so hungry that she could not feed him.

So the fisherman's wife placed her baby at her breast, and went to see the wiseman in the village, anxious about her small but starving baby, frightened by his curious change.

The wiseman listened carefully to her story, silently shaking his head.

'You have not your own bairn, but a fairy changeling,' he said finally.

The wife of the fisherman balked, for there in front of her was the very shape and likeness of her baby, and the cry was as shrill as ever. She refused to be-lieve him.

'Take him, then, to your cottage, and leave him in his cradle. Shut the door, but do not go. Spy upon him there and you will be sure.'

And so the fisherman's wife returned to her cottage, and laid the baby upon his bed, shutting the door firmly behind her, but skulking back to peer in the window. And suddenly her baby sat up and drew from under the mattress a chanter, which he began to play. And instead of her baby there was an old fairy bodach.

She fairly flew back to the wiseman, and implored him to help her get rid of the changeling, sickened at the thought of having suckled that gnarled old creature. Calmly the wiseman told her what to do.

The very next day, the wife of the fisherman took her changeling baby and laid him on a rock by the sea, busying herself by collecting seaweed as she did on every day that passed, and comforted by this routine, the baby, or the fairy bodach as she now knew he was, fell asleep. As he slept the tide drew in, licking at the rock on which he slept, until the waters began to dampen his wrappings, and he woke with a start. When he realized that he could not reach the fisherman's wife without swimming he rose to his full height, and a little fairy man once more he began to stamp his feet and howl, shaking his fist at the fisherman's wife who stood entranced as the waters threatened to engulf the fierce fairy.

And so it was that ten or twelve small fairies appeared to rescue their kin, but since fairies cannot swim, they danced helplessly on the shore while the water grew higher and higher about the rock. The fisherman's wife was smug, and she said, 'I shall leave him there, until you return my baby.'

And the fairies disappeared and returned with her baby, who had grown in his time away from his mother, and whose cheeks were roses, whose white skin held the bloom of good health. And she thanked the fairies, and returned their bodach to them.

So the fisherman's wife, flushed with her good fortune, went back to her cosy cottage, protected from the winds which blew cold and damp from the sea. She lived there with her blossoming baby, by day combing the sands for sea-weed, and at night nestling warm in her bed with her son, silently thanking the little people who had made him strong.

The Brewery of Egg-Shells

MRS. SULLIVAN fancied that her youngest child had been exchanged by 'fairies theft', and certainly appearances warranted such a conclusion; for in one night her healthy, blue-eyed boy had become shrivelled up into almost nothing, and never ceased squalling and crying. This naturally made poor Mrs. Sullivan very unhappy; and all the neighbours, by way of comforting her, said that her own child was, beyond any kind of doubt, with the good people, and that one of themselves was put in his place.

Mrs. Sullivan of course could not disbelieve what every one told her, but she did not wish to hurt the thing; for although its face was so withered, and its body wasted away to a mere skeleton, it had still a strong resemblance to her own boy. She, therefore, could not find it in her heart to roast it alive on the griddle, or to burn its nose off with the red-hot tongs, or to throw it out in the snow on the road-side, notwithstanding these, and several like proceedings, were strongly recommended to her for the recovery of her child.

One day who should Mrs. Sullivan meet but a cunning woman, well known about the country by the name of Ellen Leah (or Grey Ellen). She had the gift, however she got it, of telling where the dead were, and what was good for the rest of their souls; and could charm away warts and wens, and do a great many wonderful things of the same nature.

"You're in grief this morning, Mrs. Sullivan," were the first words of Ellen Leah to her.

"You may say that, Ellen," said Mrs. Sullivan, "and good cause I have to be in grief, for there was my own fine child whipped of from me out of his cradle, without as much as 'by your leave' or 'ask your pardon', and an ugly dony bit of a shrivelled-up fairy put in his place; no wonder, then, that you see me in grief, Ellen."

"Small blame to you, Mrs. Sullivan," said Ellen Leah, "but are you sure 'tis a fairy?"

"Sure!" echoed Mrs. Sullivan, "sure enough I am to my sorrow, and can I doubt my own two eyes? Every mother's soul must feel for me!"

"Will you take an old woman's advice?" said Ellen Leah, fixing her wild and mysterious gaze upon the unhappy mother; and, after a pause, she added, "but maybe you'll call it foolish?"

"Can you get me back my child, my own child, Ellen?" said Mrs. Sullivan with great energy.

"If you do as I bid you," returned Ellen Leah, "you'll know." Mrs. Sullivan was silent in expectation, and Ellen continued, "Put down the big pot, full of water, on the fire, and make it boil like mad; then get a dozen new-laid eggs, break them, and keep the shells, but throw away the rest; when that is done, put the shells in the pot of boiling water, and you will soon know whether it is your own boy or a fairy. If you find that it is a fairy in the cradle, take the red-hot poker and cram it down his ugly throat, and you will not have much trouble with him after that, I promise you."

Home went Mrs. Sullivan, and did as Ellen Leah desired. She put the pot on the fire, and plenty of turf under it, and set the water boiling at such a rate, that if ever water was red-hot, it surely was.

The child was lying, for a wonder, quite easy and quiet in the cradle, every now and then cocking his eye, that would twinkle as keen as a star in a frosty night, over at the great fire, and the big pot upon it; and he looked on with great attention at Mrs. Sullivan breaking the eggs and putting down the egg-shells to boil. At last he asked, with the voice of a very old man, "What are you doing, mammy?"

Mrs. Sullivan's heart, as she said herself, was up in her mouth ready to choke her, at hearing the child speak. But she contrived to put the poker in the fire, and to answer, without making any wonder at the words, "I'm brewing, a vick (my son)".

"And what are you brewing, mammy?" said the little imp, whose supernatural gift of speech now proved beyond question that he was a fairy substitute.

"I wish the poker was red," thought Mrs. Sullivan; but it was a large one, and took a long time heating; so she determined to keep him in talk until the poker was in a proper state to thrust down his throat, and therefore repeated the question.

"Is it what I'm brewing, a vick," said she, "you want to know?"

"Yes, mammy: what are you brewing?" returned the fairy.

"Egg-shells, a vick," said Mrs. Sullivan.

"Oh!" shrieked the imp, starting up in the cradle, and clapping his hands together, "I'm fifteen hundred years in the world, and I never saw a brewery of egg-shells before!" The poker was by this time quite red, and Mrs. Sullivan, seizing it, ran furiously towards the cradle; but somehow or other her foot slipped, and she fell flat on the floor, and the poker flew out of her hand to the other end of the house. However, she got up without much loss of time and went to the cradle, intending to pitch the wicked thing that was in it into the pot of boiling water, when there she saw her own child in a sweet sleep, one of his soft round arms rested upon the pillow – his features were as placid as if their repose had never been disturbed, save the rosy mouth, which moved with a gentle and regular breathing.

The Golden Spears

ONCE UPON A TIME there lived in a little house under a hill a little old woman and her two children, whose names were Connla and Nora. Right in front of the door of the little house lay a pleasant meadow, and beyond the meadow rose up to the skies a mountain whose top was sharp-pointed like a spear. For more than half-way up it was clad with heather, and when the heather was in bloom it looked like a purple robe falling from the shoulders of the mountain down to its feet. Above the heather it was bare and grey, but when the sun was sinking in the sea, its last rays rested on the bare mountain top and made it gleam like a spear of gold, and so the children always called it the 'Golden Spear'.

In summer days they gambolled in the meadow, plucking the sweet wild grasses – and often and often they clambered up the mountain side, knee deep in the heather, searching for frechans and wild honey, and sometimes they found a bird's nest – but they only peeped into it, they never touched the eggs or allowed their breath to fall upon them, for next to their little mother they loved the mountain, and next to the mountain they loved the wild birds who made the spring and summer weather musical with their songs.

Sometimes the soft white mist would steal through the glen, and creeping up the mountain would cover it with a veil so dense that the children could not see it, and then they would say to each other: "Our mountain is gone away from us." But when the mist would lift and float off into the skies, the children would clap their hands, and say: "Oh, there's our mountain back again."

In the long nights of winter they babbled of the spring and summertime to come, when the birds would once more sing for them, and never a day passed that they didn't fling crumbs outside their door, and on the borders of the wood that stretched away towards the glen.

When the spring days came they awoke with the first light of the morning, and they knew the very minute when the lark would begin to sing, and when the thrush and the blackbird would pour out their liquid notes, and when the robin would make the soft, green, tender leaves tremulous at his song.

It chanced one day that when they were resting in the noontide heat, under the perfumed shade of a hawthorn in bloom, they saw on the edge of the meadow, spread out before them, a speckled thrush cowering in the grass.

"Oh, Connla! Connla! Look at the thrush – and, look, look up in the sky, there is a hawk!" cried Nora.

Connla looked up, and he saw the hawk with quivering wings, and he knew that in a second it would pounce down on the frightened thrush. He jumped to his feet, fixed a stone in his sling, and before the whirr of the stone shooting through the air was silent, the stricken hawk tumbled headlong in the grass.

The thrush, shaking its wings, rose joyously in the air, and perching upon an elm-tree in sight of the children, he sang a song so sweet that they left the hawthorn shade and walked along together until they stood under the branches of the elm; and they listened and listened to the thrush's song, and at last Nora said:

"Oh, Connla! Did you ever hear a song so sweet as this?"

"No," said Connla, "and I do believe sweeter music was never heard before."

"Ah," said the thrush, "that's because you never heard the nine little pipers playing. And now, Connla and Nora, you saved my life today."

"It was Nora saved it," said Connla, "for she pointed you out to me, and also pointed out the hawk which was about to pounce on you."

"It was Connla saved you," said Nora, "for he slew the hawk with his sling."

"I owe my life to both of you," said the thrush. "You like my song, and you say you have never heard anything so sweet; but wait till you hear the nine little pipers playing."

"And when shall we hear them?" said the children.

"Well," said the thrush, "sit outside your door tomorrow evening, and wait and watch until the shadows have crept up the heather, and then, when the mountain top is gleaming like a golden spear, look at the line where the shadow on the heather meets the sunshine, and you shall see what you shall see."

And having said this, the thrush sang another song sweeter than the first, and then saying "goodbye", he flew away into the woods.

The children went home, and all night long they were dreaming of the thrush and the nine little pipers; and when the birds sang in the morning, they got up and went out into the meadow to watch the mountain.

The sun was shining in a cloudless sky, and no shadows lay on the mountain, and all day long they watched and waited, and at last, when the birds were singing their farewell song to the evening star, the children saw the shadows marching from the glen, trooping up the mountainside and dimming the purple of the heather.

And when the mountain top gleamed like a golden spear, they fixed their eyes on the line between the shadow and the sunshine.

"Now," said Connla, "the time has come."

"Oh, look! Look!" said Nora, and as she spoke, just above the line of shadow a door opened out, and through its portals came a little piper dressed in green and gold. He stepped down, followed by another and another, until they were nine in all, and then the door slung back again. Down through the heather marched the pipers in single file, and all the time they played a music so sweet that the birds, who had gone to sleep in their nests, came out upon the branches to listen to them and then they crossed the meadow, and they went on and on until they disappeared in the leafy woods.

While they were passing the children were spell-bound, and couldn't speak, but when the music had died away in the woods, they said:

"The thrush is right, that is the sweetest music that was ever heard in all the world."

And when the children went to bed that night the fairy music came to them in their dreams. But when the morning broke, and they looked out upon their mountain and could see no trace of the door above the heather, they asked each other whether they had really seen the little pipers, or only dreamt of them.

That day they went out into the woods, and they sat beside a stream that pattered along beneath the trees, and through the leaves tossing in the breeze the sun flashed down upon the streamlet, and shadow and sunshine danced upon it. As the children watched the water sparkling where the sunlight fell, Nora said:

"Oh, Connla, did you ever see anything so bright and clear and glancing as that?"

"No," said Connla, "I never did."

"That's because you never saw the crystal hall of the fairy of the mountains," said a voice above the heads of the children.

And when they looked up, who should they see perched on a branch but the thrush.

"And where is the crystal hall of the fairy?" said Connla.

"Oh, it is where it always was, and where it always will be," said the thrush. "And you can see it if you like."

"We would like to see it," said the children.

"Well, then," said the thrush, "if you would, all you have to do is to follow the nine little pipers when they come down through the heather, and cross the meadow tomorrow evening."

And the thrush having said this, flew away.

Connla and Nora went home, and that night they fell asleep talking of the thrush and the fairy and the crystal hall.

All the next day they counted the minutes, until they saw the shadows thronging from the glen and scaling the mountain side. And, at last, they saw the door springing open, and the nine little pipers marching down.

They waited until the pipers had crossed the meadow and were about to enter the wood. And then they followed them, the pipers marching on before them and playing all the time. It was not long until they had passed through the wood, and then, what should the children see rising up before them but another mountain, smaller than their own, but, like their own, clad more than half-way up with purple heather, and whose top was bare and sharp-pointed, and gleaming like a golden spear.

Up through the heather climbed the pipers, up through the heather the children clambered after them, and the moment the pipers passed the heather a door opened and they marched in, the children following, and the door closed behind them.

Connla and Nora were so dazzled by the light that hit their eyes, when they had crossed the threshold, that they had to shade them with their hands; but, after a moment or two, they became able to bear the splendour, and when they looked around they saw that they were in a noble hall, whose crystal roof was supported by two rows of crystal pillars rising from a crystal floor; and the walls were of crystal, and along the walls were crystal couches, with coverings and cushions of sapphire silk with silver tassels.

Over the crystal floor the little pipers marched; over the crystal floor the children followed, and when a door at the end of the hall was opened to let the pipers pass, a crowd of colours came rushing in, and floor, and ceiling, and stately pillars, and glancing couches, and shining walls, were stained with a thousand dazzling hues.

Out through the door the pipers marched; out through the door the children followed, and when they crossed the threshold they were treading on clouds of amber, of purple, and of gold.

"Oh, Connla," said Nora, "we have walked into the sunset!"

And around and about them everywhere were soft, fleecy clouds, and over their heads was the glowing sky, and the stars were shining through it, as a lady's eyes shine through a veil of gossamer. And the sky and stars seemed so near that Connla thought he could almost touch them with his hand.

When they had gone some distance, the pipers disappeared, and when Connla and Nora came up to the spot where they had seen the last of them, they found themselves at the head of a ladder, all the steps of which were formed of purple and amber clouds that descended to what appeared to be a vast and shining plain, streaked with purple and gold. In the spaces between the streaks of gold and purple they saw soft, milk-white stars. And the children thought that the great plain, so far below them, also belonged to cloudland.

They could not see the little pipers, but up the steps was borne by the cool, sweet air the fairy music; and lured on by it step by step they travelled down the fleecy stairway. When they were little more than half-way down there came mingled with the music a sound almost as sweet – the sound of waters toying in the still air with pebbles on a shelving beach, and with the sound came the odorous brine of the ocean. And then the children knew that what they thought was a plain in the realms of cloudland was the sleeping sea unstirred by wind or tide, dreaming of the purple clouds and stars of the sunset sky above it.

When Connla and Nora reached the strand they saw the nine little pipers marching out towards the sea, and they wondered where they were going to. And they could hardly believe their eyes when they saw them stepping out upon the level ocean as if they were walking upon the land; and away the nine little pipers marched, treading the golden line cast upon the waters by the setting sun. And as the music became fainter and fainter as the pipers passed into the glowing distance, the children began to wonder what was to become of themselves. Just at that very moment they saw coming towards them from the sinking sun a little white horse, with flowing mane and tail and golden hoofs. On the horse's back was a little man dressed in shining green silk. When the horse galloped on to the strand the little man doffed his hat, and said to the children:

"Would you like to follow the nine little pipers?" The children said, "Yes."

"Well, then," said the little man, "come up here behind me; you, Nora, first, and Connla after."

Connla helped up Nora, and then climbed on to the little steed himself; and as soon as they were properly seated the little man said "swish", and away went the steed, galloping over the sea without wetting hair or hoof. But fast as he galloped the nine little pipers were always ahead of him, although they seemed to be going only at a walking pace. When at last he came up rather close to the hindmost of them the nine little pipers disappeared, but the children heard the music playing beneath the waters. The white steed pulled up suddenly, and wouldn't move a step further.

"Now," said the little man to the children, "clasp me tight, Nora, and do you, Connla, cling on to Nora, and both of you shut your eyes."

The children did as they were bidden, and the little man cried:

"Swish! Swash!"

And the steed went down and down until at last his feet struck the bottom.

"Now open your eyes," said the little man.

And when the children did so they saw beneath the horse's feet a golden strand, and above their heads the sea like a transparent cloud between them and the sky. And once more they heard the fairy music, and marching on the strand before them were the nine little pipers.

"You must get off now," said the little man, "I can go no farther with you."

The children scrambled down, and the little man cried "swish", and himself and the steed shot up through the sea, and they saw him no more. Then they set out after the nine little pipers, and it wasn't long until they saw rising up from the golden strand and pushing their heads up into the sea above, a mass of dark grey rocks. And as they were gazing at them they saw the rocks opening, and the nine little pipers disappearing through them.

The children hurried on, and when they came up close to the rocks they saw sitting on a flat and polished stone a mermaid combing her golden hair, and singing a strange sweet song that brought the tears to their eyes, and by the mermaid's side was a little sleek brown otter.

When the mermaid saw them she flung her golden tresses back over her snow-white shoulders, and she beckoned the children to her. Her large eyes were full of sadness; but there was a look so tender upon her face that the children moved towards her without any fear.

"Come to me, little one," she said to Nora, "come and kiss me," and in a second her arms were around the child. The mermaid kissed her again and again, as the tears rushed to her eyes, she said:

"Oh, Nora, avourneen, your breath is as sweet as the wild rose that blooms in the green fields of Erin, and happy are you, my children, who have come so lately from the pleasant land. Oh, Connla! Connla! I get the scent of the dew of the Irish grasses and of the purple heather from your feet. And you both can soon return to Erin of the Streams, but I shall not see it till three hundred years have passed away, for I am Liban the Mermaid, daughter of a line of kings. But I may not keep you here. The Fairy Queen is waiting for you in her snow-white palace and her fragrant bowers. And now kiss me once more, Nora, and kiss me, Connla. May luck and joy go with you, and all gentleness be upon you both."

Then the children said good-bye to the mermaid, and the rocks opened for them and they passed through, and soon they found themselves in a meadow starred with flowers, and through the meadow sped a sunlit stream. They followed the stream until it led them into a garden of roses, and beyond the garden, standing on a gentle hill, was a palace white as snow. Before the palace was a crowd of fairy maidens pelting each other with rose-leaves. But when they saw the children they gave over their play, and came trooping towards them.

"Our queen is waiting for you," they said; and then they led the children to the palace door. The children entered, and after passing through a long corridor they found themselves in a crystal hall so like the one they had seen in the mountain of the golden spear that they thought it was the same. But on all the crystal couches fairies, dressed in silken robes of many colours, were sitting, and at the end of the hall, on a crystal throne, was seated the fairy queen, looking lovelier than the evening star. The queen descended from her throne to meet the children, and taking them by the hands, she led them up the shining steps. Then, sitting down, she made them sit beside her, Connla on her right hand and Nora on her left.

Then she ordered the nine little pipers to come before her, and she said to them:

"So far you have done your duty faithfully, and now play one more sweet air and your task is done."

And the little pipers played, and from the couches at the first sound of the music all the fairies rose, and forming partners, they danced over the crystal floor as lightly as the young leaves dancing in the wind.

Listening to the fairy music, and watching the wavy motion of the dancing fairies, the children fell asleep. When they awoke next morning and rose from their silken beds they were no longer children. Nora was a graceful and stately maiden, and Connla a handsome and gallant youth. They looked at each other for a moment in surprise, and then Connla said:

"Oh, Nora, how tall and beautiful you are!"

"Oh, not so tall and handsome as you are, Connla," said Nora, as she flung her white arms round his neck and kissed her brother's lips.

Then they drew back to get a better look of each other, and who should step between them but the fairy queen.

"Oh, Nora, Nora," said she, "I am not as high as your knee, and as for you, Connla, you look as straight and as tall as one of the round towers of Erin."

"And how did we grow so tall in one night?" said Connla.

"In one night!" said the fairy queen. "One night, indeed! Why, you have been fast asleep, the two of you, for the last seven years!"

"And where was the little mother all that time?" said Connla and Nora together.

"Oh, the little mother was all right. She knew where you were; but she is expecting you today, and so you must go off to see her, although I would like to keep you – if I had my way – all to myself here in the fairyland under the sea. And you will see her today; but before you go here is a necklace for you, Nora; it is formed out of the drops of the ocean spray, sparkling in the sunshine. They were caught by my fairy nymph, for you, as they skimmed the sunlit billows under the shape of sea-birds, and no queen or princess in the world can match their lustre with the diamonds won with toil from the caves of earth. As for you, Connla, see here's a helmet of shining gold fit for a king of Erin – and a king of Erin you will be yet; and here's a spear that will pierce any shield, and here's a shield that no spear can pierce and no sword can cleave as long as you fasten your warrior cloak with this brooch of gold."

And as she spoke she flung round Connla's shoulders a flowing mantle of yellow silk, and pinned it at his neck with a red gold brooch.

"And now, my children, you must go away from me. You, Nora, will be a warrior's bride in Erin of the Streams. And you, Connla, will be king yet over the loveliest province in all the land of Erin; but you will have to fight for your crown, and days of battle are before you. They will not come for a long time after you have left the fairyland under the sea, and until they come lay aside your helmet, shield, and spear, and warrior's cloak and golden brooch. But when the time comes when you will be called to battle, enter not upon it without the golden brooch I give you fastened in your cloak, for if you do harm will come to you. Now, kiss me, children; your little mother is waiting for you at the foot of the golden spear, but do not forget to say goodbye to Liban the Mermaid, exiled from the land she loves, and pining in sadness beneath the sea."

Connla and Nora kissed the fairy queen, and Connla, wearing his golden helmet and silken cloak, and carrying his shield and spear, led Nora with him. They passed from the palace through the garden of roses, through the flowery meadow, through the dark grey rocks, until they reached the golden strand; and there, sitting and singing the strange, sweet song, was Liban the Mermaid.

"And so you are going up to Erin," she said, "up through the covering waters. Kiss me, children, once again; and when you are in Erin of the Streams, sometimes think of the exile from Erin beneath the sea."

And the children kissed the mermaid, and with sad hearts, bidding her goodbye, they walked along the golden strand. When they had gone what seemed to them a long way, they began to feel weary; and just then they saw coming towards them a little man in a red jacket leading a coal-black steed.

When they met the little man, he said: "Connla, put Nora up on this steed; then jump up before her."

Connla did as he was told, and when both of them were mounted –

"Now, Connla," said the little man, "catch the bridle in your hands, and you, Nora, clasp Connla round the waist, and close your eyes."

They did as they were bidden, and then the little man said, "Swash, swish!" and the steed shot up from the strand like a lark from the grass, and pierced the covering sea, and went bounding on over the level waters; and when his hoofs struck the hard ground, Connla and Nora opened their eyes, and they saw that they were galloping towards a shady wood.

On went the steed, and soon he was galloping beneath the branches that almost touched Connla's head. And on they went until they had passed through the wood, and then they saw rising up before them the 'Golden Spear'.

"Oh, Connla," said Nora, "we are at home at last."

"Yes," said Connla, "but where is the little house under the hill?"

And no little house was there; but in its stead was standing a lime-white mansion.

"What can this mean?" said Nora.

But before Connla could reply, the steed had galloped up to the door of the mansion, and, in the twinkling of an eye, Connla and Nora were standing on the ground outside the door, and the steed had vanished.

Before they could recover from their surprise the little mother came rushing out to them, and flung her arms around their necks, and kissed them both again and again.

"Oh, children! Children! You are welcome home to me; for though I knew it was all for the best, my heart was lonely without you."

And Connla and Nora caught up the little mother in their arms, and they carried her into the hall and set her down on the floor.

"Oh, Nora!" said the little mother, "you are a head over me; and as for you, Connla, you look almost as tall as one of the round towers of Erin."

"That's what the fairy queen said, mother," said Nora.

"Blessings on the fairy queen," said the little mother. "Turn round, Connla, till I look at you."

Connla turned round, and the little mother said:

"Oh, Connla, with your golden helmet and your spear, and your glancing shield, and your silken cloak, you look like a king. But take them off, my boy, beautiful as they are. Your little mother would like to see you, her own brave boy, without any fairy finery."

And Connla laid aside his spear and shield, and took off his golden helmet and his silken cloak. Then he caught the little mother and kissed her, and lifted her up until she was as high as his head. And said he:

"Don't you know, little mother, I'd rather have you than all the world."

And that night, when they were sitting down by the fire together, you may be sure that in the whole world no people were half as happy as Nora, Connla, and the little mother.

The Seal-Killer's Adventure

THERE WAS ONCE UPON A TIME a man who lived upon the northern coasts, not far from 'Taigh Jan Crot Callow' (John-o'-Groat's House), and he gained his livelihood by catching and killing fish, of all sizes and denominations. He had a particular liking for the killing of those wonderful beasts, half dog half fish, called 'Roane,' or seals, no doubt because he got a long price for their skins, which are not less curious than they are valuable. The truth is, that the most of these animals are neither dogs nor cods, but downright fairies, as this narration will show; and, indeed, it is easy for any man to convince himself of the fact by a simple examination of his *tobacco-spluichdan*, for the dead skins of those beings are never the same for four-and-twenty hours together. Sometimes the *spluichdan* will erect its bristles almost perpendicularly, while, at other times, it reclines them even down; one time it resembles a bristly sow, at another time a *sleekit cat*; and what dead skin, except itself, could perform such cantrips? Now, it happened one day, as this notable fisher had returned from the prosecution of his calling, that he was called upon by a man who seemed a great stranger, and who said he had been despatched for him by a person who wished to contract for a quantity of seal-skins, and that the fisher must accompany him (the stranger) immediately to see the person who wished to contract for the skins, as it was necessary that he should be served that evening. Happy in the prospect of making a good bargain, and never suspecting any duplicity, he instantly complied. They both mounted a steed belonging to the stranger, and took the road with such velocity that, although the direction of the wind was towards their backs, yet the fleetness of their movement made it appear as if it had been in their faces. On reaching a stupendous precipice which overhung the sea, his guide told him they had now reached their destination.

"Where is the person you spoke of!" inquired the astonished seal-killer.

"You shall see that presently," replied the guide. With that they immediately alighted, and, without allowing the seal-killer much time to indulge the frightful suspicions that began to pervade his mind, the stranger seized him with irresistible force, and plunged headlong with him into the sea. After sinking down, down, nobody knows how far, they at length reached a door, which, being open, led them into a range of apartments, filled with inhabitants – not people, but seals, who could nevertheless speak and feel like human folk; and how much was the seal-killer surprised to find that he himself had been unconsciously transformed into the like image. If it were not so, he would probably have died from the want of breath. The nature of the poor fisher's thoughts may be more easily conceived than described. Looking at the nature of the quarters into which he had landed, all hopes of escape from them appeared wholly chimerical, whilst the degree of comfort, and length of life which the barren scene promised him were far from being flattering. The 'Roane,' who all seemed in very low spirits, appeared to feel for him, and endeavoured to soothe the distress which he evinced by the amplest assurances of personal safety. Involved in sad meditation on his evil fate, he was quickly roused from his stupor by his guide's producing a huge gully or joctaleg, the object of which he supposed was to put an end to all his earthly cares. Forlorn as was his situation, however, he did not wish to be killed; and, apprehending instant destruction, he fell down, and earnestly implored for mercy. The poor generous animals did not mean him any harm, however much his former conduct deserved it, and he was accordingly desired to pacify himself, and cease his cries.

"Did you ever see that knife before?" said the stranger to the fisher.

The latter instantly recognized his own knife, which he had that day stuck into a seal, and with which it had escaped, and acknowledged it was formerly his own, for what would be the use of denying it?

"Well," rejoined the guide, "the apparent seal which made away with it is my father, who has lain dangerously ill ever since, and no means can stay his fleeting breath without your aid. I have been obliged to resort to the artifice I have practised to bring you hither, and I trust that my filial duty to my father will readily excuse me."

Having said this, he led into another apartment the trembling seal-killer, who expected every minute to be punished for his own ill-treatment of the father. There he found the identical seal with which he had had the encounter in the morning, suffering most grievously from a tremendous cut in its hind-quarter. The seal-killer was then desired, with his hand, to cicatrise the wound, upon doing which it immediately healed, and the seal arose from its bed in perfect health. Upon this the scene changed from mourning to rejoicing – all was mirth and glee. Very different, however, were the feelings of the unfortunate seal-catcher, who expected no doubt to be metamorphosed into a seal for the remainder of his life. However, his late guide accosting him, said –

"Now, sir, you are at liberty to return to your wife and family, to whom I am about to conduct you; but it is on this express condition, to which you must bind yourself by a solemn oath, viz. that you will never maim or kill a seal in all your lifetime hereafter."

To this condition, hard as it was, he joyfully acceded; and the oath being administered in all due form, he bade his new acquaintance most heartily and sincerely a long farewell. Taking hold of his guide, they issued from the place and swam up, till they regained the surface of the sea, and, landing at the said stupendous pinnacle, they found their former steed ready for a second canter. The guide breathed upon the fisher, and they became like men. They mounted their horse, and fleet as had been their course towards the precipice, their return from it was doubly swift; and the honest seal-killer was laid down at his own door-cheek, where his guide made him such a present as would have almost reconciled him to another similar expedition, such as rendered his loss of profession, in so far as regarded the seals, a far less intolerable hardship than he had at first considered it.

Hilda's Mermaid

LITTLE HILDA'S FATHER was a sailor and went away on long voyages. Hilda lived in a little cottage on the shore and used to spin and knit while her father was away, for her mother was dead and she had to be the housekeeper. Some days she would go out in her boat and fish, for Hilda was fond of the water. She was born and had always lived on the shore. When the water was very calm Hilda would look down into the blue depths and try to see a mermaid. She was very anxious to see one, she had heard her father tell such wonderful stories about them – how they sang, and combed their beautiful long hair.

One night when the wind was blowing and the rain was beating hard upon her window Hilda could hear the horn warning the sailors off the rocks. Hilda lighted her father's big lantern and ran down to the shore and hung it on the mast of a wreck which lay there, so the sailors would not run their ships upon it. Little Hilda was not afraid, for she had seen many such storms. When she returned to her cottage she found the door was unlatched, but thought the wind had blown it open. When she entered she found a little girl with beautiful hair sitting on the floor. She was a little frightened at first, for the girl wore a green dress and it was wound around her body in the strangest manner.

"I saw your light," said the child, "and came in. The wind blew me far up on shore. I should not have come up on a night like this, but a big wave looked so tempting I thought I would jump on it and have a nice ride, but it was nearer the shore than I thought it, and it landed me right near your door."

"Oh, my!" How Hilda's heart beat, for she knew this child must be a mermaid. Then she saw what she had thought a green dress was really her body and tail curled up on the floor, and it was beautiful as the lamp fell upon it and made it glisten.

"Will you have some of my supper?" asked Hilda, for she wanted to be hospitable, although she had not the least idea what mermaids ate.

"Thank you," answered the mermaid. "I am not very hungry, but if you could give me a seaweed sandwich I should like it."

Poor Hilda did not know what to do, but she went to the closet and brought out some bread, which she spread with nice fresh butter, and filled a glass with milk. She told her she was sorry, but she did not have any seaweed sandwiches, but she hoped she would like what she had prepared. The little mermaid ate it and Hilda was pleased.

"Do you live here all the time?" she asked Hilda. "I should think you would be very warm and want to be in the water part of the time."

Hilda told her she could not live in the water as she did, because her body was not like hers.

"Oh, I am so sorry!" replied the mermaid. "I hoped you would visit me some time; we have such good times, my sisters and I, under the sea."

"Tell me about your home," said Hilda.

"Come and sit beside me and I will," she replied.

Hilda sat upon the floor by her side. The mermaid felt of Hilda's clothes and thought it must be a bother to have so many clothes.

"How can you swim?" she asked.

Hilda told her she put on a bathing-suit, but the mermaid thought that a nuisance.

"I will tell you about our house first," she began. "Our father, Neptune, lives in a beautiful castle at the bottom of the sea. It is built of mother-of-pearl. All around the castle grow beautiful green things, and it has fine white sand around it also. All my sisters live there, and we are always glad to get home after we have been at the top of the ocean, it is so nice and cool in our home. The wind never blows there and the rain does not reach us."

"You do not mind being wet by the rain, do you?" asked Hilda.

"Oh no!" said the mermaid, "but the rain hurts us. It falls in little sharp points and feels like pebbles."

"How do you know how pebbles feel?" Hilda asked.

"Oh, sometimes the nereids come and bother us; they throw pebbles and stir up the water so we cannot see."

"Who are the nereids?" asked Hilda.

"They are the sea-nymphs; but we make the dogfish drive them away. We are sirens, and they are very jealous of us because we are more beautiful than they," said the mermaid.

Hilda thought she was rather conceited, but the little mermaid seemed to be quite unconscious she had conveyed that impression.

"How do you find your way home after you have been at the top of the ocean?" asked Hilda.

"Oh, when Father Neptune counts us and finds any missing he sends a whale to spout; sometimes he sends more than one, and we know where to dive when we see that."

"What do you eat besides seaweed sandwiches?" asked Hilda.

"Fish eggs, and very little fish," answered the mermaid. "When we have a party we have cake."

Hilda opened her eyes. "Where do you get cake?" she asked.

"We make it. We grind coral into flour and mix it with fish eggs; then we put it in a shell and send a mermaid to the top of the ocean with it and she holds it in the sun until it bakes. We go to the Gulf Stream and gather grapes and we have sea-foam and lemonade to drink."

"Lemonade?" said Hilda. "Where do you get your lemons?"

"Why, the sea-lemon!" replied the mermaid; "that is a small mussel-fish the colour of a lemon."

"What do you do at your parties – you cannot dance?" said Hilda.

"We swim to the music, circle around and dive and glide."

"But the music – where do you get musicians?" Hilda continued.

"We have plenty of music," replied the mermaid. "The sea-elephant trumpets for us; then there is the pipefish, the swordfish runs the scales of the sea-adder with his sword, the sea-shells blob, and altogether we have splendid music. But it is late, and we must not talk any more."

So the little mermaid curled herself up and soon they were asleep.

The sun shining in the window awakened Hilda next morning and she looked about her. The mermaid was not there, but Hilda was sure it had not been a dream, for she found pieces of seaweed on the floor, and every time she goes out in her boat she looks for her friend, and when the whales spout she knows they are telling the mermaids to come home.

LOVE, DEATH & TRAGEDY

Introduction

"IF YOU WILL give up half of your own life to Pramadvara, she will rise up again." So says the heavenly messenger to Ruru in the Indian tale, 'The Call of Yama, King of the Dead'. The young Brahman has fallen head-over-heels in love with this beautiful maiden but, bitten by a snake, she's died before they can be wed. Ruru's bride is resurrected, at the cost of a shortened life to come for him, but he is well contented with his bargain. Some sacrifice is needed, after all, to make any relationship work: that's the mundane reality underlined by the magic here. Myth may be extravagant in its storylines and symbolism but the truths it tells are basic and eternal. Love, death and tragedy are fundamental pillars of human existence. We're all going to find ourselves bumping up against them eventually. In some cases all at once, as in the Japanese story 'The Bell of Dojoji'. Anchin, an exemplary monk, falls hopelessly for the nature-spirit Kiohimé, Magic Lady of the Mere. Repenting of his sinful passion, he tries to escape her clutches, only to be burned alive in the great bronze temple bell.

The Story of Satyavati

ONE DAY THE FAIR GODDESS briefly returned to Shantanu. She brought with her a fair and noble son, who was endowed with the virtues of the Vasus. Then she departed never to come again. The heart of king Shantanu was moved towards the child, who became a handsome and powerful youth, and was named Satanava.

When Shantanu had grown old, he sought to marry a young and beautiful bride whom he loved. For one day as he walked beside the Jumna river he was attracted by a sweet and alluring perfume, which drew him through the trees until he beheld a maiden of celestial beauty with luminous black eyes. The king spoke to her and said: "Who are you, and whose daughter, timid one? What are you doing here?"

The maiden blessed Shantanu and said: "I am the daughter of a fisherman, and I ferry passengers across the river in my boat."

Now, the name of this fair maiden was Satyavati. Like Shakuntala, she was of miraculous origin, and had been adopted by her reputed father. It happened that a fish once carried away in its stomach two unborn babies, a girl and a boy, whose father was a great king. This fish was caught by a fisherman, who opened it and found the children. He sent the boy to the king and kept the girl, who was reared as his own daughter. She grew to be beautiful, but a fishy odour ever clung to her.

One day, as she ferried pilgrims across the Jumna, the high and pious Brahman Parashara entered her boat. He was moved by the maiden's great beauty. He desired that she should become the mother of his son, and promised that ever afterwards an alluring perfume would emanate from her body. He then caused a cloud to fall on the boat, and it vanished from sight.

When the fisher girl became the mother of a son, he grew suddenly before her eyes, and in a brief space was a man. His name was Vyasa; he wished his mother farewell, and rushed to the depths of a forest to spend his days in holy meditation. Before he left he said to Satyavati: "If ever you have need of me, think of me, and I will come to your aid."

When this wonder had been accomplished, Satyavati became a virgin again through the power of the great sage Parashara, and a delicious odour lingered about her ever afterwards.

On this maiden King Shantanu gazed with love. Then he sought the fisherman, and said he desired the maiden to be his bride. But the man refused to give his daughter to the king in marriage until he promised that her son should be chosen as heir to the throne. Shantanu could not consent to disinherit Satanava, son of Ganga, and went away with a heavy heart.

Greatly the king sorrowed in his heart because of his love for the dark-eyed maiden, and eventually Satanava was told of his secret love. So the noble son of Ganga went to search for the beautiful daughter of the fisherman, and he found her. After he told the fisherman of his mission, the fisherman said to him: "If Satyavati bears sons, they will not inherit the kingdom, for the king already has a son, and he will succeed him."

So Satanava made a vow renouncing his claim to the throne, and said: "If you will give your daughter to my father to be his queen, I, who am his heir, will never accept the throne, nor marry a wife, or be the father of children. If, then, Satyavati will become the mother of a son, he will surely be chosen as king." After he said this, the gods and Apsaras (the mist fairies) caused flowers to fall out of heaven on to the prince's head, and a voice came down the wind, saying: "This one is Bhishma."

From that day on, the son of Ganga was called Bhishma, which signifies the 'Terrible', for the vow that he had taken was terrible indeed.

Then Satyavati was given in marriage to the king, and she bore him two sons, who were named Chitrangada and Vichitra-virya.

In time Shantanu sank under the burden of his years, and his soul departed from his body. Bhishma was left to care of the queen-mother, Satyavati, and the two princes.

When the days of mourning went past, Bhishma renounced the throne in accordance with his vow, and Chitrangada was proclaimed king. This youth was a haughty ruler, and his reign was brief. He waged war against the Gandharai of the hills for three years, and was slain in battle by their king. Then Bhishma placed Vichitra-virya on the throne, and, as he was but a boy, Bhishma ruled as regent for some years.

The Call of Yama, King of the Dead

ONCE UPON A TIME Menaka, the beautiful Apsara (celestial fairy) left her newborn baby, the daughter of the King of Gandharvas (celestial elves) beside a hermitage. A Rishi, named Sthulakesha, found the child and raised her. She was called Pramadarva, and grew to be the most beautiful and most devout of all young women. Ruru, the great grandson of Bhrigu, looked at her with eyes of love, and at the request of his father, Pramati, the virgin was betrothed to the young Brahman.

Pramadarva was spending time with her friends a few days before the morning of the nuptials. As her time had come, she trod on a serpent, and the death-compelling reptile bit her. She then fell down and died, becoming more beautiful in death than she had been in life.

Brahmans assembled around the body of Pramadarva and sorrowed. Ruru crept away alone and went to a solitary place in the forest where he wept and cried out: "The fair one, whom I love more dearly than ever, lies dead on the bare ground. If I have performed penances and attained to great ascetic merit, let the power which I have achieved restore my beloved to life again."

Suddenly an emissary from the celestial regions appeared in front of Ruru, who said: "Your prayer is of no use, Ruru. One whose days have been numbered can never get back her own life again. Therefore you should not abandon your heart to grief. But the gods have decreed a means whereby you can receive back your beloved."

Ruru pleaded with him, and said: "Tell me how I can comply with the will of the celestials, so that I may be delivered from my grief."

The messenger replied: "If you will give up half of your own life to Pramadvara, she will rise up again."

Ruru happily consented, saying: "I will give up half of my own life so that my beloved may be restored to me."

Then the king of the Gandharvas and the celestial messenger stood before Dharma-rajah (Yama) and said: "If it be your will, Oh Mighty One, let Pramadarva rise up endowed with a part of Ruru's life."

The King of the Dead responded: "So be it."

After Dharma-rajah had spoken, the serpent-bitten young woman rose from the ground, and Ruru, whose life was curtailed for her sake, obtained the sweetest wife on earth. The happy pair spent their days deeply devoted to each other, awaiting the call of Yama at the appointed time.

The Prince and the Procuress

IN THE CITY OF GOLDEN-STREETS there reigned a King, named Viravikrama, whose officer of justice was one day taking a certain Barber away for punishment, when he was stopped by a strolling beggar, who held him by the skirts, and cried out, "Punish not this man – punish them that do wrong of their own knowledge." Being asked his meaning, he recited the following verses:

"I that could not leave alone
Streak-o'-Gold', must therefore moan.
She that took the Housewife's place
Lost the nose from off her face.
Take this lesson to your heart –
Fools for folly suffer smart."

Still further questioned, he told this story:

"I am Prince Kandarpaketu, son of the King of Ceylon. Walking one day in my summer-garden, I heard a merchant-captain telling of how that out at sea, deep under water, he had seen what was like nothing but the famous tree of Paradise, and sitting under it a lady of most radiant beauty, bedecked with strings of pearls like Lakshmi herself, reclining, with a lute in her hands, on what appeared to be a golden couch encrusted with precious stones.

"At once I engaged the captain and his ship, and steered to the spot of which he told me. On reaching it I saw the beautiful apparition as he had described it, and, transported with the exquisite beauty of the lady, I leapt after her into the sea. In a moment I found myself in a city of gold; and in an apartment of a golden palace, surrounded by young and beautiful girls, I found the Sea-queen.

"She saw my approach, and sent an attendant with a courteous message to meet me. In reply to my questions, I learned that the lady was the Princess Ratnamanjari, daughter of the King of All the Spirits – and how she had made a vow that whoever should first come to see her golden city, with his own eyes, should marry her. So I married her and spent many happy days in her delightful society.

"One day she took me aside, and said, 'Dear Prince! All these delights, and I myself, are yours to enjoy; only that picture over there, of the Fairy Streak-o'-Gold, that you must never touch!' For a long time I observed this command until at last, impelled by resistless curiosity, I laid my hand on the picture of Streak-o'-Gold. In an instant her little foot, lovely as the lotus-blossom, advanced from out of the painting, and launched me through sea and air into my own country.

"Since then I have been a miserable wanderer; and passing through this city, I happened to lodge at a Cowkeeper's hut, and saw the truth of this Barber's affair. The herdsman returned at night with his cattle, and found his wife talking with the wife of the Barber, who is no better than a madam. Enraged at this, the man beat his wife, tied her to the milking-post, and fell asleep.

"In the dead of the night the Barber's wife came back, and said to the woman, 'He, whom you know, is burnt with the cruel fire of your absence, and lies near to death; therefore go and console him, and I will tie myself to the post until you return.'

"This was done, and the Cowkeeper soon awoke. 'Ah, you light thing!' he said jeeringly, 'why do you not keep your promise, and meet your gallant man?'

"The Barber's wife could not reply; so becoming incensed, the man cried out, 'What! Do you scorn to speak to me? I will cut your nose off!' And so he did, and then he lay down to sleep again.

"Very soon the Cowkeeper's wife came back and asked if all was well. 'Look at my face!' said the Barber's wife, 'and you will see if all is well.' The woman could do nothing but take her place again, while the Barber's wife, picking up the severed nose, and at a sad loss of how to account for it, went to her house.

"In the morning, before it was light, the Barber called to her to bring his box of razors. She brought one only, and he flung it away in a passion. 'Oh, the knave!' she shouted out, 'Neighbours, neighbours, he has cut my nose off!' and so she took him before the officers.

"In the meantime, the Cowkeeper, wondering at his wife's patience, made some inquiry about her nose; to which she replied, 'Cruel wretch! You cannot harm a virtuous woman. If Yama and the seven guardians of the world know me chaste, then be my face unmaimed!'

"The herdsman hurried to fetch a light, and finding her features unaltered, he flung himself at her feet, and begged forgiveness. For:

"Never tires the fire of burning, never wearies death of slaying,
Nor the sea of drinking rivers, nor the bright-eyed of betraying."

The king's officer immediately dismissed Kandarpaketu, and did justice by setting the Barber free, shaving the head of the Barber's wife, and punishing the Cowkeeper's.

The advice of this story is that people must suffer for their own mistakes.

Samvarana and Tapati

TAPATI WAS OF ALL NYMPHS the most beautiful; she was perfectly symmetrical and exquisitely attired; she had faultless features, and black, large eyes; she was chaste and exceedingly well behaved. For a time the sun god considered that no husband could be found who was worthy of his daughter; and therefore knew no peace of mind, always thinking of the person he should choose.

One day, however, King Samvarana worshipped the sun, and made offerings of flowers and sweet perfumes, and Surya resolved to bestow his daughter upon this ideal man.

It came to pass that Samvarana went hunting deer on the mountains. He rode swiftly in pursuit of a nimble-footed stag, leaving his companions behind, until his horse expired with exhaustion. Then he wandered around alone. In a secluded wood he came across a maiden of exquisite beauty; he gazed at her for a while, thinking she was a goddess or the embodiment of the rays emanating from the sun. Her body was as radiant as fire and as spotless as the crescent moon; she stood motionless like a golden statue. The flowers and the creepers round about partook of her beauty, and seemed to be converted into gold. She was Tapati, daughter of the sun.

The king's eyes were captivated, his heart was wounded by the arrows of the love god Kama; he lost his peace of mind. Eventually he spoke and said: "Who are you, fair one? Maiden of sweet smiles, why do you linger in these lonely woods? I have never seen or heard of one so beautiful as you.... The love god tortures me."

That lotus-eyed maiden made no answer; she vanished from sight like lightning in the clouds.

The king rushed through the forest, mourning for her: he searched in vain; he stood motionless in grief; he fell down on the earth and fainted.

Then, smiling sweetly, the maiden appeared again. In honeyed words she said: "Arise, you tiger among kings. It is not proper that you should lose your reason in this manner."

Samvarana opened his eyes and saw Tapati. Weak with emotion he uttered: "I am burning with love for you, you black-eyed beauty. Oh, accept me. My life is ebbing away.... I have been bitten by Kama, who is like a venomous snake. Have mercy on me.... You of striking and faultless features, you of face like the lotus or the moon, you of voice sweet as that of singing Kinnaras, my life now depends on you. Without you, timid one, I am unable to live. Please do not cast me off; I need you to relieve me from this affliction by giving me your love. At the first sight you have distracted my heart. My mind wanders. Be merciful; I am your obedient slave, your adorer. Accept me.... you of lotus eyes, the flame of desire burns within me. Extinguish that flame by throwing on it the water of your love...."

Tapati replied: "I am not mistress of my own self. I am a maiden ruled by my father. If you love me, demand me of him. My heart has been robbed by you."

Then, revealing her identity, Tapati ascended to heaven, and once again Samvarana fell on the earth and fainted.

The ministers and followers of the king came searching for him, and found him lying forsaken on the ground like a rainbow dropped from the heavens. They sprinkled his face with cool lotus-scented water. When he revived, the monarch sent away all his followers except one minister. For twelve days he constantly worshipped the sun on the mountain top. Then a great Rishi, whom he had sent for, came to him, and the Rishi ascended to the sun. Before long he returned with Tapas, the sun god, having declared that Varanasi would be a worthy husband for his daughter.

For twelve years the king lived with his fairy bride in the mountain forests, and a regent ruled over the kingdom. But although the monarch enjoyed much bliss living the life of a celestial, the people of the kingdom suffered. For twelve years no rain fell, not even a drop of dew came from the skies, and no corn grew. The people were afflicted with famine; men grew reckless, and deserted their wives and children; the capital became like a city of the dead.

Then a great Rishi brought Varanasi back to his capital with his celestial bride. And after that things became as they were before. Rain fell in abundance and corn was grown. Revived by that foremost of monarchs of virtuous soul, the capital and the country was filled with joy. A son was born to the king, and his name was Kuru.

Dushyanta and Shakuntala

ONE DAY KING DUSHYANTA, that tiger among men, left his stately palace to go hunting with a great host and many horses and elephants. He entered a deep jungle and there killed numerous wild animals; his arrows wounded tigers at a distance; he felled those that came near with his great sword. Lions fled from before him, wild elephants stampeded in terror, deer sought to escape hastily, and birds rose in the air uttering cries of distress.

The king, attended by a single follower, pursued a deer across a desert plain, and entered a beautiful forest which delighted his heart, for it was deep and shady, and was cooled by soft winds; sweet-throated birds sang in the branches, and all round about there were blossoming trees and blushing flowers; he heard the soft notes of the kokila, and beheld many a green bower carpeted with grass and canopied by many-coloured creepers.

Dushyanta, abandoning the chase, wandered on until he came to a delightful and secluded hermitage, where he saw the sacred fire of that austere and high-souled Brahman, the saintly Kanva. It was a scene of peace and beauty. Blossoms from the trees covered the ground; tall were the trunks, and the branches were far-sweeping. A silvery stream went past, breaking on the banks in milk-white foam; it was the sacred River Malini, studded with green islands, loved by water fowl, and abounding with fish.

Then the king was taken with desire to visit the holy sage, Kanva, he who is without darkness. So he relieved himself of his royal insignia and entered the sacred grove alone. Bees were humming; birds trilled their many melodies; he heard the low chanting voices of Brahmans among the trees – those holy men who can take captive all human hearts....

When he reached the home of Kanva, he found that it was empty, and called out: "Who is here?" and the forest echoed his voice.

Then a beautiful black-eyed virgin came towards him, clad in a robe of bark. She reverenced the king and said: "What do you seek? I am your servant."

Dushyanta replied to the maiden of faultless form and gentle voice: "I have come to honour the wise and blessed Kanva. Tell me, fair and amiable one, where he has gone?"

The maiden answered: "My illustrious father is gathering herbs, but if you will wait he will return before long."

Dushyanta was entranced by the beauty and sweet smiles of the gentle girl, and his heart was moved towards her. So he spoke, saying: "Who are you, fairest one? Where do you come from and why do you wander alone in the woods? Beautiful maiden, you have taken captive my heart."

The bright-eyed one answered: "I am the daughter of the holy and high-souled Kanva, the ever-wise and ever-constant."

"But," said the king, "Kanva is chaste and austere and has always been celibate. He cannot have broken his rigid vow. How could it be that you were born the daughter of such a one?"

Then the maiden, who was named Shakuntala, because of the birds (shakunta) who had nursed her, revealed to the king the secret of her birth. Her real father was Vishwamitra, the holy sage who had been a Kshatriya and was made a Brahman in reward for his austerities. It came to pass that Indra became alarmed at his growing power, and he feared that the mighty sage of blazing energy would, by reason of his penances, cast down even him, the king of the gods, from his heavenly seat. So Indra commanded Menaka, the beautiful Apsara, to disturb the holy meditations of the sage, for he had already achieved such power that he created a second world and many stars. The nymph called on the wind god and on the god of love, and they went with her towards Vishwamitra.

Menaka danced before the brooding sage; then the wind god snatched away her moon-white garments, and the love god shot his arrows at Vishwamitra, whereupon that saintly man was stricken with love for the nymph of peerless beauty, and he wooed her and won her as his bride. So was he diverted from his austerities. In time Menaka became the mother of a girl babe, whom she cast away on the river bank.

Now the forest was full of lions and tigers, but vultures gathered round the infant and protected her from harm. Then Kanva found and took pity on the child; he said: "She will be mine own daughter."

Shakuntala said: "I was that child who was abandoned by the nymph, and now you know how Kanva came to be my father."

The king said: "Blessed are your words, princess. You are of royal birth. Be my bride, beautiful maid, and you will have garlands of gold and golden earrings and white pearls and rich robes; my kingdom also will be yours, timid one."

Then Shakuntala promised to be the king's bride, on condition that he would choose her son as the heir to his throne.

"As you desire, so let it be," said Dushyanta. And the fair one became his bride.

When Dushyanta went away he promised Shakuntala that he would send a mighty host to escort her to his palace.

When Kanva returned, the maiden did not leave her hiding place to greet him; but he searched out and found her, and he read her heart. "You have not broken the law," he said.

"Dushyanta, my husband, is noble and true, and a son will be born to me who will achieve great renown."

The Nodding Tiger

JUST OUTSIDE THE WALLS of a Chinese city there lived a young woodcutter named T'ang and his old mother, a woman of seventy. They were very poor and had a tiny one-room shanty, built of mud and grass, which they rented from a neighbour. Every day young T'ang rose bright and early and went up on the mountain near their house. There he spent the day cutting firewood to sell in the city near by. In the evening he would return home, take the wood to market, sell it, and bring back food for his mother and himself. Now, though these two people were poor, they were very happy, for the young man loved his mother dearly, and the old woman thought there was no one like her son in all the world. Their friends, however, felt sorry for them and said, "What a pity we have no grasshoppers here, so that the T'angs could have some food from heaven!"

One day young T'ang got up before daylight and started for the hills, carrying his axe on his shoulder. He bade his mother good-bye, telling her that he would be back early with a heavier load of wood than usual, for the morrow would be a holiday and they must eat good food. All day long Widow T'ang waited patiently, saying to herself over and over as she went about her simple work, "The good boy, the good boy, how he loves his old mother!"

In the afternoon she began watching for his return – but in vain. The sun was sinking lower and lower in the west, but still he did not come. At last the old woman was frightened. "My poor son!" she muttered. "Something has happened to him." Straining her feeble eyes, she looked along the mountain path. Nothing was to be seen there but a flock of sheep following the shepherd. "Woe is me!" moaned the woman. "My boy! my boy!" She took her crutch from its corner and limped off to a neighbour's house to tell him of her trouble and beg him to go and look for the missing boy.

Now this neighbour was kind-hearted, and willing to help old Mother T'ang, for he felt very sorry for her. "There are many wild beasts in the mountains," he said, shaking his head as he walked away with her, thinking to prepare the frightened woman for the worst, "and I fear that your son has been carried off by one of them." Widow T'ang gave a scream of horror and sank upon the ground. Her friend walked slowly up the mountain path, looking carefully for signs of a struggle. At last when he had gone half way up the slope he came to a little pile of torn clothing spattered with blood. The woodman's axe was lying by the side of the path, also his carrying pole and some rope. There could be no mistake: after making a brave fight, the poor youth had been carried off by a tiger.

Gathering up the torn garments, the man went sadly down the hill. He dreaded seeing the poor mother and telling her that her only boy was indeed gone for ever. At the foot of the mountain he found her still lying on the ground. When she looked up and saw what he was carrying, with a cry of despair she fainted away. She did not need to be told what had happened.

Friends bore her into the little house and gave her food, but they could not comfort her. "Alas!" she cried, "of what use is it to live? He was my only boy. Who will take care of me in my old age? Why have the gods treated me in this cruel way?"

She wept, tore her hair, and beat her chest, until people said she had gone mad. The longer she mourned, the more violent she became.

The next day, however, much to the surprise of her neighbours, she set out for the city, making her way along slowly by means of her crutch. It was a pitiful sight to see her, so old, so feeble, and so lonely. Everyone was sorry for her and pointed her out, saying, "See! the poor old soul has no one to help her!"

In the city she asked her way to the public hall. When she found the place she knelt at the front gate, calling out loudly and telling of her ill-fortune. Just at this moment the mandarin, or city judge, walked into the court room to try any cases which might be brought before him. He heard the old woman weeping and wailing outside, and bade one of the servants let her enter and tell him of her wrongs.

Now this was just what the Widow T'ang had come for. Calming herself, she hobbled into the great hall of trial.

"What is the matter, old woman? Why do you raise such an uproar in front of my yamen? Speak up quickly and tell me of your trouble."

"I am old and feeble," she began; "lame and almost blind. I have no money and no way of earning money. I have not one relative now in all the empire. I depended on my only son for a living. Every day he climbed the mountain, for he was a woodcutter, and every evening he came back home, bringing enough money for our food. But yesterday he went and did not return. A mountain tiger carried him off and ate him, and now, alas! there seems to be no help for it – I must die of hunger. My bleeding heart cries out for justice. I have come into this hall to-day, to beg your worship to see that the slayer of my son is punished. Surely the law says that none may shed blood without giving his own blood in payment."

"But, woman, are you mad?" cried the mandarin, laughing loudly. "Did you not say it was a tiger that killed your son? How can a tiger be brought to justice? Of a truth, you must have lost your senses."

The judge's questions were of no avail. The Widow T'ang kept up her clamour. She would not be turned away until she had gained her purpose. The hall echoed with the noise of her howling. The mandarin could stand it no longer. "Hold! woman," he cried, "stop your shrieking. I will do what you ask. Only go home and wait until I summon you to court. The slayer of your son shall be caught and punished."

The judge was, of course, only trying to get rid of the demented mother, thinking that if she were only once out of his sight, he could give orders not to let her into the hall again. The old woman, however, was too sharp for him. She saw through his plan and became more stubborn than ever.

"No, I cannot go," she answered, "until I have seen you sign the order for that tiger to be caught and brought into this judgment hall."

Now, as the judge was not really a bad man, he decided to humour the old woman in her strange plea. Turning to the assistants in the court room he asked which of them would be willing to go in search of the tiger. One of these men, named Li-neng, had been leaning against the wall, half asleep. He had been drinking heavily and so had not heard what had been going on in the room. One of his friends gave him a poke in the ribs just as the judge asked for volunteers.

Thinking the judge had called him by name, he stepped forward, knelt on the floor, saying, "I, Li-neng, can go and do the will of your worship."

"Very well, you will do," answered the judge. "Here is your order. Go forth and do your duty." So saying, he handed the warrant to Li-neng. "Now, old woman, are you satisfied?" he continued.

"Quite satisfied, your worship," she replied.

"Then go home and wait there until I send for you."

Mumbling a few words of thanks, the unhappy mother left the building.

When Li-neng went outside the court room, his friends crowded round him. "Drunken sot!" they laughed; "do you know what you have done?"

Li-neng shook his head. "Just a little business for the mandarin, isn't it? Quite easy."

"Call it easy, if you like. What! man, arrest a tiger, a man-eating tiger and bring him to the city! Better go and say good-bye to your father and mother. They will never see you again."

Li-neng slept off his drunkenness, and then saw that his friends were right. He had been very foolish. But surely the judge had meant the whole thing only as a joke! No such order had ever been written before! It was plain that the judge had hit on this plan simply to get rid of the wailing old woman. Li-neng took the warrant back to the judgment hall and told the mandarin that the tiger could not be found.

But the judge was in no mood for joking. "Can't be found? And why not? You agreed to arrest this tiger. Why is it that to-day you try to get out of your promise? I can by no means permit this, for I have given my word to satisfy the old woman in her cry for justice."

Li-neng knelt and knocked his head on the floor. "I was drunk," he cried, "when I gave my promise. I knew not what you were asking. I can catch a man, but not a tiger. I know nothing of such matters. Still, if you wish it, I can go into the hills and hire hunters to help me."

"Very well, it makes no difference how you catch him, as long as you bring him into court. If you fail in your duty, there is nothing left but to beat you until you succeed. I give you five days."

During the next few days Li-neng left no stone unturned in trying to find the guilty tiger. The best hunters in the country were employed. Night and day they searched the hills, hiding in mountain caves, watching and waiting, but finding nothing. It was all very trying for Li-neng, since he now feared the heavy hands of the judge more than the claws of the tiger. On the fifth day he had to report his failure. He received a thorough beating, fifty blows on the back. But that was not the worst of it. During the next six weeks, try as he would, he could find no traces of the missing animal. At the end of each five days, he got another beating for his pains. The poor fellow was in despair. Another month of such treatment would lay him on his deathbed. This he knew very well, and yet he had little hope. His friends shook their heads when they saw him. "He is drawing near the wood," they said to each other, meaning that he would soon be in his coffin. "Why don't you flee the country?" they asked him. "Follow the tiger's example. You see he has escaped completely. The judge would make no effort to catch you if you should go across the border into the next province."

Li-neng shook his head on hearing this advice. He had no desire to leave his family for ever, and he felt sure of being caught and put to death if he should try to run away.

One day after all the hunters had given up the search in disgust and gone back to their homes in the valley, Li-neng entered a mountain temple to pray. The tears rained down his cheeks as he knelt before the great fierce-looking idol. "Alas! I am a dead man!" he moaned between his prayers; "a dead man, for now there is no hope. Would that I had never touched a drop of wine!"

Just then he heard a slight rustling near by. Looking up, he saw a huge tiger standing at the temple gate. But Li-neng was no longer afraid of tigers. He knew there was only one way to save himself. "Ah," he said, looking the great cat straight in the eye, "you have come to eat me, have you? Well, I fear you would find my flesh a trifle tough, since I have been beaten with four hundred blows during these six weeks. You are the same fellow that carried off the woodman last month, aren't you? This woodman was an only son, the sole support of an old mother. Now this poor woman has reported you to the mandarin, who, in turn, has had a warrant drawn up for your arrest. I have been sent out to find you and lead you to trial. For some reason or other you have acted the coward, and remained in hiding. This has been the cause of my beating. Now I don't want to suffer any longer as a result of your murder. You must come with me to the city and answer the charge of killing the woodman."

All the time Li-neng was speaking, the tiger listened closely. When the man was silent, the animal made no effort to escape, but, on the contrary, seemed willing and ready to be captured. He bent his head forward and let Li-neng slip a strong chain over it. Then he followed the man quietly down the mountain, through the crowded streets of the city, into the court room. All along the way there was great excitement. "The man-slaying tiger has been caught," shouted the people. "He is being led to trial."

The crowd followed Li-neng into the hall of justice. When the judge walked in, everyone became as quiet as the grave. All were filled with wonder at the strange sight of a tiger being called before a judge.

The great animal did not seem to be afraid of those who were watching so curiously. He sat down in front of the mandarin, for all the world like a huge cat. The judge rapped on the table as a signal that all was ready for the trial.

"Tiger," said he, turning toward the prisoner, "did you eat the woodman whom you are charged with killing?"

The tiger gravely nodded his head.

"Yes, he killed my boy!" screamed the aged mother. "Kill him! Give him the death that he deserves!"

"A life for a life is the law of the land," continued the judge, paying no attention to the forlorn mother, but looking the accused directly in the eye. "Did you not know it? You have robbed a helpless old woman of her only son. There are no relatives to support her. She is crying for vengeance. You must be punished for your crime. The law must be enforced. However, I am not a cruel judge. If you can promise to take the place of this widow's son and support the woman in her old age, I am quite willing to spare you from a disgraceful death. What say you, will you accept my offer?"

The gaping people craned their necks to see what would happen, and once more they were surprised to see the savage beast nod his head in silent agreement.

"Very well, then, you are free to return to your mountain home; only, of course, you must remember your promise."

The chains were taken from the tiger's neck, and the great animal walked silently out of the yamen, down the street, and through the gate opening towards his beloved mountain cave.

Once more the old woman was very angry. As she hobbled from the room, she cast sour glances at the judge, muttering over and over again, "Who ever heard of a tiger taking the place of a son? A pretty game this is, to catch the brute, and then to set him free." There was nothing for her to do, however, but to return home, for the judge had given strict orders that on no account was she to appear before him again.

Almost broken-hearted she entered her desolate hovel at the foot of the mountain. Her neighbours shook their heads as they saw her. "She cannot live long," they said. "She has the look of death on her wrinkled face. Poor soul! she has nothing to live for, nothing to keep her from starving."

But they were mistaken. Next morning when the old woman went outside to get a breath of fresh air she found a newly killed deer in front of her door. Her tiger-son had begun to keep his promise, for she could see the marks of his claws on the dead animal's body. She took the carcass into the house and dressed it for the market. On the city streets next day she had no trouble in selling the flesh and skin for a handsome sum of money. All had heard of the tiger's first gift, and no one was anxious to drive a close bargain.

Laden with food, the happy woman went home rejoicing, with money enough to keep her for many a day. A week later the tiger came to her door with a roll of cloth and some money in his mouth. He dropped these new gifts at her feet and ran away without even waiting for her thank-you. The Widow T'ang now saw that the judge had acted wisely. She stopped grieving for her dead son and began to love in his stead the handsome animal that had come to take his place so willingly.

The tiger grew much attached to his foster-mother and often purred contentedly outside her door, waiting for her to come and stroke his soft fur. He no longer had the old desire to kill. The sight of blood was not nearly so tempting as it had been in his younger days. Year after year he brought the weekly offerings to his mistress until she was as well provided for as any other widow in the country.

At last in the course of nature the good old soul died. Kind friends laid her away in her last resting place at the foot of the great mountain. There was money enough left out of what she had saved to put up a handsome tombstone, on which this story was written just as you have read it here. The faithful tiger mourned long for his dear mistress. He lay on her grave, wailing like a child that had lost its mother. Long he listened for the voice he had loved so well, long he searched the mountain-slopes, returning each night to the empty cottage, but all in vain. She whom he loved was gone for ever.

One night he vanished from the mountain, and from that day to this no one in that province has ever seen him. Some who know this story say that he died of grief in a secret cave which he had long used as a hiding-place. Others add, with a wise shrug of the shoulders, that, like Shanwang, he was taken to the Western Heaven, there to be rewarded for his deeds of virtue and to live as a fairy for ever afterwards.

The Bell of Dōjōji

THE MONK ANCHIN WAS YOUNG IN YEARS but old in scholarship. Every day for many hours he read the Great Books of the Good Law and never wearied, and hard characters were not hard to him.

The monk Anchin was young in years but old in holiness; he kept his body under by fastings and watchings and long prayers. He was acquainted with the blessedness of sublime meditations. His countenance was white as ivory and as smooth; his eyes were deep as a brown pool in autumn; his smile was that of a Buddha; his voice was like an angel's. He dwelt with a score of holy men in a monastery of the mountains, where he learned the mystic 'Way of the Gods.' He was bound to his order by the strictest vows, but was content, rejoicing in the shade of the great pine trees and the sound of the running water of the streams.

Now it happened that on a day in springtime, the old man, his Abbot, sent the young monk Anchin upon an errand of mercy. And he said, "My son, bind your sandals fast and tie spare sandals to your girdle, take your hat and your staff and your rosary and begging bowl, for you have far to go, over mountain and stream, and across the great plain."

So the monk Anchin made him ready.

"My son," the Abbot said, "if any wayfarer do you a kindness, forget not to commend him to the gods for the space of nine existences."

"I will remember," said the monk, and so he set forth upon his way.

Over mountain and stream he passed, and as he went his spirit was wrapped in contemplation, and he recited the Holy Sutras aloud in a singing voice. And the Wise Birds called and twittered from branch to branch of the tall trees, the birds that are beloved of Buddha. One bird chanted the grand Scripture of the Nicheten, the Praise of the Sutra of the Lotus, of the Good Law, and the other bird called upon his Master's name, for he cried:

"O thou Compassionate Mind! O thou Compassionate Mind!"

The monk smiled. "Sweet and happy bird," he said.

And the bird answered, "O thou Compassionate Mind! … O thou Compassionate Mind!"

When the monk Anchin came to the great plain, the sun was high in the heavens, and all the blue and golden flowers of the plain languished in the noontide heat. The monk likewise became very weary, and when he beheld the Marshy Mere, where were bulrush and sedge that cooled their feet in the water, he laid him down to rest under a sycamore tree that grew by the Marshy Mere.

Over the mere and upon the farther side of it there hung a glittering haze.

Long did the monk Anchin lie; and as he lay he looked through the glittering haze, and as he looked the haze quivered and moved and grew and gathered upon the farther side of the mere. At the last it drew into a slender column of vapour, and out of the vapour there came forth a very dazzling lady. She wore a robe of green and gold, interwoven, and golden sandals on her slender feet. In her hands were jewels – in each hand one bright jewel like a star. Her hair was tied with a braid of scarlet, and she had a crown of scarlet flowers. She came, skirting the Marshy Mere. She came, gliding in and out of the bulrush and the sedge. In the silence there could be heard the rustle of her green skirt upon the green grass.

The monk Anchin stumbled to his feet and, trembling, he leaned against the sycamore tree.

Nearer and nearer came the lady, till she stood before Anchin and looked into his eyes. With the jewel that was in her right hand she touched his forehead and his lips. With the jewel that was in her left hand she touched his rice-straw hat and his staff and his rosary and his begging bowl. After this she had him safe in thrall. Then the wind blew a tress of her hair across his face, and when he felt it he gave one sob.

For the rest of his journey the monk went as a man in a dream. Once a rich traveller riding on horseback threw a silver coin into Anchin's begging bowl; once a woman gave him a piece of cake made of millet; and once a little boy knelt down and tied the fastening of his sandal that had become loose. But each time the monk passed on without a word, for he forgot to commend the souls of these compassionate ones for the space of nine existences. In the tree-tops the Wise Birds of Buddha sang for him no more, only from the thicket was heard the cry of the Hototogisu, the bird lovelorn and forsaken.

Nevertheless, well or ill, he performed his errand of mercy and returned to the monastery by another way.

Howbeit, sweet peace left him from the hour in which he had seen the lady of the Marshy Mere. The Great Books of the Good Law sufficed him no longer; no more was he acquainted with the blessedness of divine meditations. His heart was hot within him; his eyes burned and his soul longed after the lady of the green and golden robe.

She had told him her name, and he murmured it in his sleep. "Kiohimé – Kiohimé!" Waking, he repeated it instead of his prayers – to the great scandal of the brethren, who whispered together and said, "Is our brother mad?"

At length Anchin went to the good Abbot, and in his ear poured forth all his tale in a passion of mingled love and grief, humbly asking what he must do.

The Abbot said, "Alack, my son, now you suffer for sin committed in a former life, for Karma must needs be worked out."

Anchin asked him, "Then is it past help?"

"Not that," said the Abbot, "but you are in a very great strait."

"Are you angry with me?" said Anchin.

"Nay, Heaven forbid, my poor son."

"Then what must I do?"

"Fast and pray, and for a penance stand in the ice-cold water of our mountain torrent an hour at sunrise and an hour at sunset. Thus shall you be purged from carnal affection and escape the perils of illusion."

So Anchin fasted and prayed, he scourged his body, and hour after hour he did penance in the ice-cold water of the torrent. Wan as a ghost he grew, and his eyes were like flames. His trouble would not leave him. A battle raged in his breast. He could not be faithful to his vows and faithful to his love.

The brethren wondered, "What can ail the monk Anchin, who was so learned and so holy – is he bewitched by a fox or a badger, or can he have a devil?"

But the Abbot said, "Let be."

Now on a hot night of summer, the monk being sleepless in his cell, he was visited by Kiohimé, the magic lady of the mere. The moonlight was on her hands and her long sleeves. Her robe was green and gold, interwoven; golden were her sandals. Her hair was braided with scarlet and adorned with scarlet flowers.

"Long, long have I waited for thee on the plains," she said. "The night wind sighs in the sedge – the frogs sing by the Marshy Mere. Come, lord...."

But he cried, "My vows that I have vowed – alas! The love that I love. I keep faith and loyalty, the bird in my bosom ... I may not come."

She smiled. "May not?" she said, and with that she lifted the monk Anchin in her arms.

But he, gathering all his strength together, tore himself from her and fled from the place. Barefooted and bareheaded he went, his white robe flying, through the dark halls of the monastery, where the air was heavy with incense and sweet with prayers, where the golden Amida rested upon her lotus, ineffably smiling. He leaped the grey stone steps that led down from her shrine and gained the pine trees and the mountain path. Down, down he fled on the rough way, the nymph Kiohimé pursuing. As for her, her feet never touched the ground, and she spread her green sleeves like wings. Down, down they fled together, and so close was she behind him that the monk felt her breath upon his neck.

"As a young goddess, she is fleet of foot..." he moaned.

At last they came to the famed temple of Dōjōji, which was upon the plains. By this Anchin sobbed and staggered as he ran; his knees failed him and his head swam.

"I am lost," he cried, "for a hundred existences." But with that he saw the great temple bell of Dōjōji that hung but a little way from the ground. He cast himself down and crept beneath it, and so deemed himself sheltered and secure.

Then came Kiohimé, the Merciless Lady, and the moonlight shone upon her long sleeves. She did not sigh, nor cry, nor call upon her love. She stood still for a little space and smiled. Then lightly she sprang to the top of the great bronze bell of Dōjōji, and with her sharp teeth she bit through the ropes that held it, so that the bell came to the ground and the monk was a prisoner. And Kiohimé embraced the bell with her arms. She crept about it, she crawled about it and her green robe flowed over it. Her green robe glittered with a thousand golden scales; long flames burst from her lips and from her eyes; a huge and fearsome Dragon, she wound and coiled herself about the bell of Dōjōji. With her Dragon's tail she lashed the bell, and lashed it till its bronze was red hot.

Still she lashed the bell, while the monk called piteously for mercy. And when he was very quiet she did not stop. All the night long the frogs sang by the Marshy Mere and the wind sighed in the sedges. But the Dragon Lady was upon the bell of Dōjōji, and she lashed it furiously with her tail till dawn.

The Enchanted Cave

A LONG, LONG TIME AGO, Prince Cuglas, master of the hounds to the high King of Erin, set out from Tara to the chase. As he was leaving the palace the light mists were drifting away from the hill-tops, and the rays of the morning sun were falling aslant on the grinan or sunny bower of the Princess Ailinn. Glancing towards it the prince doffed his plumed and jewelled hunting-cap, and the princess answered his salute by a wave of her little hand, that was as white as a wild rose in the hedges in June, and leaning from her bower, she watched the huntsman until his tossing plumes were hidden by the green waving branches of the woods.

The Princess Ailinn was over head and ears in love with Cuglas, and Cuglas was over head and ears in love with the Princess Ailinn, and he believed that never was summer morning half as bright, or as sweet, or as fair as she. The glimpse which he had just caught of her filled his heart with delight, and almost put all thought of hunting out of his head, when suddenly the tuneful cries of the hounds, answered by a hundred echoes from the groves, broke upon his ear.

The dogs had started a dappled deer that bounded away through the forest. The prince, spurring his gallant steed, pushed on in eager pursuit.

On through the forest sped the deer, through soft, green, secret ways and flowery dells, then out from the forest, up heathery hills, and over long stretches of moorland, and across brown rushing streams, sometimes in view of the hounds, sometimes lost to sight, but always ahead of them.

All day long the chase continued, and at last, when the sun was sinking, the dogs were close upon the panting deer, and the prince believed he was about to secure his game, when the deer suddenly disappeared through the mouth of a cave which opened before him. The dogs followed at his heels, and the prince endeavoured to rein in his steed, but the impetuous animal bore him on, and soon was clattering over the stony floor of the cave in perfect darkness. Cuglas could hear ahead of him the cries of the hounds growing fainter and fainter, as they increased the distance between them and him. Then the cries ceased altogether, and the only sound the prince heard was the noise of his horse's hoofs sounding in the hollow cave. Once more he endeavoured to check his career, but the reins broke in his hands, and in that instant the prince felt the horse had taken a plunge into a gulf, and was sinking down and down, as a stone cast from the summit of a cliff sinks down to the sea. At last the horse struck the ground again, and the prince was almost thrown out of his saddle, but he succeeded in regaining his seat. Then on through the darkness galloped the steed, and when he came into the light the prince's eyes were for some time unable to bear it. But when he got used to the brightness he saw he was galloping over a grassy plain, and in the distance he perceived the hounds rushing towards a wood faintly visible through a luminous summer haze. The prince galloped on, and as he approached the wood he saw coming towards him a comely champion, wearing a shining brown cloak, fastened by a bright bronze spear-like brooch, and bearing a white hazel wand in one hand, and a single-edged sword with a hilt made from the tooth of a sea-horse in the other; and the prince knew by the dress of the champion, and by his wand and sword, that he was a royal herald. As the herald came close to him the prince's steed stopped of his own accord.

"You are welcome, Cuglas," said the herald, "and I have been sent by the Princess Crede to greet you and to lead you to her court, where you have been so long expected."

"I know not how this may be," said Cuglas.

"How it has come about I shall tell you as we go along," said the herald. "The Princess Crede is the Queen of the Floating Island. And it chanced, once upon a day, when she was visiting her fairy kinsmen, who dwell in one of the pleasant hills that lie near Tara, she saw you with the high king and princes and nobles of Erin following the chase. And seeing you her heart went out to you, and wishing to bring you to her court, she sent one of her nymphs, in the form of a deer, to lure you on through the cave, which is the entrance to this land."

"I am deeply honoured by the preference shown me by the princess," said Cuglas, "but I may not tarry in her court; for above in Erin there is the Lady Ailinn, the loveliest of all the ladies who grace the royal palace, and before the princess and chiefs of Erin she has promised to be my bride."

"Of that I know not," said the herald; "but a true champion, like you, cannot, I know, refuse to come with me to the court of the Princess Crede."

As the herald had said these words the prince and he were on the verge of the wood, and they entered upon a mossy pathway that broadened out as they advanced until it was as wide as one of the great roads of Erin. Before they had gone very far the prince heard the tinkling of silver bells in the distance, and almost as soon as he heard them he saw coming up towards him a troop of warriors on coal black steeds. All the warriors wore helmets of shining silver, and cloaks of blue silk. And on the horses' breasts were crescents of silver, on which were hung tiny silver bells, shaking out music with the motion of the horses. As the prince approached the champions they lowered their spears, and dividing in two lines the prince and the herald passed between the ranks, and the champions, forming again, followed on behind the prince.

At last they passed through the wood, and they found themselves on a green plain, speckled with flowers, and they had not gone far when the prince saw coming towards him a hundred champions on snow-white steeds, and around the breasts of the steeds were crescents of gold, from which were hanging little golden bells. The warriors all wore golden helmets, and the shafts of their shining spears were of gold, and golden sandals on their feet, and yellow silken mantles fell down over their shoulders. And when the prince came near them they lowered their lances, and then they turned their horses' heads around and marched before him. And it was not long until above the pleasant jingle of the bells the prince heard the measured strains of music, and he saw coming towards him a band of harpers, dressed in green and gold, and when the harpers had saluted the prince they marched in front of the cavalcade, playing all the time, and it was not long until they came to a stream that ran like a blue riband around the foot of a green hill, on the top of which was a sparkling palace; the stream was crossed by a golden bridge, so narrow that the horsemen had to go two-by-two. The herald asked the prince to halt and to allow all the champions to go before him; and the cavalcade ascended the hill, the sunlight brightly glancing on helmet and on lance, and when it reached the palace the horsemen filed around the walls.

When at length the prince and herald crossed the bridge and began to climb the hill, the prince thought he felt the ground moving under them, and on looking back he could see no sign of the golden bridge, and the blue stream had already become as wide as a great river, and was becoming wider every second.

"You are on the floating island now," said the herald, "and before you is the palace of the Princess Crede."

At that moment the queen came out through the palace door, and the prince was so dazzled by her beauty, that only for the golden bracelet he wore upon his right arm, under the sleeve of his silken tunic, he might almost have forgotten the Princess Ailinn.

This bracelet was made by the dwarfs who dwell in the heart of the Scandinavian Mountains, and was sent with other costly presents by the King of Scandinavia to the King of Erin, and he gave it to the princess, and it was the virtue of this bracelet, that whoever was wearing it could not forget the person who gave it to him, and it could never be loosened from the arm by any art or magic spell; but if the wearer, even for a single moment, liked anyone better than the person who gave it to him, that very moment the bracelet fell off from the arm and could never again be fastened on. And when the princess promised her hand in marriage to the Prince Cuglas, she closed the bracelet on his arm.

The fairy queen knew nothing about the bracelet, and she hoped that before the prince was long in the floating island he would forget all about the princess.

"You are welcome, Cuglas," said the queen, as she held out her hand, and, Cuglas having thanked her for her welcome, they entered the palace together.

"You must be weary after your long journey," said the queen. "My page will lead you to your apartments, where a bath of the cool blue waters of the lake has been made ready for you, and when you have taken your bath the pages will lead you to the banquet hall, where the feast is spread."

At the feast the prince was seated beside the queen, and she talked to him of all the pleasures that were in store for him in fairyland, where pain, and sickness, and sorrow, and old age, are unknown, and where every rosy hour that flies is brighter than the one that has fled before it. And when the feast was ended the queen opened the dance with the prince, and it was not until the moon was high above the floating island that the prince retired to rest.

He was so tired after his journey and the dancing that he fell into a sound sleep. When he awoke the next morning the sun was shining brightly, and he heard outside the palace the jingle of bells and the music of baying hounds, and his heart was stirred by memories of the many pleasant days on which he had led the chase over the plains and through the green woods of Tara.

He looked out through the window, and he saw all the fairy champions mounted on their steeds ready for the chase, and at their head the fairy queen. And at that moment the pages came to say the queen wished to know if he would join them, and the prince went out and found his steed ready saddled and bridled, and they spent the day hunting in the forest that stretched away for miles behind the palace, and the night in feasting and dancing.

When the prince awoke the following morning he was summoned by the pages to the presence of the queen. The prince found the queen on the lawn outside the palace surrounded by her court.

"We shall go on the lake today, Cuglas," said the queen, and taking his arm she led him along the water's edge, all the courtiers following.

When she was close to the water she waved her wand, and in a second a thousand boats, shining like glass, shot up from beneath the lake and set their bows against the bank. The queen and Cuglas stepped into one, and when they were seated two fairy harpers took their places in the prow. All the other boats were soon thronged by fairies, and then the queen waved her wand again, and an awning of purple silk rose over the boat, and silken awning of various colours over the others, and the royal boat moved off from the bank followed by all the rest, and in every boat sat a harper with a golden harp, and when the queen waved her wand for the third time, the harpers struck the trembling chords, and to the sound of the delightful music the boats glided over the sunlit lake. And on they went until they approached the mouth of a gentle river sliding down between banks clad with trees. Up the river, close to the bank and under the drooping trees, they sailed, and when they came to a bend in the river, from which the lake could be no longer seen, they pushed their prows in against the bank, and the queen and Cuglas, and all the party, left the boats and went on under the trees until they came to a mossy glade.

Then the queen waved her wand, and silken couches were spread under the trees, and she and Cuglas sat on one apart from the others, and the courtiers took their places in proper order.

And the queen waved her wand again, and wind shook the trees above them, and the most luscious fruit that was ever tasted fell down into their hands; and when the feast was over there was dancing in the glades to the music of the harps, and when they were tired dancing they set out for the boats, and the moon was rising above the trees as they sailed away over the lake, and it was not long until they reached the bank below the fairy palace.

Well, between hunting in the forest, and sailing over the lake, and dancing in the greenwood glade and in the banquet hall, the days passed, but all the time the prince was thinking of the Princess Ailinn, and one moonlit night, when he was lying awake on his couch thinking of her, a shadow was suddenly cast on the floor.

The prince looked towards the window, and what should he see sitting on the sill outside but a little woman tapping the pane with a golden bodkin.

The prince jumped from his couch and opened the window, and the little woman floated on the moonbeams into the room and sat down on the floor.

"You are thinking of the Princess Ailinn," said the little woman.

"I never think of anyone else," said the prince.

"I know that," said the little woman, "and it's because of your love for each other, and because her mother was a friend to me in the days gone by, that I have come here to try and help you; but there is not much time for talking, the night advances. At the bank below a boat awaits you. Step into it and it will lead you to the mainland, and when you reach it you will find before you a path that will take you to the green fields of Erin and the plains of Tara. I know you will have to face danger. I know not what kind of danger; but whatever it may be do not draw your sword before you tread upon the mainland, for if you do you shall never reach it, and the boat will come back again to the floating island; and now go and may luck go with you;" and saying this the little woman climbed up the moonbeams and disappeared.

The prince left the palace and descended to the lake, and there before him he saw a glistening boat; he stepped into it, and the boat went on and on beneath the moon, and at last he saw the mainland, and he could trace a winding pathway going away from the shore. The sight filled his heart with joy, but suddenly the milk-white moonshine died away, and looking up to the sky he saw the moon turning fiery red, and the waters of the lake, shining like silver a moment before, took a blood-red hue, and a wind arose that stirred the waters, and they leaped up against the little boat, tossing it from side to side. While Cuglas was wondering at the change, he heard a strange, unearthly noise ahead of him, and a bristling monster, lifting its claws above the water, in a moment was beside the boat and stuck one of his claws in the left arm of the prince, and pierced the flesh to the bone. Maddened by the pain the prince drew his sword and chopped off the monster's claw. The monster disappeared beneath the lake, and, as it did so, the colour of the water changed, and the silver moonlight shone down from the sky again, but the boat no longer went on towards the mainland, but sped back towards the floating island, while forth from the island came a fleet of fairy boats to meet it, led by the shallop of the fairy queen. The queen greeted the prince as if she knew not of his attempted flight, and to the music of the harps the fleet returned to the palace.

The next day passed and the night came, and again the prince was lying on the couch, thinking of the Princess Ailinn, and again he saw the shadow on the floor and heard the tapping against the window.

And when he opened it the little woman slid into the room.

"You failed last night," she said, "but I come to give you another chance. Tomorrow the queen must set out on a visit to her fairy kinsmen, who dwell in the green hill near the plain of Tara; she cannot take you with her, for if your feet once touched the green grass that grows in the fruitful fields of Erin, she could never bring you back again. And so, when you find she has left the palace, go at once into the banquet hall and look behind the throne, and you will see a small door let down into the ground. Pull this up and descend the steps which you will see. Where they lead to I cannot tell. What dangers may be before you I do not know; but this I know, if you accept anything, no matter what it is, from anyone you may meet on your way, you shall not set foot on the soil of Erin."

And having said this the little woman, rising from the floor, floated out through the window.

The prince returned to his couch, and the next morning, as soon as he heard the queen had left the palace, he hastened to the banquet hall. He discovered the door and descended the steps, and he found himself in a gloomy and lonesome valley. Jagged mountains, black as night, rose on either side, and huge rocks seemed ready to topple down upon him at every step. Through broken clouds a watery moon shed a faint, fitful light, that came and went as the clouds, driven by a moaning wind, passed over the valley.

Cuglas, nothing daunted, pushed on boldly until a bank of cloud shut out completely the struggling moon, and closing over the valley covered it like a pall, leaving him in perfect darkness. At the same moment the moaning wind died away, and with it died away all sound. The darkness and the death-like silence sent an icy chill to the heart of Cuglas. He held his hand close to his eyes, but he saw it not. He shouted that he might hear the sound of his own voice, but he heard it not. He stamped his foot on the rocky ground, but no sound was returned to him. He rattled his sword in its brazen scabbard, but it gave no answer back to him. His heart grew colder and colder, when suddenly the cloud above him was rent in a dozen places, and lightning flashed through the valley, and the thunder rolled over the echoing mountains. In the lurid glare of the lightning Cuglas saw a hundred ghostly forms sweeping towards him, uttering as they came nearer and nearer shrieks so terrible that the silence of death could more easily be borne. Cuglas turned to escape, but they hemmed him round, and pressed their clammy hands upon his face.

With a yell of horror he drew his sword and slashed about him, and that very moment the forms vanished, the thunder ceased, the dark cloud passed, and the sun shone out as bright as on a summer day, and then Cuglas knew the forms he had seen were those of the wild people of the glen.

With renewed courage he pursued his way through the valley, and after three or four windings it took him out upon a sandy desert. He had no sooner set foot upon the desert than he heard behind him a crashing sound louder than thunder. He looked around, and he saw that the walls of mountain through which he had just passed had fallen into the valley, and filled it up so that he could no longer tell where it had been.

The sun was beating fiercely on the desert, and the sands were almost as hot as burning cinders; and as Cuglas advanced over them his body became dried up, and his tongue clove to the roof of his mouth, and when his thirst was at its height a fountain of sparkling water sprang up in the burning plain a few paces in front of him; but when he came up quite close to it and stretched out his parched hands to cool them in the limped waters, the fountain vanished as suddenly as it appeared. With great pain, and almost choking with heat and thirst, he struggled on, and again the fountain sprang up in front of him and moved before him, almost within his reach. At last he came to the end of the desert, and he saw a green hill up which a pathway climbed; but as he came to the foot of the hill, there, sitting right in his way, was a beautiful fairy holding out towards him a crystal cup, over the rim of which flowed water as clear as crystal. Unable to resist the temptation, the prince seized the cold, bright goblet, and drank the water. When he did so his thirst vanished, but the fairy, and the green hill, and the burning desert disappeared, and he was standing in the forest behind the palace of the fairy queen.

That evening the queen returned, and at the feast she talked as gaily to the prince as if she knew not of his attempt to leave the Floating Island, and the prince spoke as gaily as he could to her, although in his heart there was sadness when he remembered that if he had only dashed away the crystal cup, he would be at that moment in the royal banquet hall of Tara, sitting beside the Princess Ailinn.

And he thought the feast would never end; but it was over at last, and the prince returned to his apartments. And that night, as he lay on his couch, he kept his eyes fixed upon the window; but hours passed, and there was no sign of anyone. At long last, and when he had given up all hope of seeing her, he heard a tapping at the window, and he got up and opened it, and the little woman came in.

"You failed again today," said she – "failed just at the very moment when you were about to step on the green hills of Erin. I can give you only one chance more. It will be your last. The queen will go hunting in the morning. Join the hunt, and when you are separated from the rest of the party in the wood throw your reins upon your horse's neck and he will lead you to the edge of the lake. Then cast this golden bodkin into the lake in the direction of the mainland, and a golden bridge will be thrown across, over which you can pass safely to the fields of Erin; but take care and do not draw your sword, for if you do your steed will bear you back again to the Floating Island, and here you must remain for ever." Then handing the bodkin to the prince, and saying goodbye, the little woman disappeared.

The next morning the queen and the prince and all the court went out to hunt, and a fleet white deer started out before them, and the royal party pressed after him in pursuit. The prince's steed outstripped the others, and when he was alone the prince flung the reins upon his horse's neck, and before long he came to the edge of the lake.

Then the prince cast the bodkin on to the water, and a golden bridge was thrown across to the mainland, and the horse galloped on to it, and when the prince was more than half-way he saw riding towards him a champion wearing a silver helmet, and carrying on his left arm a silver shield, and holding in his right hand a gleaming sword. As he came nearer he struck his shield with his sword and challenged the prince to battle. The prince's sword almost leaped out of its scabbard at the martial sound, and, like a true knight of Tara, he dashed against his foe, and swinging his sword above his head, with one blow he clove the silver helmet, and the strange warrior reeled from his horse and fell upon the golden bridge. The prince, content with this achievement, spurred his horse to pass the fallen champion, but the horse refused to stir, and the bridge broke in two almost at his feet, and the part of it between him and the mainland disappeared beneath the lake, carrying with it the horse and the body of the champion, and before the prince could recover from his surprise, his steed wheeled round and was galloping back, and when he reached the land he rushed through the forest, and the prince was not able to pull him up until he came to the palace door.

All that night the prince lay awake on his couch with his eyes fixed upon the window, but no shadow fell upon the floor, and there was no tapping at the pane, and with a heavy heart he joined the hunting party in the morning. And day followed day, and his heart was sadder and sadder, and found no pleasure in the joys and delights of fairyland. And when all in the palace were at rest he used to roam through the forest, always thinking of the Princess Ailinn, and hoping against hope that the little woman would come again to him, but at last he began to despair of ever seeing her. It chanced one night he rambled so far that he found himself on the verge of the lake, at the very spot from which the golden bridge had been thrown across the waters, and as he gazed wistfully upon them a boat shot up and came swiftly to the bank, and who should he see sitting in the stern but the little woman.

"Ah, Cuglas, Cuglas," she said, "I gave you three chances, and you failed in all of them."

"I should have borne the pain inflicted by the monster's claw," said Cuglas. "I should have borne the thirst on the sandy desert, and dashed the crystal cup untasted from the fairy's hand; but I could never have faced the nobles and chiefs of Erin if I had refused to meet the challenge of the battle champion on the golden bridge."

"And you would have been no true knight of Erin, and you would not have been worthy of the wee girl who loves you, the bonny Princess Ailinn, if you had refused to meet it," said the little woman; "but for all that you can never return to the fair hills of Erin. But cheer up, Cuglas, there are mossy ways and forest paths and nestling bowers in fairyland. Lonely they are, I know, in your eyes now," said the little woman; "but maybe," she added, with a laugh as musical as the ripple on a streamlet when summer is in the air, "maybe you won't always think them so lonely."

"You think I'll forget Ailinn for the fairy queen," said Cuglas, with a sigh.

"I don't think anything of the kind," said she.

"Then what do you mean?" said the prince.

"Oh, I mean what I mean," said the little woman. "But I can't stop here all night talking to you: and, indeed, it is in your bed you ought to be yourself. So now good night; and I have no more to say, except that perhaps, if you happen to be here this night week at this very hour, when the moon will be on the waters, you will see –. But no matter what you will see," said she; "I must be off."

And before the prince could say another word the boat sped away from the bank, and he was alone. He went back to the palace, and he fell asleep that night only to dream of the Princess Ailinn.

As for the princess, she was pining away in the palace of Tara, the colour had fled from her cheeks, and her eyes, which had been once so bright they would have lighted darkness like a star, lost nearly all their lustre, and the king's leeches could do nothing for her, and at last they gave up all hope, and the king and queen of Erin and the ladies of the court watched her couch by night and by day sadly waiting for her last hour.

At length one day, when the sun was shining brightly over Tara's plain, and its light, softened by the intervening curtains, was falling in the sick chamber, the royal watchers noticed a sweet change coming over the face of the princess; the bloom of love and youth were flushing on her cheeks, and from her eyes shone out the old, soft, tender light, and they began to hope she was about to be restored to them, when suddenly the room was in darkness as if the night had swept across the sky, and blotted out the sun. Then they heard the sound of fairy music, and over the couch where the princess lay they beheld a gleam of golden light, but only for a moment; and again there was perfect darkness, and the fairy music ceased. Then, as suddenly as it came the darkness vanished, the softened sunlight once more filled the chamber, and rested upon the couch; but the couch was empty, and the royal watchers, looking at each other, said in whispers: "The fairies have carried away the Princess Ailinn to fairyland."

Well, that very day the prince roamed by himself through the forest, counting the hours until the day would fade in the sky and the moon come climbing up, and at last, when it was shining full above the waters, he went down to the verge of the lake, and he looked out over the gleaming surface watching for the vision promised by the little woman. But he could see nothing, and was about to turn away when he heard the faint sound of fairy music. He listened and listened, and the sound came nearer and clearer, and away in the distance, like drops of glistening water breaking the level of the lake, he saw a fleet of fairy boats, and he thought it was the fairy queen sailing in the moonlight. And it was the fairy queen, and soon he was able to recognise the royal shallop leading the others, and as it came close to the bank he saw the little woman sitting in the prow between the little harpers, and at the stern was the fairy queen, and by her side the lady of his heart, the Princess Ailinn. In a second the boat was against the bank, and the princess in his arms. And he kissed her again and again.

"And have you never a kiss for me," said the little woman, tapping his hand with the little gold bodkin.

"A kiss and a dozen," said Cuglas, as he caught the little fairy up in his arms.

"Oh, fie, Cuglas," said the queen.

"Oh, the princess isn't one bit jealous," said the little woman. "Are you, Ailinn?"

"Indeed I am not," said Ailinn.

"And you should not be," said the fairy queen, "for never lady yet had truer knight than Cuglas. I loved him, and I love him dearly. I lured him here hoping that in the delights of fairyland he might forget you. It was all in vain. I know now that there is one thing no fairy power above or below the stars, or beneath the waters, can ever subdue, and that is love. And here together forever shall you and Cuglas dwell, where old age shall never come upon you, and where pain or sorrow or sickness are unknown."

And Cuglas never returned to the fair hills of Erin, and ages passed away since the morning he followed the hounds into the fatal cave, but his story was remembered by the firesides, and sometimes, even yet, the herdboy watching his cattle in the fields hears the tuneful cry of hounds, and follows it till it leads him to a darksome cave, and as fearfully he listens to the sound becoming fainter and fainter he hears the clatter of hoofs over the stony floor, and to this day the cave bears the name of the prince who entered it never to return.

The Twelve Wild Geese

THERE WAS ONCE a King and Queen that lived very happily together, and they had twelve sons and not a single daughter. We are always wishing for what we haven't, and don't care for what we have, and so it was with the Queen. One day in winter, when the bawn was covered with snow, she was looking out of the parlour window, and saw there a calf that was just killed by the butcher, and a raven standing near it.

"Oh," says she, "if I had only a daughter with her skin as white as that snow, her cheeks as red as that blood, and her hair as black as that raven, I'd give away every one of my twelve sons for her." The moment she said the word, she got a great fright, and a shiver went through her, and in an instant after, a severe-looking old woman stood before her. "That was a wicked wish you made," said she, "and to punish you it will be granted. You will have such a daughter as you desire, but the very day of her birth you will lose your other children." She vanished the moment she said the words.

And that very way it turned out. When she expected her delivery, she had her children all in a large room of the palace, with guards all round it, but the very hour her daughter came into the world, the guards inside and outside heard a great whirling and whistling, and the twelve princes were seen flying one after another out through the open window, and away like so many arrows over the woods. Well, the king was in great grief for the loss of his sons, and he would be very enraged with his wife if he only knew that she was so much to blame for it.

Everyone called the little princess Snow-white-and-Rose-red on account of her beautiful complexion. She was the most loving and lovable child that could be seen anywhere. When she was twelve years old she began to be very sad and lonely, and to torment her mother, asking her about her brothers that she thought were dead, for none up to that time ever told her the exact thing that happened to them. The secret was weighing very heavy on the Queen's conscience, and as the little girl persevered in her questions, at last she told her. "Well, mother," said she, "it was on my account my poor brothers were changed into wild geese, and are now suffering all sorts of hardship; before the world is a day older, I'll be off to seek them, and try to restore them to their own shapes."

The King and Queen had her well watched, but all was no use. Next night she was getting through the woods that surrounded the palace, and she went on and on that night, and till the evening of next day. She had a few cakes with her, and she got nuts, and *mugoreens* (fruit of the sweet briar), and some sweet crabs, as she went along. At last she came to a nice wooden house just at sunset. There was a fine garden round it, full of the handsomest flowers, and a gate in the hedge. She went in, and saw a table laid out with twelve plates, and twelve knives and forks, and twelve spoons, and there were cakes, and cold wild fowl, and fruit along with the plates, and there was a good fire, and in another long room there were twelve beds. Well, while she was looking about her she heard the gate opening, and footsteps along the walk, and in came twelve young men, and there was great grief and surprise on all their faces when they laid eyes on her. "Oh, what misfortune sent you here?" said the eldest. "For the sake of a girl we were obliged to leave our father's court, and be in the shape of wild geese all day. That's twelve years ago, and we took a solemn oath that we would kill the first young girl that came into our hands. It's a pity to put such an innocent and handsome girl as you are out of the world, but we must keep our oath."

"But," said she, "I'm your only sister, that never knew anything about this till yesterday; and I stole away from our father's and mother's palace last night to find you out and relieve you if I can." Every one of them clasped his hands, and looked down on the floor, and you could hear a pin fall till the eldest cried out, "A curse light on our oath! What shall we do?"

"I'll tell you that," said an old woman that appeared at the instant among them. "Break your wicked oath, which no one should keep. If you attempted to lay an uncivil finger on her I'd change you into twelve *booliaun buis* (stalks of ragweed), but I wish well to you as well as to her. She is appointed to be your deliverer in this way. She must spin and knit twelve shirts for you out of bog-down, to be gathered by her own hands on the moor just outside of the wood. It will take her five years to do it, and if she once speaks, or laughs, or cries the whole time, you will have to remain wild geese by day till you're called out of the world. So take care of your sister; it is worth your while." The fairy then vanished, and it was only a strife with the brothers to see who would be first to kiss and hug their sister.

So for three long years the poor young princess was occupied pulling bog-down, spinning it, and knitting it into shirts, and at the end of the three years she had eight made. During all that time, she never spoke a word, nor laughed, nor cried: the last was the hardest to refrain from. One fine day she was sitting in the garden spinning, when in sprung a fine greyhound and bounded up to her, and laid his paws on her shoulder, and licked her forehead and her hair. The next minute a beautiful young prince rode up to the little garden gate, took off his hat, and asked for leave to come in. She gave him a little nod, and in he walked. He made ever so many apologies for intruding, and asked her ever so many questions, but not a word could he get out of her. He loved her so much from the first moment, that he could not leave her till he told her he was king of a country just bordering on the forest, and he begged her to come home with him, and be his wife. She couldn't help loving him as much as he did her, and though she shook her head very often, and was very sorry to leave her brothers, at last she nodded her head, and put her hand in his. She knew well enough that the good fairy and her brothers would be able to find her out. Before she went she brought out a basket holding all her bog-down, and another holding the eight shirts. The attendants took charge of these, and the prince placed her before him on his horse. The only thing that disturbed him while riding along was the displeasure his stepmother would feel at what he had done. However, he was full master at home, and as soon as he arrived he sent for the bishop, got his bride nicely dressed, and the marriage was celebrated, the bride answering by signs. He knew by her manners she was of high birth, and no two could be fonder of each other.

The wicked stepmother did all she could to make mischief, saying she was sure she was only a woodman's daughter; but nothing could disturb the young king's opinion of his wife. In good time the young queen was delivered of a beautiful boy, and the king was so glad he hardly knew what to do for joy. All the grandeur of the christening and the happiness of the parents tormented the bad woman more than I can tell you, and she determined to put a stop to all their comfort. She got a sleeping posset given to the young mother, and while she was thinking and thinking how she could best make away with the child, she saw a wicked-looking wolf in the garden, looking up at her, and licking his chops. She lost no time, but snatched the child from the arms of the sleeping woman, and pitched it out. The beast caught it in his mouth, and was over the garden fence in a minute. The wicked woman then pricked her own fingers, and dabbled the blood round the mouth of the sleeping mother.

Well, the young king was just then coming into the big bawn from hunting, and as soon as he entered the house, she beckoned to him, shed a few crocodile tears, began to cry and wring her hands, and hurried him along the passage to the bedchamber.

Oh, wasn't the poor king frightened when he saw the queen's mouth bloody, and missed his child? It would take two hours to tell you the devilment of the old queen, the confusion and fright, and grief of the young king and queen, the bad opinion he began to feel of his wife, and the struggle she had to keep down her bitter sorrow, and not give way to it by speaking or lamenting. The young king would not allow anyone to be called, and ordered his stepmother to give out that the child fell from the mother's arms at the window, and that a wild beast ran off with it. The wicked woman pretended to do so, but she told underhand to everybody she spoke to what the king and herself saw in the bedchamber.

The young queen was the most unhappy woman in the three kingdoms for a long time, between sorrow for her child, and her husband's bad opinion; still she neither spoke nor cried, and she gathered bog-down and went on with the shirts. Often the twelve wild geese would be seen lighting on the trees in the park or on the smooth sod, and looking in at her windows. So she worked on to get the shirts finished, but another year was at an end, and she had the twelfth shirt finished except one arm, when she was obliged to take to her bed, and a beautiful girl was born.

Now the king was on his guard, and he would not let the mother and child be left alone for a minute; but the wicked woman bribed some of the attendants, set others asleep, gave the sleepy posset to the queen, and had a person watching to snatch the child away, and kill it. But what should she see but the same wolf in the garden looking up and licking his chops again? Out went the child, and away with it flew the wolf, and she smeared the sleeping mother's mouth and face with blood, and then roared, and bawled, and cried out to the king and to everybody she met, and the room was filled, and everyone was sure the young queen had just devoured her own babe.

The poor mother thought now her life would leave her. She was in such a state she could neither think nor pray, but she sat like a stone, and worked away at the arm of the twelfth shirt.

The king was for taking her to the house in the wood where he found her, but the stepmother, and the lords of the court, and the judges would not hear of it, and she was condemned to be burned in the big bawn at three o'clock the same day. When the hour drew near, the king went to the farthest part of his palace, and there was no more unhappy man in his kingdom at that hour.

When the executioners came and led her off, she took the pile of shirts in her arms. There was still a few stitches wanted, and while they were tying her to the stakes she still worked on. At the last stitch she seemed overcome and dropped a tear on her work, but the moment after she sprang up, and shouted out, "I am innocent; call my husband!" The executioners stayed their hands, except one wicked-disposed creature, who set fire to the faggot next him, and while all were struck in amaze, there was a rushing of wings, and in a moment the twelve wild geese were standing around the pile. Before you could count twelve, she flung a shirt over each bird, and there in the twinkling of an eye were twelve of the finest young men that could be collected out of a thousand. While some were untying their sister, the eldest, taking a strong stake in his hand, struck the busy executioner such a blow that he never needed another.

While they were comforting the young queen, and the king was hurrying to the spot, a fine-looking woman appeared among them holding the babe on one arm and the little prince by the hand. There was nothing but crying for joy, and laughing for joy, and hugging and kissing, and when anyone had time to thank the good fairy, who in the shape of a wolf, carried the child away, she was not to be found. Never was such happiness enjoyed in any palace that ever was built, and if the wicked queen and her helpers were not torn by wild horses, they richly deserved it.

Murtough and the Witch Woman

IN THE DAYS when Murtough Mac Erca was in the High Kingship of Ireland, the country was divided between the old beliefs of paganism and the new doctrines of the Christian teaching. Part held with the old creed and part with the new, and the thought of the people was troubled between them, for they knew not which way to follow and which to forsake. The faith of their forefathers clung close around them, holding them by many fine and tender threads of memory and custom and tradition; yet still the new faith was making its way, and every day it spread wider and wider through the land.

The family of Murtough had joined itself to the Christian faith, and his three brothers were bishops and abbots of the Church, but Murtough himself remained a pagan, for he was a wild and lawless prince, and the peaceful teachings of the Christian doctrine, with its forgiveness of enemies, pleased him not at all. Fierce and cruel was his life, filled with dark deeds and bloody wars, and savage and tragic was his death, as we shall hear.

Now Murtough was in the sunny summer palace of Cletty, which Cormac, son of Art, had built for a pleasure house on the brink of the slow-flowing Boyne, near the Fairy Brugh of Angus the Ever Young, the God of Youth and Beauty. A day of summer was that day, and the King came forth to hunt on the borders of the Brugh, with all his boon companions around him. But when the high-noon came the sun grew hot, and the King sat down to rest upon the fairy mound, and the hunt passed on beyond him, and he was left alone.

There was a witch woman in that country whose name was 'Sigh, Sough, Storm, Rough Wind, Winter Night, Cry, Wail, and Groan'. Star-bright and beautiful was she in face and form, but inwardly she was cruel as her names. And she hated Murtough because he had scattered and destroyed the Ancient Peoples of the Fairy Tribes of Erin, her country and her fatherland, and because in the battle which he fought at Cerb on the Boyne her father and her mother and her sister had been slain. For in those days women went to battle side by side with men.

She knew, too, that with the coming of the new faith trouble would come upon the fairy folk, and their power and their great majesty would depart from them, and men would call them demons, and would drive them out with psalm-singing and with the saying of prayers, and with the sound of little tinkling bells. So trouble and anger wrought in the witch woman, and she waited the day to be revenged on Murtough, for he being yet a pagan, was still within her power to harm.

So when Sheen (for Sheen or 'Storm' was the name men gave to her) saw the King seated on the fairy mound and all his comrades parted from him, she arose softly, and combed her hair with her comb of silver adorned with little ribs of gold, and she washed her hands in a silver basin wherein were four golden birds sitting on the rim of the bowl, and little bright gems of carbuncle set round about the rim. And she donned her fairy mantle of flowing green, and her cloak, wide and hooded, with silvery fringes, and a brooch of fairest gold. On her head were tresses yellow like to gold, plaited in four locks, with a golden drop at the end of each long tress. The hue of her hair was like the flower of the iris in summer or like red gold after the burnishing thereof. And she wore on her breasts and at her shoulders marvellous clasps of gold, finely worked with the tracery of the skilled craftsman, and a golden twisted torque around her throat. And when she was decked she went softly and sat down beside Murtough on the turfy hunting mound. And after a space Murtough perceived her sitting there, and the sun shining upon her, so that the glittering of the gold and of her golden hair and the bright shining of the green silk of her garments, was like the yellow iris-beds upon the lake on a sunny summer's day. Wonder and terror seized on Murtough at her beauty, and he knew not if he loved her or if he hated her the most; for at one moment all his nature was filled with longing and with love of her, so that it seemed to him that he would give the whole of Ireland for the loan of one hour's space of dalliance with her; but after that he felt a dread of her, because he knew his fate was in her hands, and that she had come to work him ill. But he welcomed her as if she were known to him and he asked her wherefore she was come. "I am come," she said, "because I am beloved of Murtough, son of Erc, King of Erin, and I come to seek him here." Then Murtough was glad, and he said, "Dost thou not know me, maiden?"

"I do," she answered, "for all secret and mysterious things are known to me and thou and all the men of Erin are well known."

After he had conversed with her awhile, she appeared to him so fair that the King was ready to promise her anything in life she wished, so long as she would go with him to Cletty of the Boyne. "My wish," she said, "is that you take me to your house, and that you put out from it your wife and your children because they are of the new faith, and all the clerics that are in your house, and that neither your wife nor any cleric be permitted to enter the house while I am there."

"I will give you," said the King, "a hundred head of every herd of cattle that is within my kingdom, and a hundred drinking horns, and a hundred cups, and a hundred rings of gold, and a feast every other night in the summer palace of Cletty. But I pledge thee my word, oh, maiden, it were easier for me to give thee half of Ireland than to do this thing that thou hast asked." For Murtough feared that when those that were of the Christian faith were put out of his house, she would work her spells upon him, and no power would be left with him to resist those spells.

"I will not take thy gifts," said the damsel, "but only those things that I have asked; moreover, it is thus, that my name must never be uttered by thee, nor must any man or woman learn it."

"What is thy name," said Murtough, "that it may not come upon my lips to utter it?"

And she said, "Sigh, Sough, Storm, Rough Wind, Winter Night, Cry, Wail, Groan, this is my name, but men call me Sheen, for 'Storm' or Sheen is my chief name, and storms are with me where I come."

Nevertheless, Murtough was so fascinated by her that he brought her to his home, and drove out the clerics that were there, with his wife and children along with them, and drove out also the nobles of his own clan, the children of Niall, two great and gallant battalions. And Duivsech, his wife, went crying along the road with her children around her to seek Bishop Cairnech, the half-brother of her husband, and her own soul-friend, that she might obtain help and shelter from him.

But Sheen went gladly and light-heartedly into the House of Cletty, and when she saw the lovely lightsome house and the goodly nobles of the clan of Niall, and the feasting and banqueting and the playing of the minstrels and all the joyous noise of that kingly dwelling, her heart was lifted within her, and "Fair as a fairy palace is this house of Cletty," said she.

"Fair, indeed, it is," replied the King; "for neither the Kings of Leinster nor the Kings of mighty Ulster, nor the lords of the clans of Owen or of Niall, have such a house as this; nay, in Tara of the Kings itself, no house to equal this house of mine is found." And that night the King robed himself in all the splendour of his royal dignity, and on his right hand he seated Sheen, and a great banquet was made before them, and men said that never on earth was to be seen a woman more goodly of appearance than she. And the King was astonished at her, and he began to ask her questions, for it seemed to him that the power of a great goddess of the ancient time was in her; and he asked her whence she came, and what manner was the power that he saw in her. He asked her, too, did she believe in the God of the clerics, or was she herself some goddess of the older world? For he feared her, feeling that his fate was in her hands.

She laughed a careless and a cruel laugh, for she knew that the King was in their power, now that she was there alone with him, and the clerics and the Christian teachers gone.

"Fear me not, O Murtough," she cried; "I am, like thee, a daughter of the race of men of the ancient family of Adam and of Eve; fit and meet my comradeship with thee; therefore, fear not nor regret. And as to that true God of thine, worker of miracles and helper of His people, no miracle in all the world is there that I, by mine own unaided power, cannot work the like. I can create a sun and moon; the heavens I can sprinkle with radiant stars of night. I can call up to life men fiercely fighting in conflict, slaughtering one another. Wine I could make of the cold water of the Boyne, and sheep of lifeless stones, and swine of ferns. In the presence of the hosts I can make gold and silver, plenty and to spare; and hosts of famous fighting men I can produce from naught. Now, tell me, can thy God work the like?"

"Work for us," says the King, "some of these great wonders." Then Sheen went forth out of the house, and she set herself to work spells on Murtough, so that he knew not whether he was in his right mind or no. She took of the water of the Boyne and made a magic wine thereout, and she took ferns and spiked thistles and light puff-balls of the woods, and out of them she fashioned magic swine and sheep and goats, and with these she fed Murtough and the hosts. And when they had eaten, all their strength went from them, and the magic wine sent them into an uneasy sleep and restless slumbers. And out of stones and sods of earth she fashioned three battalions, and one of the battalions she placed at one side of the house, and the other at the further side beyond it, and one encircling the rest southward along the hollow windings of the glen. And thus were these battalions, one of them all made of men stark-naked and their colour blue, and the second with heads of goats with shaggy beards and horned; but the third, more terrible than they, for these were headless men, fighting like human beings, yet finished at the neck; and the sound of heavy shouting as of hosts and multitudes came from the first and the second battalion, but from the third no sound save only that they waved their arms and struck their weapons together, and smote the ground with their feet impatiently. And though terrible was the shout of the blue men and the bleating of the goats with human limbs, more horrible yet was the stamping and the rage of those headless men, finished at the neck.

And Murtough, in his sleep and in his dreams, heard the battle-shout, and he rose impetuously from off his bed, but the wine overcame him, and his strength departed from him, and he fell helplessly upon the floor. Then he heard the challenge a second time, and the stamping of the feet without, and he rose again, and madly, fiercely, he set on them, charging the hosts and scattering them before him, as he thought, as far as the fairy palace of the Brugh. But all his strength was lost in fighting phantoms, for they were but stones and sods and withered leaves of the forest that he took for fighting men.

Now Duivsech, Murtough's wife, knew what was going on. She called upon Cairnech to arise and to gather together the clans of the children of his people, the men of Owen and of Niall, and together they went to the fort; but Sheen guarded it well, so that they could by no means find an entrance. Then Cairnech was angry, and he cursed the place, and he dug a grave before the door, and he stood up upon the mound of the grave, and rang his bells and cursed the King and his house, and prophesied his downfall. But he blessed the clans of Owen and of Niall, and they returned to their own country.

Then Cairnech sent messengers to seek Murtough and to draw him away from the witch woman who sought his destruction, but because she was so lovely the King would believe no evil of her; and whenever he made any sign to go to Cairnech, she threw her spell upon the King, so that he could not break away. When he was so weak and faint that he had no power left, she cast a sleep upon him, and she went round the house, putting everything in readiness. She called upon her magic host of warriors, and set them round the fortress, with their spears and javelins pointed inwards towards the house, so that the King would not dare to go out amongst them. And that night was a night of Samhain-tide, the eve of Wednesday after All Souls' Day.

Then she went everywhere throughout the house, and took lighted brands and burning torches, and scattered them in every part of the dwelling. And she returned into the room wherein Murtough slept, and lay down by his side. And she caused a great wind to spring up, and it came soughing through the house from the north-west; and the King said, "This is the sigh of the winter night." And Sheen smiled, because, unwittingly, the King had spoken her name, for she knew by that that the hour of her revenge had come. "'Tis I myself that am Sigh and Winter Night," she said, "and I am Rough Wind and Storm, a daughter of fair nobles; and I am Cry and Wail, the maid of elfin birth, who brings ill-luck to men."

After that she caused a great snowstorm to come round the house; and like the noise of troops and the rage of battle was the storm, beating and pouring in on every side, so that drifts of deep snow were piled against the walls, blocking the doors and chilling the folk that were feasting within the house. But the King was lying in a heavy, unresting sleep, and Sheen was at his side. Suddenly he screamed out of his sleep and stirred himself, for he heard the crash of falling timbers and the noise of the magic hosts, and he smelled the strong smell of fire in the palace.

He sprang up. "It seems to me," he cried, "that hosts of demons are around the house, and that they are slaughtering my people, and that the house of Cletty is on fire."

"It was but a dream," the witch maiden said. Then he slept again, and he saw a vision, to wit, that he was tossing in a ship at sea, and the ship floundered, and above his head a griffin, with sharp beak and talons, sailed, her wings outspread and covering all the sun, so that it was dark as middle-night; and lo! As she rose on high, her plumes quivered for a moment in the air; then down she swooped and picked him from the waves, carrying him to her eyrie on the dismal cliff outhanging o'er the ocean; and the griffin began to pierce him and to prod him with her talons, and to pick out pieces of his flesh with her beak; and this went on awhile, and then a flame, that came he knew not whence, rose from the nest, and he and the griffin were enveloped in the flame. Then in her beak the griffin picked him up, and together they fell downward over the cliff's edge into the seething ocean; so that, half by fire and half by water, he died a miserable death.

When the King saw that vision, he rose screaming from his sleep, and donned his arms; and he made one plunge forward seeking for the magic hosts, but he found no man to answer him. The damsel went forth from the house, and Murtough made to follow her, but as he turned the flames leaped out, and all between him and the door was one vast sheet of flame. He saw no way of escape, save the vat of wine that stood in the banqueting hall, and into that he got; but the burning timbers of the roof fell upon his head and the hails of fiery sparks rained on him, so that half of him was burned and half was drowned, as he had seen in his dream.

The next day, amid the embers, the clerics found his corpse, and they took it up and washed it in the Boyne, and carried it to Tuilen to bury it. And they said, "Alas! That Mac Erca, High King of Erin, of the noble race of Conn and of the descendants of Ugaine the Great, should die fighting with sods and stones! Alas! That the Cross of Christ was not signed upon his face that he might have known the witchdoms of the maiden what they were."

As they went thus, bewailing the death of Murtough and bearing him to his grave, Duivsech, wife of Murtough, met them, and when she found her husband dead, she struck her hands together and she made a great and mournful lamentation; and because weakness came upon her she leaned her back against the ancient tree that is in Aenech Reil; and a burst of blood broke from her heart, and there she died, grieving for her husband. And the grave of Murtough was made wide and deep, and there they laid the Queen beside him, two in the one grave, near the north side of the little church that is in Tuilen.

Now, when the burial was finished, and the clerics were reciting over his grave the deeds of the King, and were making prayers for Murtough's soul that it might be brought out of hell, for Cairnech showed great care for this, they saw coming towards them across the sward a lonely woman, star-bright and beautiful, and a kirtle of priceless silk upon her, and a green mantle with its fringes of silver thread flowing to the ground. She reached the place where the clerics were, and saluted them, and they saluted her. And they marvelled at her beauty, but they perceived on her an appearance of sadness and of heavy grief. They asked of her, "Who art thou, maiden, and wherefore art thou come to the house of mourning? For a king lies buried here."

"A king lies buried here, indeed," said she, "and I it was who slew him, Murtough of the many deeds, of the race of Conn and Niall, High King of Ireland and of the West. And though it was I who wrought his death, I myself will die for grief of him."

And they said, "Tell us, maiden, why you brought him to his death, if so be that he was dear to thee?" And she said, "Murtough was dear to me, indeed, dearest of the men of the whole world; for I am Sheen, the daughter of Sige, the son of Dian, from whom Ath Sigi or the 'Ford of Sige' is called today. But Murtough slew my father, and my mother and sister were slain along with him, in the battle of Cerb upon the Boyne, and there was none of my house to avenge their death, save myself alone. Moreover, in his time the Ancient Peoples of the Fairy Tribes of Erin were scattered and destroyed, the folk of the underworld and of my fatherland; and to avenge the wrong and loss he wrought on them I slew the man I loved. I made poison for him; alas! I made for him magic drink and food which took his strength away, and out of the sods of earth and puff-balls that float down the wind, I wrought men and armies of headless, hideous folk, till all his senses were distraught. And, now, take me to thee, O Cairnech, in fervent and true repentance, and sign the Cross of Christ upon my brow, for the time of my death is come." Then she made penitence for the sin that she had sinned, and she died there upon the grave of grief and of sorrow after the King. And they digged a grave lengthways across the foot of the wide grave of Murtough and his spouse, and there they laid the maiden who had wrought them woe. And the clerics wondered at those things, and they wrote them and revised them in a book.

Oisín in Tír na N-Óg (The Land of Youth)

FINN MAC CUMAILL, the mightiest warrior of the Fianna, had no equal among mortal men and his reputation as one of the fiercest fighters in Ireland spread with each glorious victory on the battlefield. His young son, Oisín, was a particular favourite with him, for the boy showed signs of remarkable courage at an early age and had clearly inherited his father's voracious thirst for adventure. Each time Finn gazed at his golden-haired son a memory of Blaí, the boy's mother, stirred within his breast, filling him with both joy and sorrow. Blaí was now lost to him, but the child she had borne him possessed her great beauty and gift of poetry. Oisín was a true warrior and the greatest of Fenian poets. Many women had fallen in love with him, but none had yet succeeded in winning his heart. The son of Finn mac Cumaill was happiest fighting alongside his father, or roaming the dense forests that chimed with birdsong in the company of his trusty hounds.

While hunting in the middle of the woods one summer's morning, just as the silver veil of mist was rising from the shores of Loch Lein, Oisín was struck by the most enchanting vision. A young maiden appeared before him, seated majestically on a milk-white steed. Oisín had never seen her kind before, but felt certain she must have come from the fairy world. Her luxuriant golden hair, adorned by an elaborate jewelled crown, cascaded over her shoulders and she was clothed in a mantle of the finest red silk. Her saddle was made of purple and gold and her horse's hooves were placed in four shoes of gold, studded with the most precious gems. She moved gracefully towards Oisín, who was immediately entranced by her radiance and perfection. The maiden's cheeks were as delicate as the satin petals of a rose; her eyes were as bright and pure as two drops of dew on a violet; her skin was as white and delicate as the first snows of winter.

'I am Niamh [Pronounced Niav.] daughter of the great King who rules the Land of Youth,' she spoke softly. 'Your name is well known to me, brave Oisín, son of the noble Finn mac Cumaill. I have hastened here for love's sake, to woo you.'

Oisín stood bewitched before the maiden as she began to sing to him of Tír na N-Óg, the Land of Youth. Her music drifted lightly towards him like a perfumed summer breeze, and it was the sweetest sound the young warrior had ever heard.

Delightful land of honey and wine
Beyond what seems to thee most fair –
Rich fruits abound the bright year round
And flowers are found of hues most rare.
Unfailing there the honey and wine
And draughts divine of mead there be,
No ache nor ailing night or day –
Death or decay thou ne'er shalt see!

A hundred swords of steel refined,
A hundred cloaks of kind full rare,
A hundred steeds of proudest breed,
A hundred hounds – thy meed when there!

The royal crown of the King of Youth
Shall shine in sooth on thy brow most fair,
All brilliant with gems of luster bright
Whose worth aright none might declare.

All things I've named thou shalt enjoy
And none shall cloy – to endless life –
Beauty and strength and power thou'lt see
And I'll e'er be thy own true wife!
Michael Comyn, Niamh sings to Oisin

'Niamh of the Golden Hair,' Oisín spoke to her. 'I have never before met a maiden so pleasing to the eye and I long to visit the kingdom of which you sing. I would be honoured to take you as my bride and will depart this land of mortals without delay to be with you.'

Before reaching up to grasp her hand, he looked around him only once, catching a final glimpse of his father's great palace and the beautiful woodlands he had now chosen to leave behind. Bidding a valiant farewell in his heart to the men of the Fianna, he mounted the powerful horse which carried them both away towards the cliffs of the west, and further on into the crashing waves.

For five days and five nights they rode, crossing the great plains of Erin and journeying on through various kingdoms of the Otherworld. The deep sea opened up to greet them and they passed underneath the bed of the ocean into a land of golden light. Regal citadels, surrounded by luscious green lawns and exotic, vibrantly coloured blooms, gleamed in the rays of sparkling sunshine. A youthful knight, clad in a magnificent raiment of purple and silver, suddenly appeared alongside them, riding a white mare. A fair young maiden sat next to him on the saddle holding a golden apple in the palm of her hand. Niamh again told Oisín of the beauty of Tír na N-Óg, a land even more beautiful than the splendid images now before them. They journeyed onwards, passing from this luminous world through a raging, violent tempest, moving as swiftly as the howling winds and driving rains would carry them across mountains, valleys and bottomless dark lakes until the bright orb of the sun emerged in all its splendour once more.

The kingdom now before them was far more breathtaking than Oisín had ever imagined possible. A silver-pebbled stream wound its way towards a gently undulating hill dotted with purple and yellow orchids which breathed a rich, opulent fragrance into the air. A magnificent castle stood on the hilltop, shaded by giant leafy trees laden with ripe golden pears. The sound of honey-bees buzzing from flower to flower united melodiously with the singing of birds, languidly pruning their feathers in the amber glow of early twilight. A large crowd moved forward to welcome the couple. Minstrels played soothing, magical airs and delicate blossoms were strewn at their feet creating a soft carpet for them to tread on. The happy pair were escorted to the palace where the King and Queen had prepared a large wedding banquet. The King warmly embraced his new son-in-law and ordered the seven days of feasting and celebrations to commence.

As each new day dawned in the Land of Youth it brought with it an abundance of joy for Oisín and Niamh. Time stood absolutely still in this perfect world and they had only to wish for something and it would instantly appear. Before long, the couple were blessed with three healthy children: two handsome sons, and a beautiful daughter. The son of Finn mac Cumaill had won the admiration and respect of every person in the kingdom and he enthralled each and every subject with tales of his Fenian friends and the splendid adventures they had survived together. Only one thing now threatened to destroy his happiness. At night, Oisín was tormented by dreams of Erin and of his people, the Fianna. These dreams became more and more powerful with the passing of time and he ached with the desire to visit his homeland once again. Such a dreadful anxiety could not be hidden from Niamh, for she knew what troubled her husband and could not bear to see him suffer this deep sadness and unrest.

'Go, Oisín,' she told him, 'though it breaks my heart, I will not hinder you. But you must promise me, in the name of our love for each other and for our children, that you will not dismount on Erin's soil, for time has autonomy in the land of Erin. Hear my warning that if you touch the earth, you will never again return to the Land of Youth.'

Having listened carefully to these words of caution, Oisín rode away, guided by his magical steed across the plains leading back to his beloved country. After five long days, he arrived in his native land and made his way to the home of his father. Cheered by memories of his youth and the joyous welcome home he knew he would soon receive, he rode to the far side of the forest and waited anxiously for the thick mist to clear so that the great house would be revealed in all its regal splendour. Yet when the drizzling clouds finally dispersed, Oisín was shocked to discover only a pile of crumbling stones where the stronghold of Finn mac Cumaill had once stood firm. Utterly distressed and bewildered, he turned his horse swiftly around and galloped away in search of any mortal creature who might bring him news of the Fianna.

After what seemed an eternity, he spotted on the horizon a strange band of men toiling and sweating in their efforts to lift a slab of granite from the ground. Oisín marvelled at their small frames and their lack of strength in lifting such a trifling load.

'I am searching for the dwelling place of Finn mac Cumaill and the Fianna,' he shouted to the men.

'We have often heard of Finn,' replied a stooped, wizened figure, the eldest of the group. 'But it has been many hundreds of years since the great battle of Gabra where he and the last of the Fianna lost their lives.'

'I can see you possess the blood of such mighty ancestors,' added another of the band. 'Can you lend us your strength to shift this stone?'

Niamh's words of counsel to Oisín had not been forgotten, but he was angered by these men of Erin who stood before him so weak and feeble. Filled with a great pride in his own strength and ability, he bent forward from his horse to assist in the lifting of the slab. But the angle at which he had leaned towards the men, added to the weight of the stone, caused the animal's saddle-girth to snap and Oisín could not save himself from falling to the ground. In an instant, his steed had disappeared into thin air, his royal garments had turned to grimy sackcloth and his youthful warrior's face had become creased and lined as the burden of three hundred years of mortal life fell on him. Withered and blind, he reached out with his bony arms, grasping in the dark for some form of comfort. A wretched, pitiful cry escaped his lips and he heard again Niamh's parting words to him. As he lay helpless on the cold, damp earth, he began to weep inconsolably for the wife and children to whom he could never now return in the Land of Eternal Youth.

Wee Johnnie in the Cradle

THERE ONCE WAS A MAN and his wife who lived on a farm on the edge of a wood where fairies were known to lay their small hats. They were a young man and wife and they had not been married long before a child was born to them, a child they called Johnnie. Now wee Johnnie was an unhappy baby, and from the beginning he cried so loudly that the birds ceased their flight over the farmer's cottage, and the creatures of the woodland kept a surly distance. The man's wife longed for the days when she could tend the fields with her husband, and chat to him of things which those who are newly wed have to chat of, and to go to market, where they would share a dram and have a carry-on like they had in the days before wee Johnnie was born.

But Johnnie was there now, and their cosy cottage became messy and damp, and some days the hearth was not lit because the man and his wife were so intent on silencing the squalling boy, and some days they could not even look one another in the eye, so unhappy and disillusioned they had become.

And then, perchance, a kindly neighbour, a tailor by trade, took pity on the man and his wife, who grew ever thinner and ever more hostile as the cries of wee Johnnie grew wilder and lustier as he grew larger and stronger.

'I'll take yer bairn and ye can take yer wife to market,' he said to the farmer one day, and the man and his wife eagerly agreed and set off for the day.

They had not been gone longer than a minute or two, when the kindly tailor, who had placed himself beside the fire and was bracing himself for an afternoon of wailing, was startled from his reverie by a deep voice.

'Fetch me a glass o' that whiskey, there, in the press,' it said. And the tailor looked about him in amazement, the room empty but for the wee Johnnie in the cradle who was mercifully silent.

'I said to ye, fetch me a glass,' and up from the cradle of wee Johnnie popped wee Johnnie's head, and from the mouth on that head came that deep and bossy voice.

The tailor rose and did as he was bidden, and when the baby had drained the glass, and then another, and let out a belch that was very unbabyish indeed, he said to the wee bairn, 'You aren't Johnnie, are ye, ye are a fairy without a doubt.'

'And if I am,' said the fairy changeling, 'what will ye say to them, me mam and da?'

'I, I dunna know,' said the tailor carefully, settling himself back into his chair to watch the fairy more carefully.

'Get me some pipes,' said Johnnie the fairy, 'I like a bit of music with me drink.'

'I haven't any ... and I dunna play,' said the tailor, crossing himself and moving further from the loathsome baby.

'Fetch me a straw then,' he replied. And when the tailor complied, the fairy Johnnie played a song which was so exquisite, so effortlessly beautiful that the tailor was quite calmed. Never before had he heard music so haunting, and he would remember that melody until his dying day, although he could never repeat it himself or pass it on. But he was broken from his reverie, for wee Johnnie was speaking.

'Me mam and da, when will they be back?' he whispered.

The tailor looked startled, for the day had been pulled from under him, and it was time indeed for the farmer and his wife to return. He looked anxiously from the window and as they drew up he heard wee Johnnie begin to howl with all the vigour of a slaughtered beast, and he watched as a deep frown furrowed the brow of the farmer's wife, and a dull shadow cast itself across the face of her husband.

He must tell them, for the cruel fairy was manipulating them, taunting them with his tortuous cries. And their own wee bairn was somewhere lost to them.

He pulled the farmer aside as his wife went to tend to the wailing bairn, and told him of the fairy. A bemused look crossed his face and he struggled to keep his composure. 'My wife, she'll not believe it,' he said finally.

But the tailor had a plan. He told the farmer to pretend to leave for market the following day, and he, the tailor, would step in to look after the bairn once again. But the farmer and his wife were not really to leave, they should hide themselves outside the cottage walls and watch when the wee Johnnie thought them gone.

And so it happened that the next day the man and his wife set out for market again, but drove their horses only round the grassy bend, returning stealthily to look through the windows of their cottage. And there was wee Johnnie, sipping on a glass of their best whiskey, puffing idly on a straw pipe that played a song which was so exquisite, so effortlessly beautiful that they were quite calmed. Never before had they heard music so haunting, and they would remember that melody until their dying day, although they could never repeat it.

But when they heard that wee Johnnie's coarse voice demanding more drink, they were snapped from their reverie, and they flew into the cottage and thrust the changeling intruder on the burning griddle which the tailor had prepared for that purpose.

And the scream that ensued was not that of their own baby, and the puff of sickening smoke which burst from the fairy as he disappeared renewed their determination.

And then there was silence, an empty peace that caused the man and his wife to look at one another in dismay, for what had they done to cause their baby to be stolen from them, and where was their own wee Johnnie now?

Then a gurgle burst forth, and there was a movement in the corner of the room where the tiny cradle lay. They rushed to its side, and there lay Johnnie, brought back from his fairy confinement, smiling and waving tiny fat arms, with cheeks like pink buttons, and a smile so merry that the cottage of the man and his wife was warmed once again.

The tailor left them then, a grin on his face as he whistled to himself a tune which was so exquisite, so effortlessly beautiful that he was quite calmed.

A Dead Wife Among the Fairies

THERE ONCE WAS A MAN who lived with a wife he loved. They had been married for many years, and they made their home in a lighthouse, on the rocky coast by the sea. The waves threw up a spray but never dampened them, for they were sealed tight in their little world inside that lighthouse, and they lived happily there together, needing little else but the other. And so they lived, working together and talking all the day, lighting their beacon in the mists and fogs which fell over the sea like a woollen blanket.

Then one day, the good wife died, and she was buried in the hillside, under the rocks. And on those rocks the man sat each day, never lighting his beacon when the mists and fogs fell over the sea, staring instead at the rock which marked her grave, which marked the end of his life too. And so it was that he became a little mad, and went to see a witch, a fairy midwife who practised the magic of the earth and who could tell him how to get her back, his wife that he loved so well.

He saw her in her cottage, over the hill and across the brae, and she shook her head, and warned him to leave the dead with the fairies, for after death there can be no real life on earth, where the light would turn into dust any mortal who tried to return. But for the poor widowed man there could be no real life either, and so he begged the fairy witch to tell him her secrets and at last she did.

He was to go, she said, to a cave at the brae of Versabreck, on the night of a full moon, and he should take with him a black cat, and a Bible, and a thick wooden staff. There he must cry for his wife, and read to her from the psalms, and when he heard her voice once more, he must throw in the black cat and wait quietly for her to appear. Now the fairy folk would never let a mortal who had died pass back to his own land, so they would rally round her, and fight to keep her in their dust-webbed cave, which led to the Land of Light. The staff was to beat them with, for they could be sent back into their cave by the force of his will.

The moon waned and then it waxed again, and soon the night of the full moon arrived. The man was shivering with the fear of seeing his wife once more, yet he longed to touch her body, to feel her warmth, to hear her tender voice, so he steeled his quivering nerves and set off for the cave at the brae of Versabreck, and under his arm he held a black cat, and a Bible and a thick wooden staff. There he cried for his wife, and he read to her from the psalms, and when he heard her voice once more, he threw in the black cat and waited quietly for her to appear.

Now the fairy folk fought for their mortal princess, and struggled to keep her in their dust-webbed cave, which led to the Land of Light, but he beat them with his staff, and sent them back into their cave by the force of his will.

And there was his wife, paler to be sure, and nothing more than skin and bones, but she smiled her same familiar smile, and although her body held no warmth and she smelled rather sour, he held her to him once again and heard her tender voice. And together they walked to their lighthouse home, snug in a warm embrace, and they lit their beacon in the mists and fogs which fell over the sea like a woollen blanket. When day broke, his wife was safe in the fairy cave again, for light would turn to dust any mortal who tried to return from the dead. And so her husband would watch carefully as the moon waned and then waxed, when they could meet again.

The Wooing of Etain

MIDHIR THE PROUD WAS KING of the Daoine Sidhe, the fairy people of the Tuatha De Danann, and he dwelt at the grand palace in the Hollow Hills of Brí Leíth. He had a wife named Fuamnach with whom he had lived quite contentedly for a good many years. One day, however, while Midhir was out hunting with a group of his companions, he stumbled across the fairest maiden he had ever before laid eyes on, resting by a mountain stream. She had begun to loosen her hair to wash it and her chestnut tresses fell about her feet, shimmering magnificently in the sunlight. The King was enraptured by her perfect beauty and grace and he could not prevent himself from instantly falling in love with her. Nothing could persuade him to abandon the thought of returning to the palace with the maiden and making her his new wife. He boldly confessed to her this desire, hopeful that his noble bearing and royal apparel would not fail to win her approval. The maiden told him that her name was Etain. She was both honoured and delighted that the fairy king had requested her hand in marriage and agreed at once to return with him to Brí Leíth.

Within a short time, Etain's beauty had won her great fame throughout the land and the words 'as fair as Etain' became the highest compliment any man could bestow on a woman. Midhir had soon forgotten about his former wife and spent his days in the company of his new bride whom he doted on and could not bear to be parted from. Fuamnach was distressed and enraged to see them together, but her desire to be comforted and loved once more was entirely overlooked by her husband. When she could bear her cruel treatment no longer, she sought the help of the druid, Bressal, who was well known to the royal palace. Bressal heard Fuamnach's story and took great pity on her. That evening, as Etain lay in bed, they both entered her chamber. A great tempest began to rage around them as the druid waved his wand over the sleeping woman and delivered his curse in grave, commanding tones. As soon as he had uttered his final words, the beautiful Etain was changed into a butterfly and swiftly carried off by the howling winds through the open window far beyond the palace of Midhir the Proud.

For seven long years, Etain lived a life of intolerable misery. She could find no relief from her endless flight and her delicate wings were tattered and torn by the fiery gusts that tossed and buffeted her throughout the length and breadth of the country. One day, when she had almost abandoned hope of ever finding rest again, a chance flurry thrust her through a window of the fairy palace of Aengus Óg, the Danann god of love. All deities of the Otherworld possessed the ability to recognize their own kind, and Etain was immediately revealed to Aengus, despite her winged appearance. He could not entirely undo the druid's sorcery, but he took Etain into his care and conjured up a spell to return her to her human form every day, from dusk until dawn. During the daytime, Aengus set aside the sunniest corner of the palace gardens for her private use and planted it with the most colourful, fragrant flowers and shrubs. In the evening, when Etain was transformed once again into a beautiful maiden, she gave Aengus her love and they grew to treasure each other's company, believing they would spend many happy years together.

It was not long, however, before Fuamnach came to discover Etain's place of refuge. Still bent on revenge, she appeared at the palace of Aengus Óg in the form of a raven and alighted on an apple tree in the centre of the garden. She soon caught sight of a dainty butterfly resting on some rose petals and with a sudden swoop she opened her beak and lifted the fragile creature into the air. Once they were outside of the palace walls, a magic tempest began to blow around Etain. She found herself being carried away from the fairy mounds during the fierce storm, to the unfamiliar plains of Erin above ground where very few of the fairy people had ever dared to emerge.

As soon as he discovered that Etain had been outwitted by Fuamnach, Aengus sprinkled a magic potion into the air and called upon the gods to end the beautiful maiden's torturous wanderings above the earth's surface. A short time afterwards, Etain became trapped in a terrible gale and was hurled through the castle windows of an Ulster Chieftain named Etar. A great feast was in progress and all the noblemen of the province were gathered together for an evening of merry-making and dancing. Etar's wife sat at his right hand and she held a goblet of wine to her lips. Weary and thirsty from her flight, Etain came to rest on the rim of the vessel intending to sip some of the refreshing liquid. But as she leaned forward, she fell into the drinking-cup and was passed down the throat of the noblewoman as soon as she swallowed her next draught.

Several weeks after the great feast, Etar's wife was overjoyed to discover that she was carrying a child. The gods had fulfilled their promise and had caused Etain to nestle in her womb until the time when she could be reborn as a mortal child. After nine months, the Chieftain and his wife were blessed with a daughter and they gave her the name of Etain. She grew to become one of the most beautiful maidens in Ulster and although she bore the same name as before, she could remember nothing of her former life with the Daoine Sidhe.

It was at about this time that a distinguished warrior known as Eochaid Airem was crowned High King of Erin. One of the first tasks he set himself was to organize a splendid annual feast, gathering together all of the kingdom's noblemen to the royal palace for a month of glorious festivity. But the king was soon disappointed to discover that a great number of his noblemen would not accept his generous invitation. Deeply puzzled by this turn of events, he ordered several of them to appear before him and demanded an explanation.

'We cannot attend such a feast,' they told him, 'since the absence of a queen by your side would make it unwholesome. The people of Erin have never before served a king who does not possess a queen. There are many among us with daughters young and fair who would be more than willing to help restore your honour.'

The King was now made to realize that his integrity rested on securing a wife, and he immediately sent out horsemen to the four corners of Erin in search of a maiden who would make for him a suitable queen. Within a few days, a group of his messengers returned with the news that they had found the fairest creature in the land. Eochaid set forth at once to view with his own eyes the maiden his men had found for him. He rode for some distance until at last he happened upon four nymph-like figures laughing and dancing in the sunshine at the edge of a small, meandering brook. One of them was indeed far more beautiful than the others. She was clothed in a mantel of bright purple which was clasped over her bosom with a brooch of bright, glittering gold. Underneath, she wore a tunic of the finest emerald silk, intricately decorated with silver fringes and sparkling jewels. Her skin was as white and smooth as snow, her eyes were as blue as hyacinths and her lips as red as the finest rubies. Two tresses of chestnut hair rested on her head. Each one was plaited into four strands and fastened at the ends with tiny spheres of gold. Eochaid shyly approached the maiden and began to question her softly:

'Who are you,' he inquired, 'and who was it created so rare and beautiful a vision as you?'

'I am Etain, daughter of Etar,' said the maiden. 'Your messengers warned me of your visit Eochaid and I have heard noble tales of you since I was a little child.'

'Will you allow me to woo you then, fair Etain,' asked the King, 'for I cannot conceive of any greater pleasure left to me.'

'It is you I have waited for,' replied Etain, 'and I will only be truly fulfilled if you take me with you to Tara where I will serve you well as queen.'

Overwhelmed with joy at these words, Eochaid grasped Etain's hand and lifted her onto the saddle next to him. They rode speedily towards the palace at Tara where news of the king's betrothal had already reached the ears of his subjects. A hearty welcome awaited the couple as they approached the great gates and they were married that same afternoon to the jubilant sounds of chiming bells and shouts of approval from the large crowd that had gathered to wish them well.

The Royal Assembly of Tara was now the grand occasion everybody looked forward to and preparations began in earnest for the series of lavish banquets and pageants that were to take place in the grounds of the palace. On the morning of first day of the Assembly, Etain made ready to welcome Eochaid's guests and she rode to the top of the hill beyond the gates to catch a glimpse of the first to arrive. After a time, a young warrior on horseback appeared in the distance making his way steadily towards her. He wore a robe of royal purple and his hair, which tumbled below his shoulders, was golden yellow in colour. His face was proud and radiant and his eyes lustrous and gentle. In his left hand, he held a five-pointed spear and in his right, a circular shield, laden with white gold and precious gems. The warrior came forward and Etain welcomed him zealously:

'We are honoured by your presence, young warrior,' said Etain. 'A warm reception awaits you at the palace where I shall be pleased to lead you.'

But the warrior hesitated to accompany her and began to speak in a pained, anxious voice.

'Do you not know me, Etain?' he asked. 'For years I have been searching every corner of the land for you. I am your husband, Midhir the Proud, from the fairy kingdom of the Ever Young.'

'My husband is Eochaid Airem, High King of Erin,' replied Etain. 'Are you not deceived by your own eyes? You are a stranger to me and I have never before heard of your kingdom.'

'Fuamnach is dead and it is now safe for you to return to your home,' Midhir told her. 'It was the sorcery of Fuamnach and Bressal that drove us apart, Etain. Will you come with me now to a land full of music, where men and women remain eternally fair and without blemish. There, in the land of your birth, we may again live happily as man and wife.'

'I will not readily abandon the King of Erin for a man unknown to me,' answered Etain. 'I would never seek to depart with you without the King's consent and I know he will not give it, since his love for me deepens with every passing day.'

Hearing these words, Midhir bowed his head in defeat. It was not in his nature to take Etain by force and he sadly bade her farewell, galloping furiously across the plains of Erin, his purple cloak billowing around him in the breeze.

Throughout the winter months that followed, Etain remained haunted by the image of the stranger who had visited her on the hill. She began to dream of a land filled with sunshine and laughter where she frequently appeared seated on a throne, smiling happily. She could not explain these dreams and did not dare to confide in her husband. Often, however, she would ride to the place where she had met with Midhir the Proud and gaze outwards towards the flat, green carpet of land, secretly entertaining the hope that a rider on a white horse might suddenly appear on the horizon.

One fair summer's morning as Eochaid Airem peered out of the palace window, he noticed a young warrior in a purple cloak riding towards the Hill of Tara. The King was intrigued by the sight and ordered his horse to be saddled so that he might personally greet the stranger and establish the purpose of his visit to the palace.

'I am known to all as Midhir,' said the warrior. 'I have journeyed here to meet with Eochaid Airem, for I am told he is the finest chess-player in the land. I have with me a chessboard with which to test his skill if he is willing to meet my challenge.'

The warrior then produced from beneath his mantel a solid gold chessboard with thirty-two silver pieces, each one encrusted with the finest sapphires and diamonds.

'I would be more than delighted to play a game of chess with you,' replied the King, and he led the way to a brightly-lit chamber where they placed the board on a sturdy round table and sat down to play the first game. The King was not long in proving his reputation as a champion player and, as the young warrior seemed disappointed with his own performance, it was decided that they should play a second game. Again, the King was victorious and the warrior appeared to become more and more agitated. But it was Midhir's intention all along to win Eochaid's sympathy and to lure him into a false sense of security.

'Perhaps it would be best,' suggested the King, 'if we decided on a wager for our third and final game. Name your stake, choose any treasure you desire, and it will be forfeited to you if you are triumphant over me.'

'That is very generous of you,' replied Midhir, 'but I have more than enough wealth and possessions to satisfy me. Perhaps you have a wife, however, who would not protest too loudly if I stole from her a single kiss as my prize?'

'I am sure she would not object,' answered Eochaid cheerfully, for he felt certain that Etain would never have to deliver such a trophy.

The two played on, but this time the King struggled to keep control of the game and at length he was beaten by the younger man. Eochaid now fell silent and began to regret that he had so carelessly offered his wife as prize. In desperation and despair, he begged his opponent to surrender his claim to the pledged kiss. But Midhir insisted firmly on the forfeit and the King was forced to honour his part of the bargain.

'Perhaps you will find it in your heart to show me a little kindness,' Eochaid pleaded, 'and allow me time to reconcile myself to the dispatch of such a precious reward. Return to this palace one month from today and what you have asked for will not be denied you.'

'Your request is not unreasonable,' replied Midhir, 'and it leads me to believe that a kiss from your wife must be worth the long wait.'

Then Eochaid Airem appointed a day at the end of the month when Midhir would return to collect his prize and the young warrior departed the palace, his heart lighter than it had been for a very long time.

As the days passed by and the time approached for Etain to deliver her kiss, the King became more and more protective of his beautiful wife. Fearing that his handsome rival would appear at any moment, he gave the order for the palace to be surrounded by a great host of armed men and instructed them not to allow any stranger to enter the grounds. Once he had made certain that the outer courtyards were protected and that the doors to the inner chambers were properly guarded, Eochaid began to feel more at ease and decided to invite his closest friends to dine with him later that evening in the banqueting hall. Etain appeared next to him in a gown of shimmering silver and a row of servants carried trays of the most exotic food and flagons of the finest wine through to the long table. While the queen poured the wine for her hosts, the hall began to fill with laughter and conversation and it was not long before Eochaid called for his musicians to begin playing.

In the midst of this happy atmosphere, nobody noticed the tall, elegant figure enter the room and make his way towards the King, his face noble and determined, his spear held proudly in his left hand. Etain suddenly raised her eyes and saw before her the young rider whose image had filled her sleeping hours since their meeting on the Hill of Tara. He appeared more beautiful and resplendent than ever, more eloquent and powerful than her memory had allowed for. A wonderful feeling of warmth and affection stirred within Etain's breast as Midhir gazed tenderly upon her and she felt that somehow she had always known and loved the man who stood before her. Then Midhir addressed the King and his words were purposeful and resolute:

'Let me collect what has been promised me,' he said to Eochaid, 'It is a debt that is due and the time is ripe for payment.'

The King and his party looked on helplessly as Midhir encircled the fair Etain in his arms. As their lips met, a thick veil of mist appeared around them, and they were lifted gracefully into the air and out into the night. Eochaid and his noblemen rushed from the banqueting hall in pursuit of the couple, but all they could see were two white swans circling the star-filled sky above the royal palace. Eochaid wept bitterly for his loss and swore solemnly that he would not rest a single moment until every fairy mound in the land had been dug up and destroyed in his search for Midhir the Proud.

Echo and Narcissus

ECHO WAS A WOOD NYMPH who danced and sang in the forest. She told engaging stories to anyone who would listen, and although she was adored by the other nymphs her headstrong ways meant that none of her playmates had the last word. Echo would skip and frolic among the trees, charming the small creatures and befriending the forest folk as she played.

Hera was enchanted by the nubile young nymph, and she came daily to hear Echo's tales of adventure, of fairies and of far-off places, stories that grew ever more complicated with each telling. One day Hera left earlier than usual, inspired to see her husband Zeus by Echo's romantic tales. It was on this day that Hera was presented with evidence of her husband's philanderings, and discovered that Echo had been involved in the subterfuge, receiving a wage from Zeus to occupy his lovely wife.

Hera flew into a rage which resounded through the Kingdom, and the victim of her wrath was Echo, who was stripped of her power of speech, able only to echo the last words spoken by any person. Echo fled deep into the forest, tortured by her speechlessness, drained of her life and vitality.

Now in this same forest lived a handsome young man named Narcissus, a Thespian and the son of the blue nymph Leirope and the River-god Cephisus. When Narcissus was but a child, his mother consulted the seer Tiresias to learn of his fortune. Would he live to old age? she longed to know.

'If he never knows himself,' said the wise man.

Tales of Narcissus' beauty had spread far and wide and it was not long before a he grew conceited and self-satisfied. Lovers came and went, but Narcissus' heart grew colder, frosted by the knowledge that none could match his charm and grace.

Echo had been drawn to the youth for many months, and secretly followed him in the forest, begging him silently to speak so she could make her presence known. One day her wish was granted, and Narcissus, who had lost his companions in the forest, called out, 'Is anyone here?"

'Here,' cried the young nymph with delight.

'Come!' replied Narcissus, his face a haughty mask.

'Come!' repeated Echo.

'Why do you avoid me?' asked Narcissus, a surprised look crossing his face.

'Why do you avoid me?' said Echo.

'Let us come together,' he shouted, with careless confidence. He looked purposefully around, his manly brow furrowed with intrigue.

'Let us come together.' And as the words tumbled from Echo's tender lips, she leapt from her hiding place, and threw herself against the comely young man.

He stepped back in horror, roughly detaching himself from her grasp, and snarling, 'I will die before you ever lay with me!' Summoning up the arrogance of his youth, he cast Echo aside and left the clearing, failing to hear her pleading 'Lay with me ...' as he stalked away.

Echo grew cold with misery, and unable to draw breath, she lay still and pined for her lost love, the vessel for her childish hopes and aspirations. There Echo laid until she was no more than her voice, her tiny body becoming one with the woodland floor.

Narcissus quickly forgot this uneasy encounter, and carried on his relentless search for love. One day, deep in the forest, he stopped his hunting in order to take a drink from a pure, clear stream. As he leant over the crystal waters he was caught by such a sight of beauty that his breath escaped in a stunned gasp. There, in this magical current, was a face of such perfect loveliness that Narcissus was unable to move, to call out.

He whispered to the dazzling illusion, but though the lips of this creature moved, too, no sound was uttered. Narcissus was enchanted.

He reached forwards to the elegant face, the princely features, but alas, with every movement the object of his passion disappeared in a kaleidoscope of colour.

Narcissus had fallen in love with his own reflection, and he was held captive by its magnificence. He reclined by the stream, unable to move, and there he laid without food or water until he too pined away, to become one with the forest. The last words to slip from his aristocratic lips were,

'O youth beloved in vain. Farewell.' To which the spirit of the love-sickened nymph Echo replied, 'Farewell.'

Those who had once swooned for Narcissus prepared his funeral pyre, but his body had disappeared. In its place grew a slim and elegant flower with a blood-red heart, which gazed piteously at its reflection as it dipped over the water. Today, this flower can be found by the waters of certain streams, a flower known for its beauty, which gazes eternally at its own reflection.

The spirit of Echo is often heard, for she fled that forest, and wanders far from the shores of that stream, ever searching for her lost love, and, of course, her voice.

The Rose Beauty

IN OLDEN TIMES, when the camel was a horse-dealer, the mouse a barber, the cuckoo a tailor, the tortoise a baker, and the ass still a servant, there was a miller who had a black cat. Besides this miller, there was a Padishah who had three daughters, aged respectively forty, thirty, and twenty years. The eldest went to the youngest and made her write a letter to her father in these terms:

"Dear father, one of my sisters is forty, the other thirty, and they have not yet married. Take notice that I will not wait so long before I get a husband."

The Padishah, on reading the letter, sent for his daughters and thus addressed them: "Here are a bow and arrow for each of you; go and shoot, and wherever your arrows fall, there you will find your future husbands."

Taking the weapons from their father, the three maidens went forth. The eldest shot first, and her arrow fell in the palace of the Vezir's son; she was accordingly united to him. The second daughter's arrow fell in the palace of the son of the Sheikh-ul-Islam, and him she got for a husband. When the youngest shot, however, her arrow fell into the hut of a wood-cutter. "That doesn't count," cried everybody; and she shot again. The second time the arrow fell in the same spot; and a third attempt met no better success.

The Shah was wrathful with his daughter on account of her letter, and exclaimed: "You foolish creature, that serves you right. Your elder sisters have waited patiently and are rewarded. You, the youngest, have dared to write me that impertinent letter: you are justly punished. Take your woodcutter and be off with you." So the poor girl left her father's palace to be the wife of the woodcutter.

In the course of time a beautiful girl-baby was born to them. The wood-cutter's wife bitterly lamented the fact that her child must have so poor a home, but even while she wept, three wonderful fairies stepped through the wall of the hut into the dismal room where the child lay. Standing by her cot, each in turn stretched out a hand over the sleeping infant.

Said the first fairy: "Rose-Beauty shall she be called; and instead of tears, pearls shall she shed."

Said the second fairy: "When she smiles, roses shall blossom." Said the third: "Wherever her foot falls shall grass spring up!" Then the three disappeared as they had come.

Years passed away. The child grew and attained her twelfth year, developing such loveliness as none had ever seen before. To gaze once upon her was to be filled with love for her. When she smiled roses blossomed; when she wept pearls fell from her eyes, and grass grew wherever her feet trod. The fame of her beauty spread far and wide.

The mother of a certain Prince heard of Rose-Beauty and resolved that this maiden and no other should become her son's bride. She called her son to her and told him that in the town was a maiden who smiled roses, wept pearls, and under whose feet grass grew; he must see her.

The fairies had already shown the maid to the Prince in a dream, and thus kindled in him the fire of love; but before his mother he was shy and refused to seek the object of his passion. The Sultana therefore insisted, and finally ordered a lady of the palace to accompany him on his quest. They entered the hut, explained the purpose of their visit, and in the name of Allah demanded the maiden for the Shahzada. The poor people were overcome with joy at their good fortune; they promised their daughter, and commenced preparations for her departure.

Now this palace-dame had a daughter, who somewhat resembled the Rose-Beauty, and she was displeased that the Prince should marry a poor girl instead of her own daughter. Accordingly she concocted a scheme to deceive the people and bring about the Prince's marriage to her own child. On the wedding-day she gave the woodcutter's daughter salt food to eat, and took a jug of water and a large basket and put them in the bridal coach wherein the Rose-Beauty, herself, and her daughter were about to set out for the palace.

On the way the maiden, complaining of thirst, asked for a drink of water. The palace-dame answered: "I shall give you no water unless you give me an eye in exchange." Nearly dying of thirst, the maiden took out one of her eyes and gave it to the cruel woman for a drink of water.

As they proceeded the torments of thirst again overcame the poor maiden, and again she asked for water. "I will give you drink, but only in exchange for your other eye," answered the woman. So great was her agony that the victim yielded her other eye. No sooner had the woman got it in her possession than she took the now sightless Rose-Beauty, bound her in the basket, and had her carried to the top of a mountain.

The woman now hastened to the palace and presented her daughter, clad in a gorgeous wedding garment, to the Prince, saying: "Here is your bride." The marriage was accordingly celebrated with great festivity; but when the Prince came to lift his wife's veil he saw that she was not the one revealed to him in his dream. As, however, she resembled the dream-bride somewhat, he held his peace.

The Prince knew that the maiden of his dream wept pearls, smiled roses, and that the grass grew under her feet; from this one, however, came neither pearls, roses, nor grass. He suspected more than ever that he had been deceived, but "I will soon find out," he thought to himself, and spoke no word on the subject to anyone.

Meanwhile the poor Rose-Beauty on the mountaintop wept and moaned, pearls rolling down her cheeks from her sightless eye-sockets until the basket in which she lay bound was filled to overflowing. A scavenger at work on the road heard the sounds of grief and cried out in fear: "Who is that, a spirit or a fairy?" The maiden answered: "Neither a spirit nor a fairy, but a human being like yourself."

The scavenger, reassured, approached the basket, opened it, and saw the blind girl and the pearls she had shed. He took her home to his miserable hovel, and being alone in the world, adopted her as his own child. But the maiden constantly bemoaned the loss of her eyes, and as she was always weeping, the man now had nothing else to do but gather the pearls she shed and go out and sell them. Time rolled on. In the palace was merriment, in the scavenger's hovel grief and pain. One day as the Rose-Beauty was sitting at the door, she smiled at some pleasant recollection, and forthwith a rose appeared. Said the maiden to the scavenger: "Father, here is a rose; take it to the Prince's palace and say thou hast a rose of a rare kind to sell. When the palace dame appears, say it cannot be sold for money, but for a human eye." The man took the rose, went to the palace and cried aloud: "A rose for sale; the only one of its kind in the world."

Indeed, it was not the season for roses. The palace-dame, hearing the scavenger's cry, resolved to buy the rose for her daughter, thinking that when the Prince saw the flower in his wife's possession his suspicions would be set at rest. Calling the poor man aside, she inquired the price of the rose. "Money cannot buy it," replied the scavenger, "but I will part with it for a human eye." Hereupon the woman produced one of the Rose-Beauty's eyes and gave it in exchange for the rose. Carrying the flower immediately to her daughter, she fixed it in her hair, and when the Prince saw her he began to fancy that she might after all be the maiden the fairies had showed him in his dream, though he was by no means sure. He consoled himself with the thought that soon the matter would be cleared up.

The old man took the eye and gave it to the Rose-Beauty. Praising Allah, she fixed it in its place, and had the joy of being able to see quite well once more. In her newfound happiness the maiden smiled so much that ere long there were quite a number of roses. One of these she gave to the scavenger that he might go with it to the palace and secure her remaining eye. Scarcely had he arrived at the palace than the woman saw him with the rose and thought to herself: "All is coming right; the Prince is already beginning to love my daughter. I will buy this other rose, and as his love strengthens he will soon forget the woodcutter's child." She called the scavenger and demanded the rose, which the man said could only be sold on the same terms as the first. The woman willingly gave him the other eye and hastened with the flower to her daughter, while the old man went home with his prize.

The Rose-Beauty, now in possession of both her eyes, was even lovelier than before. As now she smilingly took her walks abroad, roses and grass transformed the barren hillside into a veritable Eden. One day while the maiden was walking in the neighbourhood, the palace-dame saw her and was dismayed. What would be her daughter's fate if the truth became known? She inquired for the scavenger's dwelling, hastened to him, and frightened the old man out of his wits by accusing him of harbouring a witch. In his fright he asked the woman what he should do. "Ask her about her talisman," she advised; "then I can soon settle the matter." So when the girl came in, the first thing her foster-father did was to ask her how it was that, being human, she could work such magic.

Suspecting no harm, she informed him that at her birth the fairies gave her a talisman whereby she could bring forth pearls, roses, and grass as long as the talisman lived. "What is your talisman?" inquired the old man. "A young stag that lives on the mountain; when it dies I must die too," answered the maiden.

Next day the palace-dame came secretly to the scavenger, and learned from him what the talisman was. With this precious knowledge she hastened joyfully home, imparted the information to her daughter, and advised her to ask the Prince for the stag. Without delay the young wife complained to her lord of indisposition, saying she must have the heart of a certain mountain stag to eat. The Prince sent out his hunters, who ere long returned with the animal, slaughtered it and took out its heart, which was cooked for the pretended invalid.

At that same instant the Rose-Beauty also died. The scavenger buried her, and mourned for her long and sincerely.

Now in the stag's heart was a red coral, that escaped observation; and when the Prince's wife was eating, it fell to the floor and rolled under the stairs.

A year later there was born to the Prince a daughter who wept pearls, smiled roses, and under whose tiny feet grass grew. When the Prince saw that his child was a Rose-Beauty, he easily persuaded himself that his wife was really the right one. But one night in a dream the Rose-Beauty appeared to him and said: "Oh, Prince, my own bridegroom, my soul is under the palace-stairs, my body in the cemetery, thy daughter is my daughter, my talisman the little coral."

As soon as the Prince awoke he went to the stairs and searched for and found the coral. He carried it to his room and laid it on the table. When his little daughter came in she took up the coral, and hardly had her fingers touched it than both vanished. The three fairies conveyed the child to her mother, the Rose-Beauty, who, as the coral fell into her mouth, awakened to a new life.

The Prince, in his restless state, went to the cemetery. Behold! there he found the Rose-Beauty of his dreams with his child in her arms. They cordially embraced, and as mother and daughter wept for joy, pearls streamed from the eyes of both; when they smiled roses blossomed, and grass sprang up wherever their feet touched.

The palace-dame and her daughter were severely punished, and the old scavenger was invited to live with the Rose-Beauty and the Prince at their palace. The reunited lovers had a magnificent wedding-feast and their happiness lasted forever.

Beauty and the Beast

ONCE UPON A TIME, in a very far-off country, there lived a merchant who had been so fortunate in all his undertakings that he was enormously rich. As he had, however, six sons and six daughters, he found that his money was not too much to let them all have everything they fancied, as they were accustomed to do.

But one day a most unexpected misfortune befell them. Their house caught fire and was speedily burnt to the ground, with all the splendid furniture, the books, pictures, gold, silver, and precious goods it contained; and this was only the beginning of their troubles. Their father, who had until this moment prospered in all ways, suddenly lost every ship he had upon the sea, either by dint of pirates, shipwreck, or fire. Then he heard that his clerks in distant countries, whom he trusted entirely, had proved unfaithful; and at last from great wealth he fell into the direst poverty.

All that he had left was a little house in a desolate place at least a hundred leagues from the town in which he had lived, and to this he was forced to retreat with his children, who were in despair at the idea of leading such a different life. Indeed, the daughters at first hoped that their friends, who had been so numerous while they were rich, would insist on their staying in their houses now they no longer possessed one. But they soon found that they were left alone, and that their former friends even attributed their misfortunes to their own extravagance, and showed no intention of offering them any help. So nothing was left for them but to take their departure to the cottage, which stood in the midst of a dark forest, and seemed to be the most dismal place upon the face of the earth. As they were too poor to have any servants, the girls had to work hard, like peasants, and the sons, for their part, cultivated the fields to earn their living. Roughly clothed, and living in the simplest way, the girls regretted unceasingly the luxuries and amusements of their former life; only the youngest tried to be brave and cheerful. She had been as sad as anyone when misfortune overtook her father, but, soon recovering her natural gaiety, she set to work to make the best of things, to amuse her father and brothers as well as she could, and to try to persuade her sisters to join her in dancing and singing. But they would do nothing of the sort, and, because she was not as doleful as themselves, they declared that this miserable life was all she was fit for. But she was really far prettier and cleverer than they were; indeed, she was so lovely that she was always called Beauty. After two years, when they were all beginning to get used to their new life, something happened to disturb their tranquillity. Their father received the news that one of his ships, which he had believed to be lost, had come safely into port with a rich cargo. All the sons and daughters at once thought that their poverty was at an end, and wanted to set out directly for the town; but their father, who was more prudent, begged them to wait a little, and, though it was harvest time, and he could ill be spared, determined to go himself first, to make inquiries. Only the youngest daughter had any doubt but that they would soon again be as rich as they were before, or at least rich enough to live comfortably in some town where they would find amusement and gay companions once more. So they all loaded their father with commissions for jewels and dresses which it would have taken a fortune to buy; only

Beauty, feeling sure that it was of no use, did not ask for anything. Her father, noticing her silence, said: "And what shall I bring for you, Beauty?"

"The only thing I wish for is to see you come home safely," she answered.

But this only vexed her sisters, who fancied she was blaming them for having asked for such costly things. Her father, however, was pleased, but as he thought that at her age she certainly ought to like pretty presents, he told her to choose something.

"Well, dear father," she said, "as you insist upon it, I beg that you will bring me a rose. I have not seen one since we came here, and I love them so much."

So the merchant set out and reached the town as quickly as possible, but only to find that his former companions, believing him to be dead, had divided between them the goods which the ship had brought; and after six months of trouble and expense he found himself as poor as when he started, having been able to recover only just enough to pay the cost of his journey. To make matters worse, he was obliged to leave the town in the most terrible weather, so that by the time he was within a few leagues of his home he was almost exhausted with cold and fatigue. Though he knew it would take some hours to get through the forest, he was so anxious to be at his journey's end that he resolved to go on; but night overtook him, and the deep snow and bitter frost made it impossible for his horse to carry him any further. Not a house was to be seen; the only shelter he could get was the hollow trunk of a great tree, and there he crouched all the night which seemed to him the longest he had ever known. In spite of his weariness the howling of the wolves kept him awake, and even when at last the day broke he was not much better off, for the falling snow had covered up every path, and he did not know which way to turn.

At length he made out some sort of track, and though at the beginning it was so rough and slippery that he fell down more than once, it presently became easier, and led him into an avenue of trees which ended in a splendid castle. It seemed to the merchant very strange that no snow had fallen in the avenue, which was entirely composed of orange trees, covered with flowers and fruit. When he reached the first court of the castle he saw before him a flight of agate steps, and went up them, and passed through several splendidly furnished rooms. The pleasant warmth of the air revived him, and he felt very hungry; but there seemed to be nobody in all this vast and splendid palace whom he could ask to give him something to eat. Deep silence reigned everywhere, and at last, tired of roaming through empty rooms and galleries, he stopped in a room smaller than the rest, where a clear fire was burning and a couch was drawn up closely to it. Thinking that this must be prepared for someone who was expected, he sat down to wait till he should come, and very soon fell into a sweet sleep.

When his extreme hunger wakened him after several hours, he was still alone; but a little table, upon which was a good dinner, had been drawn up close to him, and, as he had eaten nothing for twenty-four hours, he lost no time in beginning his meal, hoping that he might soon have an opportunity of thanking his considerate entertainer, whoever it might be. But no one appeared, and even after another long sleep, from which he awoke completely refreshed, there was no sign of anybody, though a fresh meal of dainty cakes and fruit was prepared upon the little table at his elbow. Being naturally timid, the silence began to terrify him, and he resolved to search once more through all the rooms; but it was of no use. Not even a servant was to be seen; there was no sign of life in the palace! He began to wonder what he should do, and to amuse himself by pretending that all the treasures he saw were his own, and considering how he would divide them among his children. Then he went down into the garden, and though it was winter everywhere else, here the sun shone, and the birds sang, and the flowers bloomed, and the air was soft and sweet. The merchant, in ecstacies with all he saw and heard, said to himself:

"All this must be meant for me. I will go this minute and bring my children to share all these delights."

In spite of being so cold and weary when he reached the castle, he had taken his horse to the stable and fed it. Now he thought he would saddle it for his homeward journey, and he turned down the path which led to the stable. This path had a hedge of roses on each side of it, and the merchant thought he had never seen or smelt such exquisite flowers. They reminded him of his promise to Beauty, and he stopped and had just gathered one to take to her when he was startled by a strange noise behind him. Turning round, he saw a frightful Beast, which seemed to be very angry and said, in a terrible voice:

"Who told you that you might gather my roses? Was it not enough that I allowed you to be in my palace and was kind to you? This is the way you show your gratitude, by stealing my flowers! But your insolence shall not go unpunished." The merchant, terrified by these furious words, dropped the fatal rose, and, throwing himself on his knees, cried: "Pardon me, noble sir. I am truly grateful to you for your hospitality, which was so magnificent that I could not imagine that you would be offended by my taking such a little thing as a rose." But the Beast's anger was not lessened by this speech.

"You are very ready with excuses and flattery," he cried; "but that will not save you from the death you deserve."

"Alas!" thought the merchant, "if my daughter could only know what danger her rose has brought me into!"

And in despair he began to tell the Beast all his misfortunes, and the reason of his journey, not forgetting to mention Beauty's request.

"A king's ransom would hardly have procured all that my other daughters asked." he said: "but I thought that I might at least take Beauty her rose. I beg you to forgive me, for you see I meant no harm."

The Beast considered for a moment, and then he said, in a less furious tone:

"I will forgive you on one condition – that is, that you will give me one of your daughters."

"Ah!" cried the merchant, "if I were cruel enough to buy my own life at the expense of one of my children's, what excuse could I invent to bring her here?"

"No excuse would be necessary," answered the Beast. "If she comes at all she must come willingly. On no other condition will I have her. See if any one of them is courageous enough, and loves you well enough to come and save your life. You seem to be an honest man, so I will trust you to go home. I give you a month to see if either of your daughters will come back with you and stay here, to let you go free. If neither of them is willing, you must come alone, after bidding them good-by for ever, for then you will belong to me. And do not imagine that you can hide from me, for if you fail to keep your word I will come and fetch you!" added the Beast grimly.

The merchant accepted this proposal, though he did not really think any of his daughters could be persuaded to come. He promised to return at the time appointed, and then, anxious to escape from the presence of the Beast, he asked permission to set off at once. But the Beast answered that he could not go until next day.

"Then you will find a horse ready for you," he said. "Now go and eat your supper, and await my orders."

The poor merchant, more dead than alive, went back to his room, where the most delicious supper was already served on the little table which was drawn up before a blazing fire. But he was too terrified to eat, and only tasted a few of the dishes, for fear the Beast should be angry if he did not obey his orders. When he had finished he heard a great noise in the next room, which he knew meant that the Beast was coming. As he could do nothing to escape his visit, the only thing that remained was to seem as little afraid as possible; so when the Beast appeared and asked roughly if he had supped well, the merchant answered humbly that he had, thanks to his host's kindness. Then the Beast warned him to remember their agreement, and to prepare his daughter exactly for what she had to expect.

"Do not get up to-morrow," he added, "until you see the sun and hear a golden bell ring. Then you will find your breakfast waiting for you here, and the horse you are to ride will be ready in the courtyard. He will also bring you back again when you come with your daughter a month hence. Farewell. Take a rose to Beauty, and remember your promise!"

The merchant was only too glad when the Beast went away, and though he could not sleep for sadness, he lay down until the sun rose. Then, after a hasty breakfast, he went to gather Beauty's rose, and mounted his horse, which carried him off so swiftly that in an instant he had lost sight of the palace, and he was still wrapped in gloomy thoughts when it stopped before the door of the cottage.

His sons and daughters, who had been very uneasy at his long absence, rushed to meet him, eager to know the result of his journey, which, seeing him mounted upon a splendid horse and wrapped in a rich mantle, they supposed to be favourable. He hid the truth from them at first, only saying sadly to Beauty as he gave her the rose:

"Here is what you asked me to bring you; you little know what it has cost."

But this excited their curiosity so greatly that presently he told them his adventures from beginning to end, and then they were all very unhappy. The girls lamented loudly over their lost hopes, and the sons declared that their father should not return to this terrible castle, and began to make plans for killing the Beast if it should come to fetch him. But he reminded them that he had promised to go back. Then the girls were very angry with Beauty, and said it was all her fault, and that if she had asked for something sensible this would never have happened, and complained bitterly that they should have to suffer for her folly.

Poor Beauty, much distressed, said to them:

"I have, indeed, caused this misfortune, but I assure you I did it innocently. Who could have guessed that to ask for a rose in the middle of summer would cause so much misery? But as I did the mischief it is only just that I should suffer for it. I will therefore go back with my father to keep his promise."

At first nobody would hear of this arrangement, and her father and brothers, who loved her dearly, declared that nothing should make them let her go; but Beauty was firm. As the time drew near she divided all her little possessions between her sisters, and said good-by to everything she loved, and when the fatal day came she encouraged and cheered her father as they mounted together the horse which had brought him back. It seemed to fly rather than gallop, but so smoothly that Beauty was not frightened; indeed, she would have enjoyed the journey if she had not feared what might happen to her at the end of it. Her father still tried to persuade her to go back, but in vain. While they were talking the night fell, and then, to their great surprise, wonderful coloured lights began to shine in all directions, and splendid fireworks blazed out before them; all the forest was illuminated by them, and even felt pleasantly warm, though it had been bitterly cold before. This lasted until they reached the avenue of orange trees, where were statues holding flaming torches, and when they got nearer to the palace they saw that it was illuminated from the roof to the ground, and music sounded softly from the courtyard. "The Beast must be very hungry," said Beauty, trying to laugh, "if he makes all this rejoicing over the arrival of his prey."

But, in spite of her anxiety, she could not help admiring all the wonderful things she saw.

The horse stopped at the foot of the flight of steps leading to the terrace, and when they had dismounted her father led her to the little room he had been in before, where they found a splendid fire burning, and the table daintily spread with a delicious supper.

The merchant knew that this was meant for them, and Beauty, who was rather less frightened now that she had passed through so many rooms and seen nothing of the Beast, was quite willing to begin, for her long ride had made her very hungry. But they had hardly finished their meal when the noise of the Beast's footsteps was heard approaching, and Beauty clung to her father in terror, which became all the greater when she saw how frightened he was. But when the Beast really appeared, though she trembled at the sight of him, she made a great effort to hide her terror, and saluted him respectfully.

This evidently pleased the Beast. After looking at her he said, in a tone that might have struck terror into the boldest heart, though he did not seem to be angry:

"Good-evening, old man. Good-evening, Beauty."

The merchant was too terrified to reply, but Beauty answered sweetly: "Good-evening, Beast."

"Have you come willingly?" asked the Beast. "Will you be content to stay here when your father goes away?"

Beauty answered bravely that she was quite prepared to stay.

"I am pleased with you," said the Beast. "As you have come of your own accord, you may stay. As for you, old man," he added, turning to the merchant, "at sunrise to-morrow you will take your departure. When the bell rings get up quickly and eat your breakfast, and you will find the same horse waiting to take you home; but remember that you must never expect to see my palace again."

Then turning to Beauty, he said:

"Take your father into the next room, and help him to choose everything you think your brothers and sisters would like to have. You will find two travelling-trunks there; fill them as full as you can. It is only just that you should send them something very precious as a remembrance of yourself."

Then he went away, after saying, "Good-by, Beauty; good-by, old man;" and though Beauty was beginning to think with great dismay of her father's departure, she was afraid to disobey the Beast's orders; and they went into the next room, which had shelves and cupboards all round it. They were greatly surprised at the riches it contained. There were splendid dresses fit for a queen, with all the ornaments that were to be worn with them; and when Beauty opened the cupboards she was quite dazzled by the gorgeous jewels that lay in heaps upon every shelf. After choosing a vast quantity, which she divided between her sisters – for she had made a heap of the wonderful dresses for each of them – she opened the last chest, which was full of gold.

"I think, father," she said, "that, as the gold will be more useful to you, we had better take out the other things again, and fill the trunks with it." So they did this; but the more they put in the more room there seemed to be, and at last they put back all the jewels and dresses they had taken out, and Beauty even added as many more of the jewels as she could carry at once; and then the trunks were not too full, but they were so heavy that an elephant could not have carried them!

"The Beast was mocking us," cried the merchant; "he must have pretended to give us all these things, knowing that I could not carry them away."

"Let us wait and see," answered Beauty. "I cannot believe that he meant to deceive us. All we can do is to fasten them up and leave them ready."

So they did this and returned to the little room, where, to their astonishment, they found breakfast ready. The merchant ate his with a good appetite, as the Beast's generosity made him believe that he might perhaps venture to come back soon and see Beauty. But she felt sure that her father was leaving her for ever, so she was very sad when the bell rang sharply for the second time, and warned them that the time had come for them to part. They went down into the courtyard, where two horses were waiting, one loaded with the two trunks, the other for him to ride. They were pawing the ground in their impatience to start, and the merchant was forced to bid Beauty a hasty farewell; and as soon as he was mounted he went off at such a pace that she lost sight of him in an instant. Then Beauty began to cry, and wandered sadly back to her own room. But she soon found that she was very sleepy, and as she had nothing better to do she lay down and instantly fell asleep. And then she dreamed that she was walking by a brook bordered with trees, and lamenting her sad fate, when a young prince, handsomer than anyone she had ever seen, and with a voice that went straight to her heart, came and said to her, "Ah, Beauty! you are not so unfortunate as you suppose. Here you will be rewarded for all you have suffered elsewhere. Your every wish shall be gratified. Only try to find me out, no matter how I may be disguised, as I love you dearly, and in making me happy you will find your own happiness. Be as true-hearted as you are beautiful, and we shall have nothing left to wish for."

"What can I do, Prince, to make you happy?" said Beauty.

"Only be grateful," he answered, "and do not trust too much to your eyes. And, above all, do not desert me until you have saved me from my cruel misery."

After this she thought she found herself in a room with a stately and beautiful lady, who said to her:

"Dear Beauty, try not to regret all you have left behind you, for you are destined to a better fate. Only do not let yourself be deceived by appearances."

Beauty found her dreams so interesting that she was in no hurry to awake, but presently the clock roused her by calling her name softly twelve times, and then she got up and found her dressing-table set out with everything she could possibly want; and when her toilet was finished she found dinner was waiting in the room next to hers. But dinner does not take very long when you are all by yourself, and very soon she sat down cosily in the corner of a sofa, and began to think about the charming Prince she had seen in her dream.

"He said I could make him happy," said Beauty to herself.

"It seems, then, that this horrible Beast keeps him a prisoner. How can I set him free? I wonder why they both told me not to trust to appearances? I don't understand it. But, after all, it was only a dream, so why should I trouble myself about it? I had better go and find something to do to amuse myself."

So she got up and began to explore some of the many rooms of the palace.

The first she entered was lined with mirrors, and Beauty saw herself reflected on every side, and thought she had never seen such a charming room. Then a bracelet which was hanging from a chandelier caught her eye, and on taking it down she was greatly surprised to find that it held a portrait of her unknown admirer, just as she had seen him in her dream. With great delight she slipped the bracelet on her arm, and went on into a gallery of pictures, where she soon found a portrait of the same handsome Prince, as large as life, and so well painted that as she studied it he seemed to smile kindly at her. Tearing herself away from the portrait at last, she passed through into a room which contained every musical instrument under the sun, and here she amused herself for a long while in trying some of them, and singing until she was tired. The next room was a library, and she saw everything she had ever wanted to read, as well as everything she had read, and it seemed to her that a whole lifetime would not be enough to even read the names of the books, there were so many. By this time it was growing dusk, and wax candles in diamond and ruby candlesticks were beginning to light themselves in every room.

Beauty found her supper served just at the time she preferred to have it, but she did not see anyone or hear a sound, and, though her father had warned her that she would be alone, she began to find it rather dull.

But presently she heard the Beast coming, and wondered tremblingly if he meant to eat her up now.

However, as he did not seem at all ferocious, and only said gruffly:

"Good-evening, Beauty," she answered cheerfully and managed to conceal her terror. Then the Beast asked her how she had been amusing herself, and she told him all the rooms she had seen.

Then he asked if she thought she could be happy in his palace; and Beauty answered that everything was so beautiful that she would be very hard to please if she could not be happy. And after about an hour's talk Beauty began to think that the Beast was not nearly so terrible as she had supposed at first. Then he got up to leave her, and said in his gruff voice:

"Do you love me, Beauty? Will you marry me?"

"Oh! what shall I say?" cried Beauty, for she was afraid to make the Beast angry by refusing.

"Say 'yes' or 'no' without fear," he replied.

"Oh! no, Beast," said Beauty hastily.

"Since you will not, good-night, Beauty," he said.

And she answered, "Good-night, Beast," very glad to find that her refusal had not provoked him. And after he was gone she was very soon in bed and asleep, and dreaming of her unknown Prince. She thought he came and said to her:

"Ah, Beauty! why are you so unkind to me? I fear I am fated to be unhappy for many a long day still."

And then her dreams changed, but the charming Prince figured in them all; and when morning came her first thought was to look at the portrait, and see if it was really like him, and she found that it certainly was.

This morning she decided to amuse herself in the garden, for the sun shone, and all the fountains were playing; but she was astonished to find that every place was familiar to her, and presently she came to the brook where the myrtle trees were growing where she had first met the Prince in her dream, and that made her think more than ever that he must be kept a prisoner by the Beast. When she was tired she went back to the palace, and found a new room full of materials for every kind of work – ribbons to make into bows, and silks to work into flowers. Then there was an aviary full of rare birds, which were so tame that they flew to Beauty as soon as they saw her, and perched upon her shoulders and her head.

"Pretty little creatures," she said, "how I wish that your cage was nearer to my room, that I might often hear you sing!"

So saying she opened a door, and found, to her delight, that it led into her own room, though she had thought it was quite the other side of the palace.

There were more birds in a room farther on, parrots and cockatoos that could talk, and they greeted Beauty by name; indeed, she found them so entertaining that she took one or two back to her room, and they talked to her while she was at supper; after which the Beast paid her his usual visit, and asked her the same questions as before, and then with a gruff "good-night" he took his departure, and Beauty went to bed to dream of her mysterious Prince. The days passed swiftly in different amusements, and after a while Beauty found out another strange thing in the palace, which often pleased her when she was tired of being alone. There was one room which she had not noticed particularly; it was empty, except that under each of the windows stood a very comfortable chair; and the first time she had looked out of the window it had seemed to her that a black curtain prevented her from seeing anything outside. But the second time she went into the room, happening to be tired, she sat down in one of the chairs, when instantly the curtain was rolled aside, and a most amusing pantomime was acted before her; there were dances, and coloured lights, and music, and pretty dresses, and it was all so gay that Beauty was in ecstacies. After that she tried the other seven windows in turn, and there was some new and surprising entertainment to be seen from each of them, so that Beauty never could feel lonely any more. Every evening after supper the Beast came to see her, and always before saying good-night asked her in his terrible voice:

"Beauty, will you marry me?"

And it seemed to Beauty, now she understood him better, that when she said, "No, Beast," he went away quite sad. But her happy dreams of the handsome young Prince soon made her forget the poor Beast, and the only thing that at all disturbed her was to be constantly told to distrust appearances, to let her heart guide her, and not her eyes, and many other equally perplexing things, which, consider as she would, she could not understand.

So everything went on for a long time, until at last, happy as she was, Beauty began to long for the sight of her father and her brothers and sisters; and one night, seeing her look very sad, the Beast asked her what was the matter. Beauty had quite ceased to be afraid of him. Now she knew that he was really gentle in spite of his ferocious looks and his dreadful voice. So she answered that she was longing to see her home once more. Upon hearing this the Beast seemed sadly distressed, and cried miserably.

"Ah! Beauty, have you the heart to desert an unhappy Beast like this? What more do you want to make you happy? Is it because you hate me that you want to escape?"

"No, dear Beast," answered Beauty softly, "I do not hate you, and I should be very sorry never to see you any more, but I long to see my father again. Only let me go for two months, and I promise to come back to you and stay for the rest of my life."

The Beast, who had been sighing dolefully while she spoke, now replied:

"I cannot refuse you anything you ask, even though it should cost me my life. Take the four boxes you will find in the room next to your own, and fill them with everything you wish to take with you. But remember your promise and come back when the two months are over, or you may have cause to repent it, for if you do not come in good time you will find your faithful Beast dead. You will not need any chariot to bring you back. Only say good-by to all your brothers and sisters the night before you come away, and when you have gone to bed turn this ring round upon your finger and say firmly: 'I wish to go back to my palace and see my Beast again.' Good-night, Beauty. Fear nothing, sleep peacefully, and before long you shall see your father once more."

As soon as Beauty was alone she hastened to fill the boxes with all the rare and precious things she saw about her, and only when she was tired of heaping things into them did they seem to be full.

Then she went to bed, but could hardly sleep for joy. And when at last she did begin to dream of her beloved Prince she was grieved to see him stretched upon a grassy bank, sad and weary, and hardly like himself.

"What is the matter?" she cried.

He looked at her reproachfully, and said:

"How can you ask me, cruel one? Are you not leaving me to my death perhaps?"

"Ah! don't be so sorrowful," cried Beauty; "I am only going to assure my father that I am safe and happy. I have promised the Beast faithfully that I will come back, and he would die of grief if I did not keep my word!"

"What would that matter to you?" said the Prince "Surely you would not care?"

"Indeed, I should be ungrateful if I did not care for such a kind Beast," cried Beauty indignantly. "I would die to save him from pain. I assure you it is not his fault that he is so ugly."

Just then a strange sound woke her – someone was speaking not very far away; and opening her eyes she found herself in a room she had never seen before, which was certainly not nearly so splendid as those she was used to in the Beast's palace. Where could she be? She got up and dressed hastily, and then saw that the boxes she had packed the night before were all in the room. While she was wondering by what magic the Beast had transported them and herself to this strange place she suddenly heard her father's voice, and rushed out and greeted him joyfully. Her brothers and sisters were all astonished at her appearance, as they had never expected to see her again, and there was no end to the questions they asked her. She had also much to hear about what had happened to them while she was away, and of her father's journey home. But when they heard that she had only come to be with them for a short time, and then must go back to the Beast's palace for ever, they lamented loudly. Then Beauty asked her father what he thought could be the meaning of her strange dreams, and why the Prince constantly begged her not to trust to appearances. After much consideration, he answered: "You tell me yourself that the Beast, frightful as he is, loves you dearly, and deserves your love and gratitude for his gentleness and kindness; I think the Prince must mean you to understand that you ought to reward him by doing as he wishes you to, in spite of his ugliness."

Beauty could not help seeing that this seemed very probable; still, when she thought of her dear Prince who was so handsome, she did not feel at all inclined to marry the Beast. At any rate, for two months she need not decide, but could enjoy herself with her sisters. But though they were rich now, and lived in town again, and had plenty of acquaintances, Beauty found that nothing amused her very much; and she often thought of the palace, where she was so happy, especially as at home she never once dreamed of her dear Prince, and she felt quite sad without him.

Then her sisters seemed to have got quite used to being without her, and even found her rather in the way, so she would not have been sorry when the two months were over but for her father and brothers, who begged her to stay, and seemed so grieved at the thought of her departure that she had not the courage to say good-by to them. Every day when she got up she meant to say it at night, and when night came she put it off again, until at last she had a dismal dream which helped her to make up her mind. She thought she was wandering in a lonely path in the palace gardens, when she heard groans which seemed to come from some bushes hiding the entrance of a cave, and running quickly to see what could be the matter, she found the Beast stretched out upon his side, apparently dying. He reproached her faintly with being the cause of his distress, and at the same moment a stately lady appeared, and said very gravely:

"Ah! Beauty, you are only just in time to save his life. See what happens when people do not keep their promises! If you had delayed one day more, you would have found him dead."

Beauty was so terrified by this dream that the next morning she announced her intention of going back at once, and that very night she said good-by to her father and all her brothers and sisters, and as soon as she was in bed she turned her ring round upon her finger, and said firmly, "I wish to go back to my palace and see my Beast again," as she had been told to do.

Then she fell asleep instantly, and only woke up to hear the clock saying "Beauty, Beauty" twelve times in its musical voice, which told her at once that she was really in the palace once more. Everything was just as before, and her birds were so glad to see her! But Beauty thought she had never known such a long day, for she was so anxious to see the Beast again that she felt as if suppertime would never come.

But when it did come and no Beast appeared she was really frightened; so, after listening and waiting for a long time, she ran down into the garden to search for him. Up and down the paths and avenues ran poor Beauty, calling him in vain, for no one answered, and not a trace of him could she find; until at last, quite tired, she stopped for a minute's rest, and saw that she was standing opposite the shady path she had seen in her dream. She rushed down it, and, sure enough, there was the cave, and in it lay the Beast – asleep, as Beauty thought. Quite glad to have found him, she ran up and stroked his head, but, to her horror, he did not move or open his eyes.

"Oh! he is dead; and it is all my fault," said Beauty, crying bitterly.

But then, looking at him again, she fancied he still breathed, and, hastily fetching some water from the nearest fountain, she sprinkled it over his face, and, to her great delight, he began to revive.

"Oh! Beast, how you frightened me!" she cried. "I never knew how much I loved you until just now, when I feared I was too late to save your life."

"Can you really love such an ugly creature as I am?" said the Beast faintly. "Ah! Beauty, you only came just in time. I was dying because I thought you had forgotten your promise. But go back now and rest, I shall see you again by and by."

Beauty, who had half expected that he would be angry with her, was reassured by his gentle voice, and went back to the palace, where supper was awaiting her; and afterward the Beast came in as usual, and talked about the time she had spent with her father, asking if she had enjoyed herself, and if they had all been very glad to see her.

Beauty answered politely, and quite enjoyed telling him all that had happened to her. And when at last the time came for him to go, and he asked, as he had so often asked before, "Beauty, will you marry me?"

She answered softly, "Yes, dear Beast."

As she spoke a blaze of light sprang up before the windows of the palace; fireworks crackled and guns banged, and across the avenue of orange trees, in letters all made of fire-flies, was written: 'Long live the Prince and his Bride.'

Turning to ask the Beast what it could all mean, Beauty found that he had disappeared, and in his place stood her long-loved Prince! At the same moment the wheels of a chariot were heard upon the terrace, and two ladies entered the room. One of them Beauty recognized as the stately lady she had seen in her dreams; the other was also so grand and queenly that Beauty hardly knew which to greet first.

But the one she already knew said to her companion:

"Well, Queen, this is Beauty, who has had the courage to rescue your son from the terrible enchantment. They love one another, and only your consent to their marriage is wanting to make them perfectly happy."

"I consent with all my heart," cried the Queen. "How can I ever thank you enough, charming girl, for having restored my dear son to his natural form?"

And then she tenderly embraced Beauty and the Prince, who had meanwhile been greeting the Fairy and receiving her congratulations.

"Now," said the Fairy to Beauty, "I suppose you would like me to send for all your brothers and sisters to dance at your wedding?"

And so she did, and the marriage was celebrated the very next day with the utmost splendour, and Beauty and the Prince lived happily ever after.

The Tragedy of the Gnomes

MANY, MANY AGES AGO this fair old world of ours wore a solemn and forbidding aspect; no carpet of thick, green grass eased the footfall of man as he climbed the hills; no human voice was heard amid the desolation – ice, ice everywhere – from the North Pole to the centre of that which is now the temperate zone, and only such life peopled this region as could endure the rigour of a more than arctic condition. Vast sheets of ice, in depth immeasurable, covered the surface of the hills and valleys, broken toward the tropics into serrated edges – the verdure running up an occasional valley, as though in laughing derisions of its neighbours the ice-imprisoned mountains.

In those days there existed only hideous animals and reptiles of size great and awful; animals whose terrible voice shook the mountains like an earthquake; slimy or scaly reptiles who walked on many feet, or dragged a hideous length along the ice-covered rocks. It seemed as if the great Creator must have fashioned all existent things in an hour of wrath, or that man, having existed, had been for some sin exterminated by that icy inundation, and that animal creation had so displeased him that he had fashioned them in grotesque caricature upon all grace and beauty.

Man esteems himself higher than all other created things; who shall say that the great, buzzing bluebottle fly does not think the same of himself, and perhaps, with as much reason; it is at most but a grade of intelligence; and what do we understand of that intelligence which is above us?

In one of the green valleys running up into the foothills of what is now called the Rocky Mountains, frisked and played a band of gnomes. These were but a fairy people, differing only from the fairies of woodland glade and dell in this; those fairy folk were things of beauty like imprisoned sunbeams; lighter than gossamer, they floated hither and thither, always trending toward the tropics, where the sun shone radiantly warm, and the silvery moon lighted the verdant carpet of grass, and the sweet south wind rang the lily bells in merry chime; there they idled away each sunny day – creatures of light and frivolity.

These gnomes were a sturdier, darker folk, short in stature, but with a breadth of shoulder, a depth of chest, and muscles fit for giants. Though for an occasional frolic they danced and roughly tossed each other about in the valley, they better loved their homes in the heart of the ice-covered mountains, where they forged beautiful things from the yellow metal, or decked their cavern homes with softly glowing, or fiery-eyed jewels; thus from earnest labour their faces gained a look of firmness and determination; they were homely, but were good to look upon, lighted as their faces were by love and kindliness.

One among them was wondrously fair: Lilleela they called her. Her hair was like silk as it winds from the cocoon; her eyes were blue as the sky when it shows between the fleecy clouds of summer; her cheeks were as though they had been kissed by the wild rose blooms, which left their dainty stains upon the fair skin. She was as sweet and pure as the breath of the dawn.

Walado was her lover; a short, deep-chested giant, with a face like a ripe walnut – all seams and puckers; not with age, but with jolly laughter, and intent, hard work. Lilleela must have the finest of rubies, on strings of beaten gold; tiny silver bells must be made, to ring their sweet chimes with every joyous movement; dainty chains of gold – set with amethyst, rubies and diamonds – must be wrought to bind the floating cloud of hair. Away down in the heart of the mountain Walado plied his little hammer of polished stone – clink-clink-clink all day long like a refrain it accompanied his happy song.

One fair day the troop of gnomes went down into the green valley for a holiday.

Walado objected: "No, no! You can go, but I must finish this golden girdle for my Lilleela, and then, there are sandals of gold to be set with precious stones for her feet – they are too sweet and fair to be bruised by the rocks," he had answered, screwing up his face into a funny little smile.

"Oh, do come, Walado! The girdle and sandals can wait! The sun is so cold and sorrowful up here, but down in the valley it is so beautiful!" pleaded Lilleela.

Her blue eyes moulded his will like warm wax, and over the ice they sped away many, many miles, to where its broken edges lay like icicles flattened out with huge rollers; some having sharp, sword-like points, others rounded and scalloped, as though in fanciful adornment. All along the border of the valley, reaching in places high up on the mountain side – wherever there were breaks in the ice – hardy trees had planted their feet, and lifted their heads to catch a breath of the warmer air of the tropics; some few, essaying to climb still higher, or being less hardy – reached their dead arms abroad, or pointed with ghostly fingers toward the icy desolation in warning to their kind.

These happy, childlike beings, instead of walking, had a gliding movement which carried them over the ground very rapidly; laughing, tumbling, pushing one another in merry sport, they sped on as though wings were attached to their feet. Hand in hand went Walado and Lilleela; his nut-brown face drawing into a nest of comical wrinkles, which were so many happy smiles; her look was like the sun, bright and warm.

Of a sudden she stopped and shivered: "Oh, my Walado, what was that?" From off the mountain height had come a long, low wail, and a chill was borne with it which froze them with fear.

Walado gathered her in his embrace, and shading his eyes with one hand, looked back over the mountain: "Fear not, my Lilleela, 'tis but the voice of the storm on its way from the far north. See! We shall soon be in the beautiful valley, where he cannot come!"

"Let us hasten, then, for in my heart I feel a chill which is like death."

Walado gathered her closer to him: "Little sun beam! Am I not able to shield you from the shadow of the dark cloud?"

She patted his brown face with her wee, rose-leaf palms, and kissed the wrinkles on his brown cheeks lovingly.

"Yes, my Walado; your arm is as strong as your heart is brave, but—" she broke off abruptly: "Let us fly!" she finished with a sound between a laugh and a sob as the wailing came borne from the mountain heights once more.

Turning their affrighted glance backward, they saw the tall pines at the foot of the hills swaying wildly; some which stood so tall and straight were snatched off like a brittle weed and tossed down the mountain side.

Lilleela shivered again, remembering the look the fearful Ice King had given her as he rode above the mountain height upon which she stood at twilight hour; he was seated upon a cloud of inky blackness; his eyes shot forth red and yellow flame, like the terrible light which streamed up from the far north; his lips were blue and hideous, and his matted hair, and long, tangled beard, were a mixture of frost and ice. He pointed a finger at her which looked as though belonging to the hand of one long since dead – so rigid and bloodless it appeared – the nails showed blue and ghastly. With a voice like the whistling north wind, he said, "You'll make a bonny bride for the Ice King! Your youth will warm my old blood finely! o-We-ee, Y-e-ss!" The cloud passed on, and bore him from her view, but the deadly chill remained, for well Lilleela knew that his love meant death, as his hate meant destruction.

For this reason the wailing sound shook her with an awful fear, but she dared not tell Walado; she feared that he would turn and seek the terrible monarch whose simple touch was death; once more she caught Walado's hand, crying gayly, "Come, come, before the storm god overtakes us!"

They romped and played through all that happy day; they climbed the steep inclines, and sitting on the glittering ice dashed down to the valley below, tumbling over and over, with laughter sweet as the tinkling of silver bells; it seemed strange to hear such sweet and musical sounds issuing from those queer little bodies, but the sound fitfully represented the sweet harmonious souls within.

At last, worn out with play, they climbed the long, icy hills; they wound around the towering rocks, they clung to dizzy precipices; they crept by the lairs of horrible animals with noiseless tread; ever upward and onward toward the North Pole, where life had grown old and dead, while the new life had slipped down toward the equator.

"Oh, why do we journey so far to-night, Walado?" said Lilleela wearily.

"There is a mountain lying in the light of the northern star, which is filled with yellow gold; its caverns are lined with jewels; I seek them for you, my Lilleela."

As he ceased speaking, again that wailing sound filled with awful menace smote their ears: "o-o-W-ee" a sound that rose from fretful discontent into fiercest anger, then died away like a long sigh of satisfied hate.

"I am afraid, Walado! Oh do return!" cried Lilleela in terror.

"'Tis but the wind, beloved one," answered Walado stoutly, though he too shivered.

"Nay! nay! It is the Ice King passing by in his chariot of storm, and drawn by his slaves – the winds of the hurricane," she cried frantically, fear making her pallid lips tremble.

Walado's wrinkled visage grew stern – all the pleasant lines drawn out of it; he understood more than her words told him.

"Has he dared to look upon you, with a desire to possess you? Knows he not that you are mine? I am not worthy of you – except as love for you makes me worthy—" his voice dropping into tender cadence, "but he – the monarch of all cruelty – is not of our kind. His very kiss is death; let him find a bride in his own frozen empire – the North Pole!" He shook his clinched hand in the direction of the swift rushing shadow, which so depressed them all: "Haste! haste, men and maidens! Let us flee to our own mountain home, where we can defy the monster! Our Lilleela has just cause for fear, for none upon whom he has looked with the desire for possession ever escaped him; and it is only by speedily reaching our caverns that we may hope for safety."

They turned about, and like a flock of frightened birds they flitted away, with no more noise than would be made by the rustle of a bat's wing, and were lost in the gloom.

The moon shone out cold and pale, as though grieving over the dread desolation and lighted up the angry face of the Ice King with a pallid luster; he puffed out his gaunt cheeks menacingly; his eyes darted flame like the quick thrusts of a sword blade in deadly battle; as he saw that the gnomes had fled he shrieked in wrath. He swayed the tall trees, and tossed their dead branches in every direction; he fiercely threw the rocks from the lofty mountain summits, and as they went crashing down, down, with thunderous noise, they splintered and tore up the ice like a silver foam, which glittered and flashed with pale prismatic glow as it caught the moon's sad, cold ray.

Faster, faster flew the tiny band; closer clung Lilleela to Walado's hand as that wrathful shriek reached their ears; dashing wildly past the brow of the darkly towering mountain, as the crashing of rocks smote them with wild affright; leaping across the roaring torrent, to slip and sprawl on the glassy ice of the further bank; up and away, bruised and sore; past lifeless trees, whose dead branches were falling all about them, until at last they reached a mountain home seldom used by them. Nothing was to be seen save a tiny crevice between the rocks; one after another they lay down, and silently slid through; then, and not until then, Walado spoke:

"We are safe! Even the Ice King cannot enter here! We are safe, quite safe!"

"Are you sure? Ah, my Walado, he is so vengeful!" sighed Lilleela. Walado laughed, all his funny little puckers laughing as well:

"He knows nothing of our hiding place, and he could not force his great rigid body through the narrow opening. Oh, we are quite safe!" he reiterated gleefully.

But Lilleela sighed.

Walado felt the hopelessness of that sound, and it grieved his tender heart; he passed his rugged, brown hand over her flossy hair, with a touch as soft as the brushing of a butterfly's wing.

"My treasure, if ill befall us here in this our vaulted hall, there are still the lower caverns, where none can possibly come save 'we who know.'"

They soon regained confidence, and joked and made merry; they were such trusting, childlike beings, taking the comfort and joy of each hour at its utmost worth.

Their enjoyment was at its height, when faintly heard came that long chilling wail. Two of their number had gone outside unnoticed by Walado; they came shooting in through the entrance, their brown faces bleached an ashen grey, their teeth chattering, their eyes protruding. All sprang up in wild affright.

"Where have you been? What is the matter?" cried Walado, as sternly as the gentle soul could speak.

"We but crept out for the birds we had snared! We thought to help out the feast!" said Tador, the hairy one.

"And I had a skin of berries that I gathered in the valley below; they were very sweet, Walado!" answered Sudana, the good.

"Tell me what you saw," replied Walado sadly, his anger melted away by their deprecating looks and words.

Sudana answered: "We saw the Ice King; his cloud chariot so low that it touched the top of the mountain, he was so angry that the frost flew in great clouds from his nostrils; his breath reached us and chilled us through."

Walado opened his lips to speak, when – "O-o-W-W-ee," filling all that vaulted chamber with the dread sound, it came borne on a wind so chill that it pierced the hearts of each with cold and fear.

These loving souls had never felt the need of a ruler, each doing his utmost through love for all, thus there had been no dissensions; now all turned instinctively to Walado for guidance. They were growing benumbed with the chill of that icy breath.

Walado silently pointed to the narrow passage leading deep into the bowels of the earth. Each took his beloved by the hand and prepared for the descent; before they had taken so much as one step, there came a crash so awful that it shook the great mountain to its centre; the falling of rocks resounded in deafening commotion; the Ice King's snarling wail echoed and re-echoed throughout the cavern; bitter, bitter cold grew the air; crash – crash – crash, came the sound of falling mountains heaped upon them; covering them deeply beneath the debris.

Then was a new horror added; the roaring and growling of many horrible beasts, as they fought and struggled for entrance through the narrow passageway, to escape the falling ruins, and the deadly cold.

There was the shrieking and tumult of the tempest; the hiss and roar of the struggling reptiles, but higher and shriller than all else was the fierce wailing menace of the angry Ice King; it shrieked to them insolently: "You defy me, do you? We'll see! We'll s-e-e!"

Grey and pallid grew the little brown faces as they silently followed Walado down into the bowels of the earth until they came to a lofty room; here they huddled silently together.

Thus they remained day after day, night after night, no ray of light to distinguish the one from the other; but as time passed on the pangs of hunger assailed them fiercely. Tador's birds were divided, and by morsels eaten; Sudana's berries were parceled out by ones and by twos, Walado adding all his share to Lilleela's, although she knew not that it was so; greyer grew his little, wrinkled face, but ever it smiled tenderly upon Lilleela, and with patient kindness he answered all questions in unselfish endeavour to comfort and cheer the others. For a time they could feel the earth quiver and vibrate as though in shuddering fear, then came a time of awful calm, when the sound of a voice smote the deadly silence with all the horror of thunder tones, until they shrank affrighted, and spoke only in awed whispers – afraid of the awful echo which answered sound. Paler and more spiritlike grew Lilleela; sadder, sadder grew Walado as he pillowed her head upon his broad breast. The sighs of all rose incessantly!

At last Tador whispered, "Shall I not descend further toward the centre of the earth? It will be warmer than it is here – it grows so very cold!" shivering.

"As you wish, Tador," replied Walado sadly.

Hearing Walado's answer all clamoured to accompany him – anything seemed preferable to this inaction.

As they prepared for the descent, Sudana said: "We do not know what we may find, Walado," trying to speak hopefully.

"Gold and jewels in plenty, but all that lies hidden in the whole mountain range, are not worth as much as one juicy berry," and he glanced at Lilleela's wan face. She was far too weak to accompany the party, and all insisted that Walado must remain with her; he silently folded her in his arms; he would not have left her.

She raised her sad eyes to his face: "Better had I have given myself to the Ice King; then I only should have perished," she said.

"No! no! no!" whispered they, as with one voice.

Wearily, wearily time passed on, but they did not return. Lilleela dozed and whispered fitfully, but Walado sat with staring eyes, and listened intently for sounds of his comrades, he was afraid to move lest he disturb his precious burden.

At last she raised herself up on her elbow, her eyes full of agony: "Oh, Walado, take me up above – I cannot breathe here! Oh, I must get one breath of air!" her chest heaving convulsively, her hollow cheeks palpitating with the struggle for inhalation.

One great tear rolled down Walado's cheek, and fell splashing on the rocky floor.

Around his waist he wore a rope made of the hide of animals, which served to hold his stone hammer and axe; with this rope he bound Lilleela to him, passing it under her arms and around his neck.

"Dear one, put your arms about my neck to steady yourself all that you are able, and I will carry you safely up."

Her chest rose and fell spasmodically; her heart fluttered faintly, or thumped with wild, irregular motion.

The walls of the shaft were covered with ice, rendering it almost impossible to obtain a foothold; inch by inch he made slow headway, every muscle strained to its utmost tension; his hands leaving stains of blood with every grasp. He could at last see a ray – scarcely of light, but a little less gloom; he was so exhausted that he was gasping for breath; he placed his hands upon a slight projection for one more effort – it may have been that his eagerness was too great, or that he grasped but brittle ice which broke off – for he fell. Down, down he slipped, with inconceivable rapidity; weak from want of food, and frightened lest he injure his beloved, he lost his presence of mind.

Lilleela recalled his wandering faculties; after one frantic scream, she made no outcry – indeed she had little breath for speech – but with her lips close to his ear she whispered: "Throw out your hands and feet against the wall, and I will do the same; we may at least break the fall!" Little by little the speed decreased, until as Walado's foot touched another projection they stopped altogether. He waited long enough to recover breath and a little strength. Lilleela's head fell over sidewise; she had fainted, and hung a dead weight about his neck; he dared not loose his hands, though he madly longed to caress the cheek which felt so cold to his trembling lips. Once more, nerved by desperation, he made an effort to reach the upper cave; slowly and carefully he climbed; resting often – a hand or foot slipping – clinging frantically as the ice became thicker, and the ascent more difficult. At last, just as his fingers were over the upper edge his foot slipped, and threw the other from its resting-place; for one breathless instant he hung suspended by his fingers – Lilleela's lifeless weight dragging him down! Sparks of fire shot before his eyes! A noise as of rushing water sounded in his ears: His breathing became laboured and stertorious! A bitter cry rose to his lips as Lilleela's cold cheek touched his drooping face; he made one supreme effort, and half unconscious he lay upon the floor of the upper cavern, Lilleela's cold form clasped in his embrace!

The chill at length restored him to consciousness; he sat up and unbound Lilleela; he struck two pieces of flint rapidly together, and ignited the punk which he carried in a bag about his neck. He observed that the cold wind had ceased blowing in, thus he knew that the Ice King must have departed, probably believing that all were dead. Well, so they were – all but himself – and – perhaps Lilleela!

He felt for her heart, but could find no pulsation; he kissed her cold cheeks, and blew his warm breath between her parted lips; at last the madness of despair took possession of him. He grovelled on the icy floor! He shrieked aloud, to be answered only by a thousand hollow echoes! He ran to the opening through which they had entered, and found the passage barred by rocks and dirt; he tore at the rubbish with his hands as an animal digs with its claws, only to fall back in despair with the tears coursing down his cheeks.

"Oh, my Lilleela! If I could but reach the air! If I could only carry you into the sunshine and let it warm your cold face! Oh, my Lilleela. Oh, my Lilleela!" he cried, gathering her once more into his arms. All the cave was now lighted with a dim, red light, from a few slivers of wood ignited with the burning punk. Water had oozed through the rocks from above and formed long, glittering icicles, frozen by the fierce breath of the Ice King; the floors and walls were likewise of ice, cold and scintillating. The sighs which had arisen from the imprisoned gnomes had congealed into forms of wonderful beauty, as pure as the white souls of the passing spirits; all over that arched ceiling hung fairy curtains of frost, wonderful jewels, each like a frozen tear, ornamented each jutting point. Walado sat down with his back against an angle of the wall, and clasped Lilleela in loving embrace; he smiled sadly yet lovingly as his eyes rested upon walls and dome: "It is a fitting tomb for thy fair body, my beloved! Thy spirit, not even the Ice King can imprison; and I – thine even in death – I go with thee, to serve thee still!"

He bowed his face against her fair hair, and as he so rested his spirit left his homely little body.

It seems almost a pity that they could not have known how fully their wrongs were avenged. Hot waves washed up from the tropic seas and melted the crust of ice with which the cruel monarch had encased all the hills; and he was driven by the south wind to his lair at the North Pole, there to remain in expiation forever. Thus the hills became fertile, and with the passing of those pure souls there sprang to life on the mountain side – the primrose, for Lilleela's pink-white skin; the columbine, for the azure of her eyes; the gentian, for the crimson of her lips; and the tall, white lily, for the stately grace of her body; and always the brown-coated robin, with his warm breast, sings lovingly by day and sleeps in their midst by night, and thus Walado's soul still faithfully serves his beloved.

Biographies & Text Sources

The stories in this book derive from a multitude of original sources, often from the nineteenth century and often based on the writer's first-hand accounts of tales narrated to them by natives, while others are their own retellings of traditional tales. Authors, works and contributors to this book include:

Dr. Jennifer Larson
Foreword
Dr. Jennifer Larson is Professor of Classics at Kent State University. She did her undergraduate work in English and Greek, and received her MA and PhD in Classics from the University of Wisconsin-Madison in 1992. Larson has published numerous books and articles on topics in ancient Greek literature and religion, including *Greek Nymphs: Myth, Cult, Lore* (Oxford, 2001) and *Ancient Greek Cults: A Guide* (Routledge, 2007).

Im Bang
The Home of the Fairies
(Originally Published in *Korean Folk Tales: Imps, Ghosts and Fairies*, 1913)
Im Bang (1640–1722) was a great scholar. He was a disciple of Song Si-yol, one of Korea's first writers. In 1719, he became governor of Seoul, and held as well the office of secretary of the Cabinet. In the year 1722, on account of a part he played in a disturbance in the government, he was exiled to North Korea, where he died. His writings have long been revered in Korea.

Joseph Bédier
The Little Fairy Bell
(Originally Published in *The Romance of Tristan and Iseult,* 1914)
Joseph Bédier (1864–1938) was a prominent French scholar of medieval French literature, known for his influential works on the *Tristan and Rolan*d epics. He was also a professor and held positions at the Collège de France.

Richard Bovet
The Fairy Boy of Leith
(Originally Published in *Pandaemonium,* 1684)
Richard Bovet is known for his book *Pandaemonium* (1684). He was born around 1641 and lived in Somerset, England. He was educated at Wadham College, Oxford, from 1657 to 1658.

Rachel Harriette Busk
La Cenorientola; The Transformation-Donkey; Scioccolone; Filagranata; The Queen and the Tripe-Seller
(Originally Published in *Roman Legends: A collection of the fables and folk-lore of Rome*, 1877)
Rachel Harriette Busk (1831–1907) is best known for *The Folk-Lore of Rome* (1874), one of the most prominent contributions to urban folklore made in the nineteenth century

and one of the very few studies from that period that paid attention to the contexts in which tales and legends were told. Busk wrote several other books on the folklore of European countries, which were inspired by her travels. However, these were assemblages of material previously published by others.

J. F. Campbell
Sanntraigh; Man; The Smith and the Fairies
(Originally Published in *Popular Tales of the West Highlands, Volume II*, 1890)
J.F. Campbell (1821–1885) was a Scottish author, folktale collector, and scholar of Celtic studies. Campbell, also known as Iain Òg Ìle, or Young John of Islay, was born on the island of Islay, in the Inner Hebrides. Throughout his life he travelled widely throughout Scotland recording traditional tales, anecdotes, and songs. He became known as an authority on the subjects of Celtic folklore and the Gaelic peoples. His best-known collection, *Popular Tales of the West Highlands*, was published in four volumes in 1890. He also published a collection of ballads entitled *Leabhar na Feinne*, which he self-published in 1872.

Marie-Catherine d'Aulnoy
The Yellow Dwarf
(Originally Published in *The Blue Fairy Book,* 1889)
Marie-Catherine d'Aulnoy (1652–1705) also known as Countess d'Aulnoy, was a French author known for her literary fairy tales. She is best known for her 1697 collection *Les Contes des Fées* (*Fairy Tales*). She is considered to have been a member of les conteuses group of French female authors.

János Erdélyi
The Three Oranges; The Invisible Shepherd Lad; The Three Princes, The Three Dragons, and The Woman with The Iron Nose
(Originally Published in *The Folk-Tales of the Magyars*, 1889)
János Erdélyi (1814 –1868) was a Hungarian poet, critic, author, philosopher and ethnographist. He began his literary career with poems written in folk style. His literary fame was made by his collection of Hungarian national poems and folktales, *Collection of Hungarian Folklore, Folk Songs and Tales.*

A. J. Glinski
The Good Ferryman and the Water Nymphs
(Originally Published in *Polish Fairy Tales,* 1862)
A.J. Glinski (1817–1866) was a Polish author and collector of folklore. He is considered the Polish equivalent to the Brothers Grimm, having collected, recorded and preserved a wealth of fairy tales and traditional stories from Polish oral tradition. He achieved this by travelling across the countryside and speaking with a range of ordinary people. These stories were published in his popular collection *Polish Fairy Tales* (1862).

Sir George Grey
The Art of Netting Learned by Kahukura from the Fairies (Ko Te Korero Mo Nga Patupaiarehe); The Voyage to New Zealand
(Originally Published in *Polynesian Mythology & Ancient Traditional History of the New Zealanders*, 1929)

Sir George Grey (1812–1898) was an explorer, writer and a British colonial administrator, who was called upon to govern in periods of crisis, most notably in New Zealand, South Australia, and the Cape Colony (South Africa).

Elizabeth Grierson

Thomas the Rhymer; The Page-Boy and the Silver Goblet; Farquhar MacNeill; Habetrot the Spinstress; The Dwarfie Stone

(Originally Published in *The Scottish Fairy Book*, 1910)

Elizabeth Grierson (1869–1943) was born on a farm near Hawick, in the Scottish Borders. Throughout the course of her life she published more than thirty books, many of which covered Scottish fairy tales and folklore. In addition to these, she also published travel guides to the cities of Edinburgh, Scotland, and Florence, Italy. Her best-known works are her collections *The Scottish Fairy Book* (1910) and *Children's Tales from Scottish Ballads* (1906).

William Elliot Griffis

The Kabouters and the Bells; The Elves and their Antics

(Originally Published in *Dutch Fairy Tales for Young Folks*, 1918)

Cat-Kin and the Queen Mother; Tokgabi and His Pranks; Old Timber Top; The Woodman and the Mountain Fairies

(Originally Published in *Korean Fairy Tales*, 1922)

Born in Philadelphia, William Elliot Griffis (1843–1928) went on to serve as a corporal during the American Civil War. He studied at Rutgers University after the war and graduated in 1869. He tutored Latin and English to a samurai from Fukui and then travelled around Europe for a year prior to studying at what is now known as the New Brunswick Theological Seminary. In 1870, Griffis went to Japan and worked in education as well as writing for many newspapers and magazines. On returning to the United States in 1874 he worked in several churches on the east coast but retired in 1903 to write. With the help of his extensive knowledge of Japanese and European culture, he produced a number of books, such as *Japanese Fairy World* (1880), *The Fire-fly's Lovers and Other Fairy Tales of Old Japan* (1908), *Dutch Fairy Tales* (1918), *Belgian Fairy Tales* (1919), *Welsh Fairy Tales* (1921), *Japanese Fairy Tales* (1922), *Korean Fairy Tales* (1922) and many more.

H.A. Guerber

Frey

(Originally Published in *Myths of the Norsemen From the Eddas and Sagas,* 1908)

Hélène Adeline Guerber (1859–1929) was an American author whose work focused mainly on retellings of myths and folklore for adult audiences. She was born in Michigan and was educated in Paris. She published more than two dozen books throughout her life, including *The Myths of Greece & Rome* (1908), *Legends of the Rhine* (1905) and *The Book of the Epic* (1913).

Mrs. A. W. Hall

Helga

(Originally Published in *Icelandic Fairy Tales,* 1897)

Mrs. A.W. Hall was a translator and editor. She is best known for her editorship and translation of the collection *Icelandic Fairy Tales*, published in 1897. The collection preserved many traditional pieces of Icelanding folklore that might otherwise have been lost. She also published under the pen-name of Angus W. Hall. Her other works include the short story collection entitled *The Giantess in the Granite Boat* (1897).

Rosetta Gage Harvey
The River Fairy
(Originally Published in *The flame tree and other folk-lore stories from Uganda,* 1925)
Rosetta Gage Harvey, who wrote under the pen name of Mrs. George Baskerville, was an English author and ethnographer. Focusing her work mainly on Uganda, Harvey collected and published traditional stories, folk-lore, and mythology from the first peoples of Uganda. Her collection, *The Flame Tree and Other Folk-Lore Stories from Uganda*, was published in 1925.

Nathaniel Hawthorne
The Gorgon's Head
(Originally Published in *A Wonder-Book for Boys and Girls,* 1851)
The prominent American writer Nathaniel Hawthorne (1804–64) was born in Salem, Massachusetts. His most famous novel *The Scarlet Letter* helped him become established as a writer in the 1850s. Most of his works were influenced by his friends Ralph Waldo Emerson and Herman Melville, as well as by his extended financial struggles. Hawthorne's works often incorporated a dark romanticism that focused on the evil and sin of humanity. Some of his most famous works detailed supernatural presences or occurrences, as in his *The House of the Seven Gables* as well as many of his short stories.

Clara H. Holmes
The Tragedy of the Gnomes
(Originally Published in *Floating Fancies Among the Weird and the Occult,* 1898)
Clara H. Holmes (1838–1927) was an American author born in Ohio. Later moving to Cripple Creek, Colorado, she began contributing to the *Midland Monthly* from 1896. Her best-known work is the collection *Floating Fancies Among the Weird and the Occult* (1898), in which 'The Tragedy of the Gnomes' appears. Her other works include *Scattered Autumn Leaves* (1926), as well as several short stories that were published in various newspapers.

Homer
Calypso's Island; Scylla and Charybdis
(Originally Published in *The Odyssey,* 8 BCE)
Little is known for certain about the life of Homer, the Greek poet credited as the author of the great epic poems *The Iliad* and *The Odyssey*, although he is believed to have been born some time between the twelfth and eighth centuries BC. *The Odyssey*, generally considered one of the most fundamental works of the literary canon, describes the trials and tribulations of the hero Odysseus on his journey home to Ithaca following the Trojan War. It has had a huge influence on Western literature, inspiring extensive translations, poems, plays and novels.

Eleanor Hull
Murtough and the Witch Woman
(Originally Published in *The Irish Fairy Book,* 1909)

Eleanor Hull (1860–1935) was and English author, journalist and scholar of Old Irish. Born in Manchester, her family relocated to Dublin, Ireland, when she was a child. Hull attended Alexandra College, Dublin from 1877 to 1882, and later took up Celtic studies in London. In 1915 she was elected president of the Irish Literary Society. She was also a co-founder of the Irish Texts Society. Her published works include *The Cuchullin Saga in Irish Literature* (1898), *The Northmen in Britain* (1913) and *A History of Ireland and Her People* (1931).

Joseph Jacobs
The Legend of Knockgrafton
(Originally Published in *Fairy Legends and Traditions of the South of Ireland*, 1825)
How Cormac Mac Art Went to Faery
(Originally Published in *More Celtic Fairy Tales*, 1894)
The Ainsel
(Originally Published in *More English Fairy Tales*, 1894)
Joseph Jacobs (1854–1916) was born in Australia and settled in New York. He is most famous for his collections of English folklore and fairytales including 'Jack and the Beanstalk' and 'The Three Little Pigs'. He also published Celtic, Jewish and Indian fairytales during his career. Jacobs was an editor for books and journals centered on folklore and a member of The Folklore Society in England.

Patrick Kennedy
The Fairy Nurse
(Originally Published in *Legendary Fictions of the Irish Celts*, 1866)
Patrick Kennedy (1801–1873) was one of the pioneers in uncovering Irish folkloric material. He made a lasting impact on the Celtic Revival movement. His stories, some of which he sent to Sheridan Le Fanu, appeared as *Leinster Folk Lore* in the *Dublin University Magazine* from 1861 till 1869. Le Fanu eventually encouraged Kennedy to publish a full collection of his stories (*Legendary Fictions of the Irish Celts*).

Charles Kingsley
How the Centaur Trained the Heroes on Pelion; How Perseus Slew the Gorgon
(Originally Published in *The heroes, or, Greek fairy tales for my children,* 1856)
Charles Kingsley (1819–1875) was an English priest, professor, social reformer, historian, novelist and poet, whose most famous works are probably the novels *Westward Ho!* (1855) and *The Water-Babies, A Fairy Tale for a Land Baby* (1863). Though he held some questionable views, his knack for storytelling is evident in *The Heroes, or Greek Fairy Tales* (1856).

Robert Kirk
The Minister and the Fairy
(Originally Published in *The Secret Commonwealth of Elves, Fauns and Fairies*, 1815)
Robert Kirk (1644–1692) was a minister, Gaelic scholar and folklorist, best known for *The Secret Commonwealth of Elves, Fauns and Fairies*. Sadly, Kirk died before he was able to publish his collection. Legends arose after his death saying he had been taken away to fairyland for revealing the secrets of the Good People. In 1815, Walter Scott published his work on fairies and Andrew Lang later gave it the popular title, *The Secret Commonwealth of Elves, Fauns and Fairies.*

János Kriza
Fairy Elizabeth
(Originally Published in *The Folk-Tales of the Magyars*, 1889)
János Kriza (1812–1875) was a Hungarian ethnographer, poet, author, and Unitarian minister. He was a significant collector of folklore in Transylvania. His passion for collecting and documenting folklore led to the Kriza János Ethnographic Society, a research institute founded in his honor in Cluj-Napoca, Romania, in 1990 to support ethnic Hungarian ethnographers and their cultural heritage.

Ignácz Kúnos
The Rose Beauty
(Originally Published in *Forty-four Turkish Fairy Tales,* 1903)
Ignácz Kúnos (1860–1945) was a Hungarian linguist, author, and Turkologist. He was a prominent scholar of Turkish folk literature and dialectology. Having studied linguistics at Budapest University and spending five years studying the Turkish language and culture in Constantinople (now Istanbul), he became professor of Turkish philology at Budapest University in 1890. He later worked as a professor at various other institutions and established the Department of Folkloristics at Istanbul University in 1925. His folktale collections include *Turkish Fairy Tales and Folk Tales* (1896) and *Forty-Four Turkish Fairy Tales* (1914).

Bertha Palmer Lane
The Leprechaun of Ardmore Tower'
(Originally Published in *Tower Legends*, 1932)
Little is known about Bertha Palmer Lane, author of *Tower Legends* (1932), a book that brings together classic tales and folklore stories about towers in myth and legend, such as 'The Leprechaun of Ardmore Tower'.

Andrew Lang
Beauty and the Beast
(Originally Published in *The Blue Fairy Book,* 1889)
Scottish writer and critic Andrew Lang (1844–1912) was born and raised in Selkirk. Although Lang worked variously as a historian, journalist, poet, and anthropologist, his greatest legacy has been his works on folklore, mythology, and religion. Among these are the Fairy Books, 25 volumes of folk and fairy tales published Lang published with his wife, including *The Arabian Nights Entertainments* (1898), their adaptation of the *One Thousand Nights and a Night folk tales.*

Edmond Leamy
The Golden Spears; The Enchanted Cave
(Originally Published in *Irish Fairy Tales,* 1907)
Edmund Leamy (1848–1904) was an Irish journalist, barrister, author of fairy tales, and nationalist politician. He entered parliament in 1880 as nationalist MP for Waterford city. In the 1885 general election he contested two seats for the Irish parliamentary party.

Rev. J. Macgowan
Sam-Chung and the Water Demon
(Originally Published in *Chinese Folk-Lore Tales,* 1910)

Rev. J. Macgowan (1835–1922) was a British missionary. He served as a missionary in China with the London Missionary Society. Macgowan wrote *Chinese Folk-Lore Tales* in 1910. Macgowan lived in China for over four decades. He wrote numerous books on Chinese culture, history, and folk-lore.

Ernest W. Marwick
The Fairy Dancers
(Originally Published in *The Folklore of Orkney and Shetland,* 1986)
Ernest W. Marwick was a leading scholar and author on Orkney folklore. His *An Orkney Folklore* was released in two volumes and encompasses only a selection of his full writings on Orkney.

Ivana Brlić-Mažuranić
Reygoch; Fisherman Plunk and His Wife
(Originally Published in *Croatian Tales of Long Ago,* 1916)
Ivana Brlić-Mažuranić (1874–1938) was a Croatian writer. She has been praised as the best Croatian writer for children. She started writing poetry, diaries and essays rather early, but her works were not published until the beginning of the 20th century. Her book *Croatian Tales of Long Ago*, published in 1916, is among the most popular today.

Elodie L. Mijatovich
The Dream of the King's Son; The Three Brothers
(Originally Published in *Serbian Fairy Tales,* 1918)
Elodie L. Mijatovich (1825–1908) was a British author who lived in Boston in the 1850s, where she was an advocate of the abolitionist movement. She translated several works from English into Serbian and published several books on Serbia in English, including *The History of Modern Serbia* (1872) and *Serbian Folk-lore* (1874).

Baroness Orczy
Uletka and the White Lizard; Forget-me-not; The Suitors of Princess Fire-Fly; The Twin Hunchbacks; The Wishing Skin
(Originally Published in *Old Hungarian Fairy Tales*, 1895)
Baroness Orczy (1865–1947) was a Hungarian-born British novelist, playwright, and artist. She moved to London and pursued a career in the arts before turning to writing, initially to supplement her husband's low income. Her successful play and novel *The Scarlet Pimpernel* established the popular "hero with a secret identity trope".

Ovid
Athena and Arachne; Echo and Narcissus
(Originally Published in *Metamorphoses,* 8 CE)
A contemporary of Virgil and Horace and alongside them ranked as one of the three canonical poets of Latin literature, Publius Ovidius Naso (43 BC–17/18 AD) was a Roman poet during the reign of Augustus and is best known for his *Metamorphoses*, an epic narrative poem dealing with the transformations of characters from Greco-Roman myth.

Julius Pap
The Fairies' Well
(Originally Published in *The Folk-Tales of the Magyars*, 1889)

Julius Pap was a Hungarian writer and folklorist known for his contributions to the collection and study of Hungarian folklore, particularly his work *Palóc Folk-Poetry*. Pap was a contributor to the 1889 anthology *The Folk-Tales of the Magyars*. This collection, compiled for the Folk-Lore Society, aimed to introduce English readers to the rich tradition of Hungarian folktales, including those of magical creatures, spirits, and heroic journeys.

Norman Hinsdale Pitman
The Phantom Vessel; Lu-San, Daughter of Heaven; The Princess Kwan-Yin; The Two Jugglers; The Nodding Tiger
(Originally Published in *A Chinese Wonder Book*, 1919)
Norman Hinsdale Pitman (1876–1925) was an author and educator, born in Lamont, Michigan. His works include: *The Lady Elect: A Chinese Romance* (1913), *A Chinese Wonder Book* (1919), *Chinese Fairy Tales* (1924) and *Dragon Lure: A Romance of Peking* (1925).

Apollonius of Rhodes
Giants and Doliones; The Golden Fleece
(Originally Published in *Argonautica,* 238 BC)
Apollonius of Rhodes (born c. 295 BC) was a Greek poet and grammarian who was the author of the *Argonautica*. His other poems, which survive only in small fragments, concerned the beginnings or foundations of cities, such as Alexandria and Cnidus- places of interest to the Ptolemies, whom he served as a scholar and librarian at the Library of Alexandria.

T. W. Rolleston
The Birth of Oisín
(Originally Published in *The High Deeds of Finn and other Bardic Romances of Ancient Ireland,* 1910)
T. W. Rolleston (1857–1920) was a prominent Irish poet, writer, and journalist known for his work on Celtic mythology, most notably his influential book *Celtic Myths and Legends*. He was educated at Trinity College Dublin and founded the *Dublin University Review*. Rolleston also wrote on German literature, translated works, and was involved in early Irish nationalism.

W.H.D. Rouse
The Goblin City
(Originally Published in *The Giant Crab and Other Tales from Old India,* 1897)
W.H.D. Rouse (1863–1950) was a pioneering British teacher who advocated the use of the "direct method" of teaching Latin and Greek. Rouse is known for his plain English prose translations of Homer's *Odyssey* (1937) and *Iliad* (1938). He is also recognized for his translations of some of Plato's dialogues, including *The Republic*, *Apology*, *Crito*, and *Phaedo*.

William H. Barker and Cecilia Sinclair
Farmer Mybrow and the Fairies
(Originally Published in *West African Folk-tales*, 1917)
William H. Barker (1882–1929) was born in Derbyshire, England. An author and missionary, Barker travelled to Africa and learned of the culture, stories, and

mythology of the Akan people of Ghana. Cecilia Sinclair, often writing under the name C. Sinclair, published several collections of stories with Barker. One of their best-known works, *West African Folk-Tales*, was published in 1917. They are also known for their collections *Anansi and Nothing* (1917) and *How We Got the Name "Spider Tales"* (1917).

Charles J. Tibbits
The Brownie
(Originally Published in *Folk-Lore and Legends: Scotland,* 1889)
Charles John Tibbits (1861–1935) was an English journalist, newspaper editor, and author. He attended Oxford University and married the novelist Annie Olive Brazier. Tibbits wrote prolifically on folk tales and legends, publishing extensive collections. One of his most popular works is the series *Folk-Lore and Legends*, which features numerous volumes of tales from cultures and societies around the world. These include folk-lore of Native American nations, Scandinavia, Russia, and Scotland, among others.

Vyasa
Dushyanta and Shakuntala
(Originally Published in *Mahabharata,* 4 CE)
Vyasa was a venerated Indian sage, and he is credited as the author of the *Mahabharata*, a Sanskrit epic of Ancient India. He is believed by many Hindus to be a partial reincarnation of the god Vishnu. Some theorise that Vyasa was not an individual but in fact a series of sages, each given the title of Vyasa upon composing a new Purana.

Abbie Phillips Walker
Hilda's Mermaid
(Originally Published in *The Sandman's Hour: Stories for Bedtime,* 1917)
Abbie Phillips Walker (1867 –1943) was a children's writer. Much of Walker's writing is encapsulated in her collection of bedtime stories titled *The Sandman's Hour: Stories for Bedtime*. Notably, her work has kindled the imaginations of numerous children across generations.

Richard Wilhelm
The Ape Sun Wu King; The Kindly Magician
(Originally Published in *The Chinese Fairy Book,* 1921)
Richard Wilhelm (1873–1930) was a German sinologist, theologian and missionary. He was born in Stuttgart and attended the University of Frankfurt. Wilhelm lived in China for 25 years and was fluent in both spoken and written Chinese. He is best known for his translation of the *I Ching*, which is considered one of the best translations, and for his translation of Chinese philosophical works into German.

William Butler Yeats
The Brewery of Egg-Shells; The Twelve Wild Geese
(Originally Published in *Fairy and Folk Tales of the Irish Peasantry,* 1888)
William Butler Yeats (1865–1939) was an Irish poet and is considered as one of the greatest writers from the twentieth century. He played an important role in the Celtic

Twilight, a revival of Irish literature focused on Gaelic heritage and Irish nationalism. Yeats was fascinated by Irish legends, including many Irish heroes in his works and focusing his poetry on Irish folklore. Alongside his poetry he is famous for writing short stories and plays. Yeats set up the Abbey Theatre in 1899, which held Irish and Celtic performances. In recognition of Yeats' important work he received a Nobel Prize in 1923.

GOTHIC FANTASY

For our books, calendars, blog
and latest special offers please see:
flametreepublishing.com